POKÉMON™ ADVENTURES

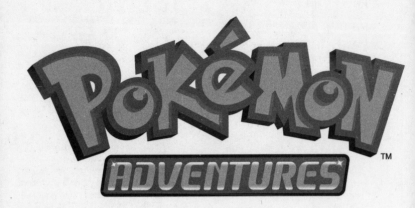

Pokémon ADVENTURES
Volume 3
VIZ Media Edition

Story by **HIDENORI KUSAKA**
Art by **MATO**

© 2009 The Pokémon Company International.
© 1995–1998 Nintendo / Creatures Inc. / GAME FREAK inc.
TM, ®, and character names are trademarks of Nintendo.
POCKET MONSTERS SPECIAL Vol. 3
by Hidenori KUSAKA, MATO
© 1997 Hidenori KUSAKA, MATO
All rights reserved.
Original Japanese edition published by SHOGAKUKAN.
English translation rights in the United States of America, Canada, the
United Kingdom, Ireland, Australia, New Zealand and India arranged with SHOGAKUKAN.

English Adaptation/Gerard Jones
Translation/Kaori Inoue
Miscellaneous Text Adaptation/Ben Costa
Touch-up & Lettering/Wayne Truman
Design/Sean D. Williams, Sam Elzway
Editor, 1st Edition/William Flanagan
Editor, VIZ Media Edition/Annette Roman

Printed in the U.S.A.

Published by VIZ Media, LLC
P.O. Box 77010
San Francisco, CA 94107

17
First printing, October 2009
Seventeenth printing, April 2019

PARENTAL ADVISORY
POKÉMON ADVENTURES is rated A
and is suitable for readers of all ages.

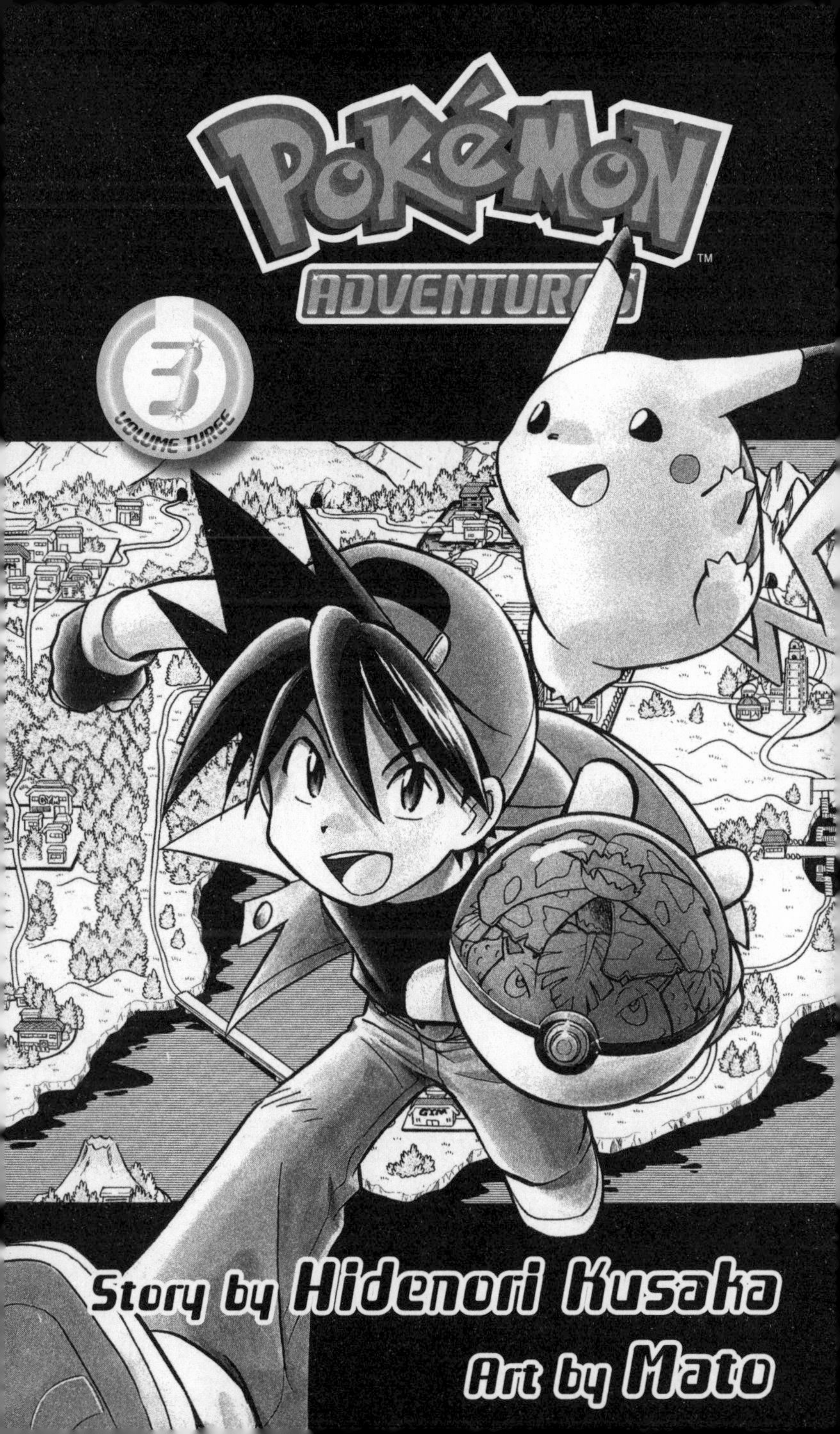
Pokémon™
Adventures
3
Volume Three
Story by Hidenori Kusaka
Art by Mato

CHARACTERS THUS FAR...

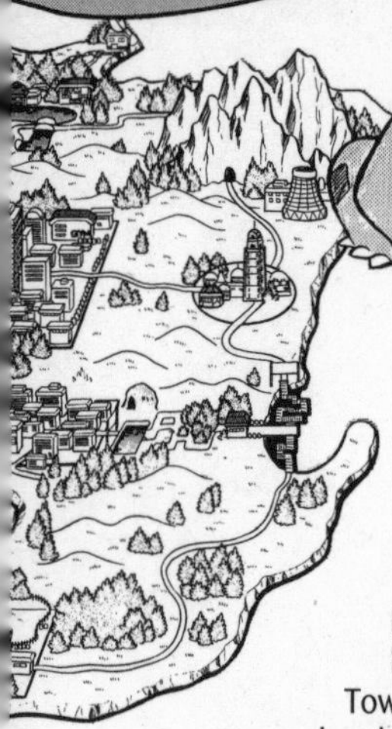

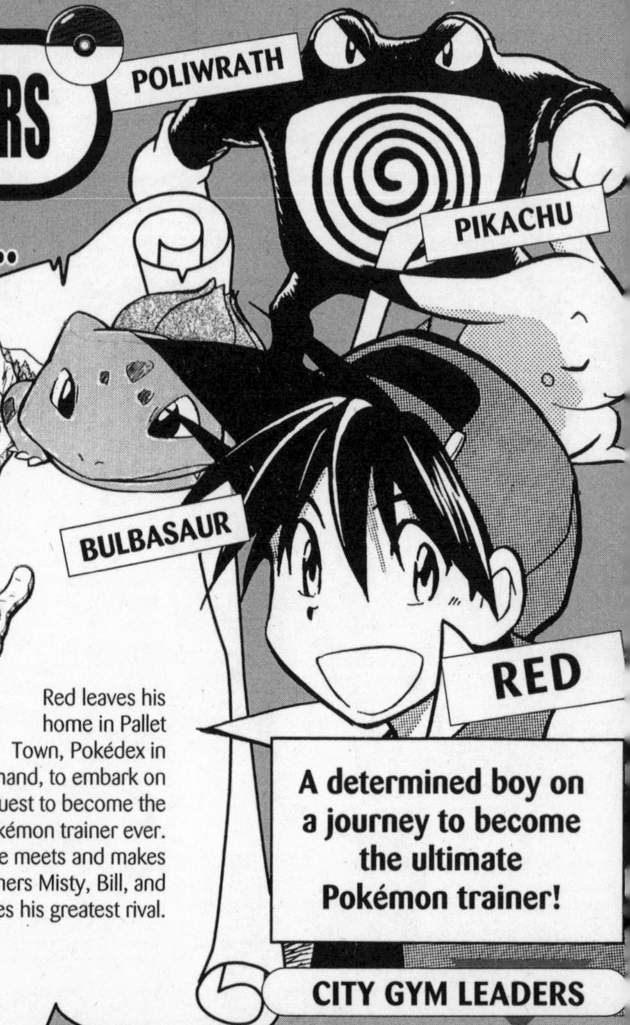
POLIWRATH
PIKACHU
BULBASAUR
RED
A determined boy on a journey to become the ultimate Pokémon trainer!

Red leaves his home in Pallet Town, Pokédex in hand, to embark on a quest to become the greatest Pokémon trainer ever. Along the way, he meets and makes friends with fellow trainers Misty, Bill, and Blue–who becomes his greatest rival.

CITY GYM LEADERS

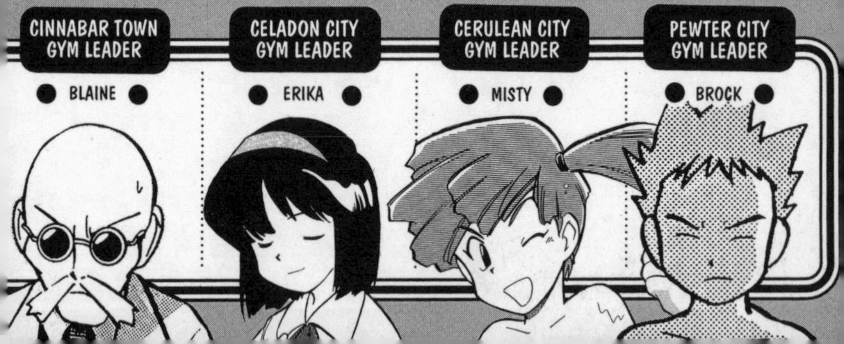
CINNABAR TOWN GYM LEADER
BLAINE
CELADON CITY GYM LEADER
ERIKA
CERULEAN CITY GYM LEADER
MISTY
PEWTER CITY GYM LEADER
BROCK

MAI

JOURNEY

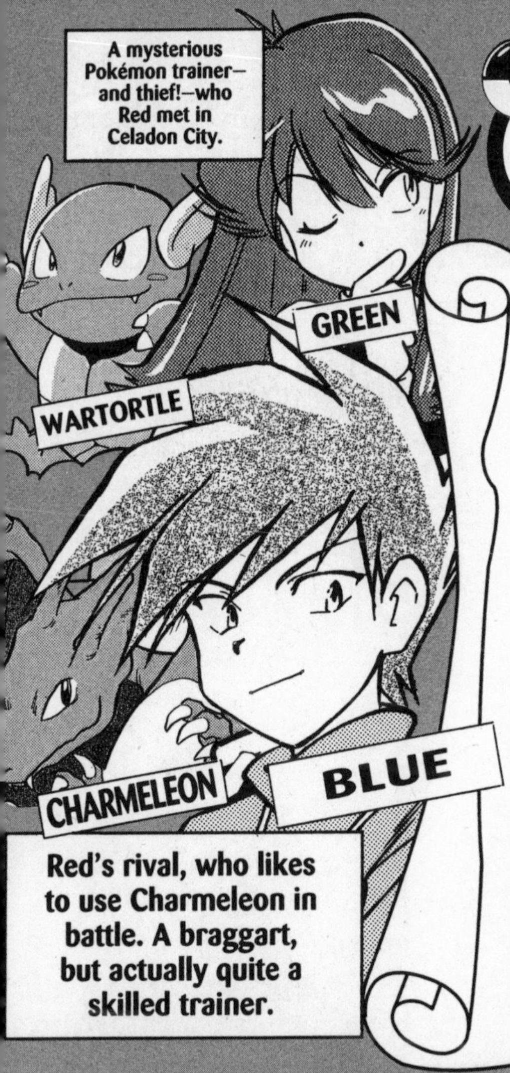

A mysterious Pokémon trainer—and thief!—who Red met in Celadon City.
GREEN
WARTORTLE
CHARMELEON
BLUE
Red's rival, who likes to use Charmeleon in battle. A braggart, but actually quite a skilled trainer.

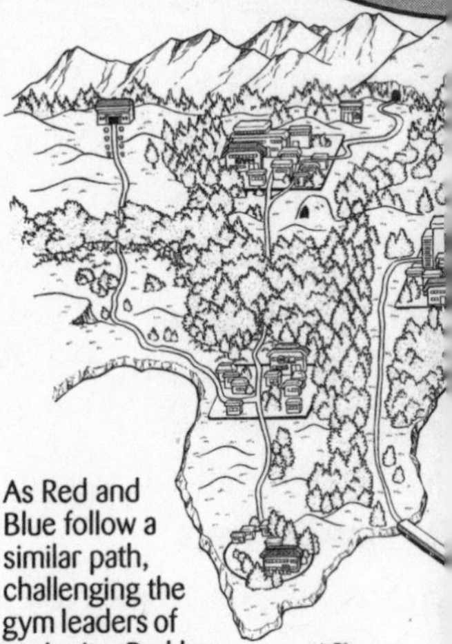

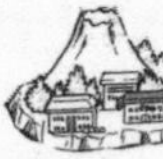

As Red and Blue follow a similar path, challenging the gym leaders of each city, Red has to either compete against Blue or join forces with him to defeat those who would stand in their way. At the top of their list of enemies is the evil organization Team Rocket, a group that secretly harbors gym leaders in its ranks!

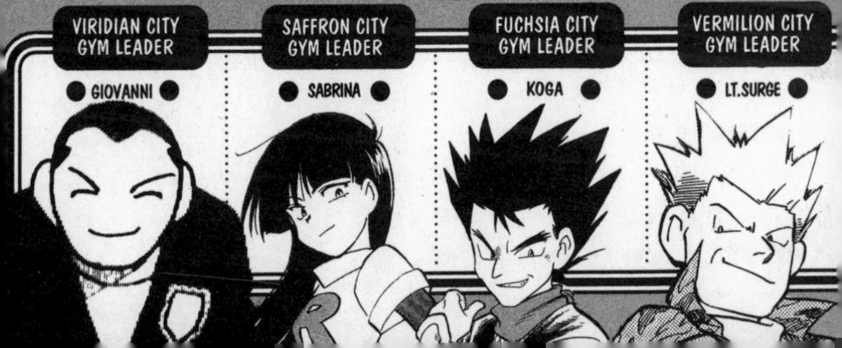

VIRIDIAN CITY GYM LEADER
GIOVANNI
SAFFRON CITY GYM LEADER
SABRINA
FUCHSIA CITY GYM LEADER
KOGA
VERMILION CITY GYM LEADER
LT.SURGE

CONTENTS

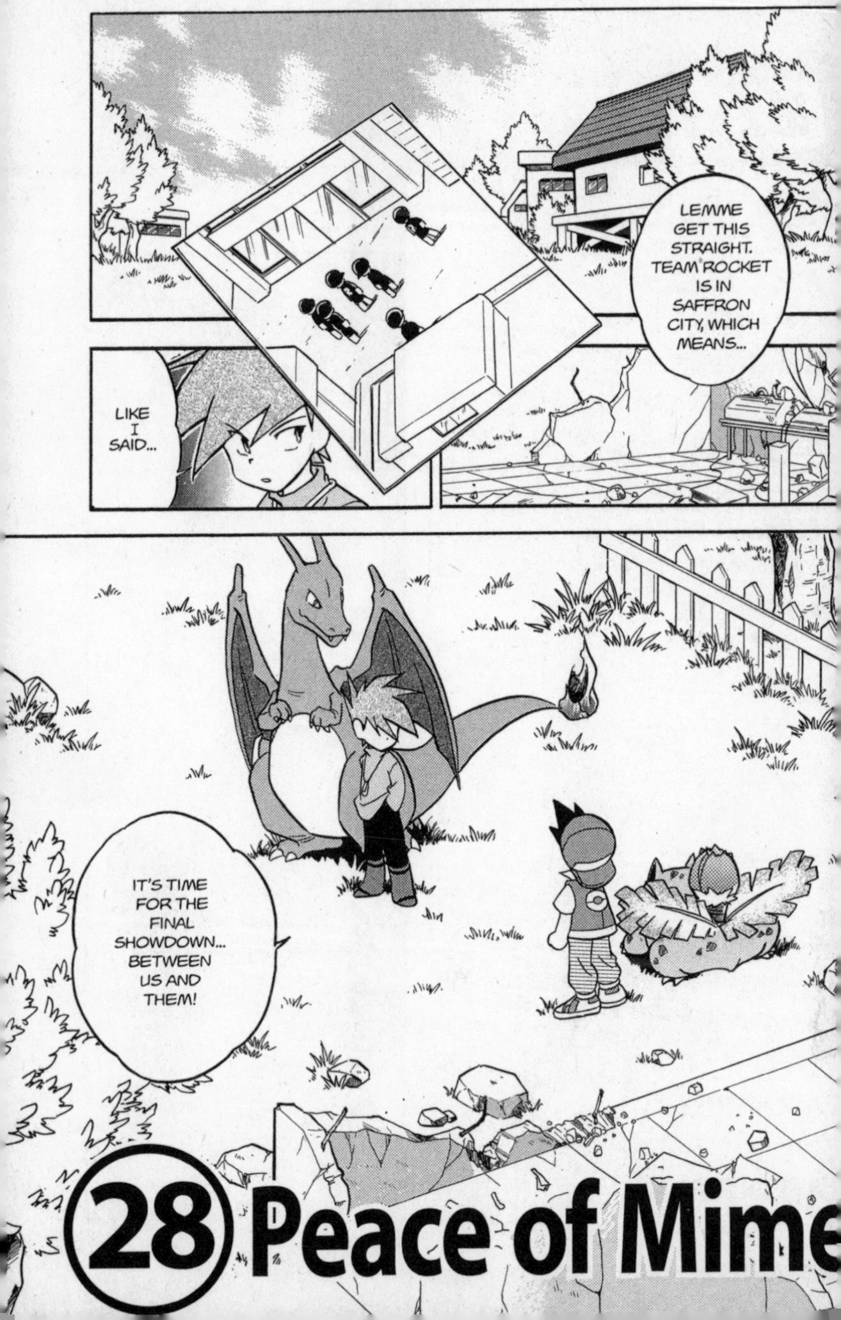
LEMME GET THIS STRAIGHT. TEAM ROCKET IS IN SAFFRON CITY, WHICH MEANS...
LIKE I SAID...
IT'S TIME FOR THE FINAL SHOWDOWN... BETWEEN US AND THEM!
28 Peace of Mime

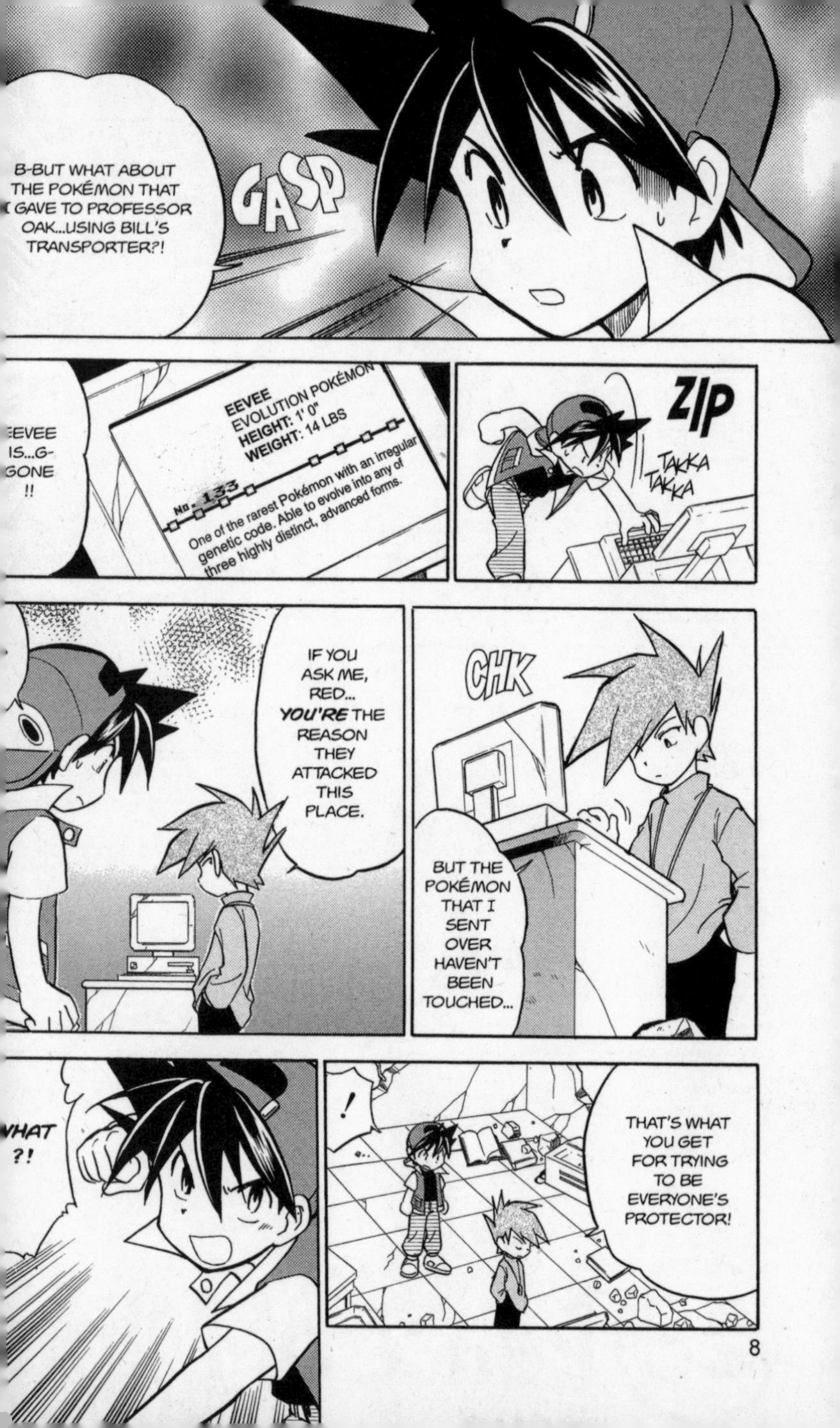
B-BUT WHAT ABOUT THE POKÉMON THAT I GAVE TO PROFESSOR OAK...USING BILL'S TRANSPORTER?!
GASP
ZIP
TAKKA TAKKA
EEVEE
EVOLUTION POKÉMON
HEIGHT: 1' 0"
WEIGHT: 14 LBS
No. 133
One of the rarest Pokémon with an irregular genetic code. Able to evolve into any of three highly distinct, advanced forms.
EEVEE IS...G-GONE!!
CHK
BUT THE POKÉMON THAT I SENT OVER HAVEN'T BEEN TOUCHED...
IF YOU ASK ME, RED... *YOU'RE* THE REASON THEY ATTACKED THIS PLACE.
!
THAT'S WHAT YOU GET FOR TRYING TO BE EVERYONE'S PROTECTOR!
WHAT?!

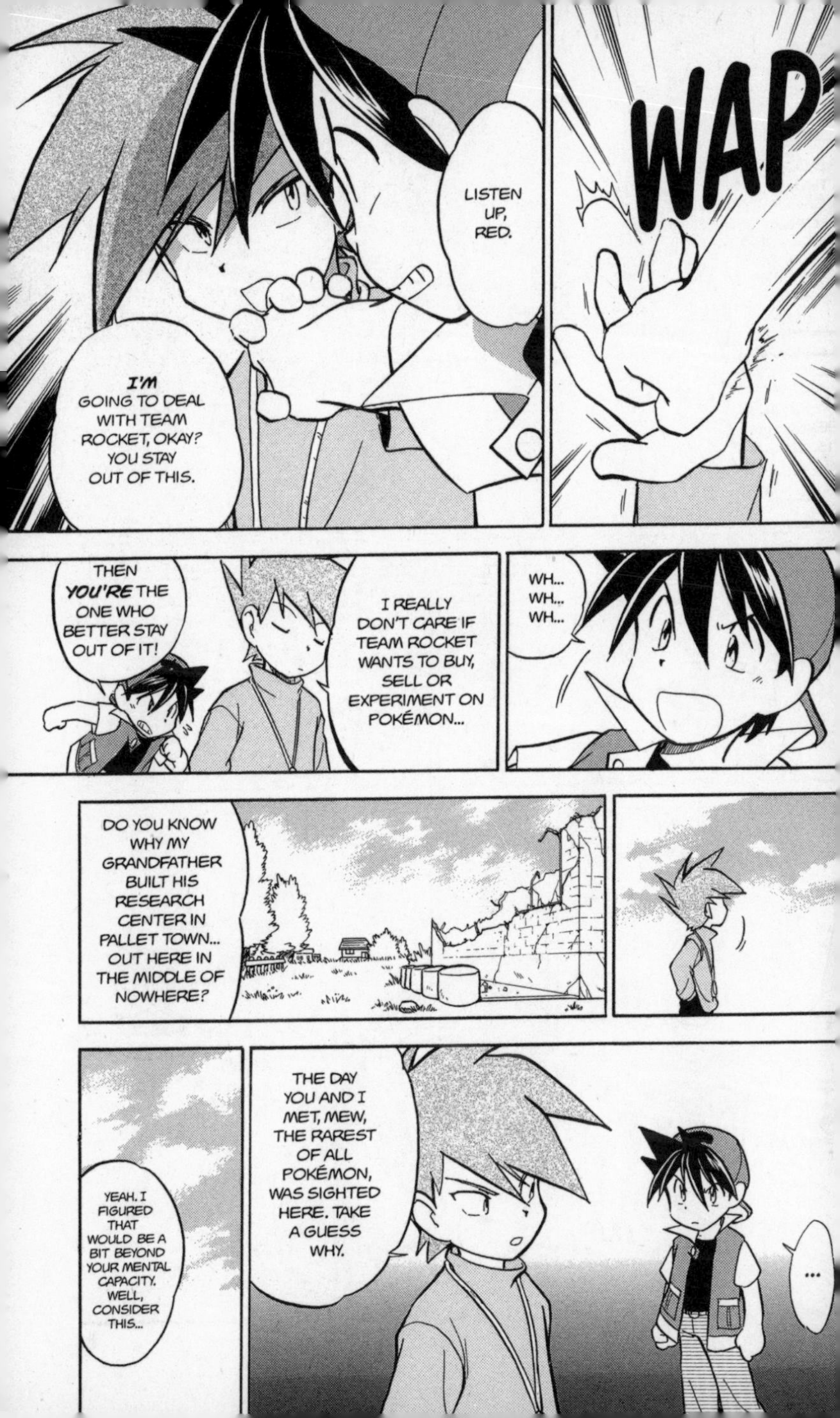
WAP
LISTEN UP, RED.
I'M GOING TO DEAL WITH TEAM ROCKET, OKAY? YOU STAY OUT OF THIS.
WH... WH... WH...
THEN YOU'RE THE ONE WHO BETTER STAY OUT OF IT!
I REALLY DON'T CARE IF TEAM ROCKET WANTS TO BUY, SELL OR EXPERIMENT ON POKÉMON...
DO YOU KNOW WHY MY GRANDFATHER BUILT HIS RESEARCH CENTER IN PALLET TOWN... OUT HERE IN THE MIDDLE OF NOWHERE?
...
THE DAY YOU AND I MET, MEW, THE RAREST OF ALL POKÉMON, WAS SIGHTED HERE. TAKE A GUESS WHY.
YEAH. I FIGURED THAT WOULD BE A BIT BEYOND YOUR MENTAL CAPACITY. WELL, CONSIDER THIS...

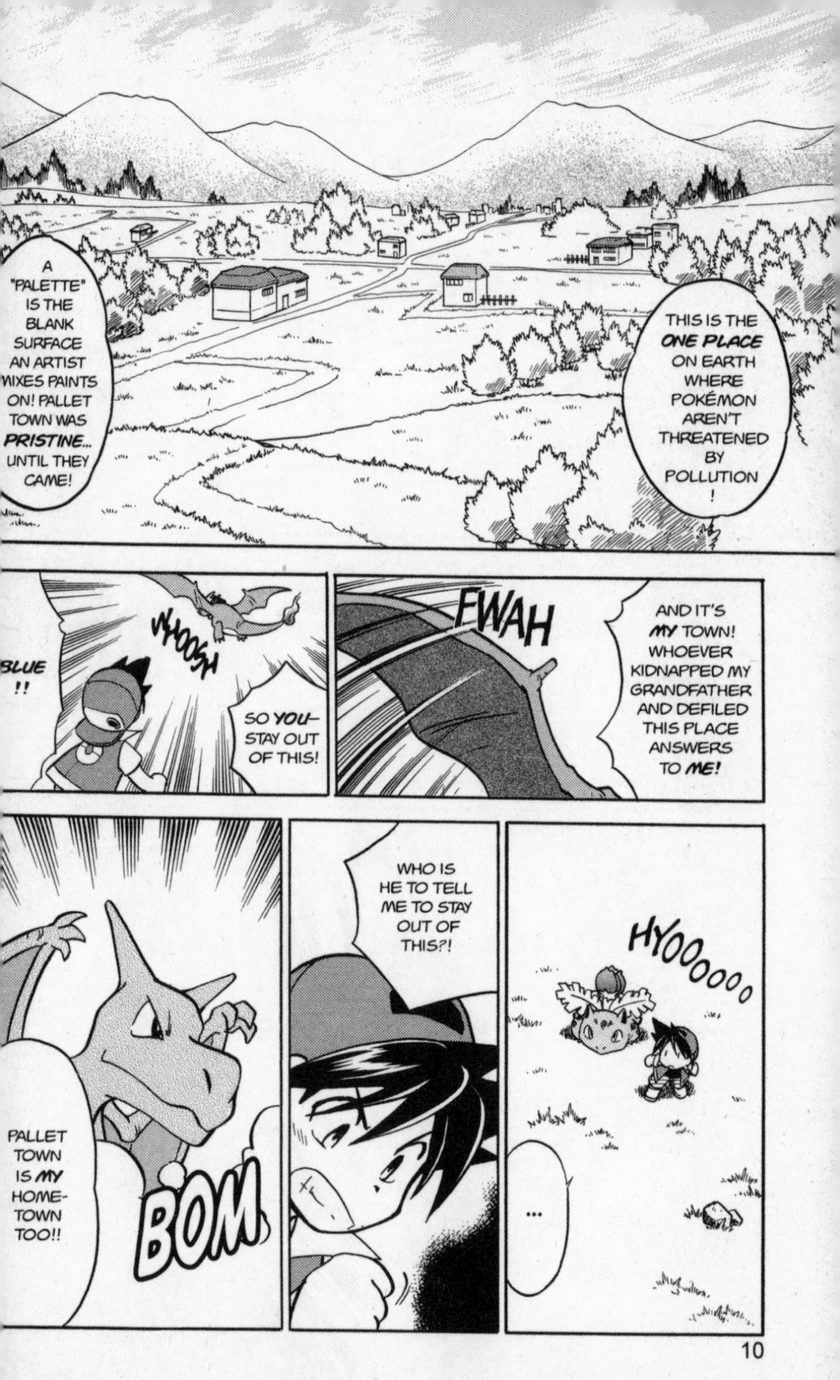
THIS IS THE ONE PLACE ON EARTH WHERE POKÉMON AREN'T THREATENED BY POLLUTION!
A "PALETTE" IS THE BLANK SURFACE AN ARTIST MIXES PAINTS ON! PALLET TOWN WAS PRISTINE... UNTIL THEY CAME!
FWAH
AND IT'S MY TOWN! WHOEVER KIDNAPPED MY GRANDFATHER AND DEFILED THIS PLACE ANSWERS TO ME!
WHOOSH
BLUE!!
SO YOU— STAY OUT OF THIS!
HYOOOOOOO
...
WHO IS HE TO TELL ME TO STAY OUT OF THIS?!
PALLET TOWN IS MY HOME-TOWN TOO!!
BOM

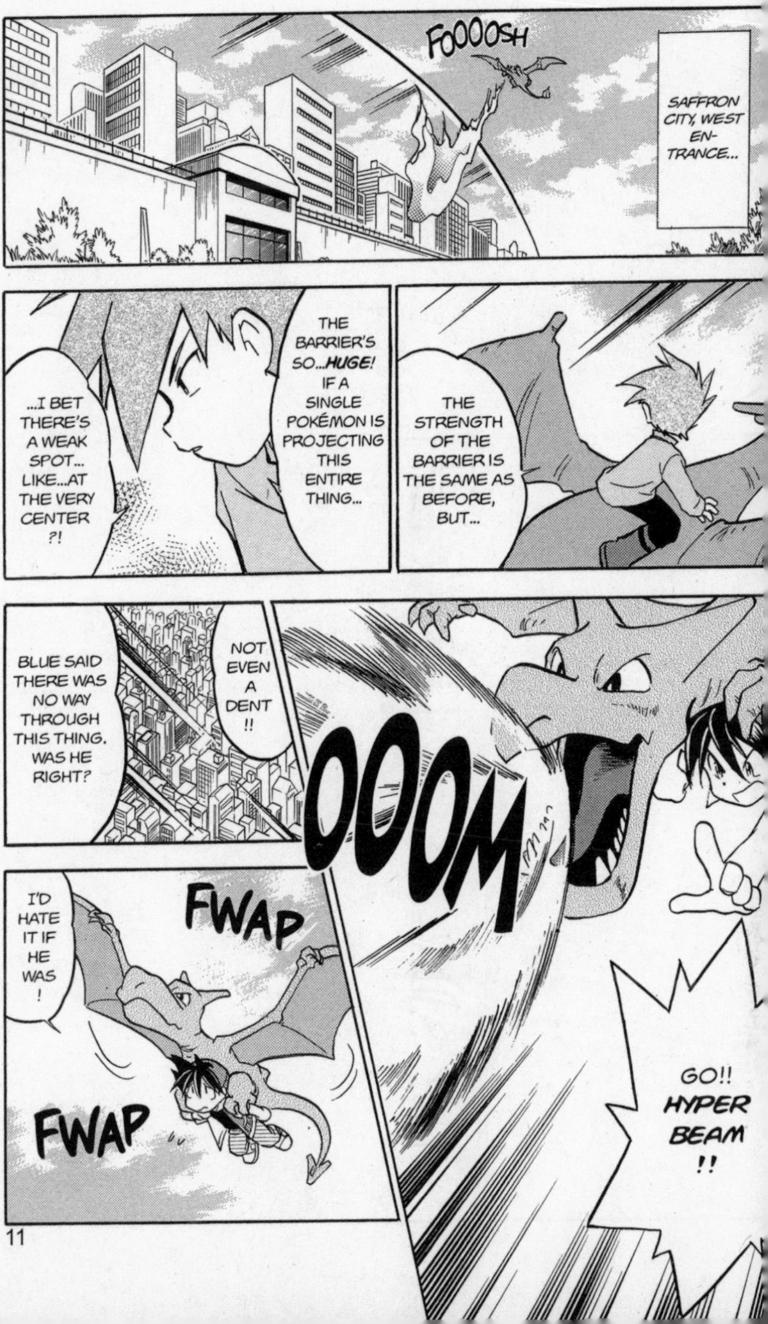
SAFFRON CITY, WEST EN-TRANCE...
FOOOOSH
THE STRENGTH OF THE BARRIER IS THE SAME AS BEFORE, BUT...
THE BARRIER'S SO...**HUGE**! IF A SINGLE POKÉMON IS PROJECTING THIS ENTIRE THING...
...I BET THERE'S A WEAK SPOT... LIKE...AT THE VERY CENTER ?!
GO!! **HYPER BEAM** !!
OOOM
NOT EVEN A DENT !!
BLUE SAID THERE WAS NO WAY THROUGH THIS THING. WAS HE RIGHT?
FWAP
I'D HATE IT IF HE WAS !
FWAP

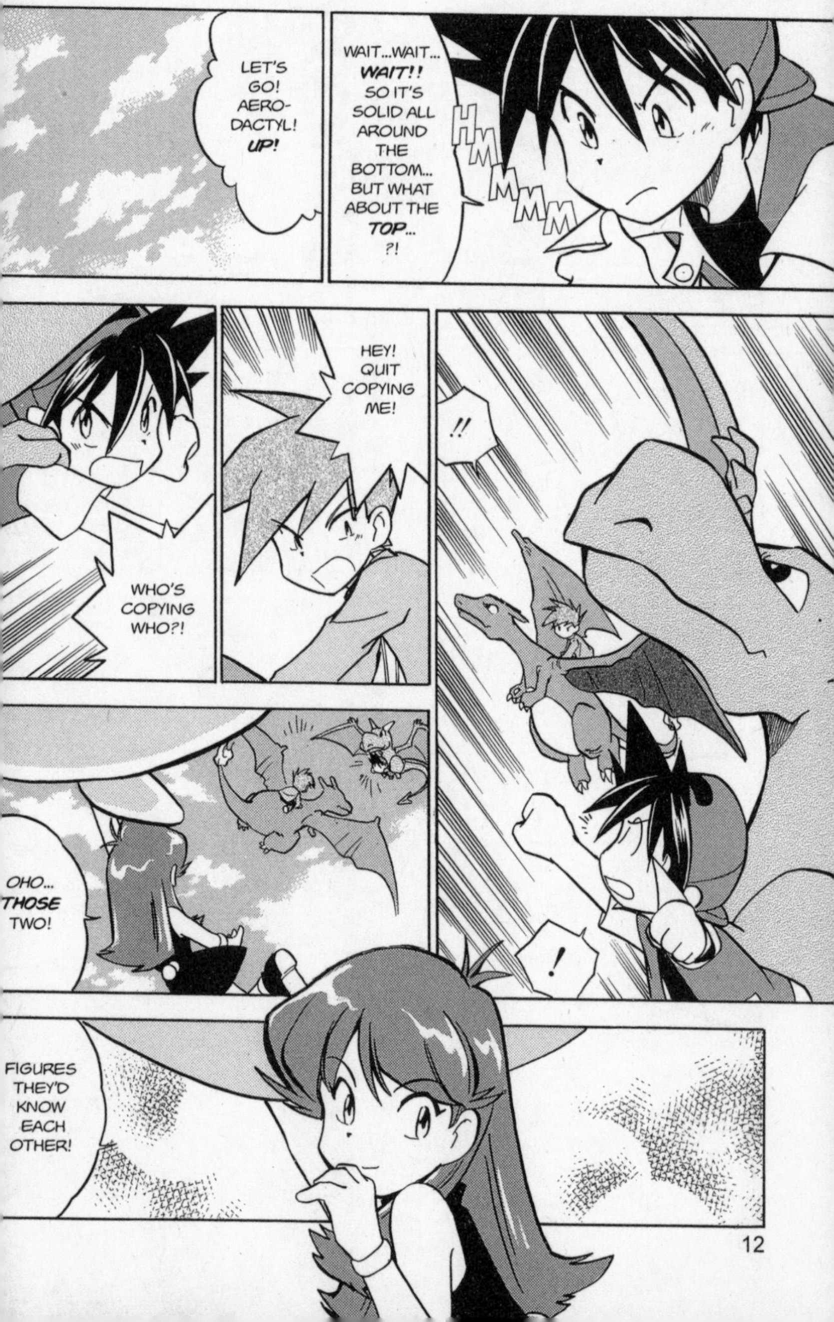
WAIT...WAIT... **WAIT!!** SO IT'S SOLID ALL AROUND THE BOTTOM... BUT WHAT ABOUT THE **TOP**... ?!
HMMMMM
LET'S GO! AERO-DACTYL! **UP!**
!!
!
HEY! QUIT COPYING ME!
WHO'S COPYING WHO?!
OHO... **THOSE** TWO!
FIGURES THEY'D KNOW EACH OTHER!

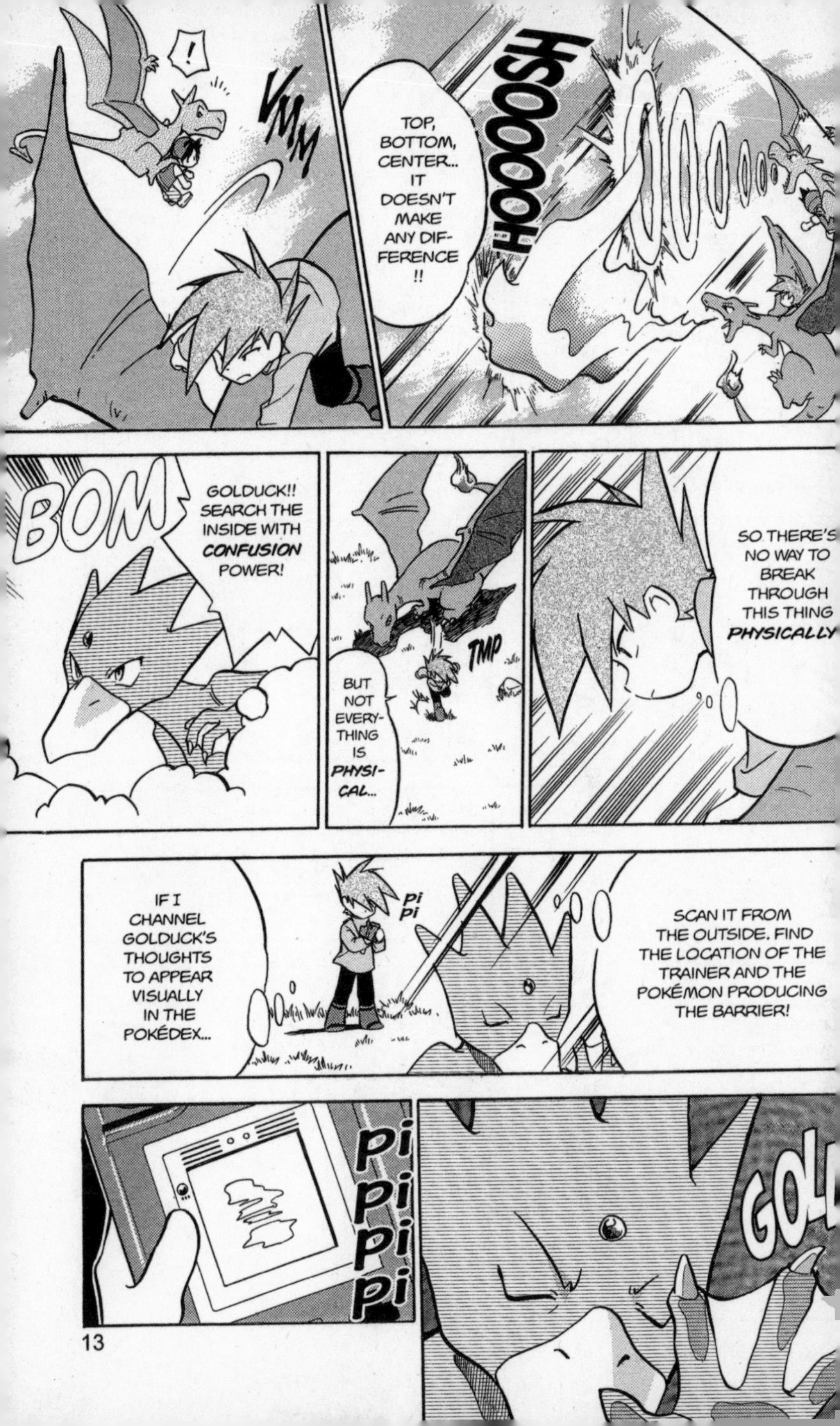
HOOOOSH
TOP, BOTTOM, CENTER... IT DOESN'T MAKE ANY DIFFERENCE !!
!
VMM
SO THERE'S NO WAY TO BREAK THROUGH THIS THING ***PHYSICALLY***
TMP
BUT NOT EVERYTHING IS ***PHYSICAL***...
BOM
GOLDUCK!! SEARCH THE INSIDE WITH ***CONFUSION*** POWER!
SCAN IT FROM THE OUTSIDE. FIND THE LOCATION OF THE TRAINER AND THE POKÉMON PRODUCING THE BARRIER!
pi pi
IF I CHANNEL GOLDUCK'S THOUGHTS TO APPEAR VISUALLY IN THE POKÉDEX...
GOL
pi pi pi pi pi pi pi pi

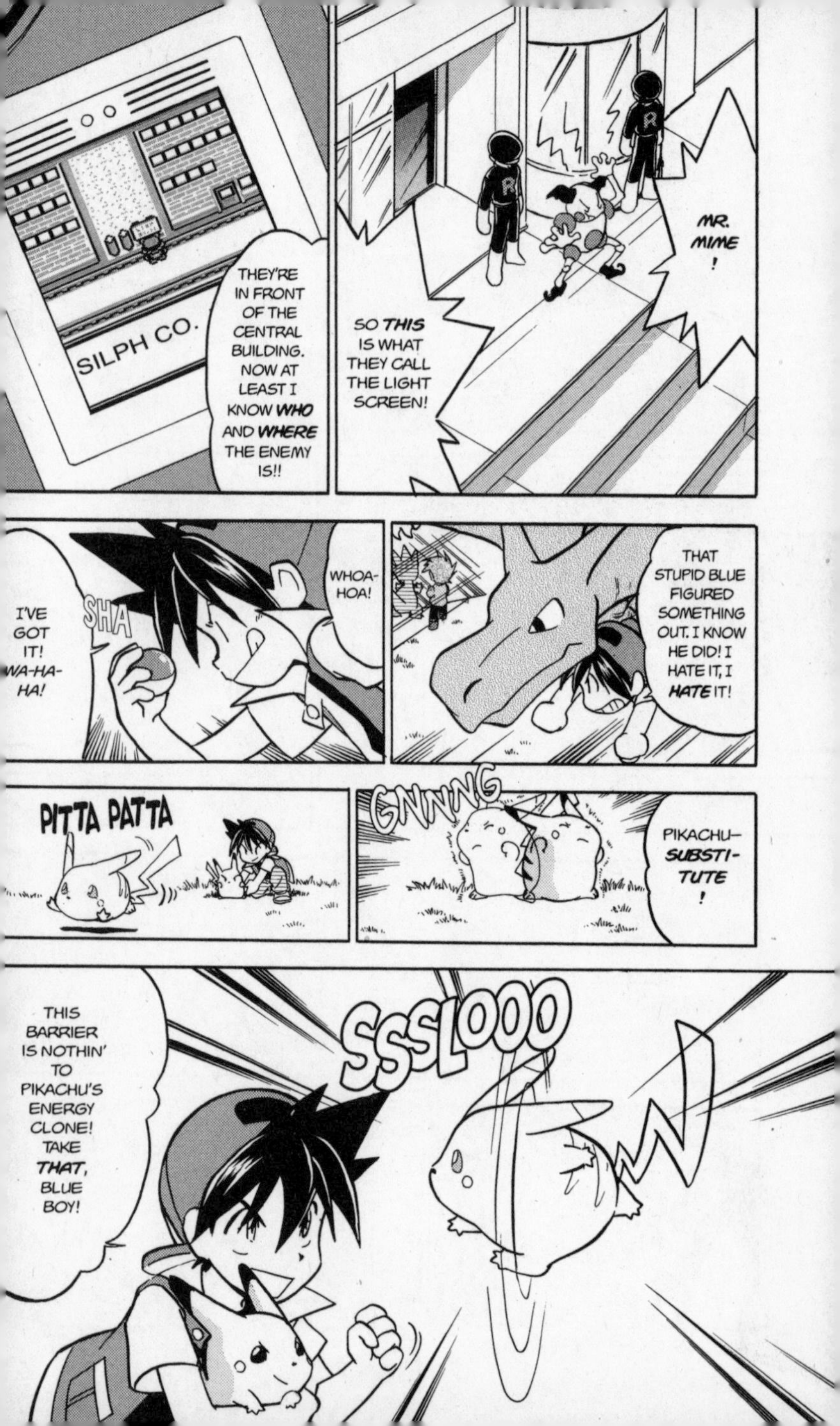
MR. MIME !
SO THIS IS WHAT THEY CALL THE LIGHT SCREEN!
SILPH CO.
THEY'RE IN FRONT OF THE CENTRAL BUILDING. NOW AT LEAST I KNOW WHO AND WHERE THE ENEMY IS!!
THAT STUPID BLUE FIGURED SOMETHING OUT. I KNOW HE DID! I HATE IT, I HATE IT!
WHOA-HOA!
SHA
I'VE GOT IT! WA-HA-HA!
PIKACHU-SUBSTI-TUTE !
GNNNG
PITTA PATTA
SSSLOOO
THIS BARRIER IS NOTHIN' TO PIKACHU'S ENERGY CLONE! TAKE THAT, BLUE BOY!

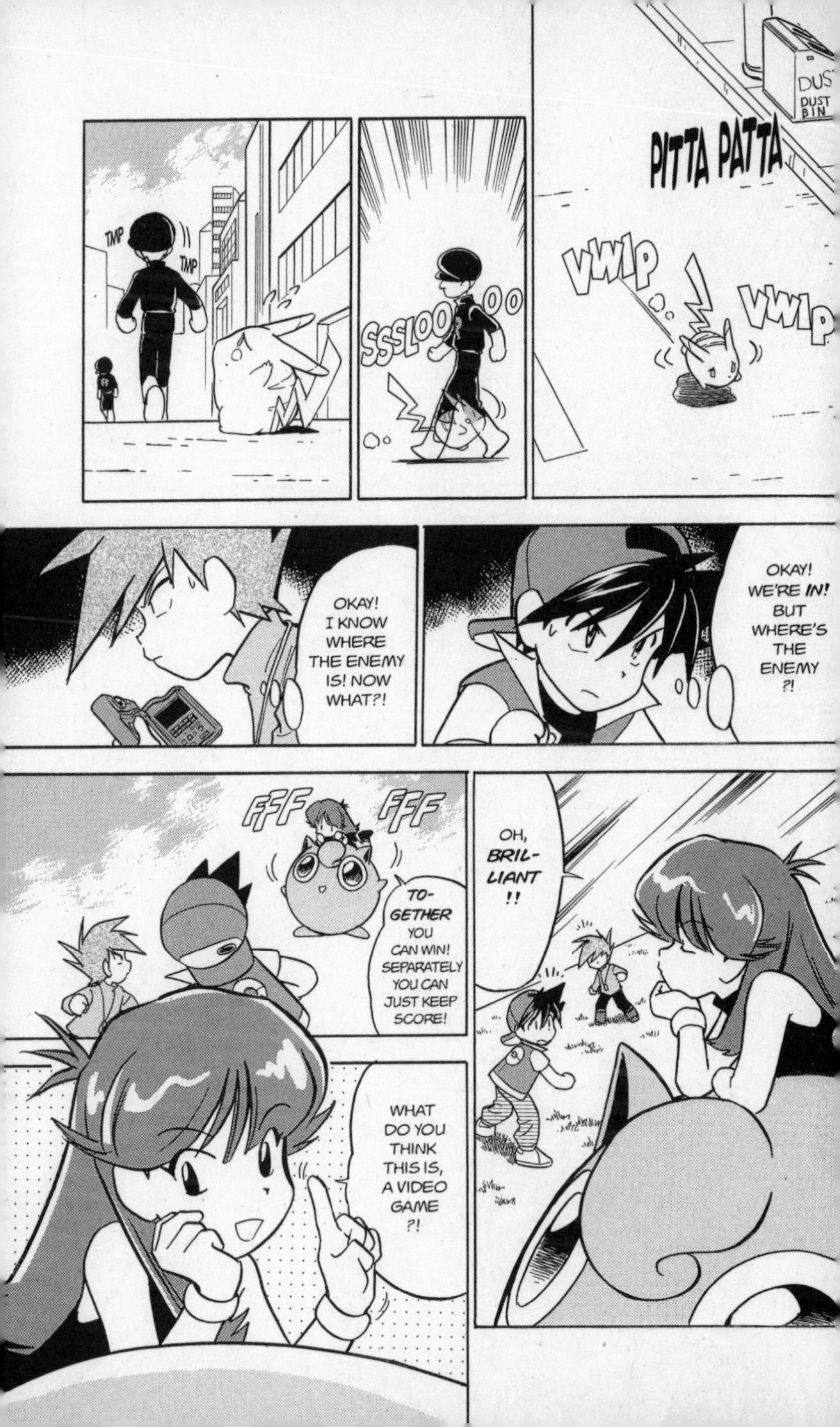
DUST
DUST BIN
PITTA PATTA
VWIP
VWIP
SSSLOO OO
TMP
TMP
OKAY! WE'RE IN! BUT WHERE'S THE ENEMY ?!
OKAY! I KNOW WHERE THE ENEMY IS! NOW WHAT?!
OH, BRIL-LIANT !!
FFF
FFF
TO-GETHER YOU CAN WIN! SEPARATELY YOU CAN JUST KEEP SCORE!
WHAT DO YOU THINK THIS IS, A VIDEO GAME ?!

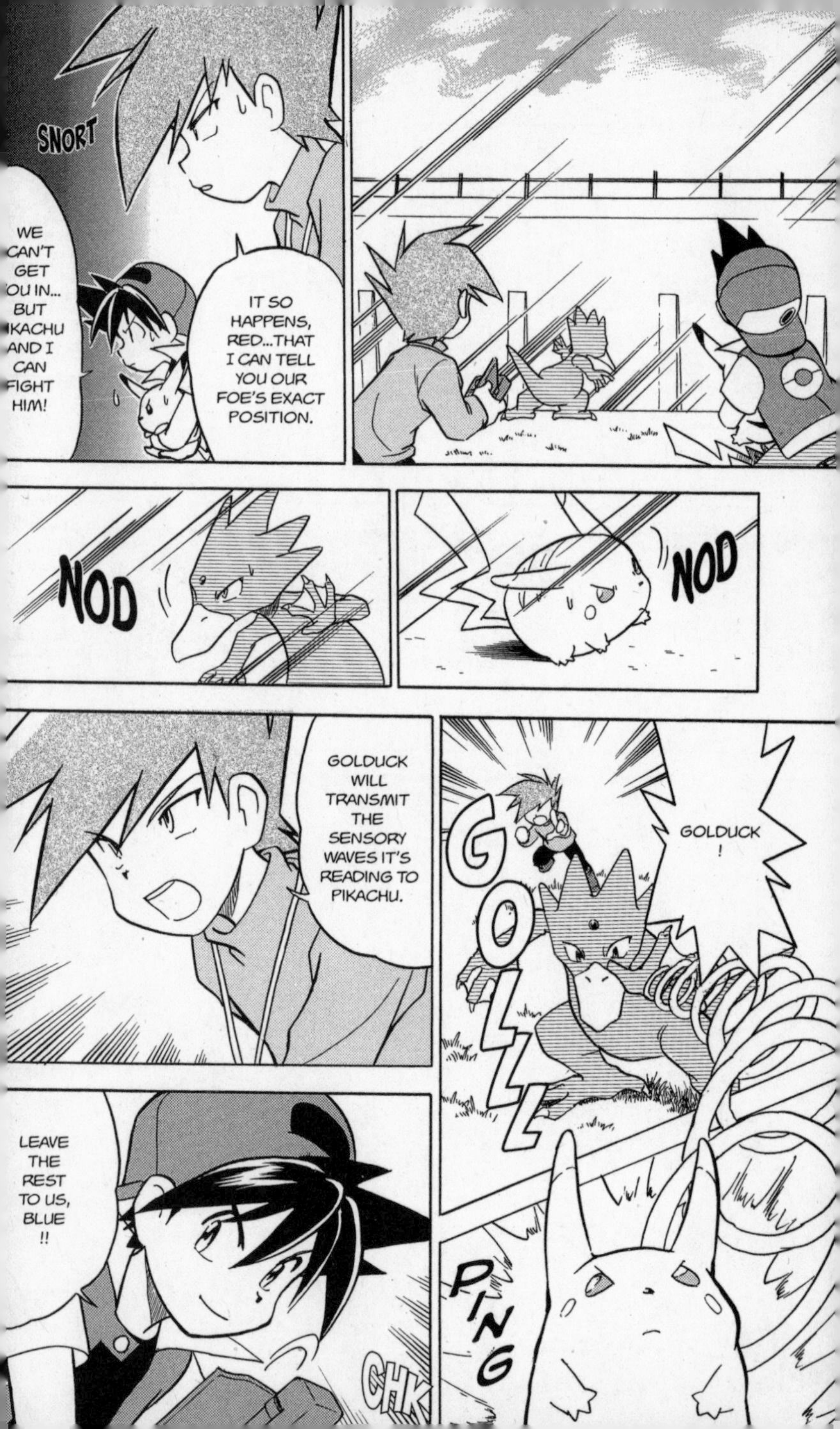

WE CAN'T GET OU IN... BUT IKACHU AND I CAN FIGHT HIM!
SNORT
IT SO HAPPENS, RED...THAT I CAN TELL YOU OUR FOE'S EXACT POSITION.
NOD
NOD
GOLDUCK !
GOLL
PING
GOLDUCK WILL TRANSMIT THE SENSORY WAVES IT'S READING TO PIKACHU.
LEAVE THE REST TO US, BLUE !!
CHK

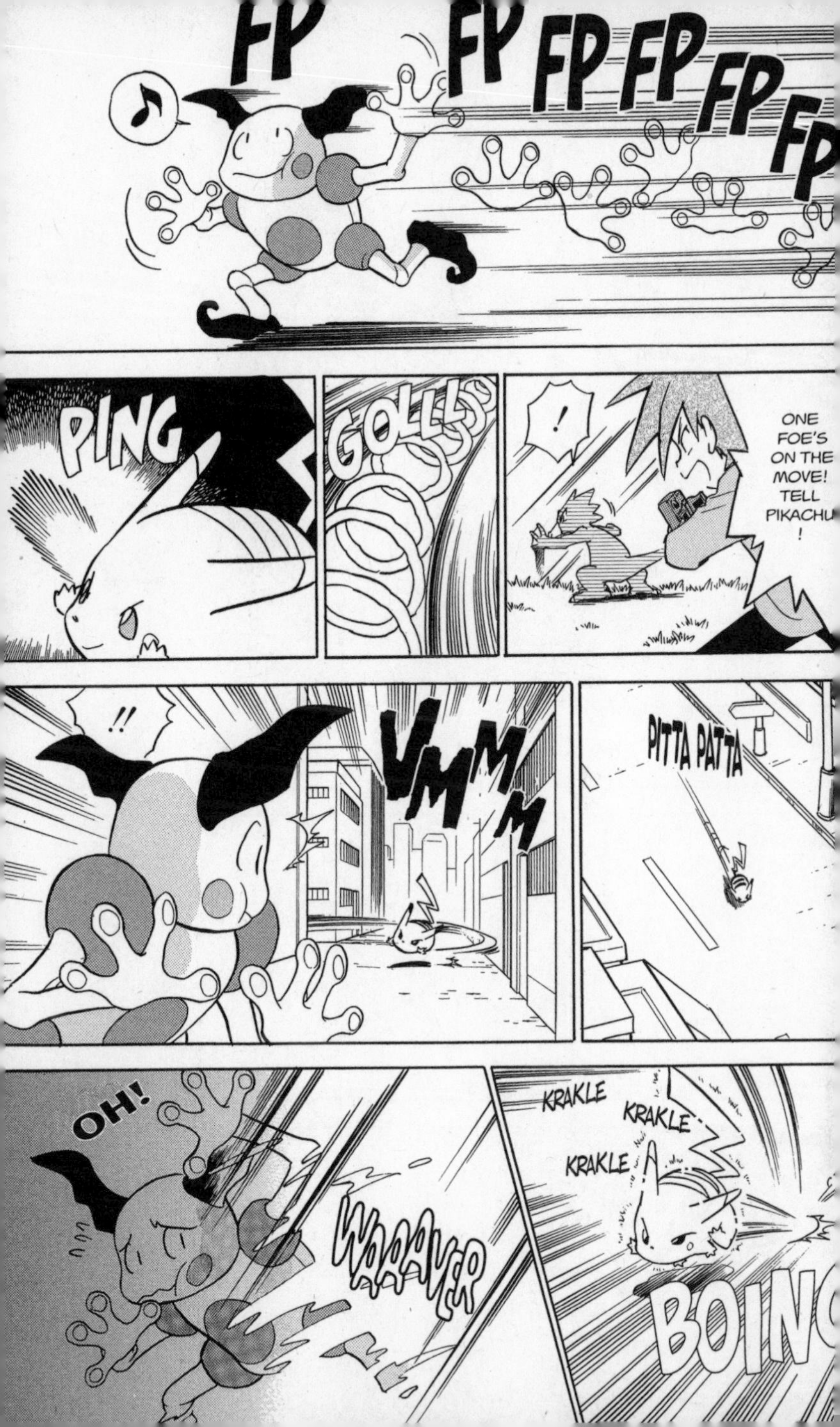

FP FP FP FP FP FP
♪
!
ONE FOE'S ON THE MOVE! TELL PIKACHU!
GOLLLS
PING
PITTA PATTA
VMMM
!!
KRAKLE
KRAKLE
KRAKLE
BOING
WAAAVER
OH!

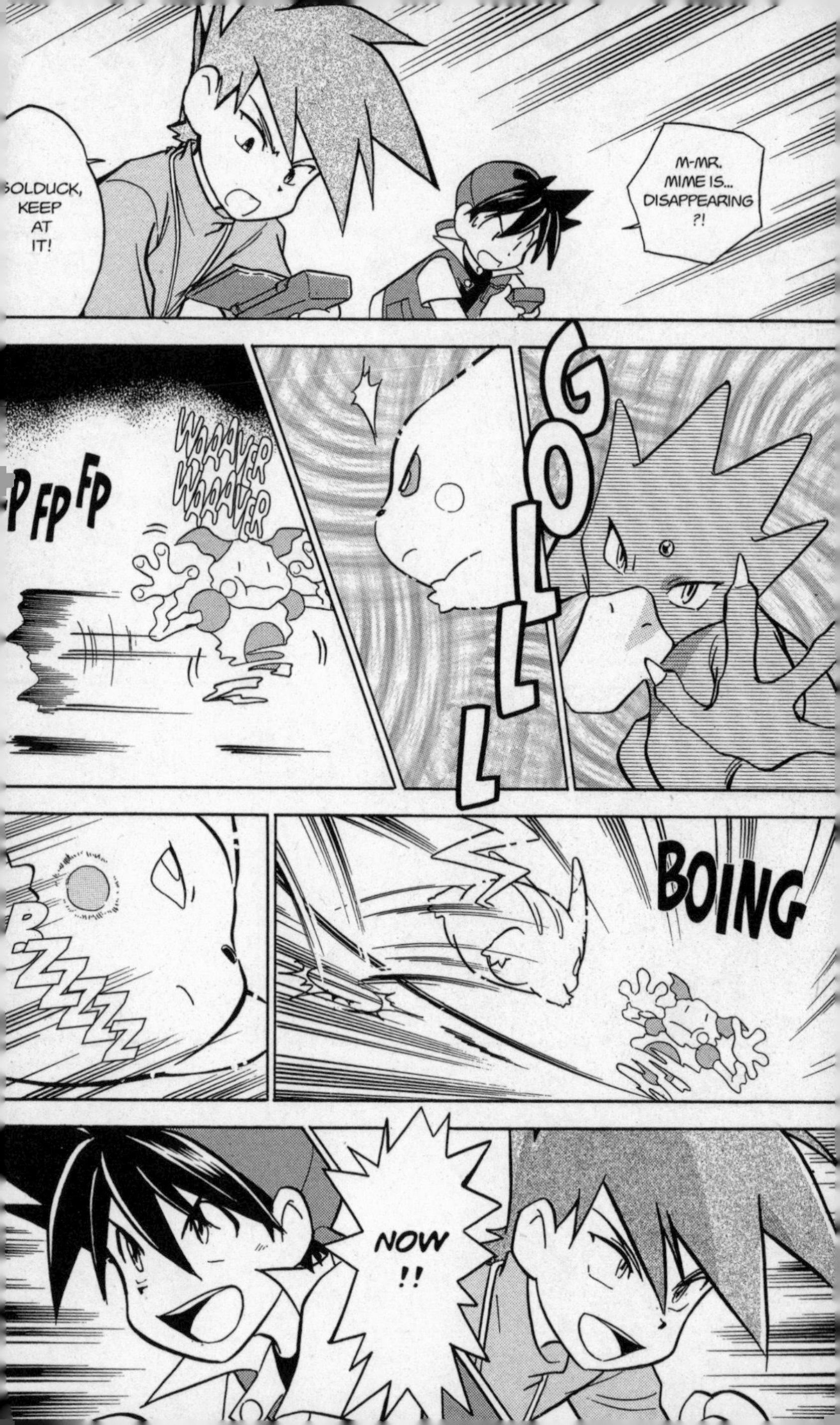

M-MR. MIME IS... DISAPPEARING ?!
OLDUCK, KEEP AT IT!
GOLLL
WAAAVER WAAAVER
P FP FP
BOING
ZZZZZ
NOW !!

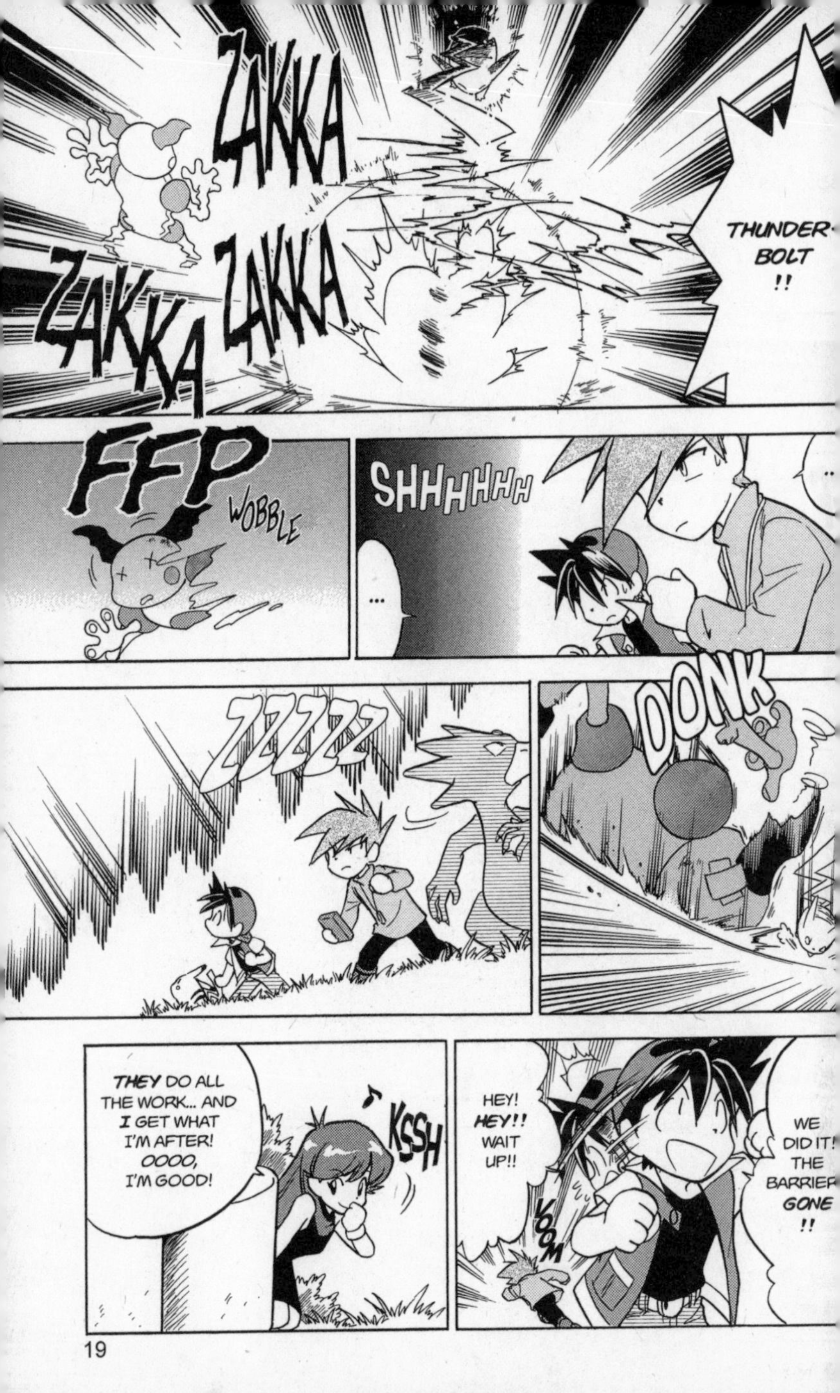

THUNDER-BOLT !!
ZAKKA
ZAKKA
ZAKKA
...
SHHHHHHH
...
FFP
WOBBLE
DONK
ZZZZZ
WE DID IT! THE BARRIER GONE !!
HEY! HEY!! WAIT UP!!
VOOM
KSSH
THEY DO ALL THE WORK... AND I GET WHAT I'M AFTER! OOOO, I'M GOOD!

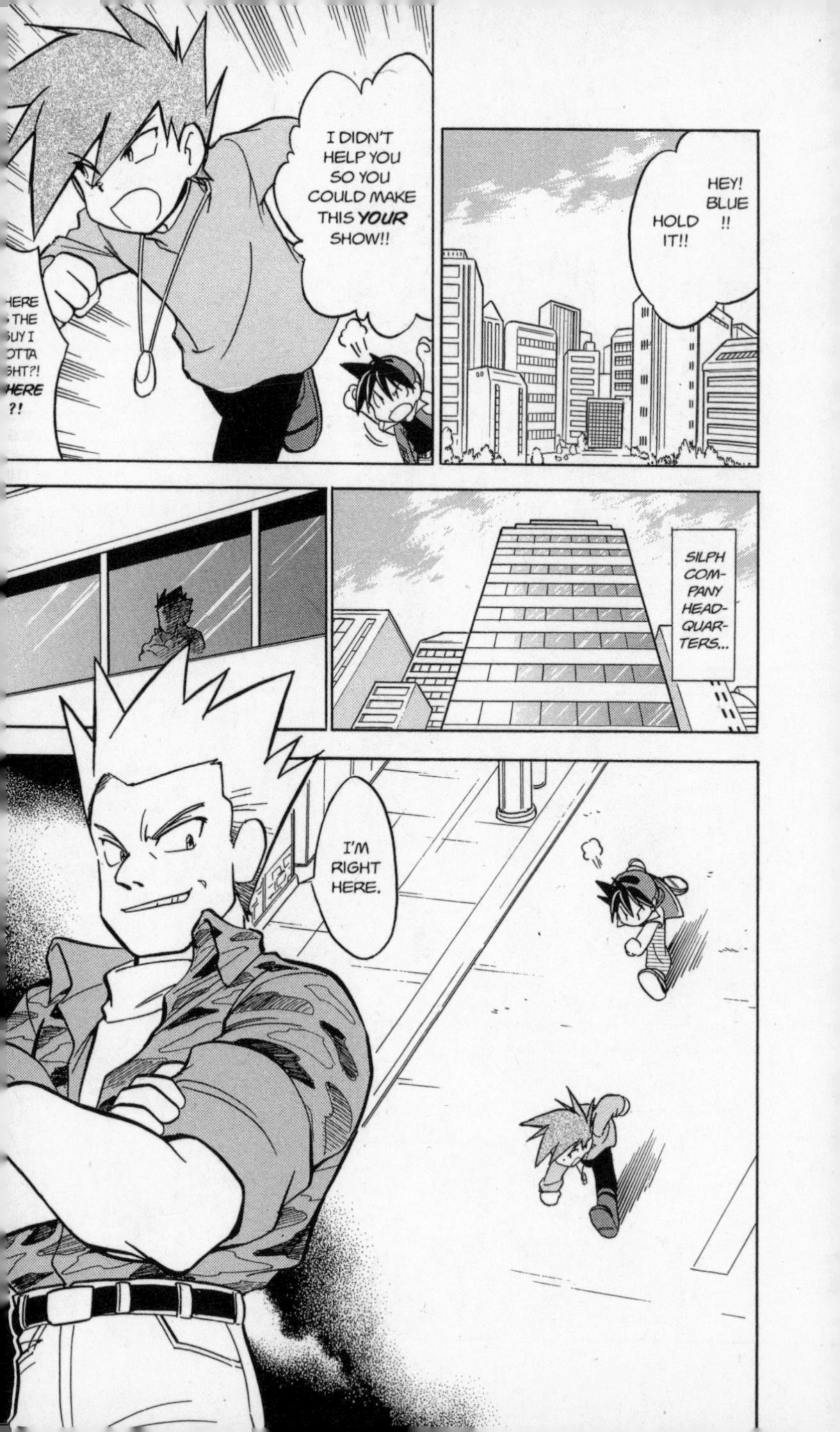
HEY! BLUE !!
HOLD IT!!
I DIDN'T HELP YOU SO YOU COULD MAKE THIS YOUR SHOW!!
SILPH COMPANY HEADQUARTERS...
I'M RIGHT HERE.

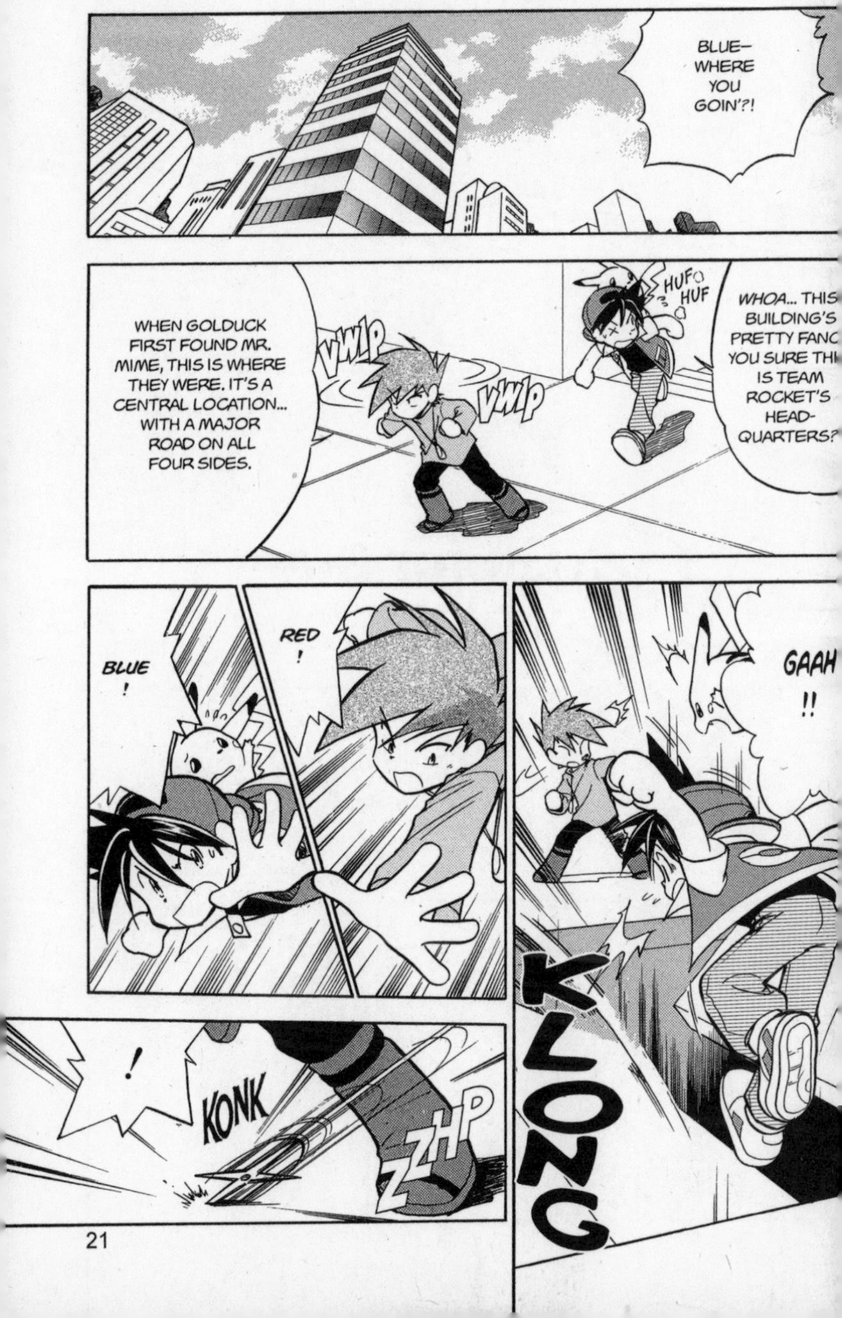
BLUE— WHERE YOU GOIN'?!
WHOA... THIS BUILDING'S PRETTY FANC YOU SURE THI IS TEAM ROCKET'S HEAD-QUARTERS?
HUF HUF
VWIP
VWIP
WHEN GOLDUCK FIRST FOUND MR. MIME, THIS IS WHERE THEY WERE. IT'S A CENTRAL LOCATION... WITH A MAJOR ROAD ON ALL FOUR SIDES.
GAAH!!
KLONG
RED!
BLUE!
KONK
ZZHP
!

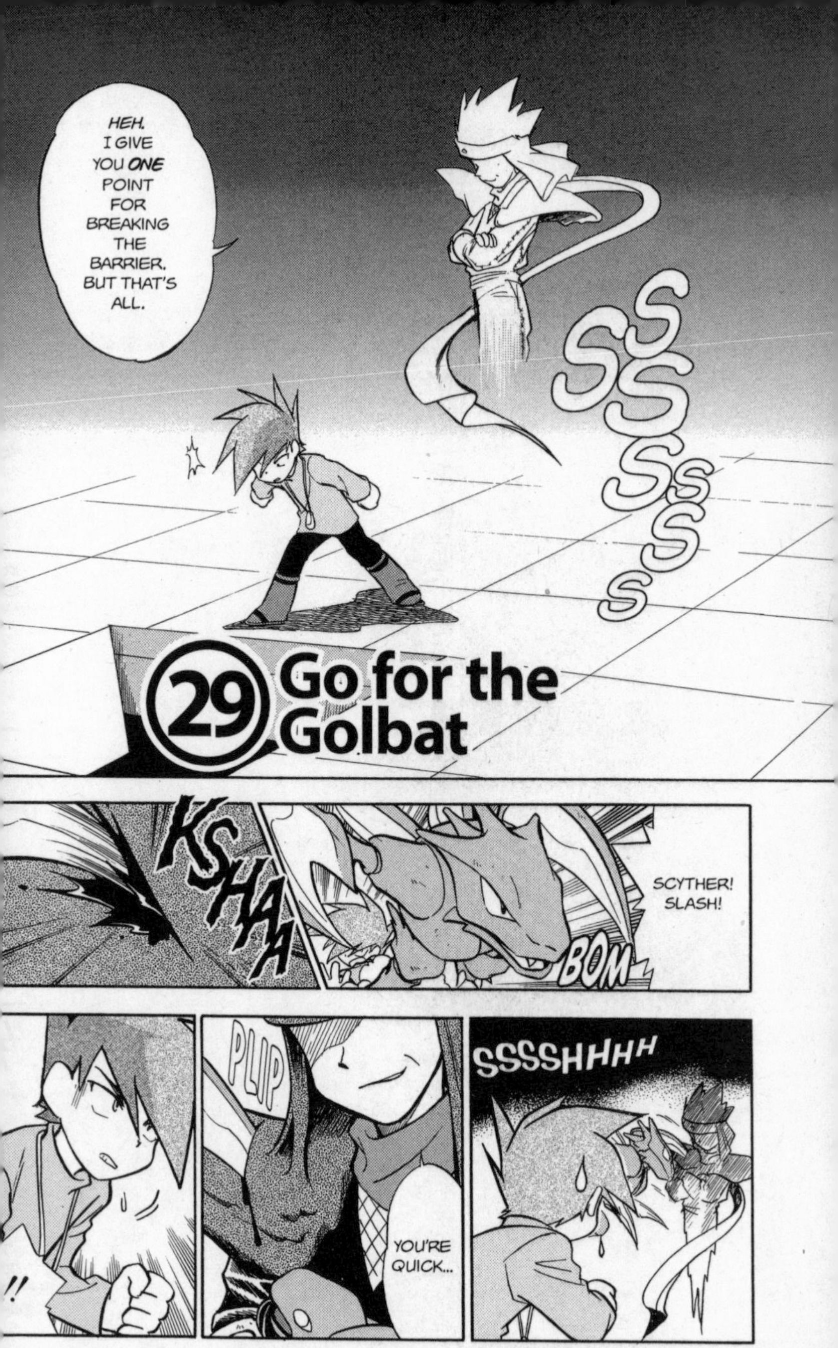
HEH. I GIVE YOU ONE POINT FOR BREAKING THE BARRIER. BUT THAT'S ALL.
SSSSSSSS
29 Go for the Golbat
SCYTHER! SLASH!
BOM
KSHAAA
SSSSHHHH
PLIP
YOU'RE QUICK...
!!

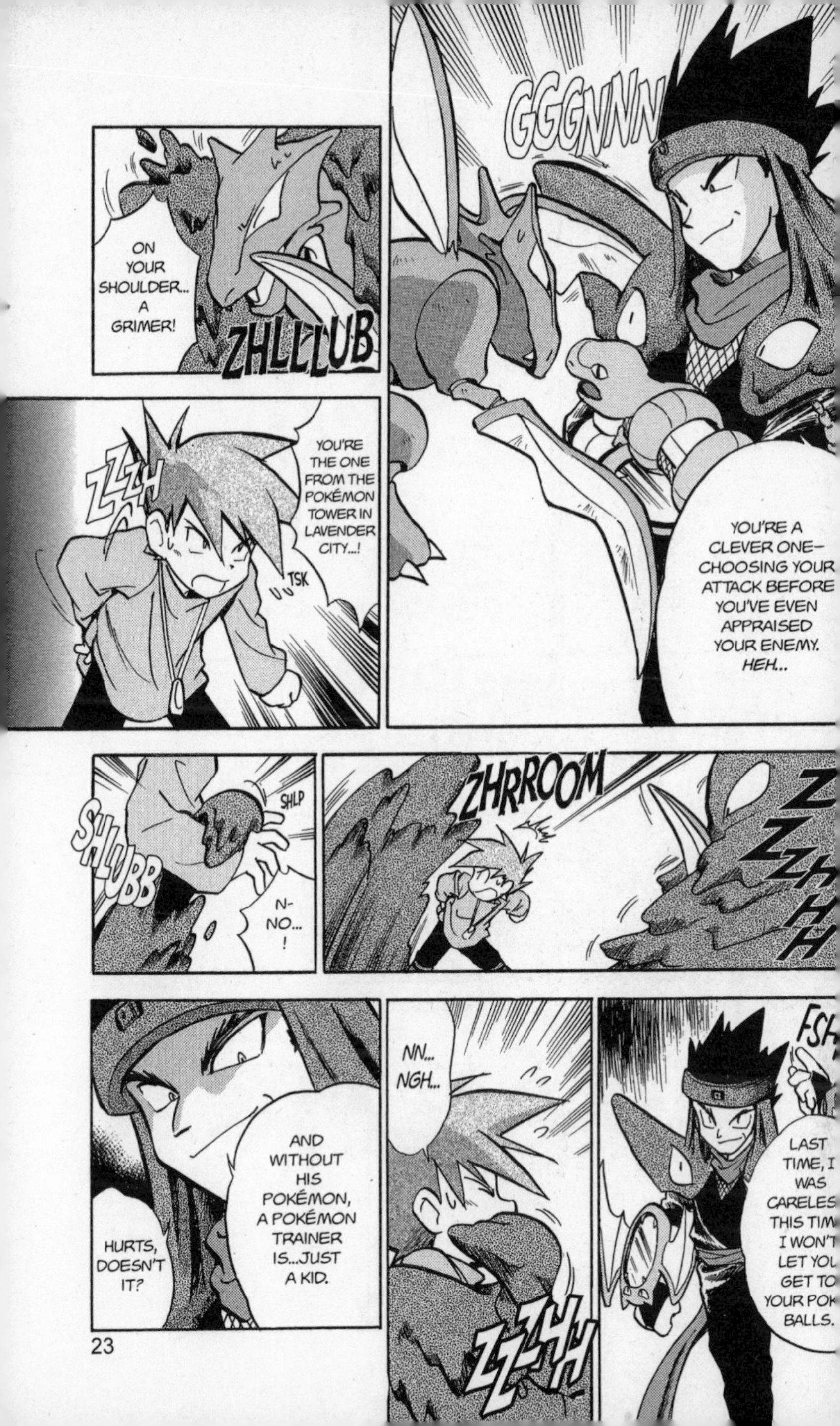
GGGNNNN
YOU'RE A CLEVER ONE—CHOOSING YOUR ATTACK BEFORE YOU'VE EVEN APPRAISED YOUR ENEMY. HEH...
ON YOUR SHOULDER... A GRIMER!
ZHLLLUB
YOU'RE THE ONE FROM THE POKÉMON TOWER IN LAVENDER CITY...!
ZZZH
TSK
ZHRROOM
ZZZHHH
SHLUBB
SHLP
N-NO... !
FSH
LAST TIME, I WAS CARELES THIS TIM I WON'T LET YOU GET TO YOUR POK BALLS.
NN... NGH...
ZZZHH
AND WITHOUT HIS POKÉMON, A POKÉMON TRAINER IS...JUST A KID.
HURTS, DOESN'T IT?

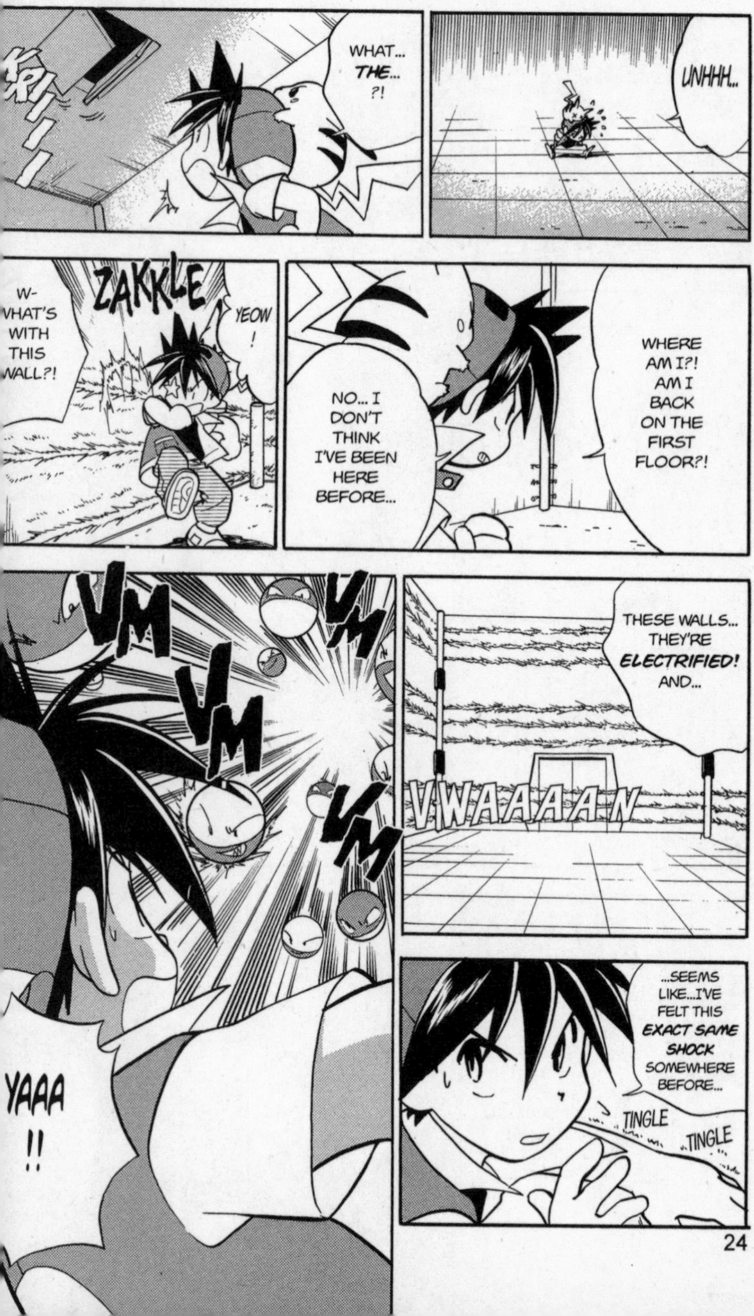
UNHHH...
WHAT... THE... ?!
KRI-I-I-I
WHERE AM I?! AM I BACK ON THE FIRST FLOOR?!
NO... I DON'T THINK I'VE BEEN HERE BEFORE...
ZAKKLE
YEOW!
W-WHAT'S WITH THIS WALL?!
THESE WALLS... THEY'RE ***ELECTRIFIED!*** AND...
VWAAAAAN
...SEEMS LIKE...I'VE FELT THIS ***EXACT SAME SHOCK*** SOMEWHERE BEFORE...
TINGLE
TINGLE
VM
VM
VM
VM
VM
YAAA!!

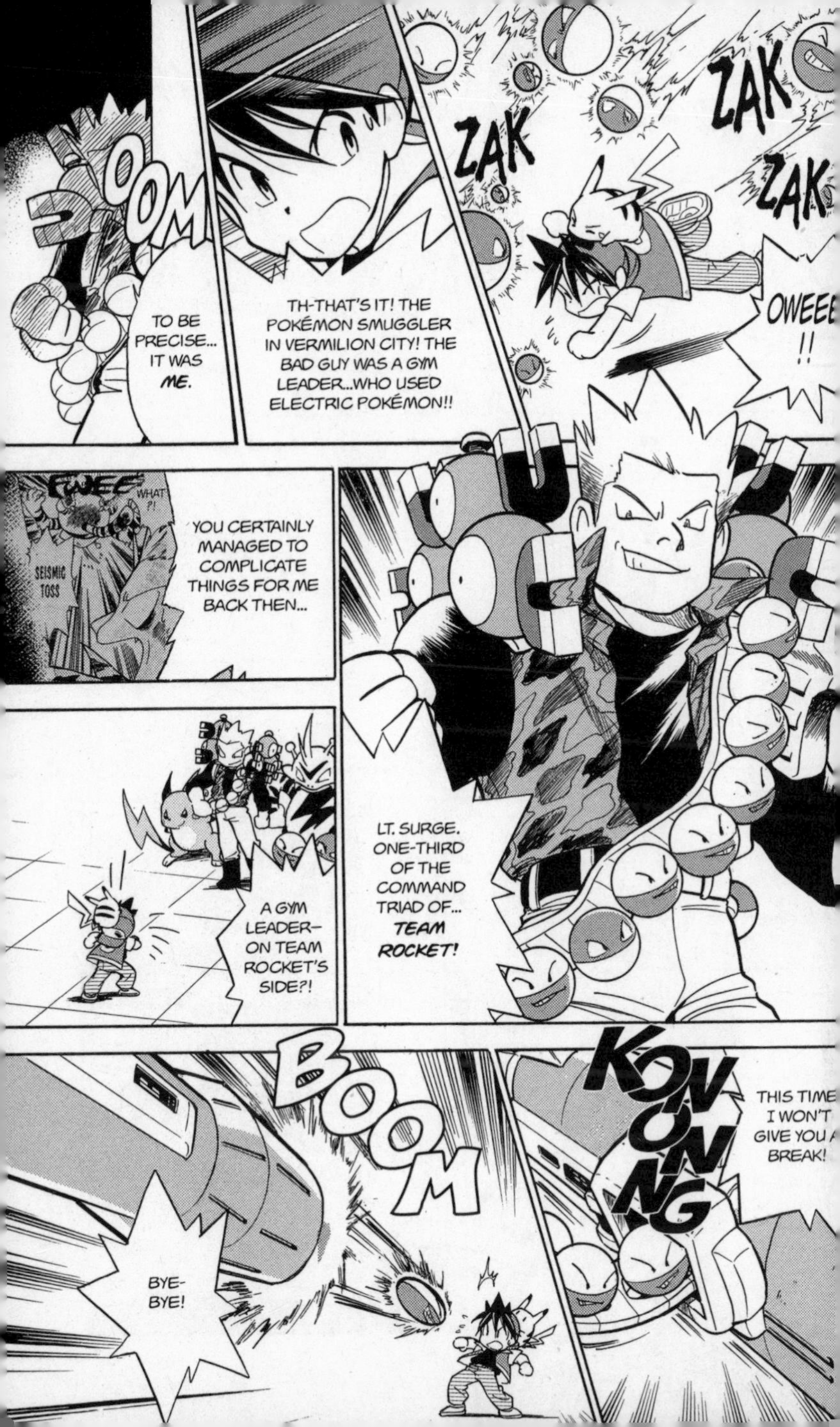
ZAK
ZAK
ZAK
OWEEE!!
TH-THAT'S IT! THE POKÉMON SMUGGLER IN VERMILION CITY! THE BAD GUY WAS A GYM LEADER...WHO USED ELECTRIC POKÉMON!!
OOOM
TO BE PRECISE... IT WAS *ME*.
LT. SURGE. ONE-THIRD OF THE COMMAND TRIAD OF... ***TEAM ROCKET!***
FWEE
WHAT?!
SEISMIC TOSS
YOU CERTAINLY MANAGED TO COMPLICATE THINGS FOR ME BACK THEN...
A GYM LEADER—ON TEAM ROCKET'S SIDE?!
THIS TIME I WON'T GIVE YOU A BREAK!
BOOOM
BYE-BYE!

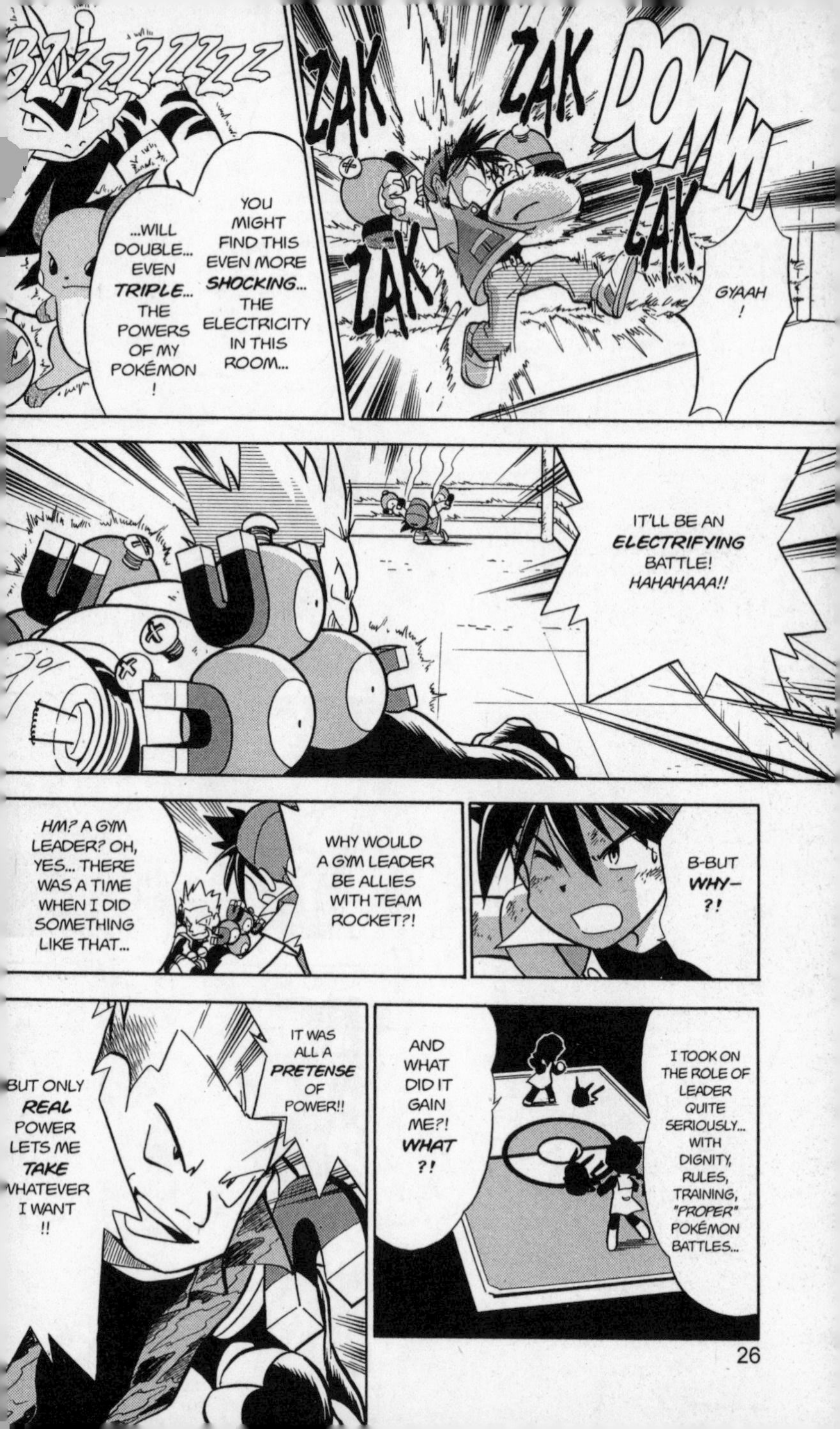
ZAK ZAK DOOM
ZAK
ZAK
GYAAH!
BZZZZZZZZ
YOU MIGHT FIND THIS EVEN MORE SHOCKING... THE ELECTRICITY IN THIS ROOM...
...WILL DOUBLE... EVEN TRIPLE... THE POWERS OF MY POKÉMON!
IT'LL BE AN ELECTRIFYING BATTLE! HAHAHAAA!!
B-BUT WHY—?!
WHY WOULD A GYM LEADER BE ALLIES WITH TEAM ROCKET?!
HM? A GYM LEADER? OH, YES... THERE WAS A TIME WHEN I DID SOMETHING LIKE THAT...
I TOOK ON THE ROLE OF LEADER QUITE SERIOUSLY... WITH DIGNITY, RULES, TRAINING, "PROPER" POKÉMON BATTLES...
AND WHAT DID IT GAIN ME?! WHAT?!
IT WAS ALL A PRETENSE OF POWER!!
BUT ONLY REAL POWER LETS ME TAKE WHATEVER I WANT!!

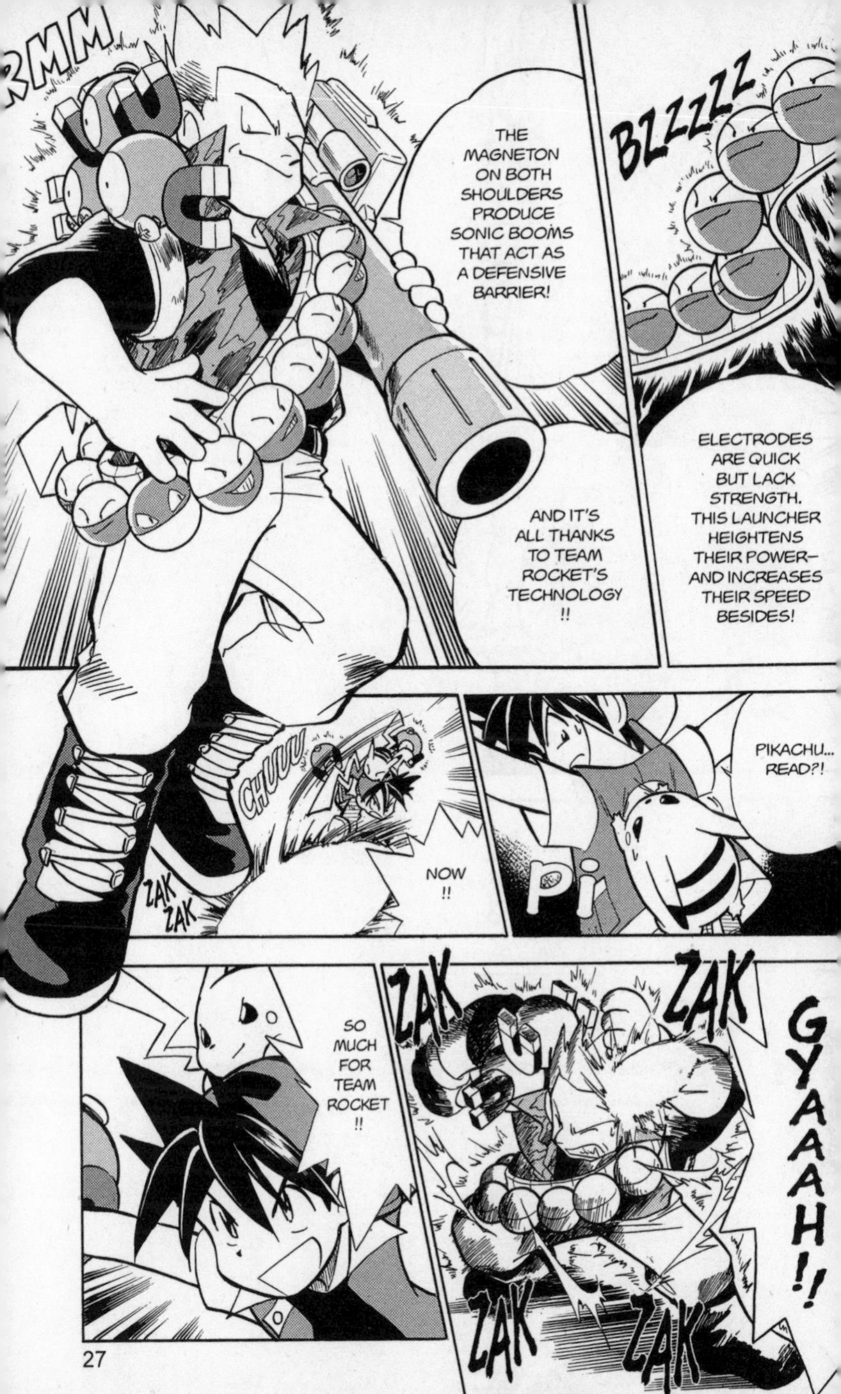
BZZZZZ
ELECTRODES ARE QUICK BUT LACK STRENGTH. THIS LAUNCHER HEIGHTENS THEIR POWER— AND INCREASES THEIR SPEED BESIDES!
RMM
THE MAGNETON ON BOTH SHOULDERS PRODUCE SONIC BOOMS THAT ACT AS A DEFENSIVE BARRIER!
AND IT'S ALL THANKS TO TEAM ROCKET'S TECHNOLOGY !!
PIKACHU... READ?!
pi
CHUUU
NOW !!
ZAK ZAK
ZAK
ZAK
GYAAAH!!
ZAK
ZAK
SO MUCH FOR TEAM ROCKET !!

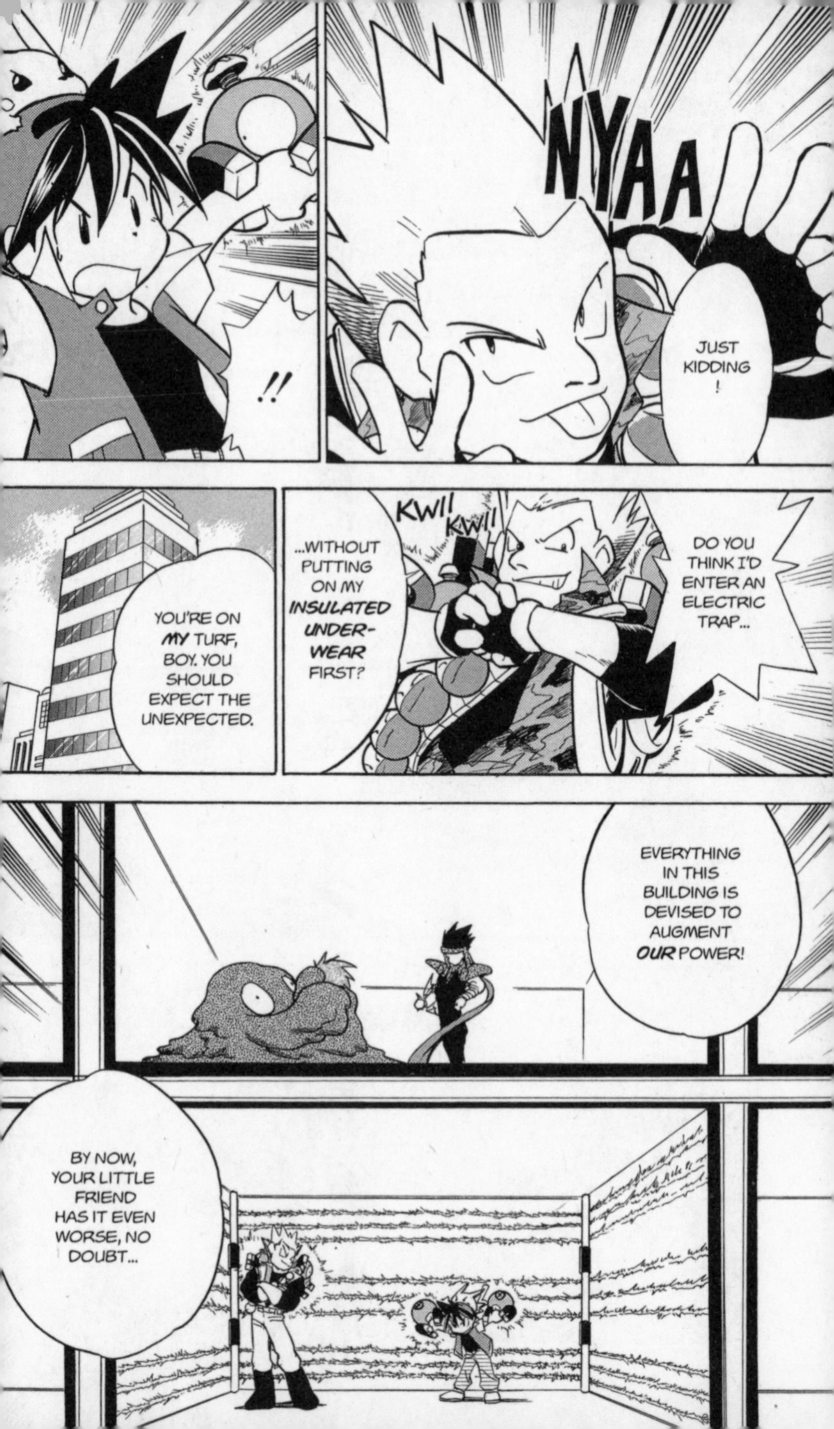
NYAA
JUST KIDDING !
!!
DO YOU THINK I'D ENTER AN ELECTRIC TRAP...
KWI! KWI!
...WITHOUT PUTTING ON MY INSULATED UNDER-WEAR FIRST?
YOU'RE ON MY TURF, BOY. YOU SHOULD EXPECT THE UNEXPECTED.
EVERYTHING IN THIS BUILDING IS DEVISED TO AUGMENT OUR POWER!
BY NOW, YOUR LITTLE FRIEND HAS IT EVEN WORSE, NO DOUBT...

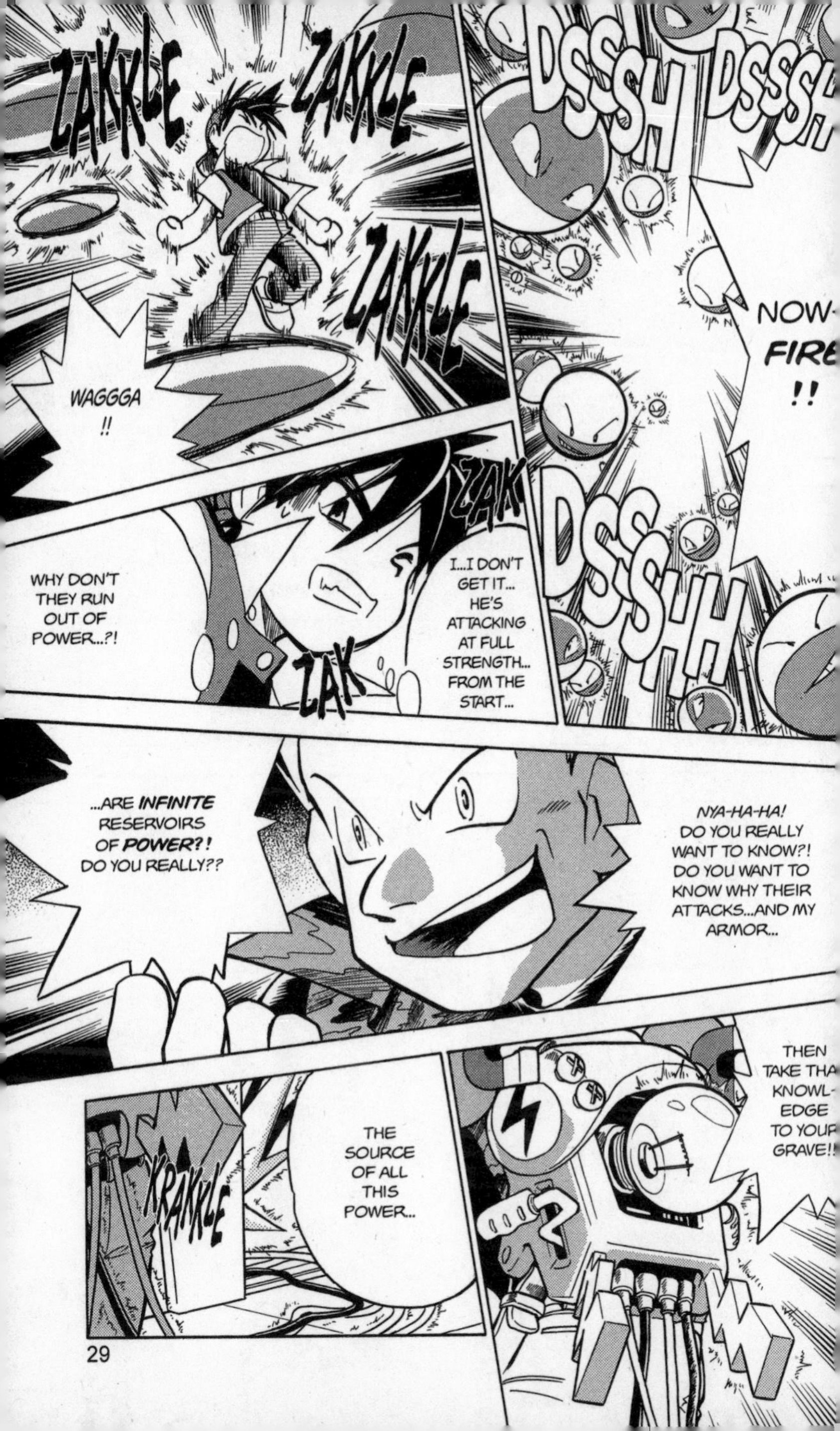
DSSSH
DSSSH
NOW-
FIRE
!!
DSSUH
ZAKKLE
ZAKKLE
ZAKKLE
WAGGGA
!!
I...I DON'T GET IT... HE'S ATTACKING AT FULL STRENGTH... FROM THE START...
ZAK
ZAK
WHY DON'T THEY RUN OUT OF POWER...?!
NYA-HA-HA! DO YOU REALLY WANT TO KNOW?! DO YOU WANT TO KNOW WHY THEIR ATTACKS...AND MY ARMOR...
...ARE *INFINITE* RESERVOIRS OF *POWER?!* DO YOU REALLY??
THEN TAKE THA KNOWL- EDGE TO YOUR GRAVE!!
THE SOURCE OF ALL THIS POWER...
KRAKKLE

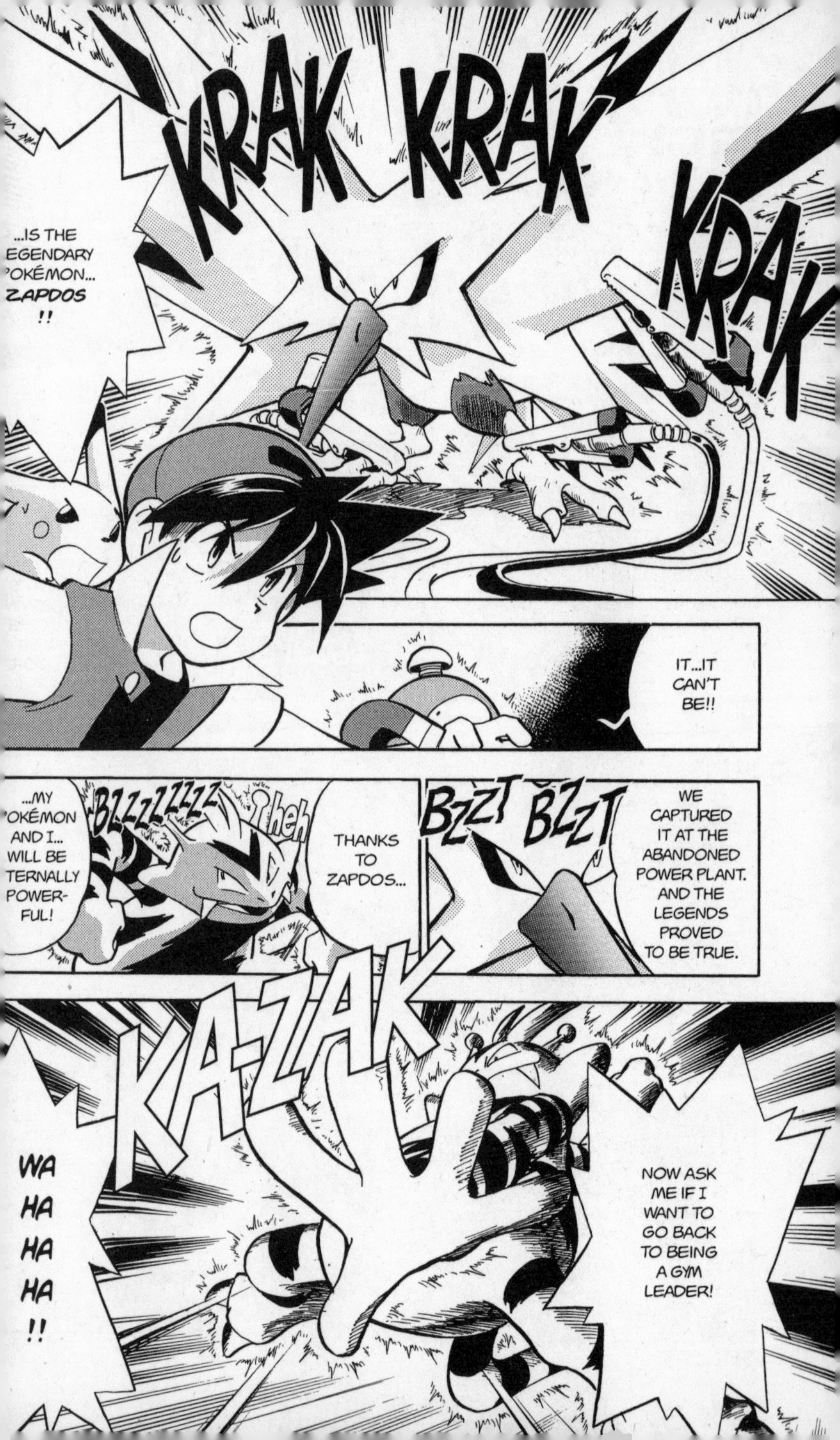
KRAK KRAK KRAK
...IS THE EGENDARY OKÉMON... ZAPDOS !!
IT...IT CAN'T BE!!
BZZT BZZT
WE CAPTURED IT AT THE ABANDONED POWER PLANT. AND THE LEGENDS PROVED TO BE TRUE.
THANKS TO ZAPDOS...
heh
BZZZZZZZZ
...MY OKÉMON AND I... WILL BE TERNALLY POWER-FUL!
KA-ZAK
NOW ASK ME IF I WANT TO GO BACK TO BEING A GYM LEADER!
WA HA HA HA !!

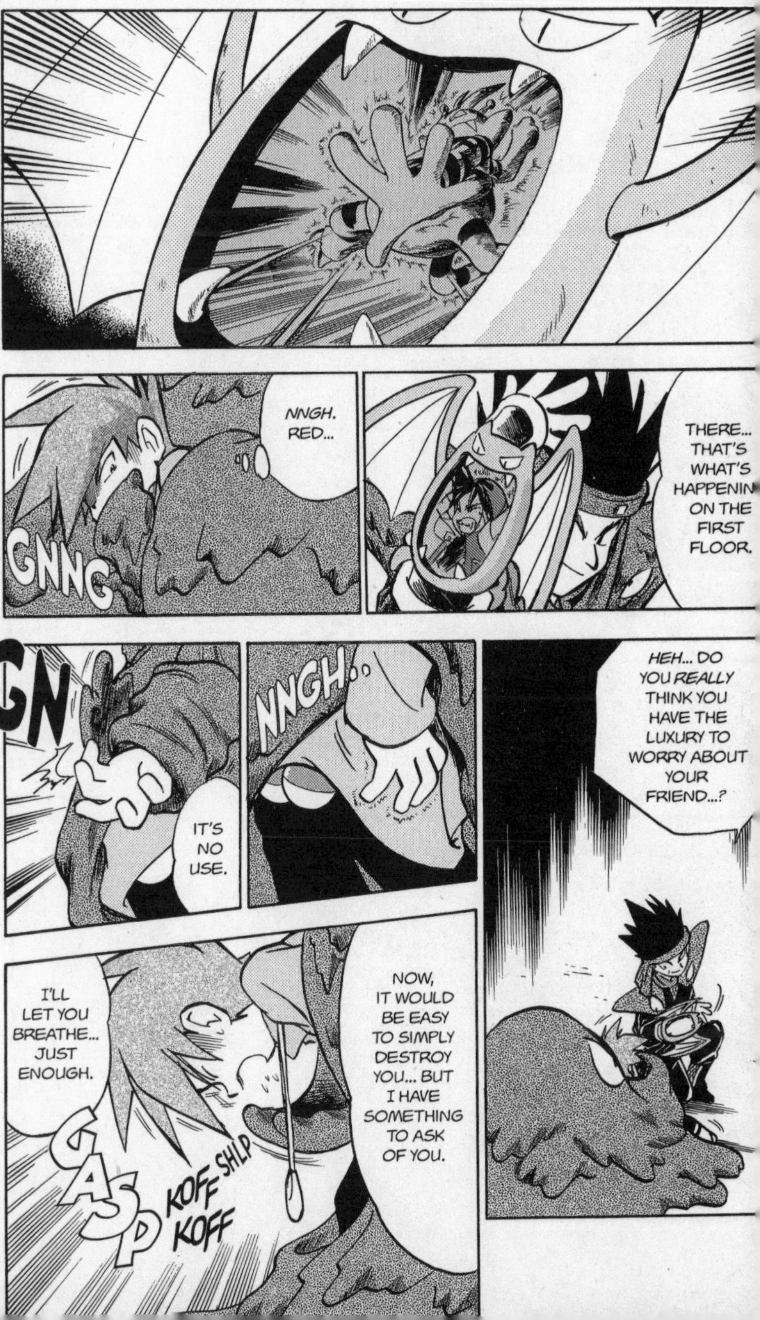
THERE... THAT'S WHAT'S HAPPENIN ON THE FIRST FLOOR.
NNGH. RED...
GNNG
HEH... DO YOU *REALLY* THINK YOU HAVE THE LUXURY TO WORRY ABOUT YOUR FRIEND...?
NNGH..
GN
IT'S NO USE.
NOW, IT WOULD BE EASY TO SIMPLY DESTROY YOU... BUT I HAVE SOMETHING TO ASK OF YOU.
I'LL LET YOU BREATHE... JUST ENOUGH.
SHLP
GASP
KOFF KOFF

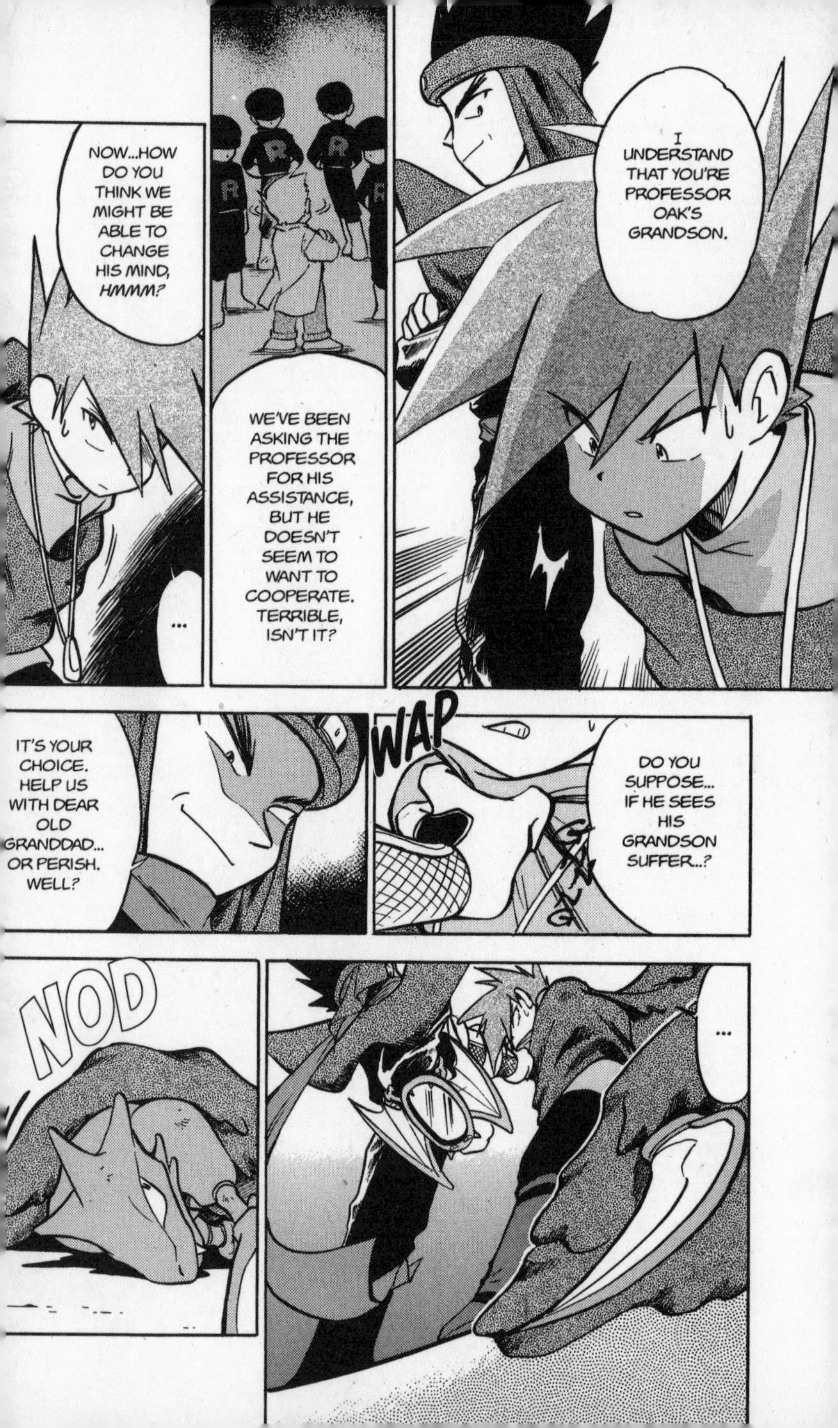
I UNDERSTAND THAT YOU'RE PROFESSOR OAK'S GRANDSON.
WE'VE BEEN ASKING THE PROFESSOR FOR HIS ASSISTANCE, BUT HE DOESN'T SEEM TO WANT TO COOPERATE. TERRIBLE, ISN'T IT?
NOW...HOW DO YOU THINK WE MIGHT BE ABLE TO CHANGE HIS MIND, *HMMM?*
...
WAP
DO YOU SUPPOSE... IF HE SEES HIS GRANDSON SUFFER...?
IT'S YOUR CHOICE. HELP US WITH DEAR OLD GRANDDAD... OR PERISH. WELL?
...
NOD

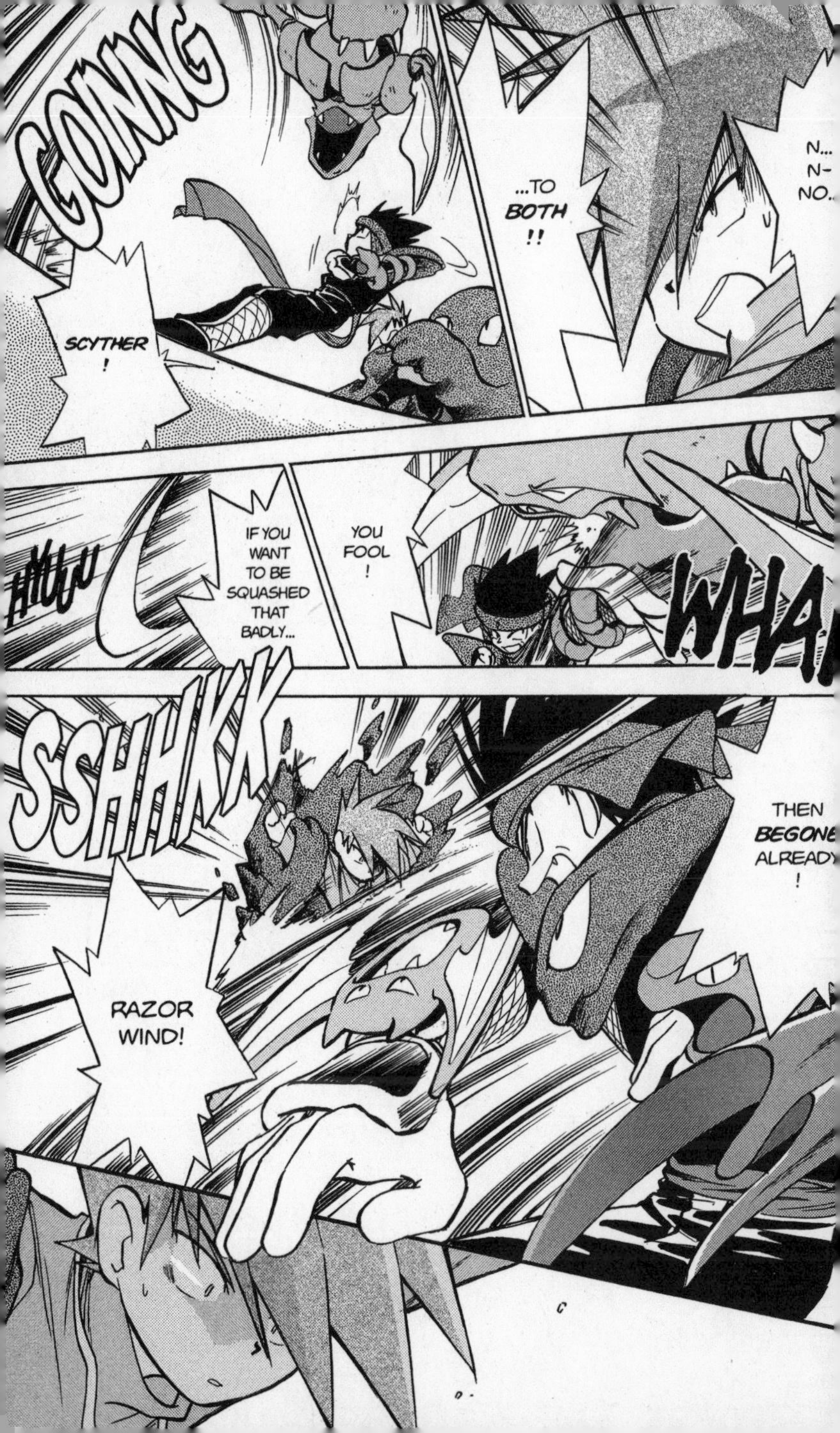
N... N- NO...
...TO BOTH !!
GOONG
SCYTHER !
WHA
YOU FOOL !
IF YOU WANT TO BE SQUASHED THAT BADLY...
THEN BEGONE ALREADY !
SSHHKK
RAZOR WIND!

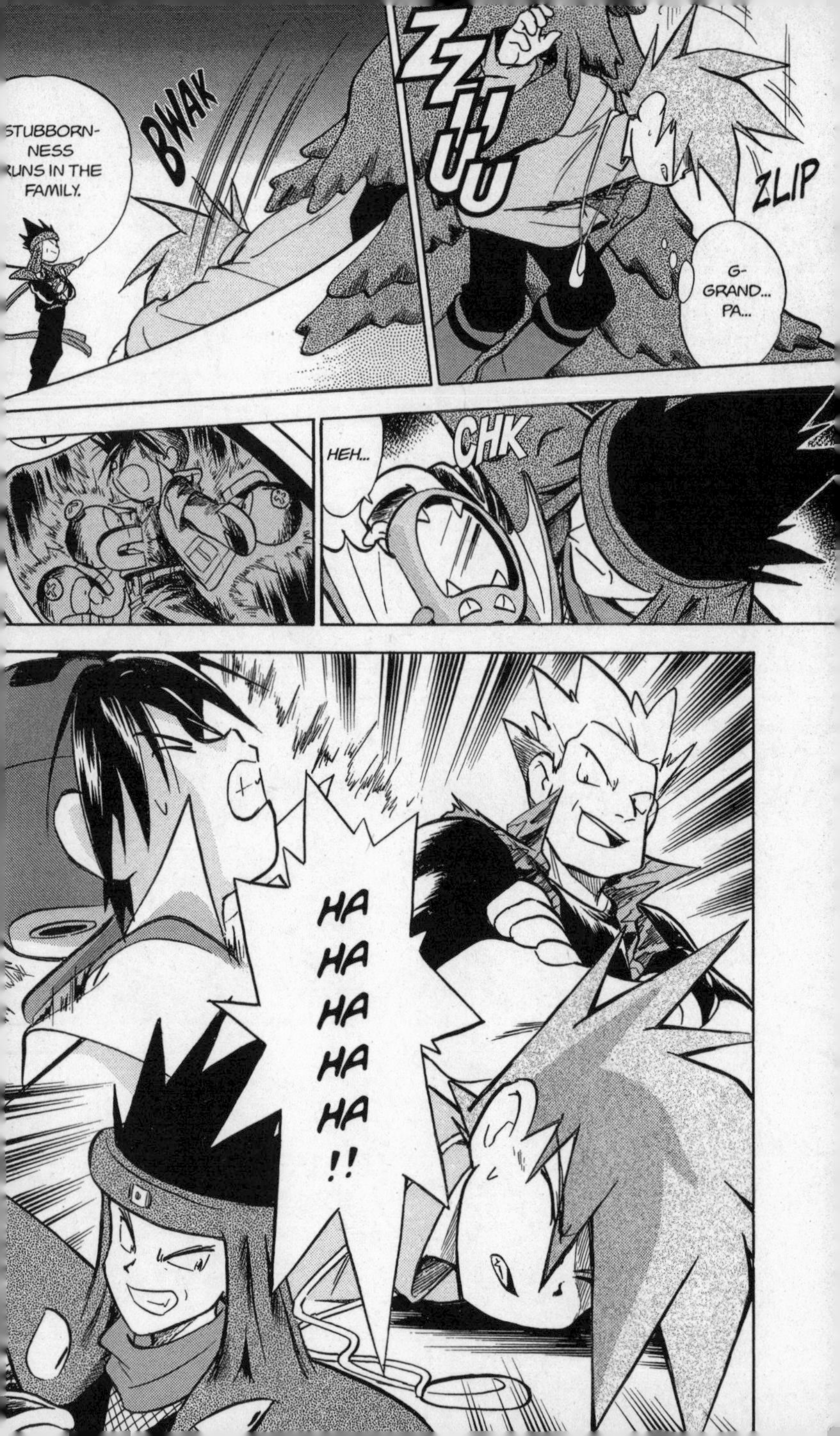
ZZUUUU
ZLIP
G-GRAND... PA...
BWAK
STUBBORN-NESS RUNS IN THE FAMILY.
CHK
HEH...
HA HA HA HA HA !!

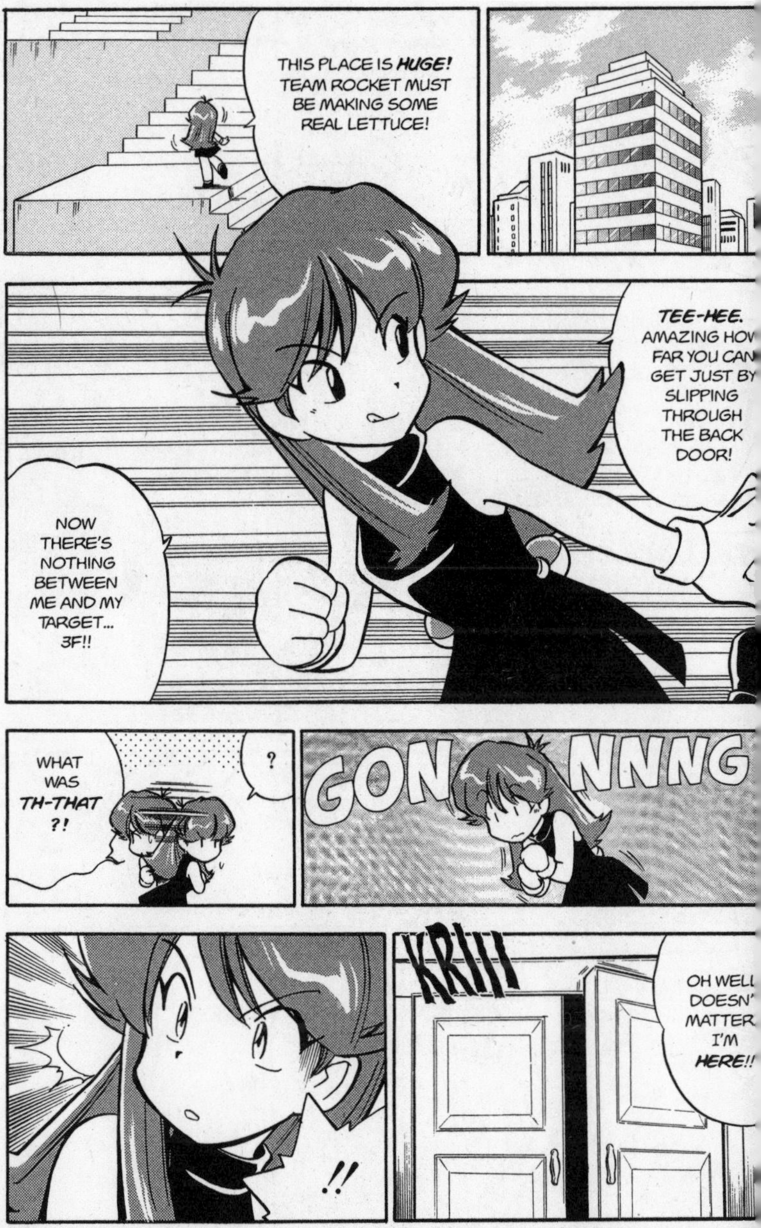
THIS PLACE IS ***HUGE!*** TEAM ROCKET MUST BE MAKING SOME REAL LETTUCE!
TEE-HEE. AMAZING HOW FAR YOU CAN GET JUST BY SLIPPING THROUGH THE BACK DOOR!
NOW THERE'S NOTHING BETWEEN ME AND MY TARGET... 3F!!
GONNNNG
?
WHAT WAS ***TH-THAT?!***
KRIII
OH WELL DOESN'T MATTER. I'M ***HERE!!***
!!

30 Zap! Zap! Zapdos!

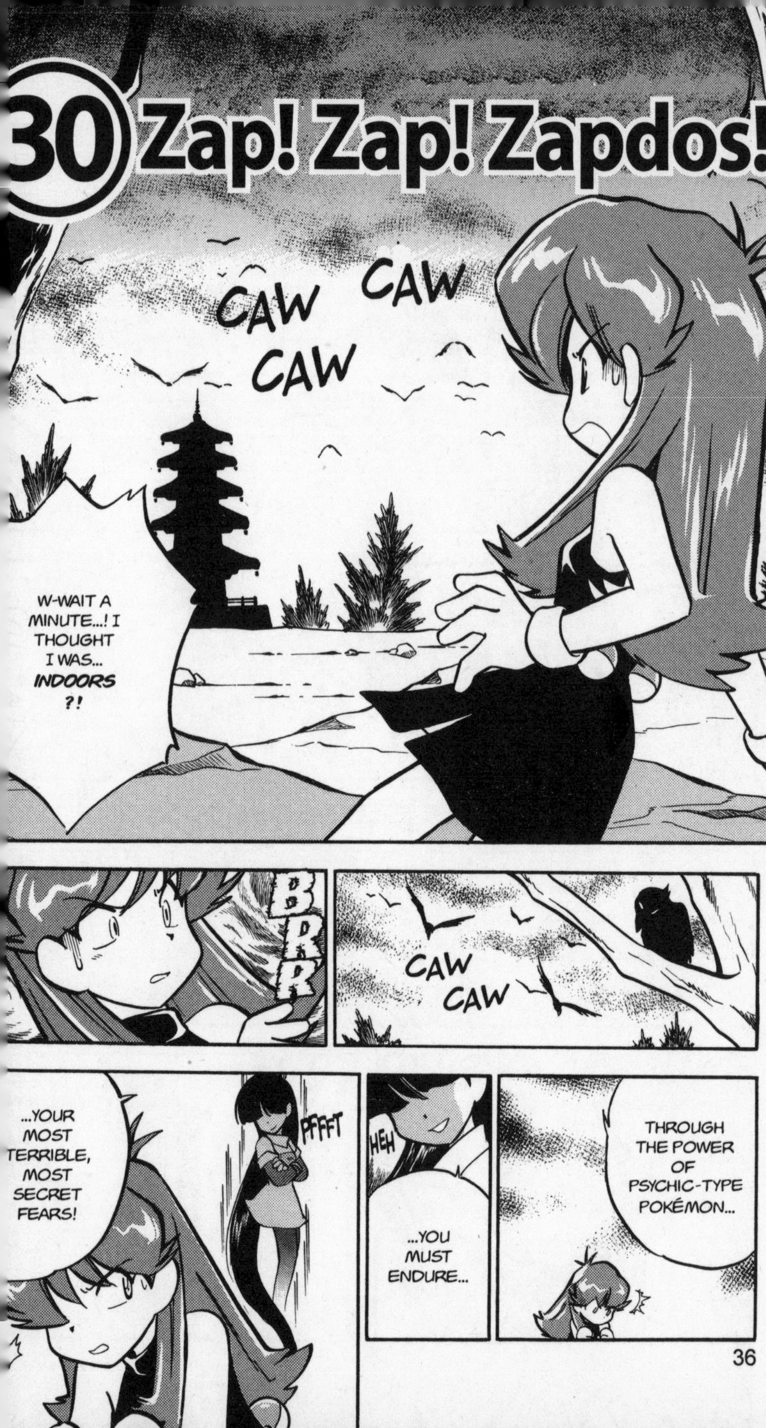
CAW CAW
CAW
W-WAIT A MINUTE...! I THOUGHT I WAS... INDOORS ?!
CAW CAW
BRR
THROUGH THE POWER OF PSYCHIC-TYPE POKÉMON...
HEH
...YOU MUST ENDURE...
PFFFT
...YOUR MOST TERRIBLE, MOST SECRET FEARS!

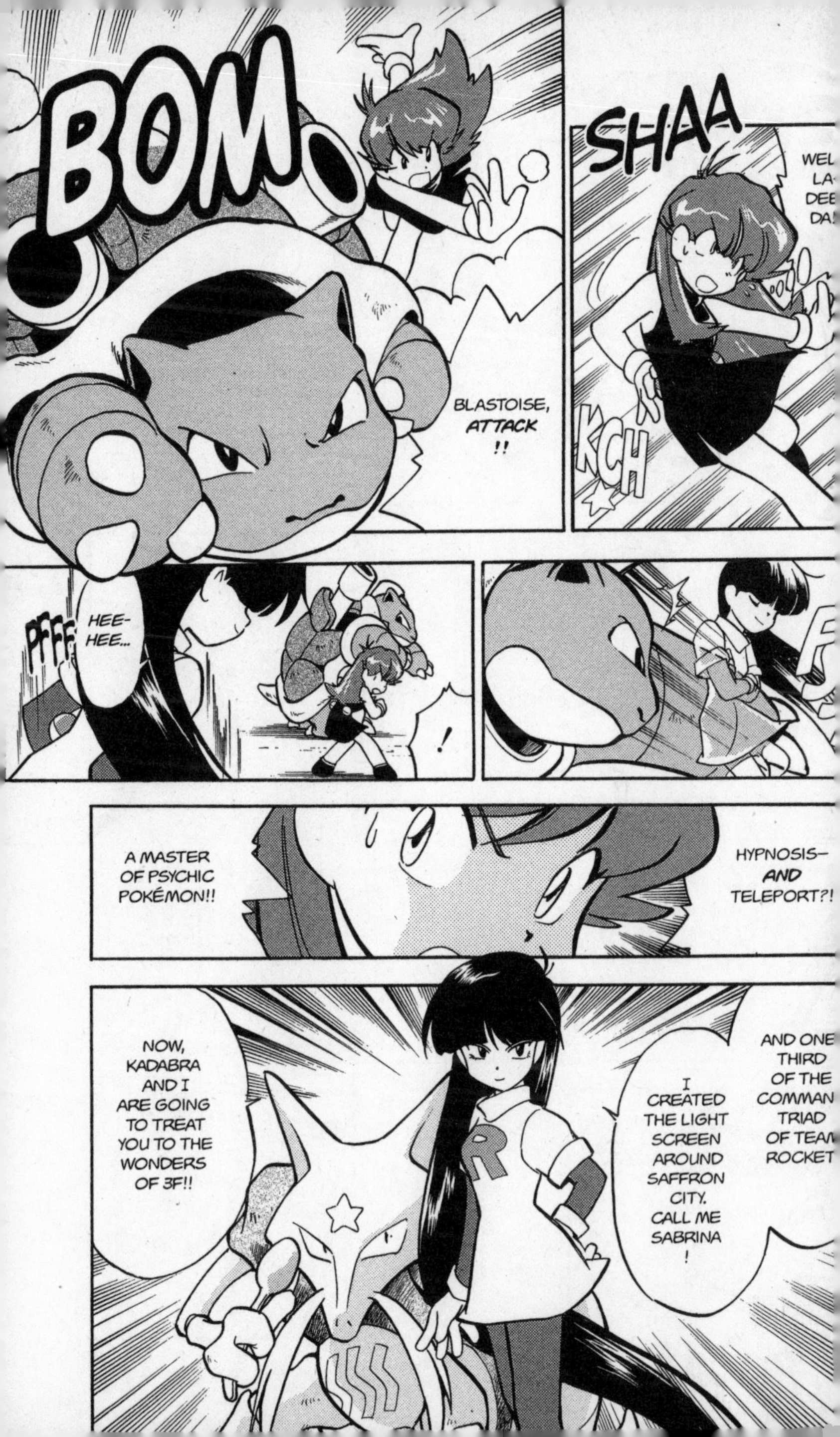
SHAA
WEL LA-DEE DA!
KCH
BOM
BLASTOISE, ATTACK!!
PFFF
HEE-HEE...
!
HYPNOSIS—AND TELEPORT?!
A MASTER OF PSYCHIC POKÉMON!!
AND ONE THIRD OF THE COMMAN TRIAD OF TEAM ROCKET
I CREATED THE LIGHT SCREEN AROUND SAFFRON CITY. CALL ME SABRINA!
NOW, KADABRA AND I ARE GOING TO TREAT YOU TO THE WONDERS OF 3F!!

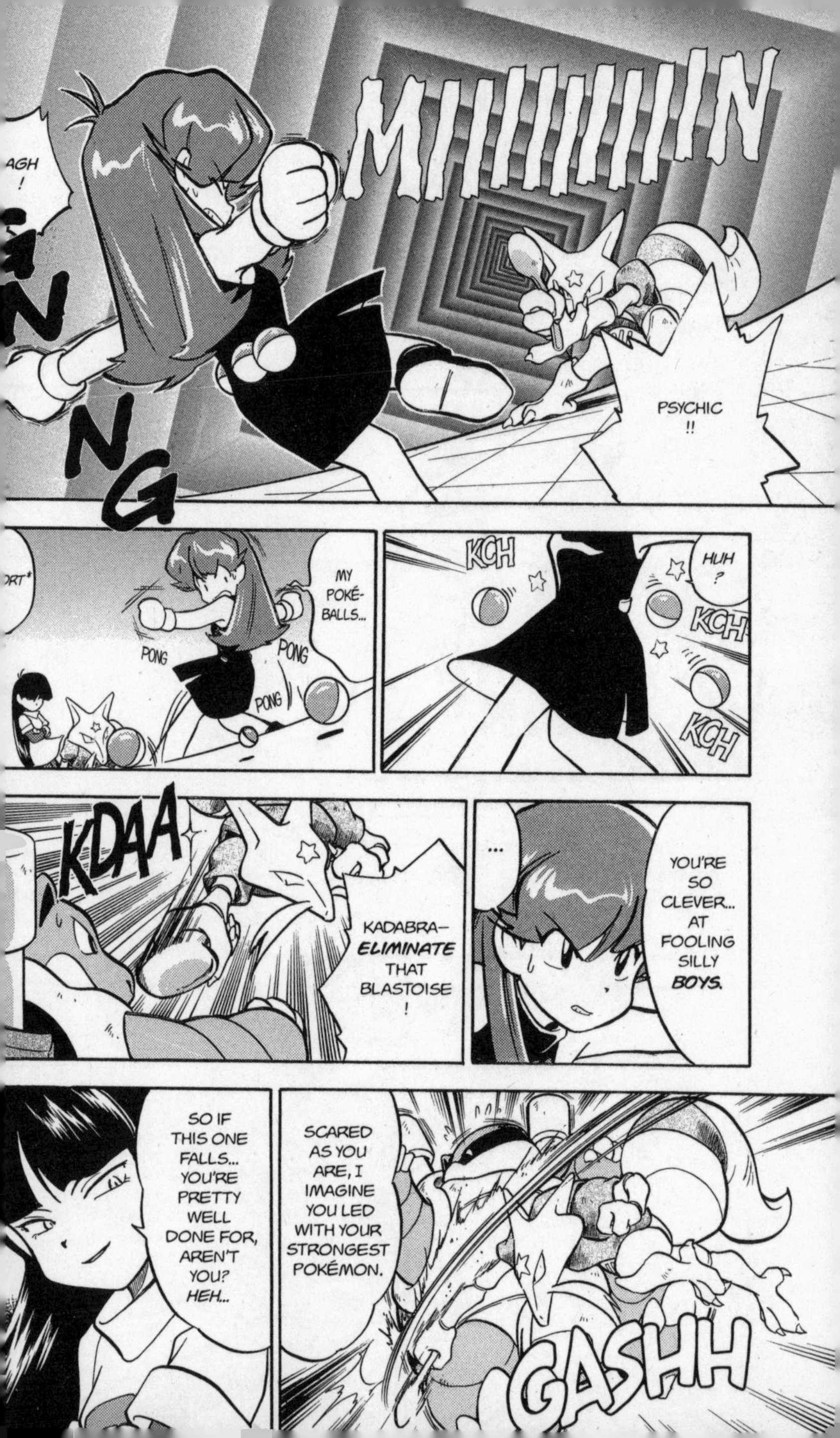
MIIIIIIIIIN
PSYCHIC !!
AGH !
HUH ?
KCH
KCH
KCH
MY POKÉ-BALLS...
PONG
PONG
PONG
YOU'RE SO CLEVER... AT FOOLING SILLY BOYS.
...
KADABRA—ELIMINATE THAT BLASTOISE !
KDAA
SCARED AS YOU ARE, I IMAGINE YOU LED WITH YOUR STRONGEST POKÉMON.
GASHH
SO IF THIS ONE FALLS... YOU'RE PRETTY WELL DONE FOR, AREN'T YOU? HEH...

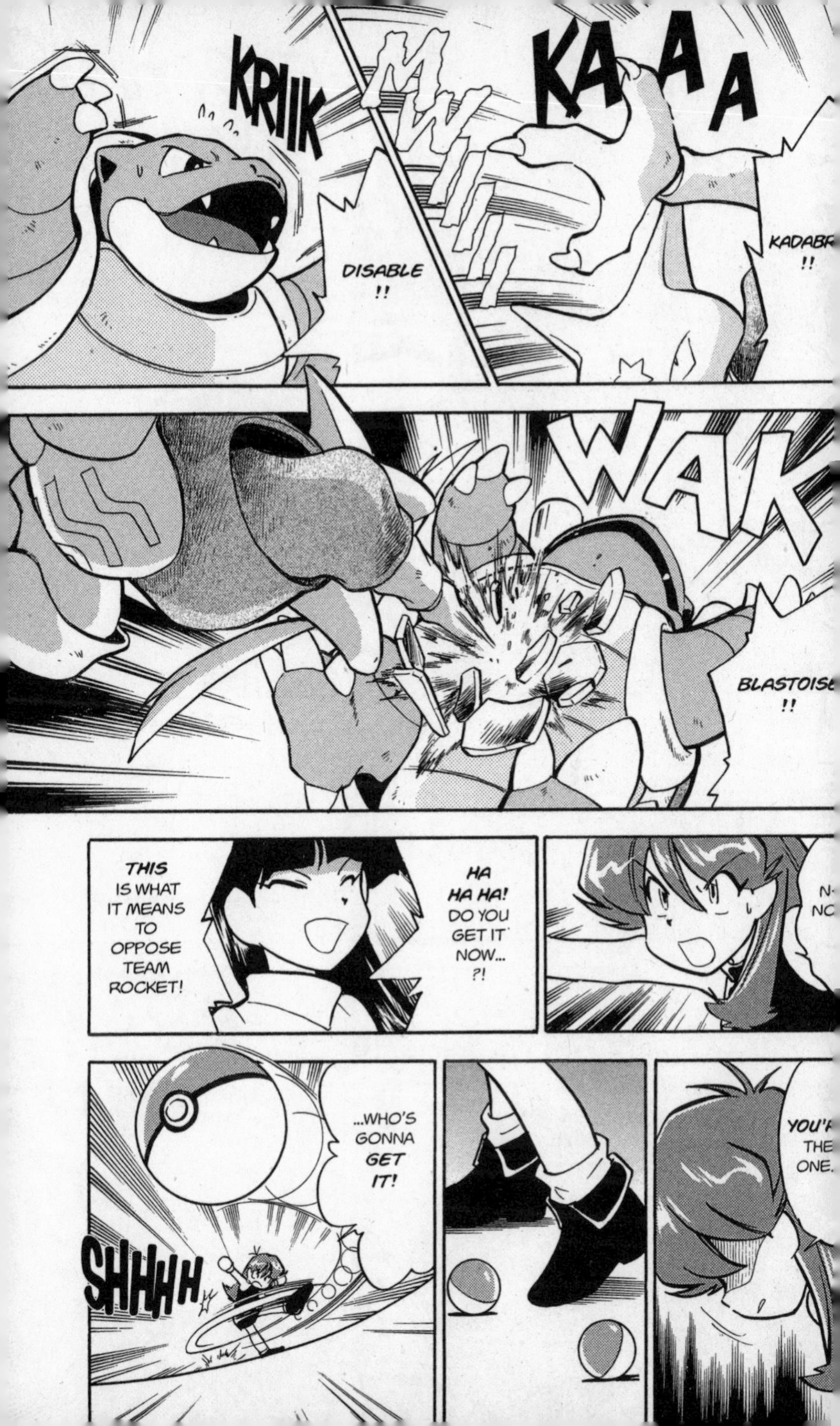
KA A A A
KADABR !!
KRIIK
DISABLE !!
WAK
BLASTOIS !!
N- NO
HA HA HA! DO YOU GET IT NOW... ?!
THIS IS WHAT IT MEANS TO OPPOSE TEAM ROCKET!
YOU'R THE ONE.
...WHO'S GONNA GET IT!
SHHHH

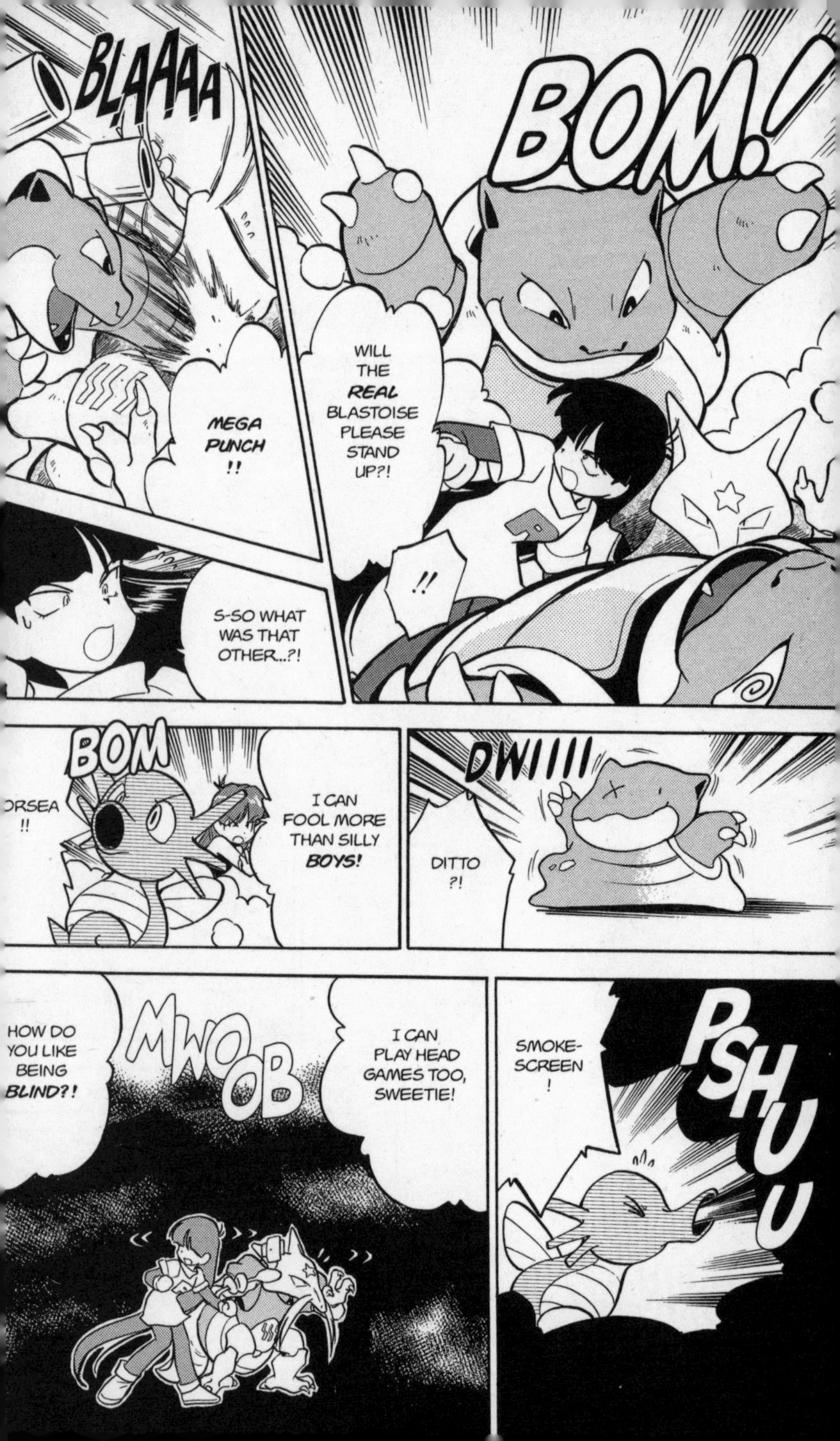
BOM!
WILL THE REAL BLASTOISE PLEASE STAND UP?!
!!
BLAAAA
MEGA PUNCH !!
S-SO WHAT WAS THAT OTHER...?!
DWIIII
DITTO ?!
I CAN FOOL MORE THAN SILLY BOYS!
BOM
ORSEA !!
PSHUUU
SMOKE-SCREEN !
I CAN PLAY HEAD GAMES TOO, SWEETIE!
MWOOB
HOW DO YOU LIKE BEING BLIND?!

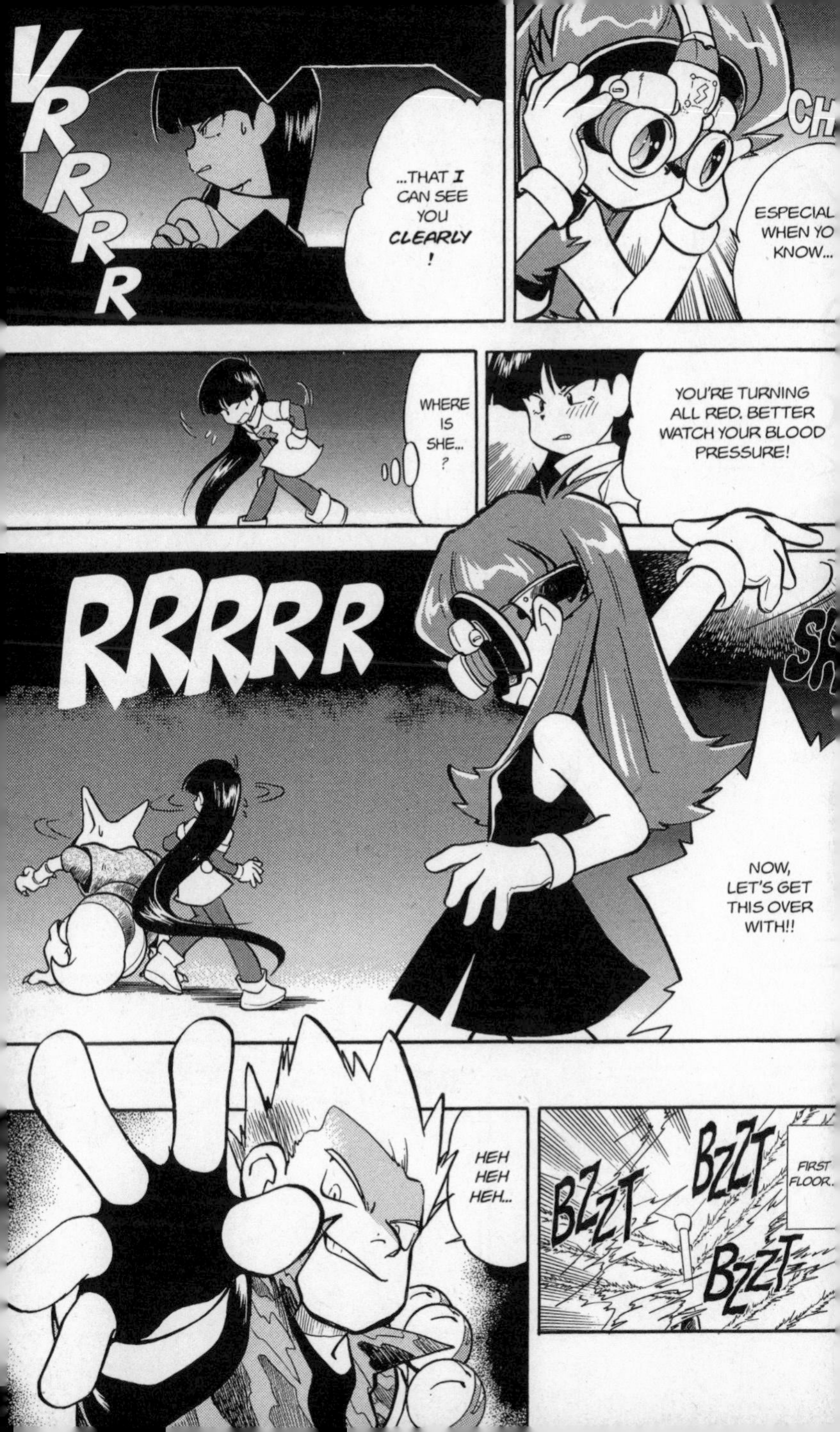

ESPECIAL
WHEN YO
KNOW...
VRRRR
...THAT I CAN SEE YOU CLEARLY!
YOU'RE TURNING ALL RED. BETTER WATCH YOUR BLOOD PRESSURE!
WHERE IS SHE...?
NOW, LET'S GET THIS OVER WITH!!
RRRRRR
FIRST FLOOR..
BZZT
BZZT
BZZT
HEH HEH HEH...

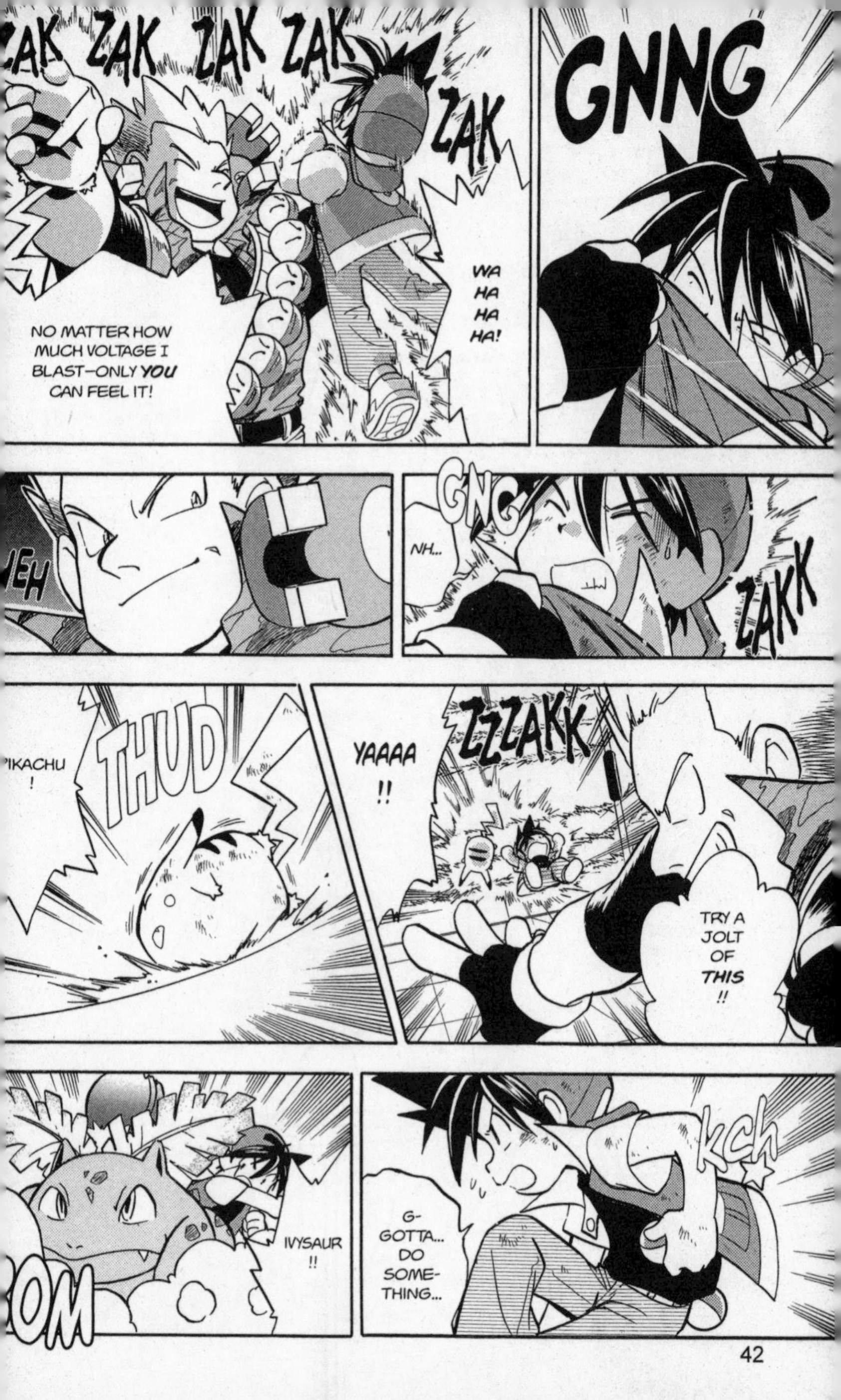
GNNG
ZAK ZAK ZAK ZAK
ZAK
WA HA HA HA!
NO MATTER HOW MUCH VOLTAGE I BLAST—ONLY **YOU** CAN FEEL IT!
GNG
NH...
ZAKK
ZZZAKK
YAAAA !!
TRY A JOLT OF **THIS** !!
THUD
PIKACHU !
kch
G- GOTTA... DO SOME-THING...
IVYSAUR !!

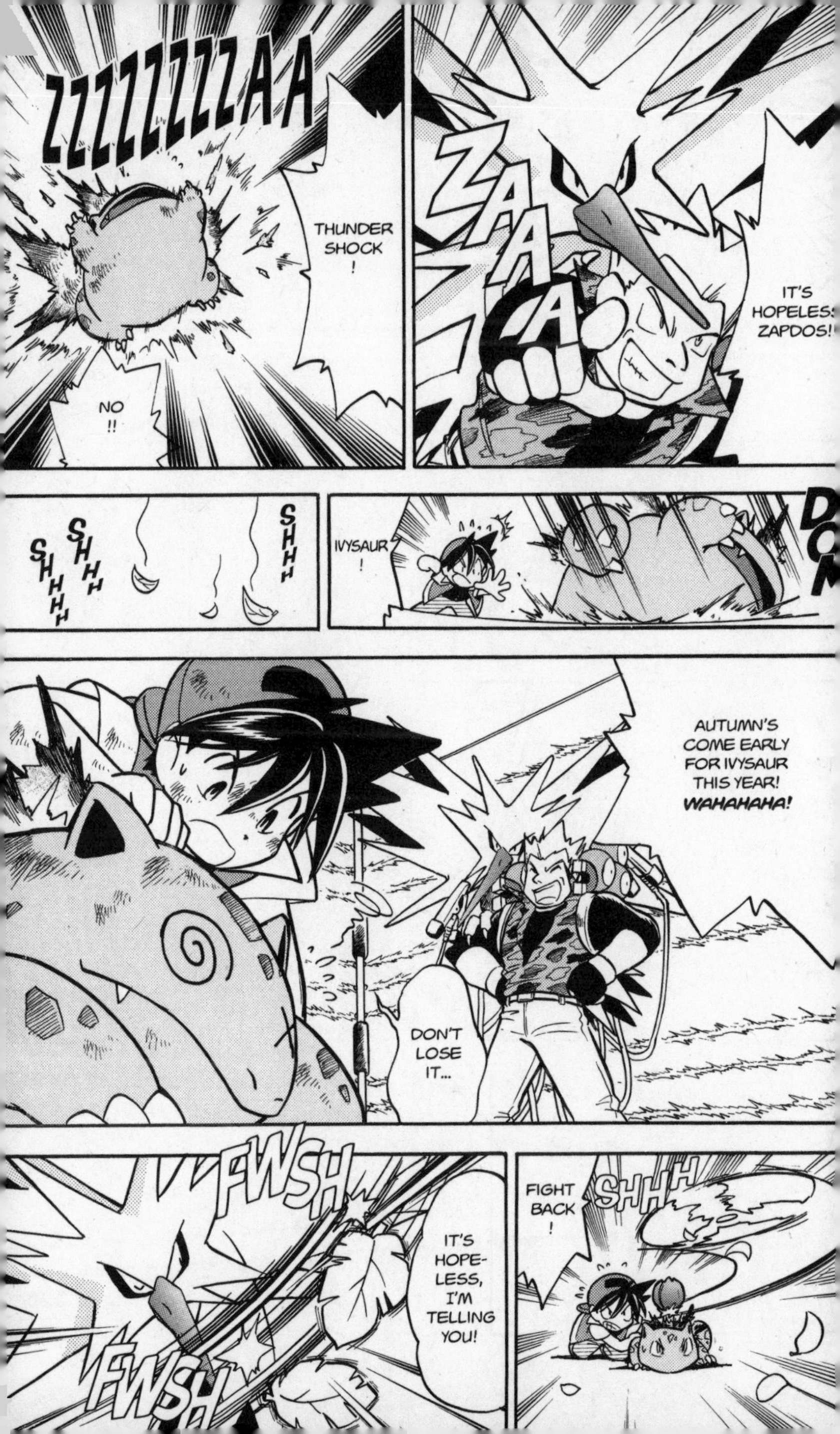
ZAAA
IT'S HOPELES ZAPDOS!
ZZZZZZZZAA
THUNDER SHOCK!
NO!!
DOM
IVYSAUR!
SHHH
SHHHH
SHHHH
AUTUMN'S COME EARLY FOR IVYSAUR THIS YEAR! WAHAHAHA!
DON'T LOSE IT...
FIGHT BACK!
SHHH
FWSH
IT'S HOPE-LESS, I'M TELLING YOU!
FWSH

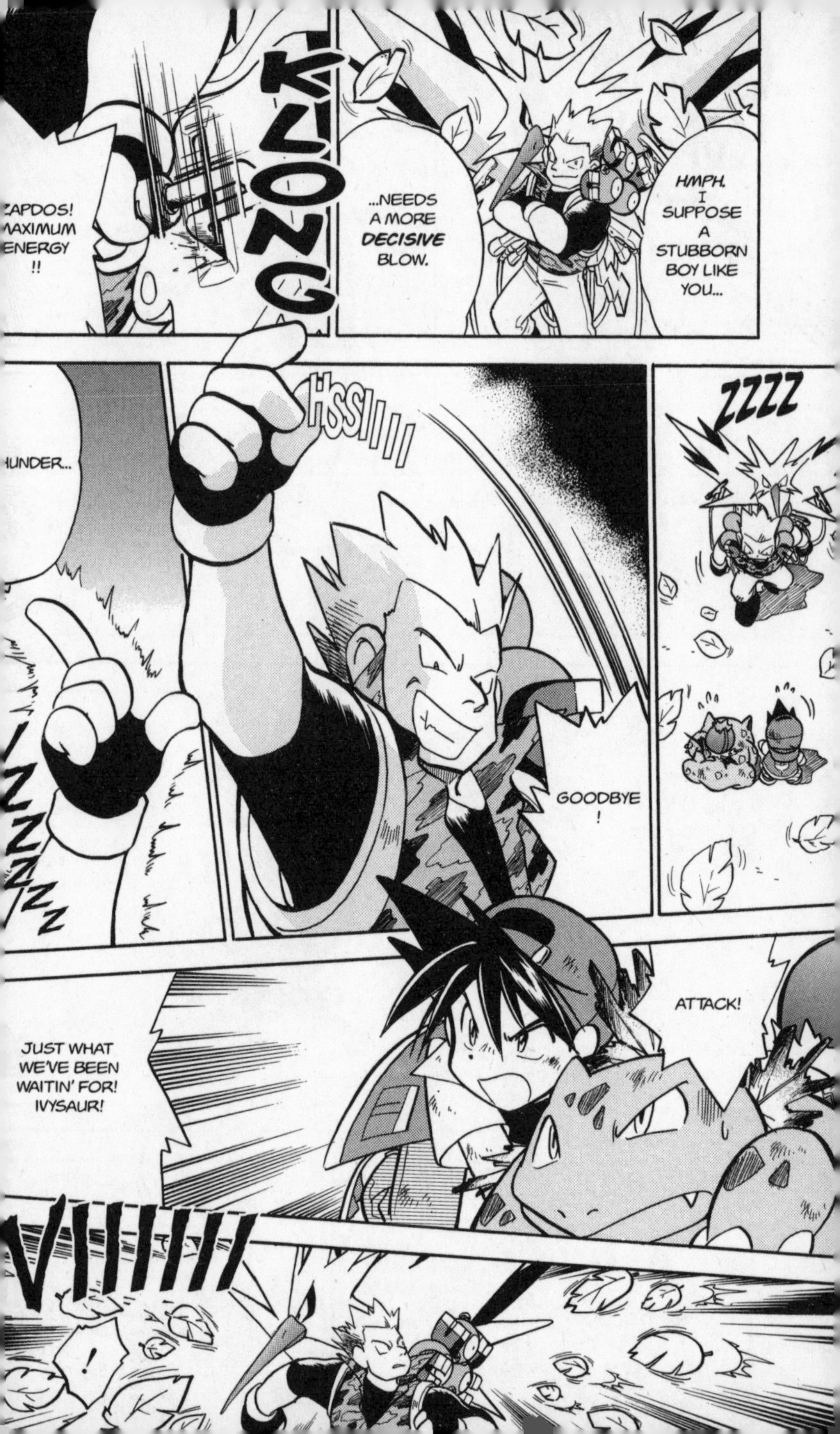
HMPH. I SUPPOSE A STUBBORN BOY LIKE YOU...
...NEEDS A MORE DECISIVE BLOW.
KLONG
ZAPDOS! MAXIMUM ENERGY !!
ZZZZ
HSSIIII
GOODBYE !
HUNDER...
ZZZZZZ
ATTACK!
JUST WHAT WE'VE BEEN WAITIN' FOR! IVYSAUR!
VIIIIII
!

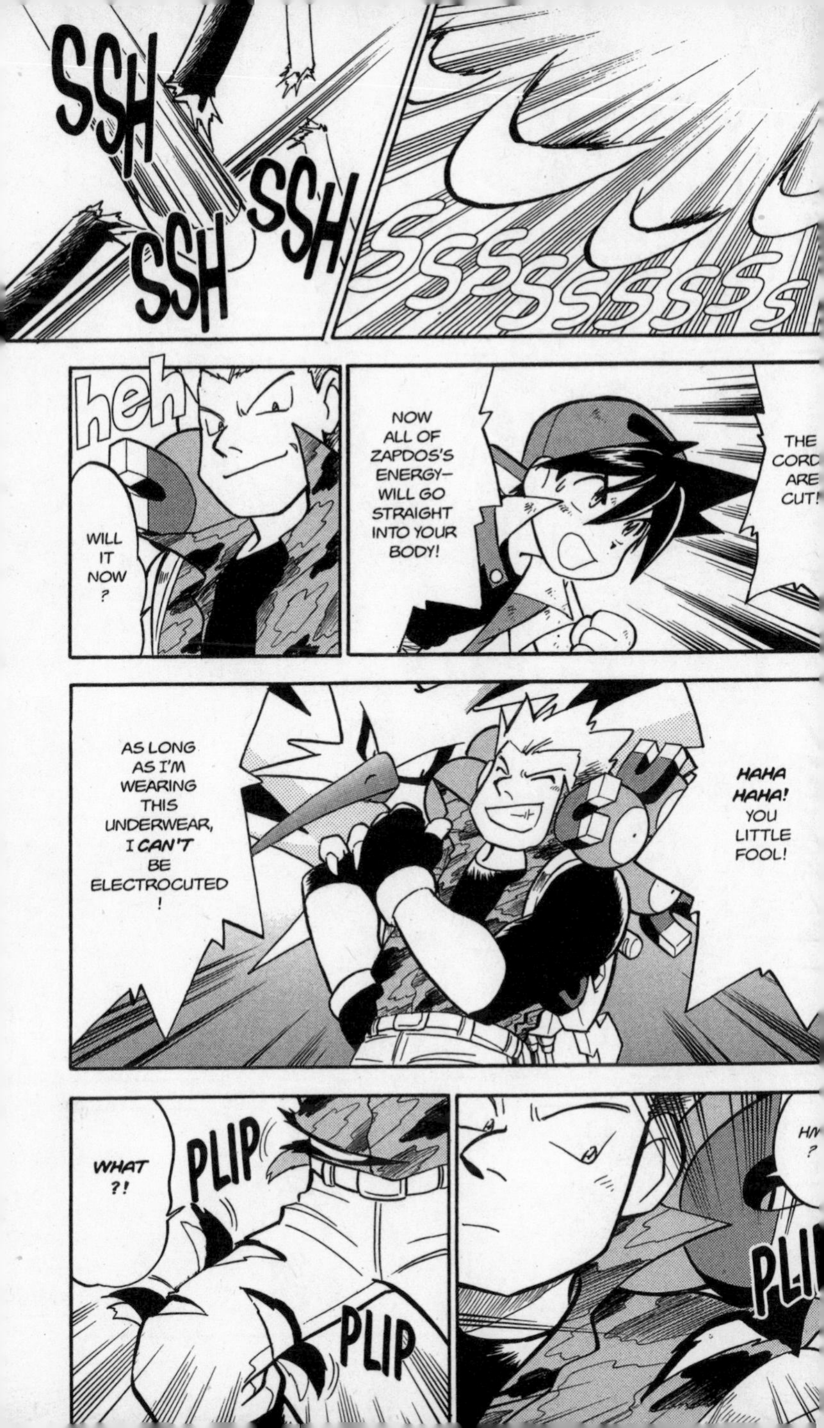
SSSSSSSSs
SSH
SSH
SSH
THE CORD ARE CUT!
NOW ALL OF ZAPDOS'S ENERGY— WILL GO STRAIGHT INTO YOUR BODY!
heh
WILL IT NOW?
HAHA HAHA! YOU LITTLE FOOL!
AS LONG AS I'M WEARING THIS UNDERWEAR, I CAN'T BE ELECTROCUTED!
HM?
PLI
PLIP
WHAT?!
PLIP

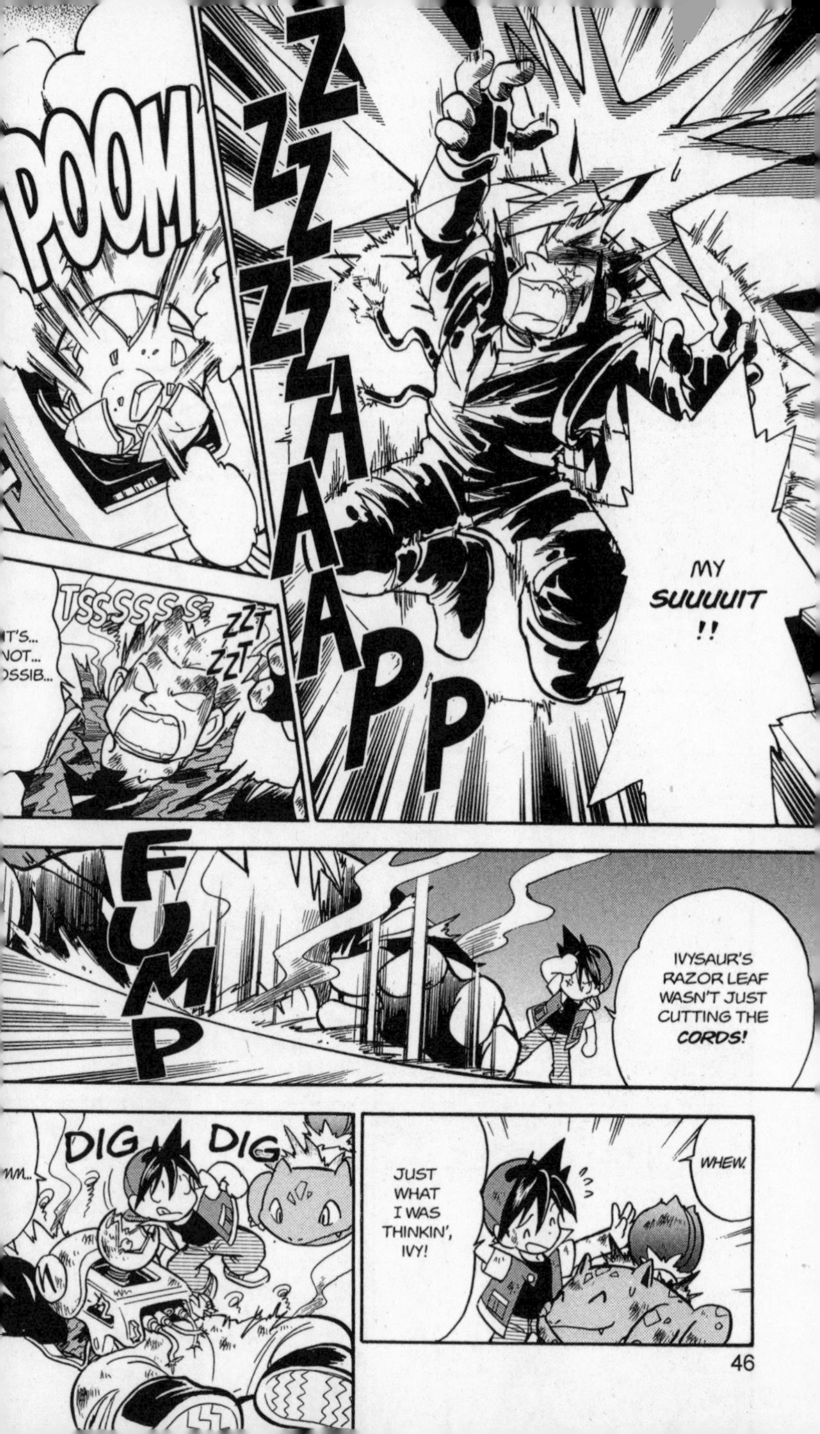
ZZZZZAAAPP
MY SUUUUIT !!
POOM
TSSSSSS
ZZT
ZZT
T'S...
NOT...
OSSIB...
IVYSAUR'S RAZOR LEAF WASN'T JUST CUTTING THE CORDS!
FUMP
WHEW.
JUST WHAT I WAS THINKIN', IVY!
DIG DIG
MM...

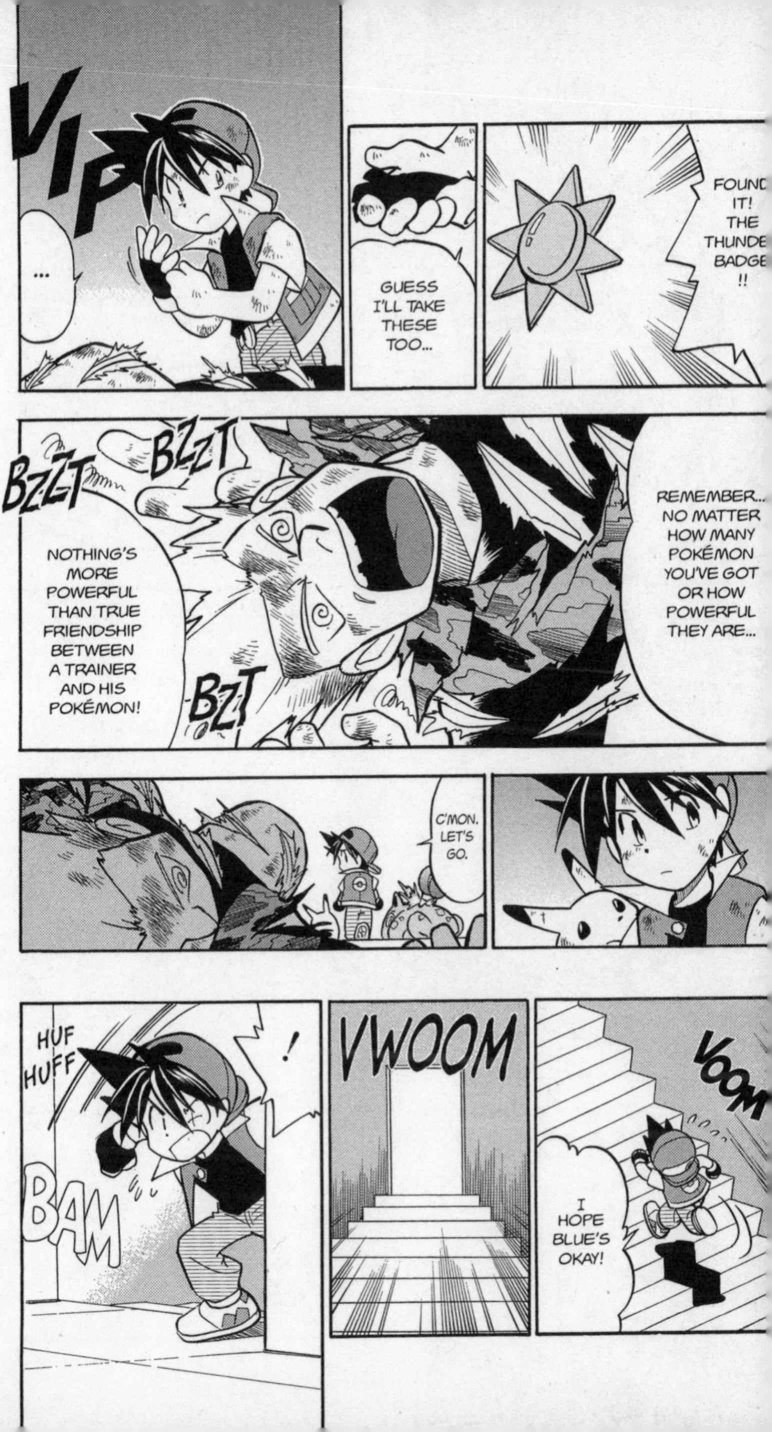
FOUND IT! THE THUNDE BADGE !!
GUESS I'LL TAKE THESE TOO...
VIP
...
REMEMBER... NO MATTER HOW MANY POKÉMON YOU'VE GOT OR HOW POWERFUL THEY ARE...
BZZT
BZZT
NOTHING'S MORE POWERFUL THAN TRUE FRIENDSHIP BETWEEN A TRAINER AND HIS POKÉMON!
BZT
C'MON. LET'S GO.
VOOM
I HOPE BLUE'S OKAY!
VWOOM
!
HUF HUFF
BAM

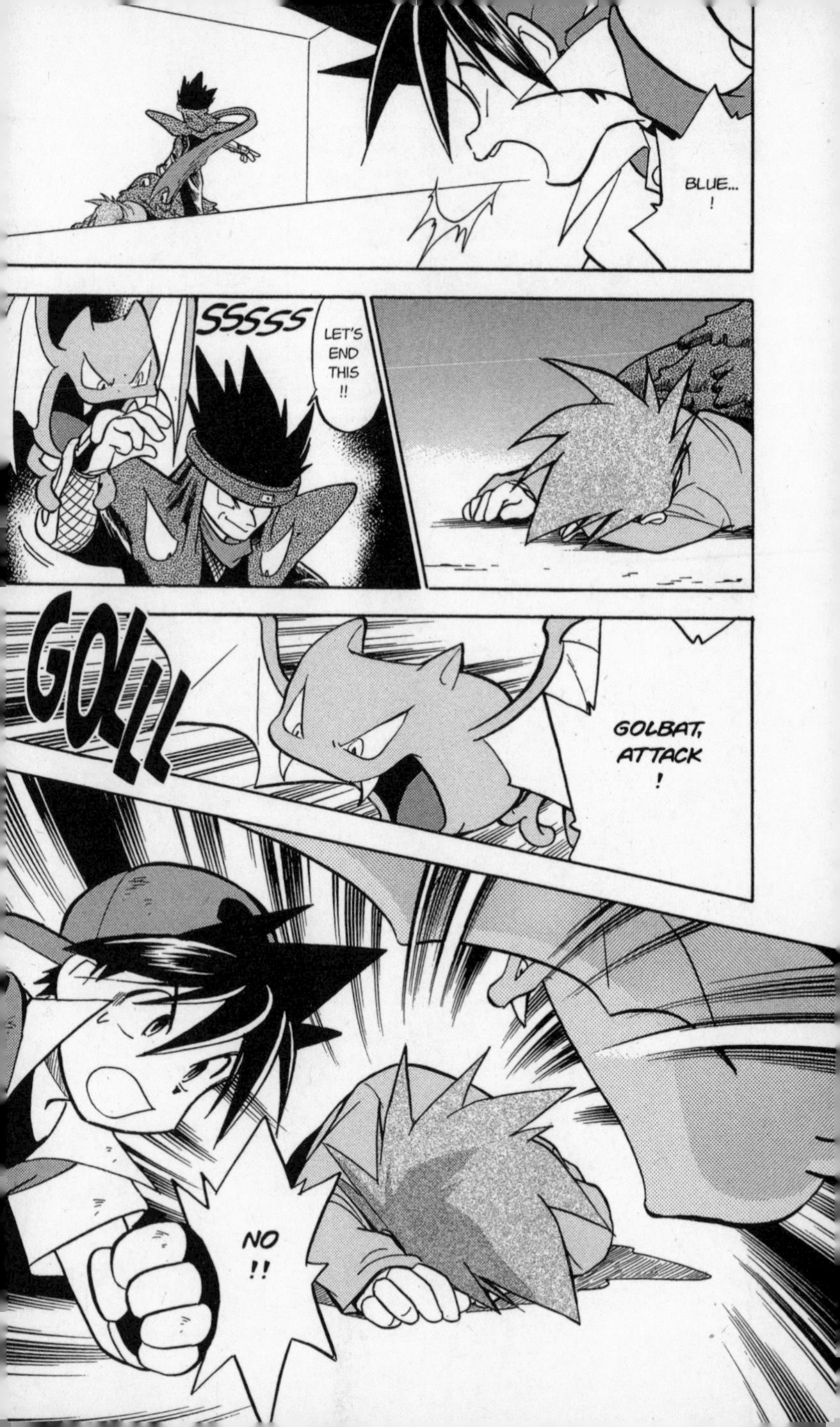
BLUE... !
LET'S END THIS !!
SSSSS
GOLBAT, ATTACK !
GO!!
NO !!

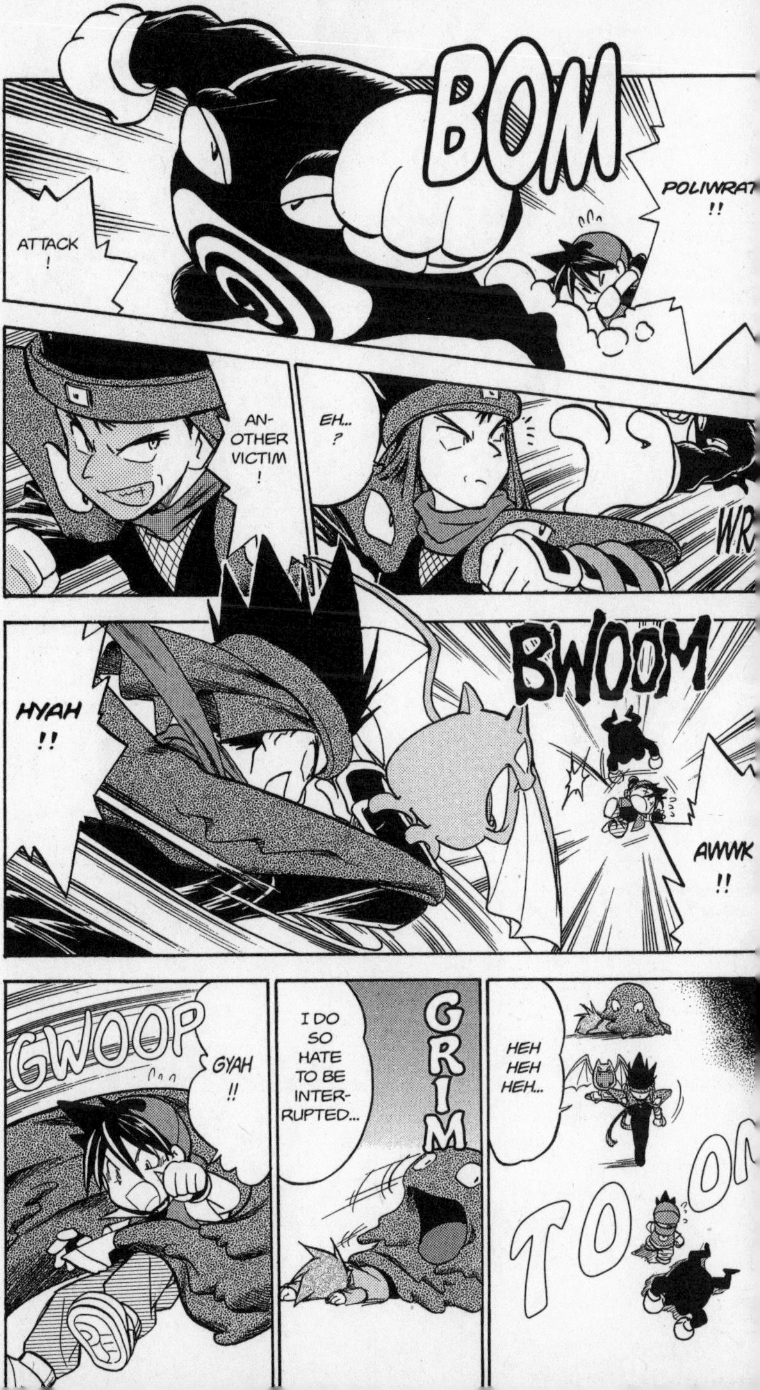
BOM
POLIWRAT !!
ATTACK !
WR
EH... ?
AN-OTHER VICTIM !
BWOOM
AWWK !!
HYAH !!
HEH HEH HEH...
TO
GRIM
I DO SO HATE TO BE INTER-RUPTED...
GWOOP
GYAH !!

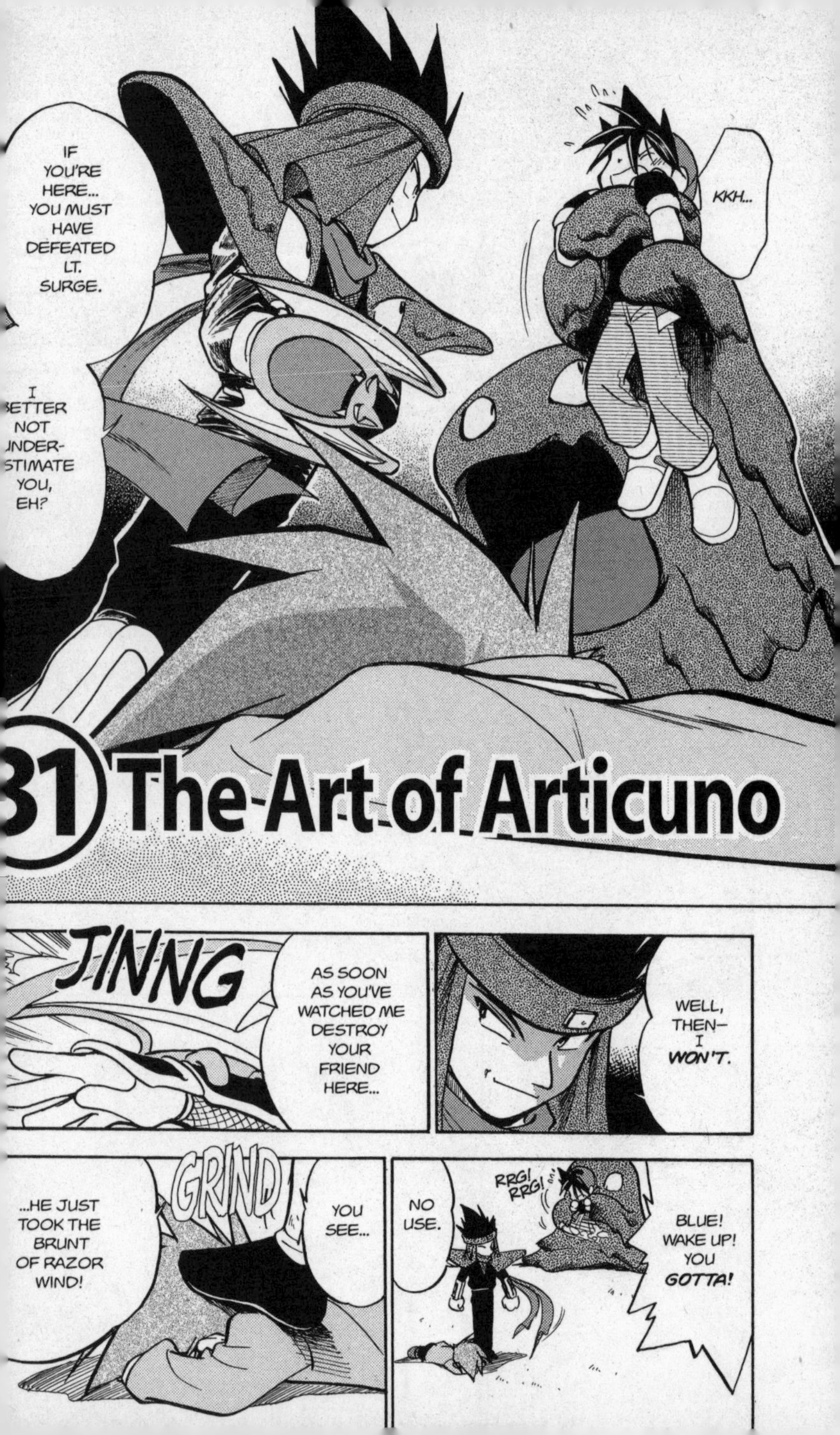
KKH...
IF YOU'RE HERE... YOU MUST HAVE DEFEATED LT. SURGE.
I ETTER NOT NDER-STIMATE YOU, EH?
31 The Art of Articuno
WELL, THEN— I *WON'T*.
JINNG
AS SOON AS YOU'VE WATCHED ME DESTROY YOUR FRIEND HERE...
BLUE! WAKE UP! YOU *GOTTA!*
RRG! RRG!
NO USE.
YOU SEE...
GRIND
...HE JUST TOOK THE BRUNT OF RAZOR WIND!

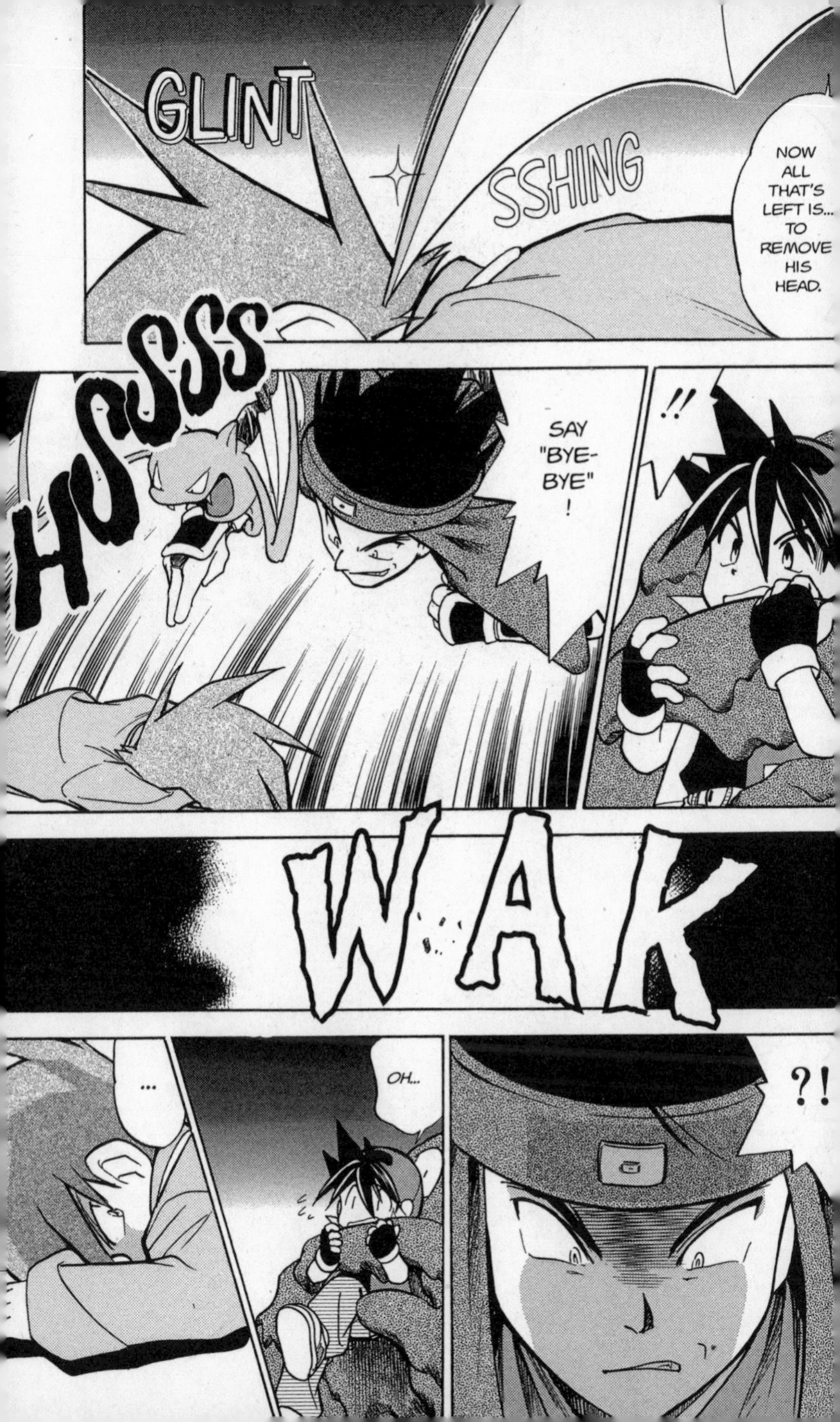
NOW ALL THAT'S LEFT IS... TO REMOVE HIS HEAD.
SSHING
GLINT
!!
SAY "BYE-BYE"!
HISSSS
WAK
?!
OH...
...

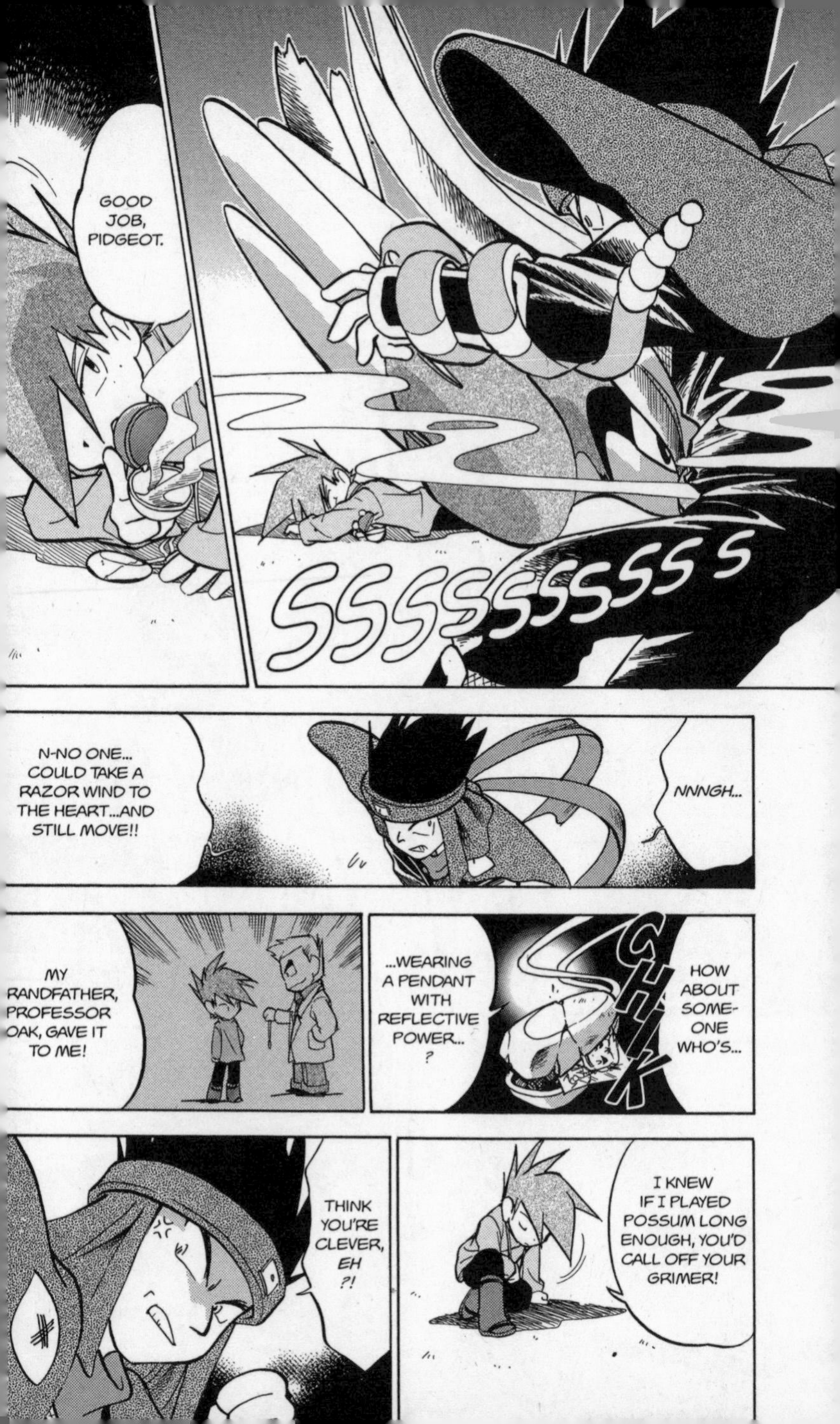
SSSSSSSSSS S
GOOD JOB, PIDGEOT.
NNNGH...
N-NO ONE... COULD TAKE A RAZOR WIND TO THE HEART...AND STILL MOVE!!
HOW ABOUT SOME-ONE WHO'S...
CHIK
...WEARING A PENDANT WITH REFLECTIVE POWER... ?
MY RANDFATHER, PROFESSOR OAK, GAVE IT TO ME!
I KNEW IF I PLAYED POSSUM LONG ENOUGH, YOU'D CALL OFF YOUR GRIMER!
THINK YOU'RE CLEVER, EH ?!

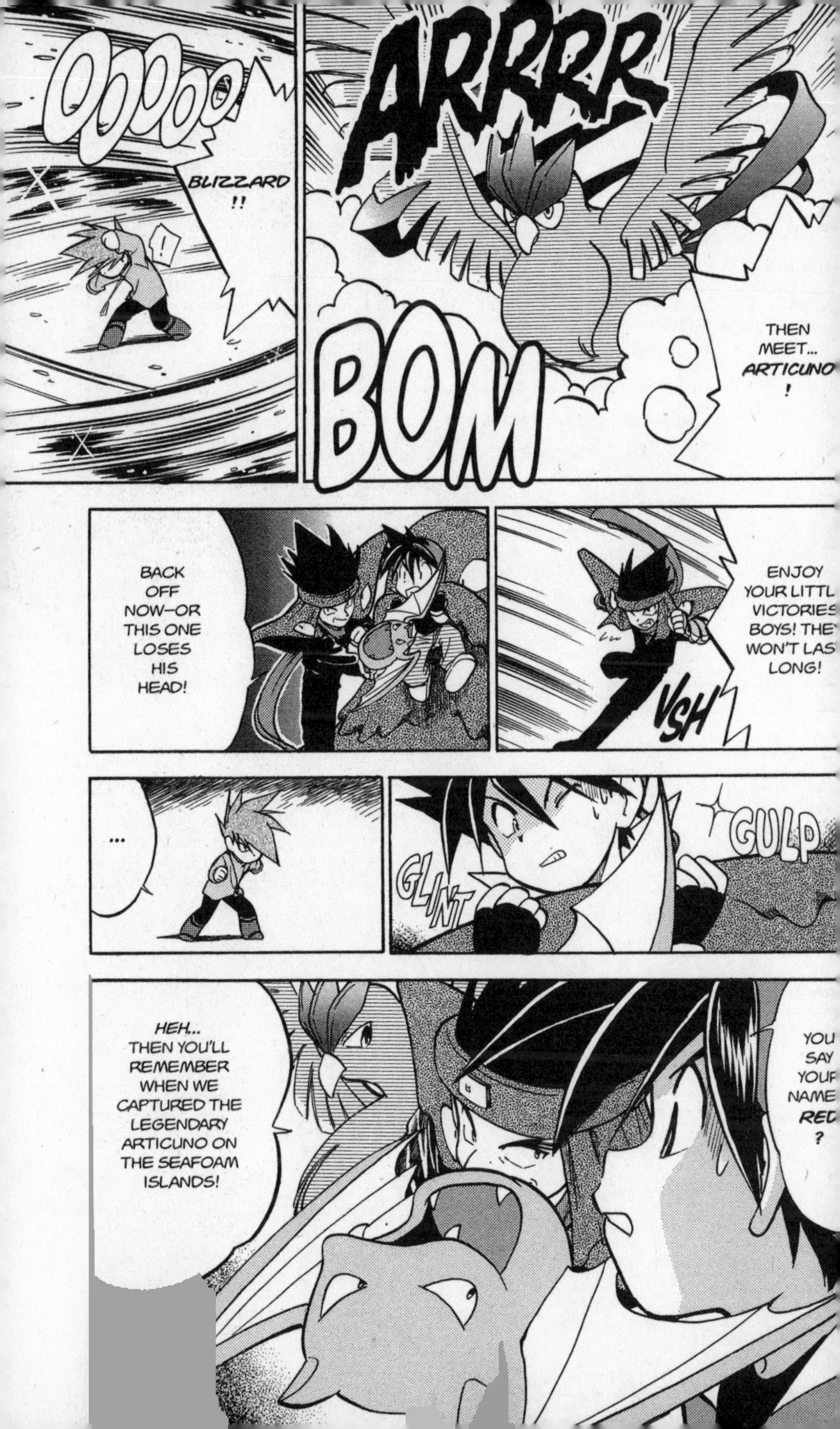
ARRRR
BOM
THEN MEET... ARTICUNO!
OOOOO
BLIZZARD!!
!
ENJOY YOUR LITTL VICTORIES BOYS! THE WON'T LAS LONG!
VSH
BACK OFF NOW—OR THIS ONE LOSES HIS HEAD!
GULP
GLINT
...
YOU SAY YOU NAME RE ?
HEH... THEN YOU'LL REMEMBER WHEN WE CAPTURED THE LEGENDARY ARTICUNO ON THE SEAFOAM ISLANDS!

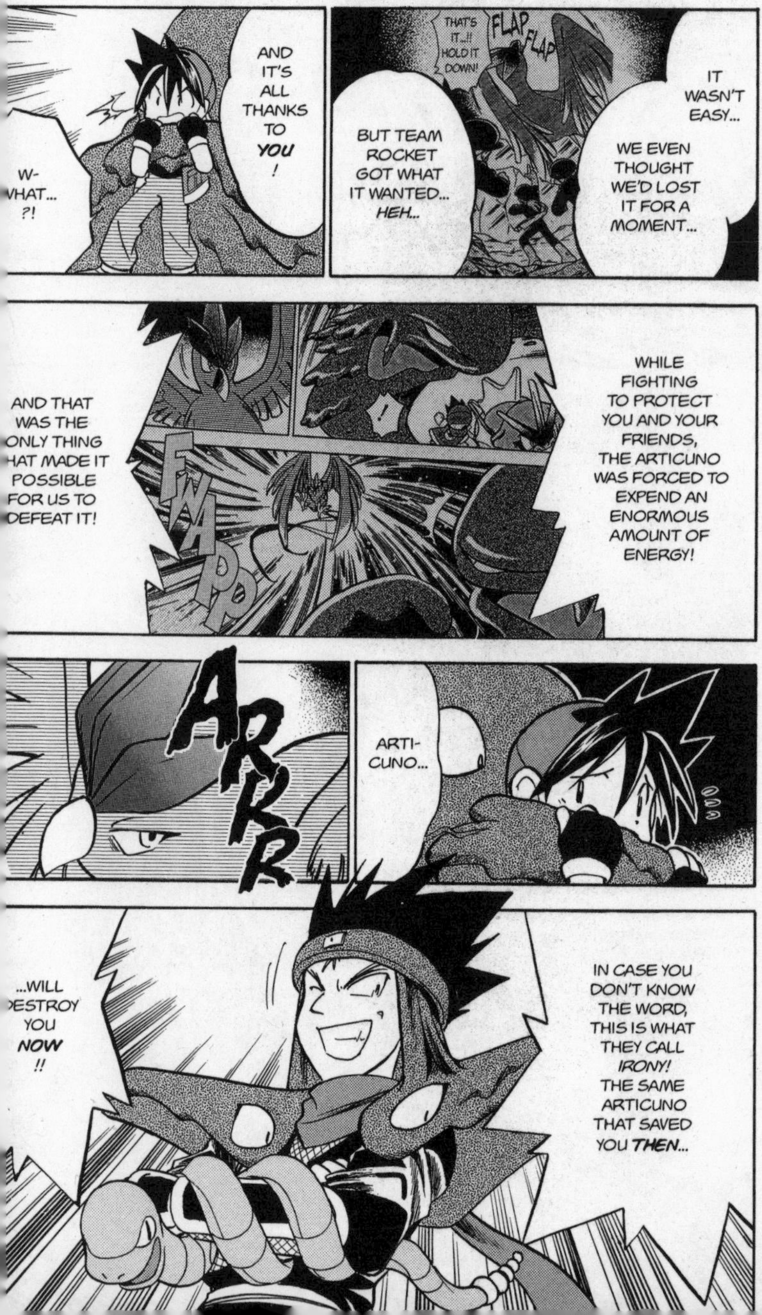
IT WASN'T EASY...
WE EVEN THOUGHT WE'D LOST IT FOR A MOMENT...
THAT'S IT...!! HOLD IT DOWN!
FLAP FLAP
BUT TEAM ROCKET GOT WHAT IT WANTED... HEH...
AND IT'S ALL THANKS TO YOU!
W-WHAT...?!
WHILE FIGHTING TO PROTECT YOU AND YOUR FRIENDS, THE ARTICUNO WAS FORCED TO EXPEND AN ENORMOUS AMOUNT OF ENERGY!
FWAPP
AND THAT WAS THE ONLY THING THAT MADE IT POSSIBLE FOR US TO DEFEAT IT!
ARTI-CUNO...
ARRR
IN CASE YOU DON'T KNOW THE WORD, THIS IS WHAT THEY CALL IRONY! THE SAME ARTICUNO THAT SAVED YOU THEN...
...WILL DESTROY YOU NOW!!

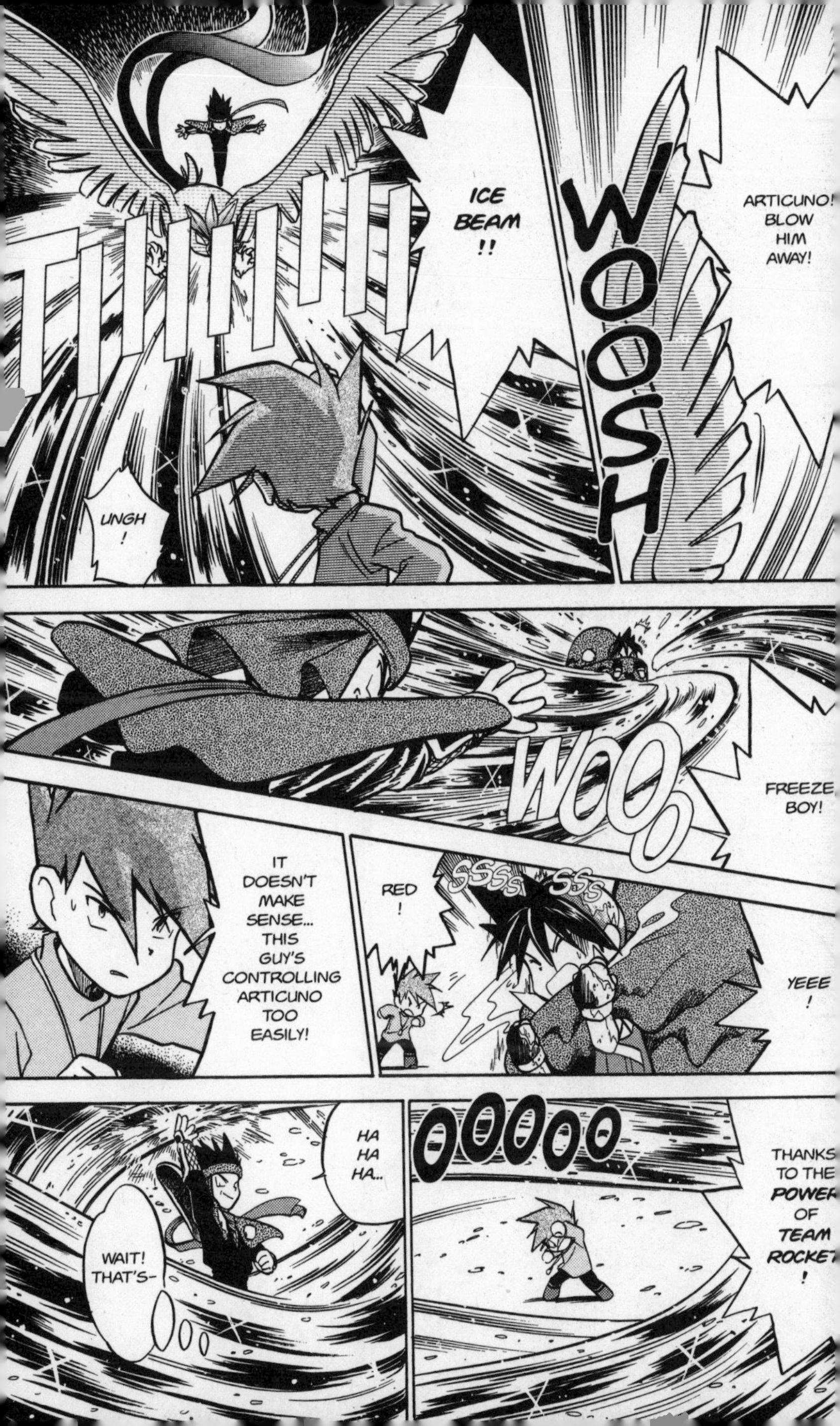
ARTICUNO! BLOW HIM AWAY!
WOOSH
ICE BEAM !!
TIIIIIII
UNGH !
FREEZE BOY!
WOOO
YEEE !
SSSS SSS
RED !
IT DOESN'T MAKE SENSE... THIS GUY'S CONTROLLING ARTICUNO TOO EASILY!
THANKS TO THE POWEF OF TEAM ROCKET !
OOOOO
HA HA HA...
WAIT! THAT'S-
OOO

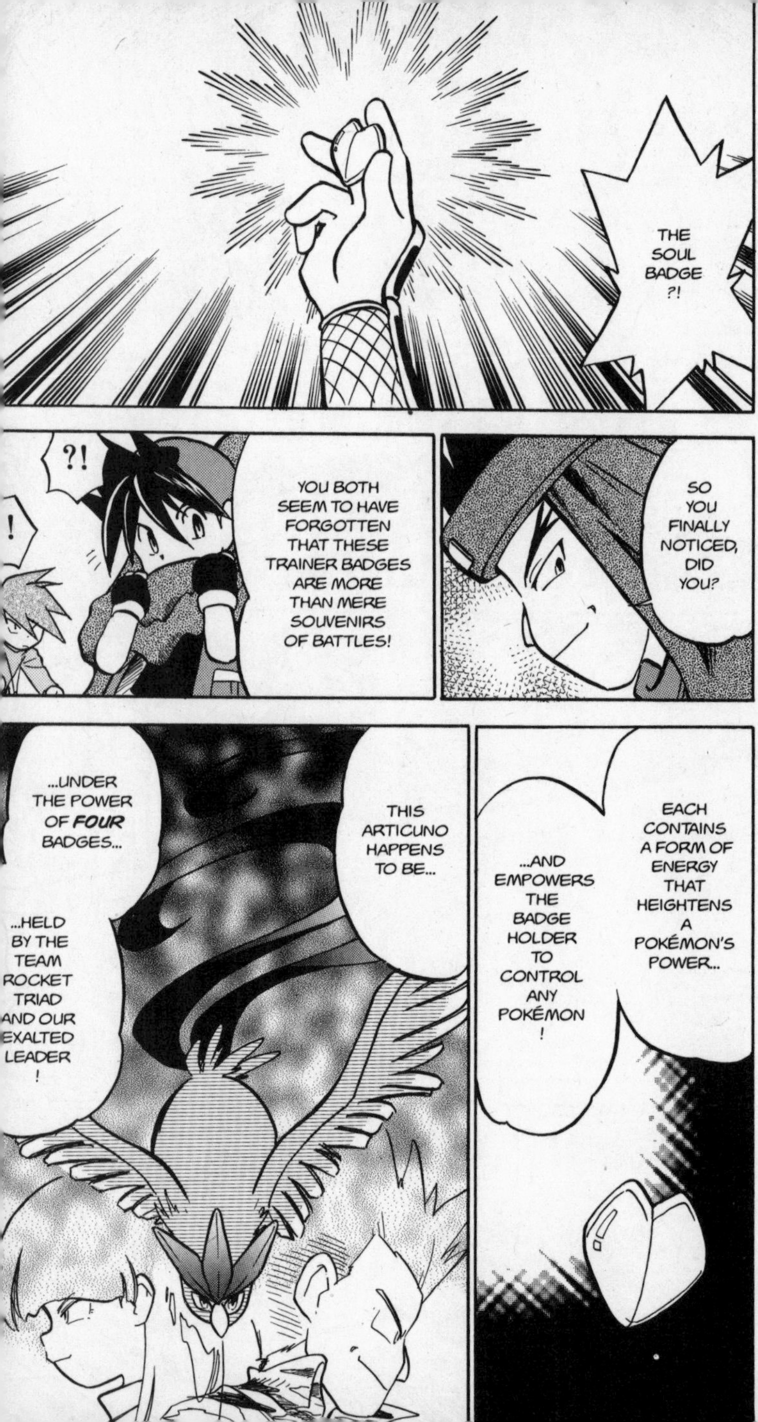
THE SOUL BADGE ?!
SO YOU FINALLY NOTICED, DID YOU?
YOU BOTH SEEM TO HAVE FORGOTTEN THAT THESE TRAINER BADGES ARE MORE THAN MERE SOUVENIRS OF BATTLES!
?!
!
EACH CONTAINS A FORM OF ENERGY THAT HEIGHTENS A POKÉMON'S POWER...
...AND EMPOWERS THE BADGE HOLDER TO CONTROL ANY POKÉMON !
THIS ARTICUNO HAPPENS TO BE...
...UNDER THE POWER OF **FOUR** BADGES...
...HELD BY THE TEAM ROCKET TRIAD AND OUR EXALTED LEADER !

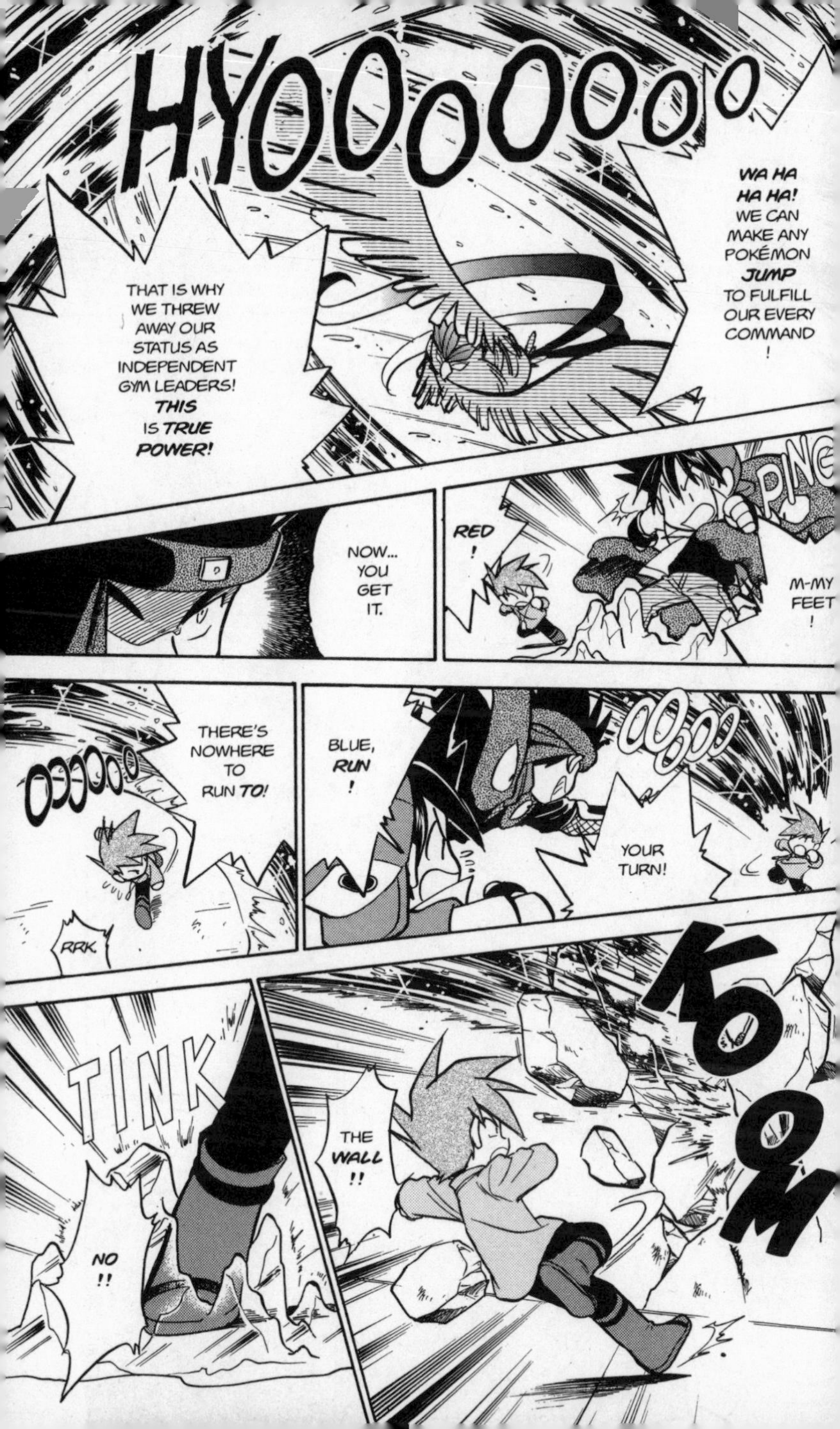
HYOOOOOOO
WA HA HA HA! WE CAN MAKE ANY POKÉMON JUMP TO FULFILL OUR EVERY COMMAND!
THAT IS WHY WE THREW AWAY OUR STATUS AS INDEPENDENT GYM LEADERS! THIS IS TRUE POWER!
PING
M-MY FEET!
RED!
NOW... YOU GET IT.
OOOOOO
BLUE, RUN!
YOUR TURN!
THERE'S NOWHERE TO RUN TO!
OOOOOO
RRK.
KBOOM
THE WALL!!
TINK
NO!!

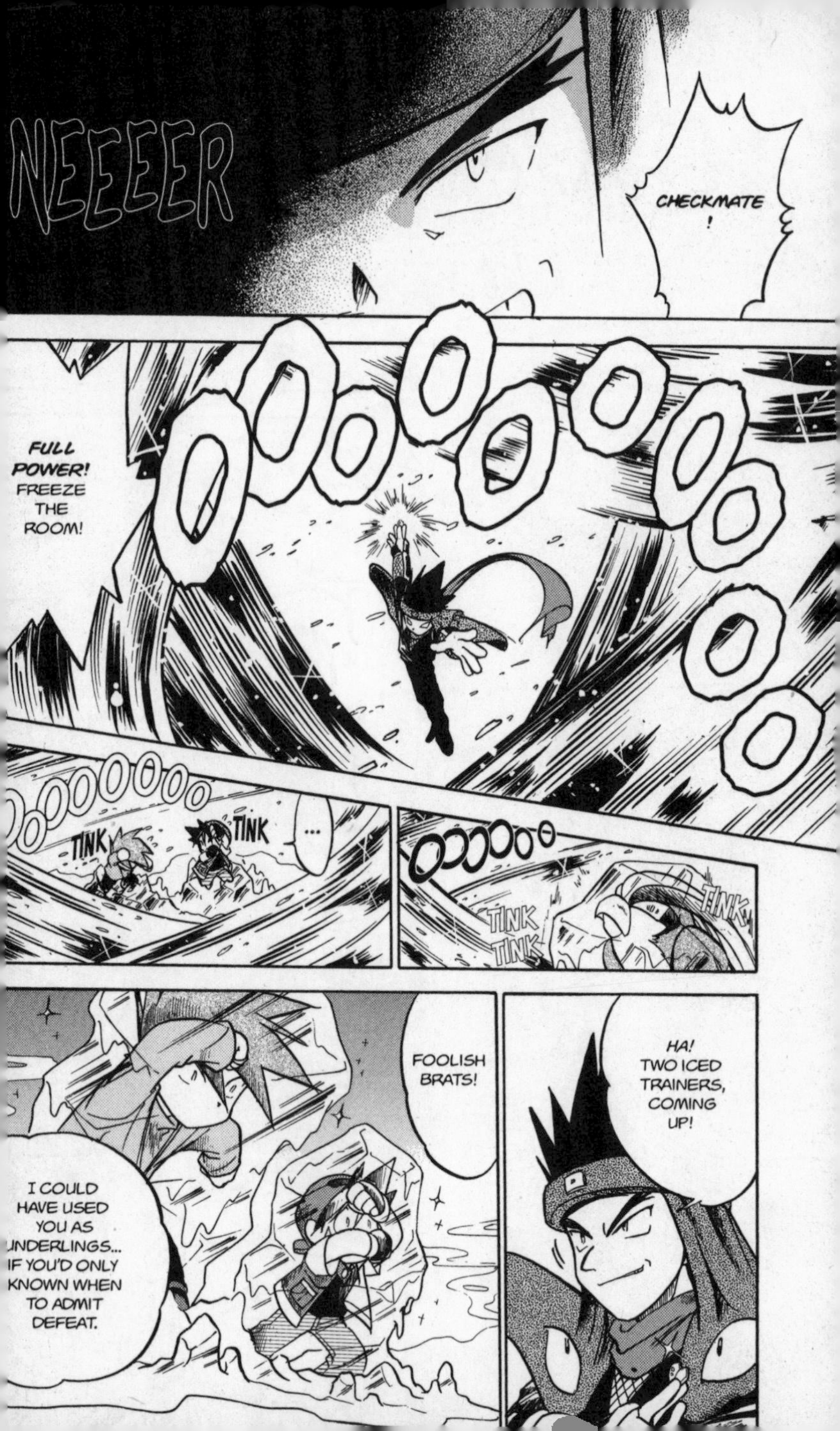
CHECKMATE!
NEEEER
FULL POWER! FREEZE THE ROOM!
TINK
TINK
TINK
TINK
TINK
...
HA! TWO ICED TRAINERS, COMING UP!
FOOLISH BRATS!
I COULD HAVE USED YOU AS UNDERLINGS... IF YOU'D ONLY KNOWN WHEN TO ADMIT DEFEAT.

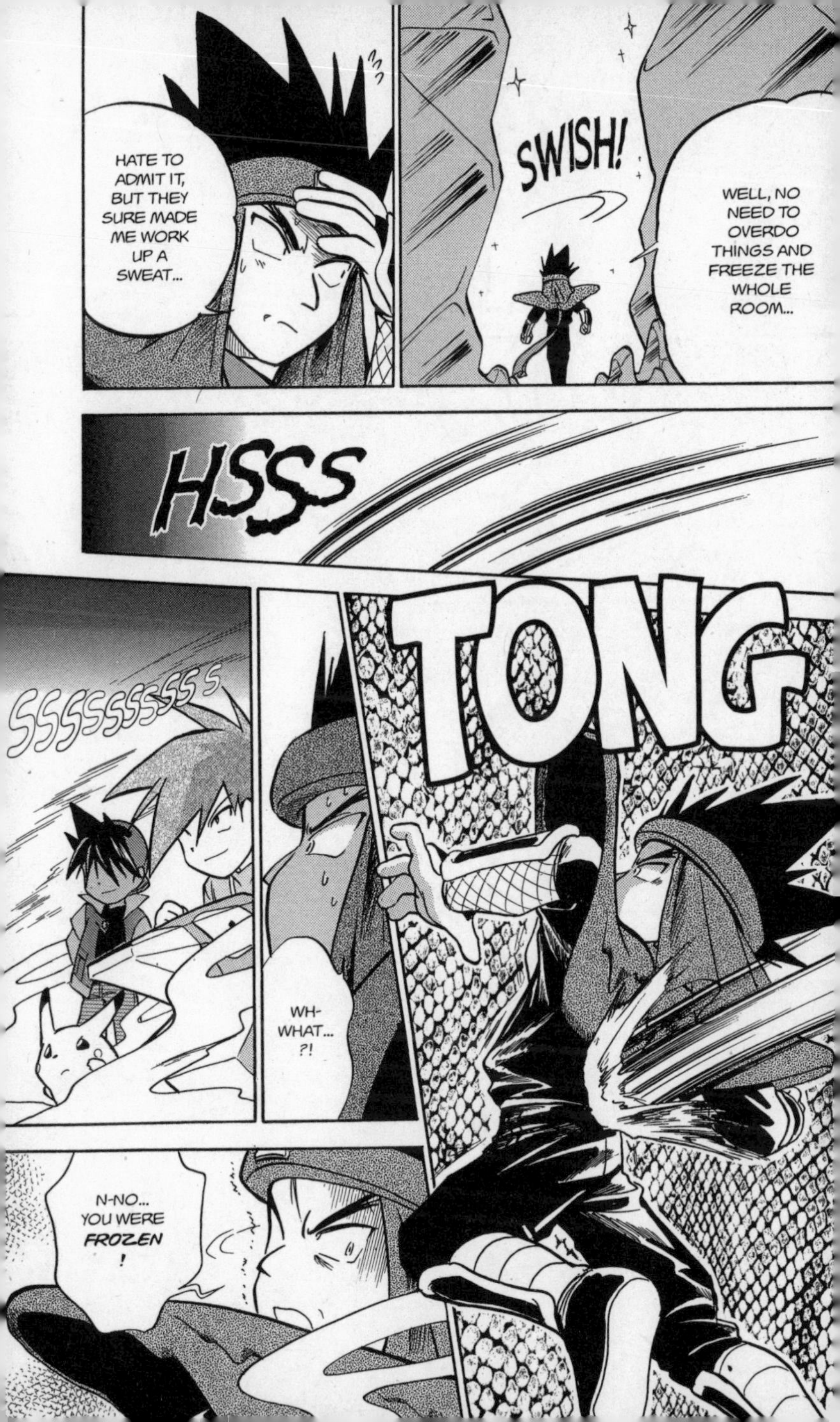
SWISH!
WELL, NO NEED TO OVERDO THINGS AND FREEZE THE WHOLE ROOM...
HATE TO ADMIT IT, BUT THEY SURE MADE ME WORK UP A SWEAT...
HSSS
TONG
WH-WHAT...?!
SSSSSSSSSS S
N-NO... YOU WERE *FROZEN*!

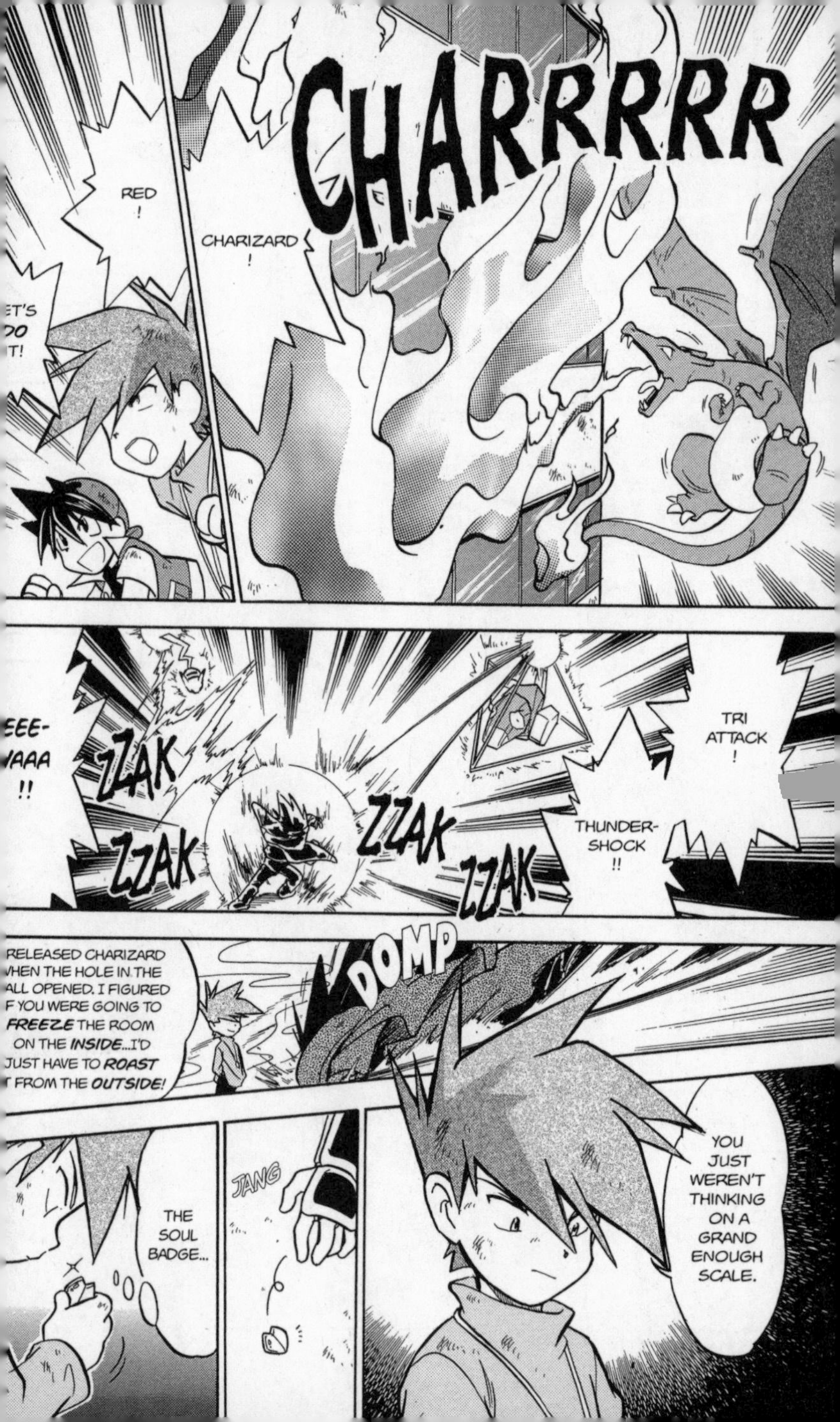
CHARRRRR
CHARIZARD!
RED!
ET'S DO T!
TRI ATTACK!
THUNDER-SHOCK!!
ZZAK
ZZAK
ZZAK
ZZAK
EEE-AAAA!!
DOMP
RELEASED CHARIZARD WHEN THE HOLE IN THE ALL OPENED. I FIGURED F YOU WERE GOING TO *FREEZE* THE ROOM ON THE *INSIDE*...I'D JUST HAVE TO *ROAST* T FROM THE *OUTSIDE*!
YOU JUST WEREN'T THINKING ON A GRAND ENOUGH SCALE.
JANG
THE SOUL BADGE...

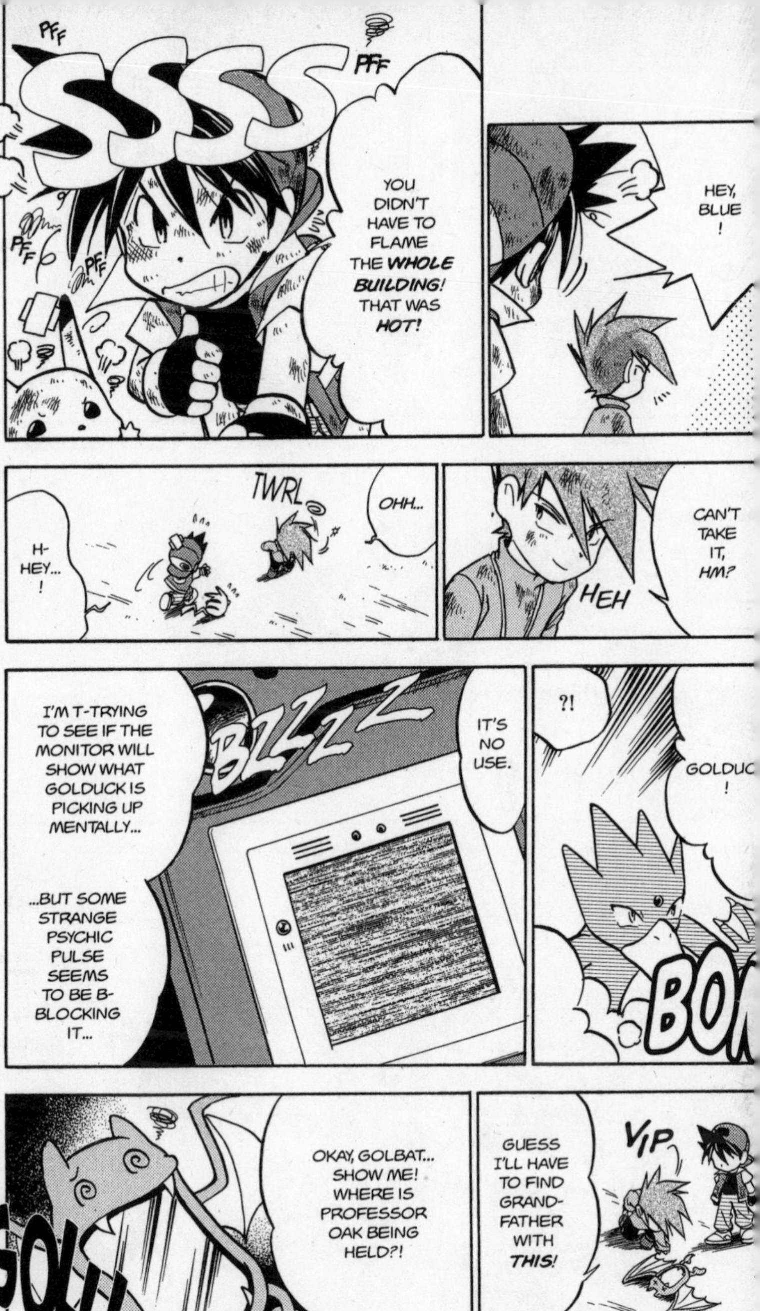
HEY, BLUE!
PFF
SSSS
PFF
PFF
PFF
YOU DIDN'T HAVE TO FLAME THE **WHOLE BUILDING**! THAT WAS **HOT**!
CAN'T TAKE IT, *HM?*
HEH
OHH...
TWRL
H-HEY...!
?!
GOLDUC!
BOM
IT'S NO USE.
BZZZ
I'M T-TRYING TO SEE IF THE MONITOR WILL SHOW WHAT GOLDUCK IS PICKING UP MENTALLY...
...BUT SOME STRANGE PSYCHIC PULSE SEEMS TO BE B-BLOCKING IT...
VIP
GUESS I'LL HAVE TO FIND GRAND-FATHER WITH ***THIS***!
OKAY, GOLBAT... SHOW ME! WHERE IS PROFESSOR OAK BEING HELD?!
GOLLL

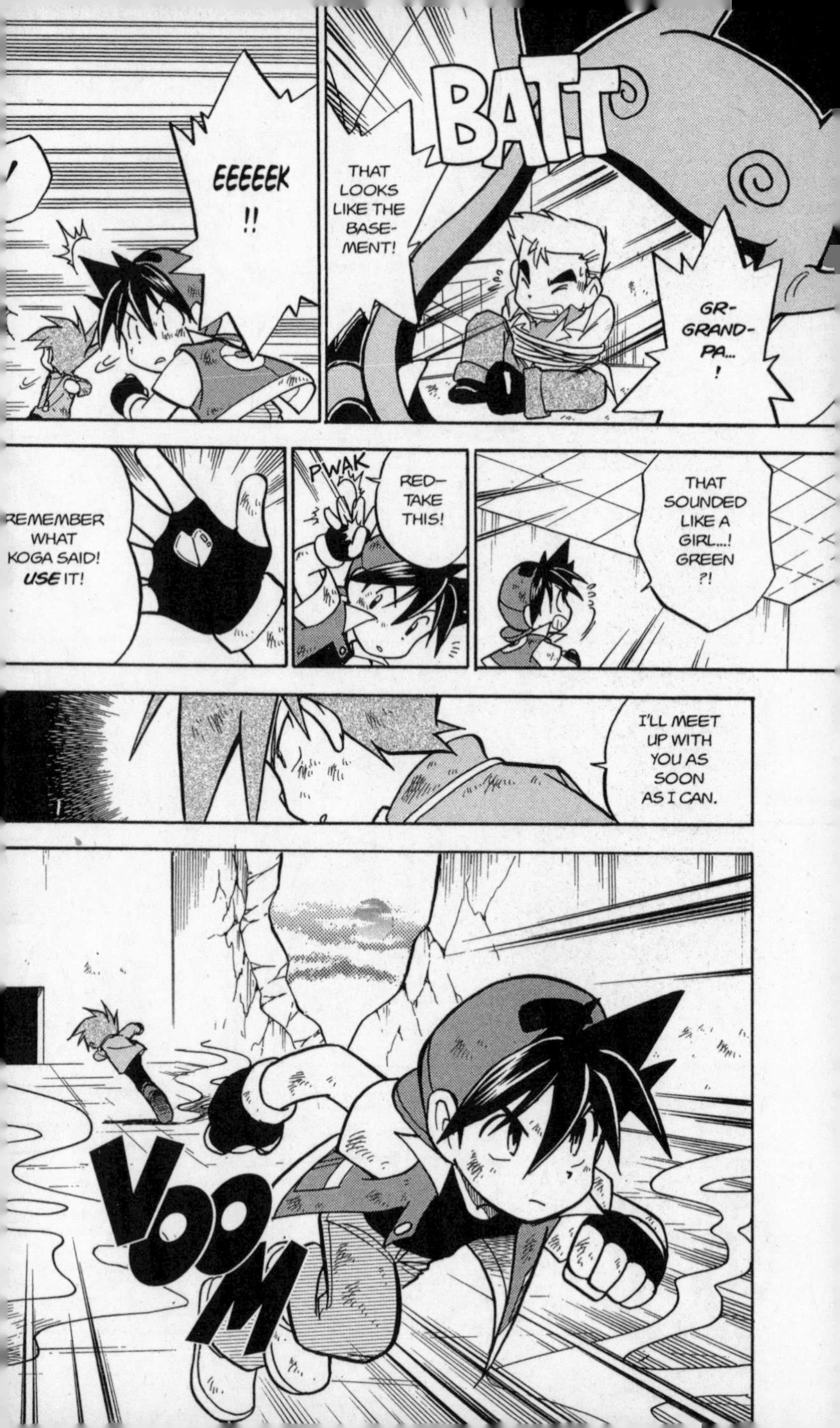

BATT
GR-GRANDPA...!
THAT LOOKS LIKE THE BASEMENT!
EEEEEK!!
THAT SOUNDED LIKE A GIRL...! GREEN?!
PWAK
RED- TAKE THIS!
REMEMBER WHAT KOGA SAID! USE IT!
I'LL MEET UP WITH YOU AS SOON AS I CAN.
VOOM

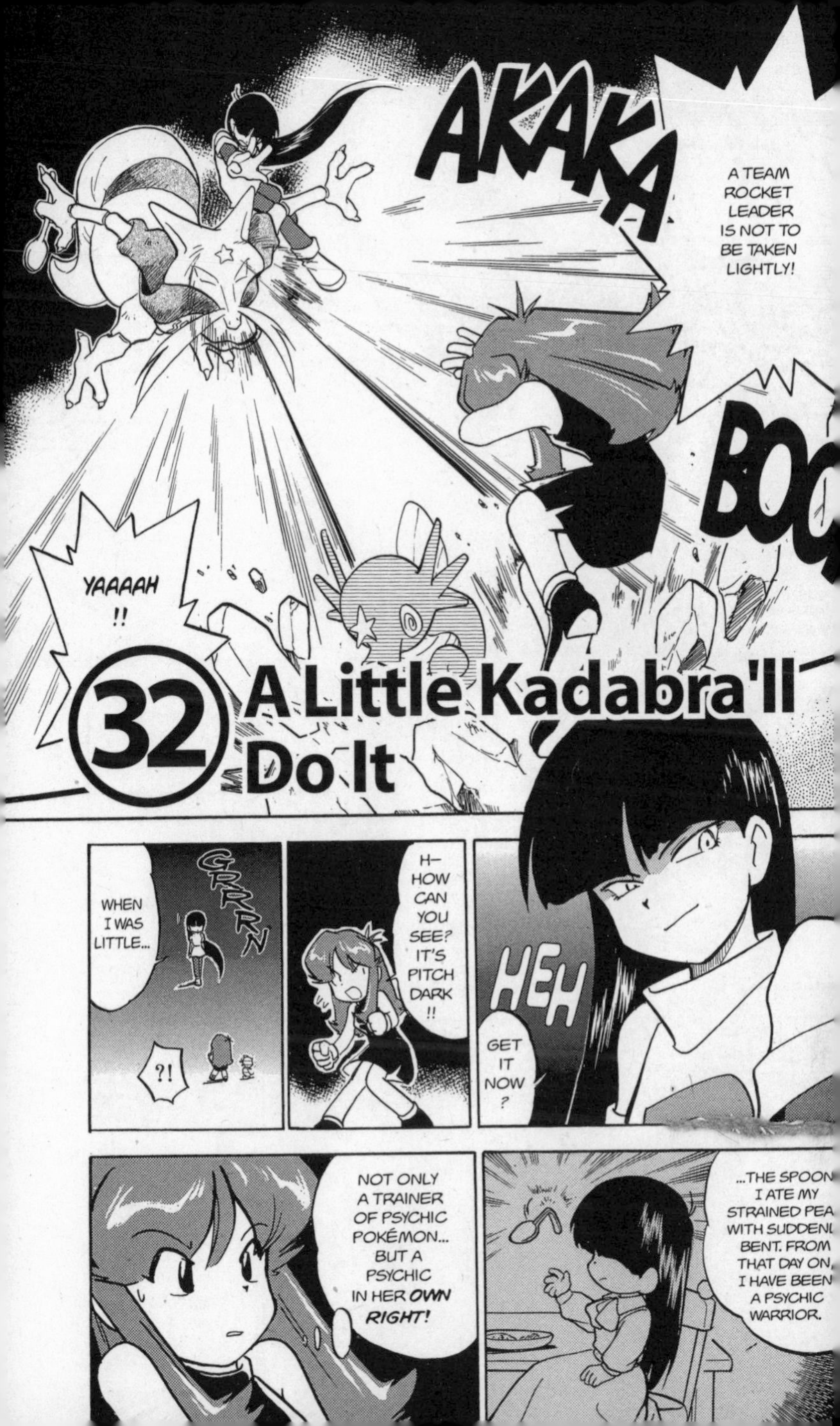
AKAKA
A TEAM ROCKET LEADER IS NOT TO BE TAKEN LIGHTLY!
BOO
YAAAAH !!
32 A Little Kadabra'll Do It
HEH
GET IT NOW?
H— HOW CAN YOU SEE? IT'S PITCH DARK !!
GRRRRN
WHEN I WAS LITTLE...
?!
...THE SPOON I ATE MY STRAINED PEA WITH SUDDENL BENT. FROM THAT DAY ON, I HAVE BEEN A PSYCHIC WARRIOR.
NOT ONLY A TRAINER OF PSYCHIC POKÉMON... BUT A PSYCHIC IN HER *OWN* *RIGHT*!

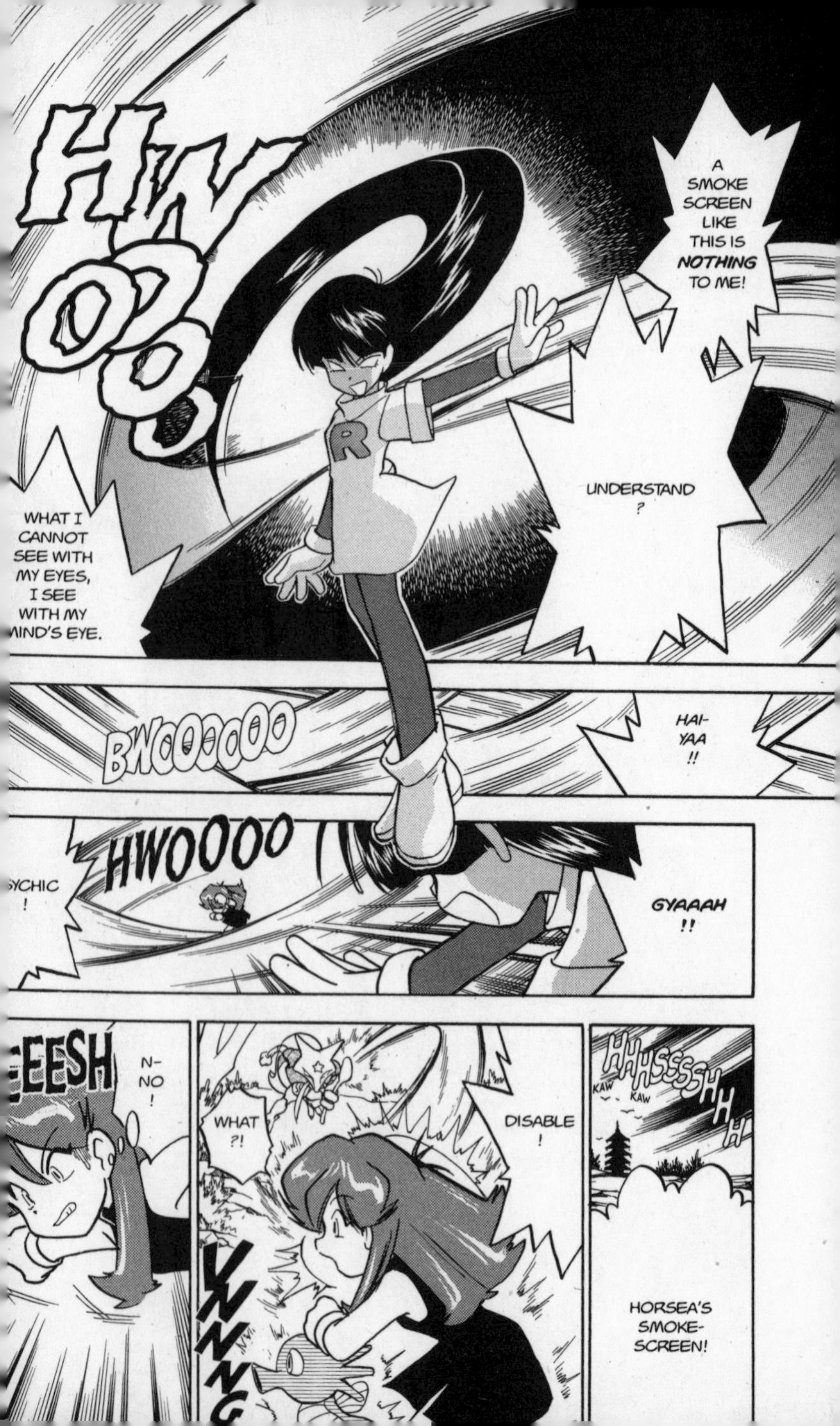
A SMOKE SCREEN LIKE THIS IS **NOTHING** TO ME!
UNDERSTAND ?
HWOOOO
WHAT I CANNOT SEE WITH MY EYES, I SEE WITH MY MIND'S EYE.
HAI-YAA !!
BWOOOOOO
GYAAAH !!
HWOOOO
SYCHIC !
HHHSSSSHHH
KAW KAW
HORSEA'S SMOKE-SCREEN!
DISABLE !
WHAT ?!
N-NO !
EESH

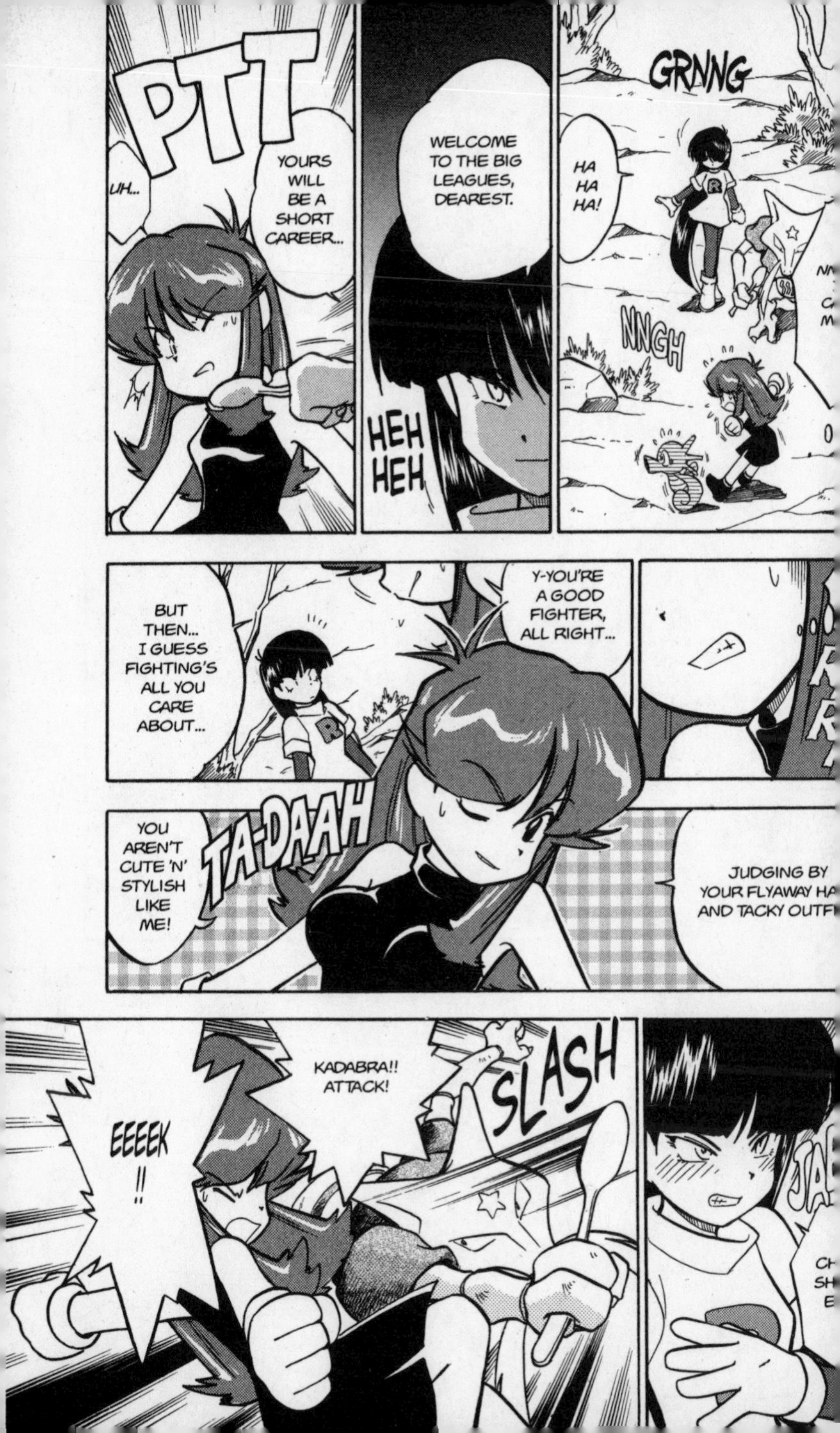
GRNNG
HA HA HA!
NNGH
WELCOME TO THE BIG LEAGUES, DEAREST.
HEH HEH
PTT
YOURS WILL BE A SHORT CAREER...
UH...
Y-YOU'RE A GOOD FIGHTER, ALL RIGHT...
BUT THEN... I GUESS FIGHTING'S ALL YOU CARE ABOUT...
JUDGING BY YOUR FLYAWAY HA
AND TACKY OUTF
TA-DAAH
YOU AREN'T CUTE 'N' STYLISH LIKE ME!
SLASH
KADABRA!! ATTACK!
EEEEK!!

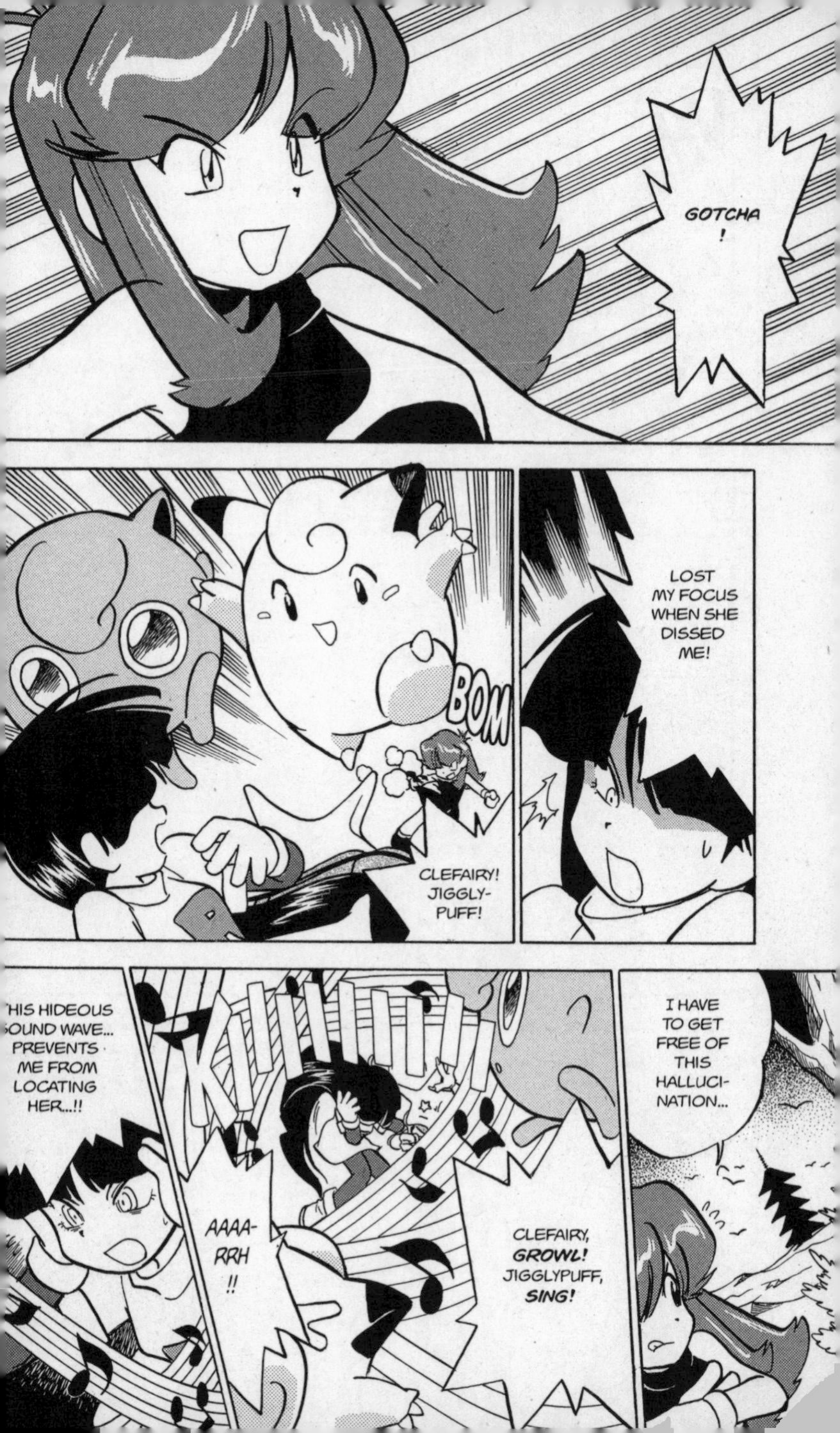
GOTCHA !
LOST MY FOCUS WHEN SHE DISSED ME!
BOM
CLEFAIRY! JIGGLY-PUFF!
I HAVE TO GET FREE OF THIS HALLUCI-NATION...
CLEFAIRY, GROWL! JIGGLYPUFF, SING!
AAAA-RRH !!
THIS HIDEOUS SOUND WAVE... PREVENTS ME FROM LOCATING HER...!!

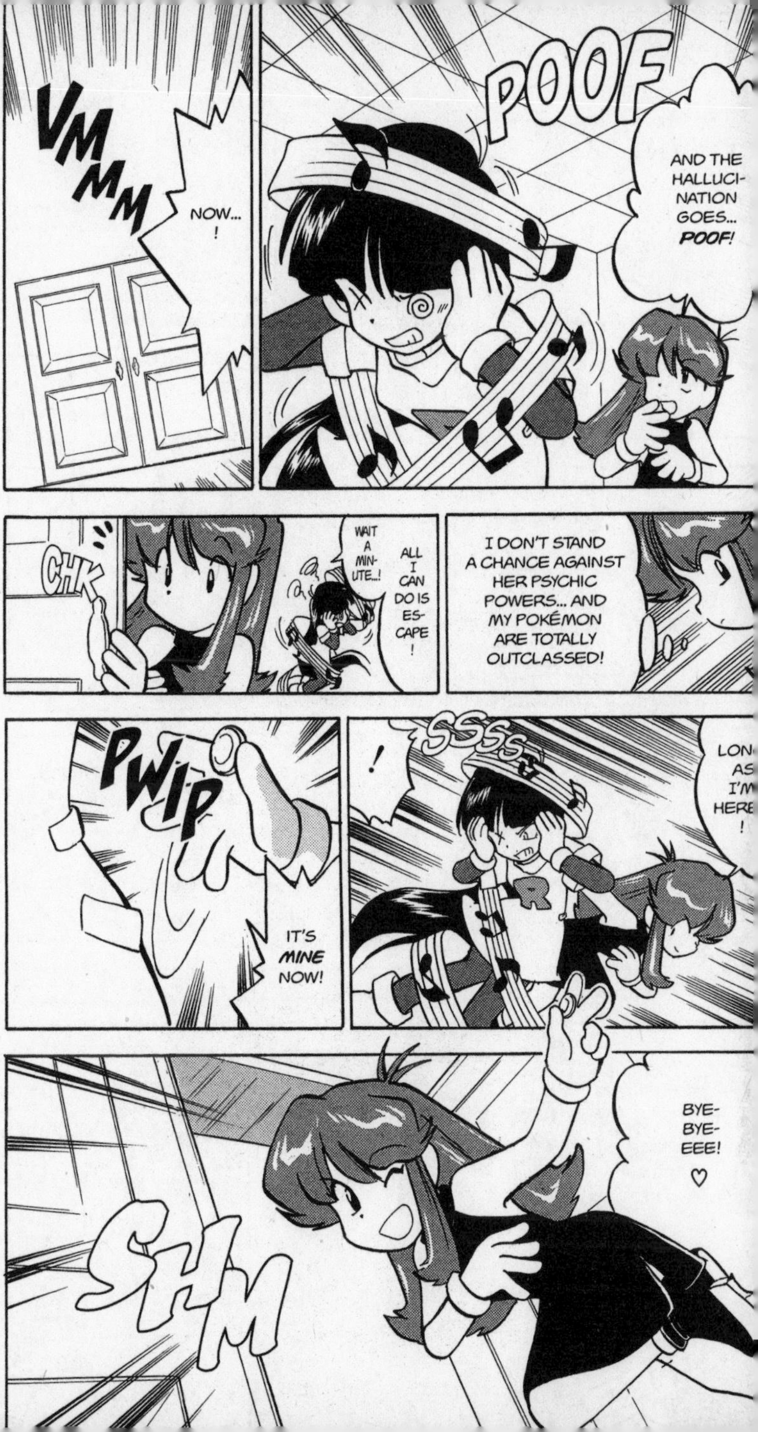
POOF
AND THE HALLUCI-NATION GOES... ***POOF!***
VMMM
NOW... !
I DON'T STAND A CHANCE AGAINST HER PSYCHIC POWERS... AND MY POKÉMON ARE TOTALLY OUTCLASSED!
ALL I CAN DO IS ES-CAPE!
WAIT A MIN-UTE..!
CHK
SSSS
LON AS I'M HERE!
!
PWIP
IT'S ***MINE*** NOW!
BYE-BYE-EEE! ♡
SHM

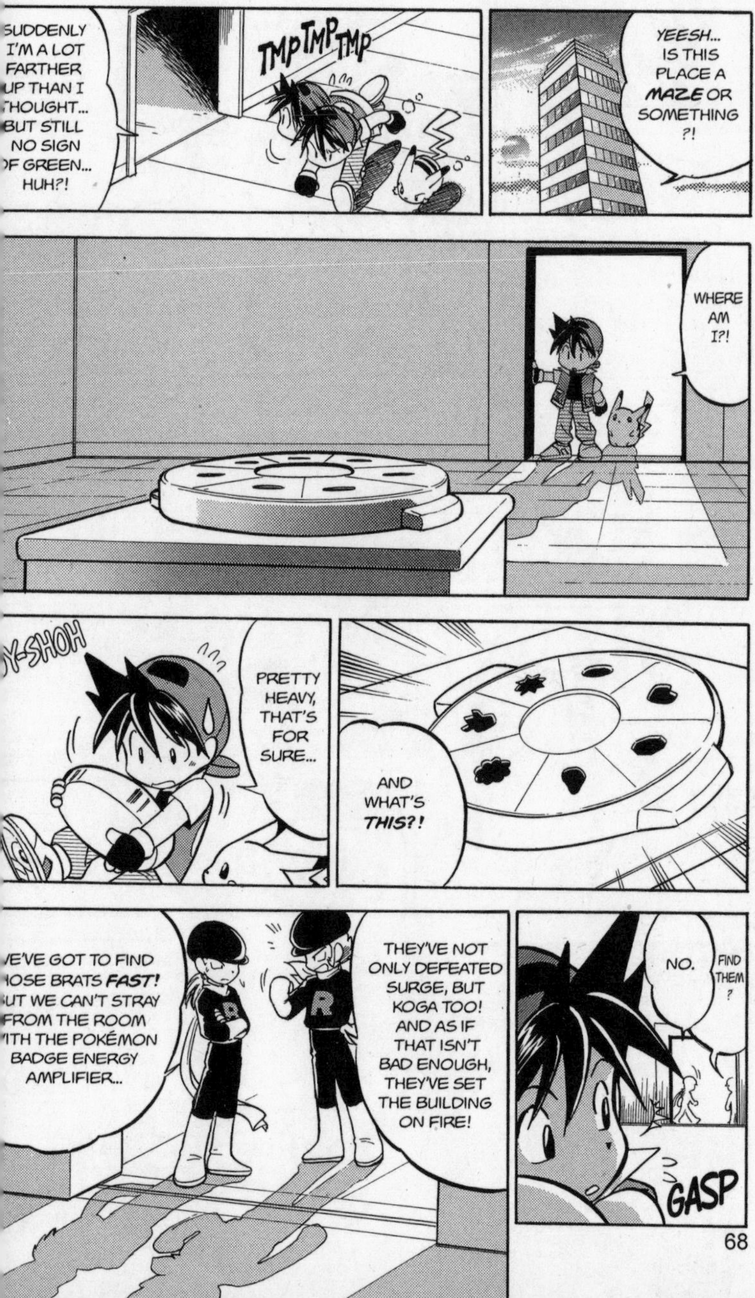
YEESH... IS THIS PLACE A MAZE OR SOMETHING ?!
SUDDENLY I'M A LOT FARTHER UP THAN I THOUGHT... BUT STILL NO SIGN OF GREEN... HUH?!
TMP TMP TMP
WHERE AM I?!
AND WHAT'S THIS?!
Y-SHOH
PRETTY HEAVY, THAT'S FOR SURE...
FIND THEM?
NO.
GASP
THEY'VE NOT ONLY DEFEATED SURGE, BUT KOGA TOO! AND AS IF THAT ISN'T BAD ENOUGH, THEY'VE SET THE BUILDING ON FIRE!
E'VE GOT TO FIND HOSE BRATS FAST! UT WE CAN'T STRAY FROM THE ROOM ITH THE POKÉMON BADGE ENERGY AMPLIFIER...

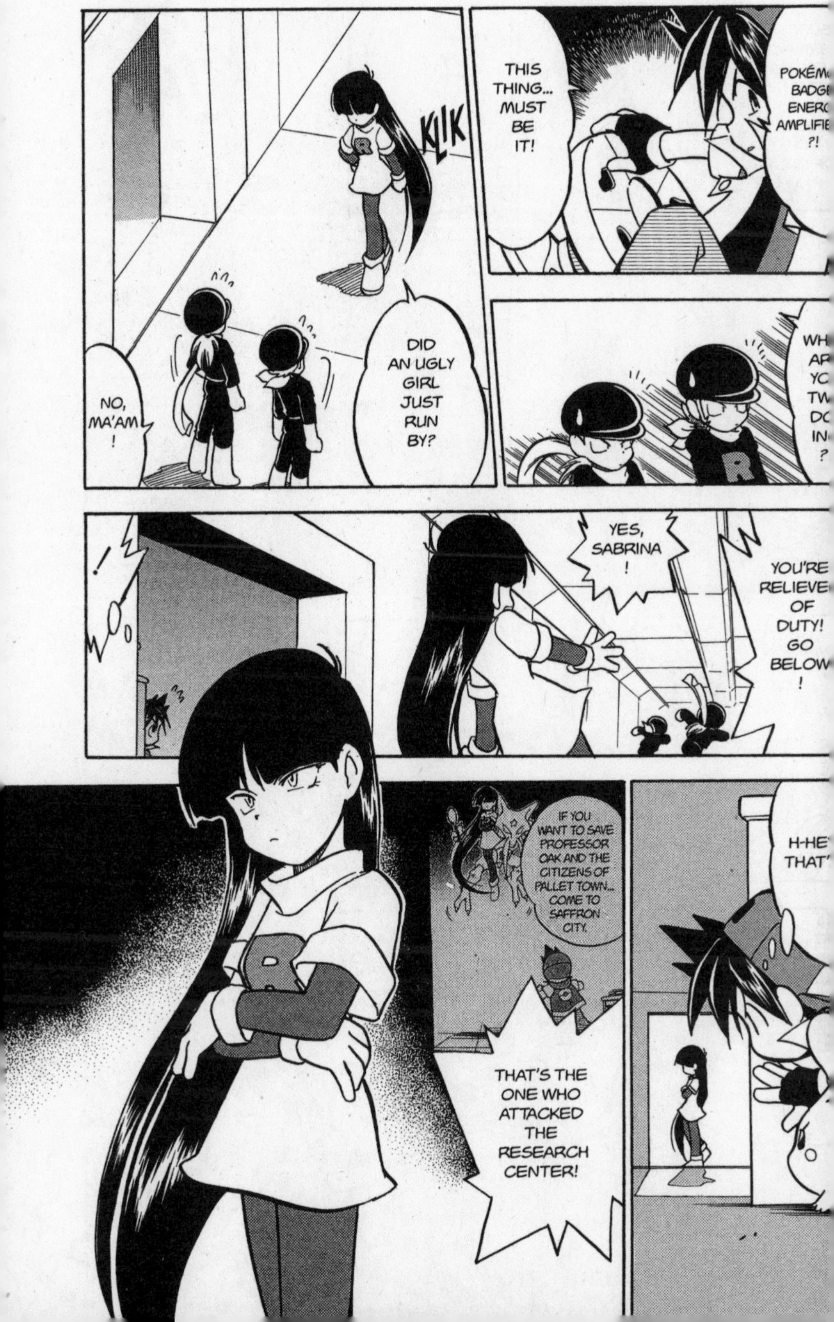
POKÉMO BADGE ENERG AMPLIFIE ?!
THIS THING... MUST BE IT!
WHA AR YO TW DO IN ?
KLIK
DID AN UGLY GIRL JUST RUN BY?
NO, MA'AM!
YOU'RE RELIEVE OF DUTY! GO BELOW!
YES, SABRINA!
!
H-HE THAT'
IF YOU WANT TO SAVE PROFESSOR OAK AND THE CITIZENS OF PALLET TOWN... COME TO SAFFRON CITY.
THAT'S THE ONE WHO ATTACKED THE RESEARCH CENTER!

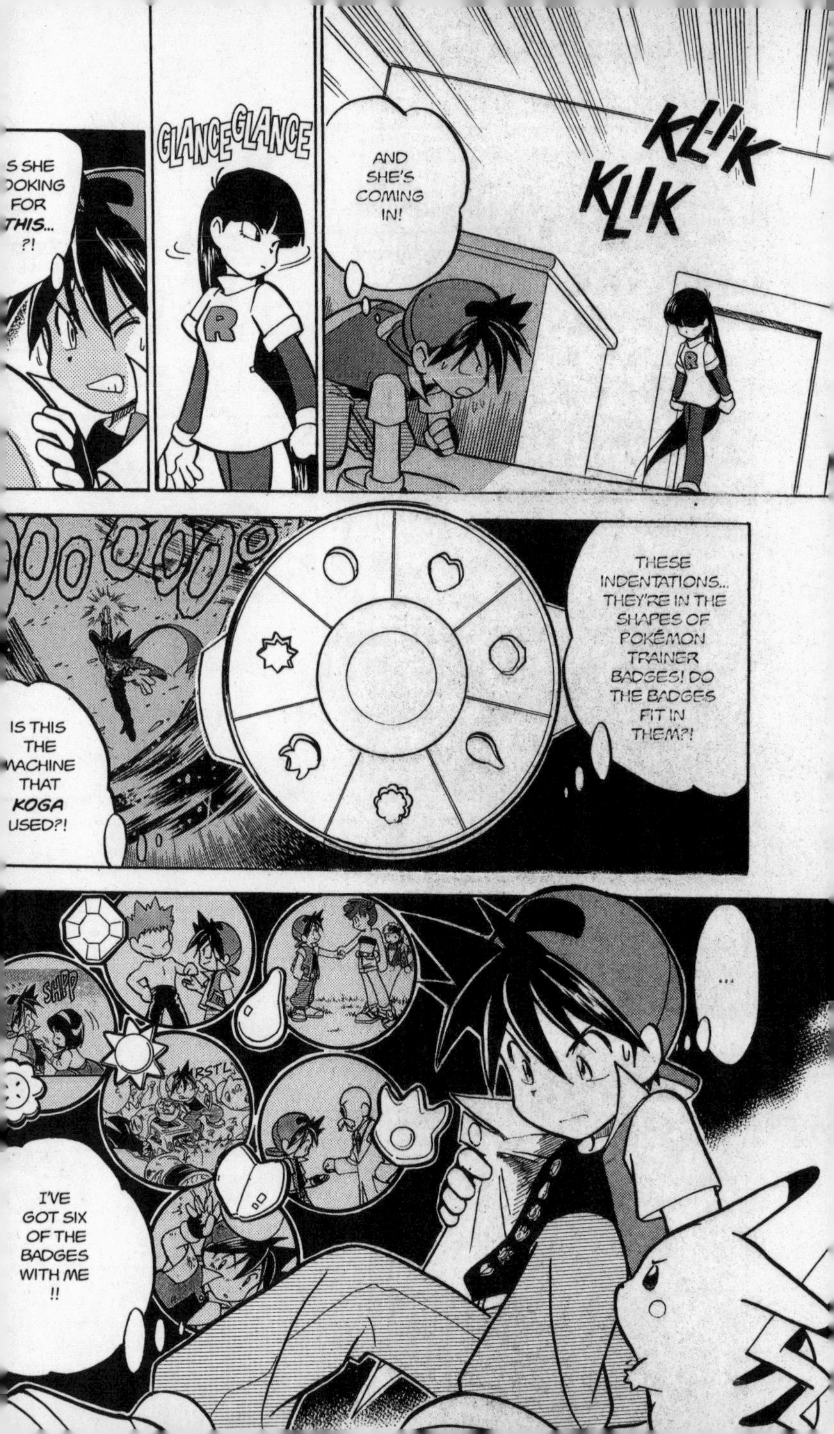
KLIK KLIK
AND SHE'S COMING IN!
GLANCE GLANCE
S SHE OOKING FOR THIS... ?!
THESE INDENTATIONS... THEY'RE IN THE SHAPES OF POKÉMON TRAINER BADGES! DO THE BADGES FIT IN THEM?!
IS THIS THE ACHINE THAT KOGA USED?!
...
SHPP
RSTL
I'VE GOT SIX OF THE BADGES WITH ME !!

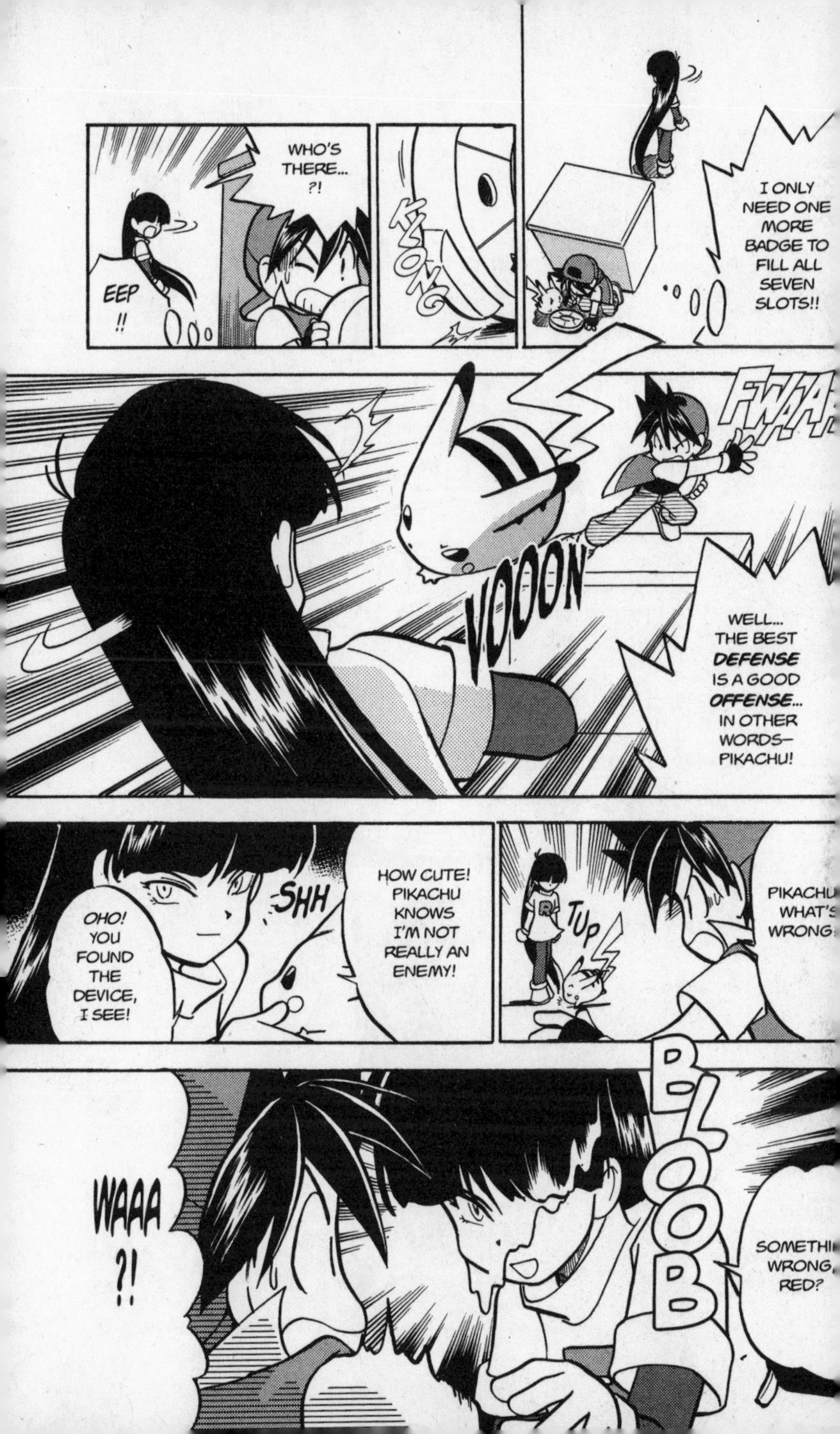
I ONLY NEED ONE MORE BADGE TO FILL ALL SEVEN SLOTS!!
KLONG
WHO'S THERE... ?!
EEP !!
FWA!
WELL... THE BEST **DEFENSE** IS A GOOD **OFFENSE**... IN OTHER WORDS— PIKACHU!
VOOON
PIKACHU WHAT'S WRONG
TUP
HOW CUTE! PIKACHU KNOWS I'M NOT REALLY AN ENEMY!
SHH
OHO! YOU FOUND THE DEVICE, I SEE!
SOMETHI WRONG, RED?
BLOOB
WAAA ?!

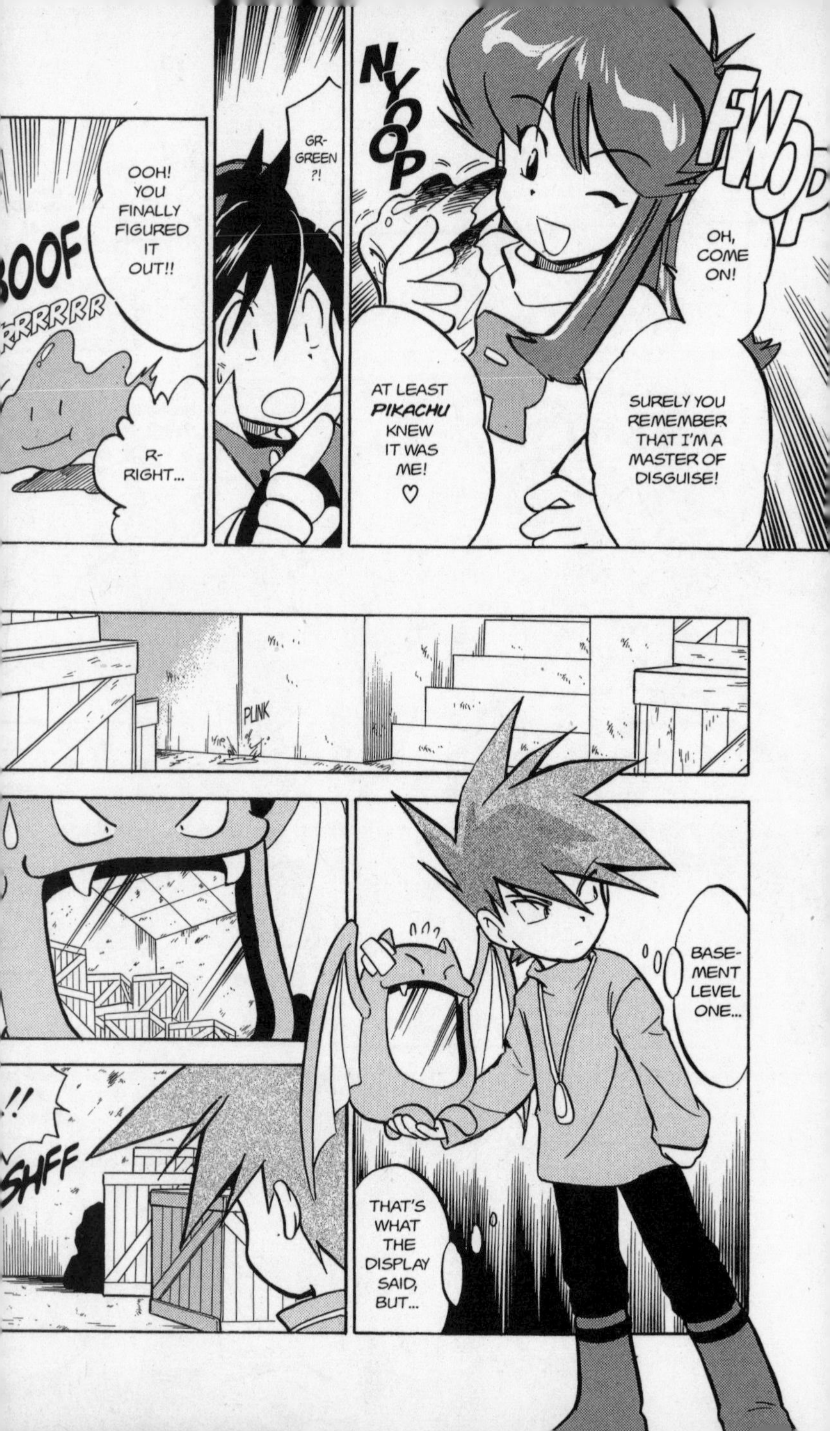
FWOOP
OH, COME ON!
SURELY YOU REMEMBER THAT I'M A MASTER OF DISGUISE!
NYOOP
AT LEAST PIKACHU KNEW IT WAS ME! ♡
GR-GREEN?!
OOH! YOU FINALLY FIGURED IT OUT!!
BOOF
RRRRRR
R-RIGHT...
PLINK
BASE-MENT LEVEL ONE...
THAT'S WHAT THE DISPLAY SAID, BUT...
!!
SHFF

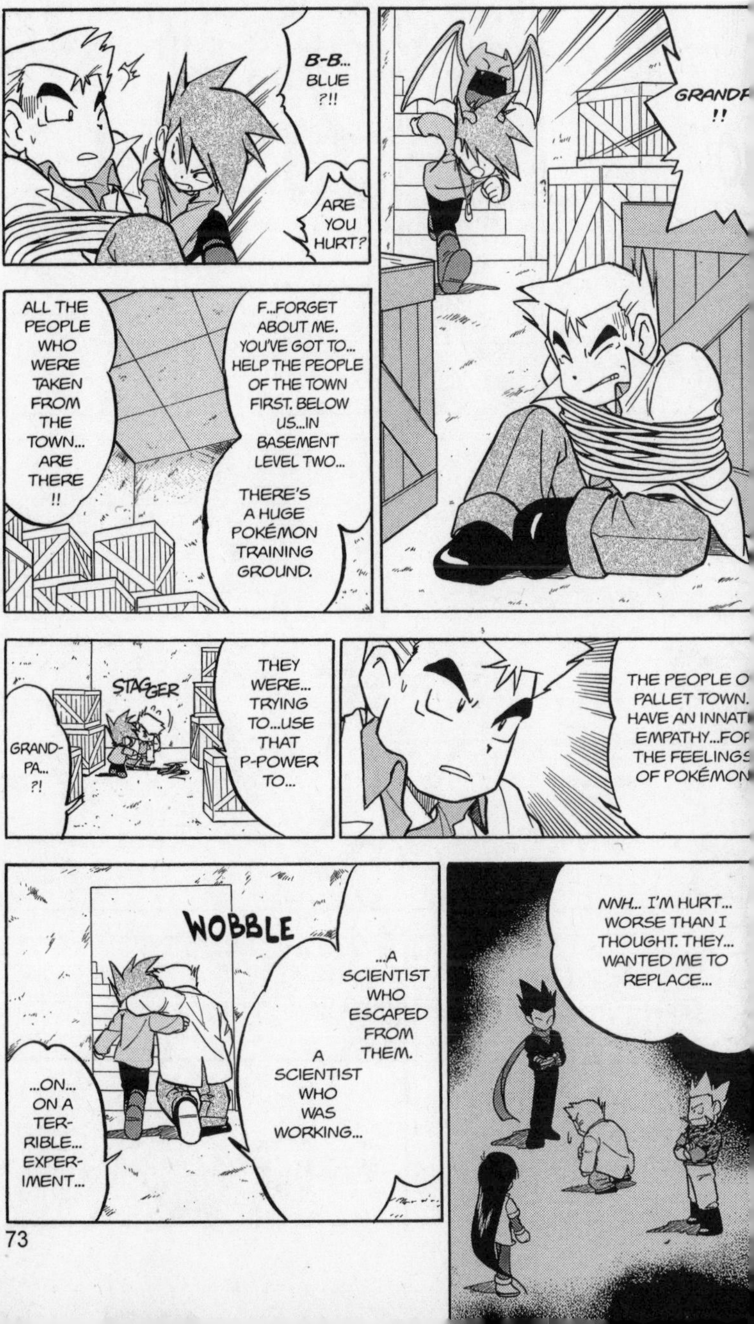
GRANDP !!
B-B... BLUE ?!!
ARE YOU HURT?
F...FORGET ABOUT ME. YOU'VE GOT TO... HELP THE PEOPLE OF THE TOWN FIRST. BELOW US...IN BASEMENT LEVEL TWO...
THERE'S A HUGE POKÉMON TRAINING GROUND.
ALL THE PEOPLE WHO WERE TAKEN FROM THE TOWN... ARE THERE !!
THE PEOPLE O PALLET TOWN. HAVE AN INNAT EMPATHY...FOF THE FEELINGS OF POKÉMON
THEY WERE... TRYING TO...USE THAT P-POWER TO...
STAGGER
GRAND-PA... ?!
NNH... I'M HURT... WORSE THAN I THOUGHT. THEY... WANTED ME TO REPLACE...
WOBBLE
...A SCIENTIST WHO ESCAPED FROM THEM.
A SCIENTIST WHO WAS WORKING...
...ON... ON A TER-RIBLE... EXPER-IMENT...

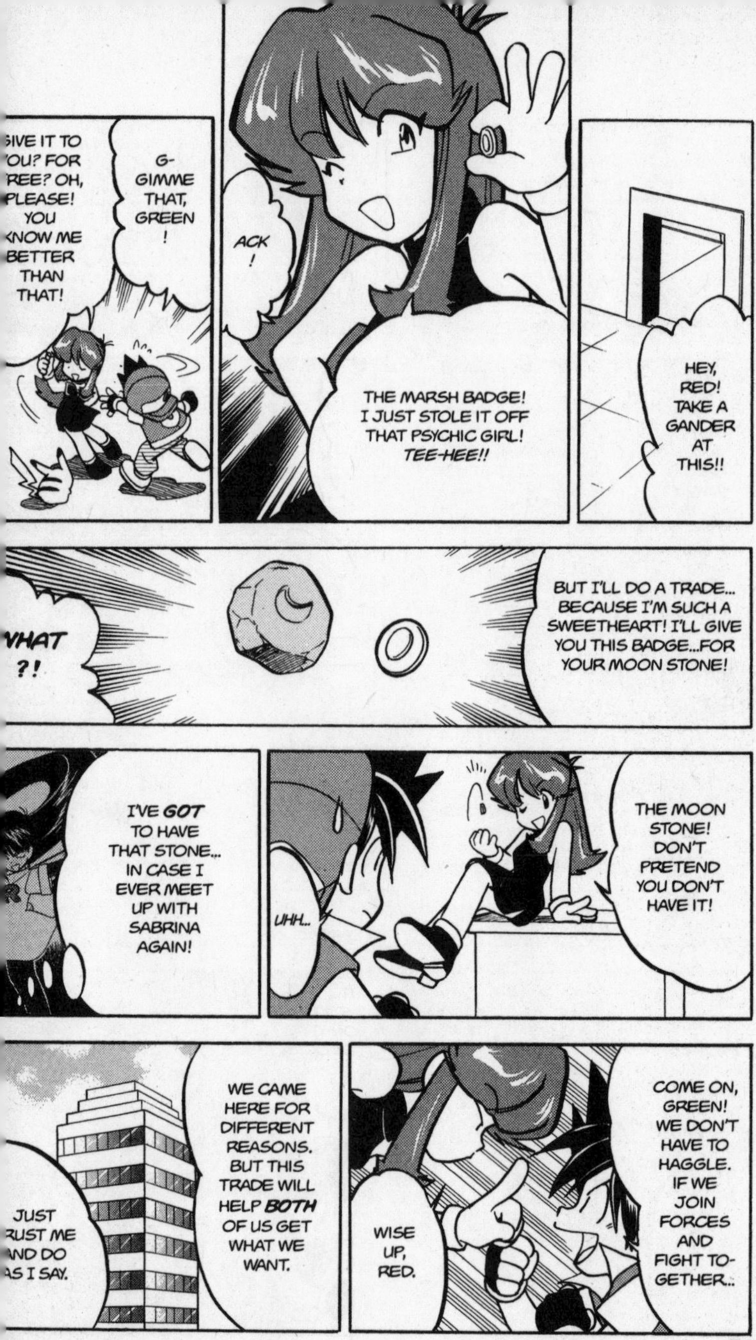
HEY, RED! TAKE A GANDER AT THIS!!
THE MARSH BADGE! I JUST STOLE IT OFF THAT PSYCHIC GIRL! *TEE-HEE!!*
ACK!
G-GIMME THAT, GREEN!
IVE IT TO OU? FOR REE? OH, PLEASE! YOU NOW ME BETTER THAN THAT!
BUT I'LL DO A TRADE... BECAUSE I'M SUCH A SWEETHEART! I'LL GIVE YOU THIS BADGE...FOR YOUR MOON STONE!
VHAT ?!
THE MOON STONE! DON'T PRETEND YOU DON'T HAVE IT!
UHH...
I'VE *GOT* TO HAVE THAT STONE... IN CASE I EVER MEET UP WITH SABRINA AGAIN!
COME ON, GREEN! WE DON'T HAVE TO HAGGLE. IF WE JOIN FORCES AND FIGHT TO-GETHER...
WISE UP, RED.
WE CAME HERE FOR DIFFERENT REASONS. BUT THIS TRADE WILL HELP *BOTH* OF US GET WHAT WE WANT.
JUST RUST ME ND DO S I SAY.

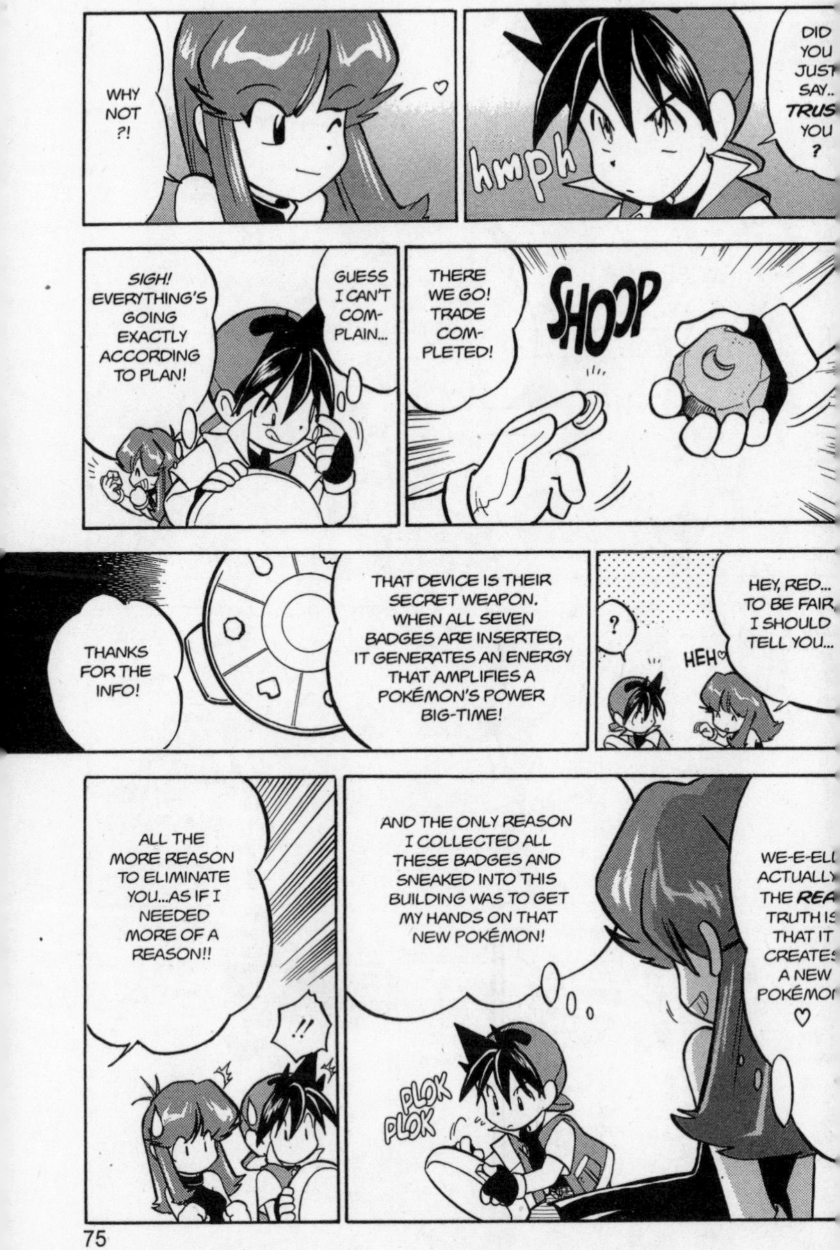

DID YOU JUST SAY.. *TRUS* YOU ?
hmph
WHY NOT ?!
THERE WE GO! TRADE COMPLETED!
SHOOP
GUESS I CAN'T COMPLAIN...
SIGH! EVERYTHING'S GOING EXACTLY ACCORDING TO PLAN!
HEY, RED... TO BE FAIR, I SHOULD TELL YOU...
HEH♡
?
THAT DEVICE IS THEIR SECRET WEAPON. WHEN ALL SEVEN BADGES ARE INSERTED, IT GENERATES AN ENERGY THAT AMPLIFIES A POKÉMON'S POWER BIG-TIME!
THANKS FOR THE INFO!
WE-E-EL ACTUALL THE *REA* TRUTH IS THAT IT CREATES A NEW POKÉMO ♡
AND THE ONLY REASON I COLLECTED ALL THESE BADGES AND SNEAKED INTO THIS BUILDING WAS TO GET MY HANDS ON THAT NEW POKÉMON!
PLOK PLOK
ALL THE MORE REASON TO ELIMINATE YOU...AS IF I NEEDED MORE OF A REASON!!
!!

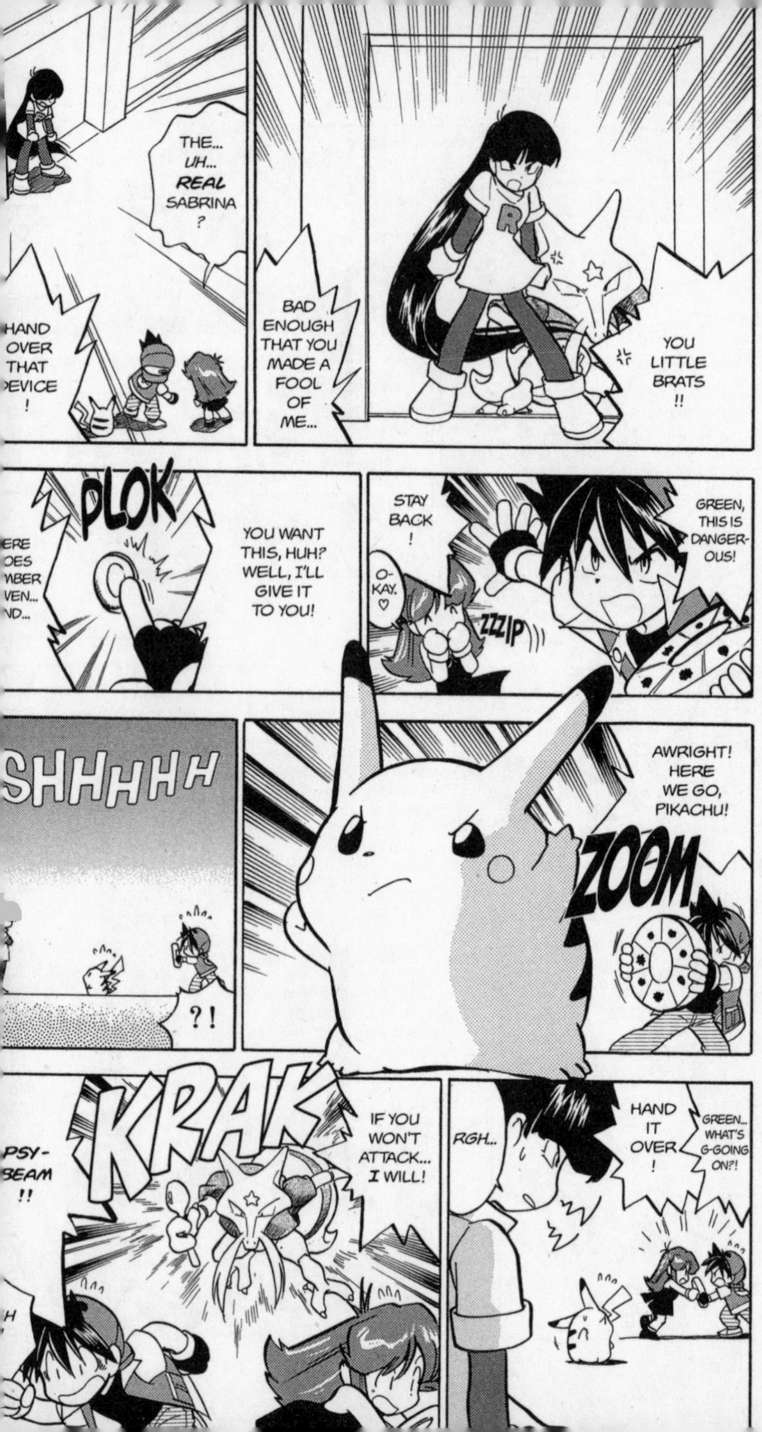
YOU LITTLE BRATS !!
BAD ENOUGH THAT YOU MADE A FOOL OF ME...
THE... UH... REAL SABRINA ?
HAND OVER THAT EVICE !
GREEN, THIS IS DANGER-OUS!
STAY BACK !
O-KAY. ♡
ZZZIP
YOU WANT THIS, HUH? WELL, I'LL GIVE IT TO YOU!
PLOK
ERE OES MBER VEN... ND...
AWRIGHT! HERE WE GO, PIKACHU!
ZOOM
SHHHHH
?!
GREEN... WHAT'S G-GOING ON?!
HAND IT OVER !
RGH...
IF YOU WON'T ATTACK... I WILL!
KRAK
PSY-BEAM !!

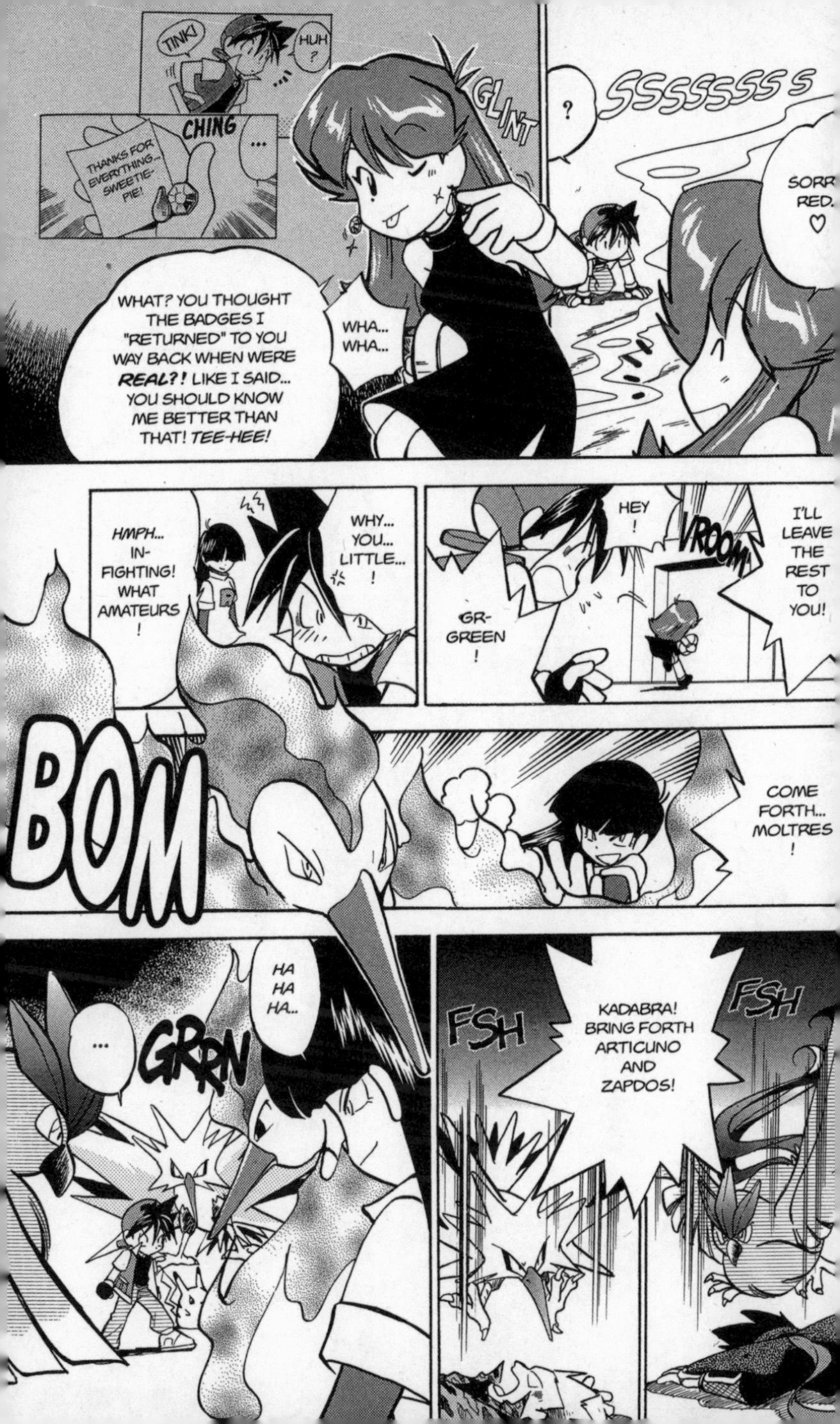
SSSSSSSS S
?
SORR
RED.
♡
HUH
?
TINK!
...
CHING
THANKS FOR EVERYTHING... SWEETIE-PIE!
GLINT
WHA... WHA...
WHAT? YOU THOUGHT THE BADGES I "RETURNED" TO YOU WAY BACK WHEN WERE *REAL?!* LIKE I SAID... YOU SHOULD KNOW ME BETTER THAN THAT! *TEE-HEE!*
I'LL LEAVE THE REST TO YOU!
VROOM
HEY!
GR-GREEN!
WHY... YOU... LITTLE...!
HMPH... IN-FIGHTING! WHAT AMATEURS!
COME FORTH... MOLTRES!
BOM
FSH
KADABRA! BRING FORTH ARTICUNO AND ZAPDOS!
FSH
HA HA HA...
GRRN
...

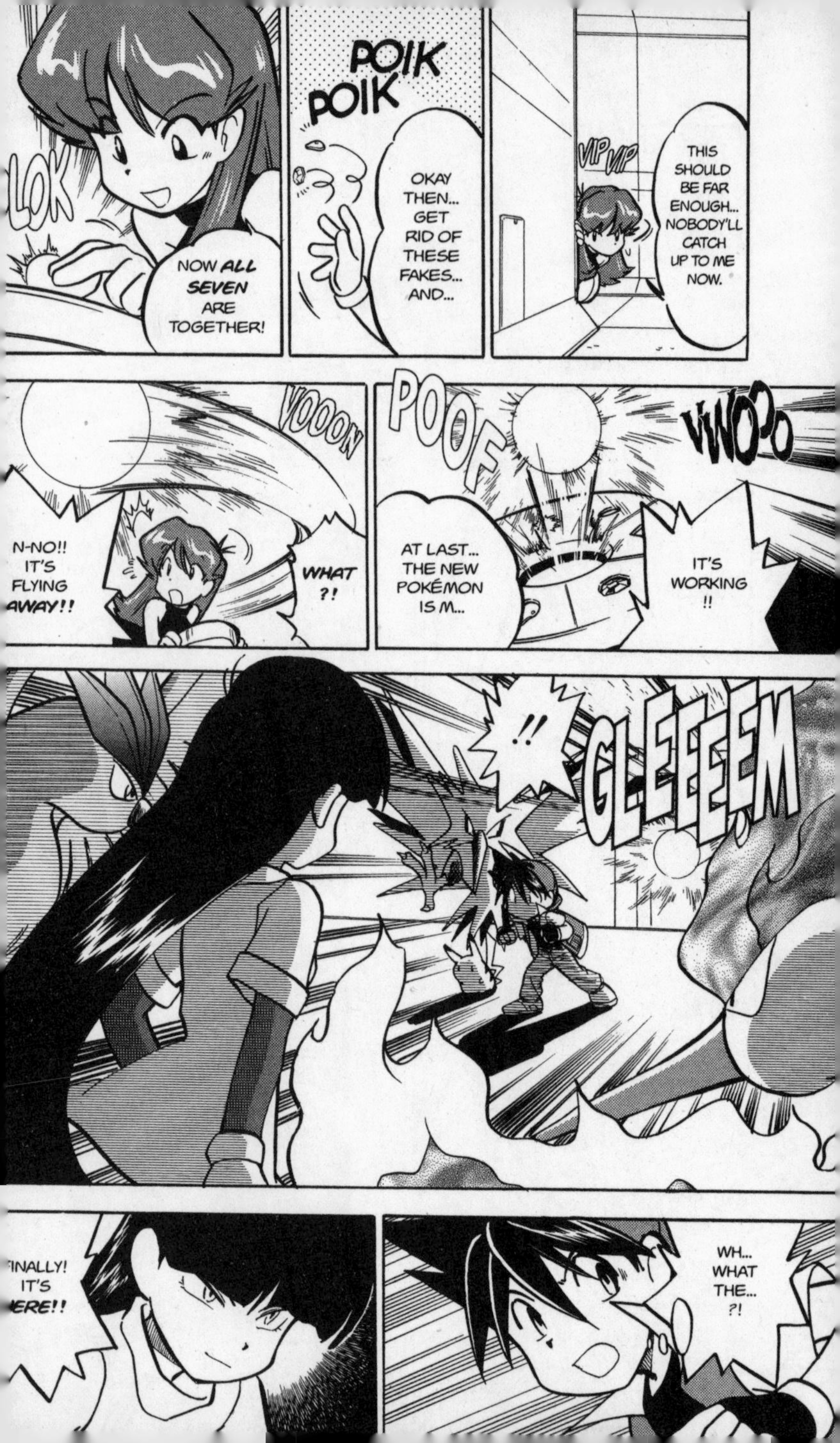
VIP VIP
THIS SHOULD BE FAR ENOUGH... NOBODY'LL CATCH UP TO ME NOW.
POIK POIK
OKAY THEN... GET RID OF THESE FAKES... AND...
LOK
NOW ALL SEVEN ARE TOGETHER!
VWOOO
IT'S WORKING !!
POOF
AT LAST... THE NEW POKÉMON IS M...
VOOOON
WHAT ?!
N-NO!! IT'S FLYING AWAY!!
GLEEEEM
!!
WH... WHAT THE... ?!
INALLY! IT'S ERE!!

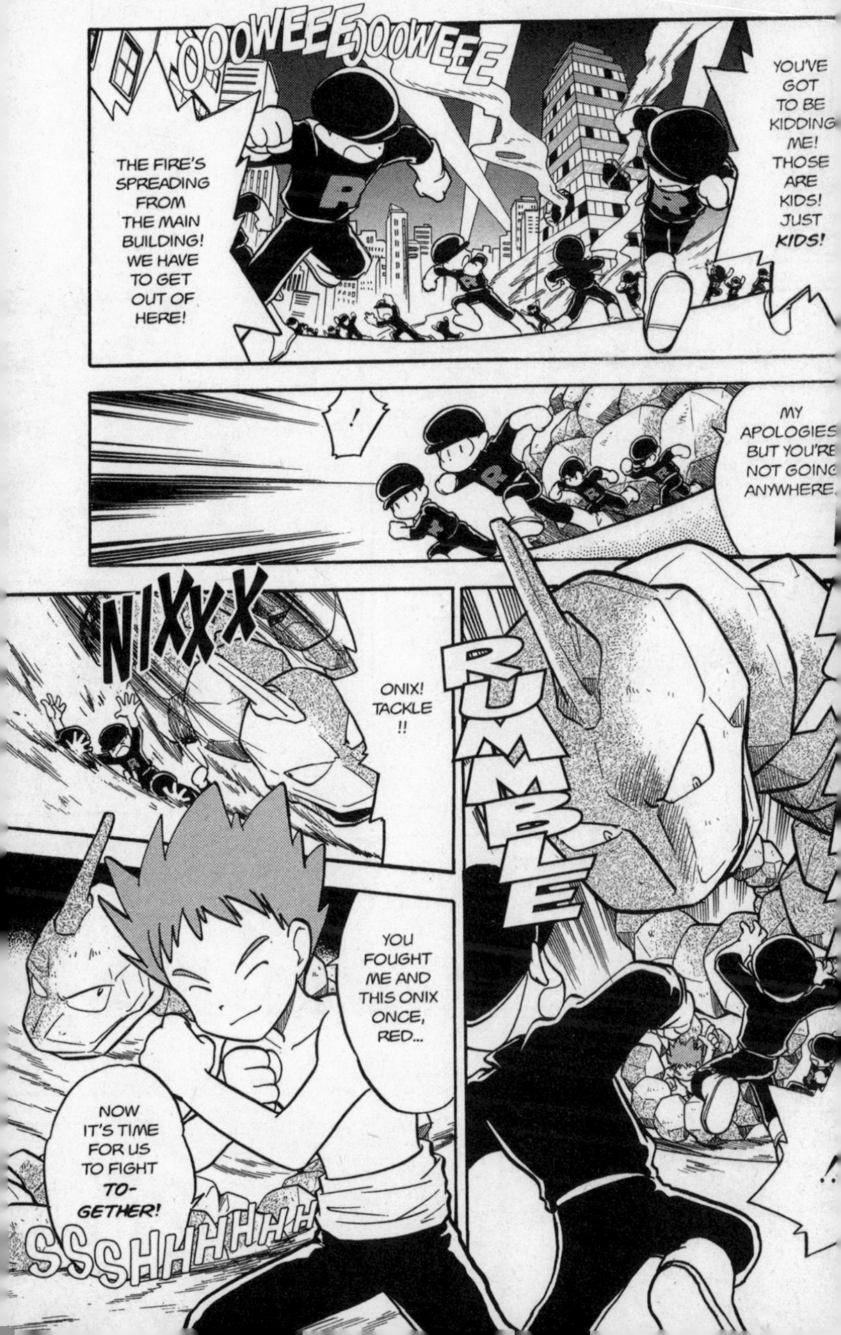
YOU'VE GOT TO BE KIDDING ME! THOSE ARE KIDS! JUST KIDS!
OOOWEEE OOOWEEE
THE FIRE'S SPREADING FROM THE MAIN BUILDING! WE HAVE TO GET OUT OF HERE!
MY APOLOGIES BUT YOU'RE NOT GOING ANYWHERE.
!
RUMBLE
NIXXX
ONIX! TACKLE !!
YOU FOUGHT ME AND THIS ONIX ONCE, RED...
NOW IT'S TIME FOR US TO FIGHT TO-GETHER!
SSSHHHHHH

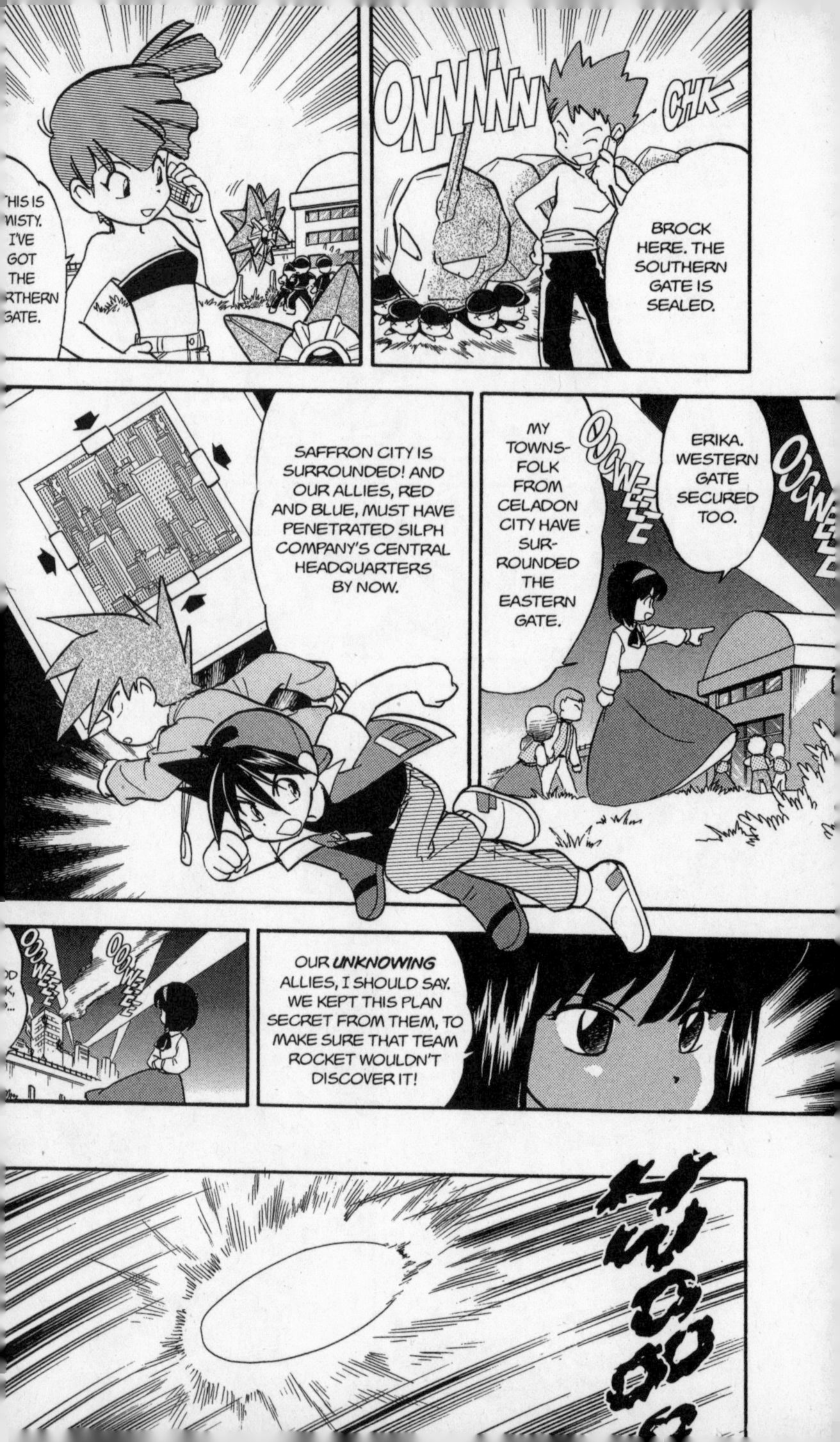
ONNNNNN
CHK
BROCK HERE. THE SOUTHERN GATE IS SEALED.
THIS IS MISTY. I'VE GOT THE RTHERN GATE.
ERIKA. WESTERN GATE SECURED TOO.
OOOWEEE
MY TOWNS-FOLK FROM CELADON CITY HAVE SUR-ROUNDED THE EASTERN GATE.
OOOWEEE
SAFFRON CITY IS SURROUNDED! AND OUR ALLIES, RED AND BLUE, MUST HAVE PENETRATED SILPH COMPANY'S CENTRAL HEADQUARTERS BY NOW.
OUR UNKNOWING ALLIES, I SHOULD SAY. WE KEPT THIS PLAN SECRET FROM THEM, TO MAKE SURE THAT TEAM ROCKET WOULDN'T DISCOVER IT!
OOOWEEE
OOOWEEE

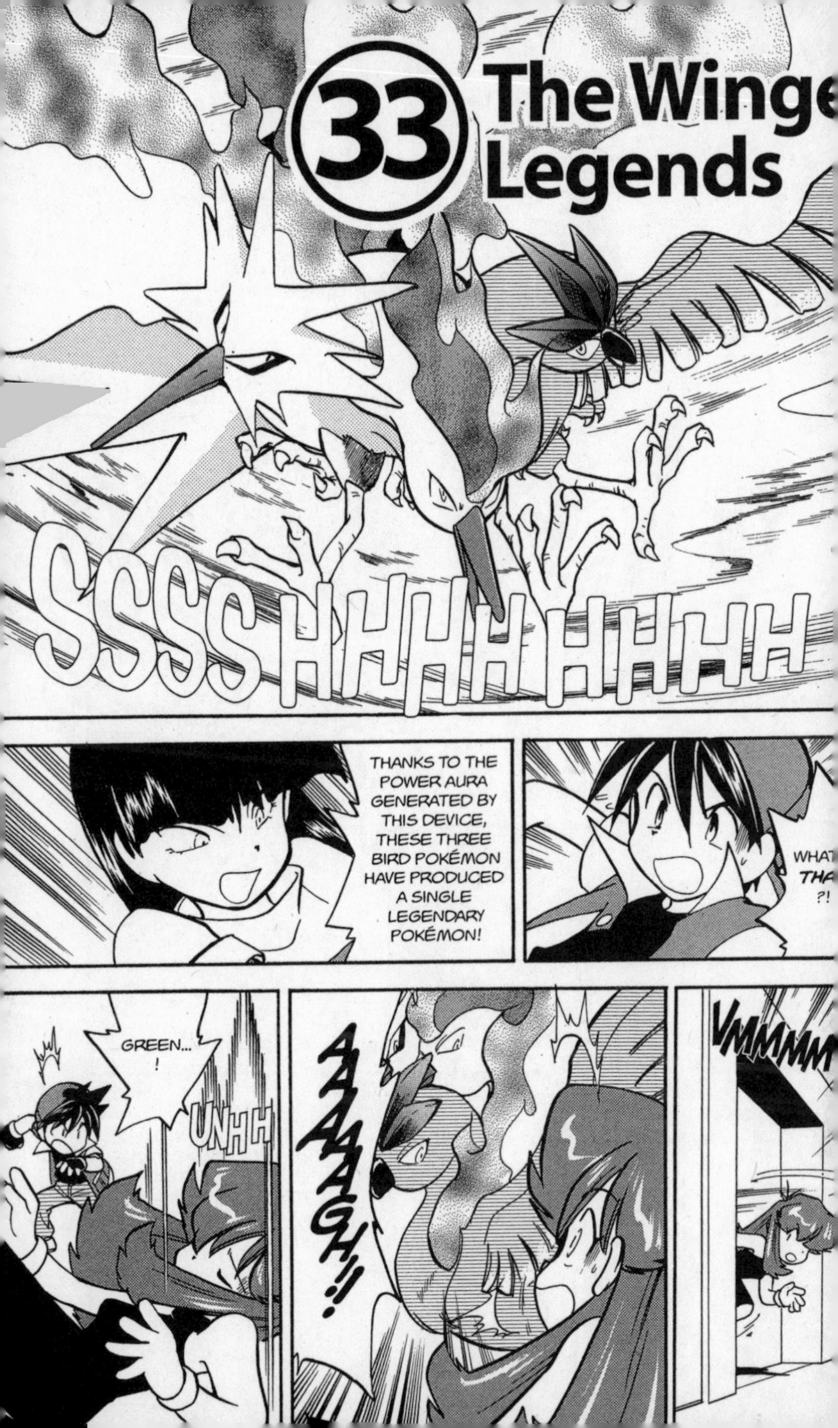
33
The Winge
Legends
SSSSHHHHHHHHH
WHAT
THA
?!
THANKS TO THE POWER AURA GENERATED BY THIS DEVICE, THESE THREE BIRD POKÉMON HAVE PRODUCED A SINGLE LEGENDARY POKÉMON!
VMMMM
AAAAAGH!!
GREEN...!
UNHH

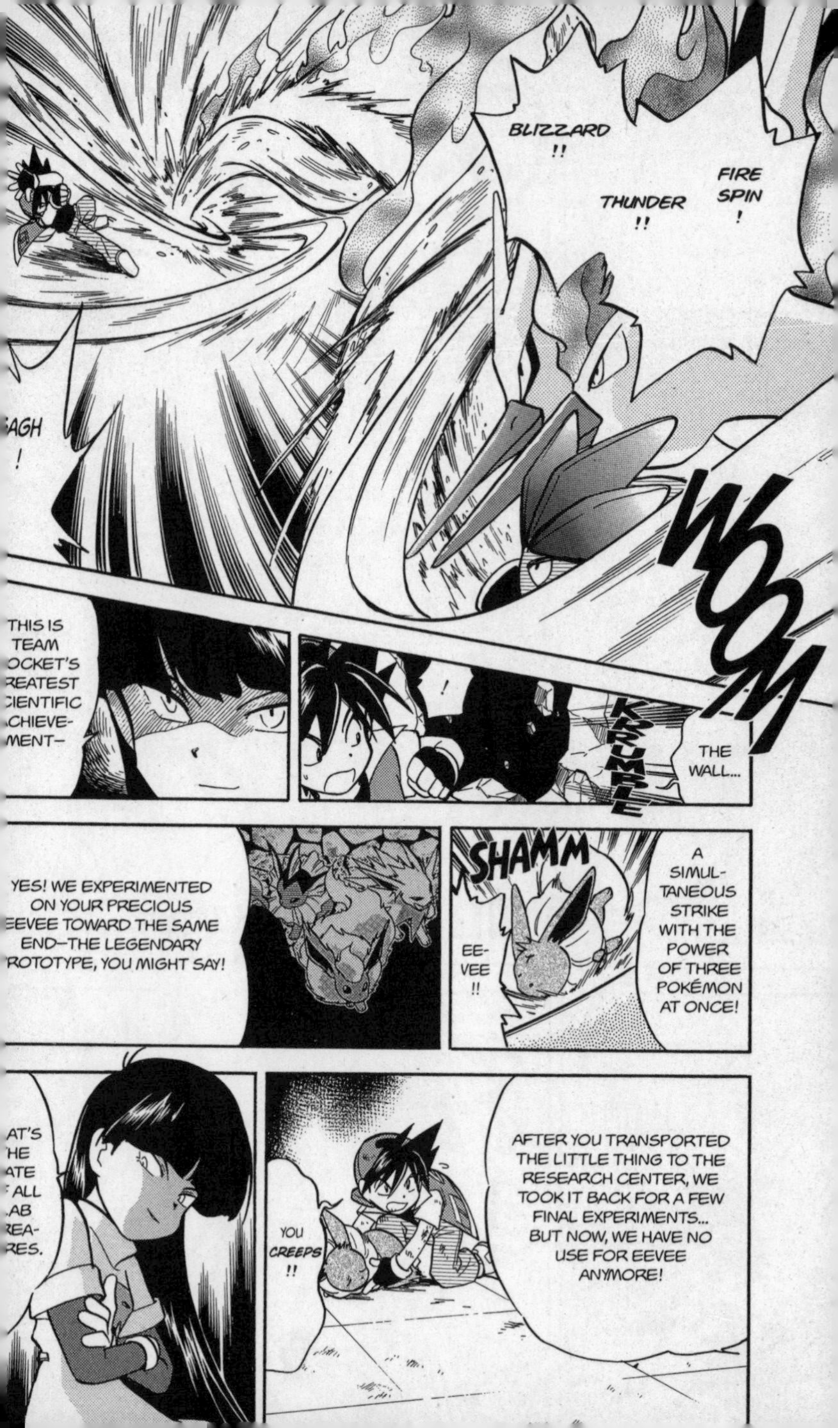
FIRE SPIN!
THUNDER!!
BLIZZARD!!
WOOM
AGH!
THE WALL...
KRRUMBLE
!
THIS IS TEAM OCKET'S REATEST CIENTIFIC CHIEVE-MENT—
A SIMUL-TANEOUS STRIKE WITH THE POWER OF THREE POKÉMON AT ONCE!
SHAMM
EE-VEE!!
YES! WE EXPERIMENTED ON YOUR PRECIOUS EEVEE TOWARD THE SAME END—THE LEGENDARY ROTOTYPE, YOU MIGHT SAY!
AFTER YOU TRANSPORTED THE LITTLE THING TO THE RESEARCH CENTER, WE TOOK IT BACK FOR A FEW FINAL EXPERIMENTS... BUT NOW, WE HAVE NO USE FOR EEVEE ANYMORE!
YOU CREEPS!!
AT'S HE ATE F ALL AB REA-RES.

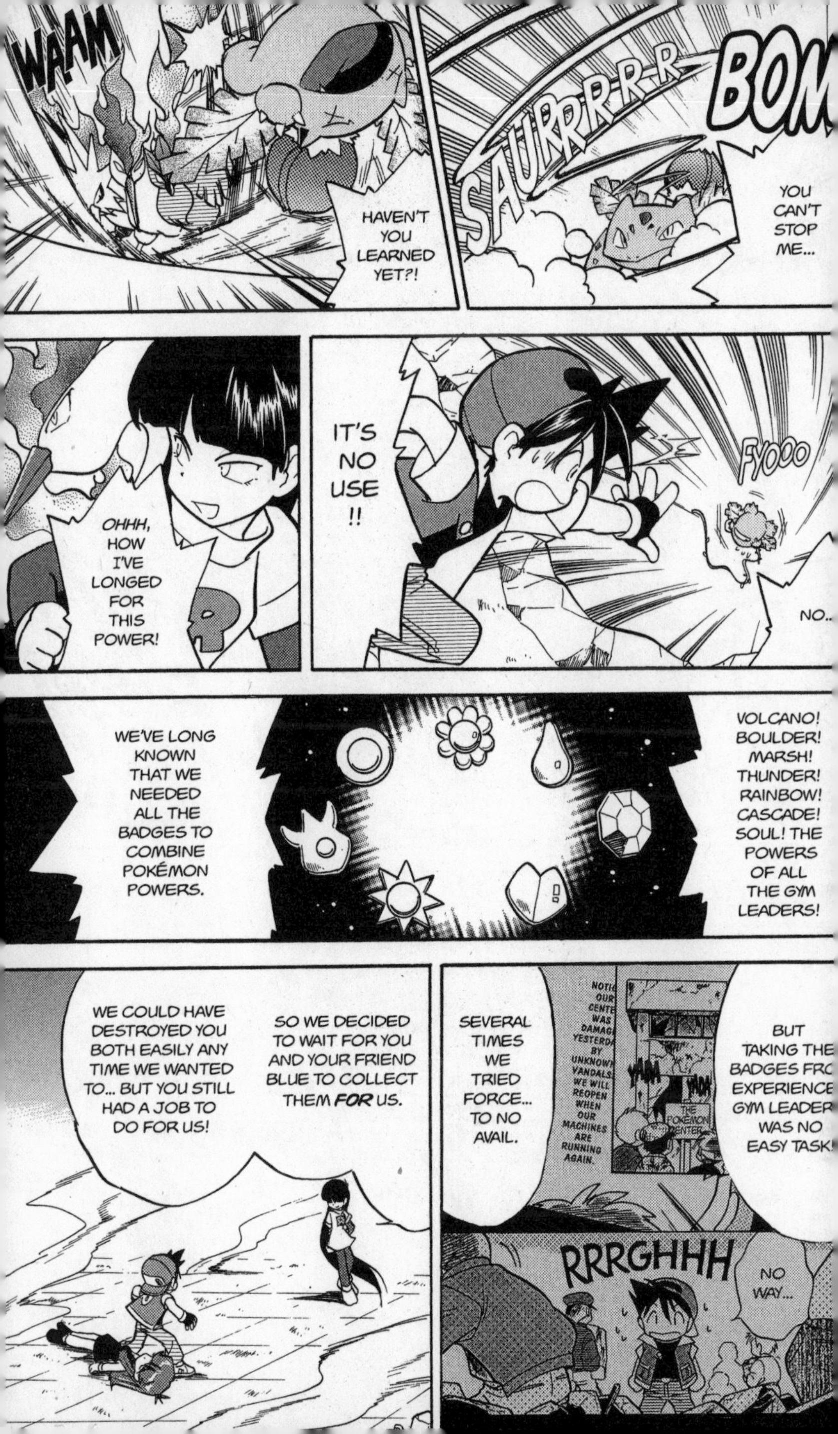
BOM
SAURRRR-R-R
YOU CAN'T STOP ME...
WAAM
HAVEN'T YOU LEARNED YET?!
FYOOO
IT'S NO USE !!
NO...
OHHH, HOW I'VE LONGED FOR THIS POWER!
VOLCANO! BOULDER! MARSH! THUNDER! RAINBOW! CASCADE! SOUL! THE POWERS OF ALL THE GYM LEADERS!
WE'VE LONG KNOWN THAT WE NEEDED ALL THE BADGES TO COMBINE POKÉMON POWERS.
BUT TAKING THE BADGES FRO EXPERIENCE GYM LEADER WAS NO EASY TASK
NOTIC OUR CENTE WAS DAMAG YESTERDA BY UNKNOWN VANDALS. WE WILL REOPEN WHEN OUR MACHINES ARE RUNNING AGAIN.
YAM
YADA
THE POKÉMON CENTER
SEVERAL TIMES WE TRIED FORCE... TO NO AVAIL.
NO WAY...
RRRGHHH
SO WE DECIDED TO WAIT FOR YOU AND YOUR FRIEND BLUE TO COLLECT THEM FOR US.
WE COULD HAVE DESTROYED YOU BOTH EASILY ANY TIME WE WANTED TO... BUT YOU STILL HAD A JOB TO DO FOR US!

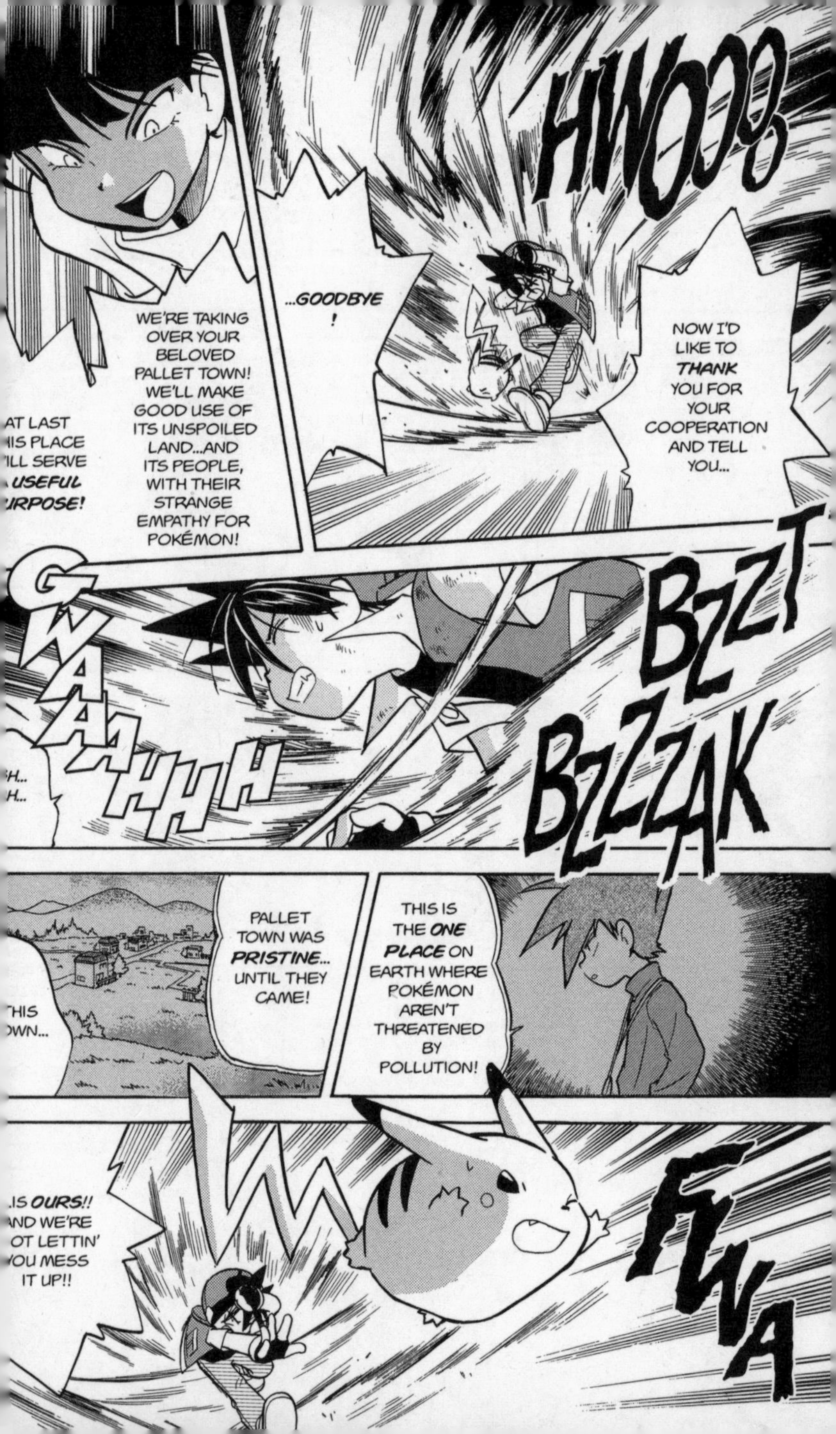
NOW I'D LIKE TO **THANK** YOU FOR YOUR COOPERATION AND TELL YOU...
...**GOODBYE**!
WE'RE TAKING OVER YOUR BELOVED PALLET TOWN! WE'LL MAKE GOOD USE OF ITS UNSPOILED LAND...AND ITS PEOPLE, WITH THEIR STRANGE EMPATHY FOR POKÉMON!
AT LAST IIS PLACE 'ILL SERVE **USEFUL** **RPOSE!**
BZZT BZZZAK
GWAAAHHHHH
H... H...
THIS IS THE **ONE PLACE** ON EARTH WHERE POKÉMON AREN'T THREATENED BY POLLUTION!
PALLET TOWN WAS **PRISTINE**... UNTIL THEY CAME!
THIS OWN...
FWA
.IS **OURS!!** ND WE'RE OT LETTIN' YOU MESS IT UP!!

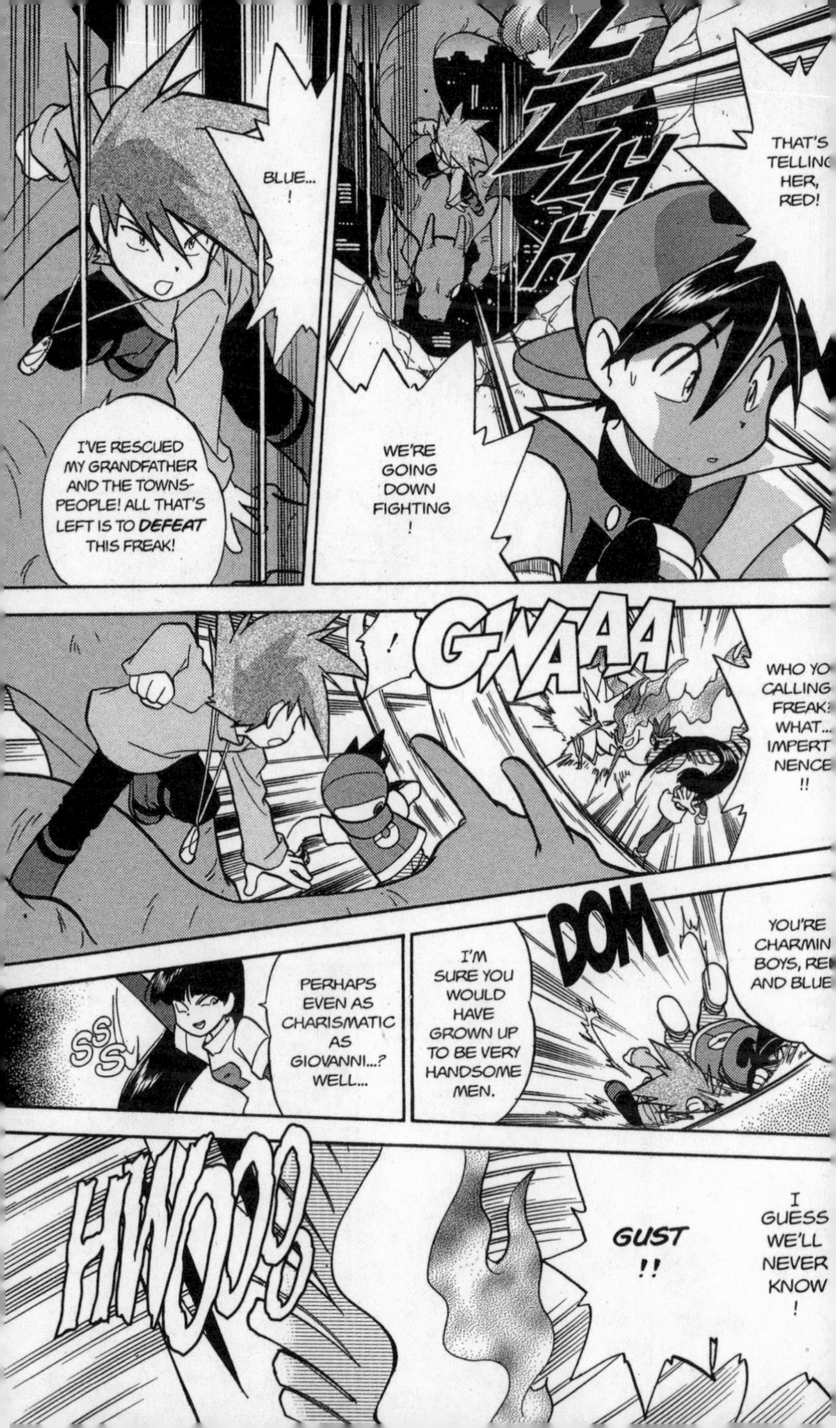
ZZZH
THAT'S TELLIN HER, RED!
WE'RE GOING DOWN FIGHTING !
BLUE... !
I'VE RESCUED MY GRANDFATHER AND THE TOWNS-PEOPLE! ALL THAT'S LEFT IS TO DEFEAT THIS FREAK!
WHO YO CALLING FREAK WHAT... IMPERT NENCE !!
GNAAA
!
YOU'RE CHARMIN BOYS, RE AND BLUE
DOM
I'M SURE YOU WOULD HAVE GROWN UP TO BE VERY HANDSOME MEN.
PERHAPS EVEN AS CHARISMATIC AS GIOVANNI...? WELL...
SSS
I GUESS WE'LL NEVER KNOW !
!
GUST !!
HWOOO

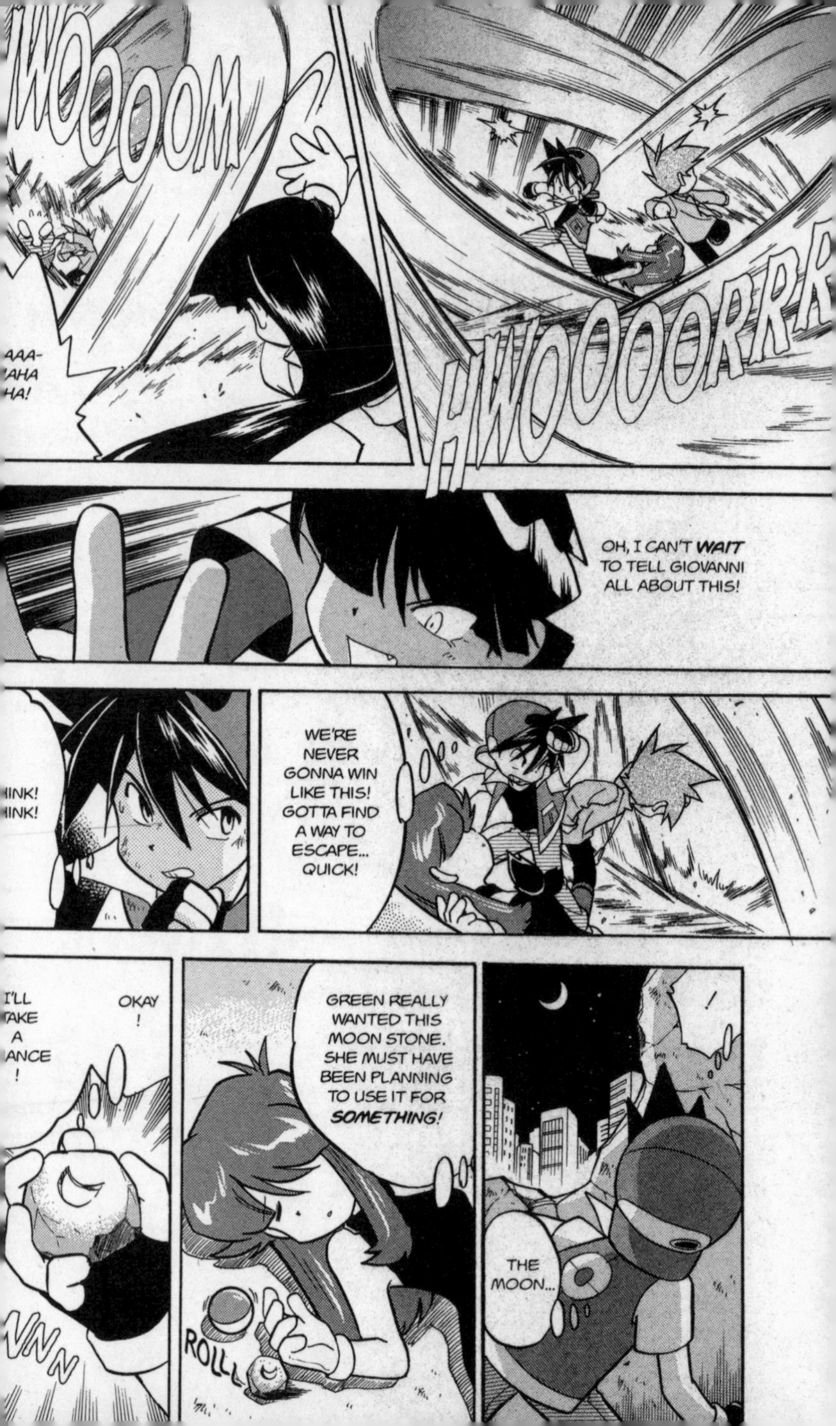
HWOOOORRR
WOOOOM
AAA- AHA HA!
OH, I CAN'T WAIT TO TELL GIOVANNI ALL ABOUT THIS!
WE'RE NEVER GONNA WIN LIKE THIS! GOTTA FIND A WAY TO ESCAPE... QUICK!
INK! INK!
!
THE MOON...
GREEN REALLY WANTED THIS MOON STONE. SHE MUST HAVE BEEN PLANNING TO USE IT FOR SOMETHING!
ROLL
OKAY!
I'LL TAKE A ANCE!
VNN

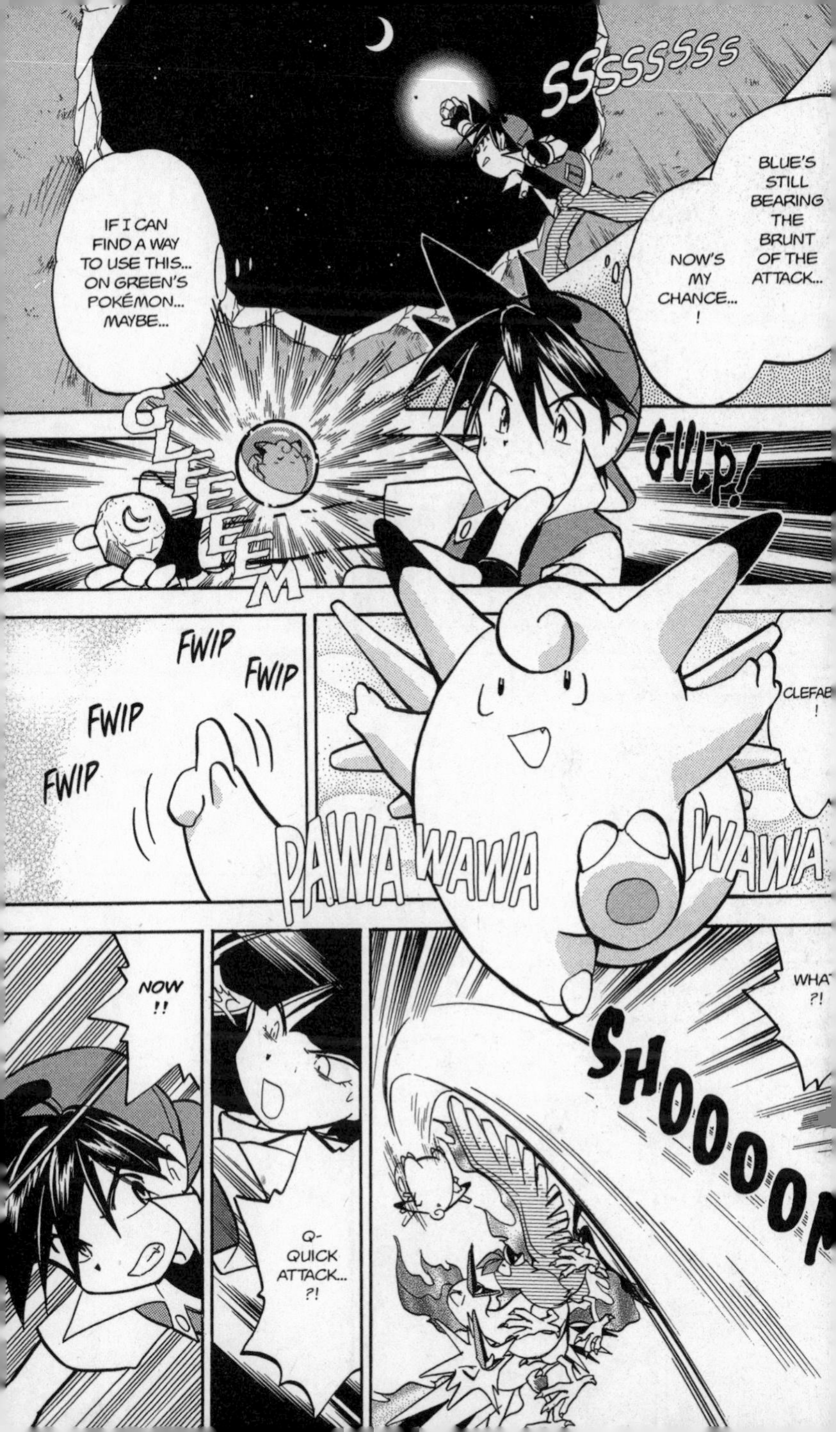
BLUE'S STILL BEARING THE BRUNT OF THE ATTACK...
NOW'S MY CHANCE... !
SSSSSSSS
IF I CAN FIND A WAY TO USE THIS... ON GREEN'S POKÉMON... MAYBE...
GULP!
GLEEEEM
CLEFAB !
PAWAWAWA WAWA
FWIP
FWIP
FWIP
FWIP
WHAT ?!
SHOOOOOP
Q- QUICK ATTACK... ?!
NOW !!

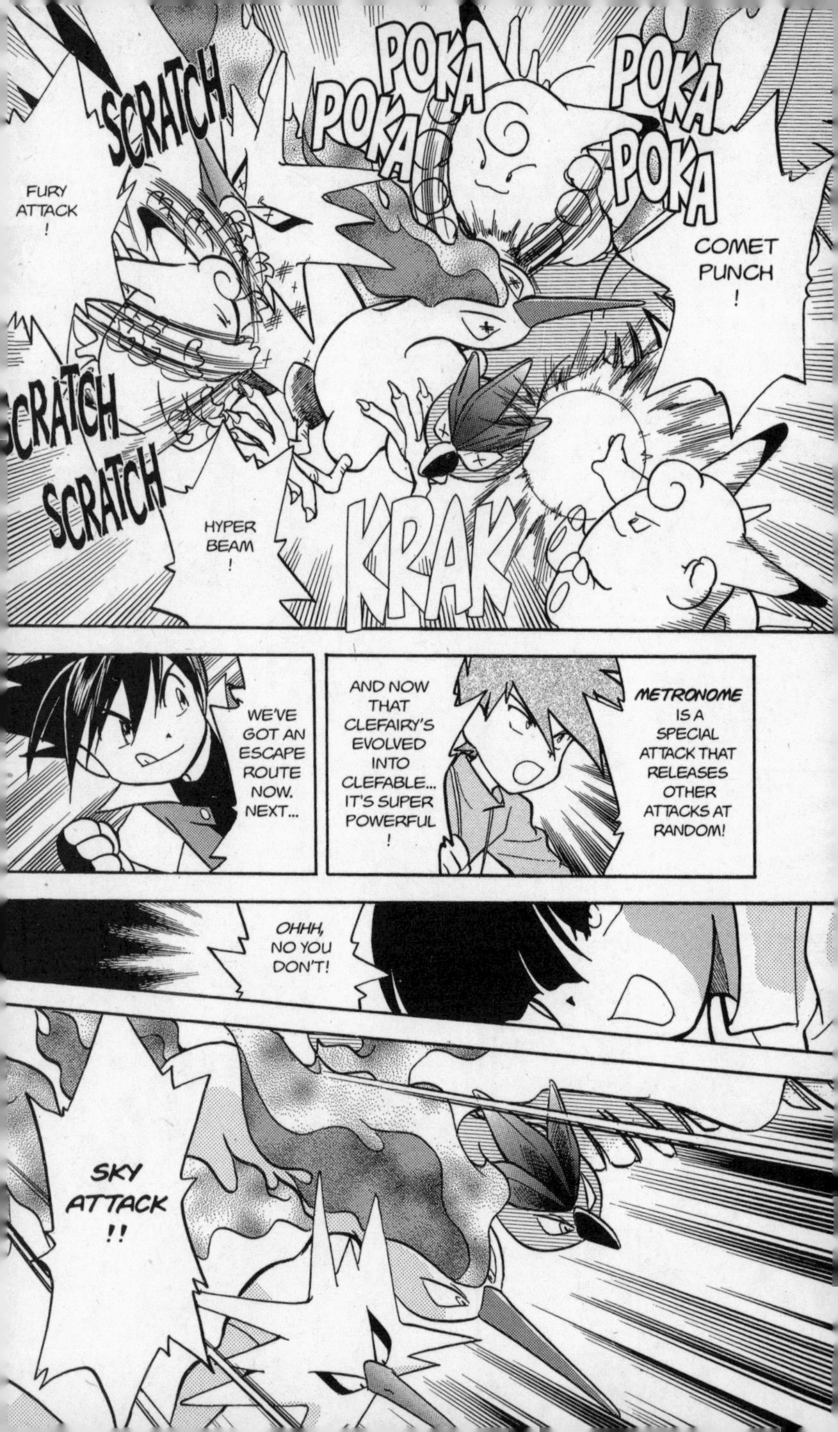
POKA POKA
COMET PUNCH!
POKA POKA
SCRATCH
FURY ATTACK!
KRAK
HYPER BEAM!
SCRATCH SCRATCH
METRONOME IS A SPECIAL ATTACK THAT RELEASES OTHER ATTACKS AT RANDOM!
AND NOW THAT CLEFAIRY'S EVOLVED INTO CLEFABLE... IT'S SUPER POWERFUL!
WE'VE GOT AN ESCAPE ROUTE NOW. NEXT...
OHHH, NO YOU DON'T!
SKY ATTACK!!

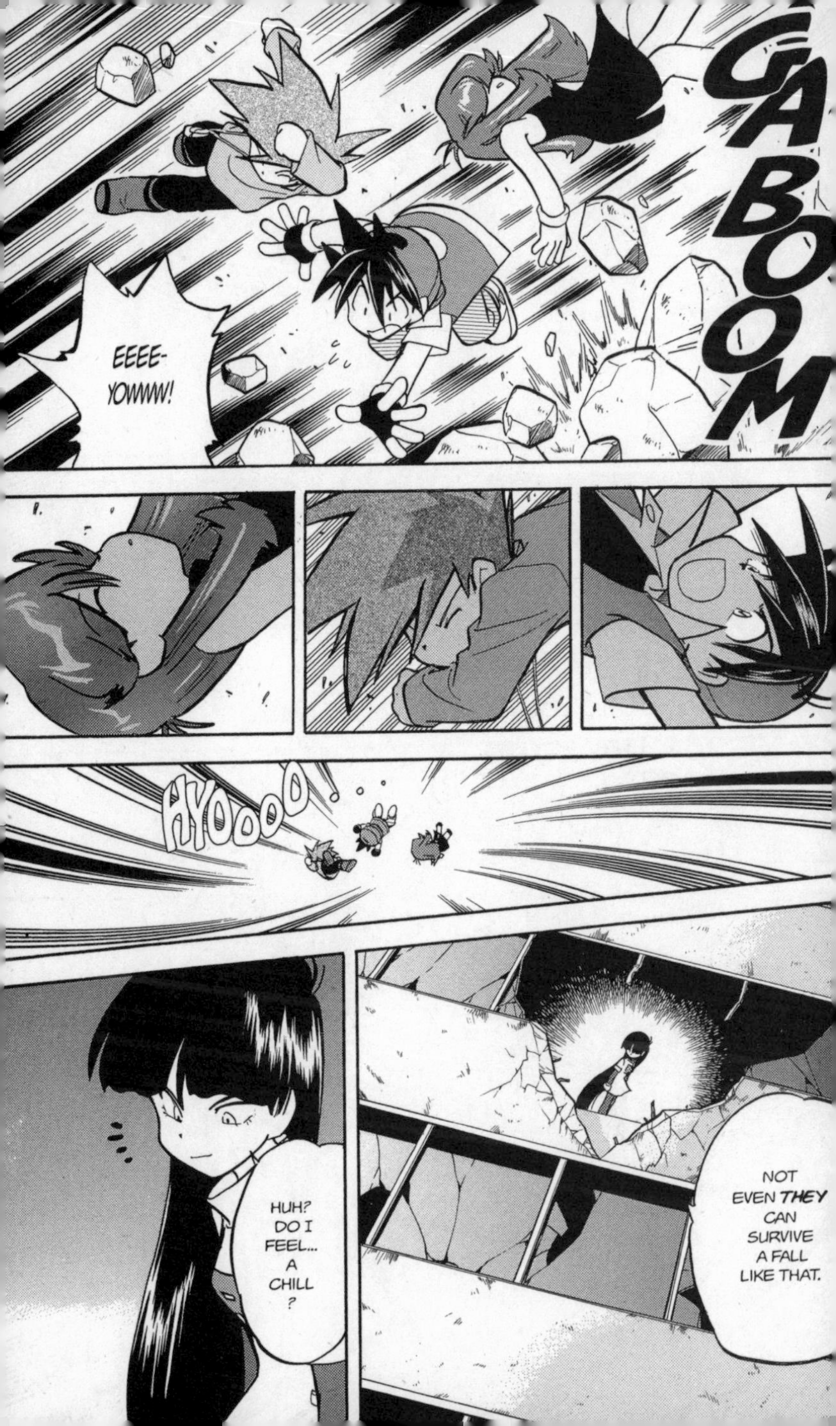
GABOOM
EEEE-YOWWW!
HYOOOO
NOT EVEN ***THEY*** CAN SURVIVE A FALL LIKE THAT.
HUH? DO I FEEL... A CHILL?

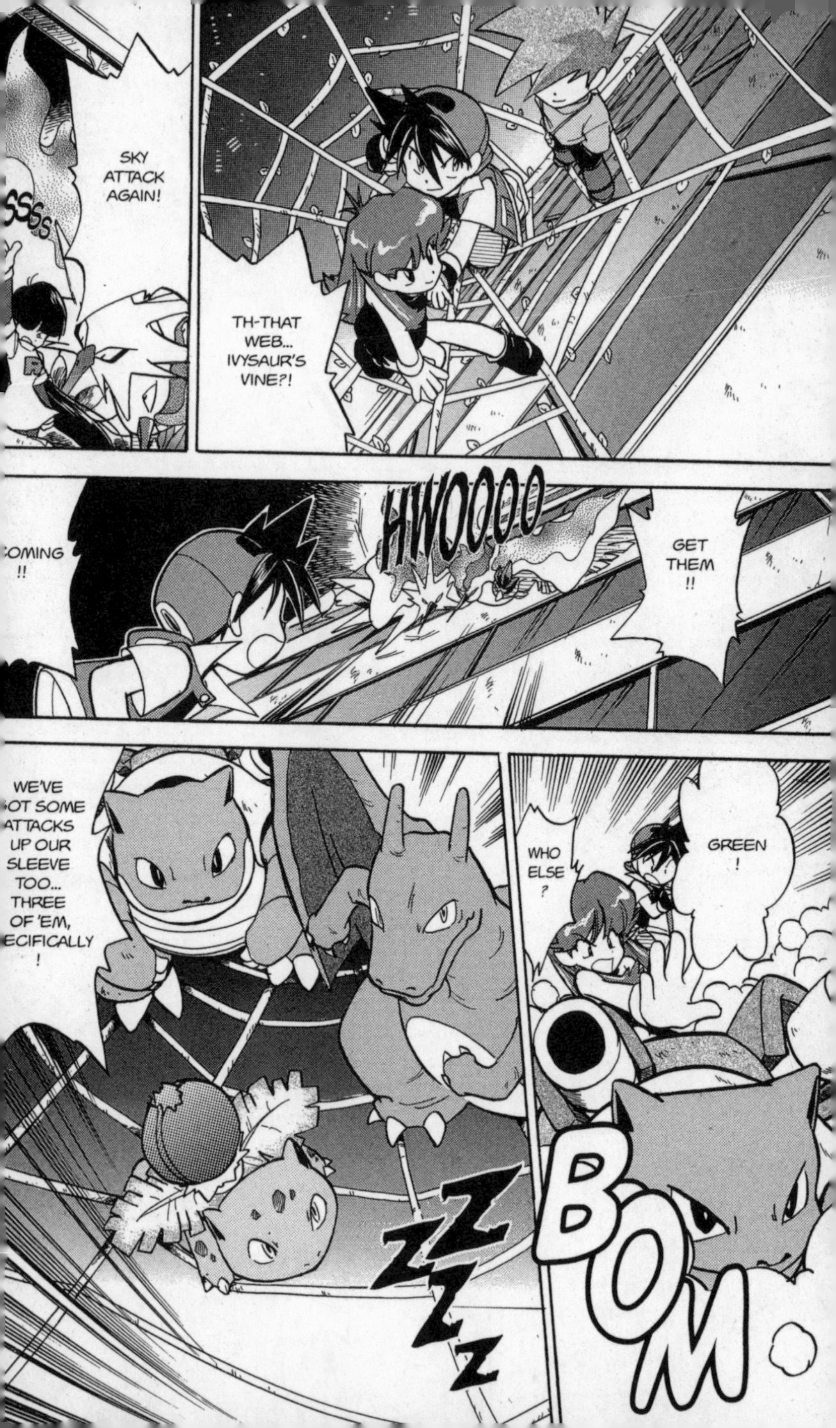

TH-THAT WEB... IVYSAUR'S VINE?!
SKY ATTACK AGAIN!
SSSSS
GET THEM !!
HWOOOO
OMING !!
GREEN !
WHO ELSE ?
BOOM
WE'VE OT SOME ATTACKS UP OUR SLEEVE TOO... THREE OF 'EM, ECIFICALLY !
ZZZ

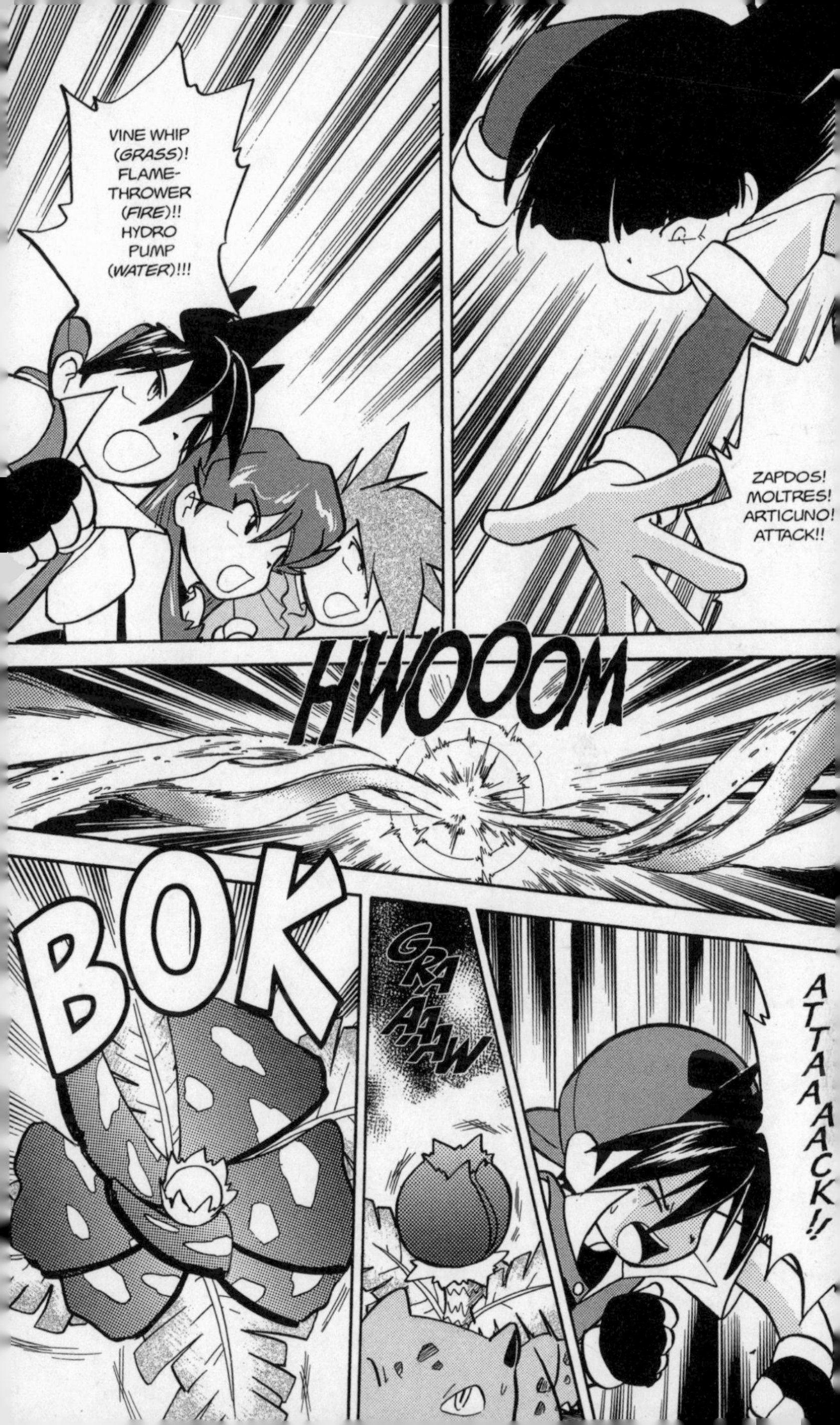
ZAPDOS! MOLTRES! ARTICUNO! ATTACK!!
VINE WHIP (GRASS)! FLAME-THROWER (FIRE)!! HYDRO PUMP (WATER)!!!
HWOOOM
ATTAAAAACK!!
GRAAAAW
BOK

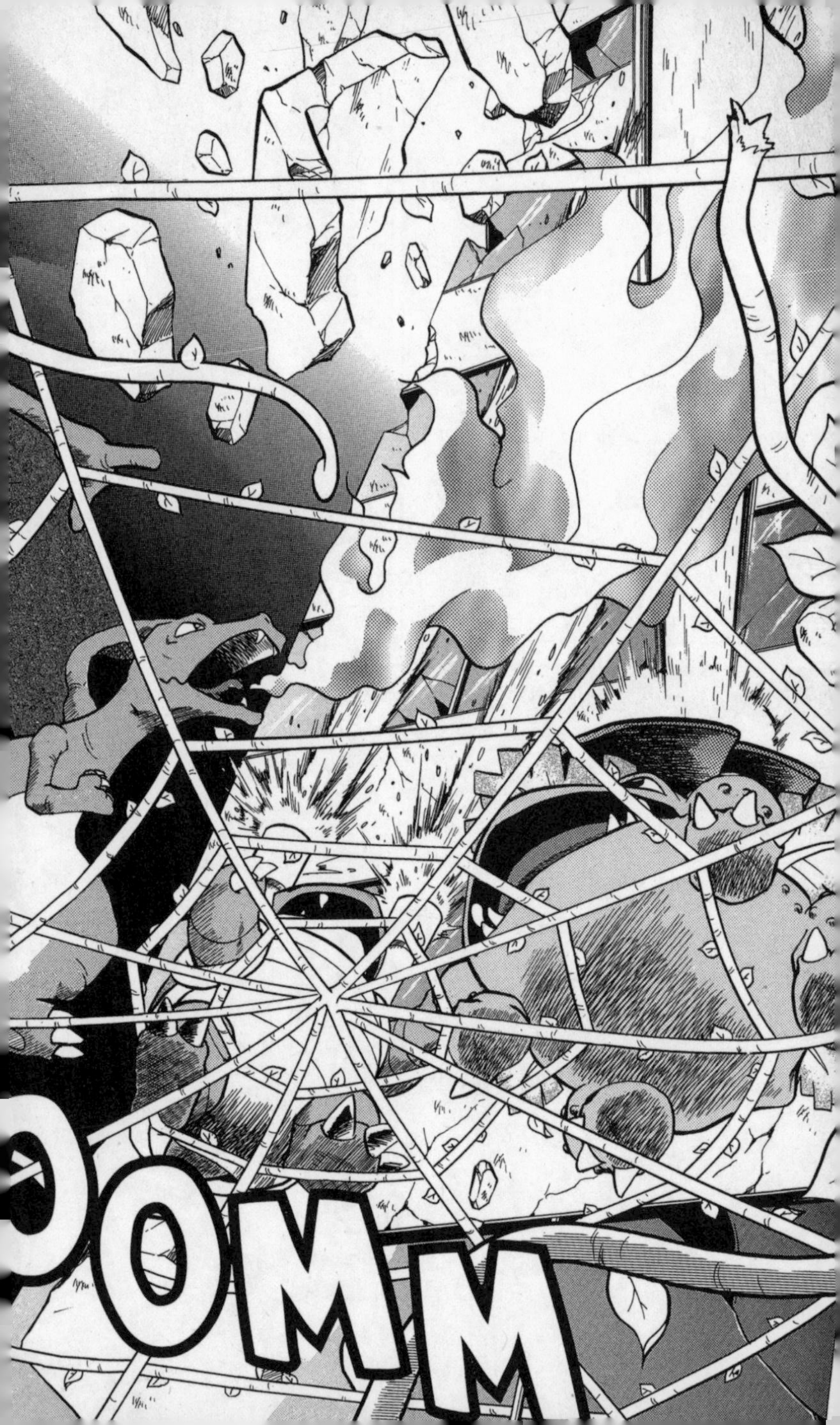
OOMM

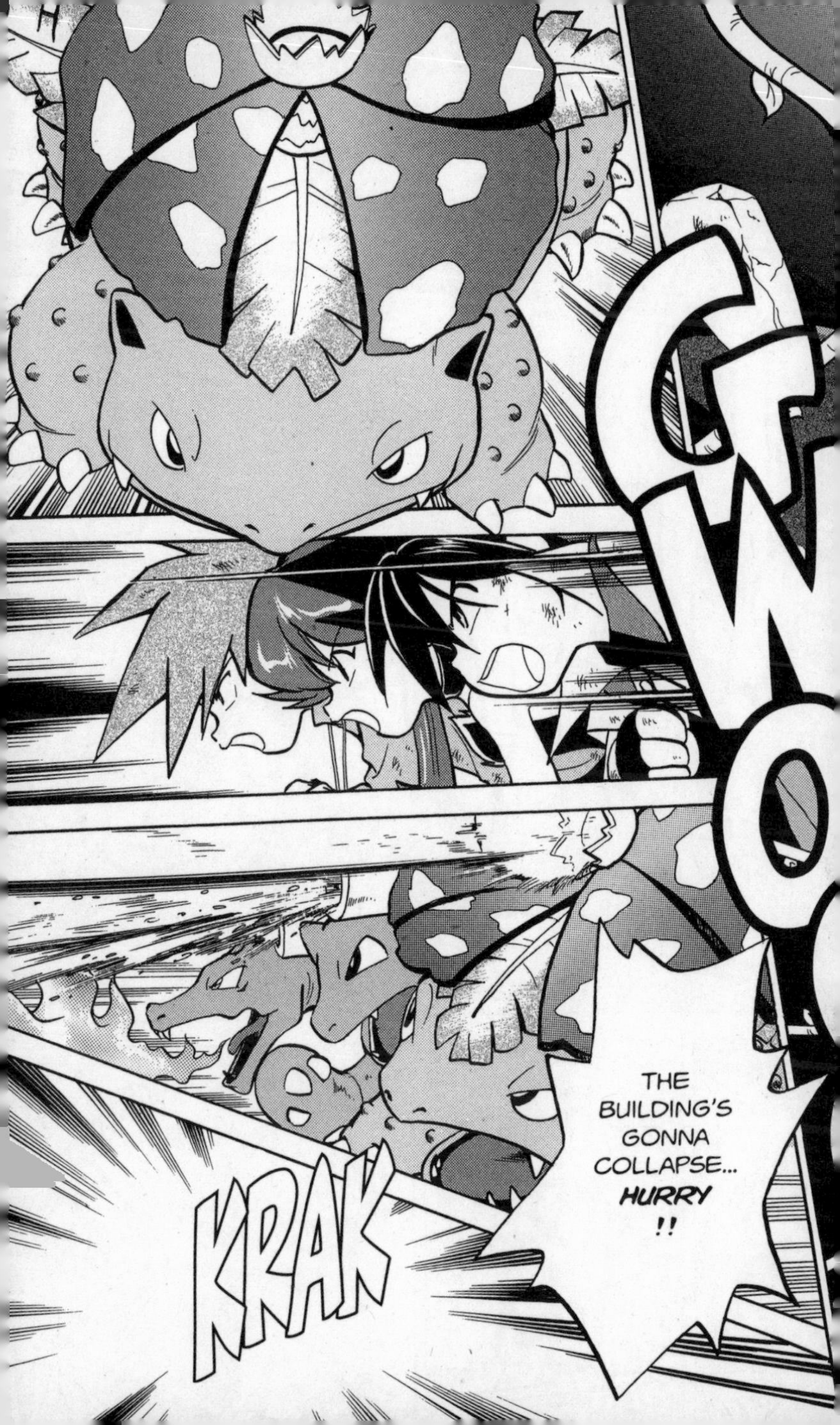
GWOO
THE BUILDING'S GONNA COLLAPSE... **HURRY** !!
KRAK

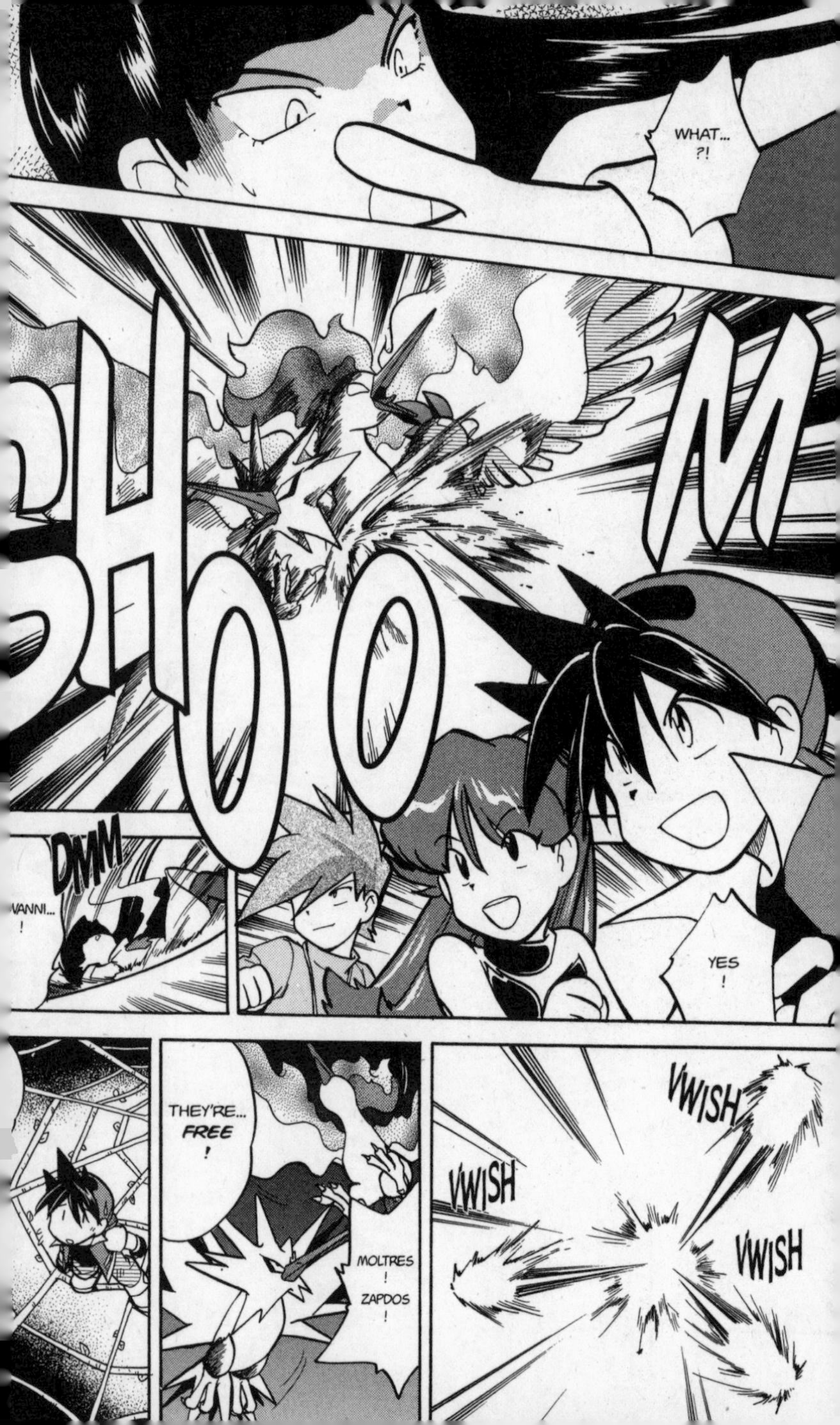
WHAT... ?!
SHOOM
YES!
DMM
WANNI... !
VWISH
VWISH
VWISH
THEY'RE... *FREE*!
MOLTRES! ZAPDOS!

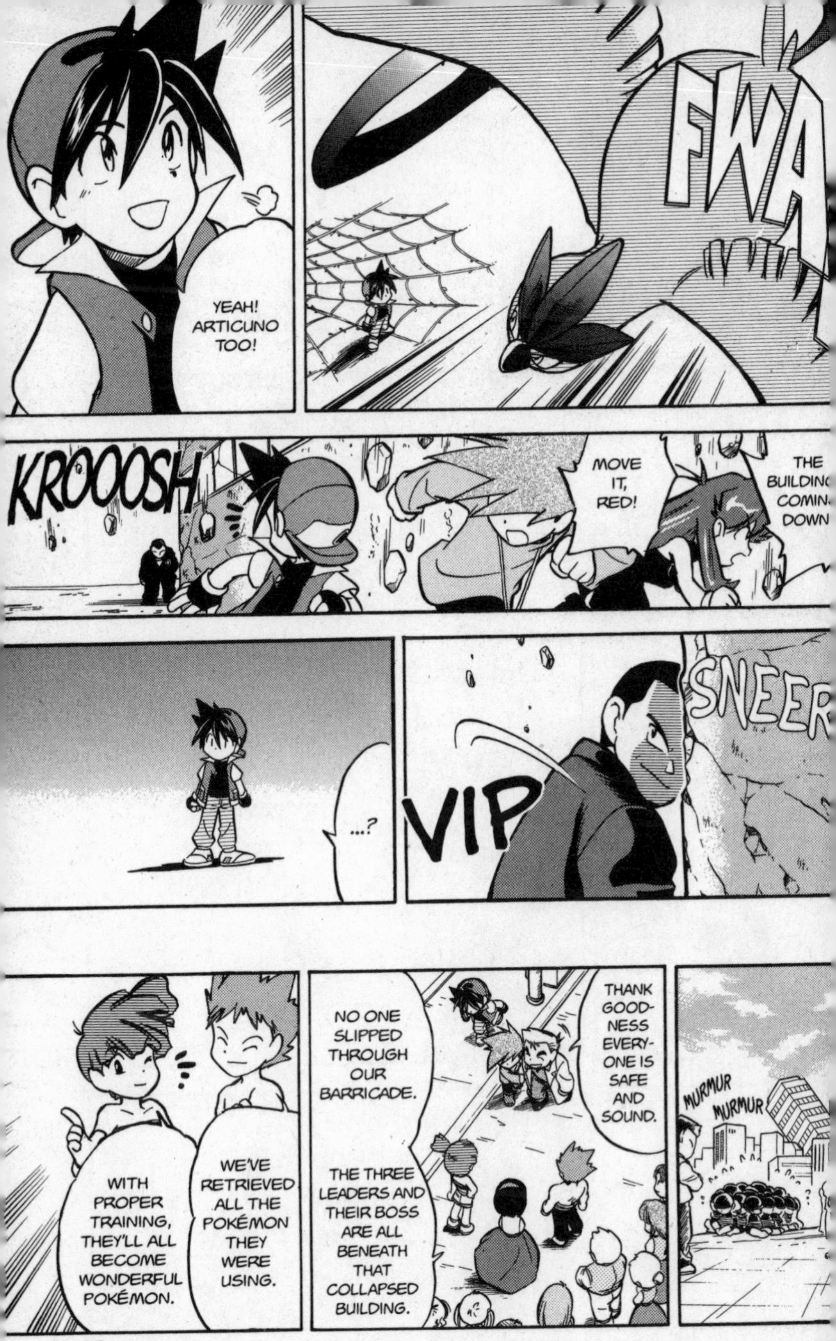
FWA
YEAH! ARTICUNO TOO!
THE BUILDIN COMIN DOWN
MOVE IT, RED!
KROOOSH
SNEER
VIP
...?
MURMUR MURMUR
THANK GOOD-NESS EVERY-ONE IS SAFE AND SOUND.
NO ONE SLIPPED THROUGH OUR BARRICADE.
THE THREE LEADERS AND THEIR BOSS ARE ALL BENEATH THAT COLLAPSED BUILDING.
WE'VE RETRIEVED ALL THE POKÉMON THEY WERE USING.
WITH PROPER TRAINING, THEY'LL ALL BECOME WONDERFUL POKÉMON.

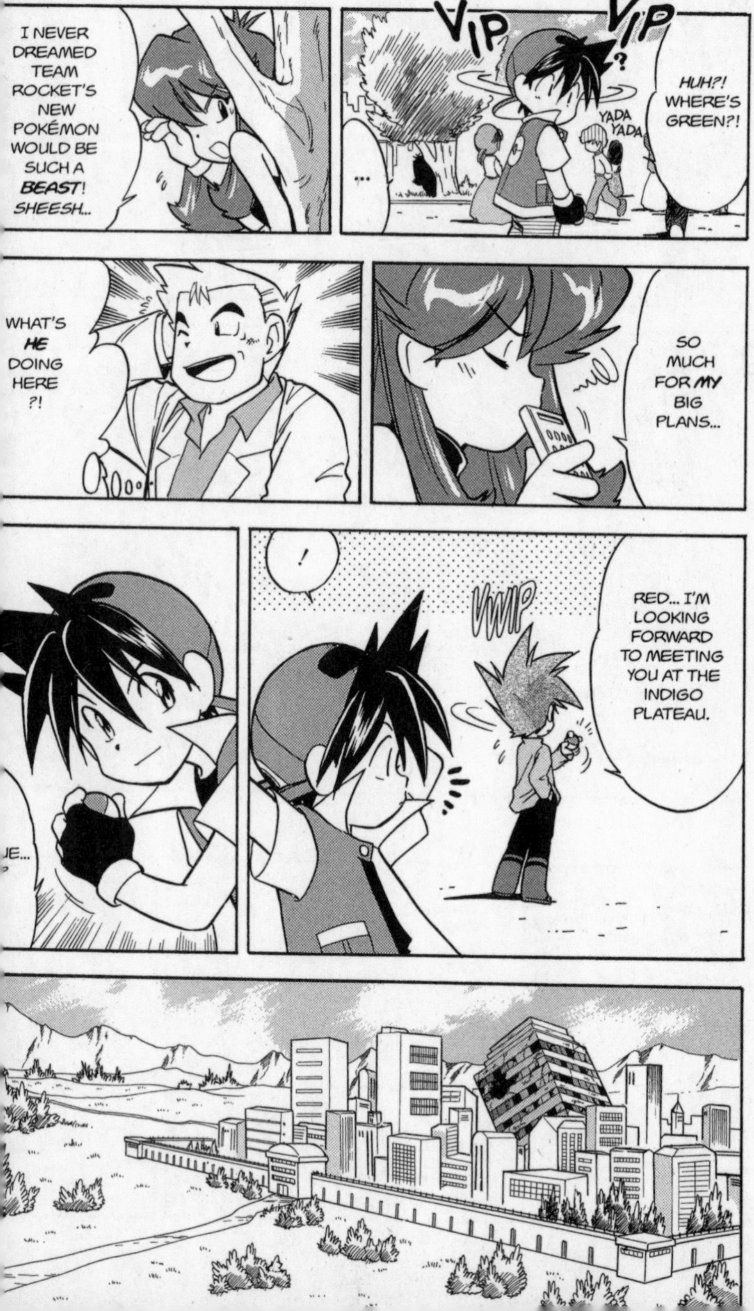
VIP
VIP
?
HUH?! WHERE'S GREEN?!
YADA YADA
...
I NEVER DREAMED TEAM ROCKET'S NEW POKÉMON WOULD BE SUCH A **BEAST**! SHEESH...
SO MUCH FOR *MY* BIG PLANS...
WHAT'S *HE* DOING HERE ?!
!
VWIP
RED... I'M LOOKING FORWARD TO MEETING YOU AT THE INDIGO PLATEAU.

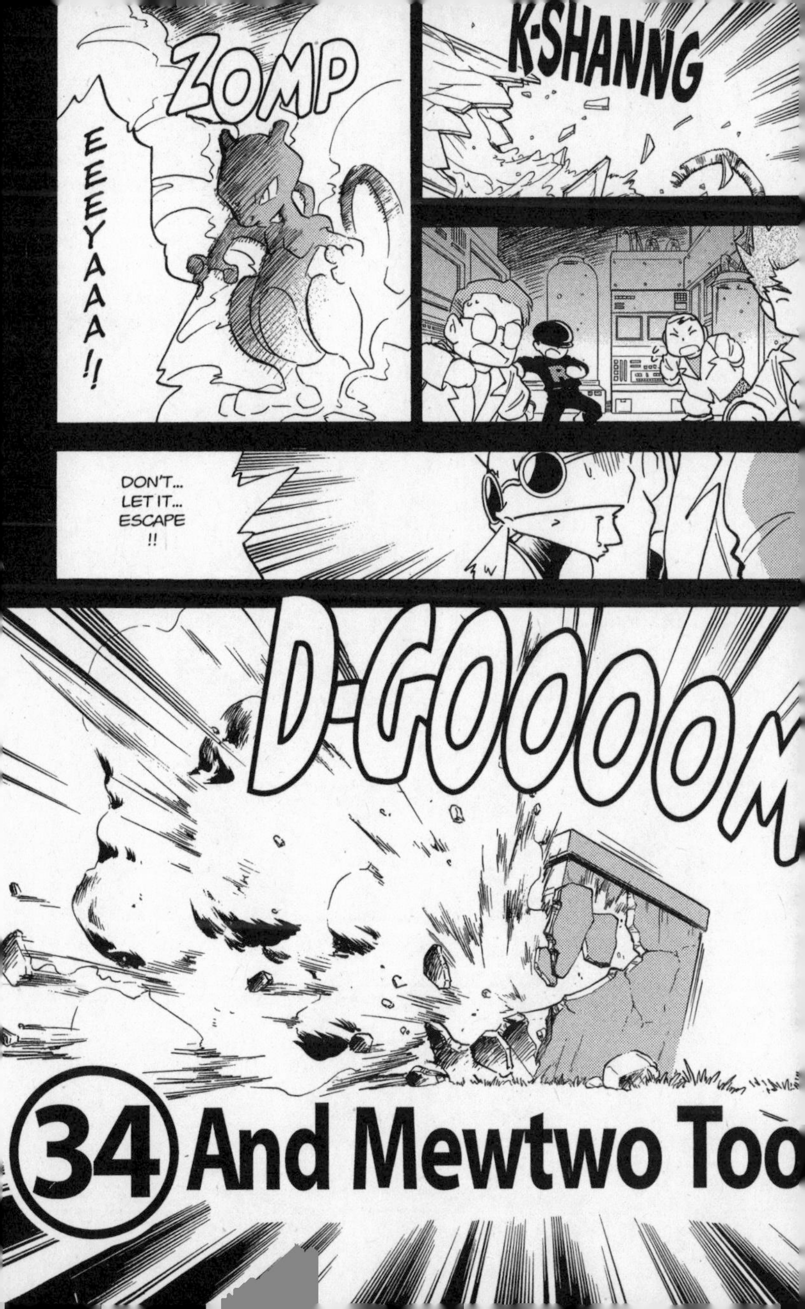
K-SHANNG
ZOMP
EEEYAAA!!
DON'T... LET IT... ESCAPE !!
D-GOOOOOM

34 And Mewtwo Too

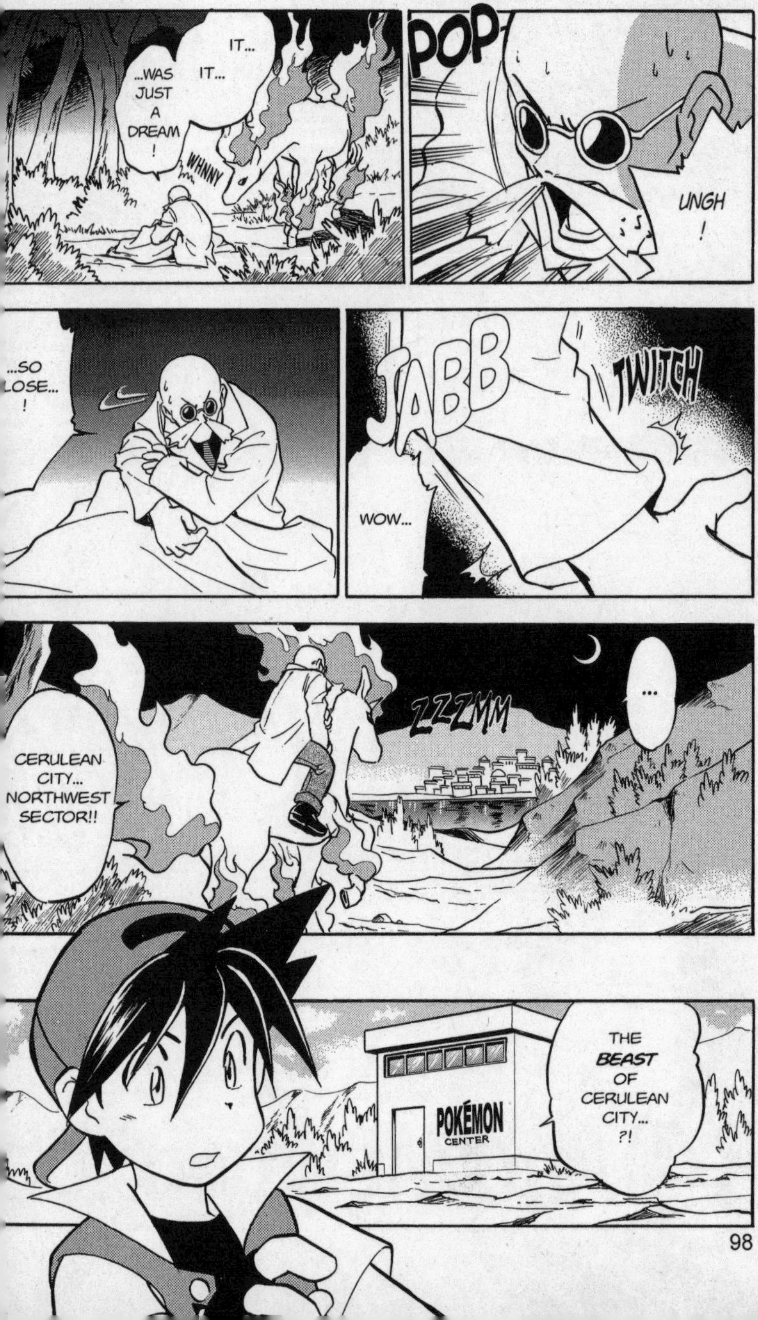
POP
UNGH!
IT... IT...
...WAS JUST A DREAM!
WHNNY
JABB
TWITCH
WOW...
...SO LOSE...!
...
ZZZMM
CERULEAN CITY... NORTHWEST SECTOR!!
THE BEAST OF CERULEAN CITY...?!
POKÉMON CENTER

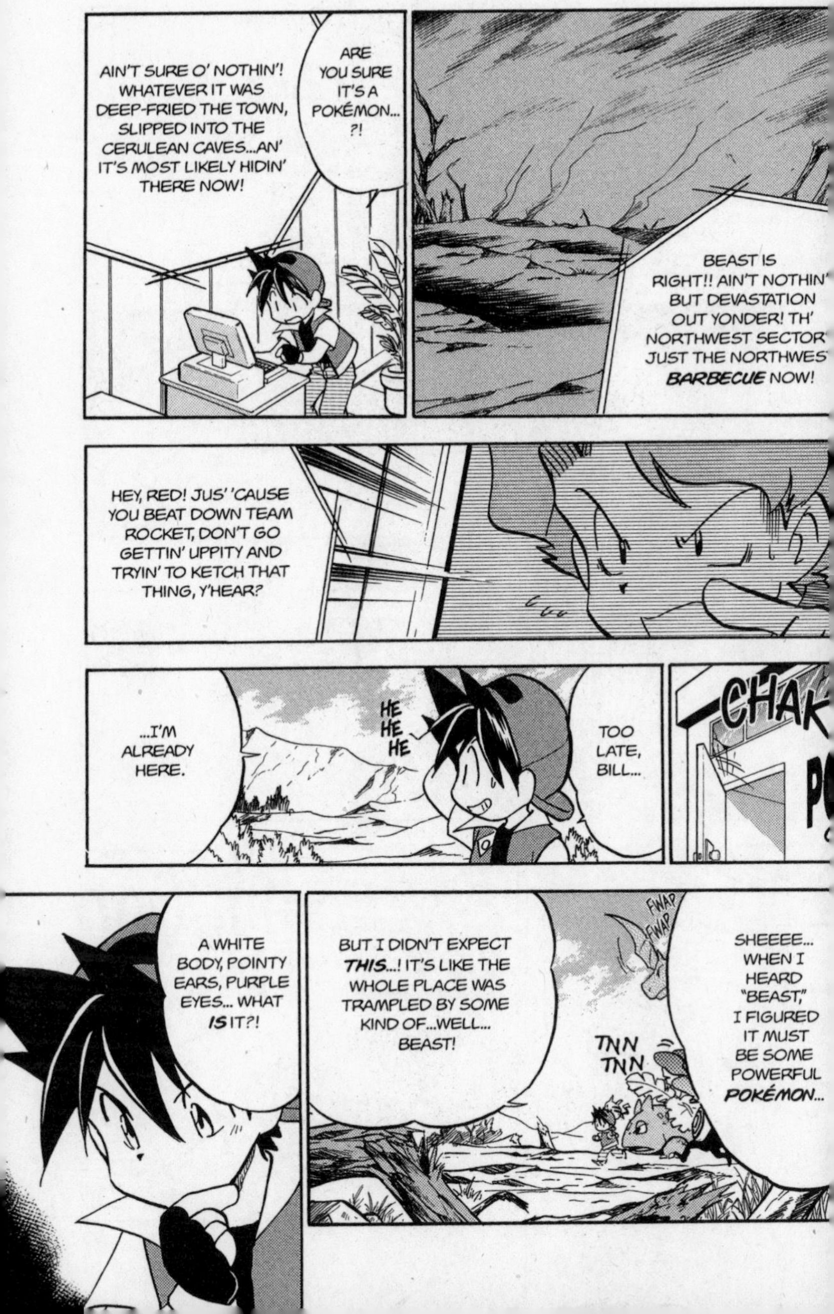

BEAST IS RIGHT!! AIN'T NOTHIN' BUT DEVASTATION OUT YONDER! TH' NORTHWEST SECTOR JUST THE NORTHWEST BARBECUE NOW!
ARE YOU SURE IT'S A POKÉMON...?!
AIN'T SURE O' NOTHIN'! WHATEVER IT WAS DEEP-FRIED THE TOWN, SLIPPED INTO THE CERULEAN CAVES...AN' IT'S MOST LIKELY HIDIN' THERE NOW!
HEY, RED! JUS' 'CAUSE YOU BEAT DOWN TEAM ROCKET, DON'T GO GETTIN' UPPITY AND TRYIN' TO KETCH THAT THING, Y'HEAR?
CHAK
TOO LATE, BILL...
HE HE HE
...I'M ALREADY HERE.
SHEEEE... WHEN I HEARD "BEAST," I FIGURED IT MUST BE SOME POWERFUL POKÉMON...
FWAP FWAP
TNN TNN
BUT I DIDN'T EXPECT THIS...! IT'S LIKE THE WHOLE PLACE WAS TRAMPLED BY SOME KIND OF...WELL... BEAST!
A WHITE BODY, POINTY EARS, PURPLE EYES... WHAT IS IT?!

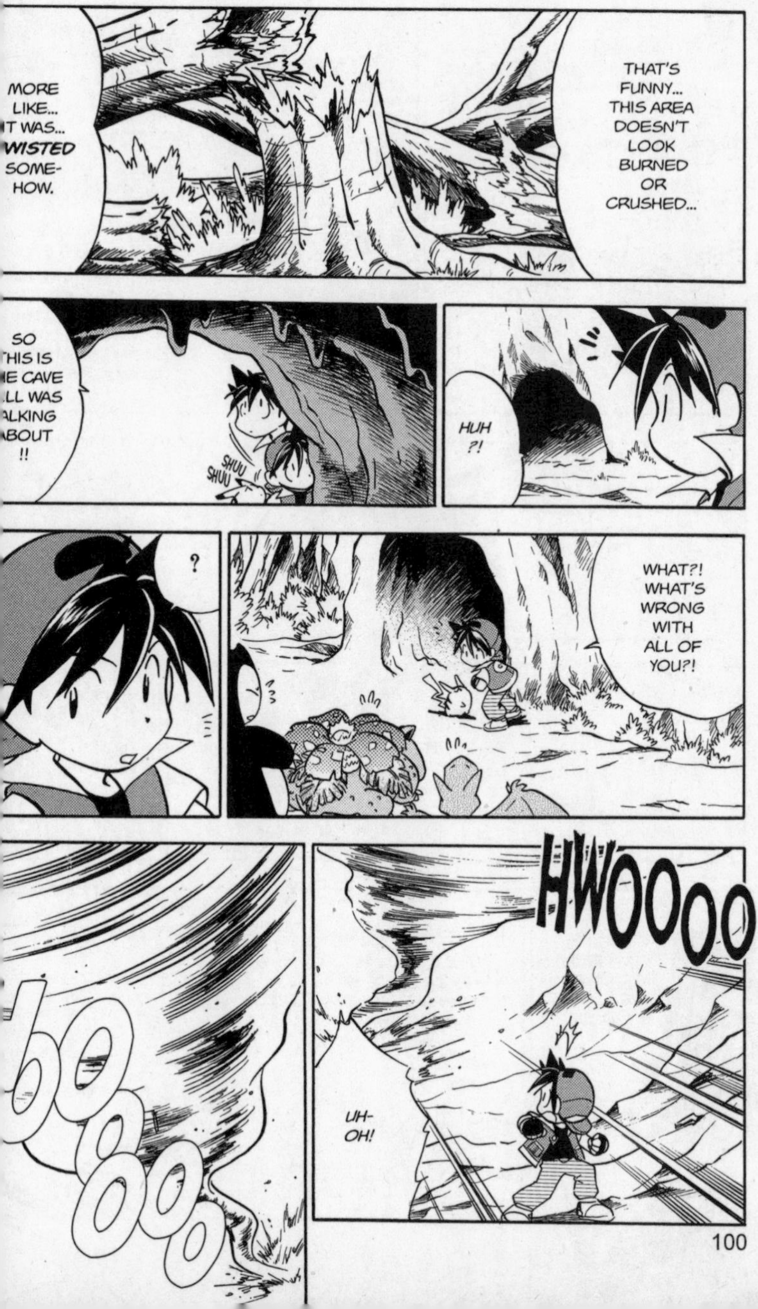
THAT'S FUNNY... THIS AREA DOESN'T LOOK BURNED OR CRUSHED...
MORE LIKE... T WAS... WISTED SOME-HOW.
HUH ?!
SO THIS IS E CAVE LL WAS ALKING BOUT !!
SHUU SHUU
WHAT?! WHAT'S WRONG WITH ALL OF YOU?!
?
HWOOOO
UH-OH!
OOOOOO

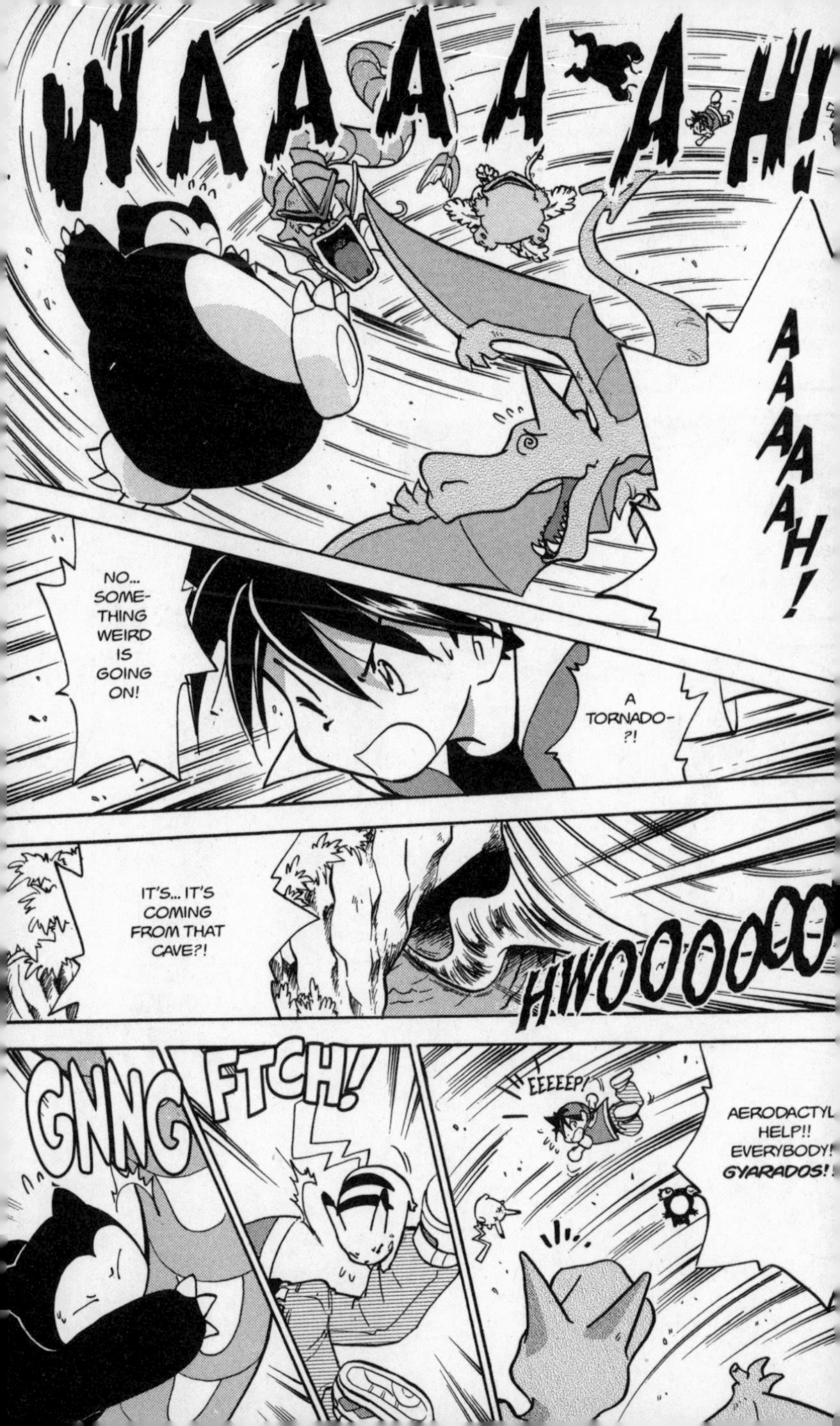
WAAAAA-AH!
AAAAAAH!
A TORNADO-?!
NO... SOME-THING WEIRD IS GOING ON!
HWOOOOOOO
IT'S... IT'S COMING FROM THAT CAVE?!
AERODACTYL! HELP!! EVERYBODY! *GYARADOS!!*
EEEEEP!
FTCH!
GNNG

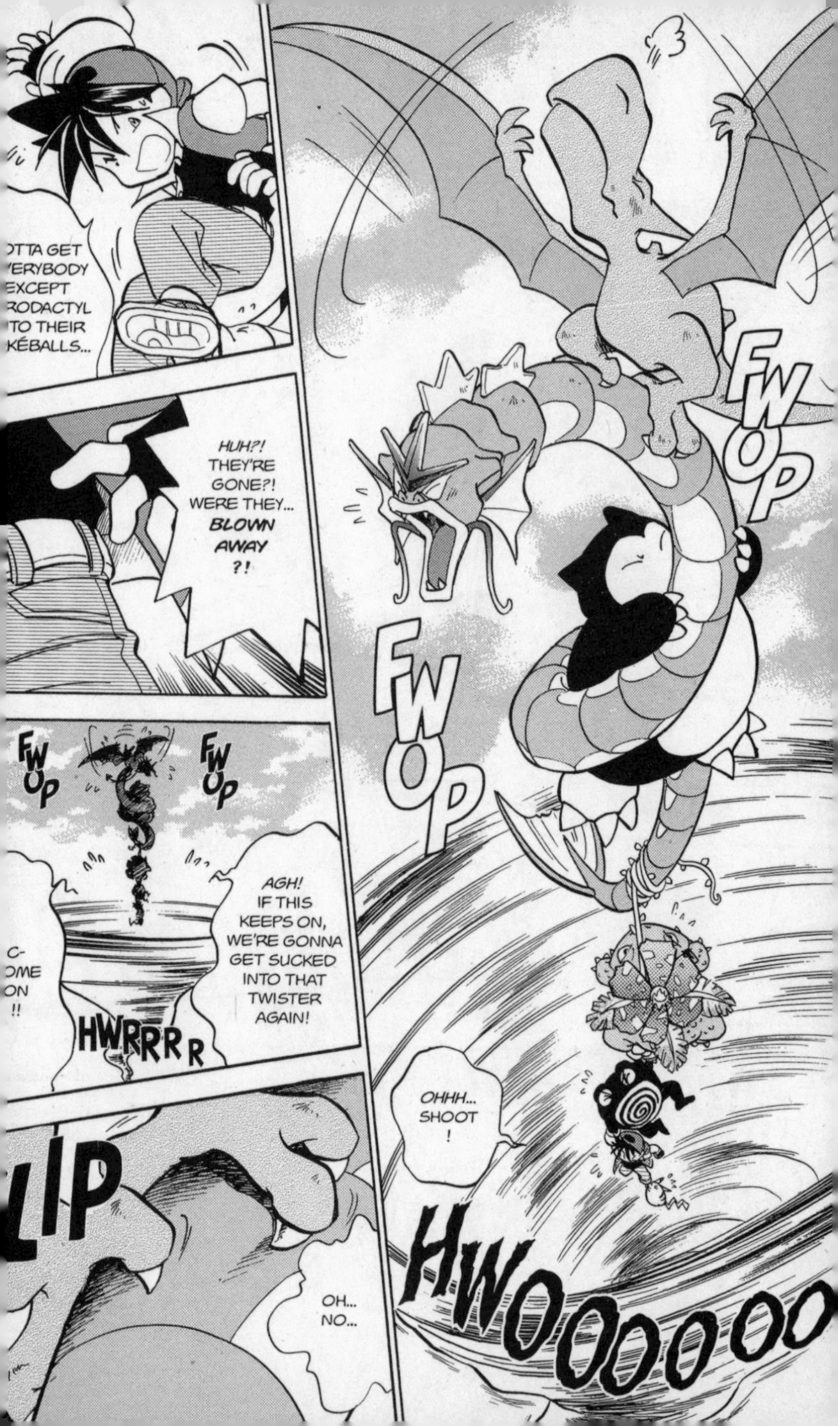
FWOP
FWOP
OHHH... SHOOT!
HWOOOOOOO
OTTA GET VERYBODY EXCEPT RODACTYL TO THEIR KÉBALLS...
HUH?! THEY'RE GONE?! WERE THEY... BLOWN AWAY?!
FWOP
FWOP
AGH! IF THIS KEEPS ON, WE'RE GONNA GET SUCKED INTO THAT TWISTER AGAIN!
C-OME ON!!
HWRRRRR
LIP
OH... NO...

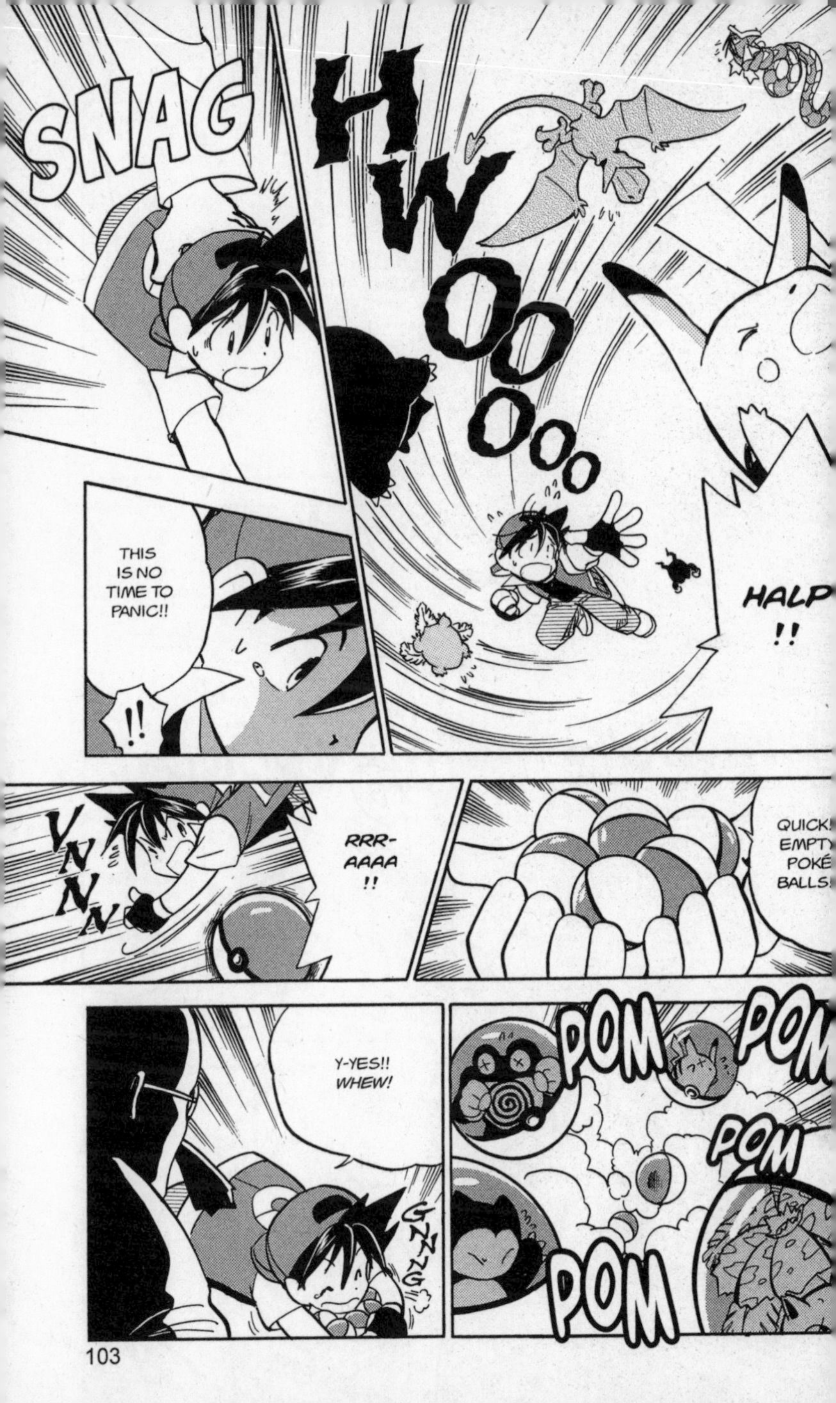
HWOOOOOO
HALP !!
SNAG
THIS IS NO TIME TO PANIC!!
!!
QUICK EMPTY POKÉ BALLS
RRR-AAAA !!
VNNN
POM
POM
POM
POM
Y-YES!! WHEW!
GNNNG

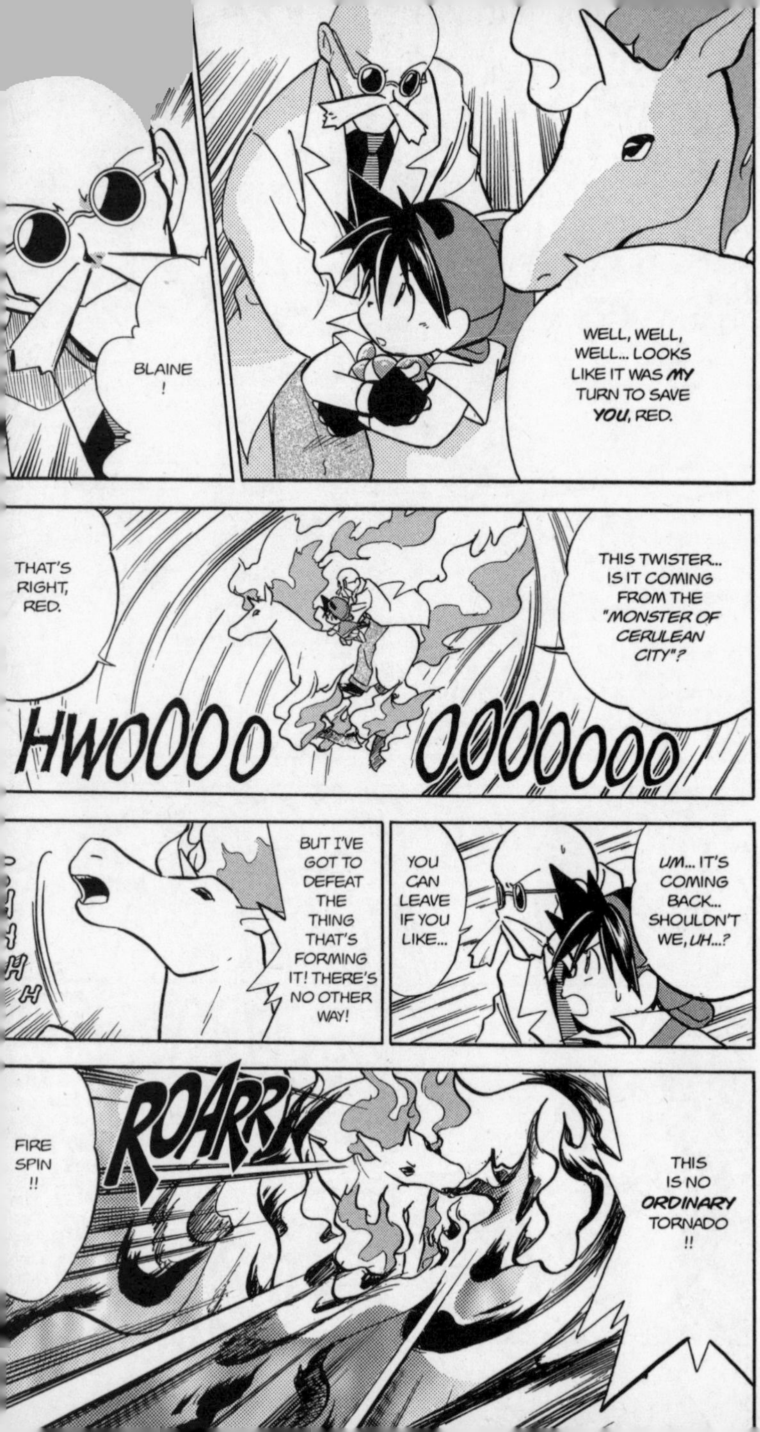
WELL, WELL, WELL... LOOKS LIKE IT WAS *MY* TURN TO SAVE *YOU*, RED.
BLAINE !
THIS TWISTER... IS IT COMING FROM THE *"MONSTER OF CERULEAN CITY"*?
THAT'S RIGHT, RED.
HWOOOO OOOOOOO
UM... IT'S COMING BACK... SHOULDN'T WE, *UH*...?
YOU CAN LEAVE IF YOU LIKE...
BUT I'VE GOT TO DEFEAT THE THING THAT'S FORMING IT! THERE'S NO OTHER WAY!
THIS IS NO *ORDINARY* TORNADO !!
ROARRW
FIRE SPIN !!

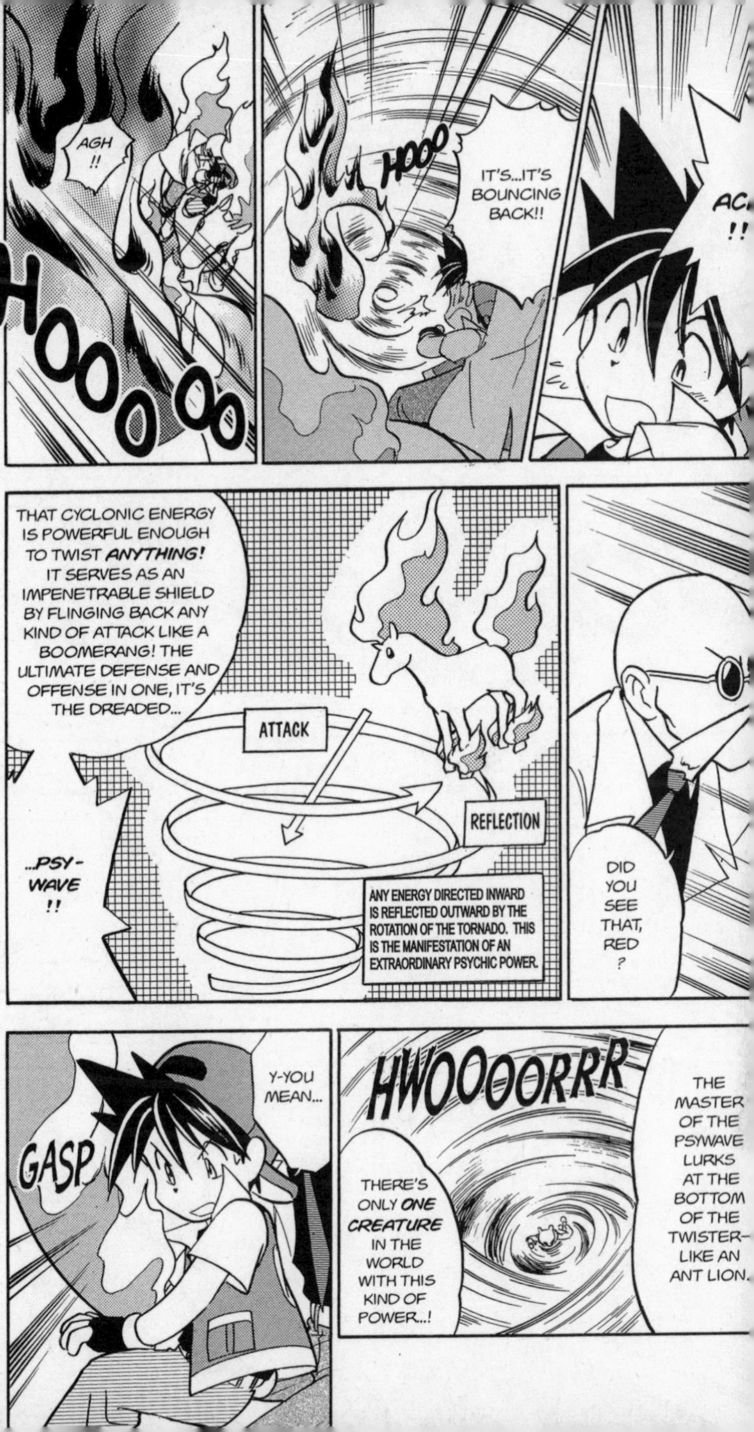
AC
!!
IT'S...IT'S BOUNCING BACK!!
HOOO
AGH !!
HOOOOO
DID YOU SEE THAT, RED ?
THAT CYCLONIC ENERGY IS POWERFUL ENOUGH TO TWIST ***ANYTHING!*** IT SERVES AS AN IMPENETRABLE SHIELD BY FLINGING BACK ANY KIND OF ATTACK LIKE A BOOMERANG! THE ULTIMATE DEFENSE AND OFFENSE IN ONE, IT'S THE DREADED...
ATTACK
REFLECTION
ANY ENERGY DIRECTED INWARD IS REFLECTED OUTWARD BY THE ROTATION OF THE TORNADO. THIS IS THE MANIFESTATION OF AN EXTRAORDINARY PSYCHIC POWER.
...PSY-WAVE !!
HWOOOORRR
THE MASTER OF THE PSYWAVE LURKS AT THE BOTTOM OF THE TWISTER—LIKE AN ANT LION.
THERE'S ONLY ***ONE CREATURE*** IN THE WORLD WITH THIS KIND OF POWER...!
Y-YOU MEAN...
GASP

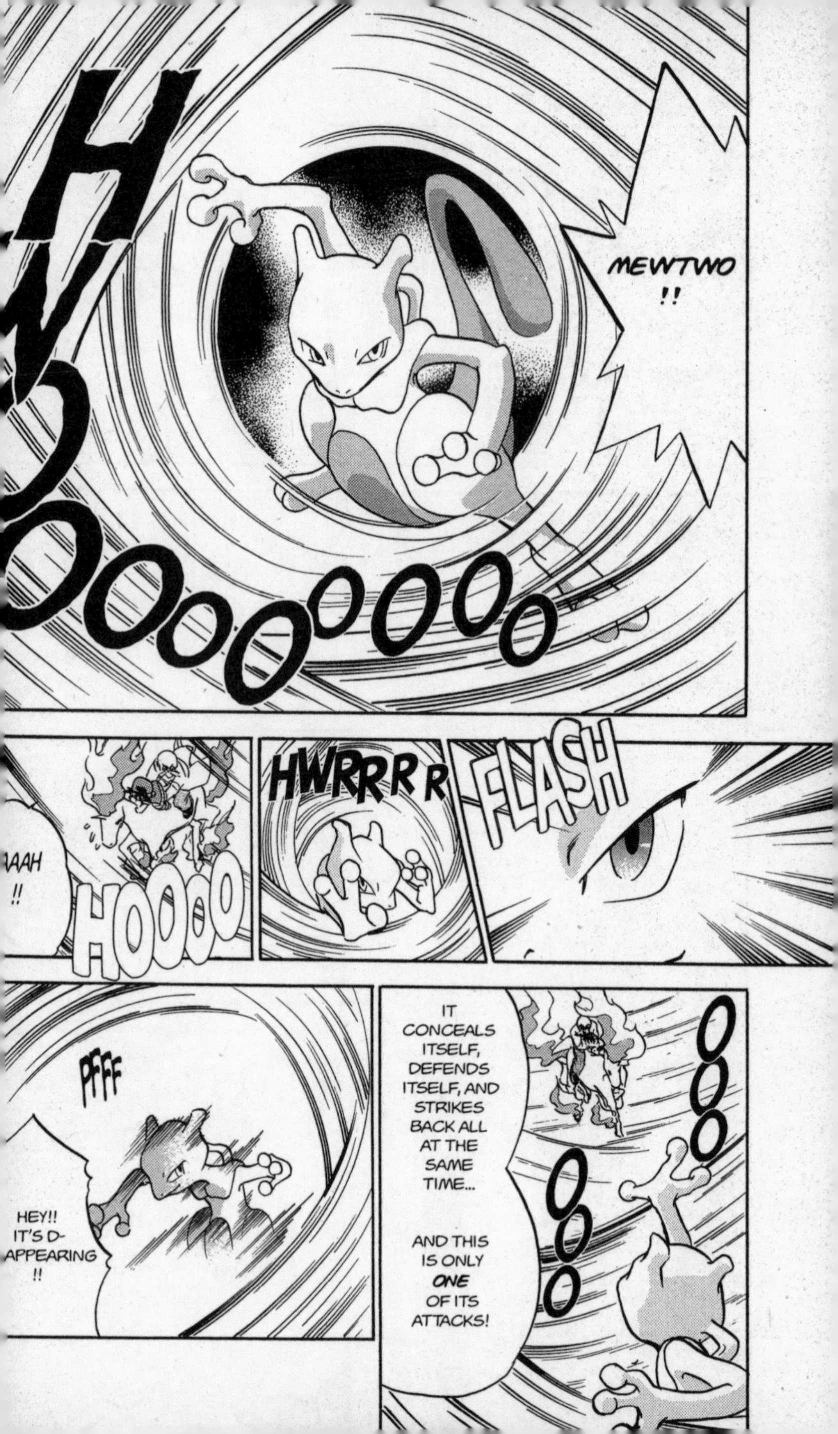

HOOOOOOOOO
MEWTWO !!
FLASH
HWRRRRR
AAAH !!
HOOOO
IT CONCEALS ITSELF, DEFENDS ITSELF, AND STRIKES BACK ALL AT THE SAME TIME...
AND THIS IS ONLY *ONE* OF ITS ATTACKS!
OOOOOO
PFFF
HEY!! IT'S D- APPEARING !!

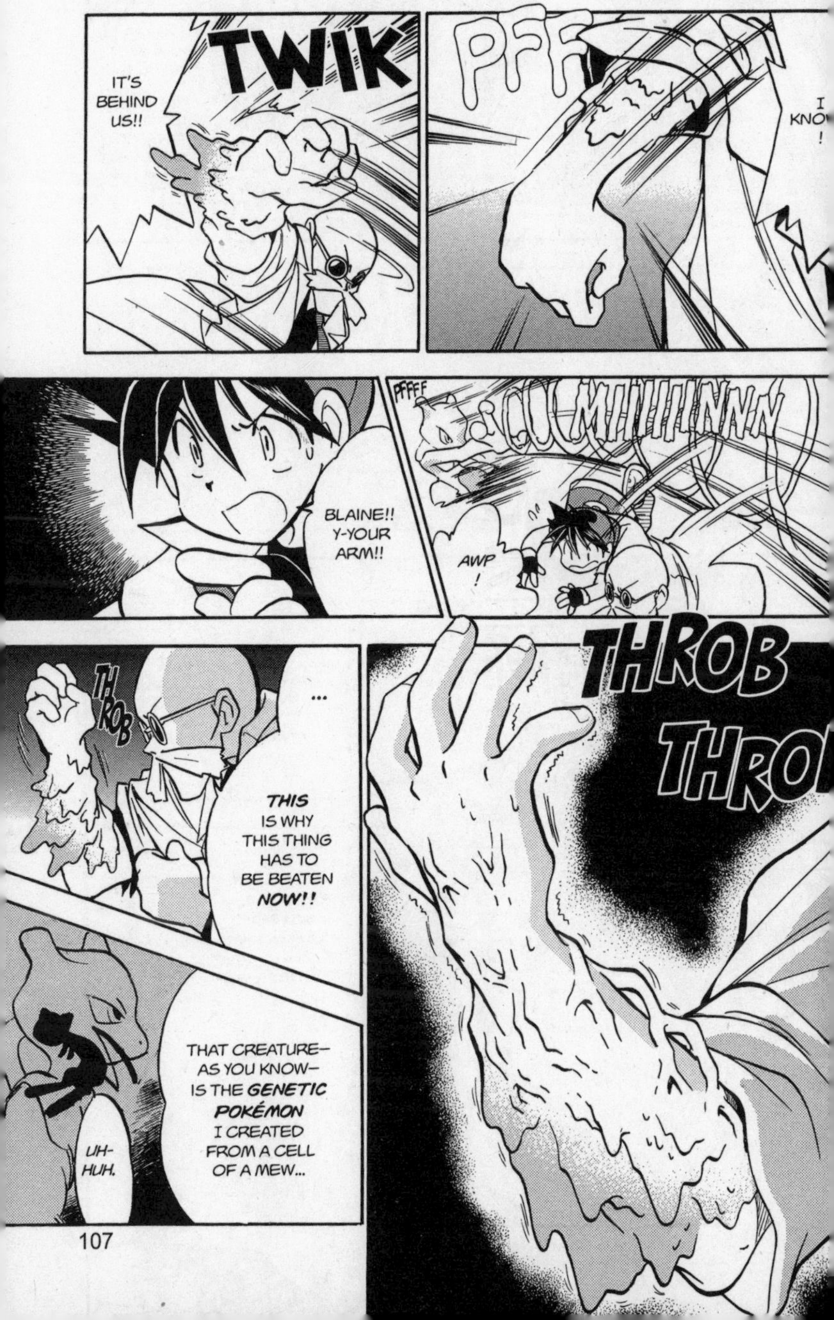
PFF
I KNO !
TWIK
IT'S BEHIND US!!
PFFFF
MIIIIINNNN
AWP !
BLAINE!! Y-YOUR ARM!!
THROB
THRO
THROB
...
THIS IS WHY THIS THING HAS TO BE BEATEN NOW!!
THAT CREATURE— AS YOU KNOW— IS THE GENETIC POKÉMON I CREATED FROM A CELL OF A MEW...
UH-HUH.

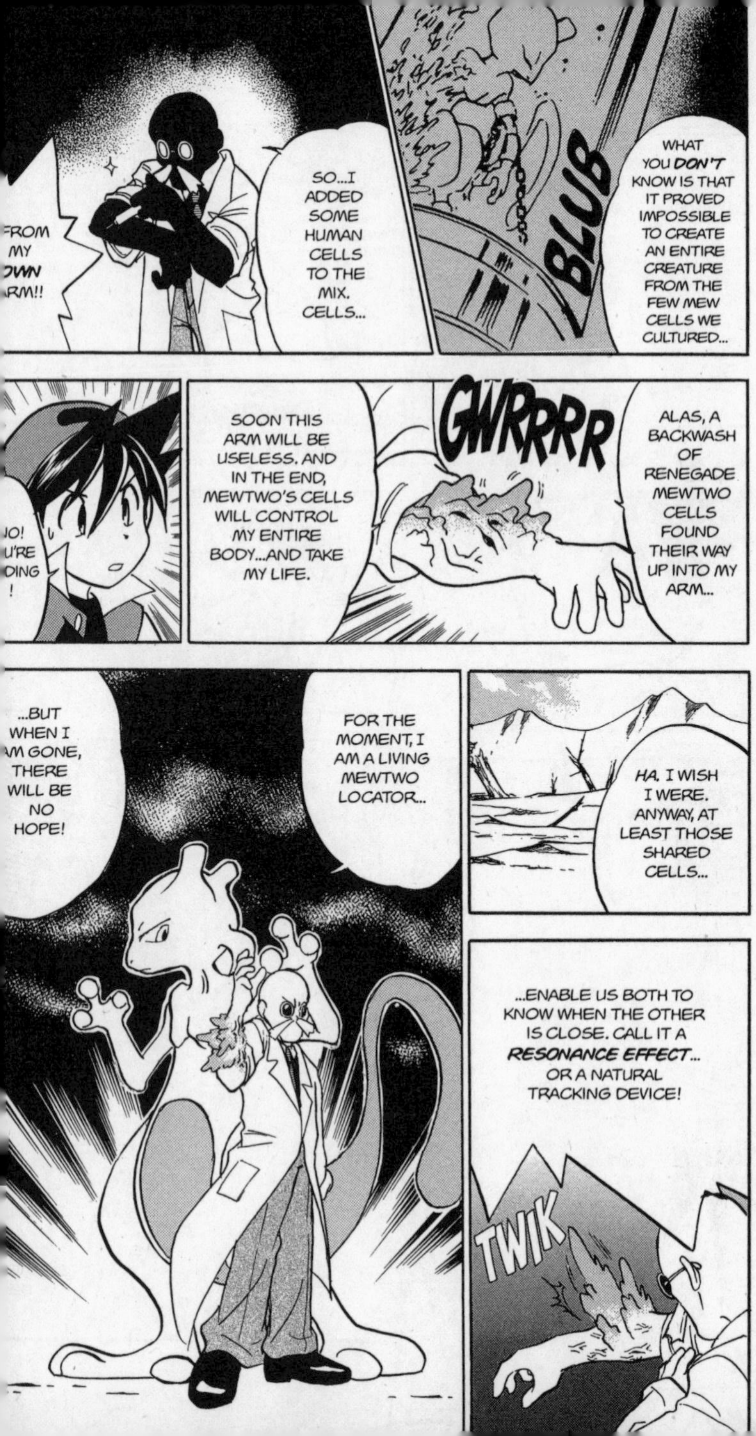
BLUB
WHAT YOU DON'T KNOW IS THAT IT PROVED IMPOSSIBLE TO CREATE AN ENTIRE CREATURE FROM THE FEW MEW CELLS WE CULTURED...
SO...I ADDED SOME HUMAN CELLS TO THE MIX. CELLS...
FROM MY
ALAS, A BACKWASH OF RENEGADE MEWTWO CELLS FOUND THEIR WAY UP INTO MY ARM...
GWRRRR
SOON THIS ARM WILL BE USELESS. AND IN THE END, MEWTWO'S CELLS WILL CONTROL MY ENTIRE BODY...AND TAKE MY LIFE.
HA. I WISH I WERE. ANYWAY, AT LEAST THOSE SHARED CELLS...
...ENABLE US BOTH TO KNOW WHEN THE OTHER IS CLOSE. CALL IT A RESONANCE EFFECT... OR A NATURAL TRACKING DEVICE!
TWIK
FOR THE MOMENT, I AM A LIVING MEWTWO LOCATOR...
...BUT WHEN I
THERE WILL BE NO HOPE!

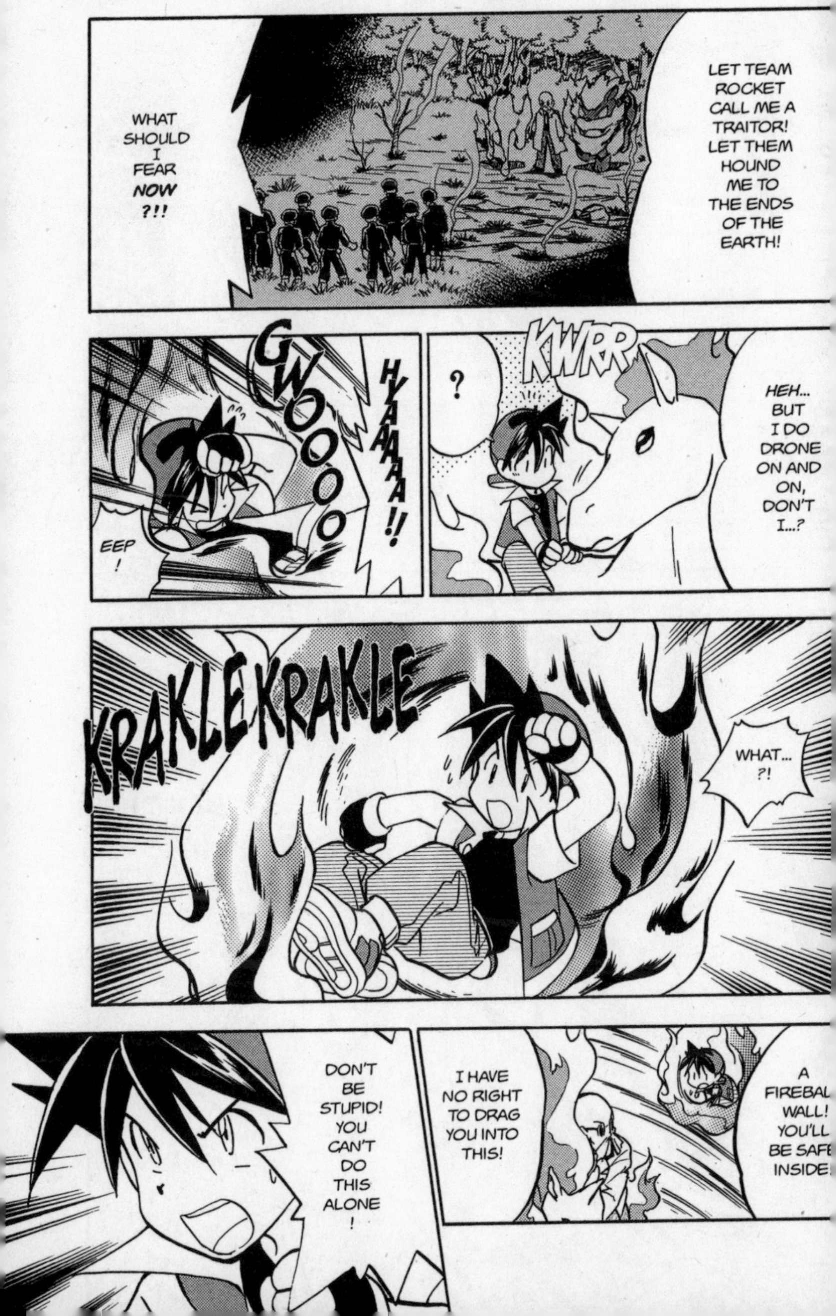
LET TEAM ROCKET CALL ME A TRAITOR! LET THEM HOUND ME TO THE ENDS OF THE EARTH!
WHAT SHOULD I FEAR NOW?!!
HEH... BUT I DO DRONE ON AND ON, DON'T I...?
KWRR
?
HYAAAAAA!!
GWOOOOO
EEP!
WHAT...?!
KRAKLE KRAKLE
A FIREBAL WALL! YOU'LL BE SAFE INSIDE
I HAVE NO RIGHT TO DRAG YOU INTO THIS!
DON'T BE STUPID! YOU CAN'T DO THIS ALONE!

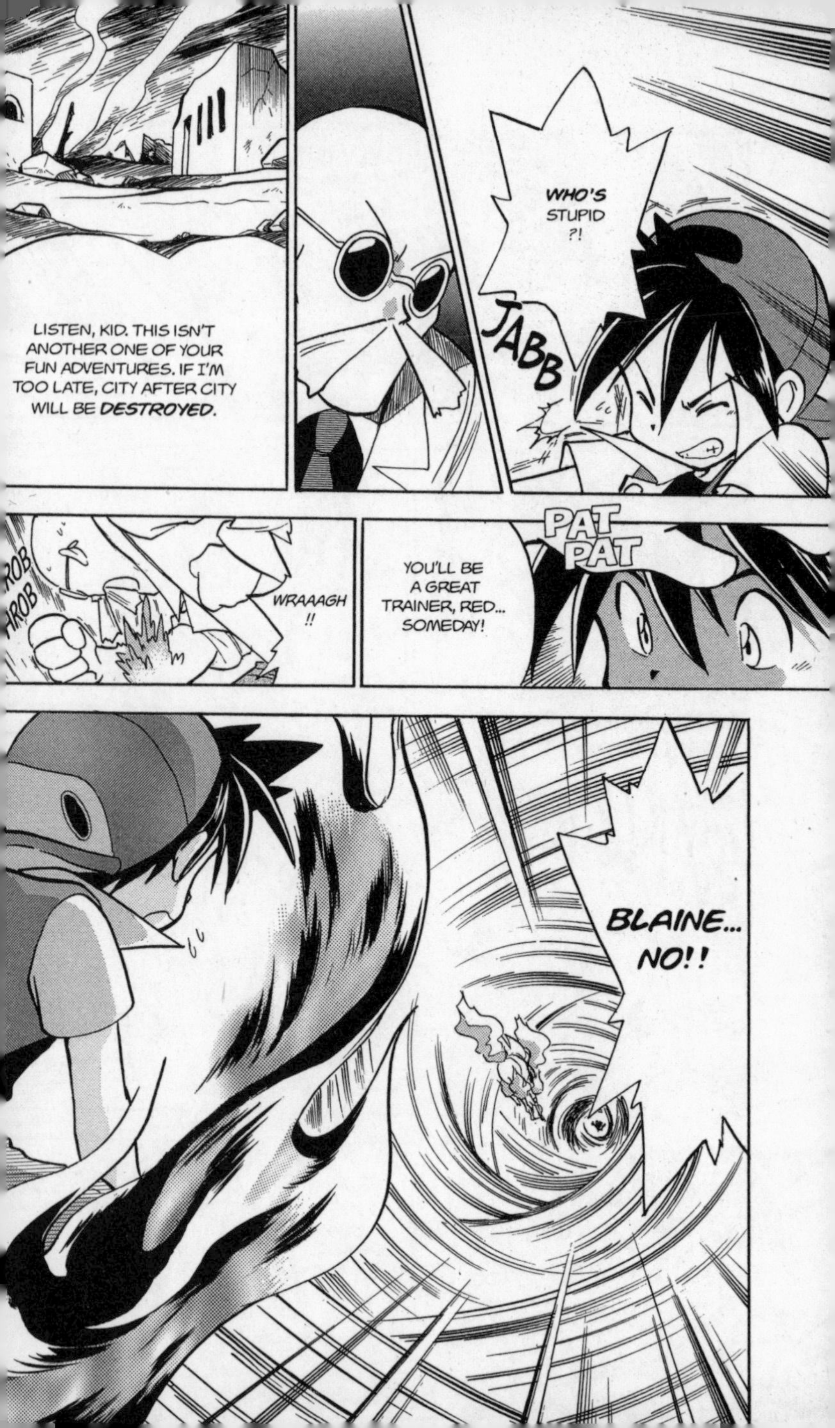
WHO'S STUPID ?!
JABB
LISTEN, KID. THIS ISN'T ANOTHER ONE OF YOUR FUN ADVENTURES. IF I'M TOO LATE, CITY AFTER CITY WILL BE ***DESTROYED***.
PAT PAT
YOU'LL BE A GREAT TRAINER, RED... SOMEDAY!
WRAAAGH !!
BLAINE... NO!!

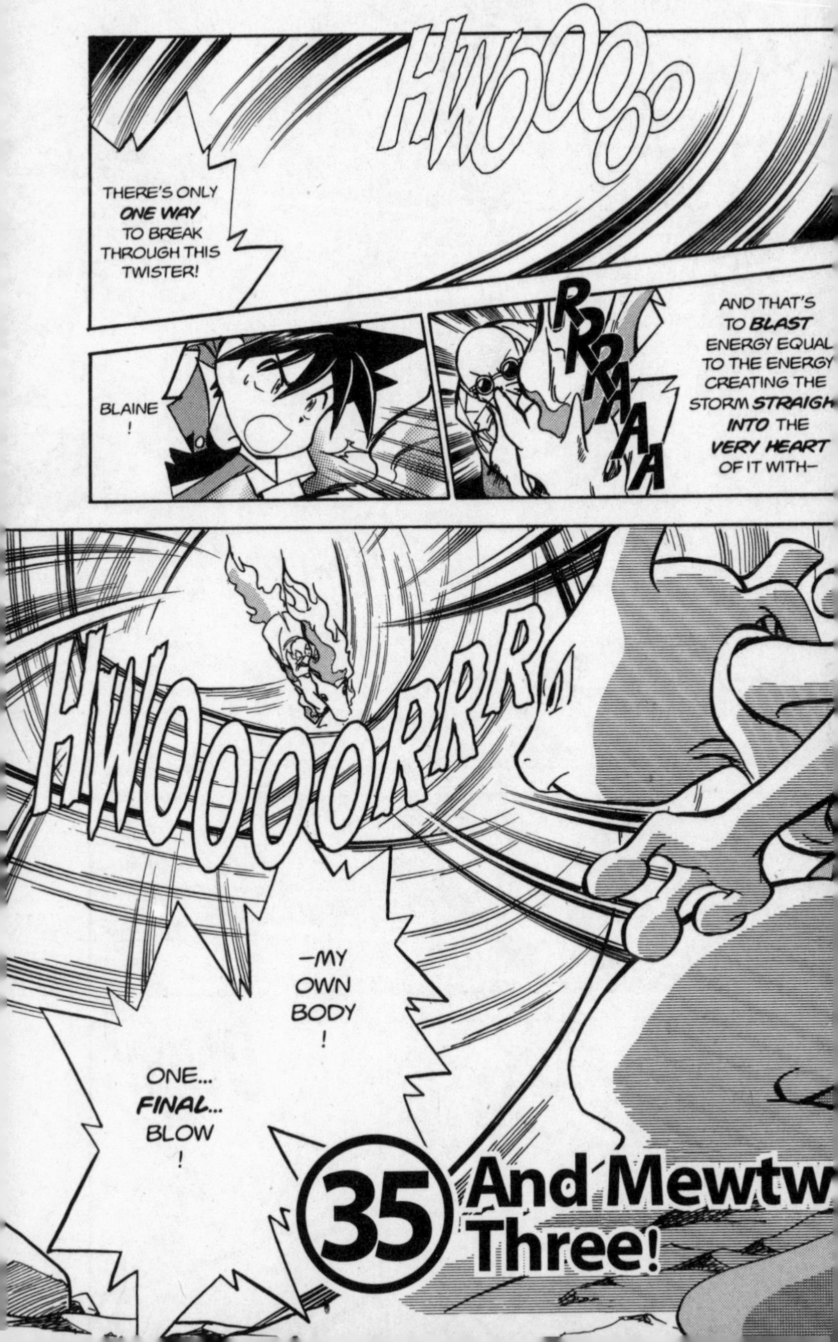
HWOOOOoo
THERE'S ONLY ONE WAY TO BREAK THROUGH THIS TWISTER!
RRRAAAA
AND THAT'S TO BLAST ENERGY EQUAL TO THE ENERGY CREATING THE STORM STRAIGH INTO THE VERY HEART OF IT WITH–
BLAINE!
HWOOOORRR
–MY OWN BODY!
ONE... FINAL... BLOW!
35 And Mewtw
Three!

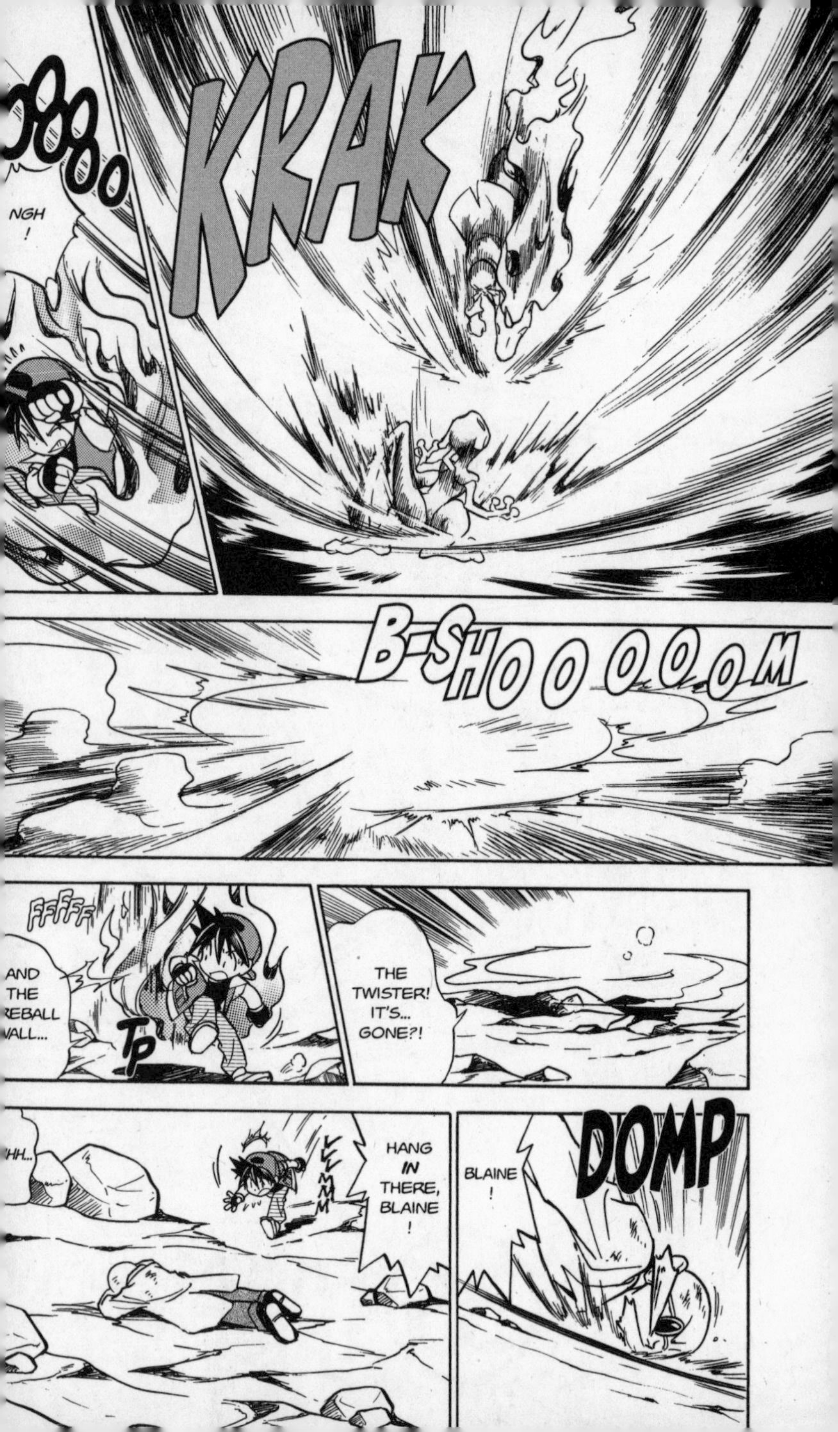
KRAK
NGH!
B-SHOOOOOOM
THE TWISTER! IT'S... GONE?!
FFFFF
AND THE REBALL WALL...
TP
DOMP
BLAINE!
HANG IN THERE, BLAINE!
HH...

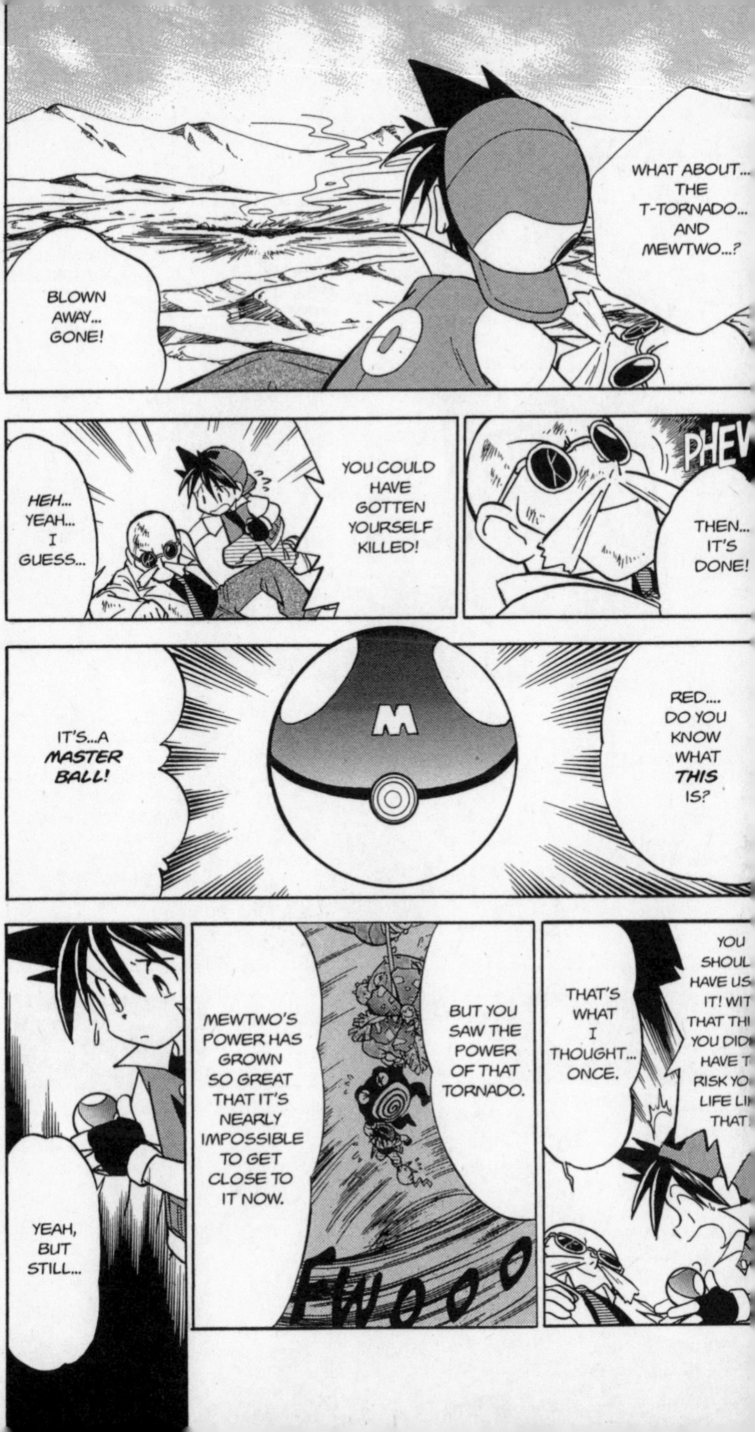
WHAT ABOUT... THE T-TORNADO... AND MEWTWO...?
BLOWN AWAY... GONE!
PHEV
THEN... IT'S DONE!
YOU COULD HAVE GOTTEN YOURSELF KILLED!
HEH... YEAH... I GUESS...
RED.... DO YOU KNOW WHAT THIS IS?
IT'S...A MASTER BALL!
YOU SHOUL HAVE US IT! WIT THAT THI YOU DID HAVE T RISK YO LIFE LI THAT!
THAT'S WHAT I THOUGHT... ONCE.
BUT YOU SAW THE POWER OF THAT TORNADO.
MEWTWO'S POWER HAS GROWN SO GREAT THAT IT'S NEARLY IMPOSSIBLE TO GET CLOSE TO IT NOW.
FWOOOO
YEAH, BUT STILL...

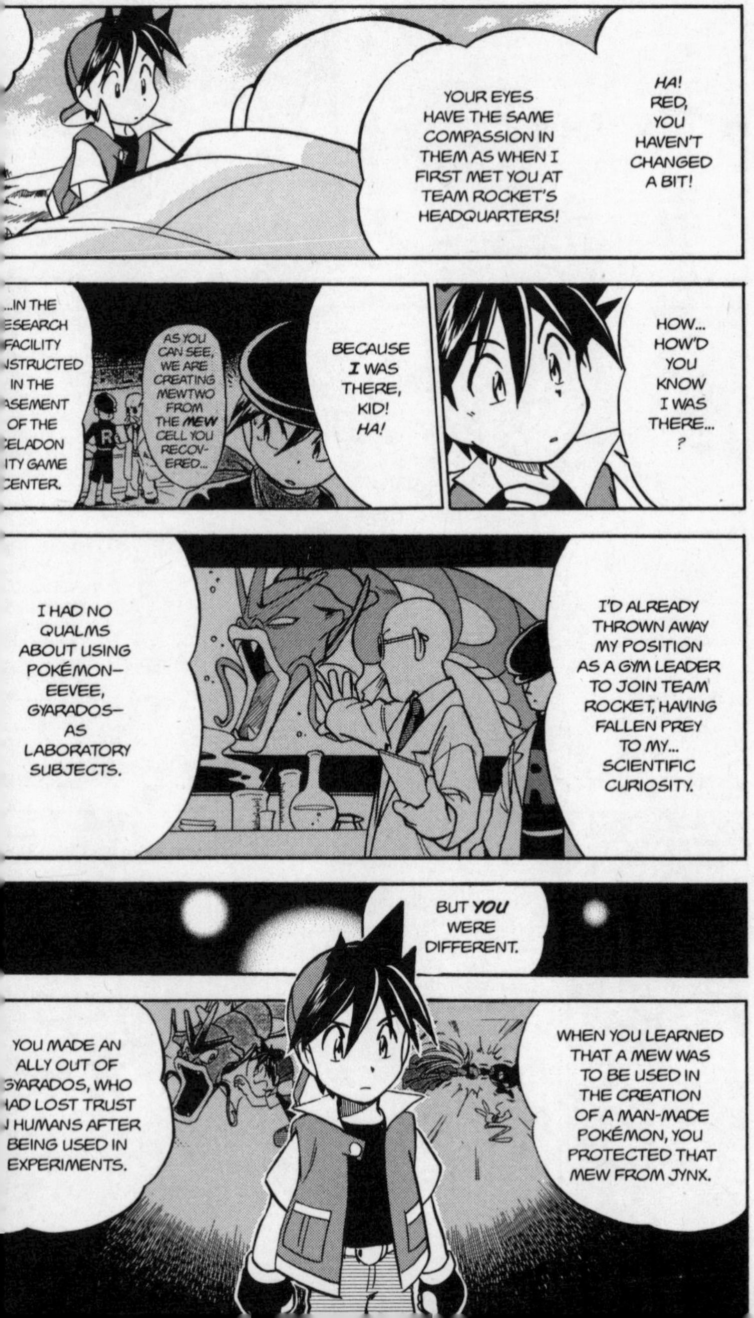
HA! RED, YOU HAVEN'T CHANGED A BIT!
YOUR EYES HAVE THE SAME COMPASSION IN THEM AS WHEN I FIRST MET YOU AT TEAM ROCKET'S HEADQUARTERS!
HOW... HOW'D YOU KNOW I WAS THERE...?
BECAUSE I WAS THERE, KID! HA!
...IN THE ESEARCH FACILITY NSTRUCTED IN THE ASEMENT OF THE ELADON ITY GAME ENTER.
AS YOU CAN SEE, WE ARE CREATING MEWTWO FROM THE MEW CELL YOU RECOVERED...
I'D ALREADY THROWN AWAY MY POSITION AS A GYM LEADER TO JOIN TEAM ROCKET, HAVING FALLEN PREY TO MY... SCIENTIFIC CURIOSITY.
I HAD NO QUALMS ABOUT USING POKÉMON— EEVEE, GYARADOS— AS LABORATORY SUBJECTS.
BUT YOU WERE DIFFERENT.
WHEN YOU LEARNED THAT A MEW WAS TO BE USED IN THE CREATION OF A MAN-MADE POKÉMON, YOU PROTECTED THAT MEW FROM JYNX.
YOU MADE AN ALLY OUT OF YARADOS, WHO AD LOST TRUST HUMANS AFTER BEING USED IN EXPERIMENTS.

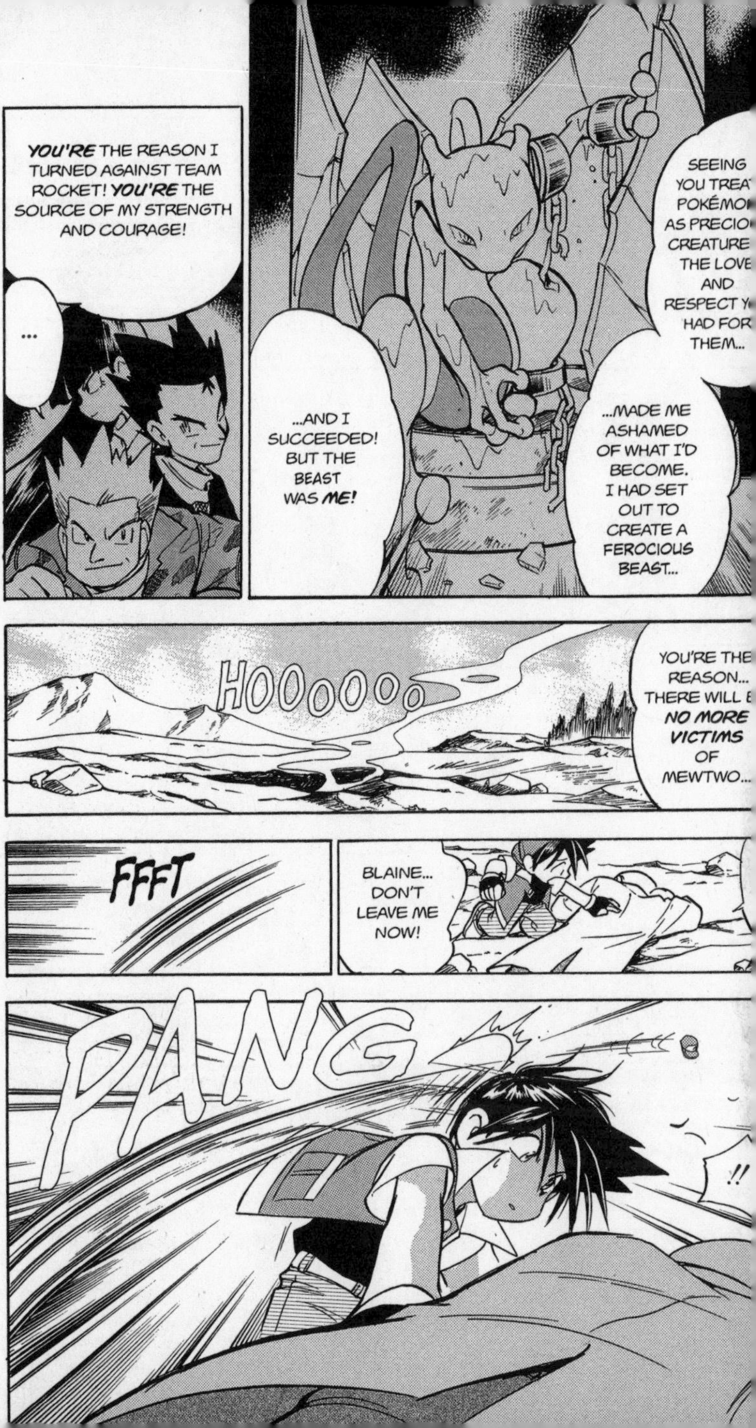
SEEING YOU TREA POKÉMO AS PRECIO CREATURE THE LOVE AND RESPECT Y HAD FOR THEM...
...MADE ME ASHAMED OF WHAT I'D BECOME. I HAD SET OUT TO CREATE A FEROCIOUS BEAST...
...AND I SUCCEEDED! BUT THE BEAST WAS *ME!*
YOU'RE THE REASON I TURNED AGAINST TEAM ROCKET! *YOU'RE* THE SOURCE OF MY STRENGTH AND COURAGE!
...
YOU'RE THE REASON... THERE WILL B *NO MORE VICTIMS* OF MEWTWO...
HOOOOOOO
BLAINE... DON'T LEAVE ME NOW!
FFFT
PANG
!!

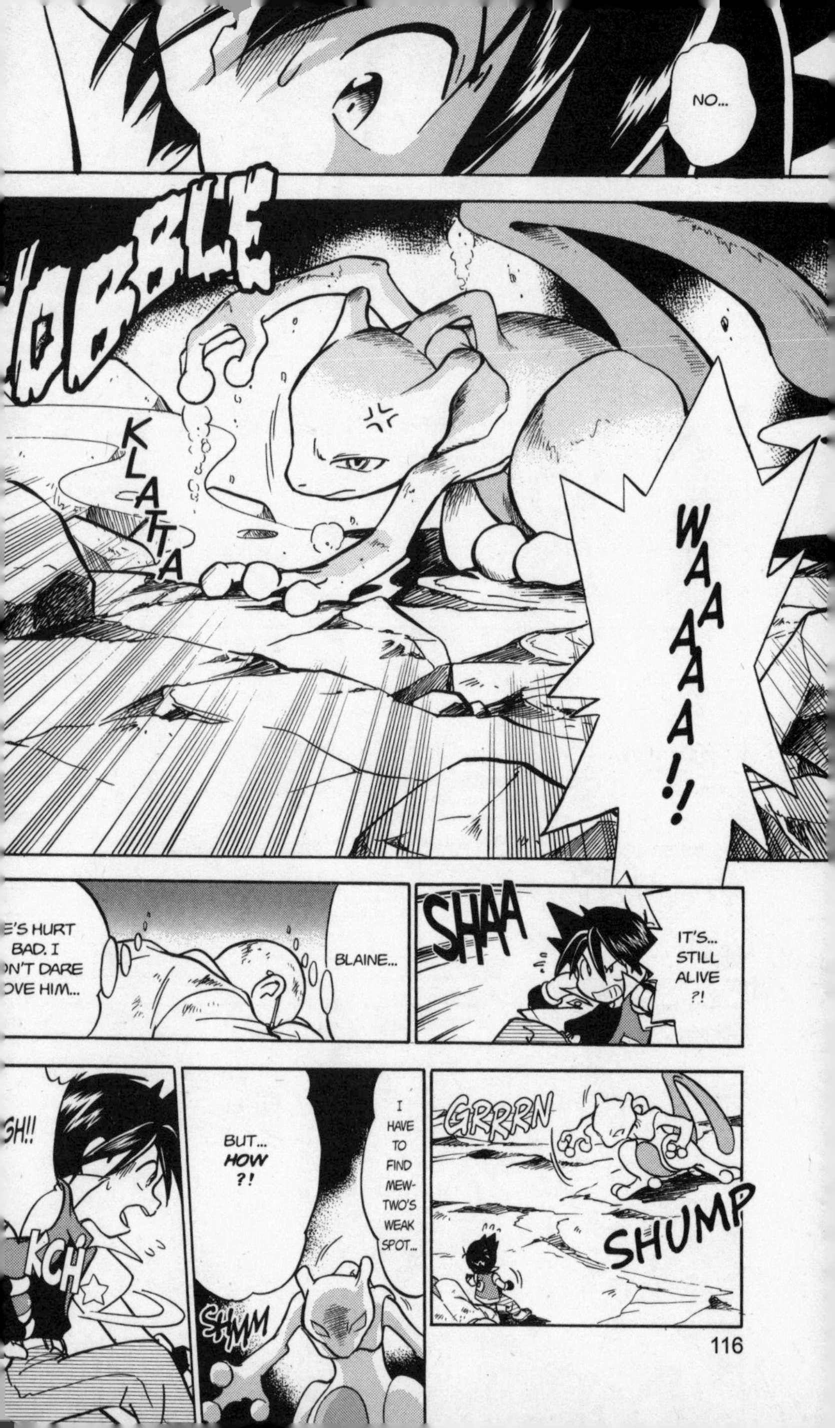
NO...
WAAAAA!!
OBBLE
KLATTA
SHAA
IT'S... STILL ALIVE ?!
BLAINE...
E'S HURT BAD. I
ON'T DARE
OVE HIM...
GRRRN
SHUMP
I HAVE TO FIND MEW-TWO'S WEAK SPOT...
BUT... **HOW** ?!
SHMM
GH!!
KCH

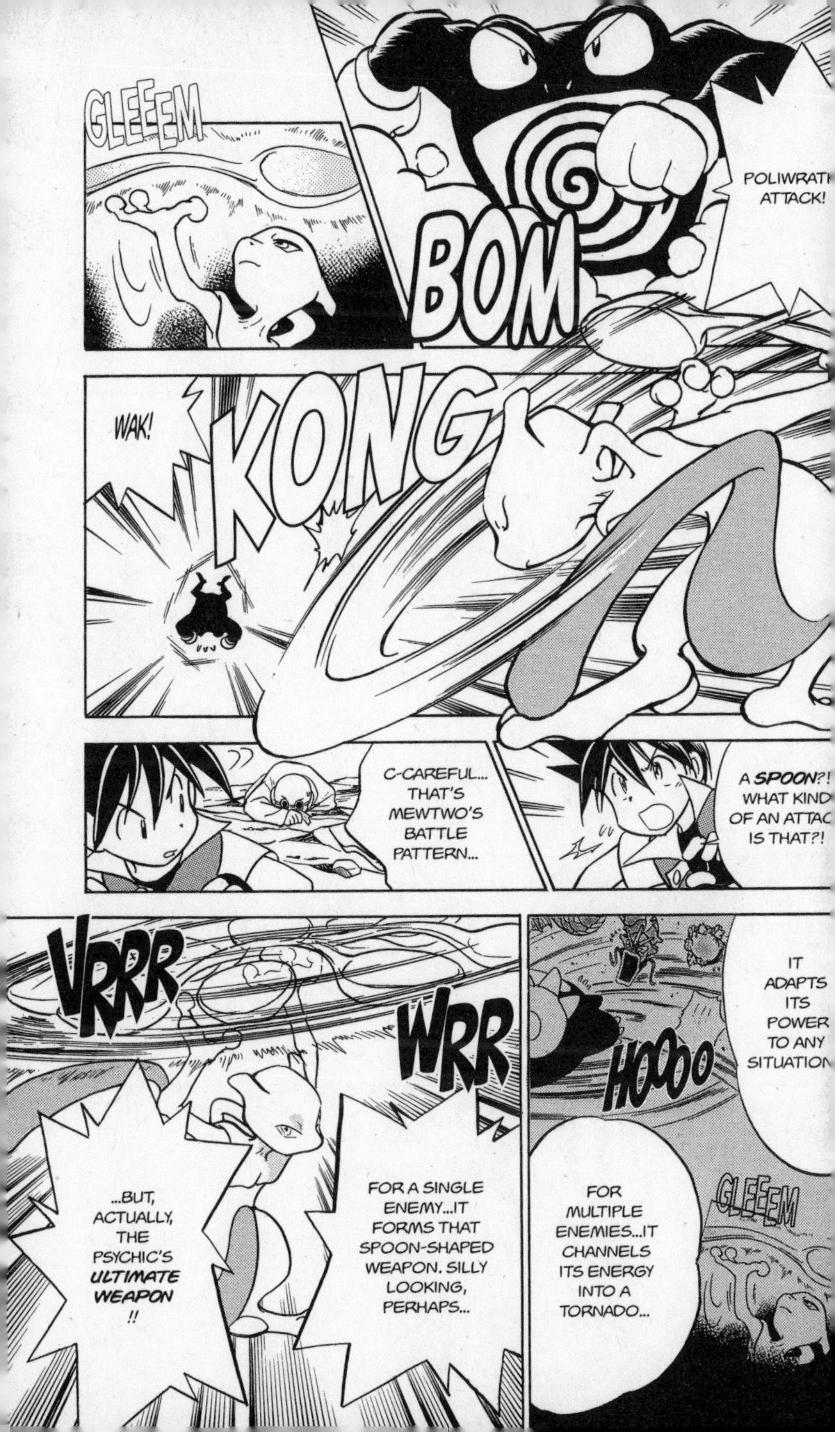
POLIWRAT ATTACK!
BOM
GLEEEM
KONG
WAK!
A **SPOON**?! WHAT KIND OF AN ATTAC IS THAT?!
C-CAREFUL... THAT'S MEWTWO'S BATTLE PATTERN...
IT ADAPTS ITS POWER TO ANY SITUATION
HOOOO
GLEEEM
FOR MULTIPLE ENEMIES...IT CHANNELS ITS ENERGY INTO A TORNADO...
WRR
VRRR
FOR A SINGLE ENEMY...IT FORMS THAT SPOON-SHAPED WEAPON. SILLY LOOKING, PERHAPS...
...BUT, ACTUALLY, THE PSYCHIC'S ***ULTIMATE WEAPON*** !!

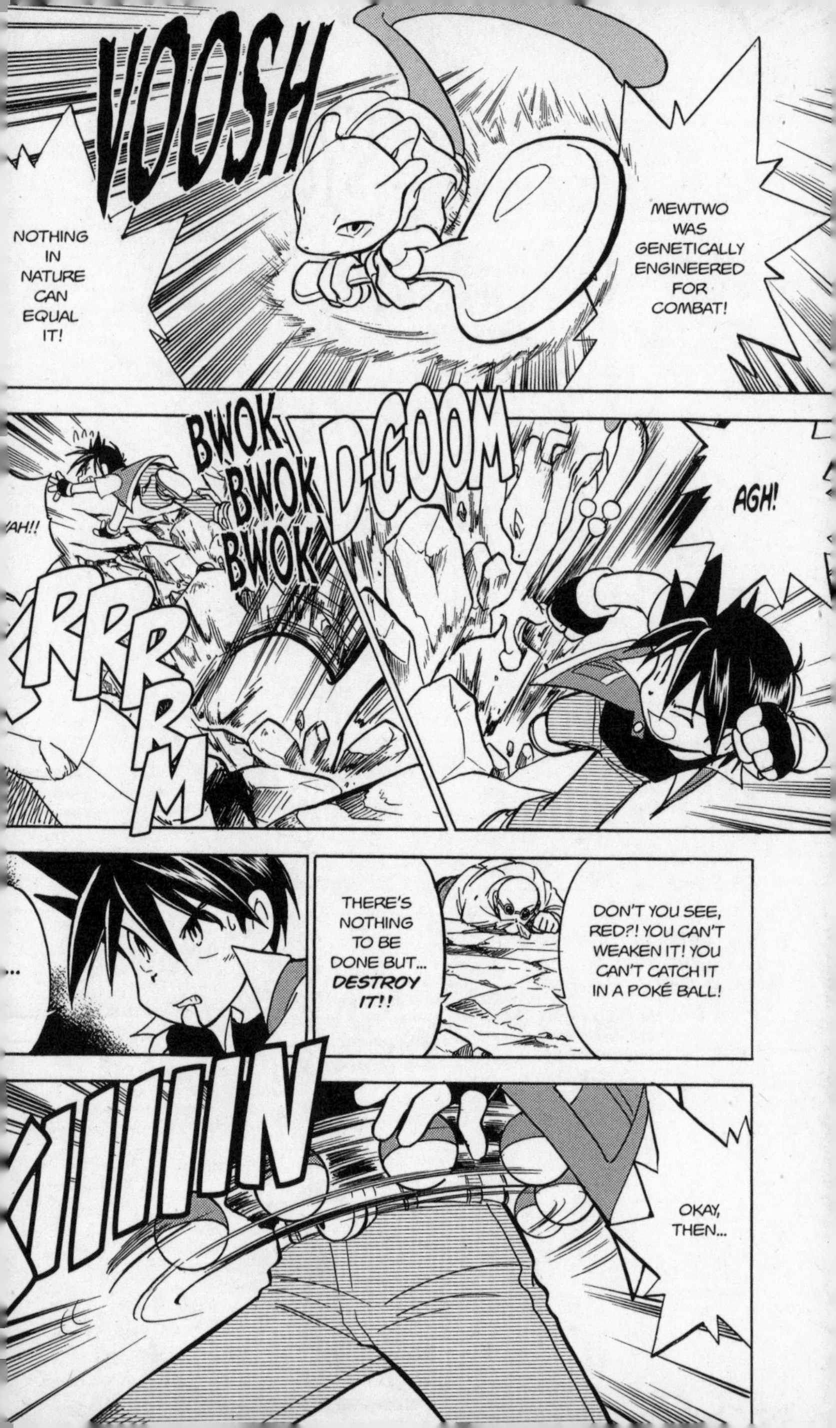
MEWTWO WAS GENETICALLY ENGINEERED FOR COMBAT!
VOOSH
NOTHING IN NATURE CAN EQUAL IT!
AGH!
D-GOOM
BWOK BWOK BWOK
YAH!!
RRRRM
DON'T YOU SEE, RED?! YOU CAN'T WEAKEN IT! YOU CAN'T CATCH IT IN A POKÉ BALL!
THERE'S NOTHING TO BE DONE BUT... ***DESTROY IT!!***
...
OKAY, THEN...

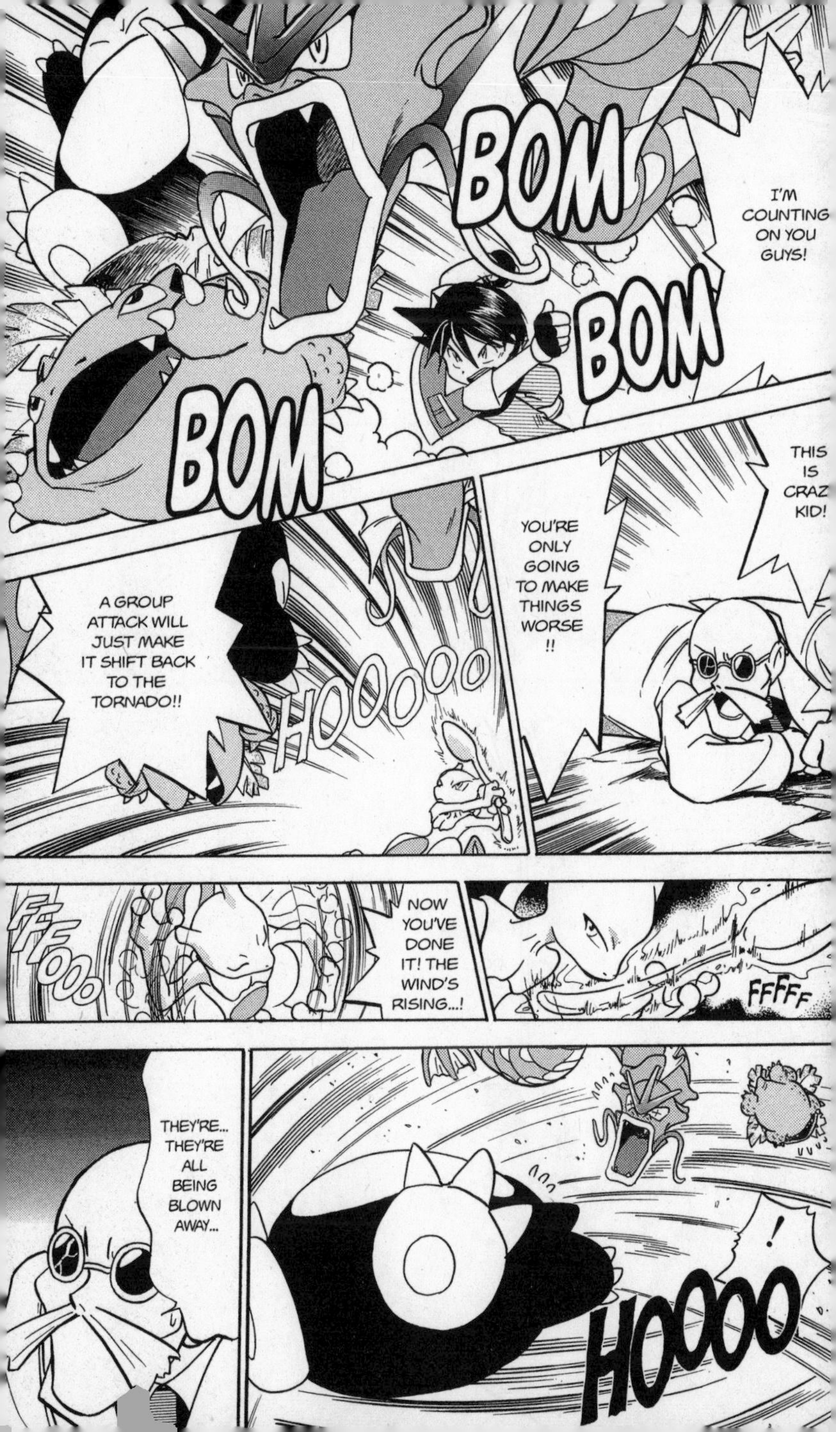
I'M COUNTING ON YOU GUYS!
BOM
BOM
BOM
THIS IS CRAZ KID!
YOU'RE ONLY GOING TO MAKE THINGS WORSE !!
A GROUP ATTACK WILL JUST MAKE IT SHIFT BACK TO THE TORNADO!!
HOOOOOO
NOW YOU'VE DONE IT! THE WIND'S RISING...!
FFFFF
FFFOoo
!
HOOOO
THEY'RE... THEY'RE ALL BEING BLOWN AWAY...

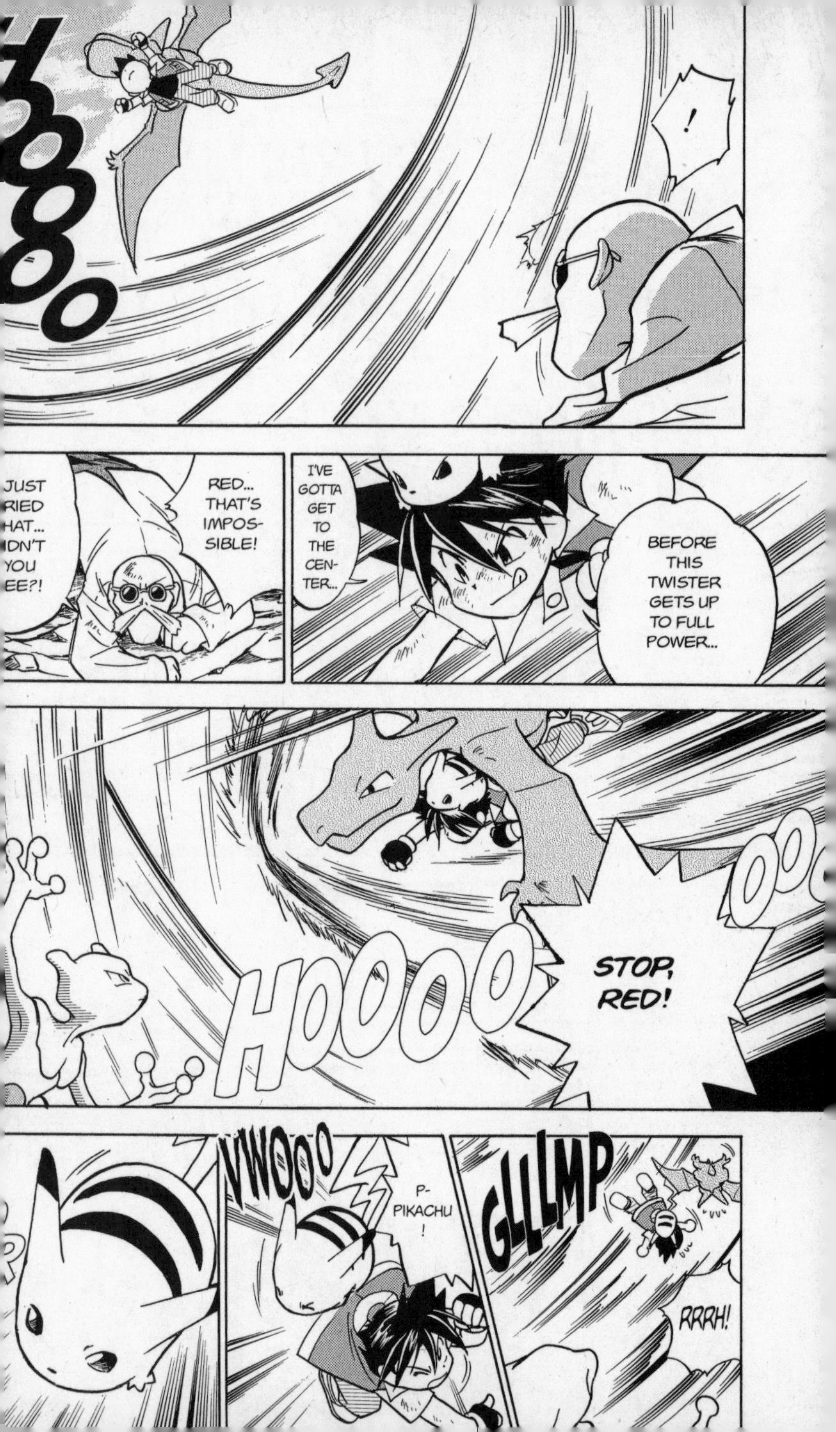
!
HOOOO
I'VE GOTTA GET TO THE CENTER...
BEFORE THIS TWISTER GETS UP TO FULL POWER...
RED... THAT'S IMPOSSIBLE!
JUST RIED HAT... IDN'T YOU EE?!
STOP, RED!
HOOOO
GLLLMP
RRRH!
P-PIKACHU!
VWOOO

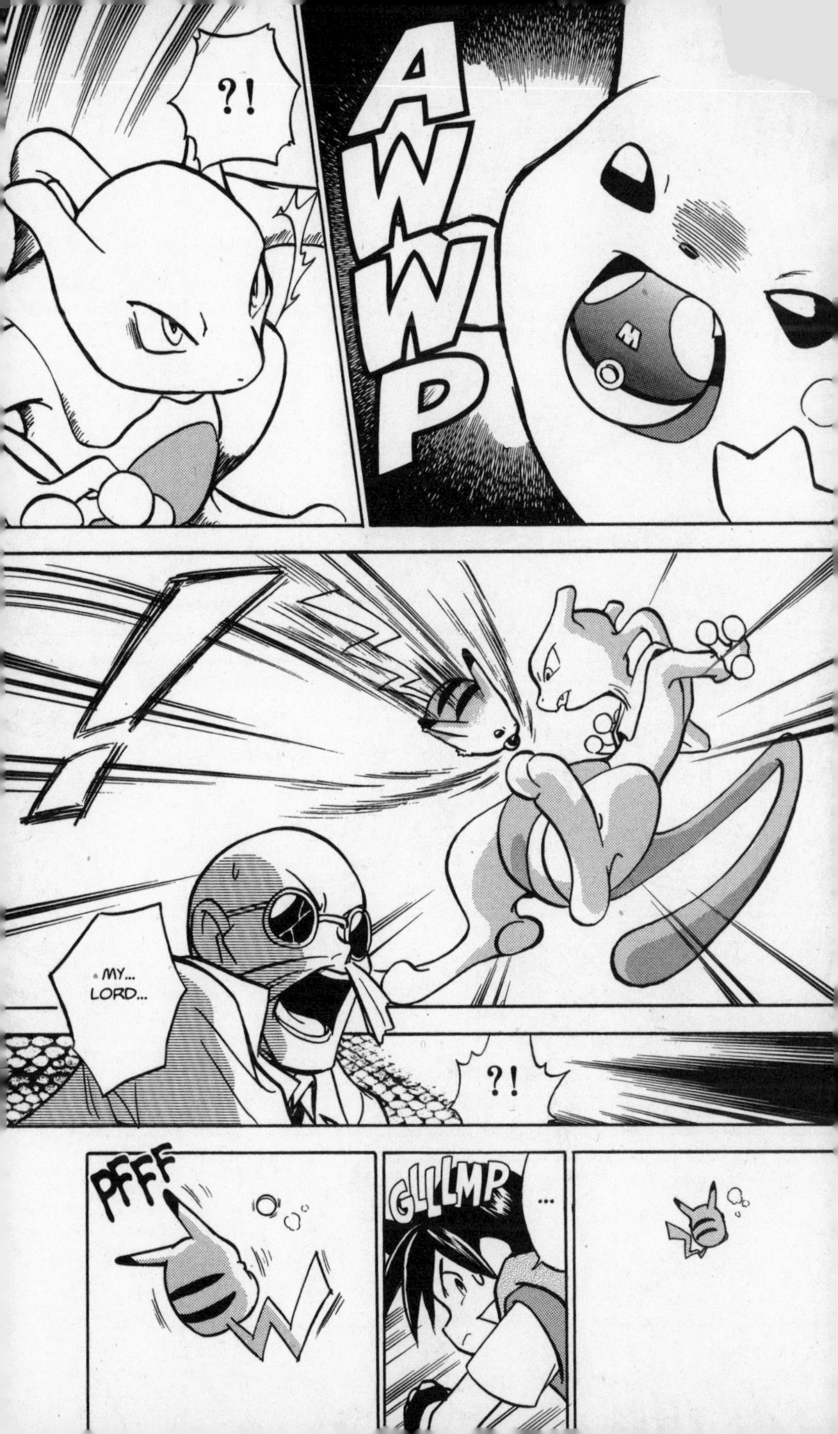
AWWWP
?!
MY... LORD...
?!
GLLLMP
...
PFFF

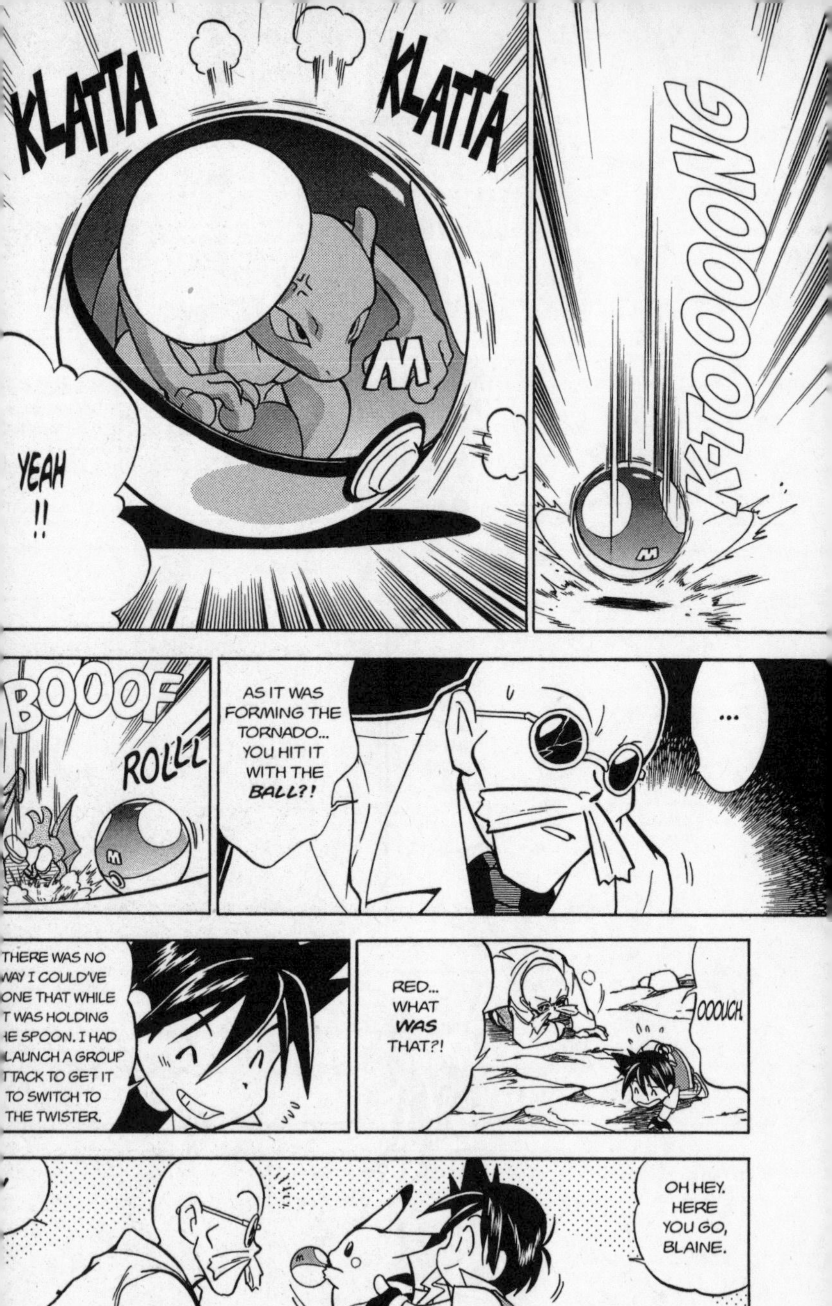
K-TOOOONG
KLATTA
KLATTA
YEAH !!
...
AS IT WAS FORMING THE TORNADO... YOU HIT IT WITH THE *BALL?!*
BOOOF
ROLLL
RED... WHAT *WAS* THAT?!
OOOUCH
THERE WAS NO WAY I COULD'VE ONE THAT WHILE T WAS HOLDING HE SPOON. I HAD LAUNCH A GROUP TTACK TO GET IT TO SWITCH TO THE TWISTER.
OH HEY. HERE YOU GO, BLAINE.

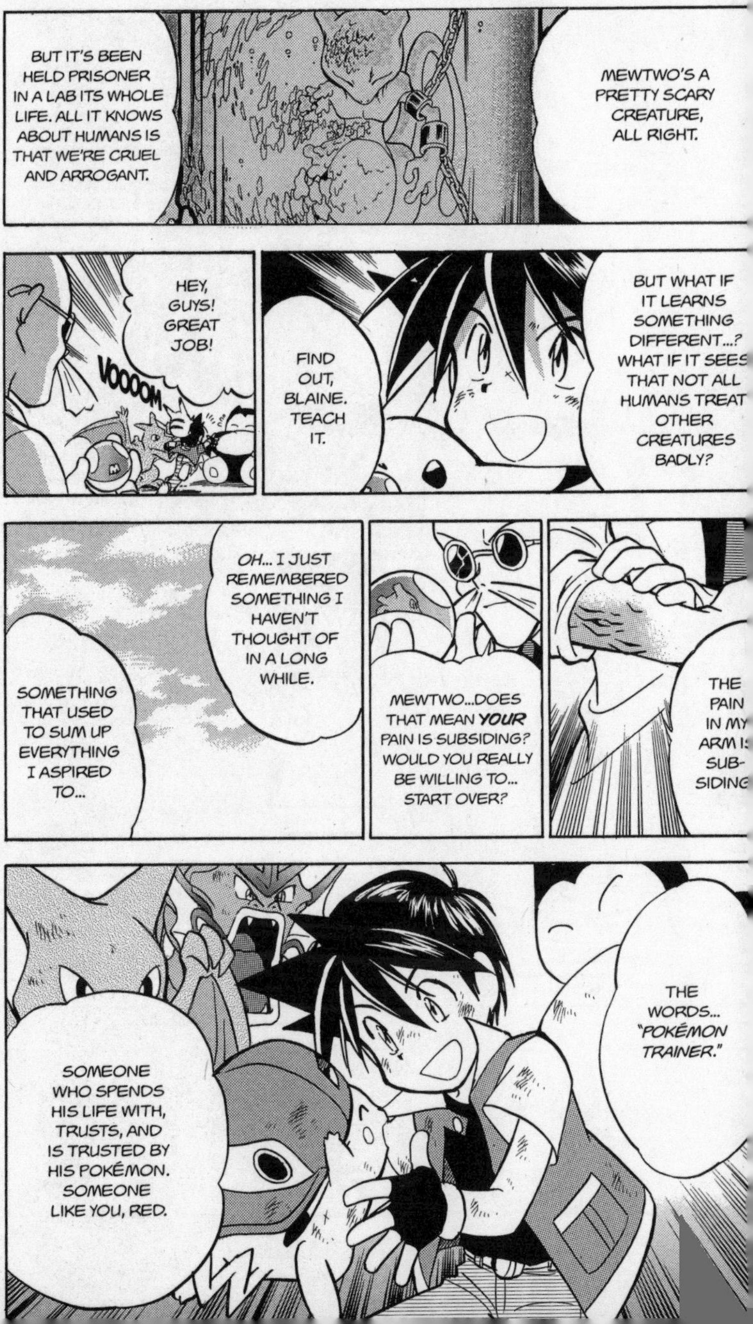
MEWTWO'S A PRETTY SCARY CREATURE, ALL RIGHT.
BUT IT'S BEEN HELD PRISONER IN A LAB ITS WHOLE LIFE. ALL IT KNOWS ABOUT HUMANS IS THAT WE'RE CRUEL AND ARROGANT.
BUT WHAT IF IT LEARNS SOMETHING DIFFERENT...? WHAT IF IT SEES THAT NOT ALL HUMANS TREAT OTHER CREATURES BADLY?
FIND OUT, BLAINE. TEACH IT.
HEY, GUYS! GREAT JOB!
VOOOOM
THE PAIN IN MY ARM IS SUB-SIDING
MEWTWO...DOES THAT MEAN *YOUR* PAIN IS SUBSIDING? WOULD YOU REALLY BE WILLING TO... START OVER?
OH... I JUST REMEMBERED SOMETHING I HAVEN'T THOUGHT OF IN A LONG WHILE.
SOMETHING THAT USED TO SUM UP EVERYTHING I ASPIRED TO...
THE WORDS... *"POKÉMON TRAINER."*
SOMEONE WHO SPENDS HIS LIFE WITH, TRUSTS, AND IS TRUSTED BY HIS POKÉMON. SOMEONE LIKE YOU, RED.

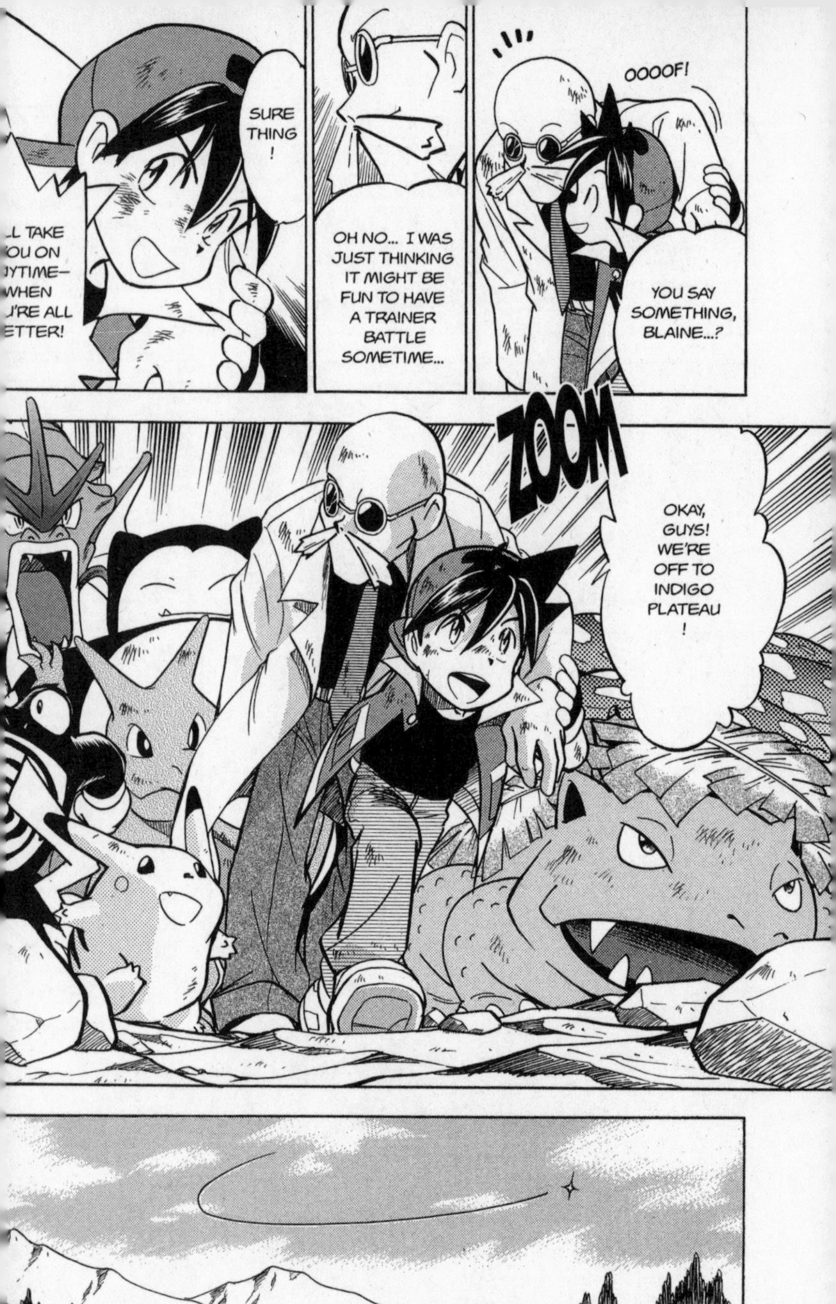
OOOOF!
YOU SAY SOMETHING, BLAINE...?
OH NO... I WAS JUST THINKING IT MIGHT BE FUN TO HAVE A TRAINER BATTLE SOMETIME...
SURE THING!
LL TAKE OU ON YTIME— WHEN 'RE ALL ETTER!
ZOOM
OKAY, GUYS! WE'RE OFF TO INDIGO PLATEAU!

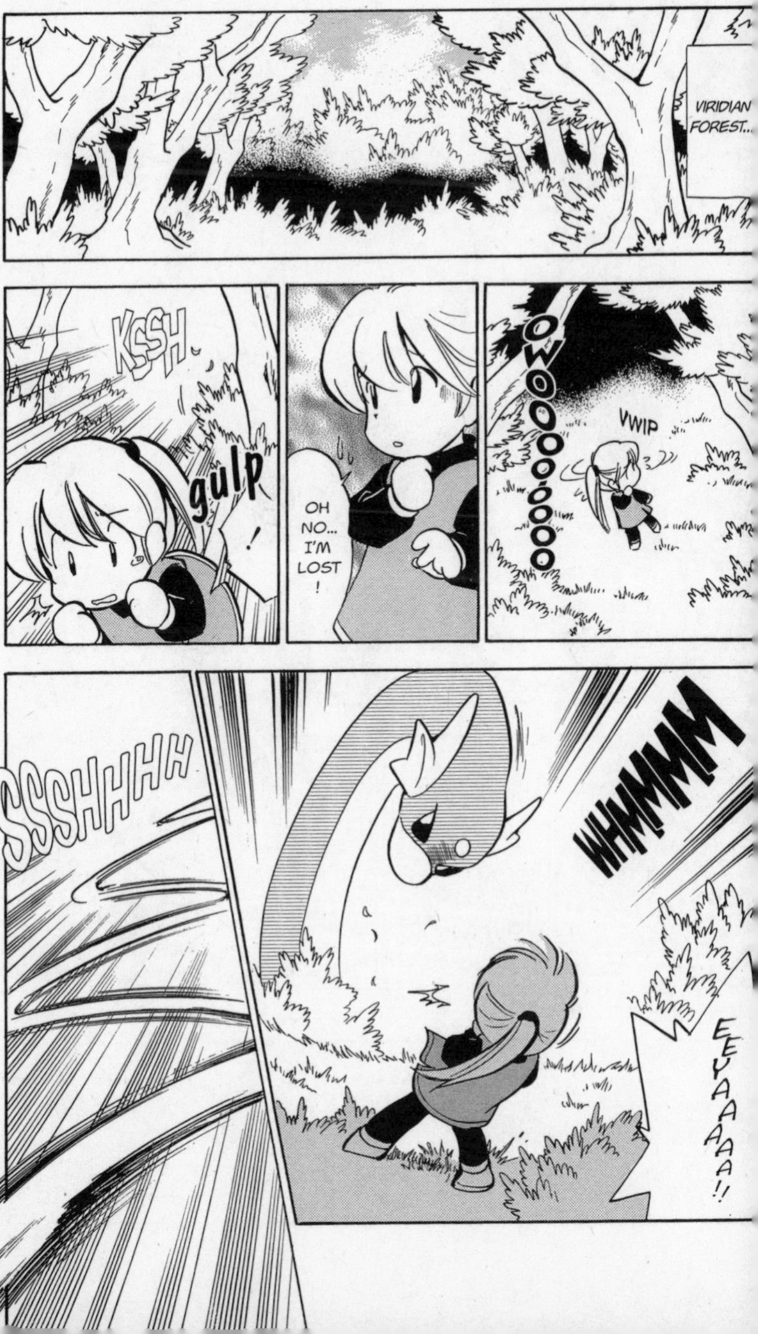
VIRIDIAN FOREST...
OWOOOOOOOOO
VWIP
OH NO... I'M LOST!
KSSH
gulp
!
WHMMMM
EEYAAAAAA!!
SSSHHHH

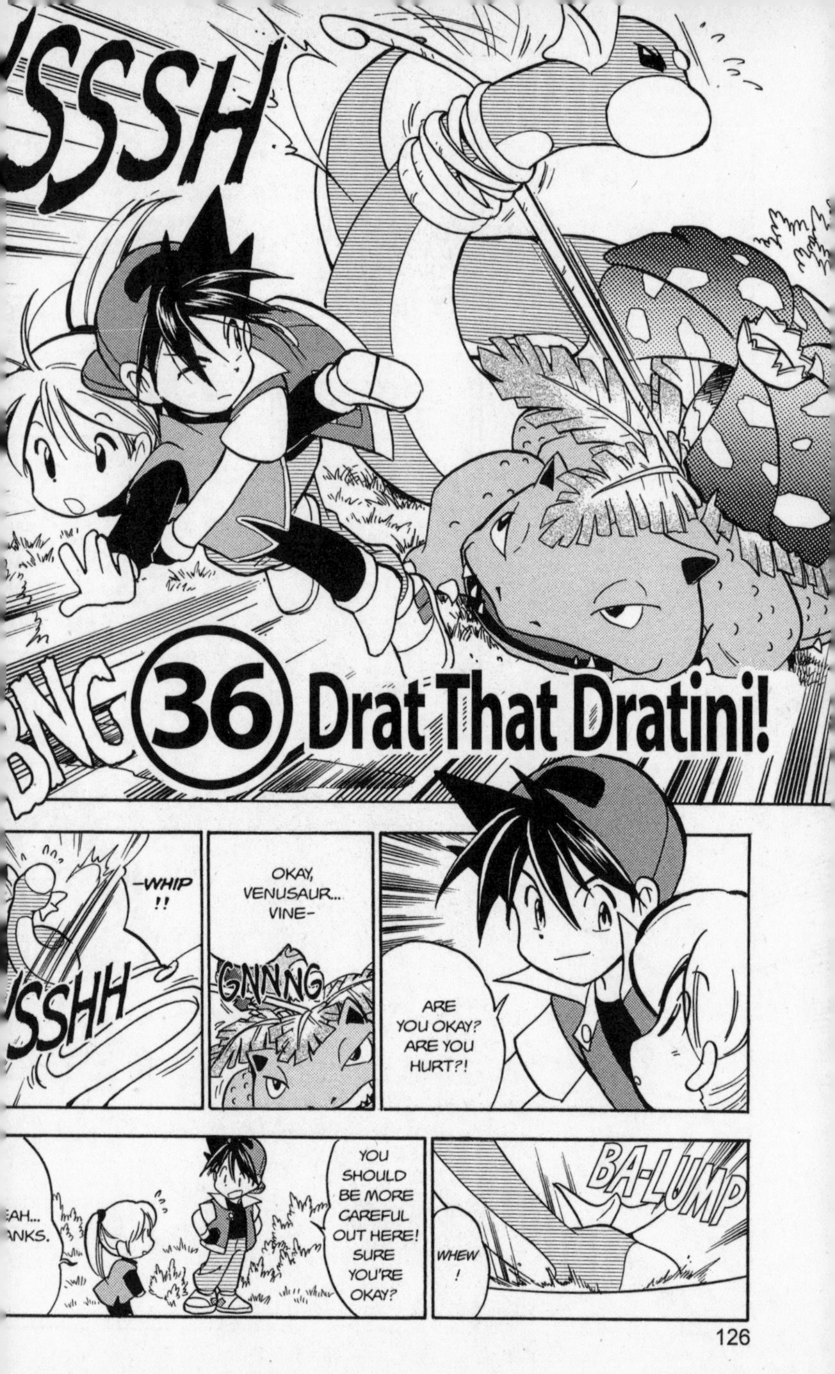
SSSH
36 Drat That Dratini!
ARE YOU OKAY? ARE YOU HURT?!
OKAY, VENUSAUR... VINE-
GNNNG
-WHIP !!
SSHH
BA-LUMP
WHEW !
YOU SHOULD BE MORE CAREFUL OUT HERE! SURE YOU'RE OKAY?
EAH... ANKS.

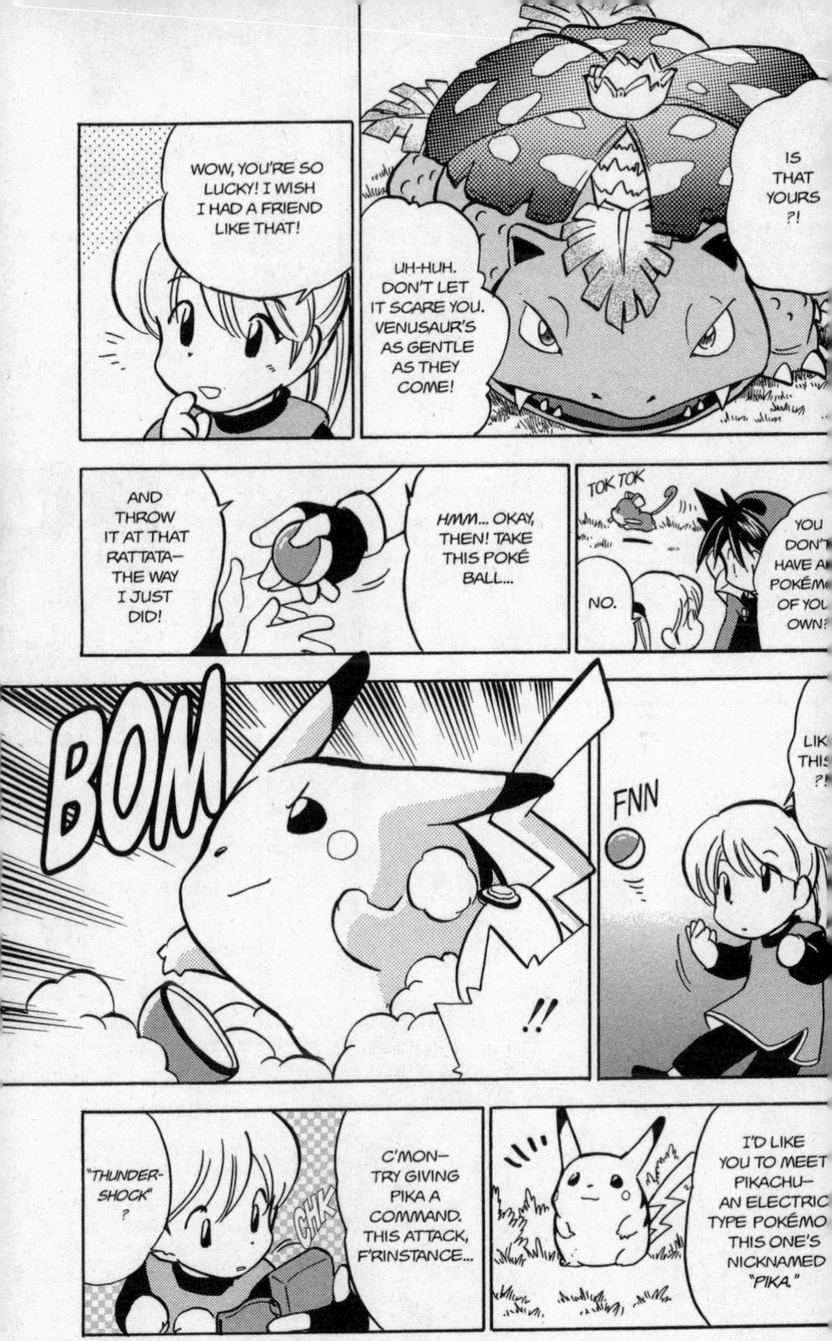
IS THAT YOURS ?!
UH-HUH. DON'T LET IT SCARE YOU. VENUSAUR'S AS GENTLE AS THEY COME!
WOW, YOU'RE SO LUCKY! I WISH I HAD A FRIEND LIKE THAT!
TOK TOK
YOU DON'T HAVE A POKÉMO OF YOU OWN?
NO.
HMM... OKAY, THEN! TAKE THIS POKÉ BALL...
AND THROW IT AT THAT RATTATA— THE WAY I JUST DID!
LIK THIS ?!
FNN
BOM
!!
I'D LIKE YOU TO MEET PIKACHU— AN ELECTRIC TYPE POKÉMO THIS ONE'S NICKNAMED "PIKA."
C'MON— TRY GIVING PIKA A COMMAND. THIS ATTACK, F'RINSTANCE...
CHK
"THUNDER-SHOCK" ?

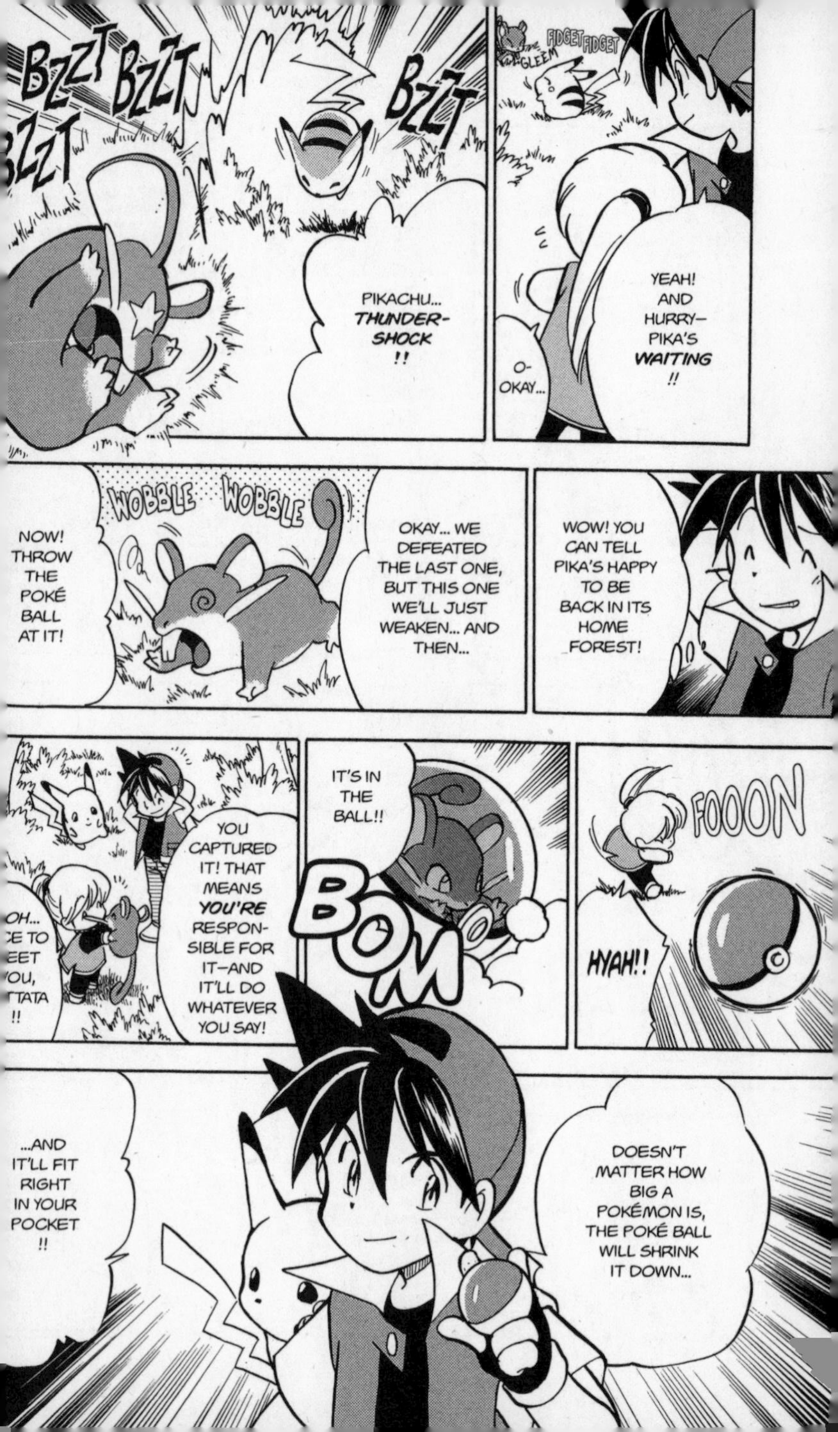
FIDGET FIDGET
GLEEM
YEAH! AND HURRY—PIKA'S WAITING!!
O-OKAY...
BZZT
PIKACHU... THUNDER-SHOCK!!
BZZT BZZT
BZZT
WOW! YOU CAN TELL PIKA'S HAPPY TO BE BACK IN ITS HOME FOREST!
OKAY... WE DEFEATED THE LAST ONE, BUT THIS ONE WE'LL JUST WEAKEN... AND THEN...
WOBBLE WOBBLE
NOW! THROW THE POKÉ BALL AT IT!
FOOON
HYAH!!
IT'S IN THE BALL!!
BOM
YOU CAPTURED IT! THAT MEANS YOU'RE RESPONSIBLE FOR IT—AND IT'LL DO WHATEVER YOU SAY!
OH... CE TO EET YOU, TTATA!!
DOESN'T MATTER HOW BIG A POKÉMON IS, THE POKÉ BALL WILL SHRINK IT DOWN...
...AND IT'LL FIT RIGHT IN YOUR POCKET!!

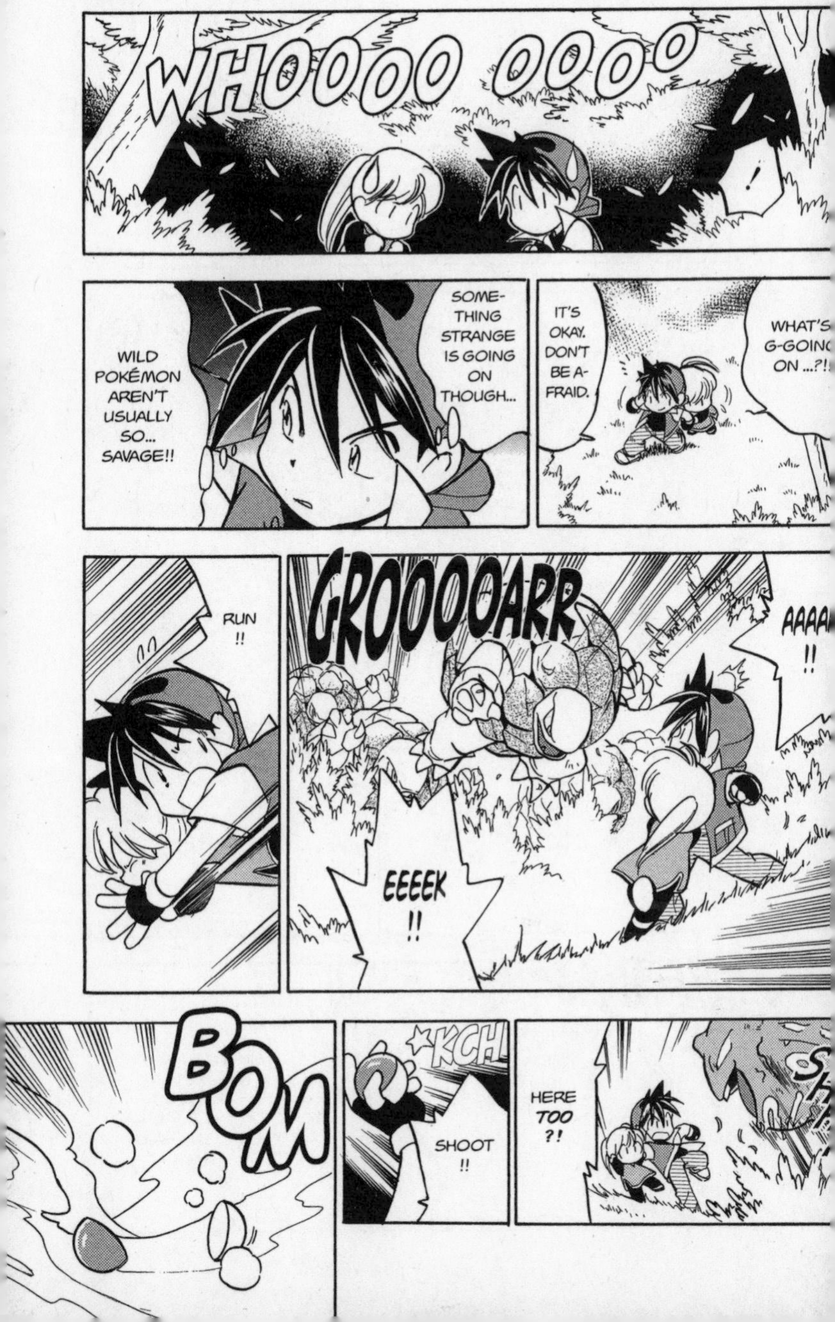
WHOOOO OOOO
!
WHAT'S G-GOIN ON ...?!
IT'S OKAY. DON'T BE AFRAID.
SOMETHING STRANGE IS GOING ON THOUGH...
WILD POKÉMON AREN'T USUALLY SO... SAVAGE!!
AAAA !!
GROOOOARR
EEEEK !!
RUN !!
HERE TOO ?!
KCH
SHOOT !!
BOM

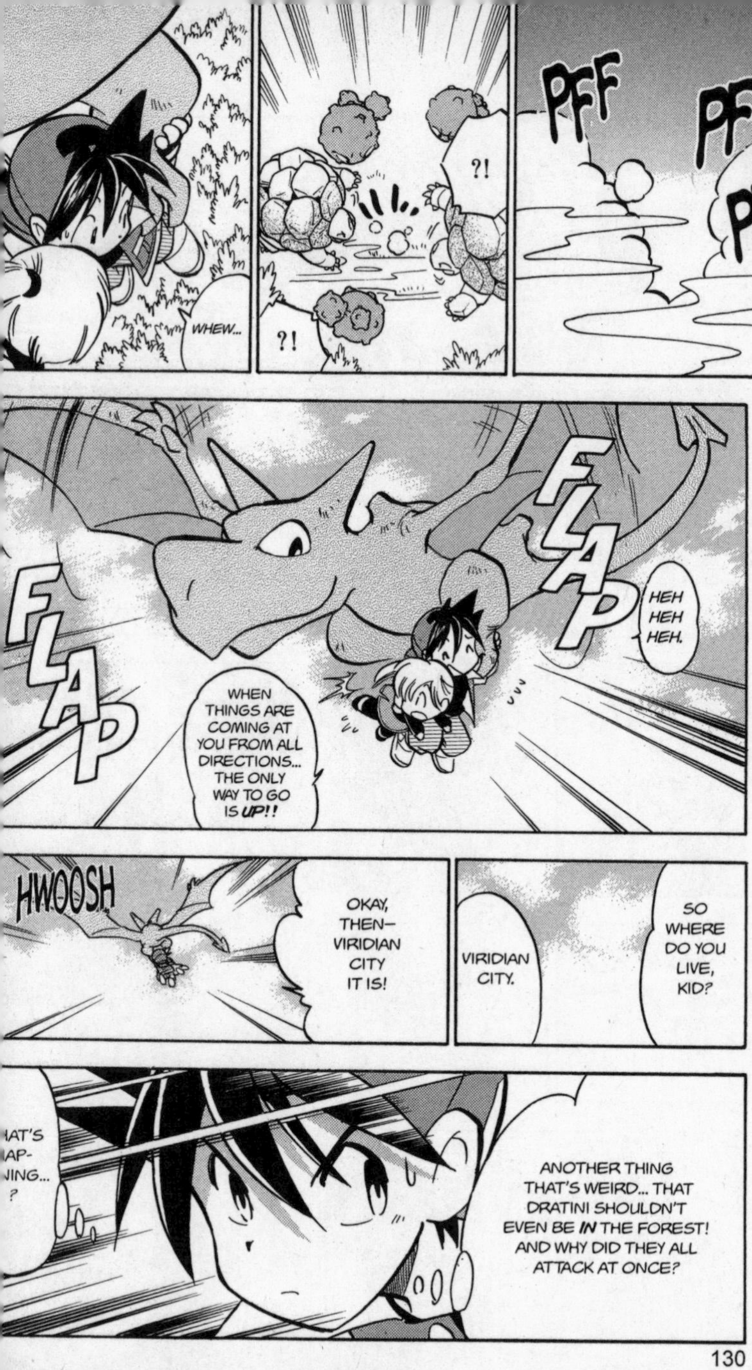
PFF
PFF
PFF
?!
?!
WHEW...
FLAP
HEH HEH HEH.
FLAP
WHEN THINGS ARE COMING AT YOU FROM ALL DIRECTIONS... THE ONLY WAY TO GO IS *UP!!*
SO WHERE DO YOU LIVE, KID?
VIRIDIAN CITY.
OKAY, THEN— VIRIDIAN CITY IT IS!
HWOOSH
ANOTHER THING THAT'S WEIRD... THAT DRATINI SHOULDN'T EVEN BE *IN* THE FOREST! AND WHY DID THEY ALL ATTACK AT ONCE?

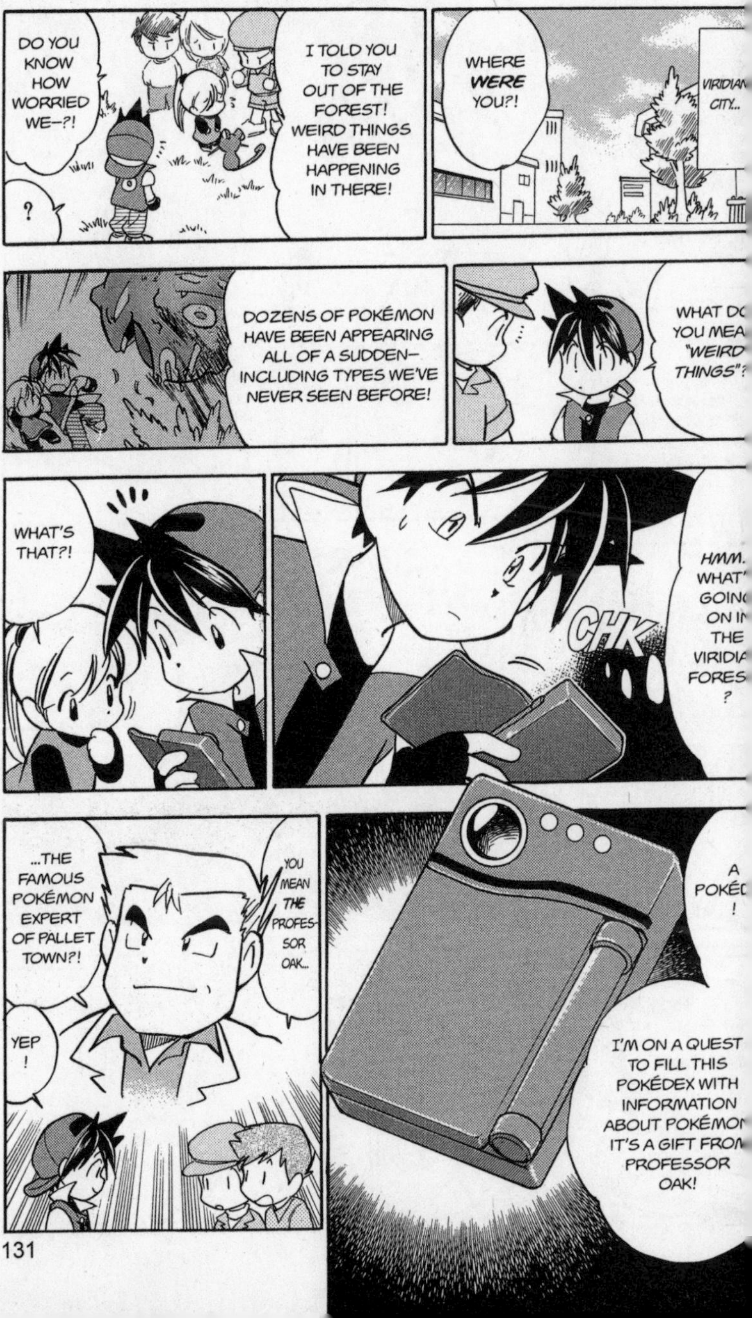
VIRIDIAN CITY...
WHERE ***WERE*** YOU?!
I TOLD YOU TO STAY OUT OF THE FOREST! WEIRD THINGS HAVE BEEN HAPPENING IN THERE!
DO YOU KNOW HOW WORRIED WE--?!
?
WHAT DC YOU MEA "WEIRD THINGS"?
DOZENS OF POKÉMON HAVE BEEN APPEARING ALL OF A SUDDEN-- INCLUDING TYPES WE'VE NEVER SEEN BEFORE!
HMM... WHAT' GOIN ON IN THE VIRIDIA FORES ?
CHK
WHAT'S THAT?!
A POKÉD !
I'M ON A QUEST TO FILL THIS POKÉDEX WITH INFORMATION ABOUT POKÉMON IT'S A GIFT FROM PROFESSOR OAK!
YOU MEAN ***THE*** PROFESSOR OAK...
...THE FAMOUS POKÉMON EXPERT OF PALLET TOWN?!
YEP!

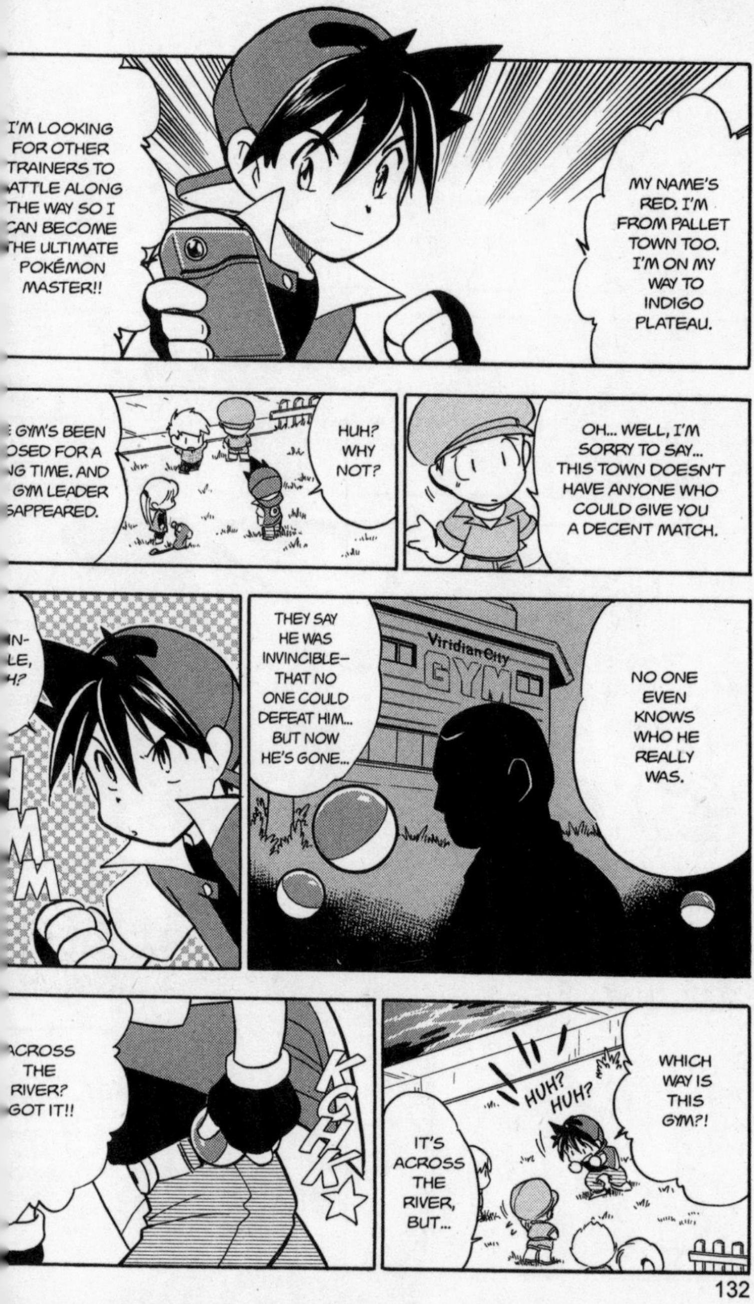
MY NAME'S RED. I'M FROM PALLET TOWN TOO. I'M ON MY WAY TO INDIGO PLATEAU.
I'M LOOKING FOR OTHER TRAINERS TO ATTLE ALONG THE WAY SO I CAN BECOME THE ULTIMATE POKÉMON MASTER!!
OH... WELL, I'M SORRY TO SAY... THIS TOWN DOESN'T HAVE ANYONE WHO COULD GIVE YOU A DECENT MATCH.
HUH? WHY NOT?
E GYM'S BEEN OSED FOR A NG TIME. AND GYM LEADER SAPPEARED.
NO ONE EVEN KNOWS WHO HE REALLY WAS.
Viridian City
GYM
THEY SAY HE WAS INVINCIBLE— THAT NO ONE COULD DEFEAT HIM... BUT NOW HE'S GONE...
IN- LE, H?
HMMM
WHICH WAY IS THIS GYM?!
HUH? HUH?
IT'S ACROSS THE RIVER, BUT...
KCHK
ACROSS THE RIVER? GOT IT!!

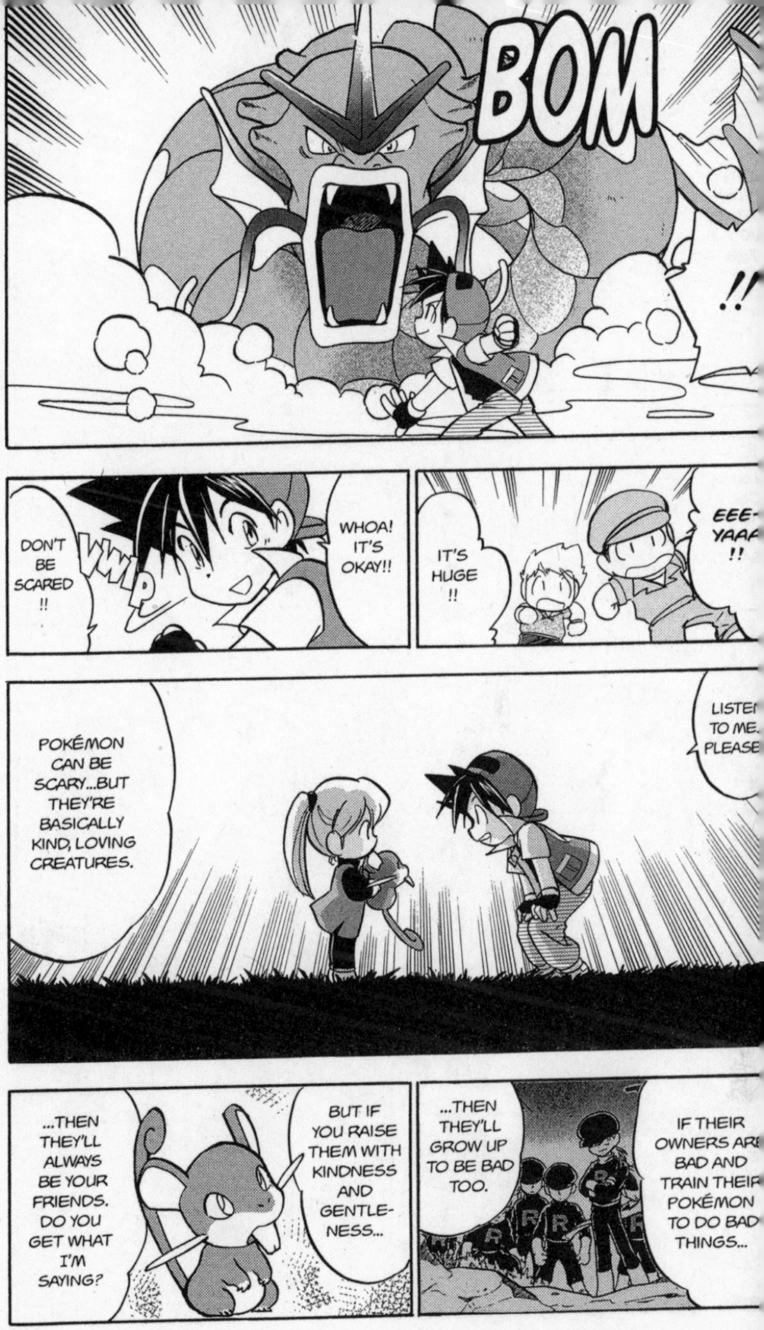
BOM
!!
EEE-YAAA!!
IT'S HUGE!!
WHOA! IT'S OKAY!!
VWIP
DON'T BE SCARED!!
LISTEN TO ME. PLEASE
POKÉMON CAN BE SCARY...BUT THEY'RE BASICALLY KIND, LOVING CREATURES.
IF THEIR OWNERS ARE BAD AND TRAIN THEIR POKÉMON TO DO BAD THINGS...
...THEN THEY'LL GROW UP TO BE BAD TOO.
BUT IF YOU RAISE THEM WITH KINDNESS AND GENTLE-NESS...
...THEN THEY'LL ALWAYS BE YOUR FRIENDS. DO YOU GET WHAT I'M SAYING?

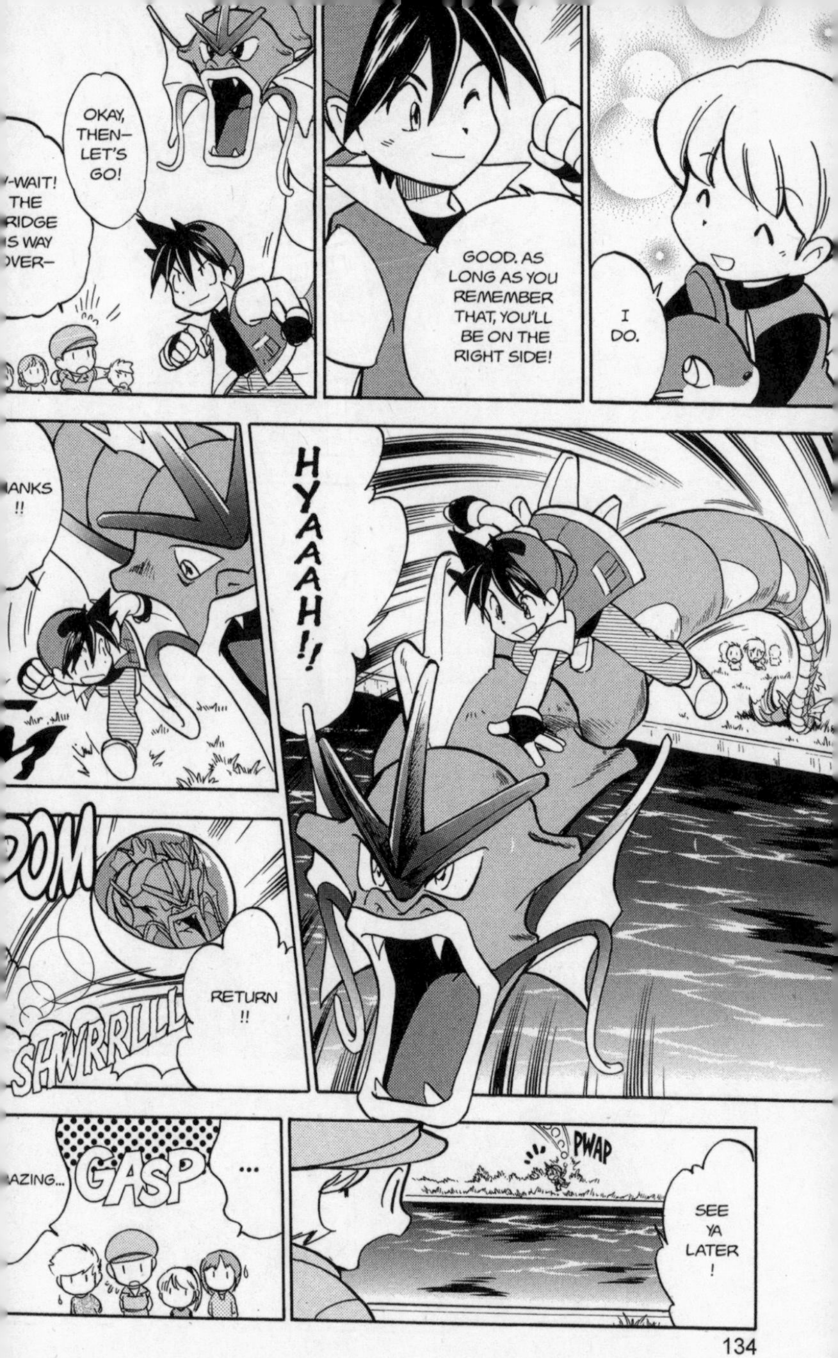
I DO.
GOOD. AS LONG AS YOU REMEMBER THAT, YOU'LL BE ON THE RIGHT SIDE!
OKAY, THEN— LET'S GO!
-WAIT! THE RIDGE S WAY OVER—
HYAAAAH!!
ANKS !!
DOM
RETURN !!
SHWRRLLL
PWAP
SEE YA LATER !
...
GASP
AZING...

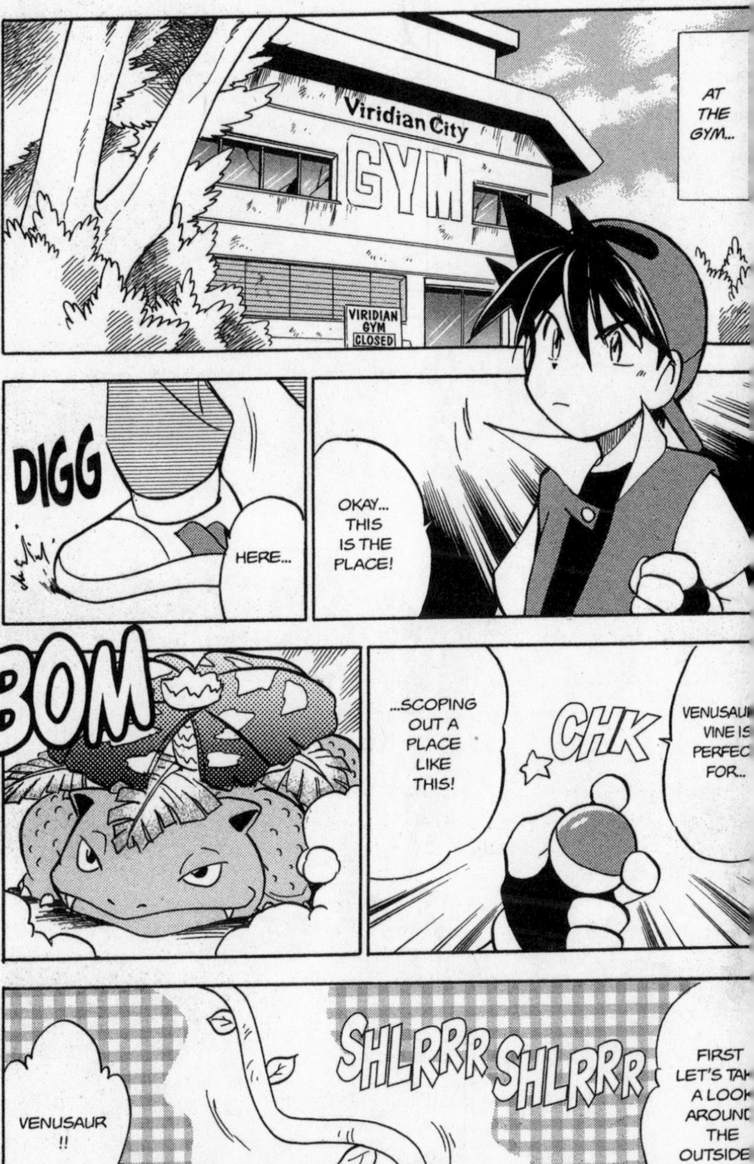
AT THE GYM...
Viridian City
GYM
VIRIDIAN GYM CLOSED
OKAY... THIS IS THE PLACE!
DIGG
HERE...
VENUSAU VINE IS PERFEC FOR...
CHK
...SCOPING OUT A PLACE LIKE THIS!
BOM
FIRST LET'S TA A LOO AROUN THE OUTSIDE
SHLRRR SHLRRR
VENUSAUR !!

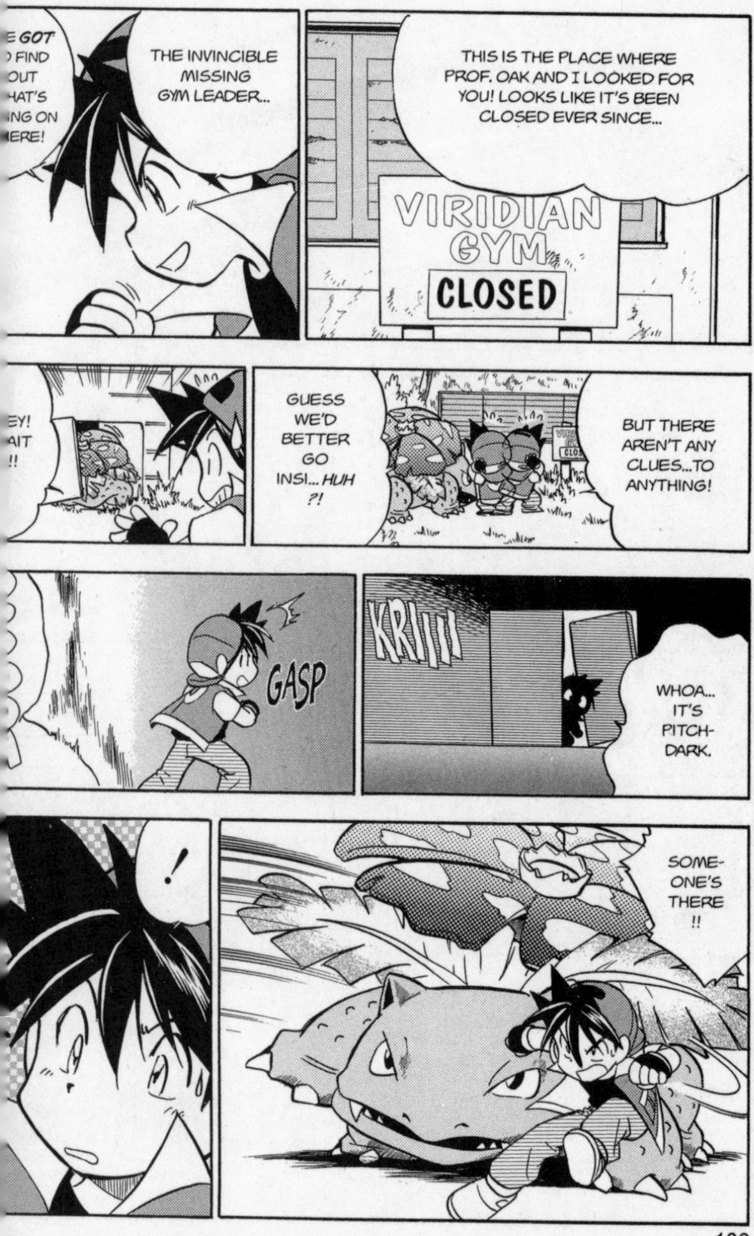
THIS IS THE PLACE WHERE PROF. OAK AND I LOOKED FOR YOU! LOOKS LIKE IT'S BEEN CLOSED EVER SINCE...
VIRIDIAN GYM
CLOSED
THE INVINCIBLE MISSING GYM LEADER...
E GOT O FIND OUT HAT'S ING ON ERE!
BUT THERE AREN'T ANY CLUES...TO ANYTHING!
GUESS WE'D BETTER GO INSI... HUH ?!
EY! AIT !!
KRIII
WHOA... IT'S PITCH-DARK.
GASP
SOME-ONE'S THERE !!
!

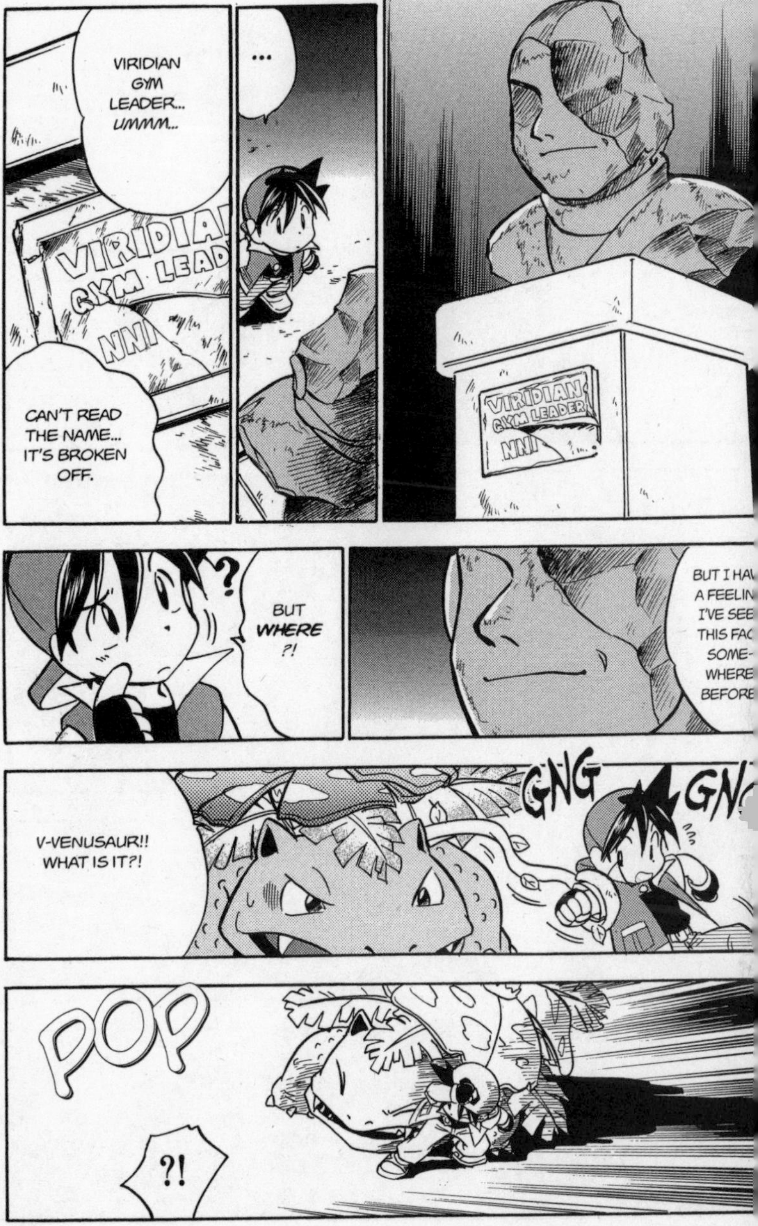
VIRIDIAN GYM LEADER NNI
...
VIRIDIAN GYM LEADER.. UMMM..
VIRIDIAN GYM LEAD NNI
CAN'T READ THE NAME... IT'S BROKEN OFF.
BUT I HAV A FEELIN I'VE SEE THIS FAC SOME-WHERE BEFORE
?
BUT WHERE ?!
GNG GNG
V-VENUSAUR!! WHAT IS IT?!
POP
?!

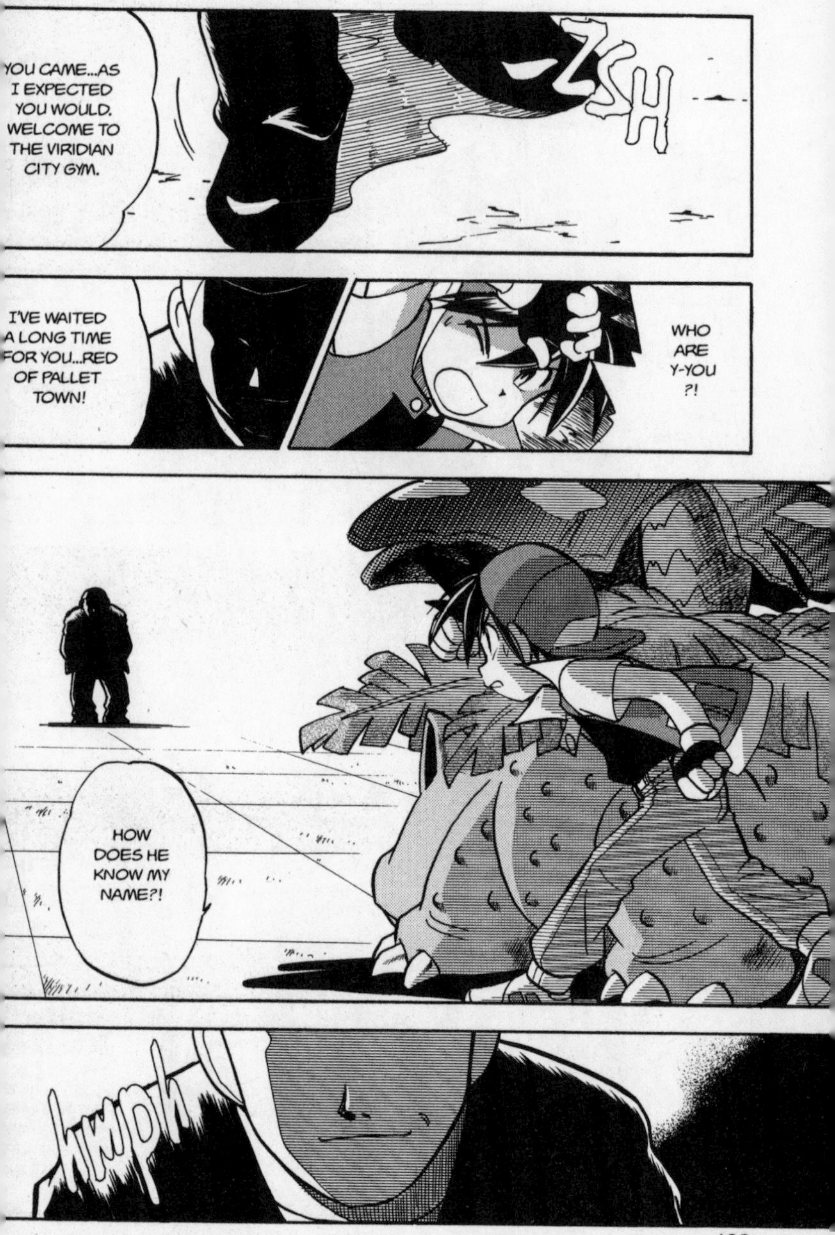
ZSH
YOU CAME...AS I EXPECTED YOU WOULD. WELCOME TO THE VIRIDIAN CITY GYM.
WHO ARE Y-YOU ?!
I'VE WAITED A LONG TIME FOR YOU...RED OF PALLET TOWN!
HOW DOES HE KNOW MY NAME?!
hmph

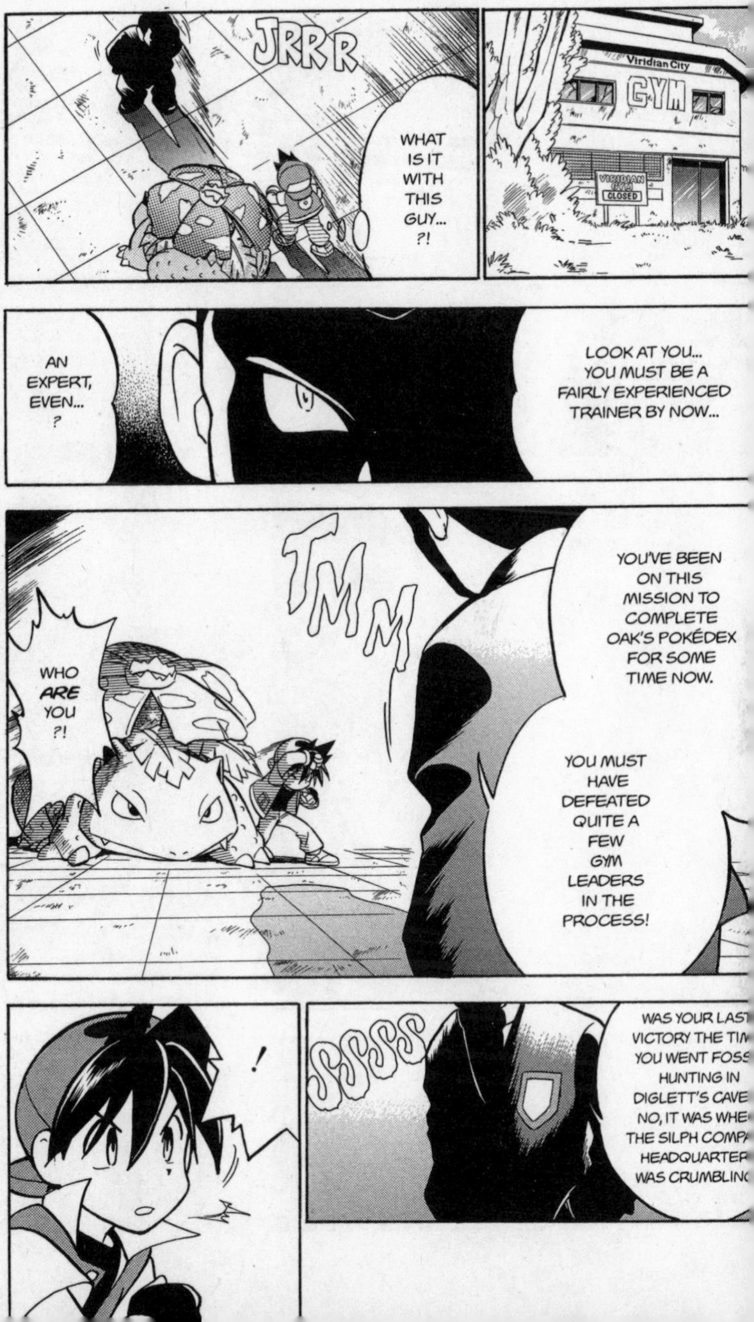

Viridian City
GYM
VIRIDIAN GYM CLOSED
JRRR
WHAT IS IT WITH THIS GUY... ?!
LOOK AT YOU... YOU MUST BE A FAIRLY EXPERIENCED TRAINER BY NOW...
AN EXPERT, EVEN... ?
YOU'VE BEEN ON THIS MISSION TO COMPLETE OAK'S POKÉDEX FOR SOME TIME NOW.
YOU MUST HAVE DEFEATED QUITE A FEW GYM LEADERS IN THE PROCESS!
TMM
WHO *ARE* YOU ?!
WAS YOUR LAST
VICTORY THE TIM
YOU WENT FOSS
HUNTING IN
DIGLETT'S CAVE
NO, IT WAS WHE
THE SILPH COMPA
HEADQUARTER
WAS CRUMBLIN
SSSSS
!

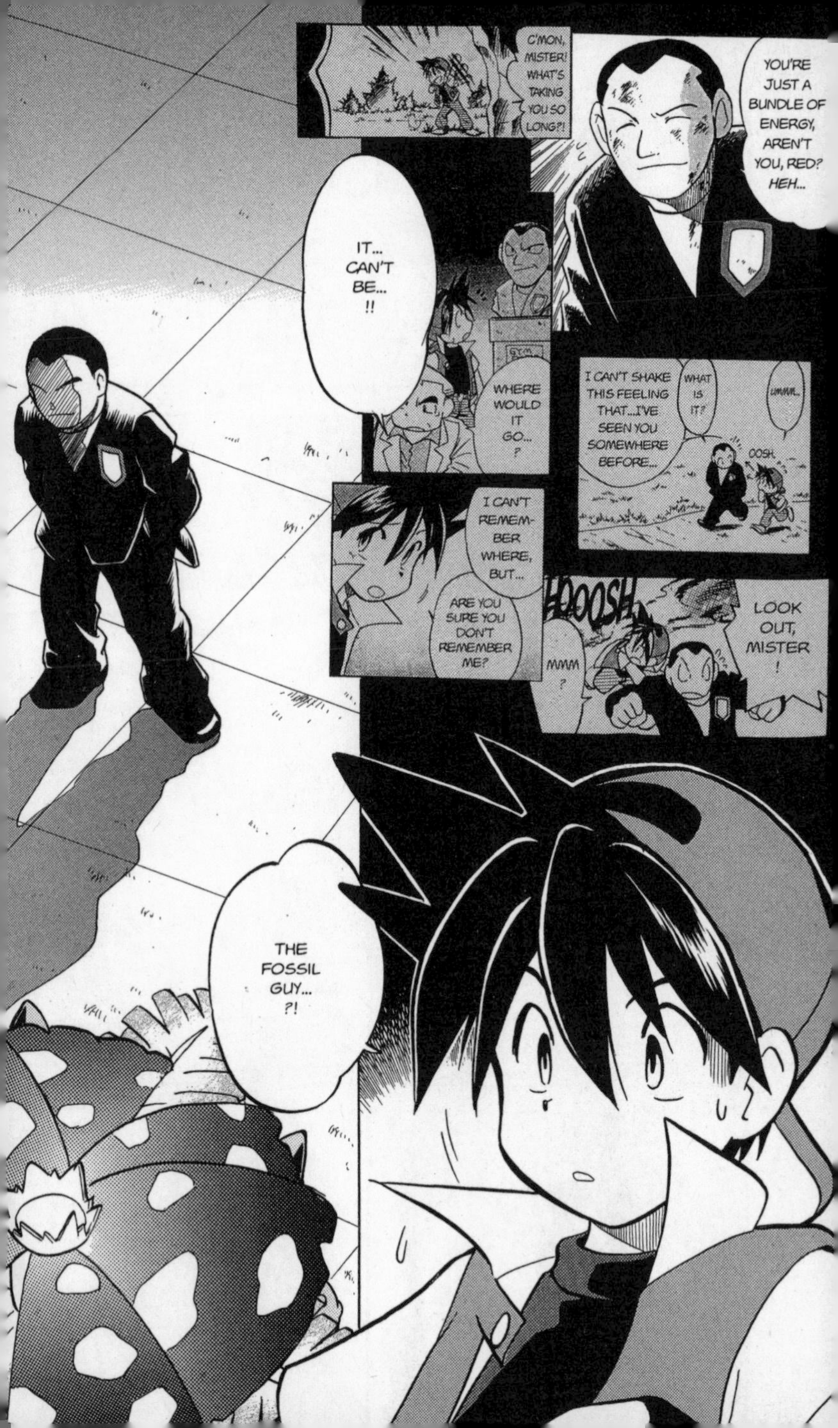

YOU'RE JUST A BUNDLE OF ENERGY, AREN'T YOU, RED? HEH...
C'MON, MISTER! WHAT'S TAKING YOU SO LONG?!
IT... CAN'T BE... !!
UMMM...
WHAT IS IT?
I CAN'T SHAKE THIS FEELING THAT...I'VE SEEN YOU SOMEWHERE BEFORE...
OOSH
WHERE WOULD IT GO... ?
LOOK OUT, MISTER !
HOOOSH
MMM ?
I CAN'T REMEMBER WHERE, BUT...
ARE YOU SURE YOU DON'T REMEMBER ME?
THE FOSSIL GUY... ?!

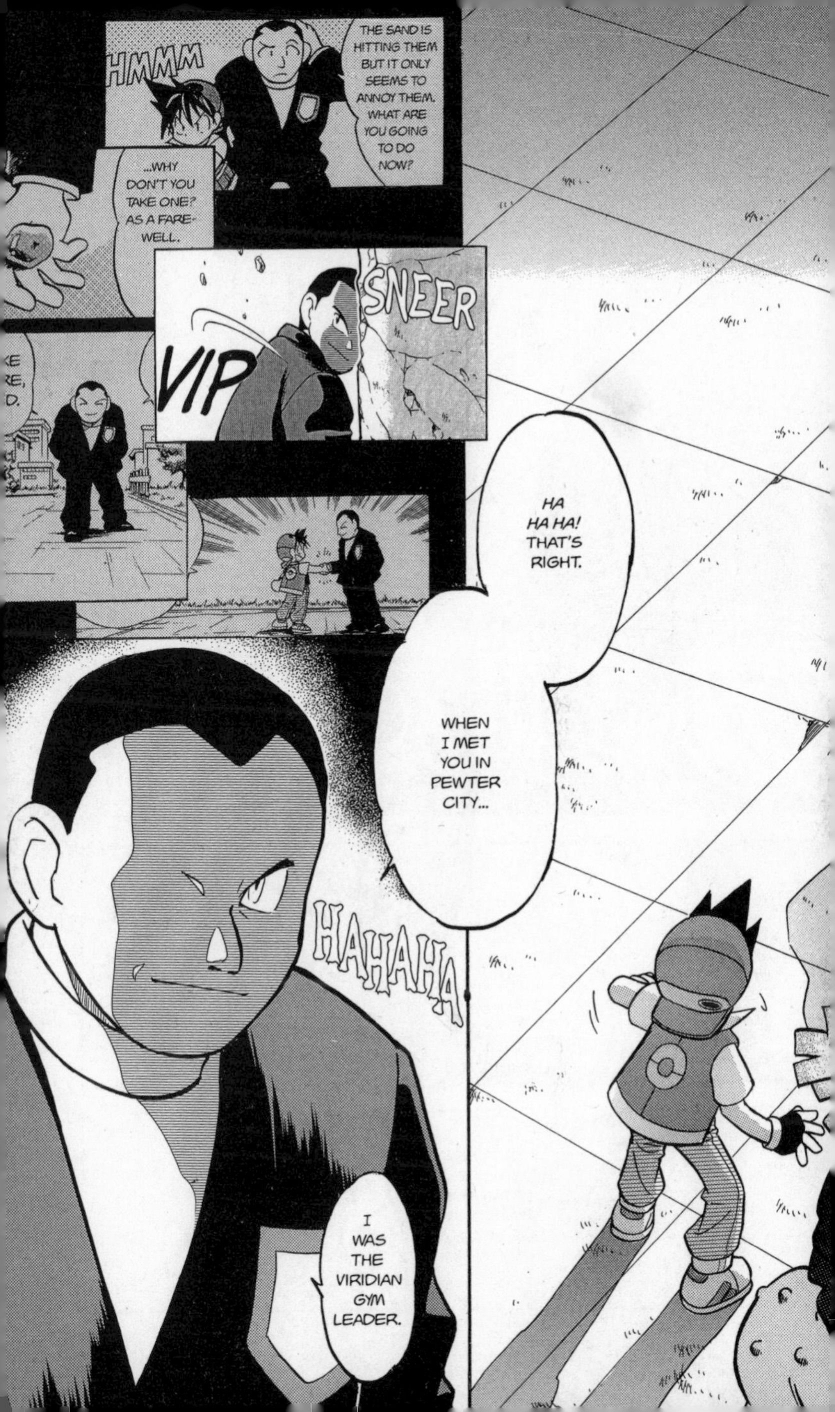
HA HA HA! THAT'S RIGHT.
WHEN I MET YOU IN PEWTER CITY...
HMMM
THE SAND IS HITTING THEM BUT IT ONLY SEEMS TO ANNOY THEM. WHAT ARE YOU GOING TO DO NOW?
...WHY DON'T YOU TAKE ONE? AS A FARE-WELL.
SNEER
VIP
HAHAHA
I WAS THE VIRIDIAN GYM LEADER.

37 Golly, Golem!

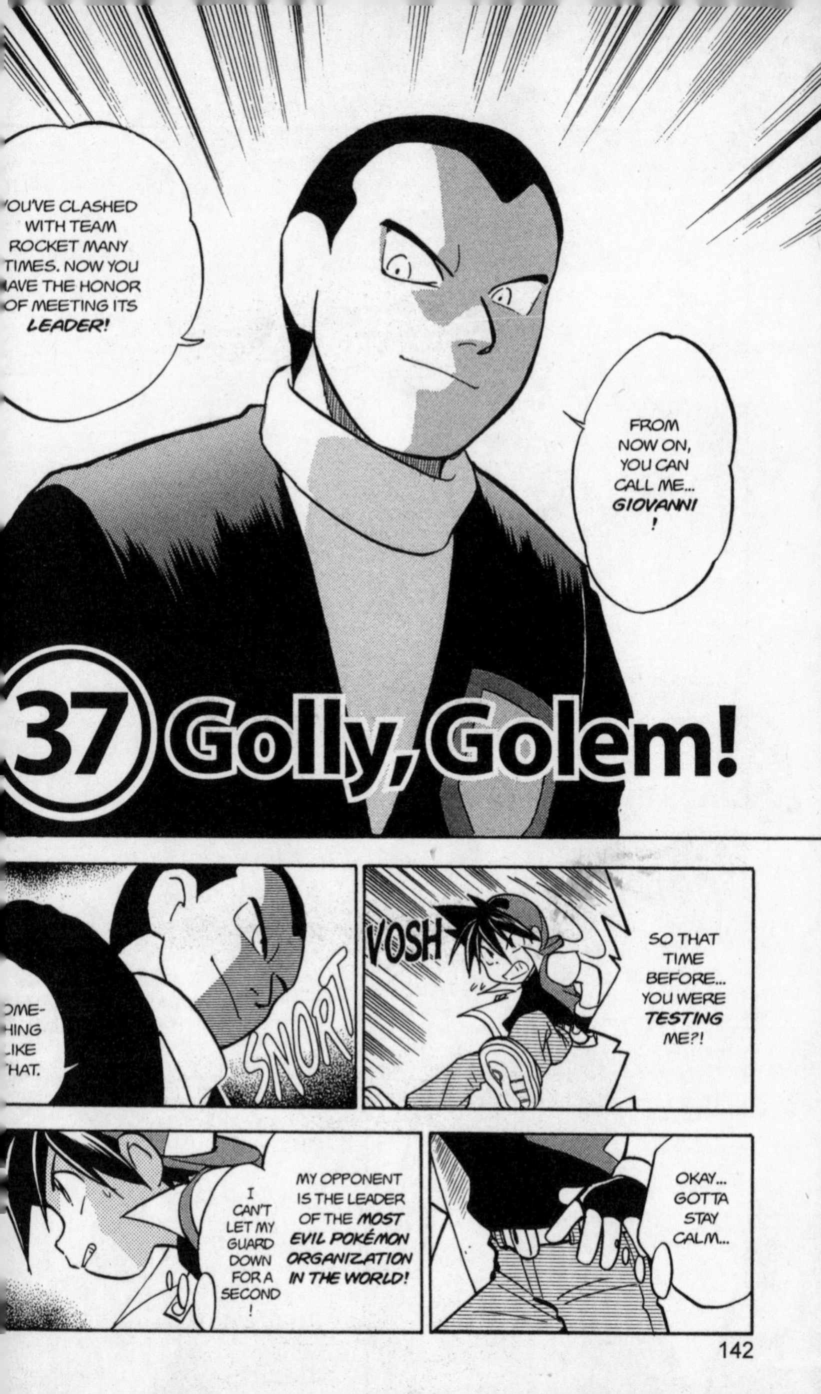

OU'VE CLASHED WITH TEAM ROCKET MANY TIMES. NOW YOU AVE THE HONOR OF MEETING ITS *LEADER!*
FROM NOW ON, YOU CAN CALL ME... *GIOVANNI!*
VOSH
SO THAT TIME BEFORE... YOU WERE *TESTING* ME?!
SNORT
OME-HING LIKE HAT.
OKAY... GOTTA STAY CALM...
MY OPPONENT IS THE LEADER OF THE *MOST EVIL POKÉMON ORGANIZATION IN THE WORLD!*
I CAN'T LET MY GUARD DOWN FOR A SECOND!

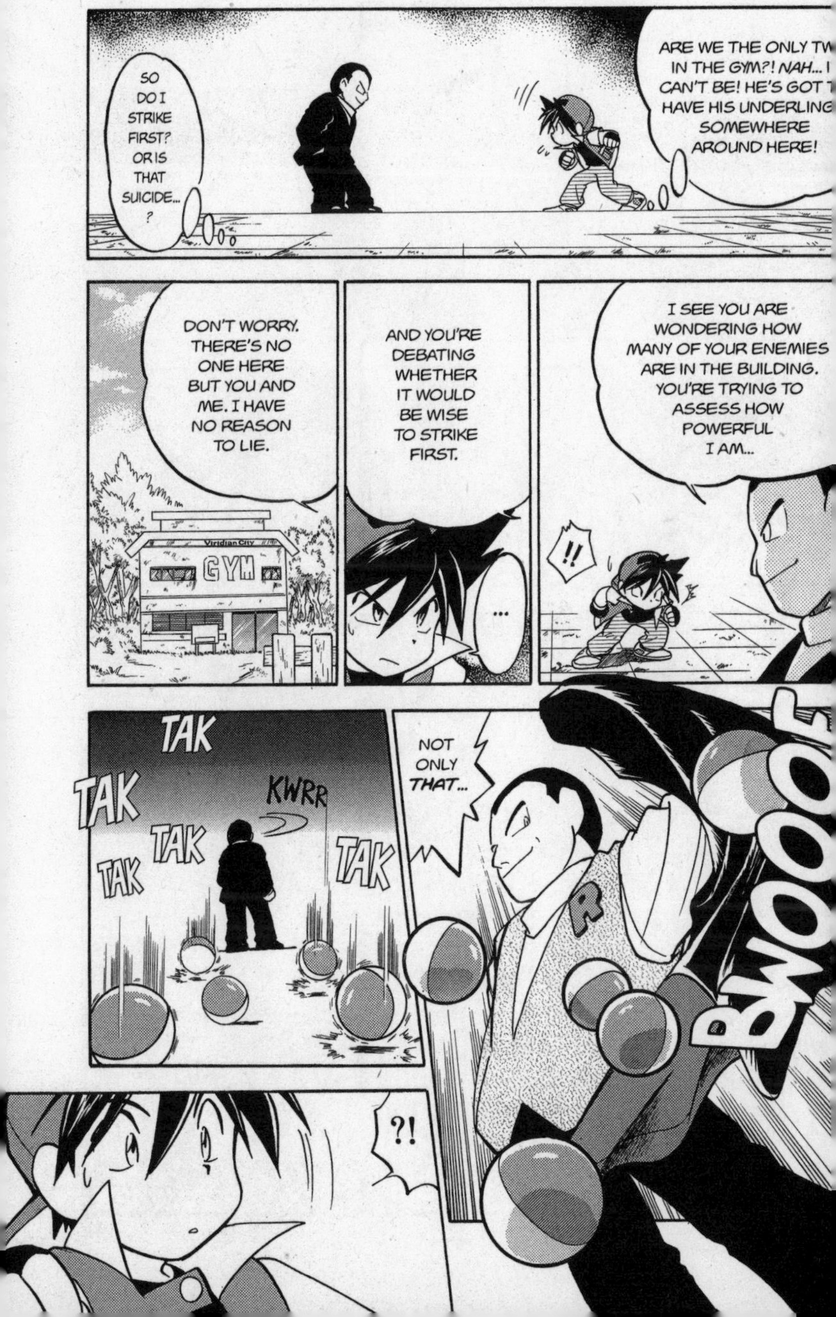
ARE WE THE ONLY TW IN THE GYM?! *NAH...* I CAN'T BE! HE'S GOT T HAVE HIS UNDERLING SOMEWHERE AROUND HERE!
SO DO I STRIKE FIRST? OR IS THAT SUICIDE... ?
I SEE YOU ARE WONDERING HOW MANY OF YOUR ENEMIES ARE IN THE BUILDING. YOU'RE TRYING TO ASSESS HOW POWERFUL I AM...
!!
AND YOU'RE DEBATING WHETHER IT WOULD BE WISE TO STRIKE FIRST.
...
DON'T WORRY. THERE'S NO ONE HERE BUT YOU AND ME. I HAVE NO REASON TO LIE.
Viridian City
GYM
NOT ONLY *THAT...*
BWOOOF
TAK
TAK
KWRR
TAK
TAK
TAK
?!

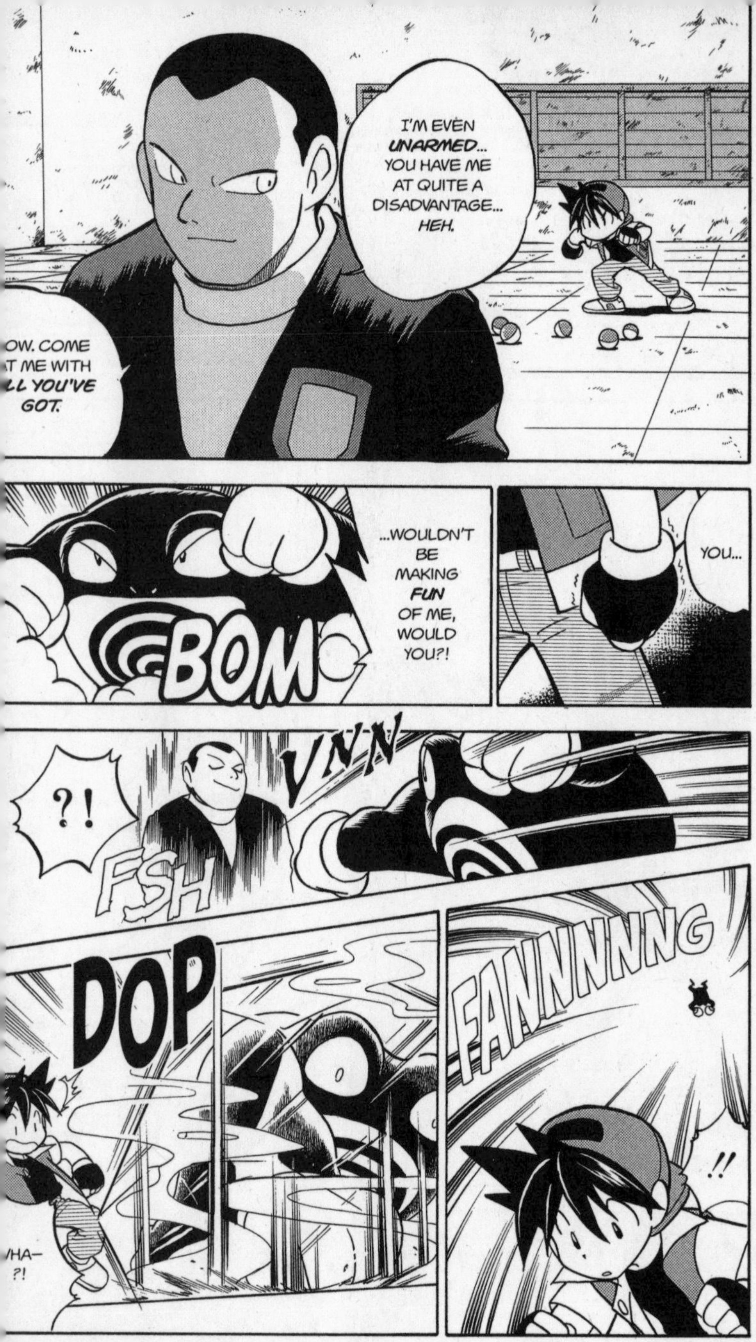
I'M EVEN UNARMED... YOU HAVE ME AT QUITE A DISADVANTAGE... HEH.
OW. COME T ME WITH LL YOU'VE GOT.
YOU...
...WOULDN'T BE MAKING FUN OF ME, WOULD YOU?!
BOM
VNN
?!
FSH
FANNNNNG
!!
DOP
WHA- ?!

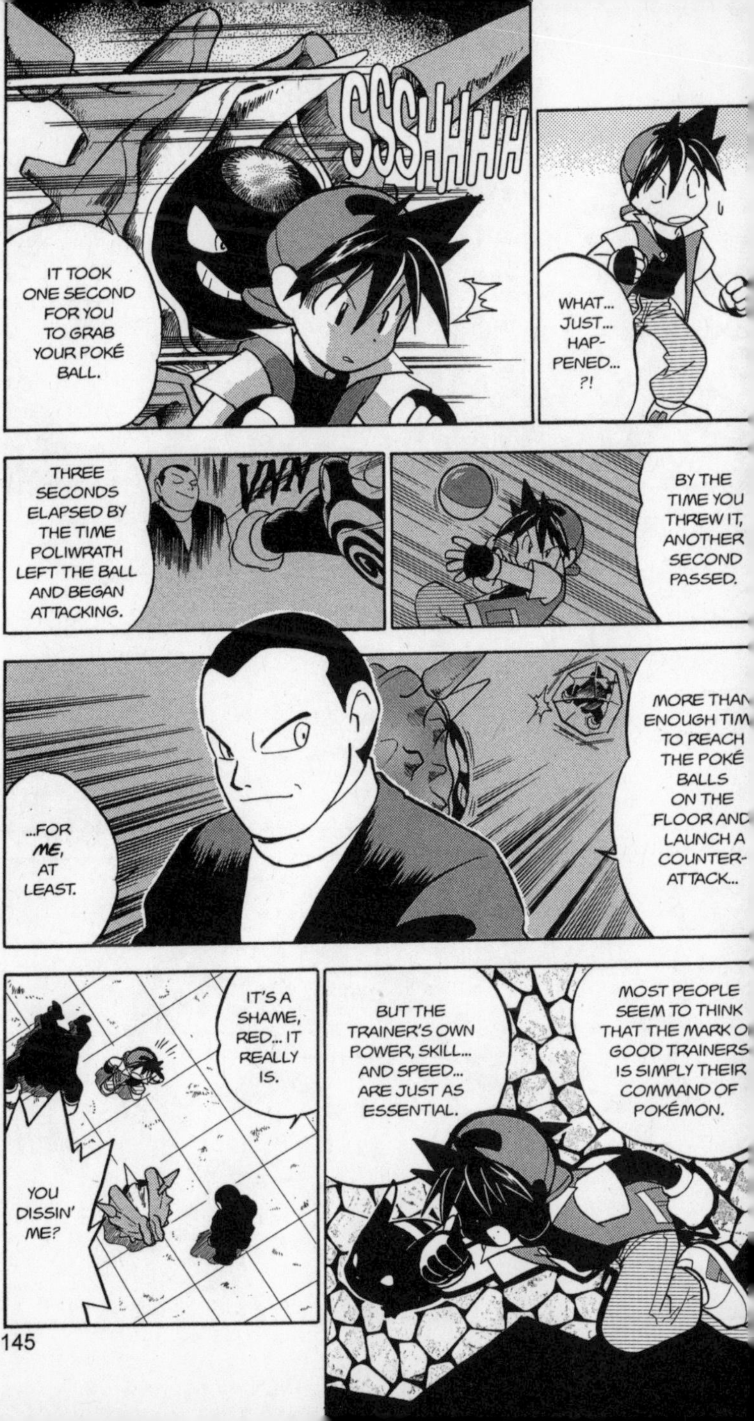
WHAT... JUST... HAP- PENED... ?!
SSSHHHHH
IT TOOK ONE SECOND FOR YOU TO GRAB YOUR POKÉ BALL.
BY THE TIME YOU THREW IT, ANOTHER SECOND PASSED.
THREE SECONDS ELAPSED BY THE TIME POLIWRATH LEFT THE BALL AND BEGAN ATTACKING.
VVN
MORE THAN ENOUGH TIM TO REACH THE POKÉ BALLS ON THE FLOOR AND LAUNCH A COUNTER- ATTACK...
...FOR *ME*, AT LEAST.
MOST PEOPLE SEEM TO THINK THAT THE MARK O GOOD TRAINERS IS SIMPLY THEIR COMMAND OF POKÉMON.
BUT THE TRAINER'S OWN POWER, SKILL... AND SPEED... ARE JUST AS ESSENTIAL.
IT'S A SHAME, RED... IT REALLY IS.
YOU DISSIN' ME?

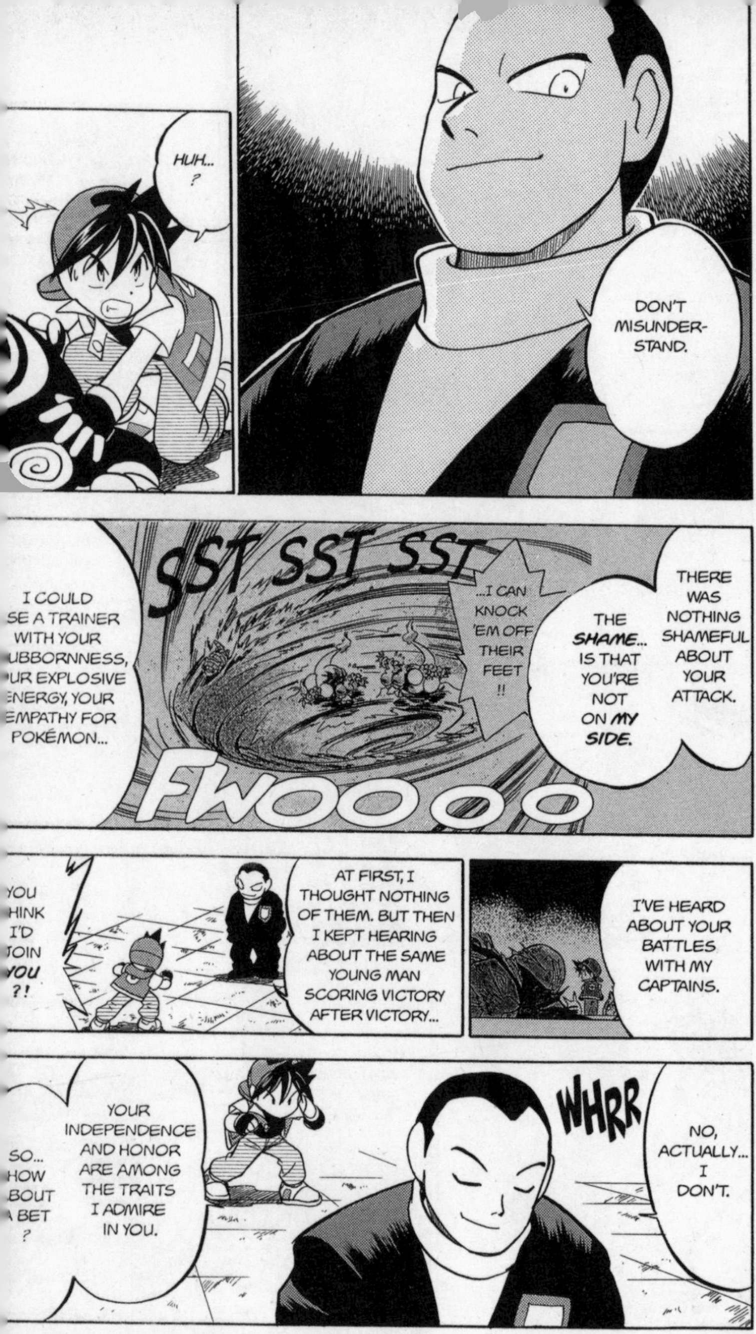
DON'T MISUNDERSTAND.
HUH... ?
THERE WAS NOTHING SHAMEFUL ABOUT YOUR ATTACK.
THE SHAME... IS THAT YOU'RE NOT ON MY SIDE.
...I CAN KNOCK 'EM OFF THEIR FEET !!
SST SST SST
I COULD SE A TRAINER WITH YOUR UBBORNNESS, UR EXPLOSIVE ENERGY, YOUR EMPATHY FOR POKÉMON...
FWOOOO
I'VE HEARD ABOUT YOUR BATTLES WITH MY CAPTAINS.
AT FIRST, I THOUGHT NOTHING OF THEM. BUT THEN I KEPT HEARING ABOUT THE SAME YOUNG MAN SCORING VICTORY AFTER VICTORY...
YOU HINK I'D OIN YOU ?!
NO, ACTUALLY... I DON'T.
WHRR
YOUR INDEPENDENCE AND HONOR ARE AMONG THE TRAITS I ADMIRE IN YOU.
SO... HOW BOUT BET ?

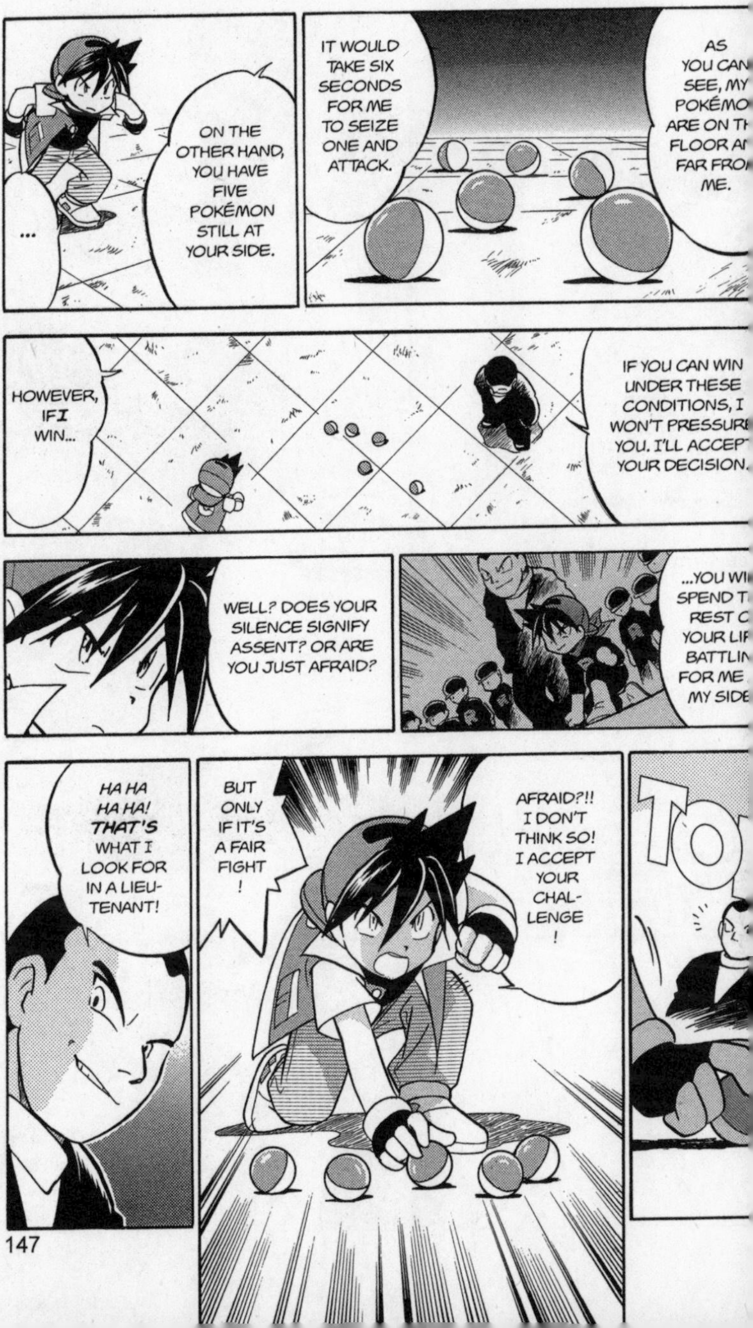
AS YOU CAN SEE, MY POKÉMO ARE ON TH FLOOR AN FAR FRO ME.
IT WOULD TAKE SIX SECONDS FOR ME TO SEIZE ONE AND ATTACK.
ON THE OTHER HAND, YOU HAVE FIVE POKÉMON STILL AT YOUR SIDE.
...
IF YOU CAN WIN UNDER THESE CONDITIONS, I WON'T PRESSUR YOU. I'LL ACCEP YOUR DECISION.
HOWEVER, IF *I* WIN...
...YOU WI SPEND T REST O YOUR LIF BATTLIN FOR ME MY SIDE
WELL? DOES YOUR SILENCE SIGNIFY ASSENT? OR ARE YOU JUST AFRAID?
TO
AFRAID?!! I DON'T THINK SO! I ACCEPT YOUR CHAL-LENGE!
BUT ONLY IF IT'S A FAIR FIGHT!
HA HA HA HA! ***THAT'S*** WHAT I LOOK FOR IN A LIEU-TENANT!

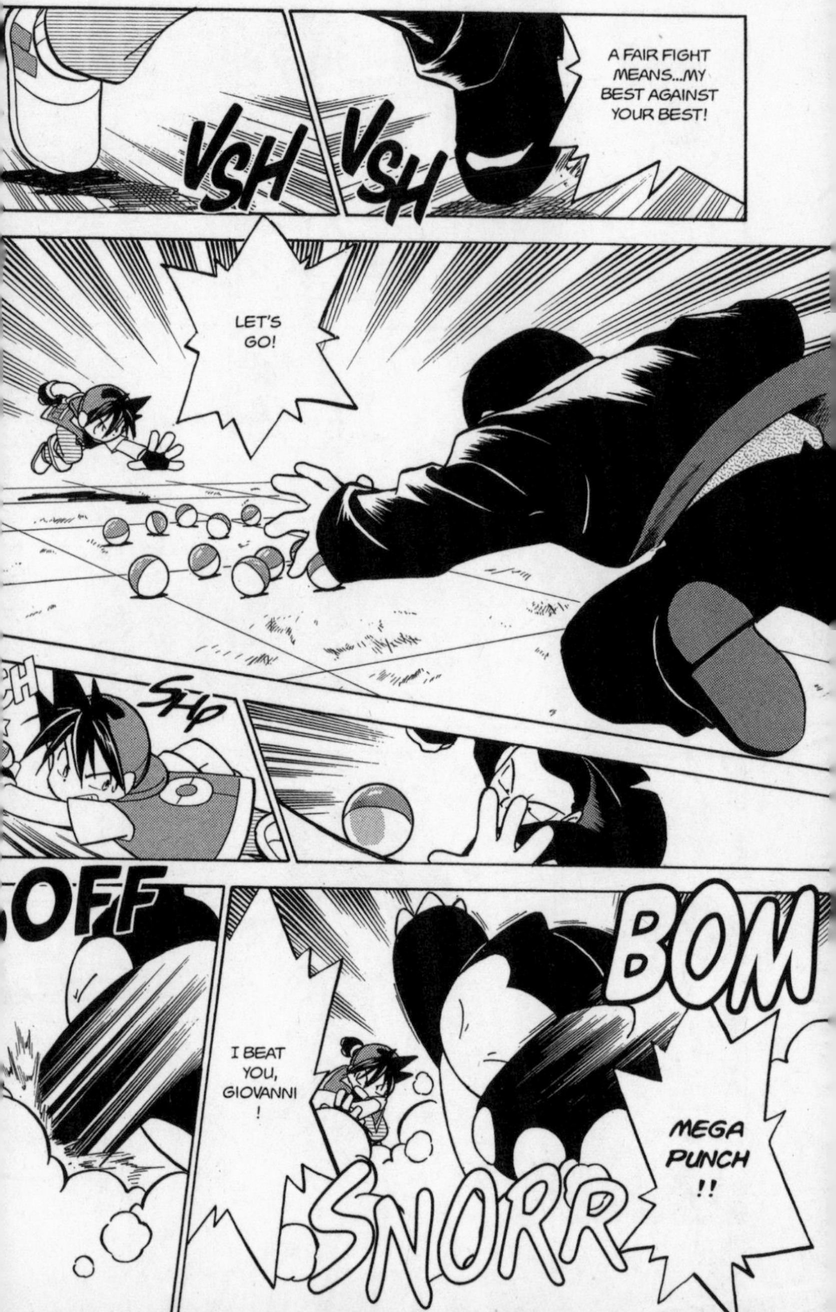
A FAIR FIGHT MEANS...MY BEST AGAINST YOUR BEST!
VSH
VSH
LET'S GO!
BOM
MEGA PUNCH !!
SNORR
I BEAT YOU, GIOVANNI !

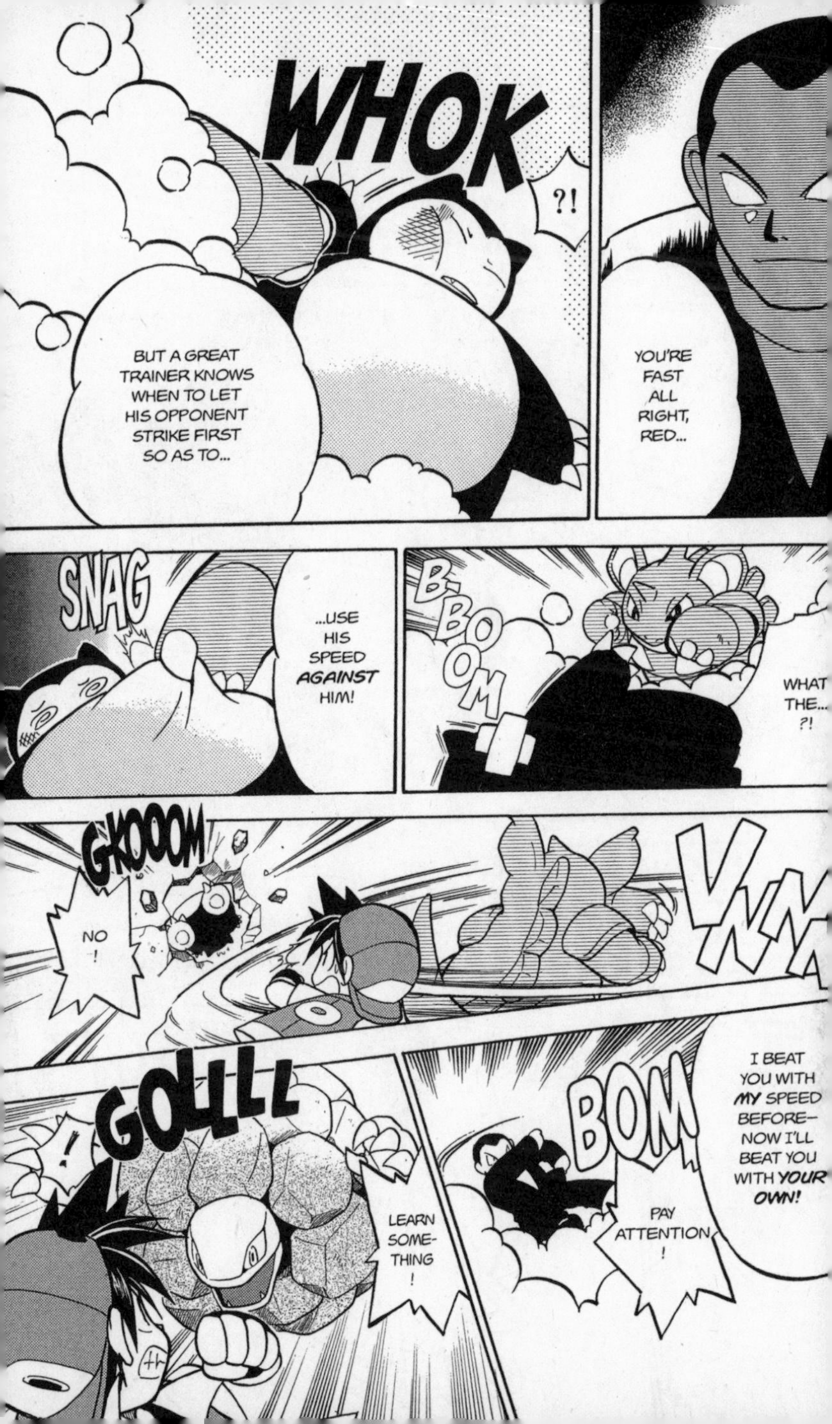

YOU'RE FAST ALL RIGHT, RED...
WHOK
?!
BUT A GREAT TRAINER KNOWS WHEN TO LET HIS OPPONENT STRIKE FIRST SO AS TO...
B-BOOM
WHAT THE...?!
...USE HIS SPEED AGAINST HIM!
SNAG
VVVN
GKOOOM
NO-!
I BEAT YOU WITH MY SPEED BEFORE—NOW I'LL BEAT YOU WITH YOUR OWN!
BOM
PAY ATTENTION!
GOLLL
!
LEARN SOME-THING!

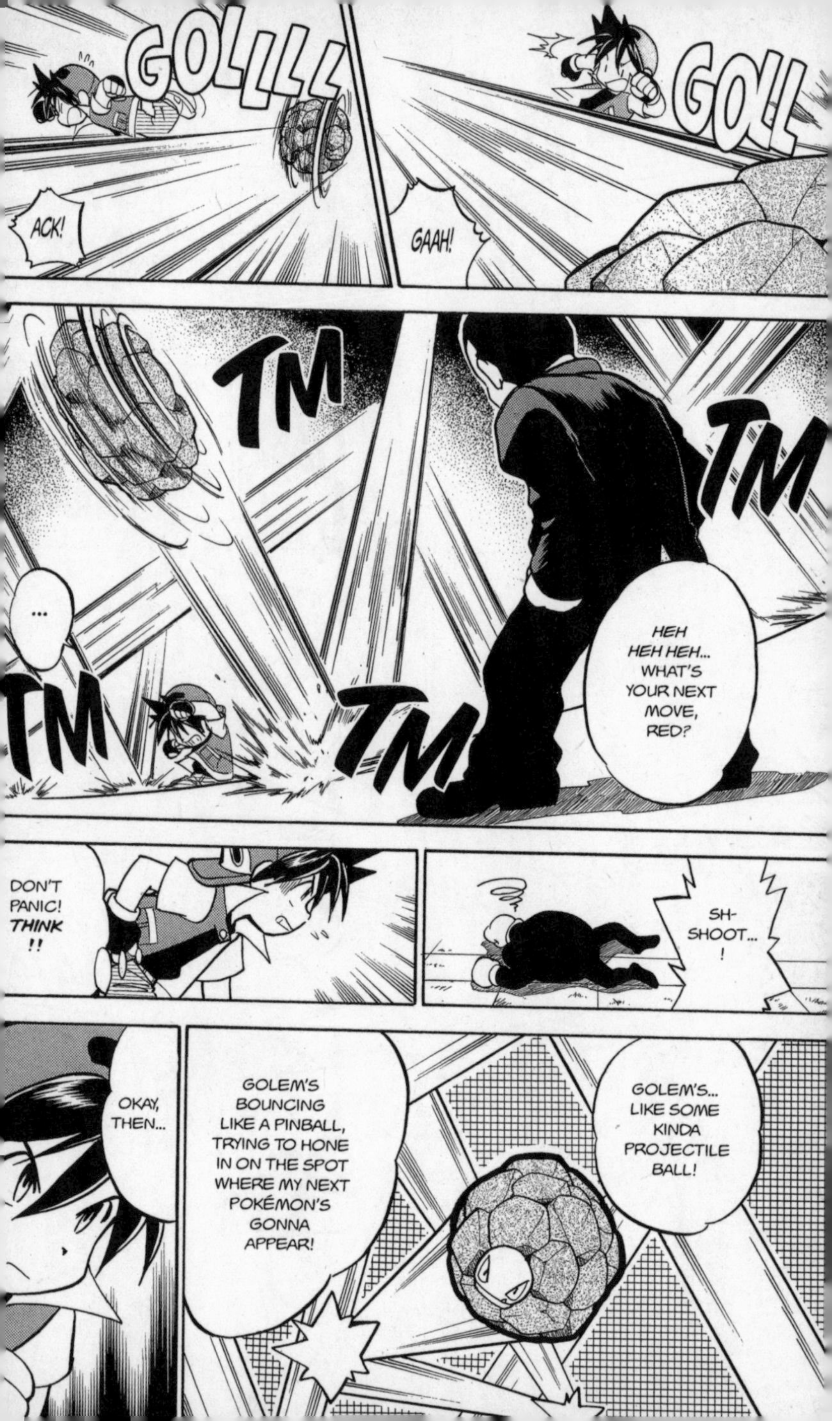
GOLL
GAAH!
GOLLLL
ACK!
TM
TM
HEH HEH HEH... WHAT'S YOUR NEXT MOVE, RED?
...
TM
TM
SH- SHOOT... !
DON'T PANIC! **THINK** !!
GOLEM'S... LIKE SOME KINDA PROJECTILE BALL!
GOLEM'S BOUNCING LIKE A PINBALL, TRYING TO HONE IN ON THE SPOT WHERE MY NEXT POKÉMON'S GONNA APPEAR!
OKAY, THEN...

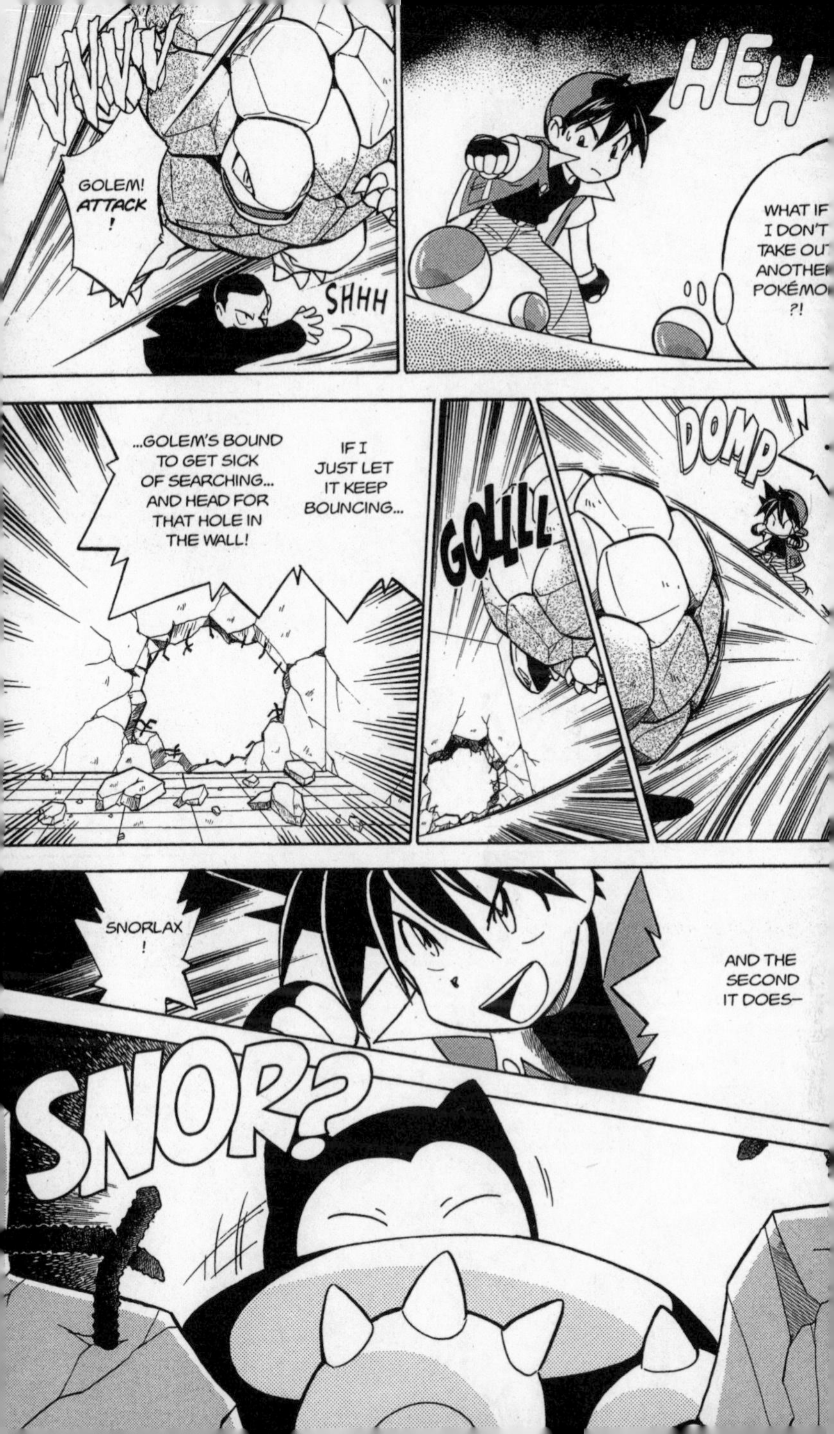
HEH
WHAT IF I DON'T TAKE OUT ANOTHE POKÉMO ?!
GOLEM! ATTACK !
SHHH
DOMP
GOLLLL
IF I JUST LET IT KEEP BOUNCING...
...GOLEM'S BOUND TO GET SICK OF SEARCHING... AND HEAD FOR THAT HOLE IN THE WALL!
AND THE SECOND IT DOES—
SNORLAX !
SNOR?

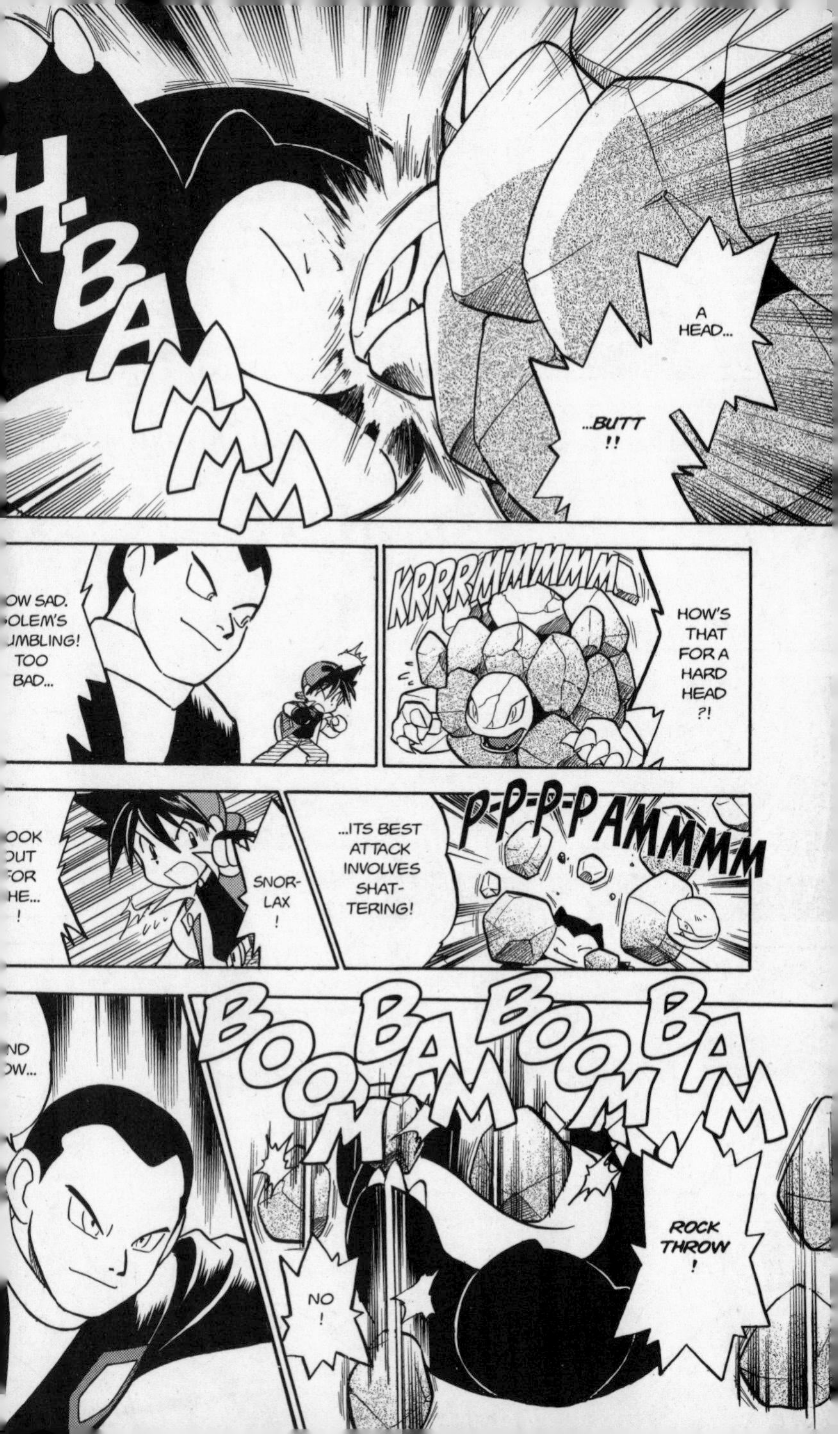

A HEAD...
...BUTT !!
H-BAMMMM
HOW'S THAT FOR A HARD HEAD ?!
KRRRMMMMMM...
OW SAD. OLEM'S UMBLING! TOO BAD...
P-P-P-PAMMMMM
...ITS BEST ATTACK INVOLVES SHAT-TERING!
SNOR-LAX !
OOK OUT FOR HE... !
BOOM BAM BOOM BAM
ROCK THROW !
NO !
ND OW...

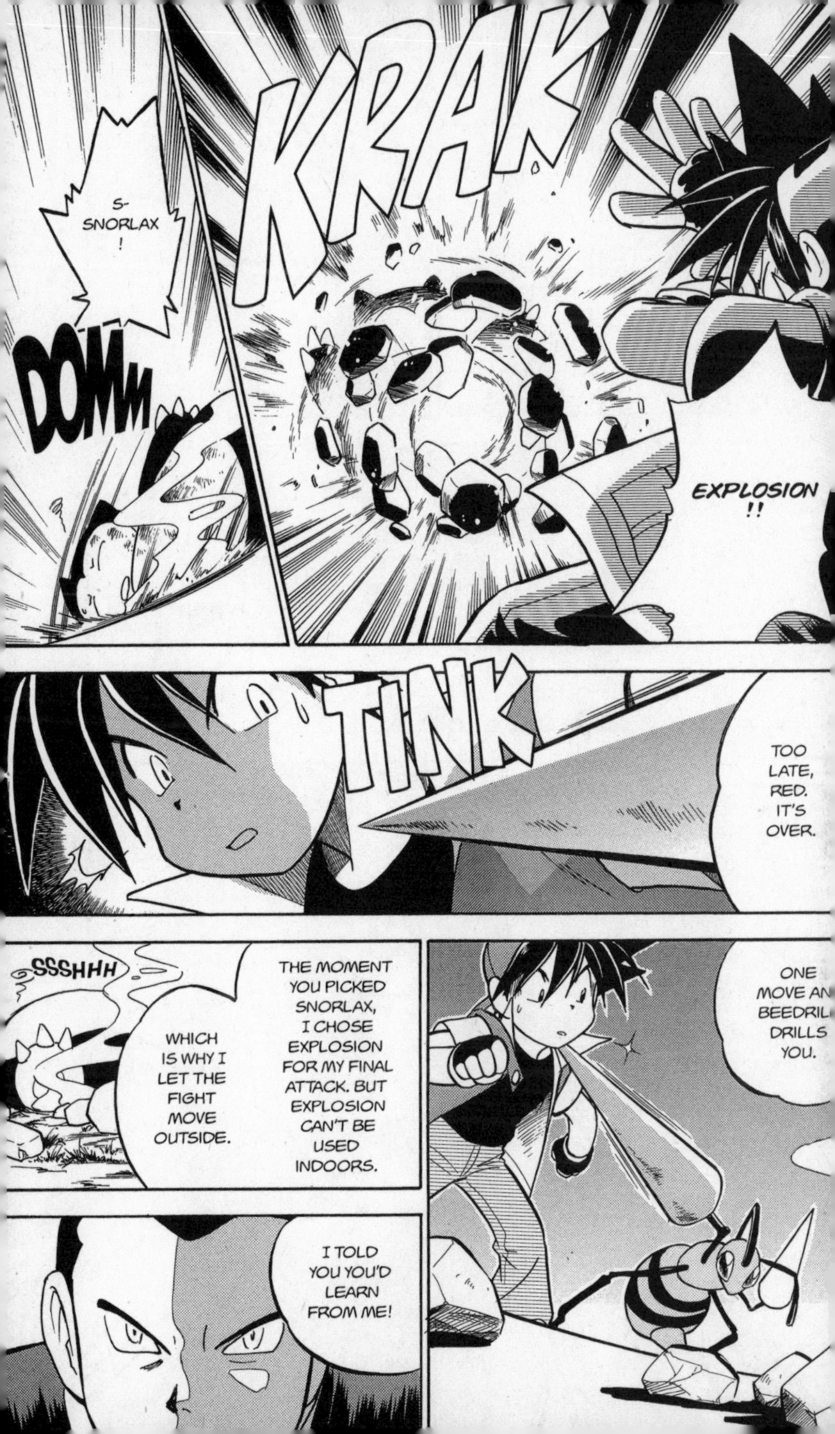
KRAK
EXPLOSION !!
S- SNORLAX !
DOMM
TINK
TOO LATE, RED. IT'S OVER.
ONE MOVE AN BEEDRIL DRILLS YOU.
SSSHHH
THE MOMENT YOU PICKED SNORLAX, I CHOSE EXPLOSION FOR MY FINAL ATTACK. BUT EXPLOSION CAN'T BE USED INDOORS.
WHICH IS WHY I LET THE FIGHT MOVE OUTSIDE.
I TOLD YOU YOU'D LEARN FROM ME!

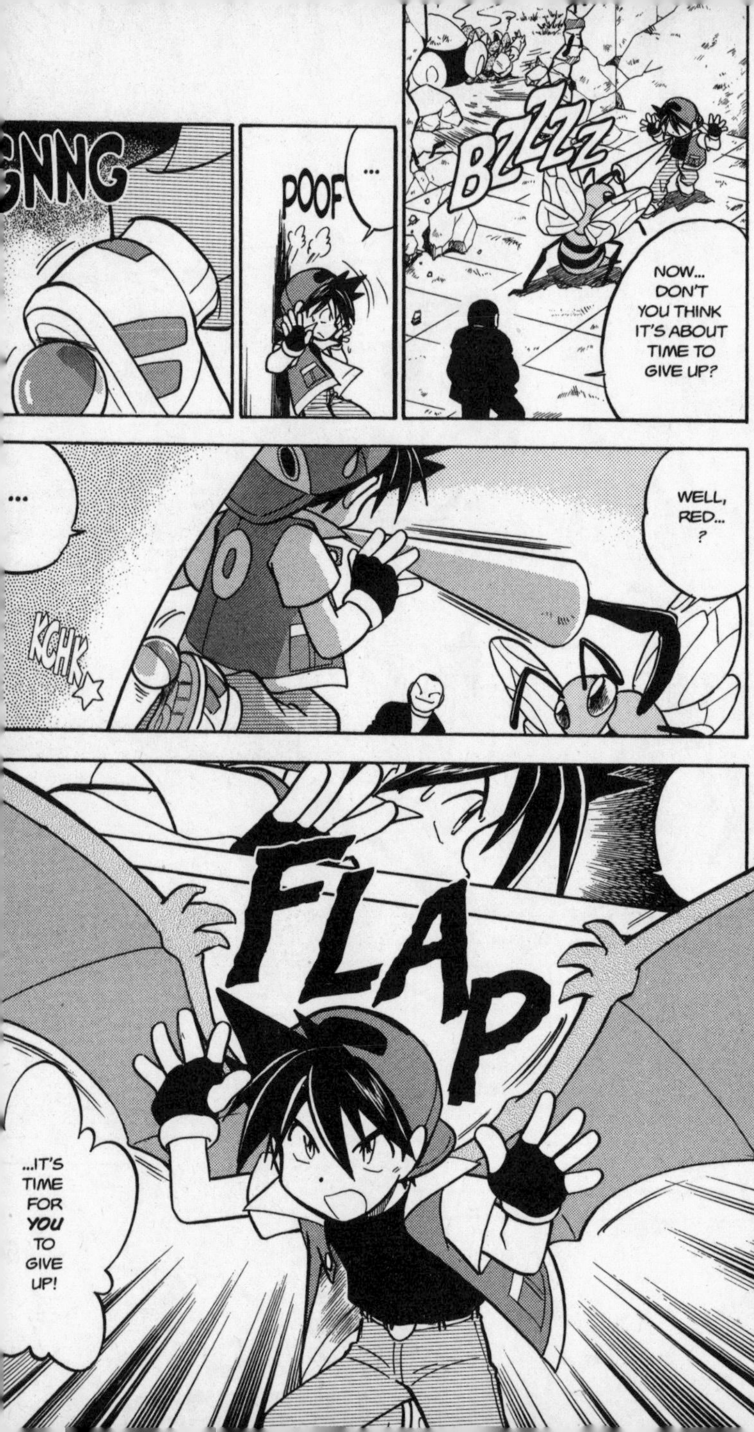
BZZZZ
NOW... DON'T YOU THINK IT'S ABOUT TIME TO GIVE UP?
POOF
...
GNNG
WELL, RED...?
...
KCHK
FLAP
...IT'S TIME FOR *YOU* TO GIVE UP!

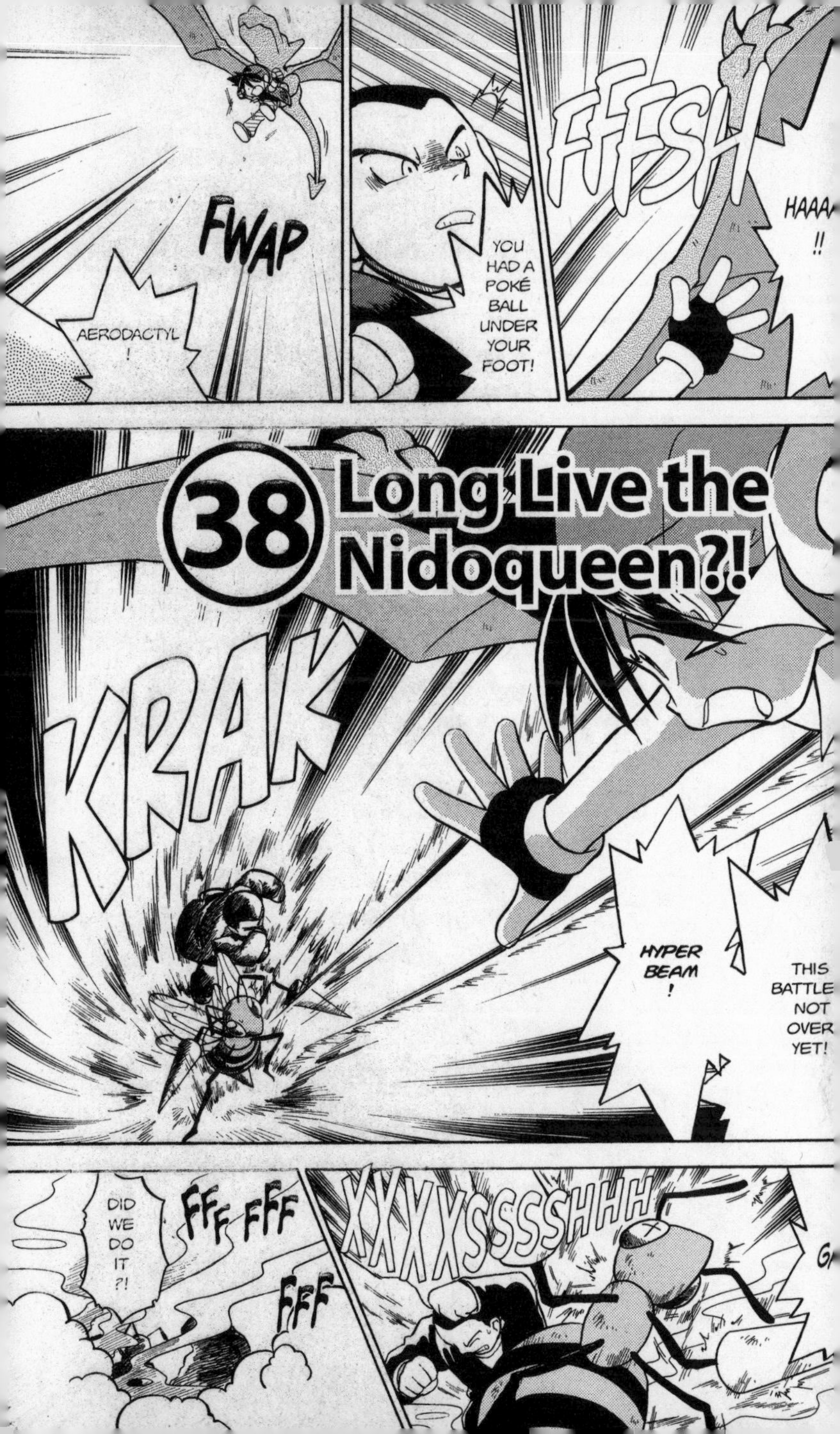
FFFSH
HAAA !!
YOU HAD A POKÉ BALL UNDER YOUR FOOT!
FWAP
AERODACTYL !
38 Long Live the Nidoqueen?!
THIS BATTLE NOT OVER YET!
HYPER BEAM !
KRAK
XXXXSSSSHHH
DID WE DO IT ?!
FFF FFF
FFF

SSSHHHHHHHH

Y'RE...
ONE
?!

?!

RRRM MM

TH-
THAT
HOLE...
!!

NO
WAY
!

VSSH

TMP

GRRRROOOOMMMM

EARTHQUAKE!
THE GYM'S
GONNA
COLLAPSE!

KRASH

VWM

NO!
P-POLI—
!!

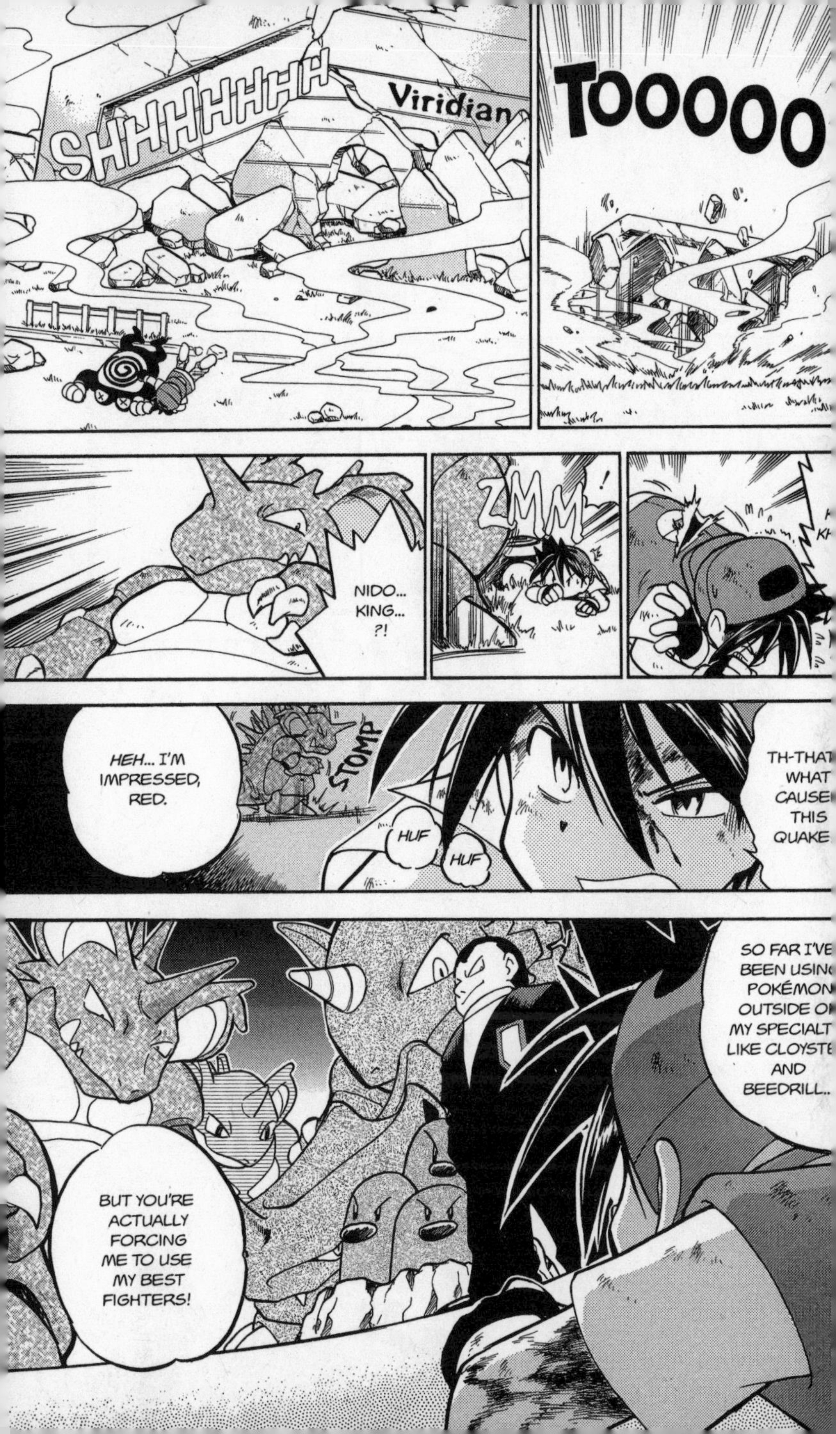
TOOOOO
SHHHHHHH
Viridian
KH
ZMM
!
NIDO... KING... ?!
TH-THAT WHAT CAUSE THIS QUAKE
STOMP
HEH... I'M IMPRESSED, RED.
HUF
HUF
SO FAR I'VE BEEN USING POKÉMON OUTSIDE O MY SPECIALT LIKE CLOYSTE AND BEEDRILL...
BUT YOU'RE ACTUALLY FORCING ME TO USE MY BEST FIGHTERS!

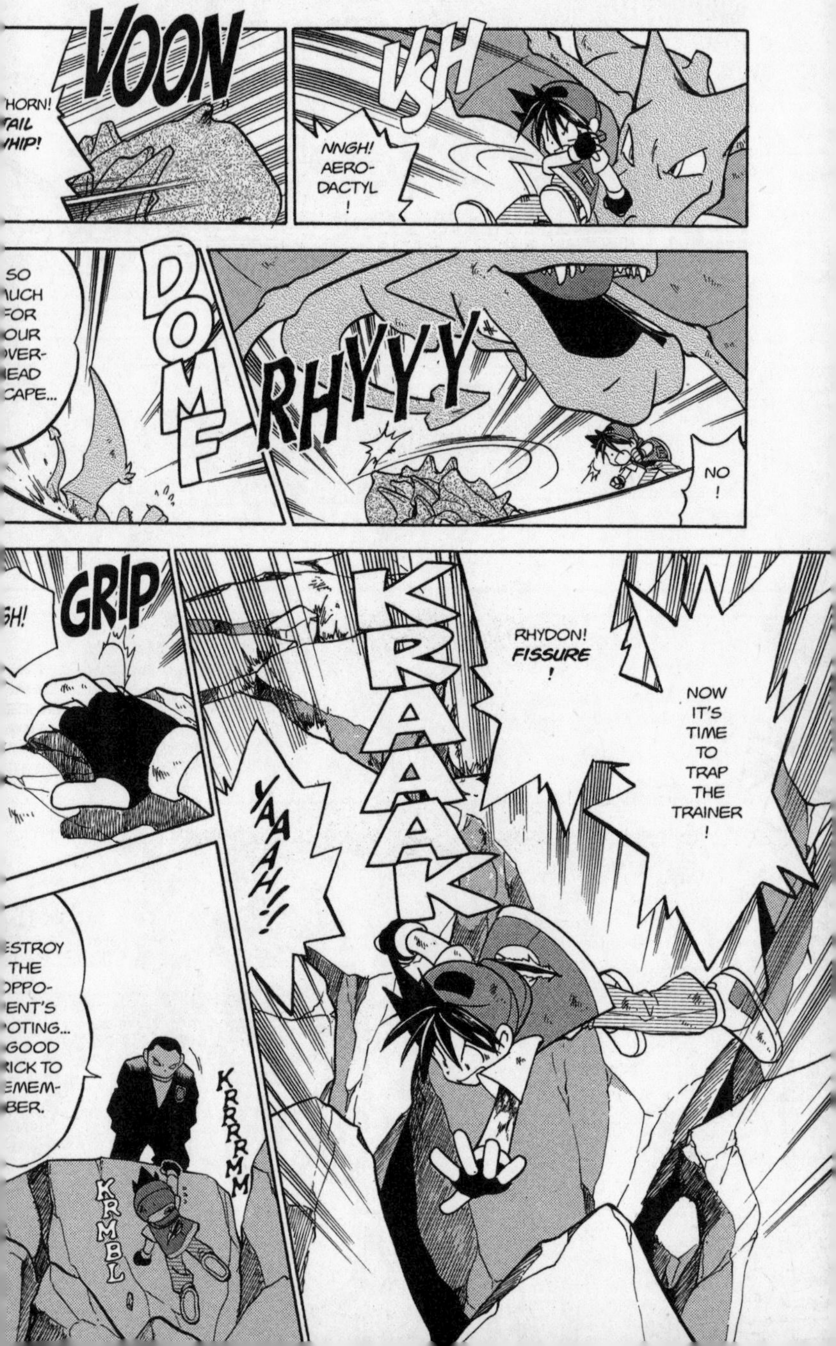
USH
NNGH! AERO-DACTYL!
VOON
HORN! TAIL HIP!
RHYYY
NO!
DOMF
SO UCH FOR OUR VER-HEAD CAPE...
RHYDON! FISSURE!
NOW IT'S TIME TO TRAP THE TRAINER!
KRAAAK
YAAAAH!!
GRIP
GH!
ESTROY THE PPO-ENT'S OTING... GOOD RICK TO EMEM-BER.
KRRRRMM
KRMBL

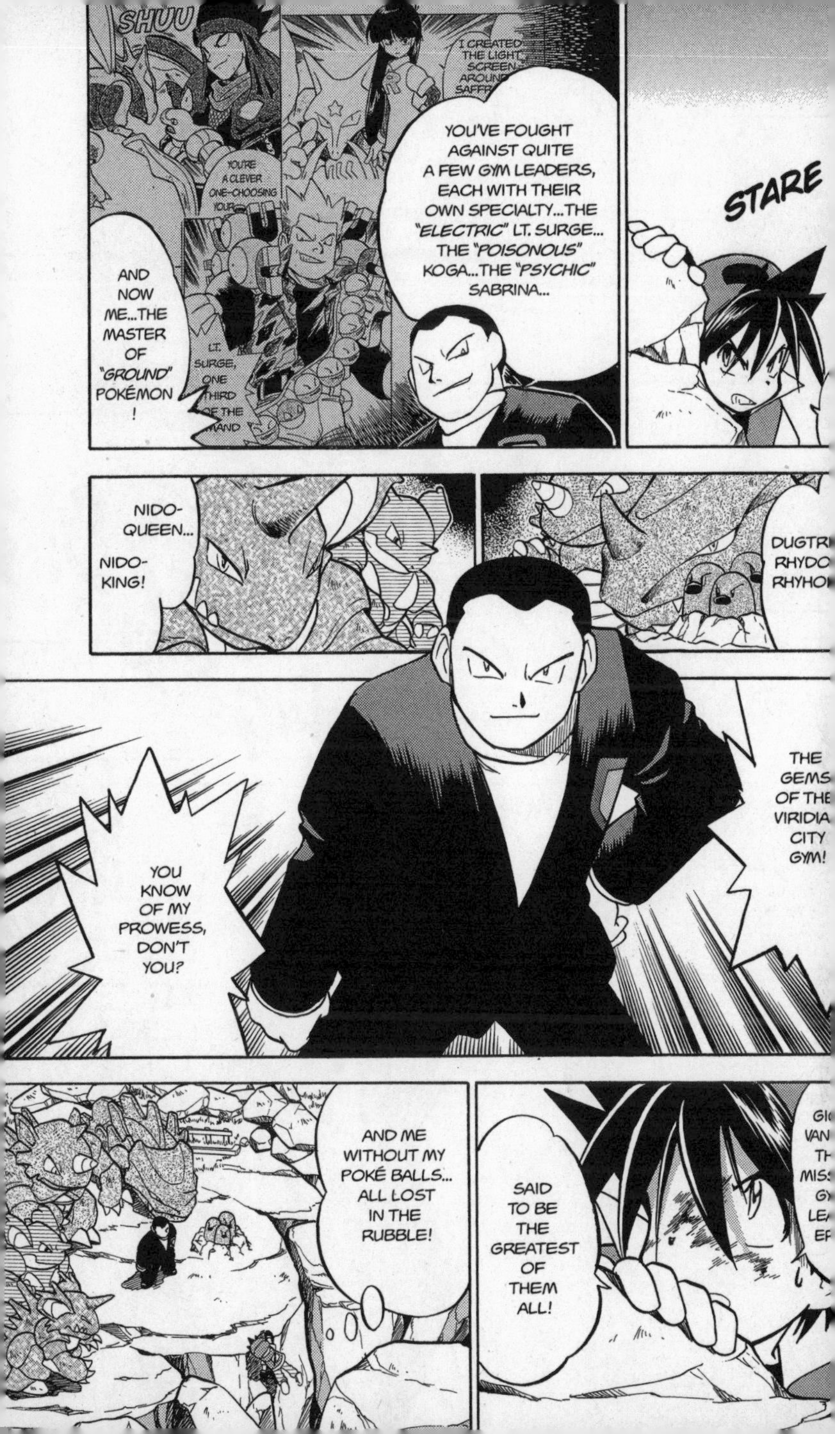
STARE
I CREATED THE LIGHT SCREEN AROUND SAFFR
SHUU
YOU'VE FOUGHT AGAINST QUITE A FEW GYM LEADERS, EACH WITH THEIR OWN SPECIALTY...THE "ELECTRIC" LT. SURGE... THE "POISONOUS" KOGA...THE "PSYCHIC" SABRINA...
YOU'RE A CLEVER ONE-CHOOSING YOUR
AND NOW ME...THE MASTER OF "GROUND" POKÉMON!
LT. SURGE, ONE THIRD OF THE HAND
DUGTRI RHYDO RHYHO
NIDO-QUEEN... NIDO-KING!
THE GEMS OF THE VIRIDIA CITY GYM!
YOU KNOW OF MY PROWESS, DON'T YOU?
GI VAN TH MISS GY LEA ER
SAID TO BE THE GREATEST OF THEM ALL!
AND ME WITHOUT MY POKÉ BALLS... ALL LOST IN THE RUBBLE!

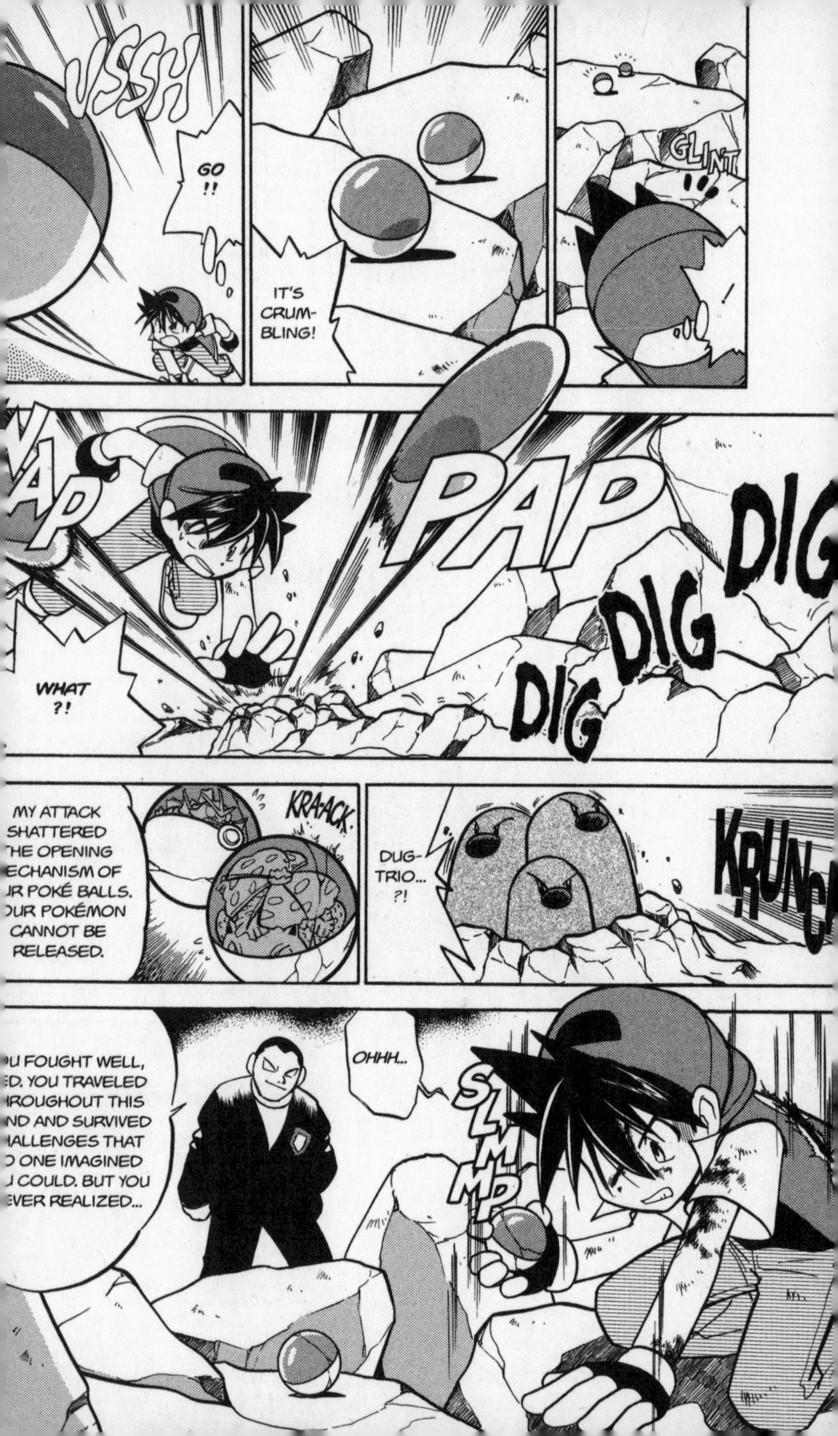
GLINT
IT'S CRUMBLING!
VSSH
GO!!
PAP
DIG
DIG
DIG
AP
WHAT ?!
DUG-TRIO... ?!
KRUNC
KRA-ACK
MY ATTACK SHATTERED THE OPENING ECHANISM OF UR POKÉ BALLS. OUR POKÉMON CANNOT BE RELEASED.
OHHH...
SLMMMP
U FOUGHT WELL, ED. YOU TRAVELED HROUGHOUT THIS ND AND SURVIVED HALLENGES THAT O ONE IMAGINED U COULD. BUT YOU EVER REALIZED...

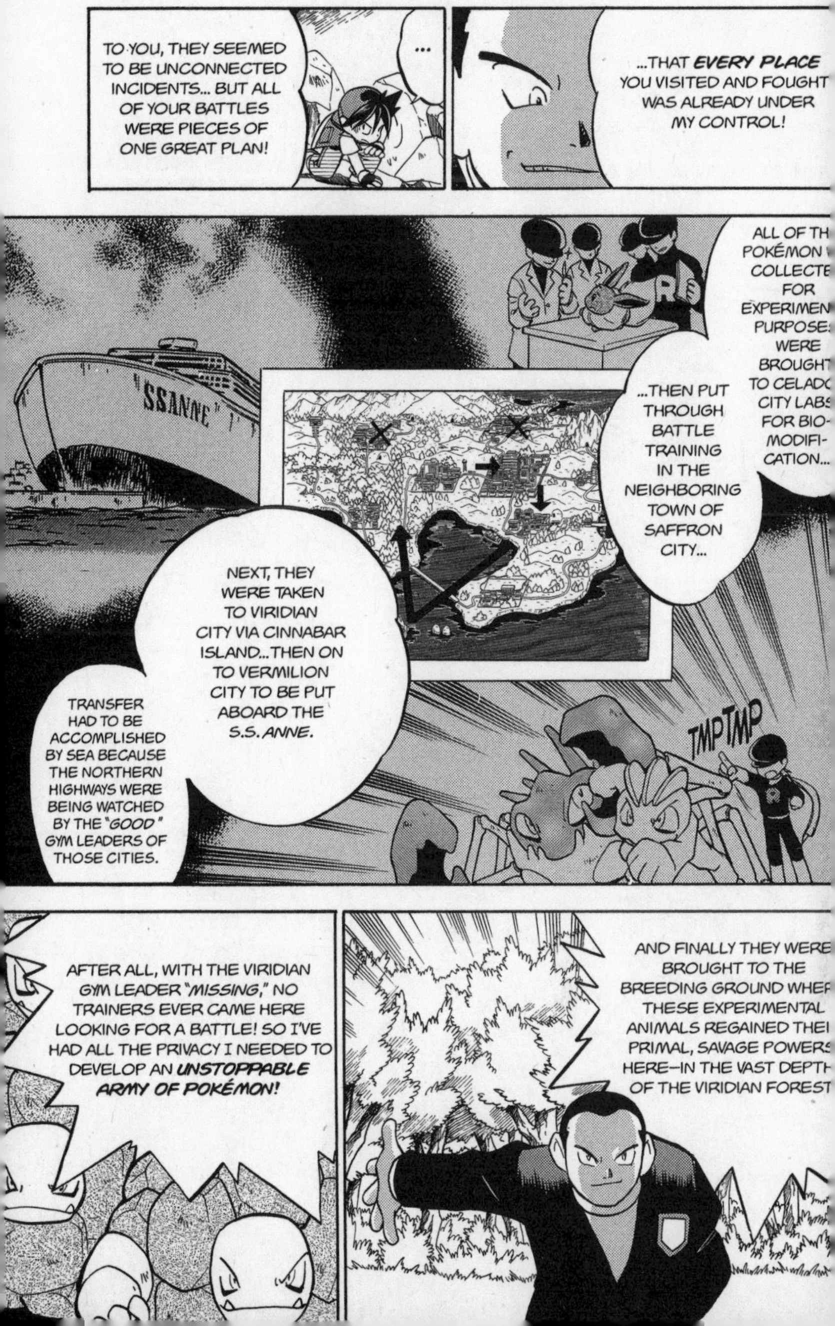
...THAT EVERY PLACE YOU VISITED AND FOUGHT WAS ALREADY UNDER MY CONTROL!
...
TO YOU, THEY SEEMED TO BE UNCONNECTED INCIDENTS... BUT ALL OF YOUR BATTLES WERE PIECES OF ONE GREAT PLAN!
ALL OF TH POKÉMON COLLECTE FOR EXPERIMEN PURPOSE WERE BROUGHT TO CELADO CITY LABS FOR BIO-MODIFI-CATION...
...THEN PUT THROUGH BATTLE TRAINING IN THE NEIGHBORING TOWN OF SAFFRON CITY...
SSANNE
TMPTMP
NEXT, THEY WERE TAKEN TO VIRIDIAN CITY VIA CINNABAR ISLAND...THEN ON TO VERMILION CITY TO BE PUT ABOARD THE S.S. ANNE.
TRANSFER HAD TO BE ACCOMPLISHED BY SEA BECAUSE THE NORTHERN HIGHWAYS WERE BEING WATCHED BY THE "GOOD" GYM LEADERS OF THOSE CITIES.
AND FINALLY THEY WERE BROUGHT TO THE BREEDING GROUND WHER THESE EXPERIMENTAL ANIMALS REGAINED THEI PRIMAL, SAVAGE POWERS HERE—IN THE VAST DEPTH OF THE VIRIDIAN FOREST
AFTER ALL, WITH THE VIRIDIAN GYM LEADER "MISSING," NO TRAINERS EVER CAME HERE LOOKING FOR A BATTLE! SO I'VE HAD ALL THE PRIVACY I NEEDED TO DEVELOP AN UNSTOPPABLE ARMY OF POKÉMON!

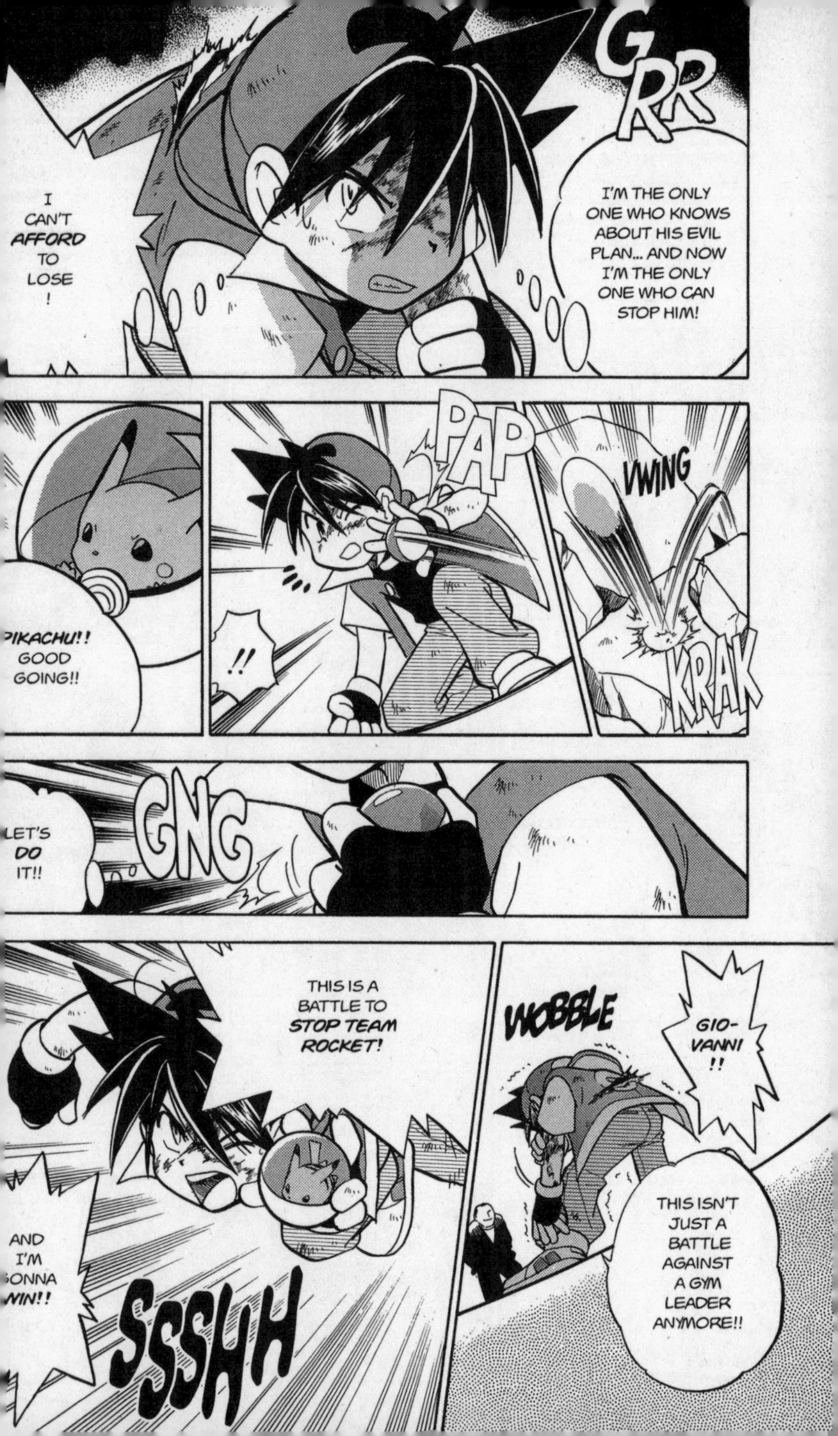
GRR
I'M THE ONLY ONE WHO KNOWS ABOUT HIS EVIL PLAN... AND NOW I'M THE ONLY ONE WHO CAN STOP HIM!
I CAN'T AFFORD TO LOSE!
VWING
KRAK
PAP
!!
PIKACHU!! GOOD GOING!!
GNG
LET'S DO IT!!
WOBBLE
GIO-VANNI!!
THIS ISN'T JUST A BATTLE AGAINST A GYM LEADER ANYMORE!!
THIS IS A BATTLE TO STOP TEAM ROCKET!
AND I'M GONNA WIN!!
SSSHH

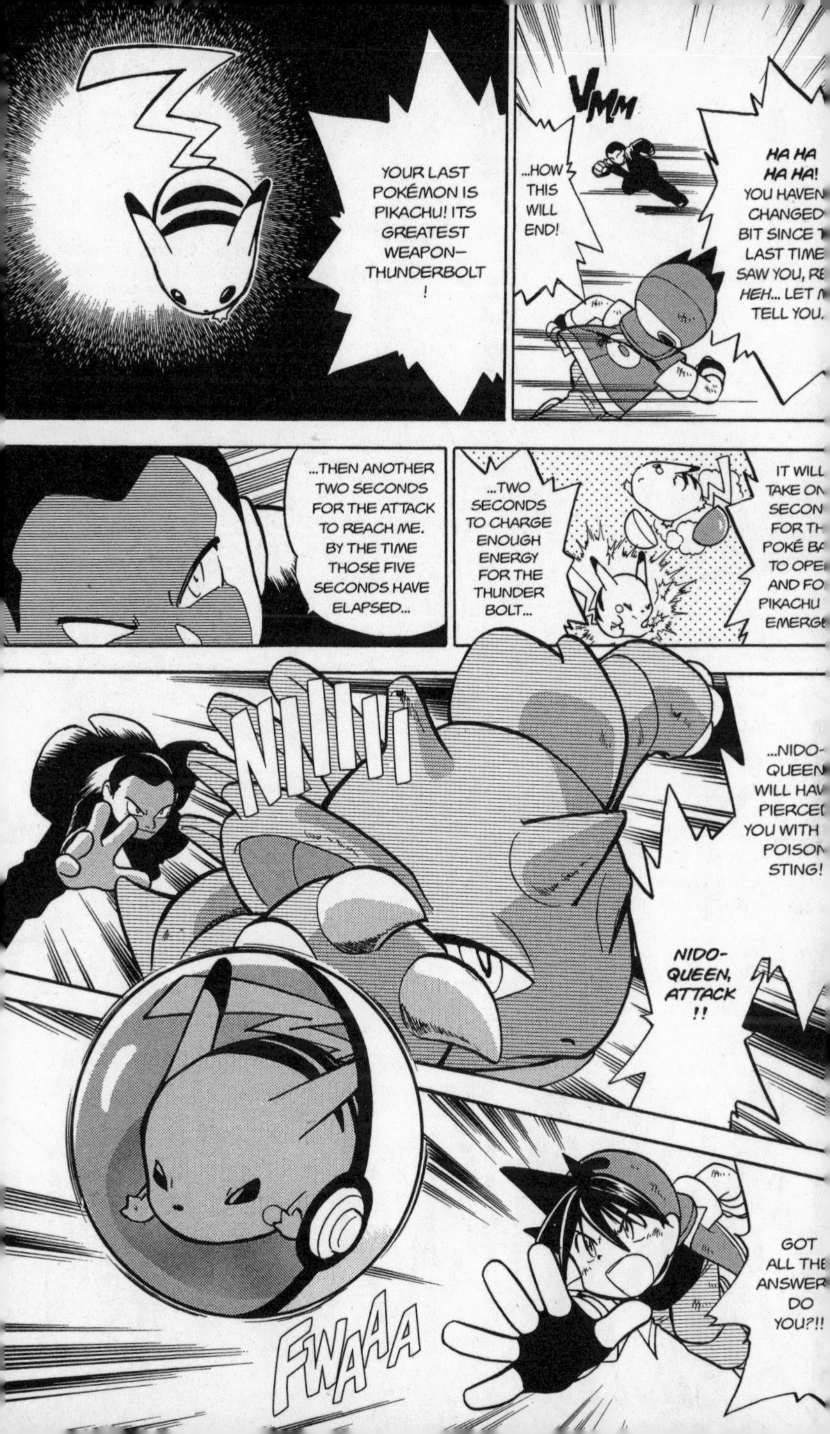
VMM
HA HA HA HA! YOU HAVEN CHANGED BIT SINCE T LAST TIME SAW YOU, RE HEH... LET M TELL YOU.
...HOW THIS WILL END!
YOUR LAST POKÉMON IS PIKACHU! ITS GREATEST WEAPON—THUNDERBOLT!
IT WILL TAKE ON SECON FOR TH POKÉ BA TO OPE AND FO PIKACHU EMERG
...TWO SECONDS TO CHARGE ENOUGH ENERGY FOR THE THUNDER BOLT...
...THEN ANOTHER TWO SECONDS FOR THE ATTACK TO REACH ME. BY THE TIME THOSE FIVE SECONDS HAVE ELAPSED...
...NIDO-QUEEN WILL HAV PIERCED YOU WITH POISON STING!
NIIIIII
NIDO-QUEEN, ATTACK!!
GOT ALL THE ANSWER DO YOU?!!
FWAAA

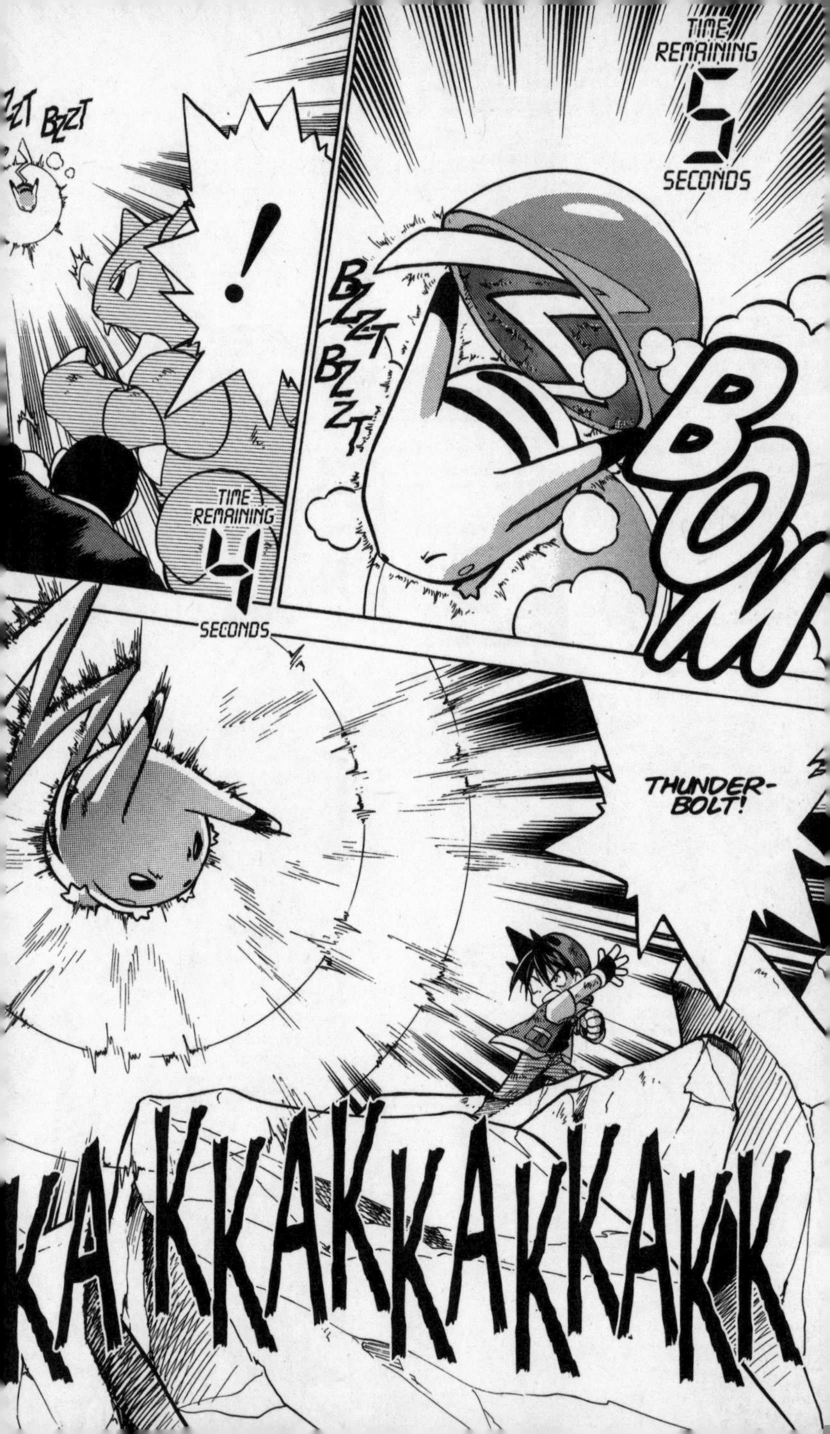
TIME REMAINING
5
SECONDS
BZZT BZZT
BOM
ZZT BZZT
!
TIME REMAINING
4
SECONDS
THUNDER-BOLT!
KAKKAKKAKK

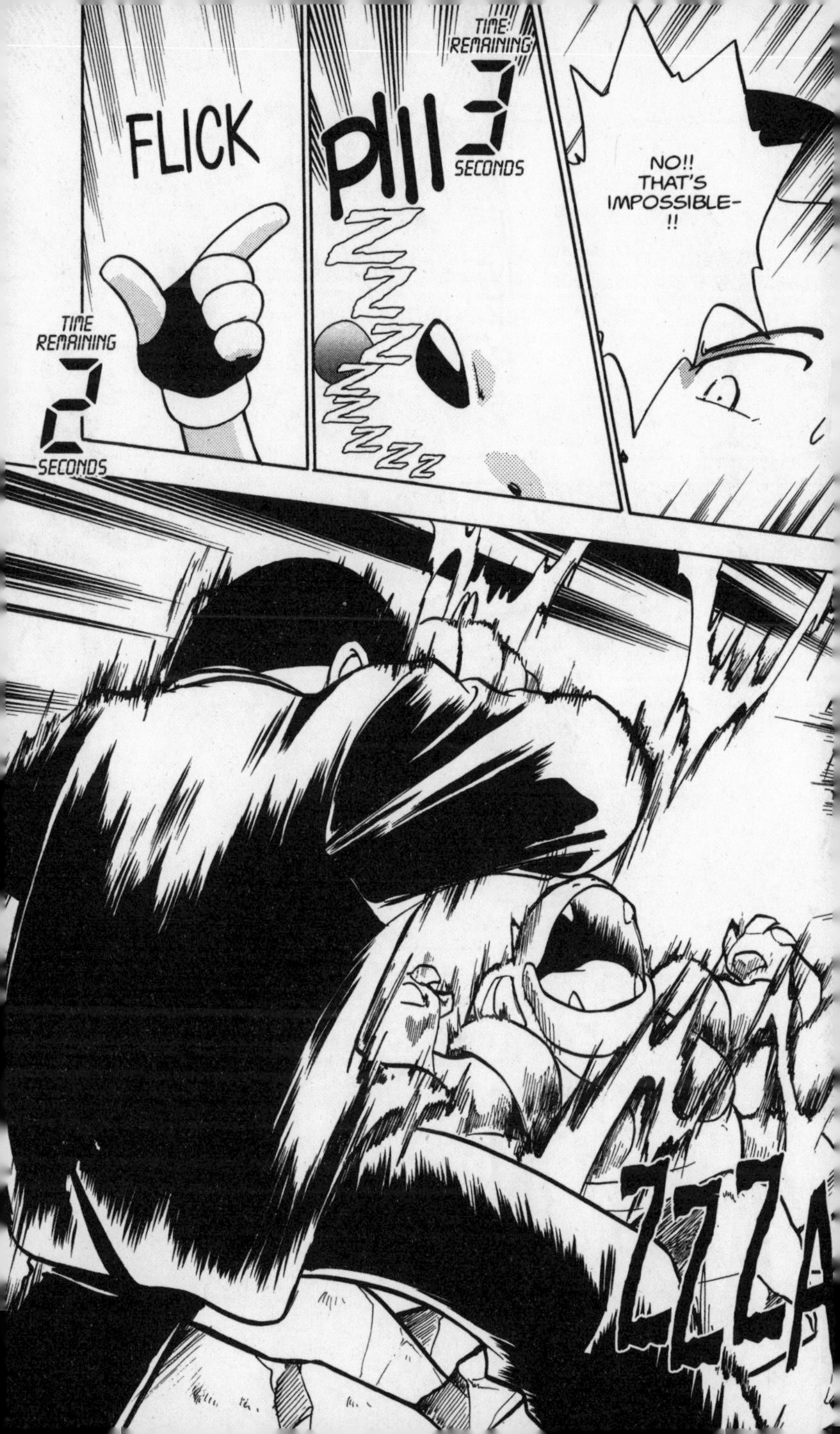
NO!! THAT'S IMPOSSIBLE-!!
TIME REMAINING 3 SECONDS
PIII
ZZZZZZZzz
FLICK
TIME REMAINING 2 SECONDS
ZZZA

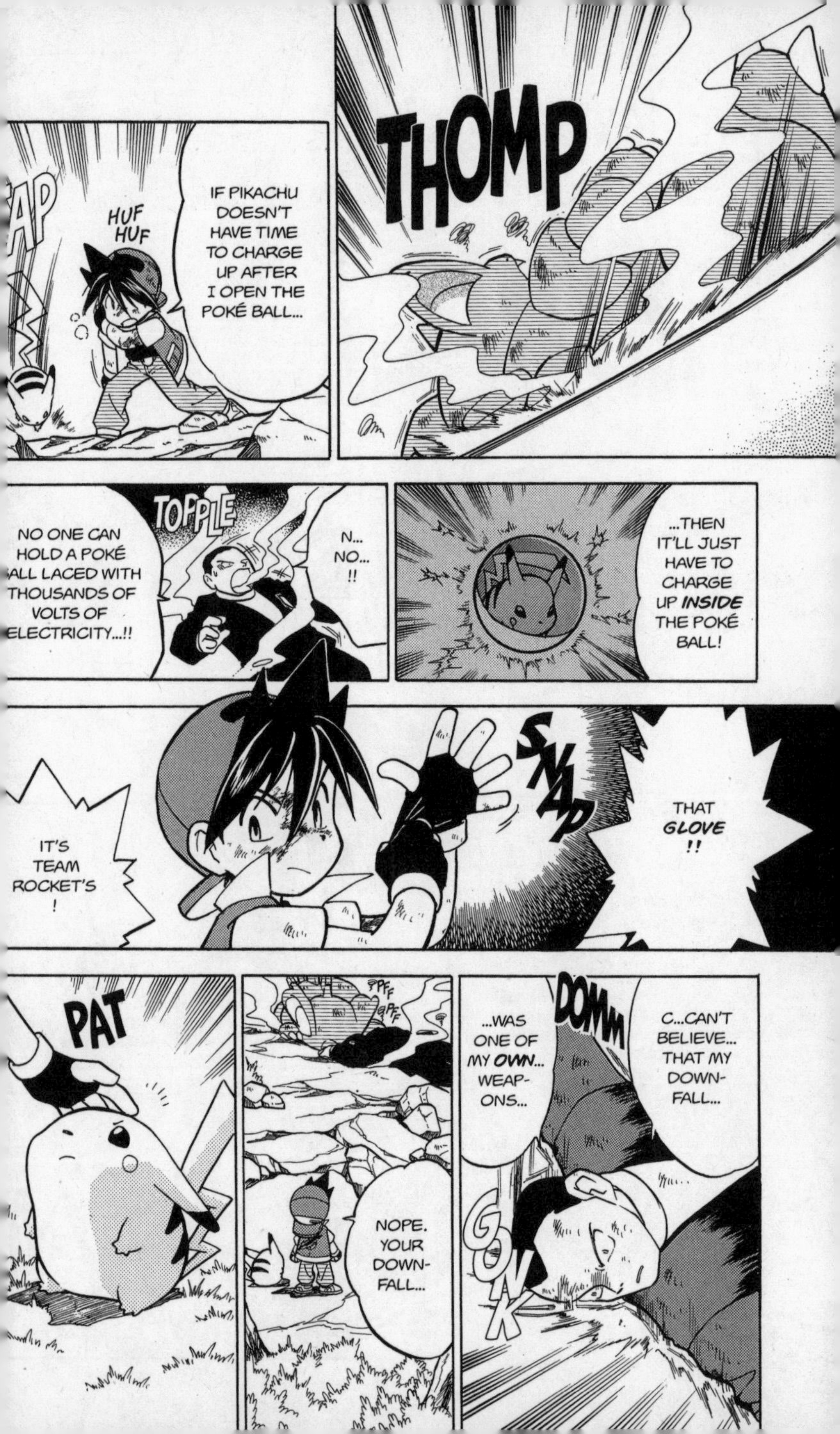
THOMP
IF PIKACHU DOESN'T HAVE TIME TO CHARGE UP AFTER I OPEN THE POKÉ BALL...
HUF HUF
...THEN IT'LL JUST HAVE TO CHARGE UP *INSIDE* THE POKÉ BALL!
N... NO... !!
TOPPLE
NO ONE CAN HOLD A POKÉ BALL LACED WITH THOUSANDS OF VOLTS OF ELECTRICITY...!!
THAT *GLOVE* !!
SNAP
IT'S TEAM ROCKET'S !
C...CAN'T BELIEVE... THAT MY DOWN-FALL...
DOMM
...WAS ONE OF MY *OWN*... WEAP-ONS...
GONK
PFF PFF
NOPE. YOUR DOWN-FALL...
PAT

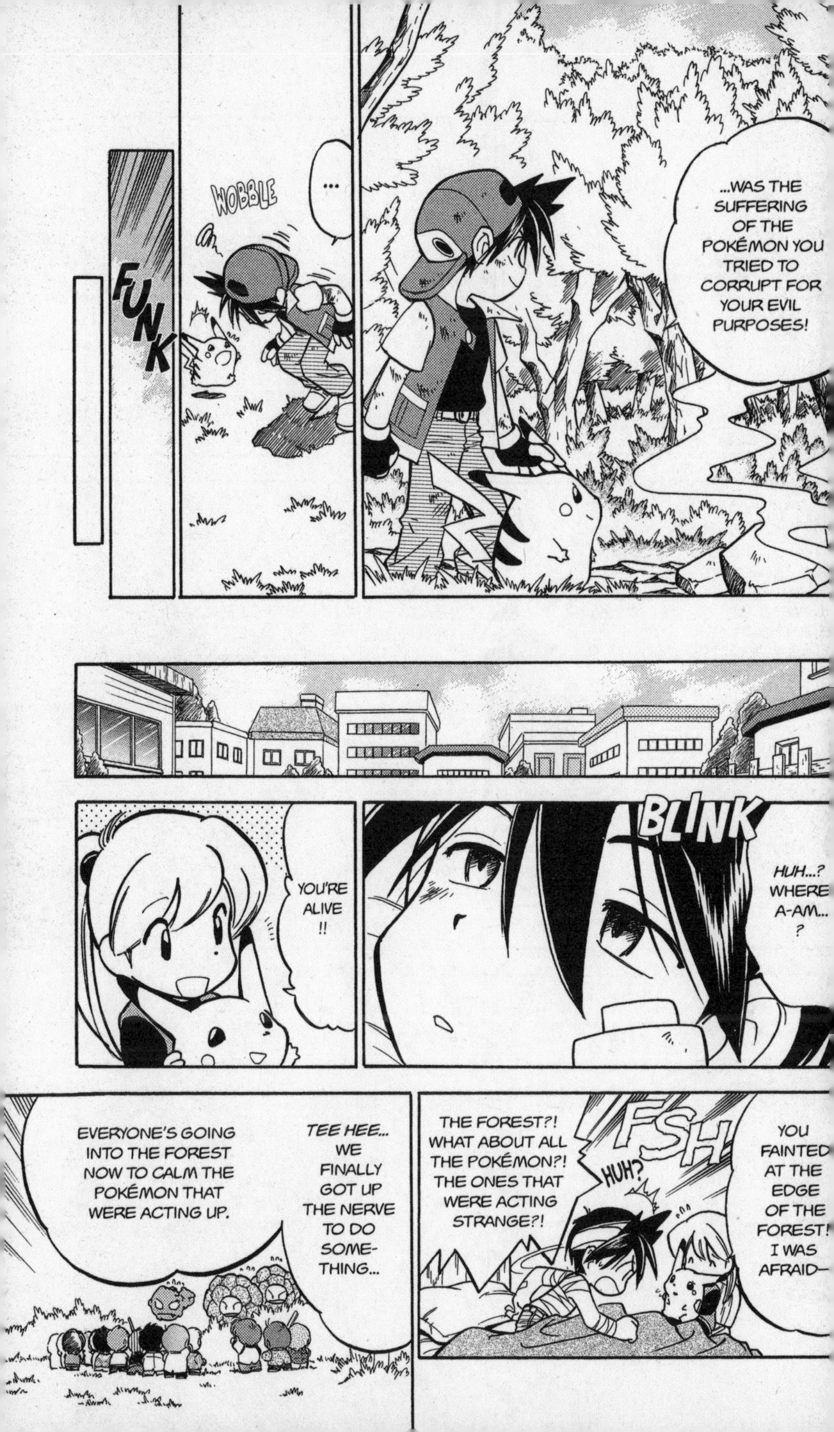
...WAS THE SUFFERING OF THE POKÉMON YOU TRIED TO CORRUPT FOR YOUR EVIL PURPOSES!
...
WOBBLE
FUNK
BLINK
HUH...? WHERE A-AM...?
YOU'RE ALIVE!!
YOU FAINTED AT THE EDGE OF THE FOREST! I WAS AFRAID—
FSH
HUH?
THE FOREST?! WHAT ABOUT ALL THE POKÉMON?! THE ONES THAT WERE ACTING STRANGE?!
TEE HEE... WE FINALLY GOT UP THE NERVE TO DO SOME-THING...
EVERYONE'S GOING INTO THE FOREST NOW TO CALM THE POKÉMON THAT WERE ACTING UP.

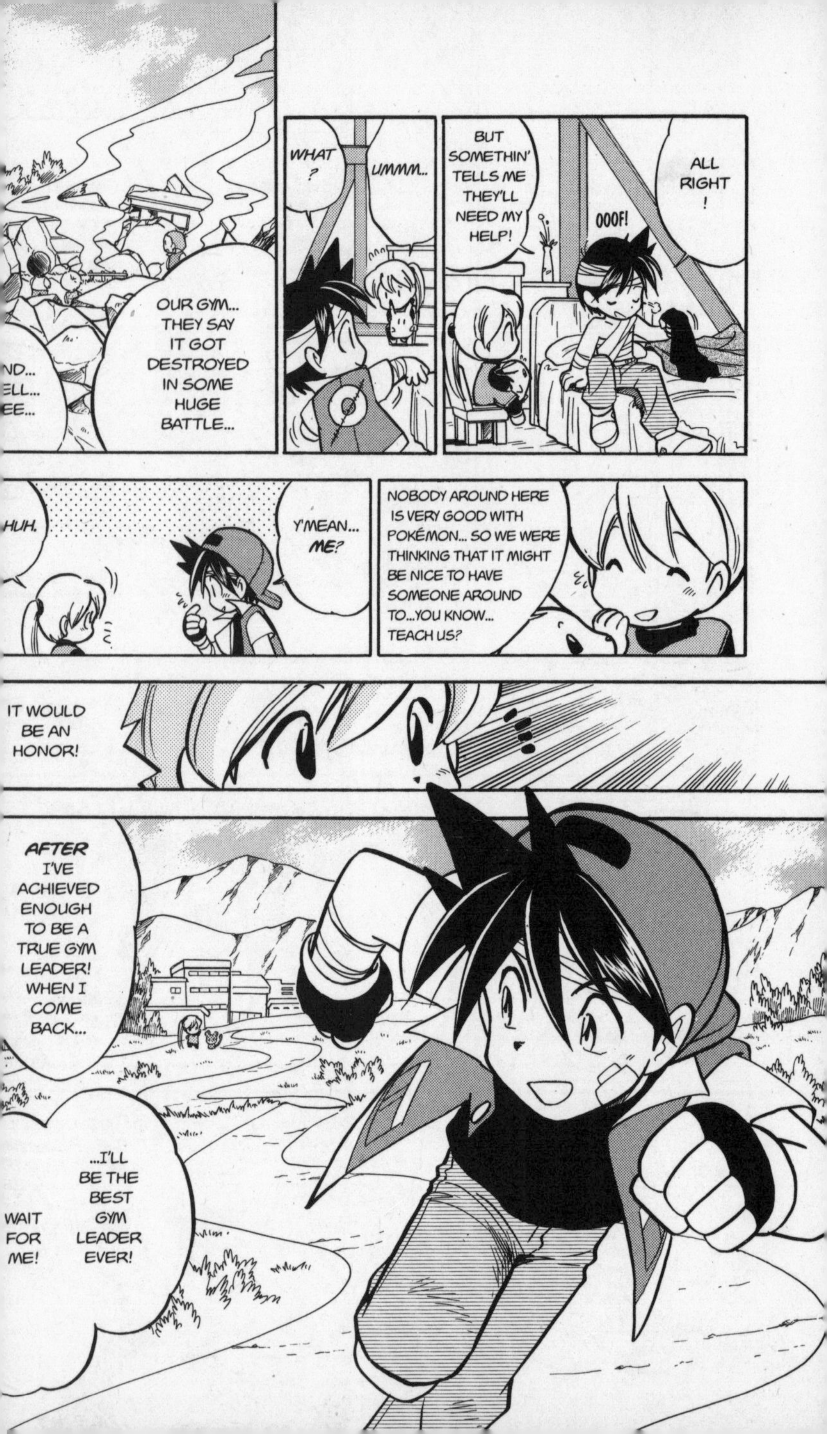

ALL RIGHT!
OOOF!
BUT SOMETHIN' TELLS ME THEY'LL NEED MY HELP!
UMMM...
WHAT?
OUR GYM... THEY SAY IT GOT DESTROYED IN SOME HUGE BATTLE...
ND... ELL... EE...
NOBODY AROUND HERE IS VERY GOOD WITH POKÉMON... SO WE WERE THINKING THAT IT MIGHT BE NICE TO HAVE SOMEONE AROUND TO...YOU KNOW... TEACH US?
Y'MEAN... *ME?*
HUH.
IT WOULD BE AN HONOR!
AFTER I'VE ACHIEVED ENOUGH TO BE A TRUE GYM LEADER! WHEN I COME BACK...
...I'LL BE THE BEST GYM LEADER EVER!
WAIT FOR ME!

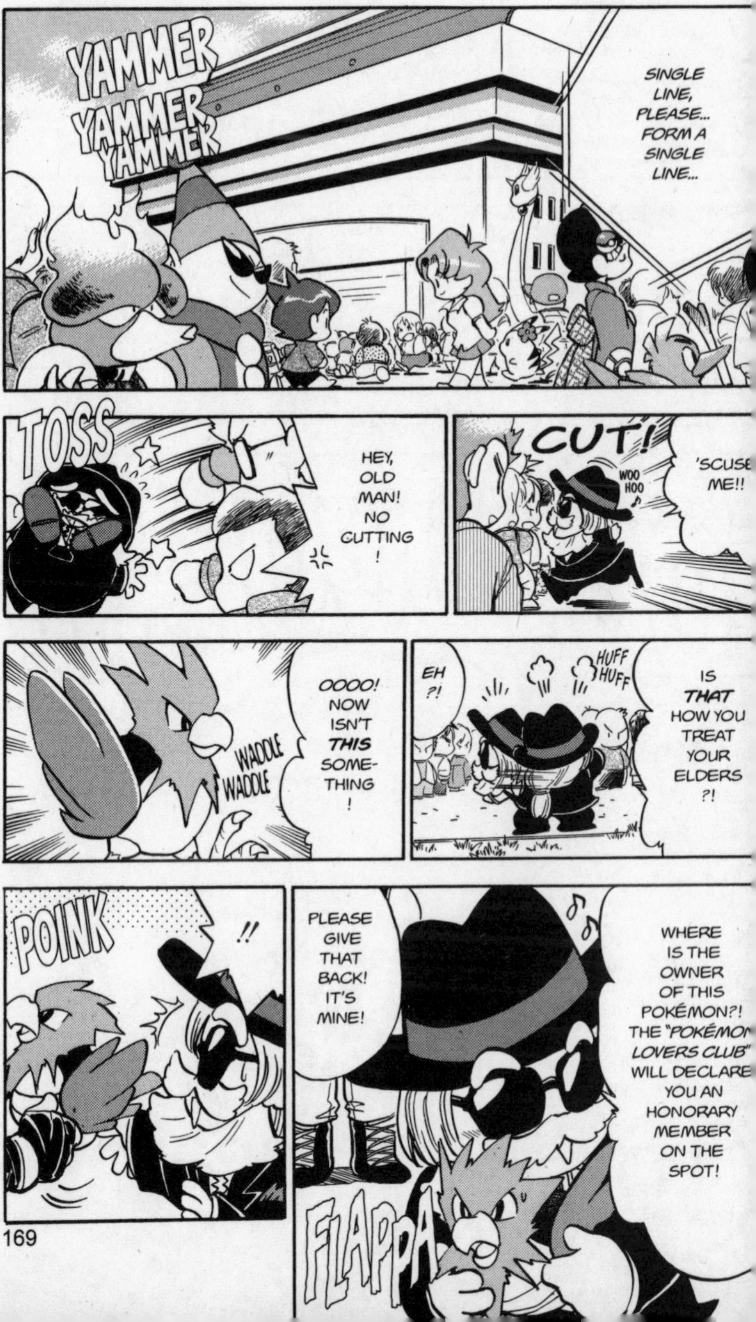
SINGLE LINE, PLEASE... FORM A SINGLE LINE...
YAMMER YAMMER YAMMER
'SCUSE ME!!
WOO HOO ♪
CUT!
HEY, OLD MAN! NO CUTTING!
TOSS
IS THAT HOW YOU TREAT YOUR ELDERS?!
HUFF HUFF
EH?!
OOOO! NOW ISN'T THIS SOMETHING!
WADDLE WADDLE
WHERE IS THE OWNER OF THIS POKÉMON?! THE "POKÉMON LOVERS CLUB" WILL DECLARE YOU AN HONORARY MEMBER ON THE SPOT!
PLEASE GIVE THAT BACK! IT'S MINE!
FLAPPA
!!
POINK

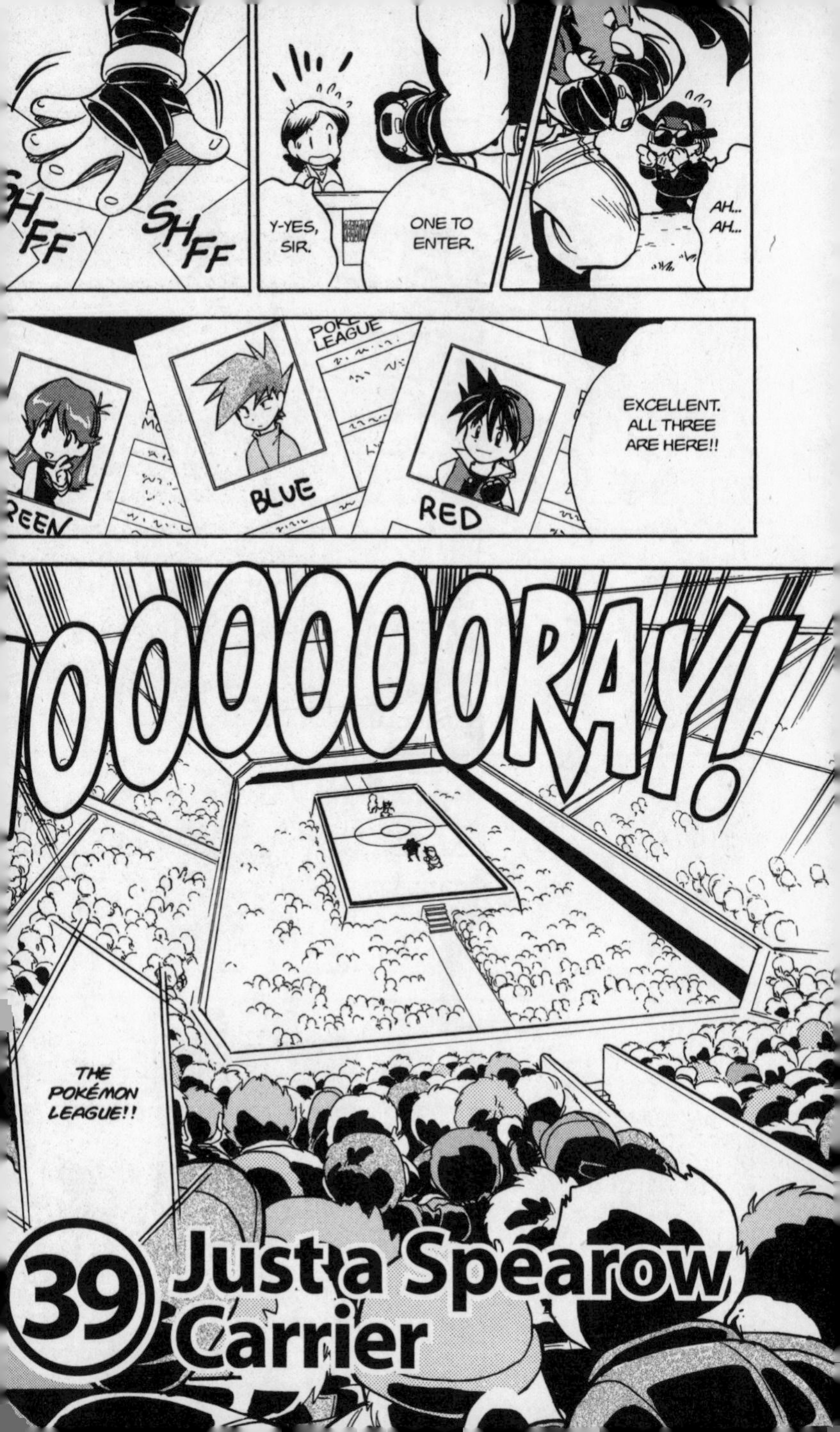
AH... AH...
ONE TO ENTER.
Y-YES, SIR.
SHFF
SHFF
EXCELLENT. ALL THREE ARE HERE!!
RED
POKé LEAGUE
BLUE
OOOOOORAY!
THE POKÉMON LEAGUE!!

39 Just a Spearow Carrier

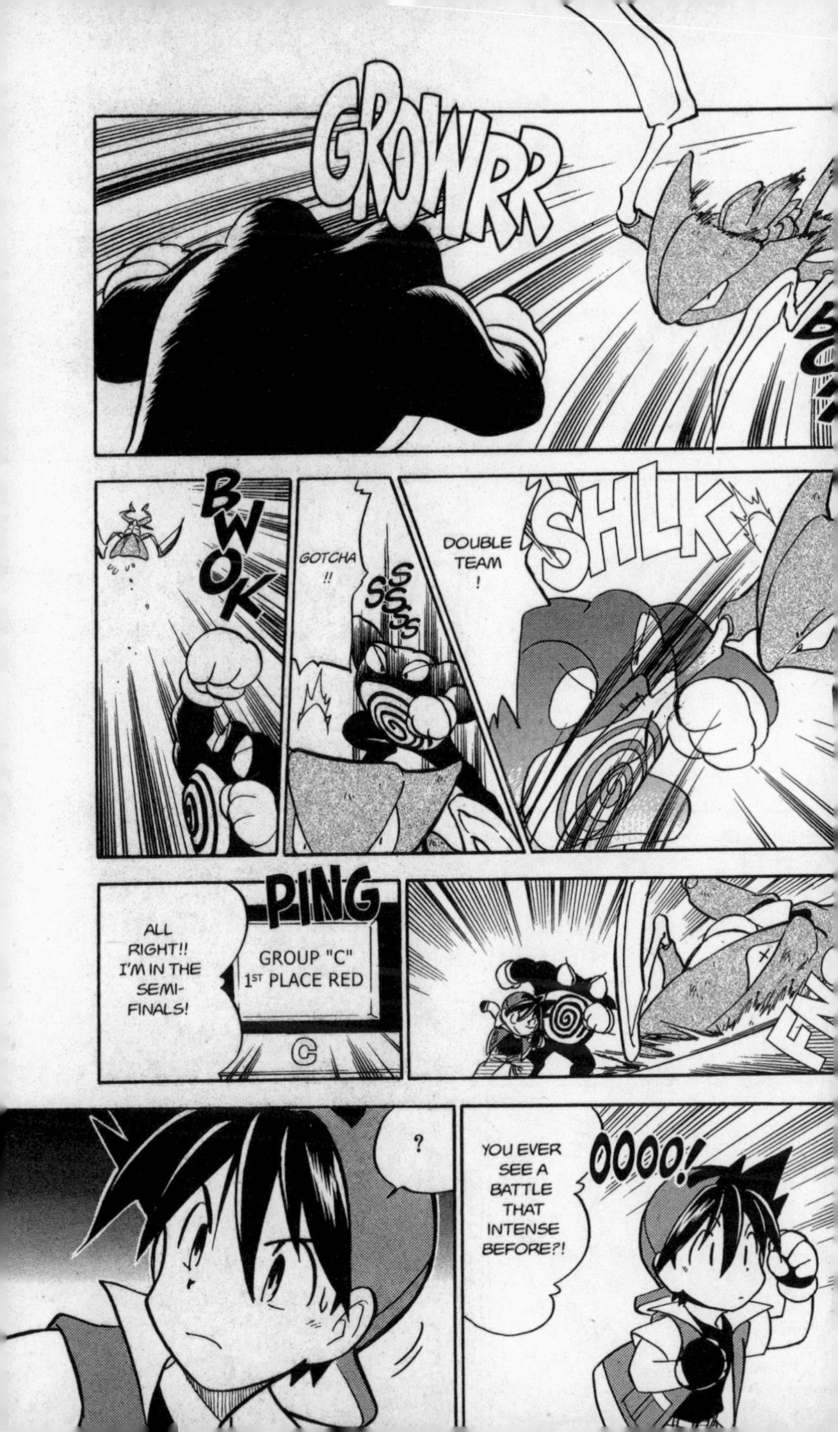
GROWRR
SHLK
DOUBLE TEAM !
GOTCHA !!
SSSSSS
BWOK
PING
GROUP "C" 1ST PLACE RED
ALL RIGHT!! I'M IN THE SEMI-FINALS!
C
OOOO!
YOU EVER SEE A BATTLE THAT INTENSE BEFORE?!
?

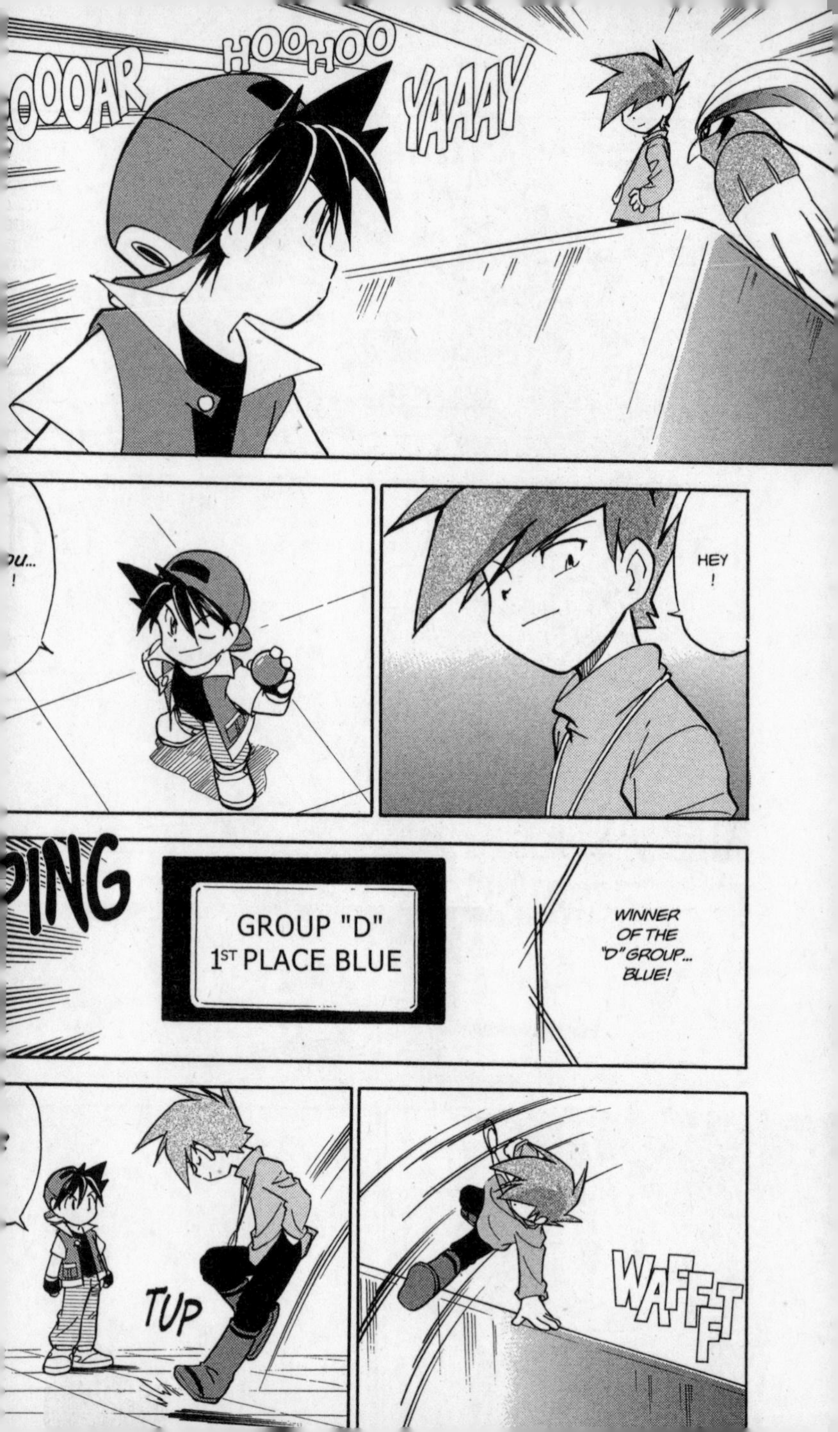
YAAAY
HOOHOO
OOOOAR
HEY !
OU... !
WINNER OF THE "D" GROUP... BLUE!
GROUP "D" 1ST PLACE BLUE
PING
WAFFT
TUP

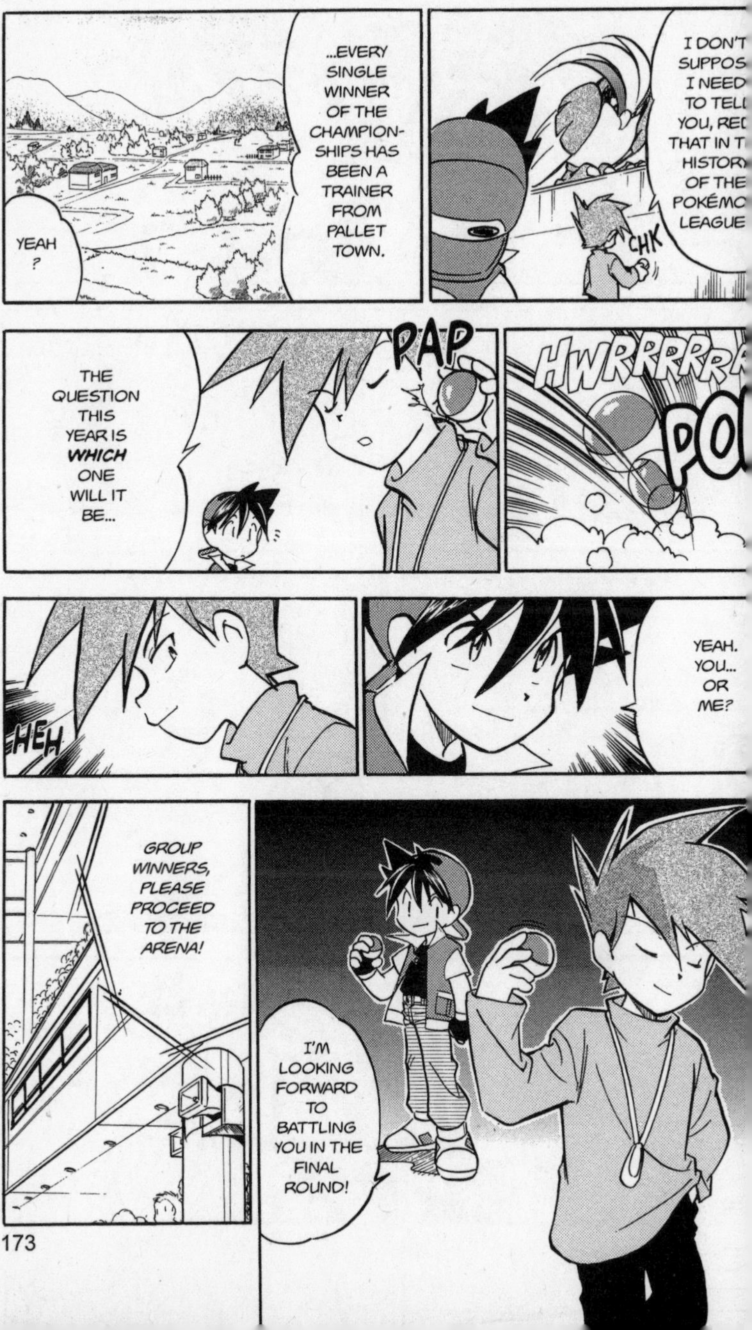
I DON'T SUPPOS I NEED TO TELL YOU, RED THAT IN T HISTORY OF THE POKÉMO LEAGUE
CHK
...EVERY SINGLE WINNER OF THE CHAMPIONSHIPS HAS BEEN A TRAINER FROM PALLET TOWN.
YEAH ?
HWRRRRR
PO
PAP
THE QUESTION THIS YEAR IS ***WHICH*** ONE WILL IT BE...
YEAH. YOU... OR ME?
HEH
I'M LOOKING FORWARD TO BATTLING YOU IN THE FINAL ROUND!
GROUP WINNERS, PLEASE PROCEED TO THE ARENA!

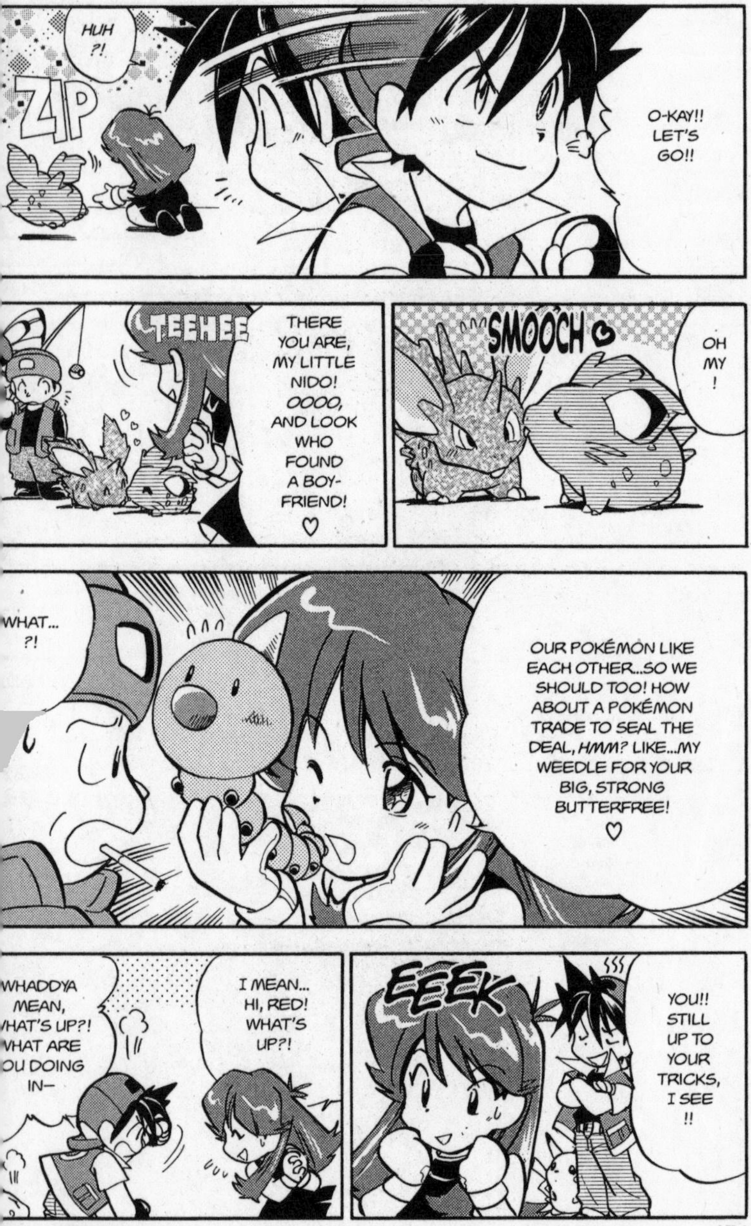
O-KAY!! LET'S GO!!
HUH ?!
ZIP
OH MY !
SMOOCH
THERE YOU ARE, MY LITTLE NIDO! *OOOO,* AND LOOK WHO FOUND A BOY-FRIEND! ♡
TEEHEE
OUR POKÉMON LIKE EACH OTHER...SO WE SHOULD TOO! HOW ABOUT A POKÉMON TRADE TO SEAL THE DEAL, *HMM?* LIKE...MY WEEDLE FOR YOUR BIG, STRONG BUTTERFREE! ♡
WHAT... ?!
YOU!! STILL UP TO YOUR TRICKS, I SEE !!
EEEK
I MEAN... HI, RED! WHAT'S UP?!
WHADDYA MEAN, HAT'S UP?! HAT ARE OU DOING IN—

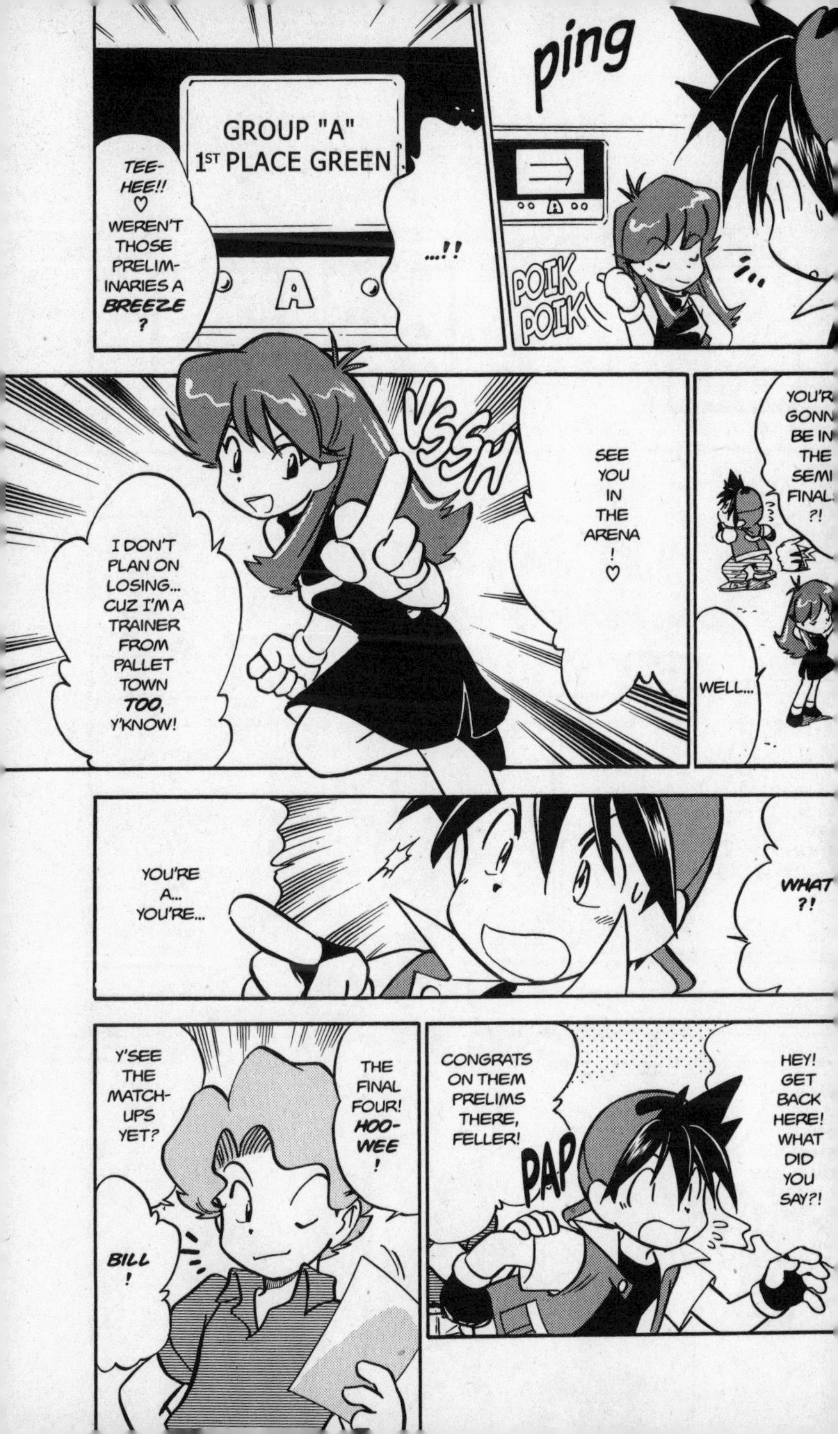

ping
POIK POIK
GROUP "A" 1ST PLACE GREEN
...!!
TEE-HEE!! ♡ WEREN'T THOSE PRELIMINARIES A BREEZE?
YOU'R GONN BE IN THE SEMI FINAL ?!
WELL...
SEE YOU IN THE ARENA! ♡
VSSH
I DON'T PLAN ON LOSING... CUZ I'M A TRAINER FROM PALLET TOWN TOO, Y'KNOW!
WHAT?!
YOU'RE A... YOU'RE...
HEY! GET BACK HERE! WHAT DID YOU SAY?!
CONGRATS ON THEM PRELIMS THERE, FELLER!
PAP
THE FINAL FOUR! HOO-WEE!
Y'SEE THE MATCH-UPS YET?
BILL!

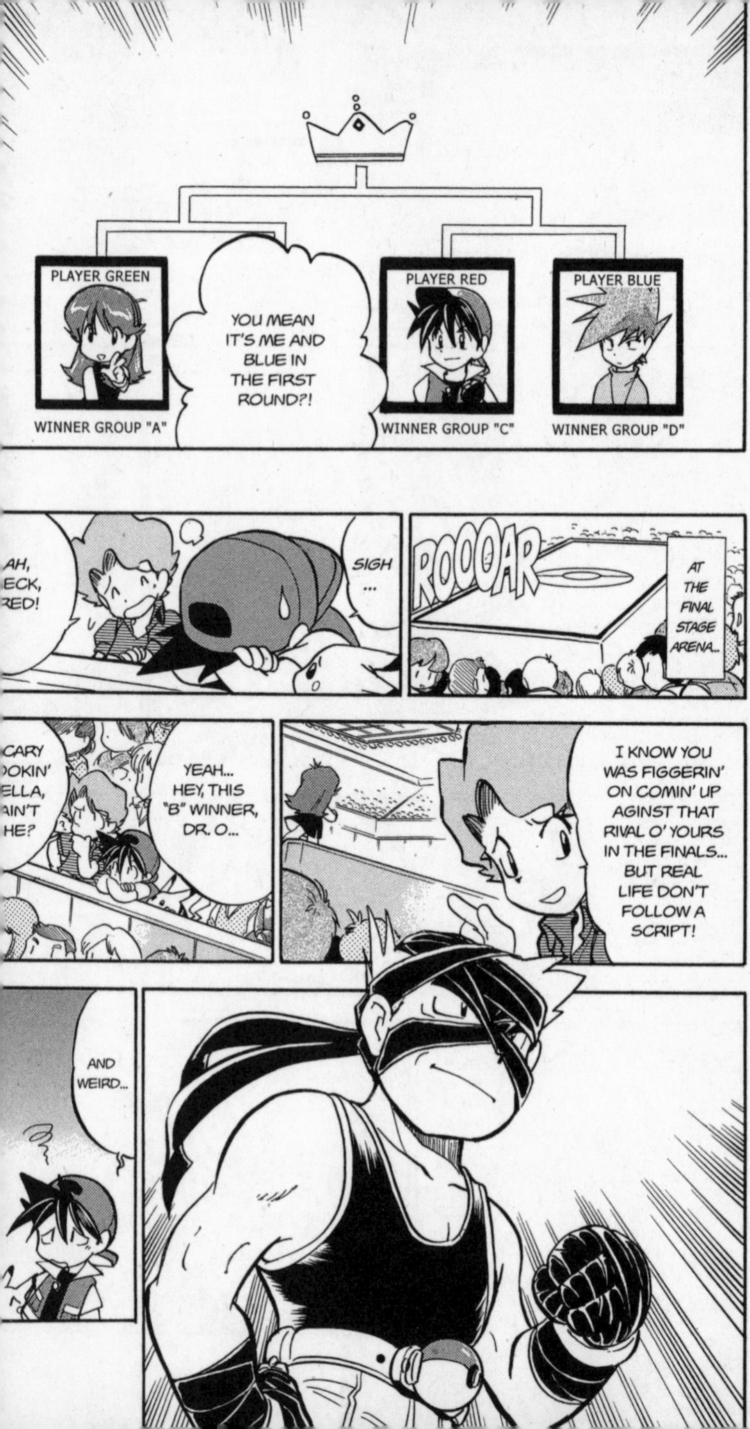
PLAYER BLUE
PLAYER RED
YOU MEAN IT'S ME AND BLUE IN THE FIRST ROUND?!
PLAYER GREEN
WINNER GROUP "D"
WINNER GROUP "C"
WINNER GROUP "A"
AT THE FINAL STAGE ARENA...
ROOOAR
SIGH ...
AH, ECK, RED!
I KNOW YOU WAS FIGGERIN' ON COMIN' UP AGINST THAT RIVAL O' YOURS IN THE FINALS... BUT REAL LIFE DON'T FOLLOW A SCRIPT!
YEAH... HEY, THIS "B" WINNER, DR. O...
CARY OOKIN' ELLA, AIN'T HE?
AND WEIRD...

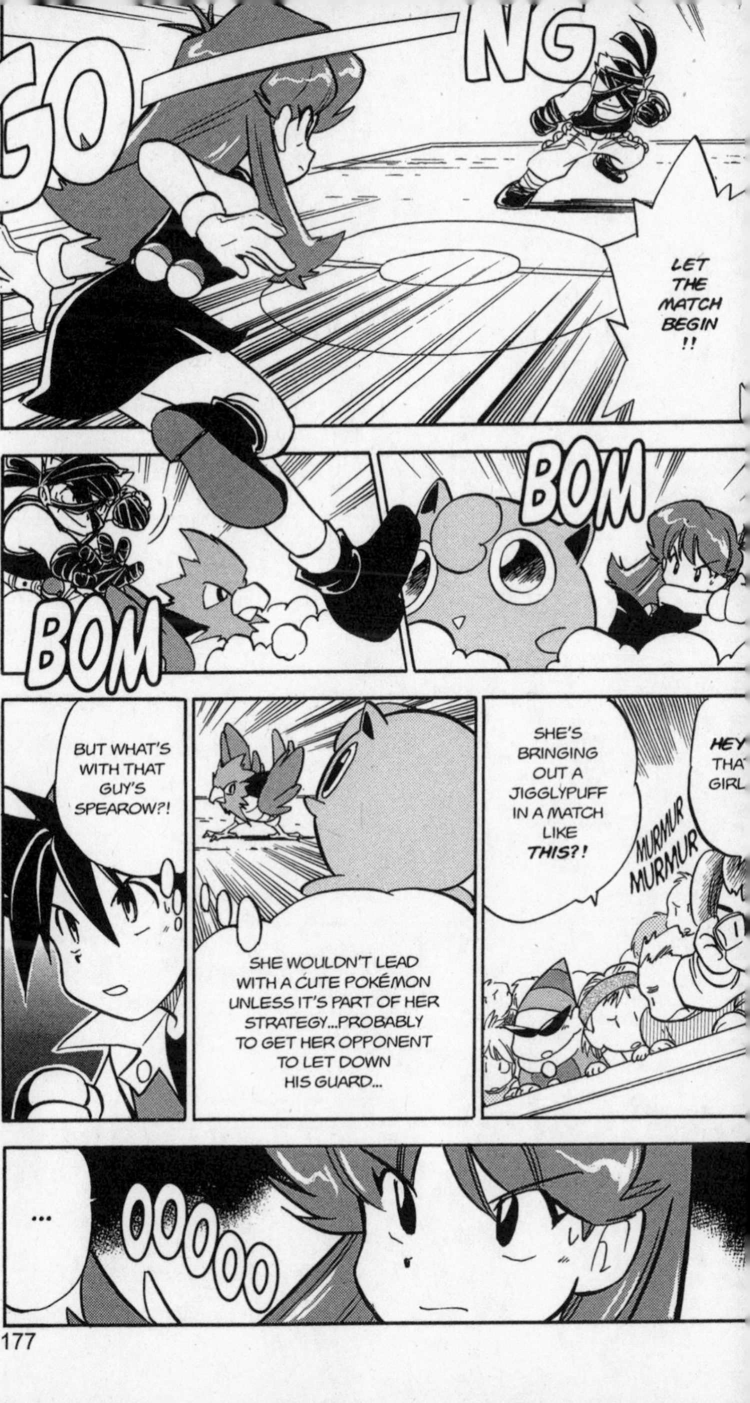
GONG
LET THE MATCH BEGIN!!
BOM
BOM
HEY THAT GIRL
SHE'S BRINGING OUT A JIGGLYPUFF IN A MATCH LIKE THIS?!
MURMUR MURMUR
SHE WOULDN'T LEAD WITH A CUTE POKÉMON UNLESS IT'S PART OF HER STRATEGY...PROBABLY TO GET HER OPPONENT TO LET DOWN HIS GUARD...
BUT WHAT'S WITH THAT GUY'S SPEAROW?!
OOOOO
...

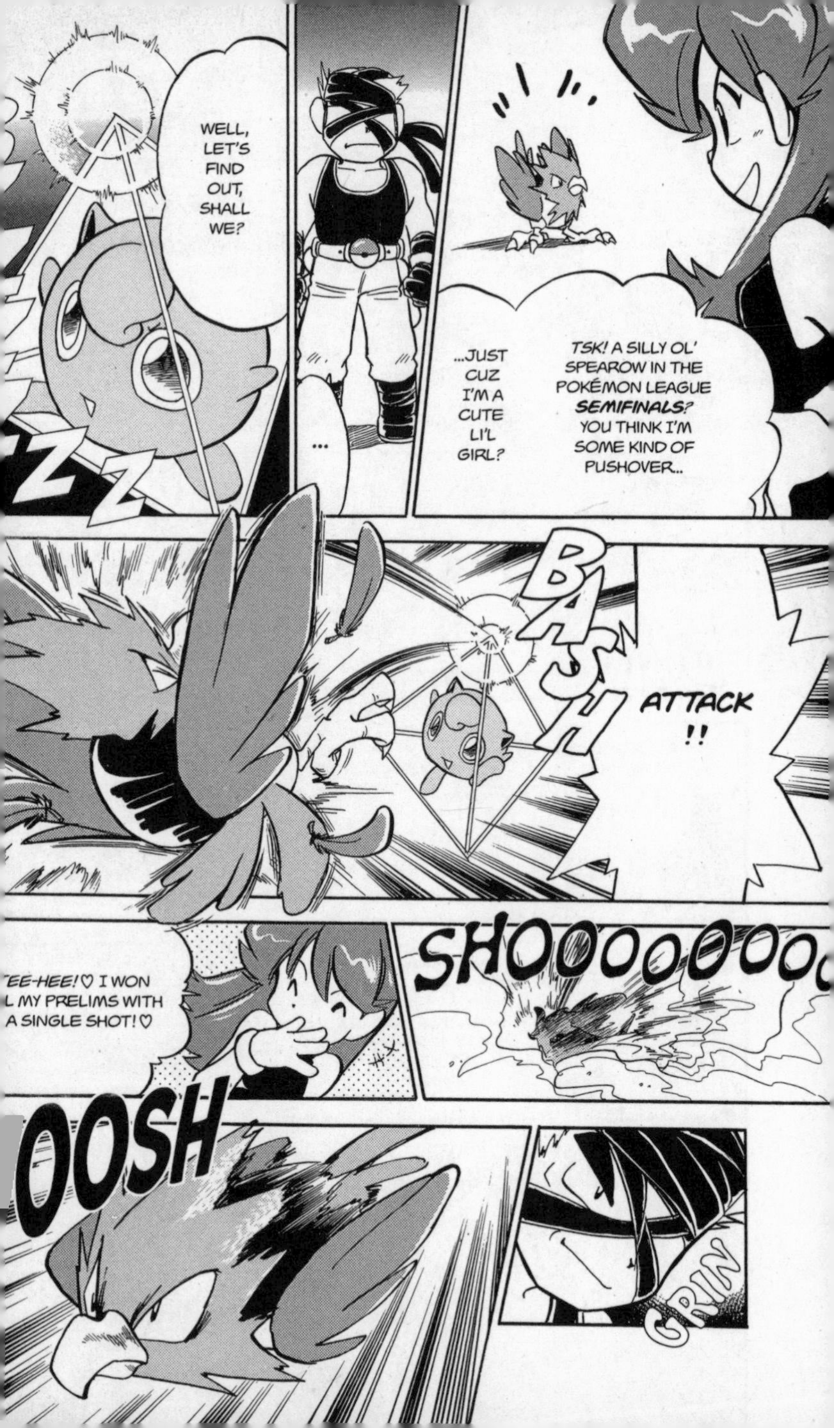

TSK! A SILLY OL' SPEAROW IN THE POKÉMON LEAGUE ***SEMIFINALS?*** YOU THINK I'M SOME KIND OF PUSHOVER...
...JUST CUZ I'M A CUTE LI'L GIRL?
...
WELL, LET'S FIND OUT, SHALL WE?
BASH
ATTACK !!
SHOOOOOOOOO
EE-HEE!♡ I WON L MY PRELIMS WITH A SINGLE SHOT!♡
GRIN
OOSH

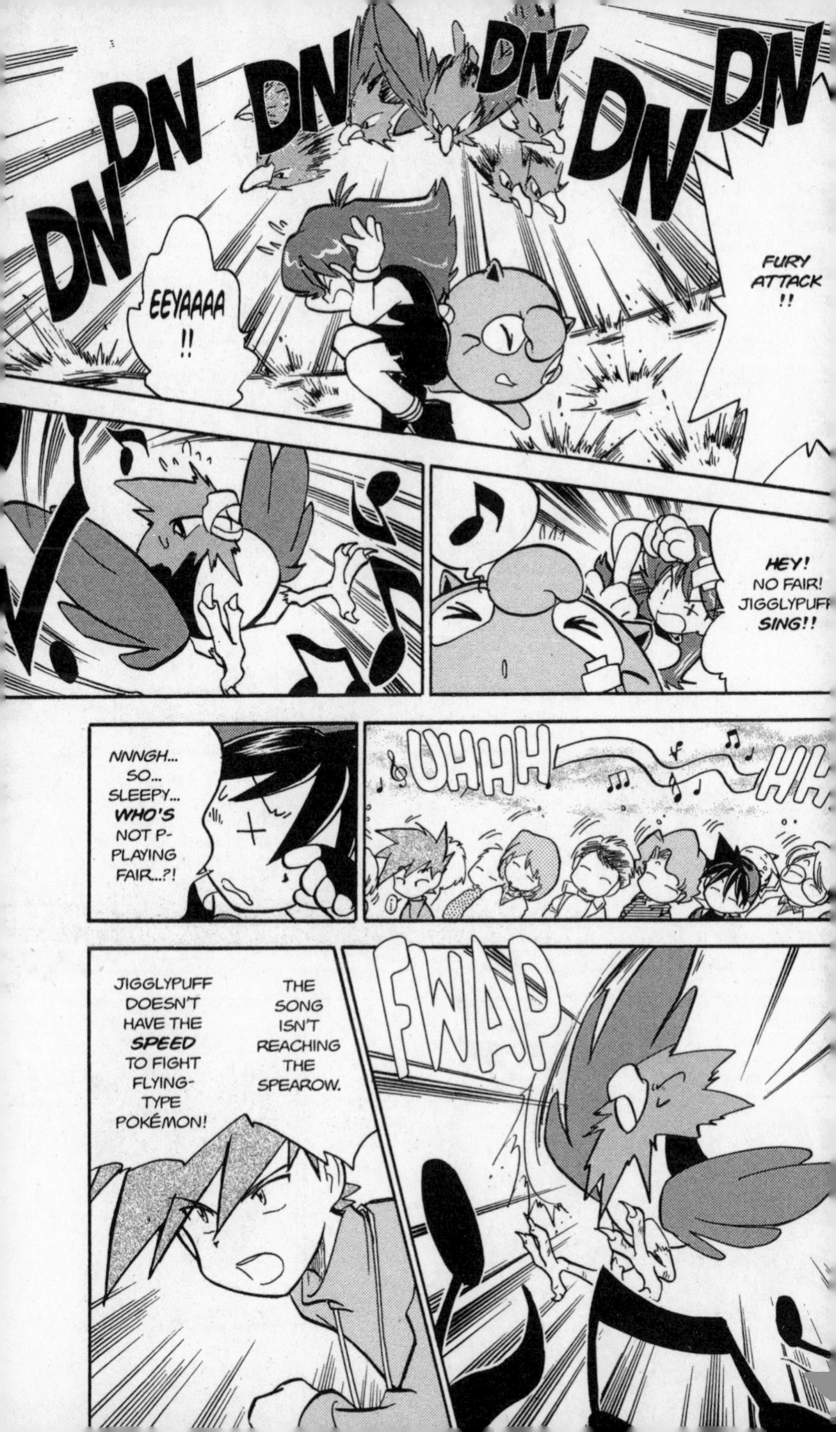
DN DN DN DN DN DN DN
FURY ATTACK!!
EEYAAAA!!
HEY! NO FAIR! JIGGLYPUFF SING!!
UHHH HH
NNNGH... SO... SLEEPY... WHO'S NOT P-PLAYING FAIR...?!
FWAP
THE SONG ISN'T REACHING THE SPEAROW.
JIGGLYPUFF DOESN'T HAVE THE SPEED TO FIGHT FLYING-TYPE POKÉMON!

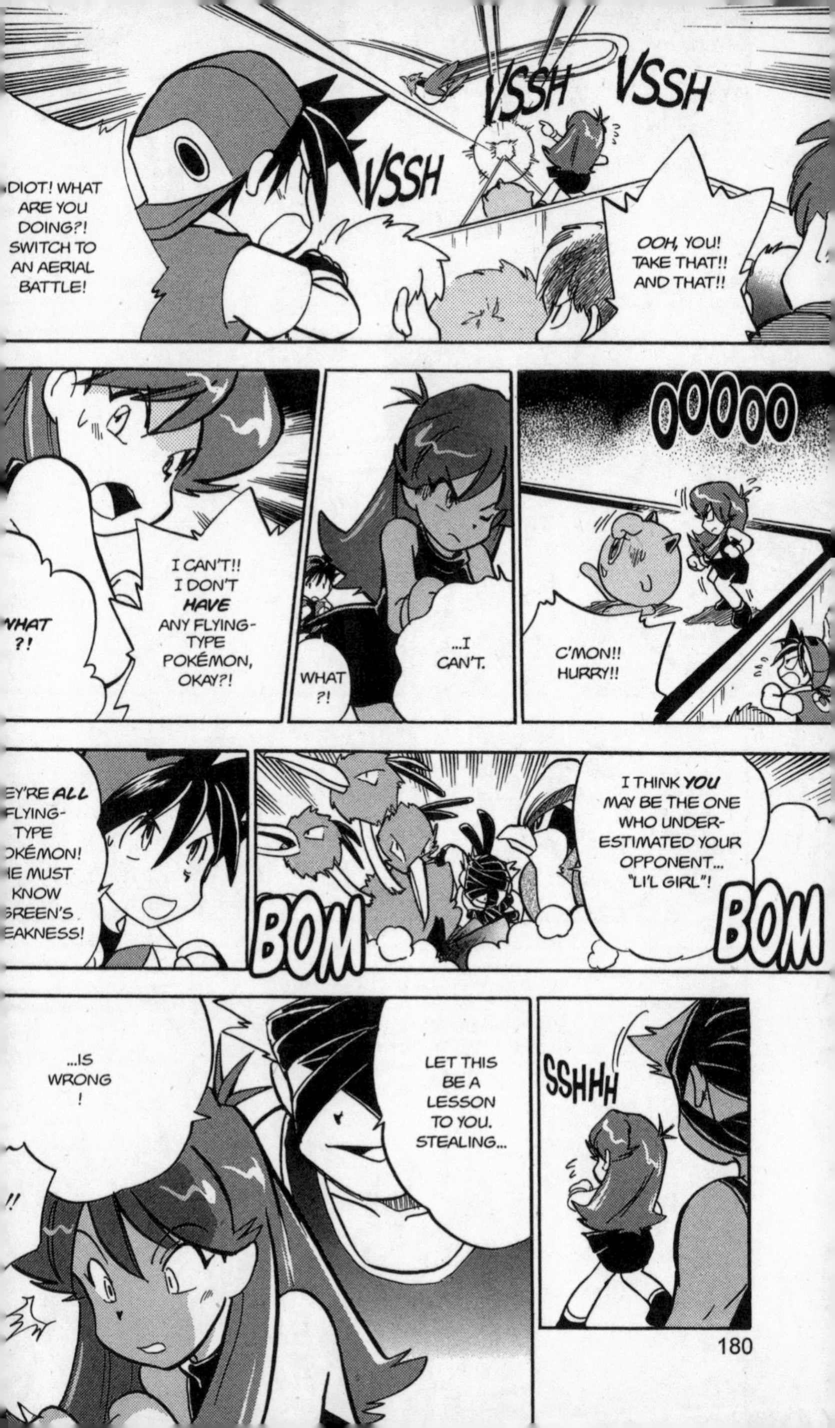
VSSH VSSH
VSSH
OOH, YOU! TAKE THAT!! AND THAT!!
DIOT! WHAT ARE YOU DOING?! SWITCH TO AN AERIAL BATTLE!
OOOOO
C'MON!! HURRY!!
...I CAN'T.
WHAT ?!
I CAN'T!! I DON'T HAVE ANY FLYING-TYPE POKÉMON, OKAY?!
VHAT ?!
I THINK YOU MAY BE THE ONE WHO UNDER-ESTIMATED YOUR OPPONENT... "LI'L GIRL"!
BOM
BOM
EY'RE ALL FLYING-TYPE OKÉMON! HE MUST KNOW GREEN'S EAKNESS!
SSHHH
LET THIS BE A LESSON TO YOU. STEALING...
...IS WRONG !
!!

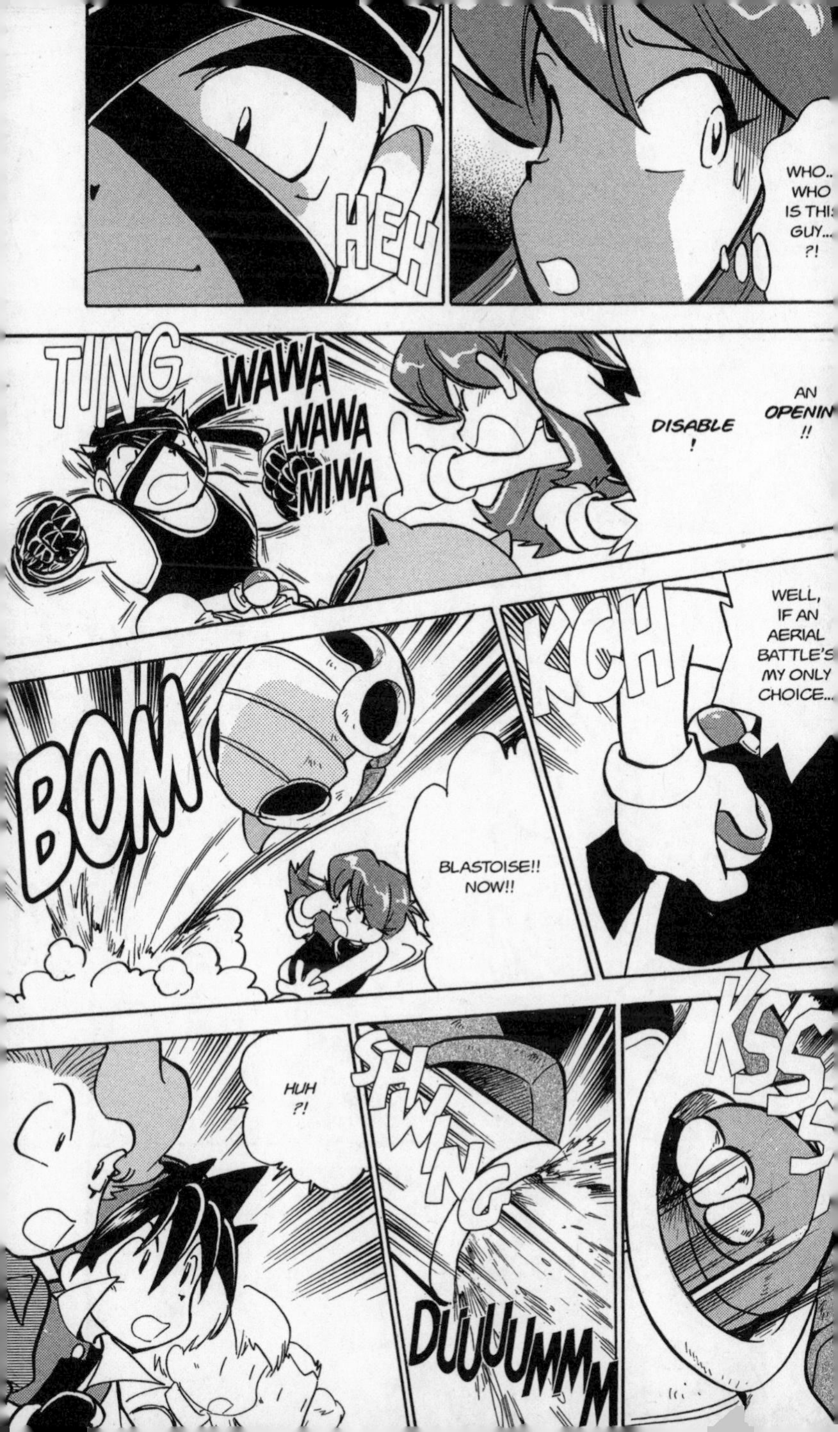
WHO.. WHO IS THIS GUY... ?!
HEH
AN OPENIN !!
DISABLE !
TING
WAWA WAWA MIWA
WELL, IF AN AERIAL BATTLE'S MY ONLY CHOICE...
KCH
BLASTOISE!! NOW!!
BOM
KSS
SHWNG
DUUUUMMM
HUH ?!

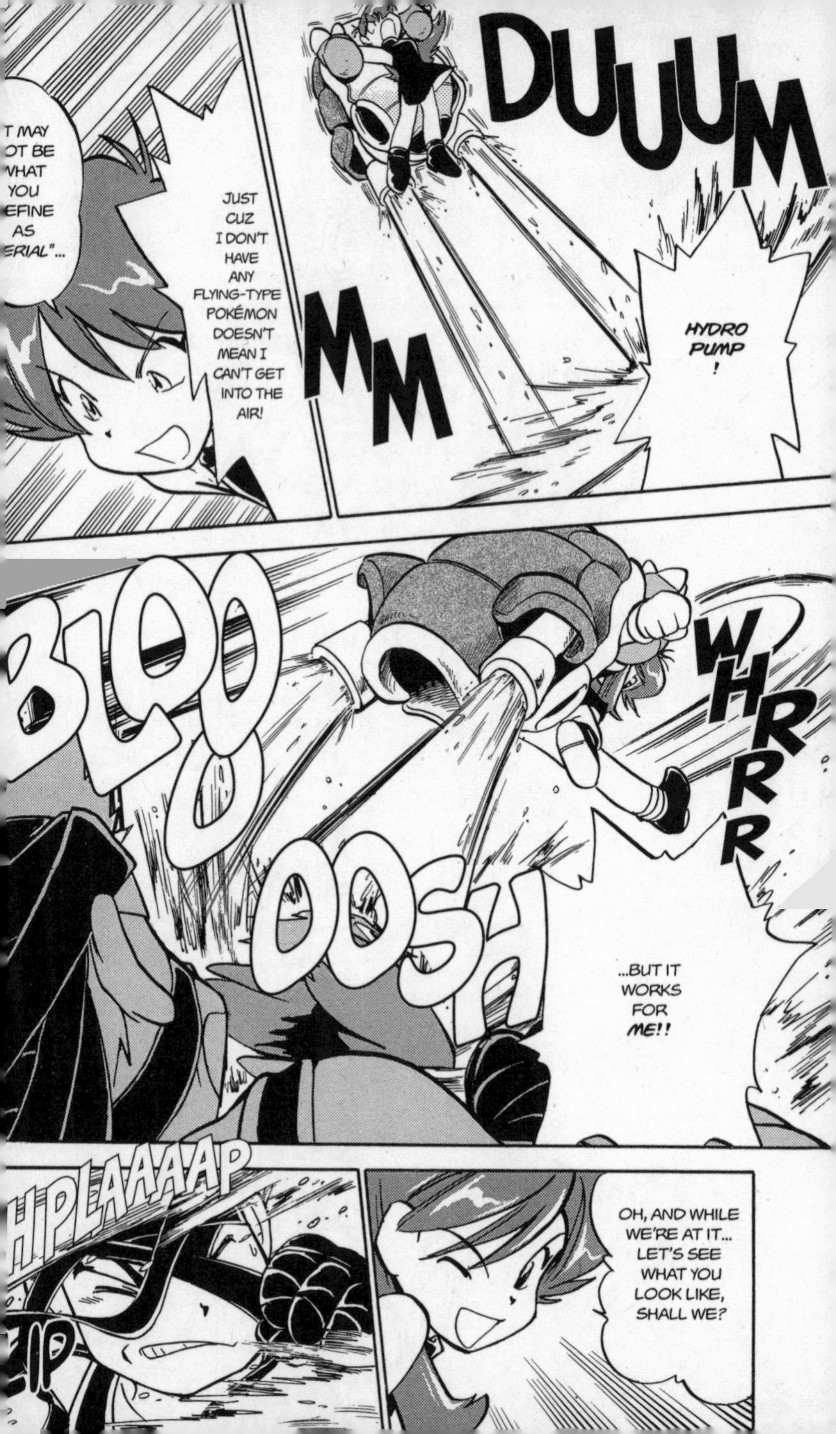
DUUUUM
MM
HYDRO PUMP!
JUST CUZ I DON'T HAVE ANY FLYING-TYPE POKÉMON DOESN'T MEAN I CAN'T GET INTO THE AIR!
T MAY OT BE WHAT YOU EFINE AS ERIAL"...
WHRRR
BLOOOOOSH
...BUT IT WORKS FOR *ME!!*
OH, AND WHILE WE'RE AT IT... LET'S SEE WHAT YOU LOOK LIKE, SHALL WE?
HIPLAAAAP
IP

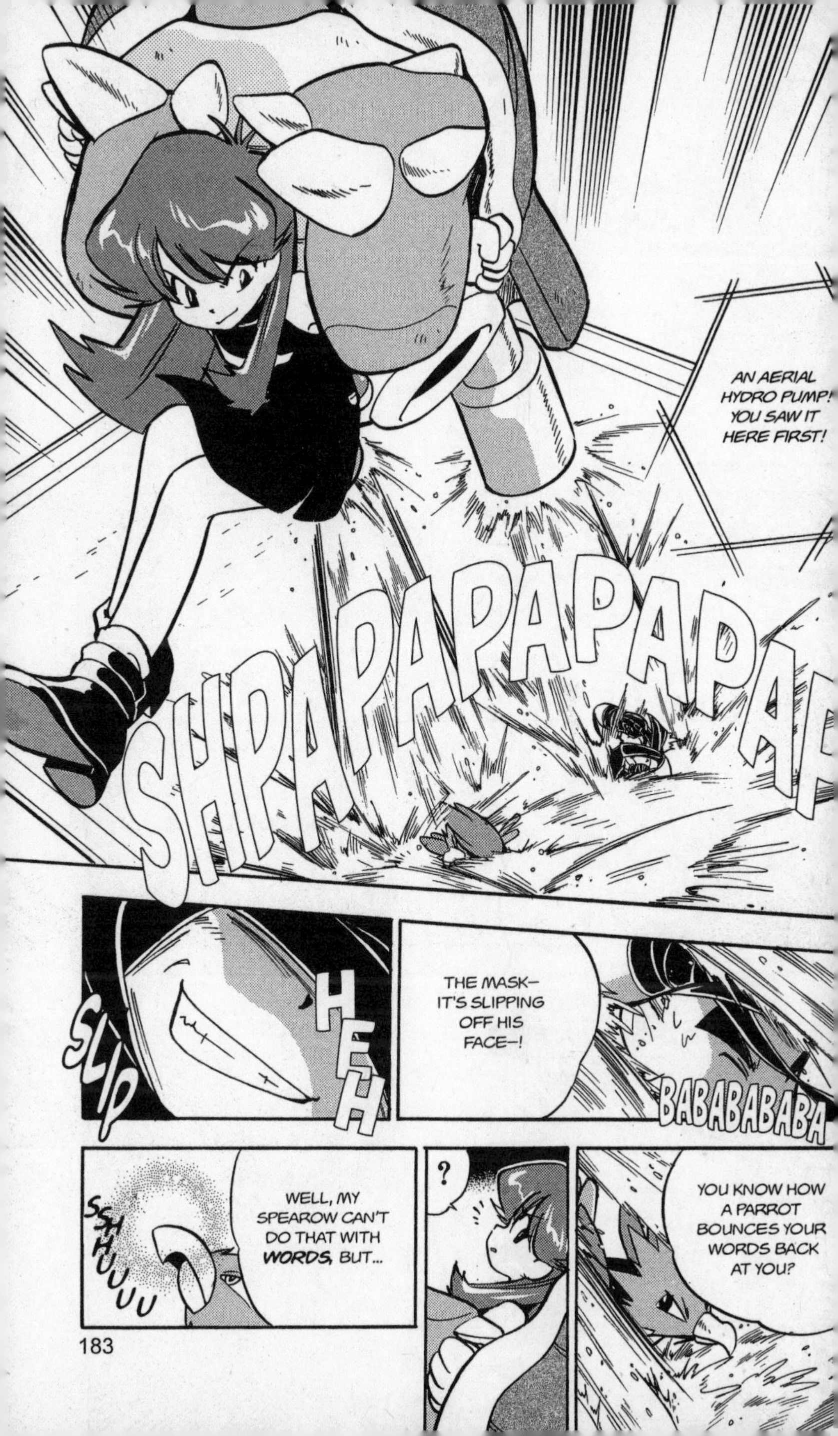
AN AERIAL HYDRO PUMP! YOU SAW IT HERE FIRST!
SHPAPAPAPAPAPAP
THE MASK— IT'S SLIPPING OFF HIS FACE—!
BABABABABA
HEH
SLIP
YOU KNOW HOW A PARROT BOUNCES YOUR WORDS BACK AT YOU?
?
WELL, MY SPEAROW CAN'T DO THAT WITH *WORDS*, BUT...
SSHUUUU

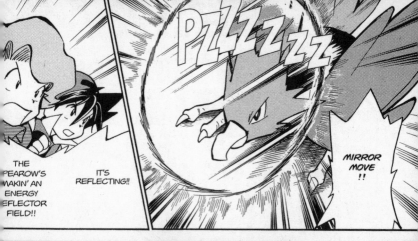

PZZZZZZ
MIRROR MOVE !!
IT'S REFLECTING!!
THE PEAROW'S MAKIN' AN ENERGY EFLECTOR FIELD!!
BLOOSH
BLOOSH
EEEP !!
BLASTOISE HP
ITS HEALTH LEVELS...
UH-HUH...
THWAP
FLUTTERRRRR
N... NO...
ZZZMM

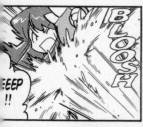

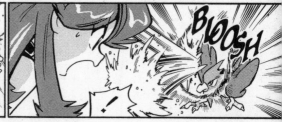

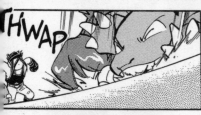

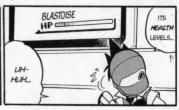

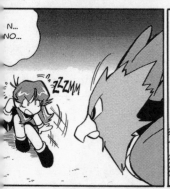

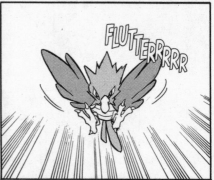

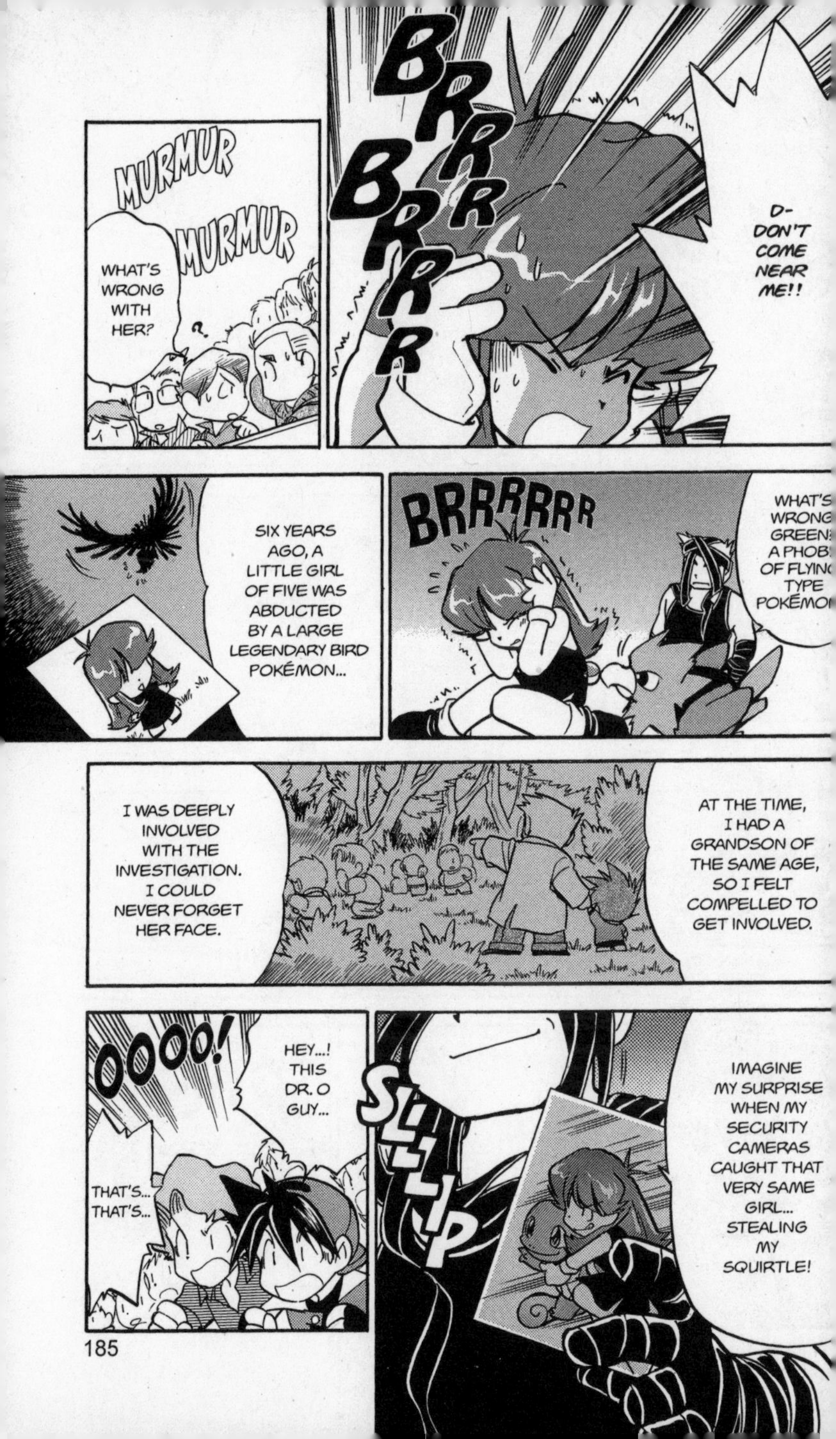
BRRRR
BRRRR
D-DON'T COME NEAR ME!!
MURMUR
MURMUR
WHAT'S WRONG WITH HER?
?
BRRRRRRR
WHAT'S WRONG GREEN A PHOB OF FLYIN TYPE POKÉMO
SIX YEARS AGO, A LITTLE GIRL OF FIVE WAS ABDUCTED BY A LARGE LEGENDARY BIRD POKÉMON...
AT THE TIME, I HAD A GRANDSON OF THE SAME AGE, SO I FELT COMPELLED TO GET INVOLVED.
I WAS DEEPLY INVOLVED WITH THE INVESTIGATION. I COULD NEVER FORGET HER FACE.
SLLIP
IMAGINE MY SURPRISE WHEN MY SECURITY CAMERAS CAUGHT THAT VERY SAME GIRL... STEALING MY SQUIRTLE!
OOOO!
HEY...! THIS DR. O GUY...
THAT'S... THAT'S...

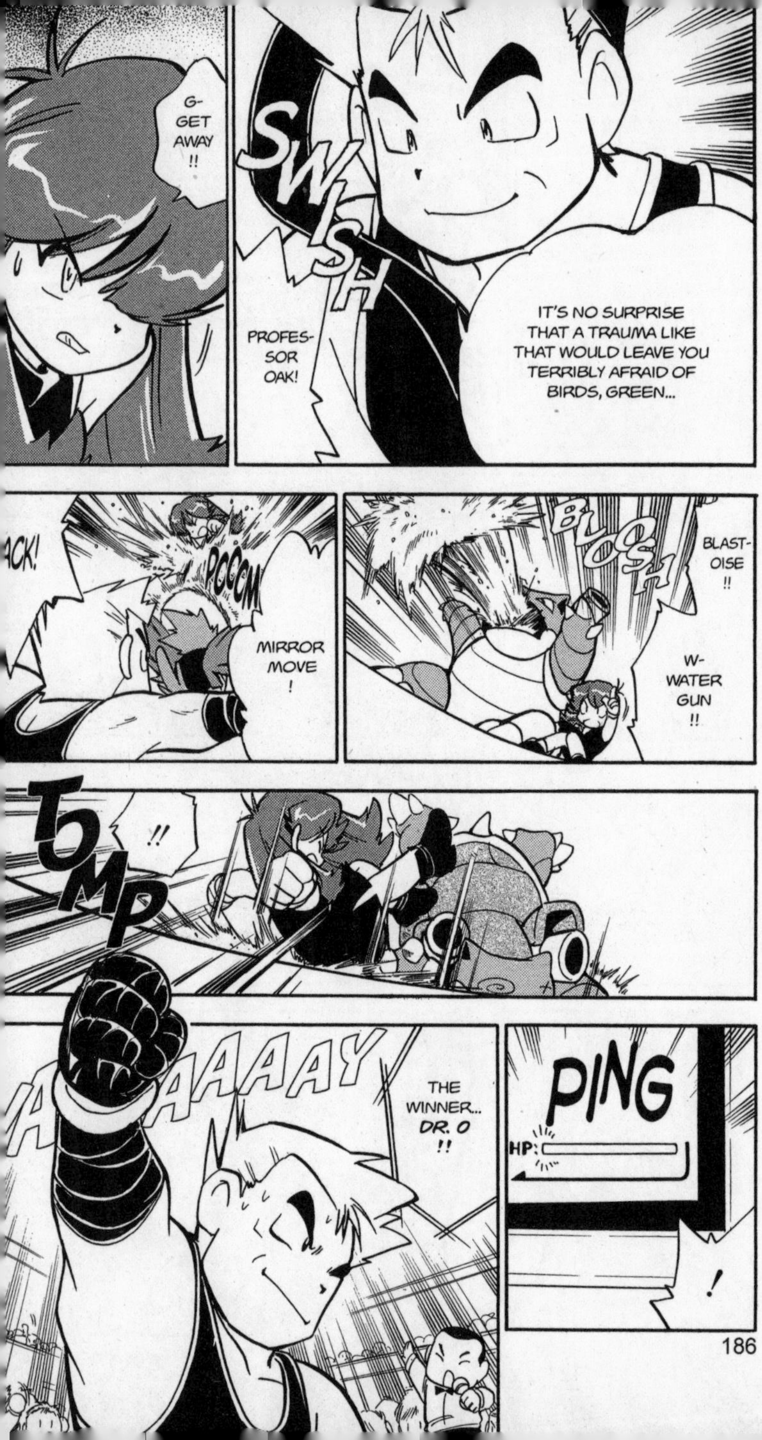
SWISH
IT'S NO SURPRISE THAT A TRAUMA LIKE THAT WOULD LEAVE YOU TERRIBLY AFRAID OF BIRDS, GREEN...
PROFES-SOR OAK!
G-GET AWAY!!
BLOSH
BLAST-OISE!!
W-WATER GUN!!
POOOM
ACK!
MIRROR MOVE!
TOMP
!!
PING
HP:
!
AAAAAY
THE WINNER... DR. O!!

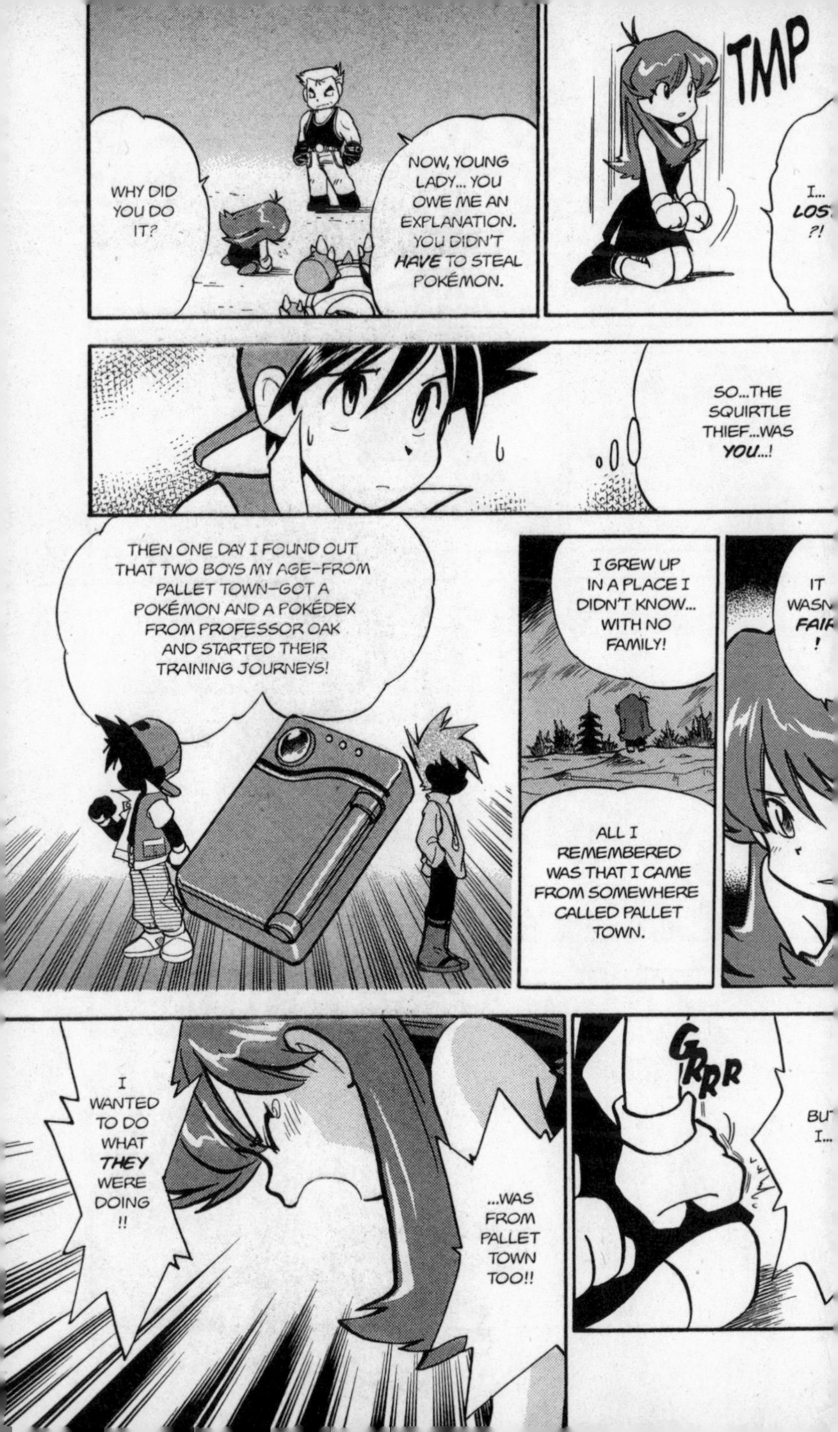

TMP
I... LOS ?!
NOW, YOUNG LADY... YOU OWE ME AN EXPLANATION. YOU DIDN'T HAVE TO STEAL POKÉMON.
WHY DID YOU DO IT?
SO...THE SQUIRTLE THIEF...WAS YOU...!
IT WASN FAIR !
I GREW UP IN A PLACE I DIDN'T KNOW... WITH NO FAMILY!
ALL I REMEMBERED WAS THAT I CAME FROM SOMEWHERE CALLED PALLET TOWN.
THEN ONE DAY I FOUND OUT THAT TWO BOYS MY AGE—FROM PALLET TOWN—GOT A POKÉMON AND A POKÉDEX FROM PROFESSOR OAK AND STARTED THEIR TRAINING JOURNEYS!
GRRR
BU I...
...WAS FROM PALLET TOWN TOO!!
I WANTED TO DO WHAT THEY WERE DOING!!

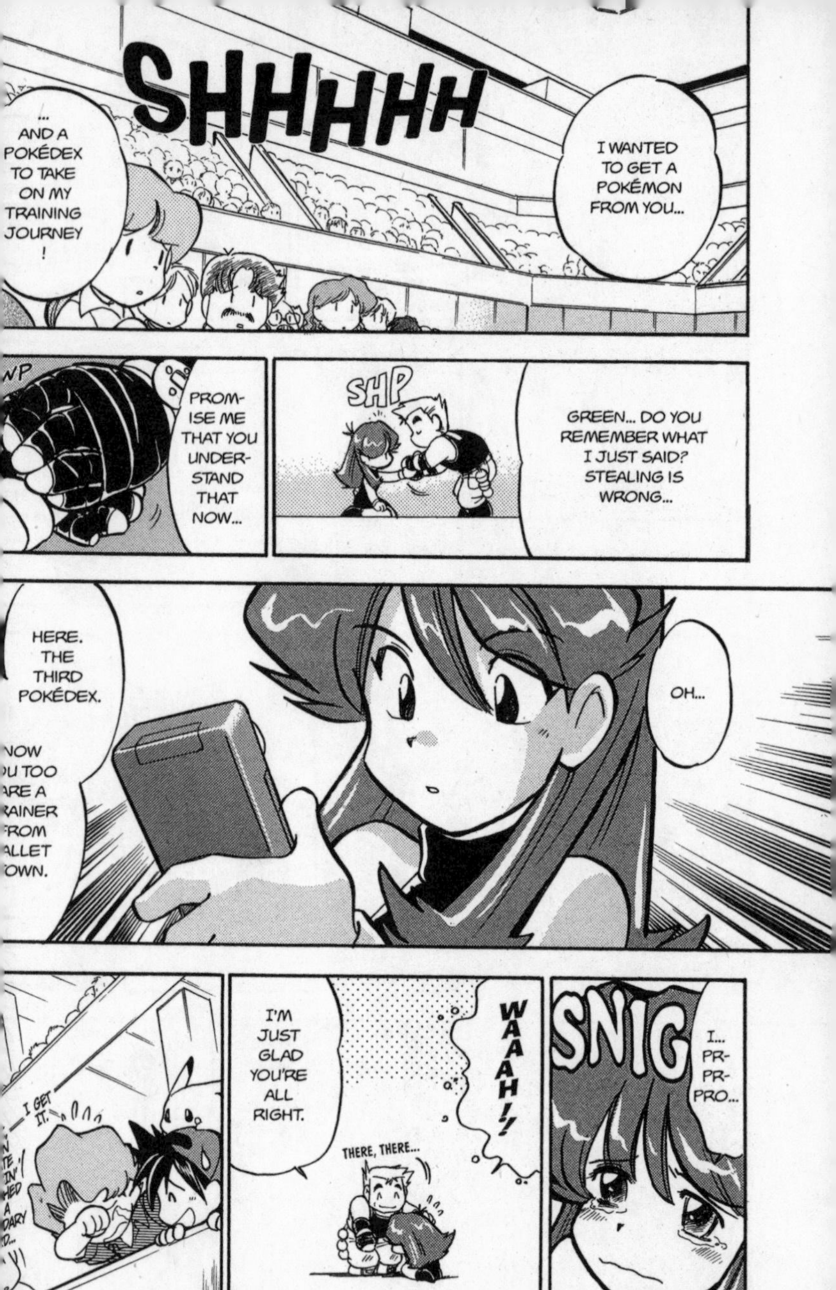
I WANTED TO GET A POKÉMON FROM YOU...
SHHHHH
... AND A POKÉDEX TO TAKE ON MY TRAINING JOURNEY!
SHP
GREEN... DO YOU REMEMBER WHAT I JUST SAID? STEALING IS WRONG...
PROMISE ME THAT YOU UNDERSTAND THAT NOW...
OH...
HERE. THE THIRD POKÉDEX.
NOW OU TOO ARE A RAINER FROM ALLET OWN.
SNIG
I... PR-PR-PRO...
WAAAH!!
I'M JUST GLAD YOU'RE ALL RIGHT.
THERE, THERE...
I GET IT.

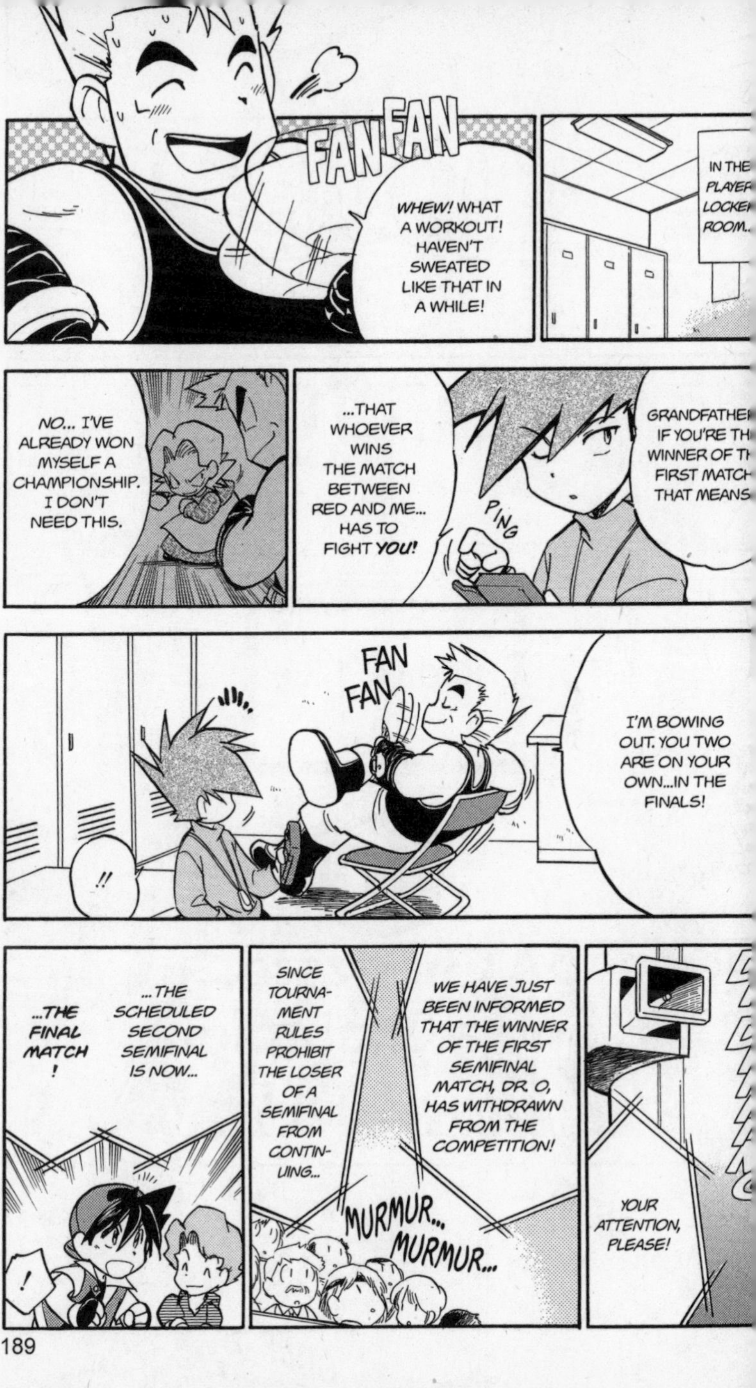

IN THE PLAYER LOCKER ROOM...
FAN FAN
WHEW! WHAT A WORKOUT! HAVEN'T SWEATED LIKE THAT IN A WHILE!
GRANDFATHER, IF YOU'RE THE WINNER OF THE FIRST MATCH THAT MEANS
...THAT WHOEVER WINS THE MATCH BETWEEN RED AND ME... HAS TO FIGHT **YOU!**
PING
NO... I'VE ALREADY WON MYSELF A CHAMPIONSHIP. I DON'T NEED THIS.
I'M BOWING OUT. YOU TWO ARE ON YOUR OWN...IN THE FINALS!
FAN FAN
!!
YOUR ATTENTION, PLEASE!
WE HAVE JUST BEEN INFORMED THAT THE WINNER OF THE FIRST SEMIFINAL MATCH, DR. O, HAS WITHDRAWN FROM THE COMPETITION!
SINCE TOURNAMENT RULES PROHIBIT THE LOSER OF A SEMIFINAL FROM CONTINUING...
MURMUR... MURMUR...
...THE SCHEDULED SECOND SEMIFINAL IS NOW...
...THE FINAL MATCH!
!

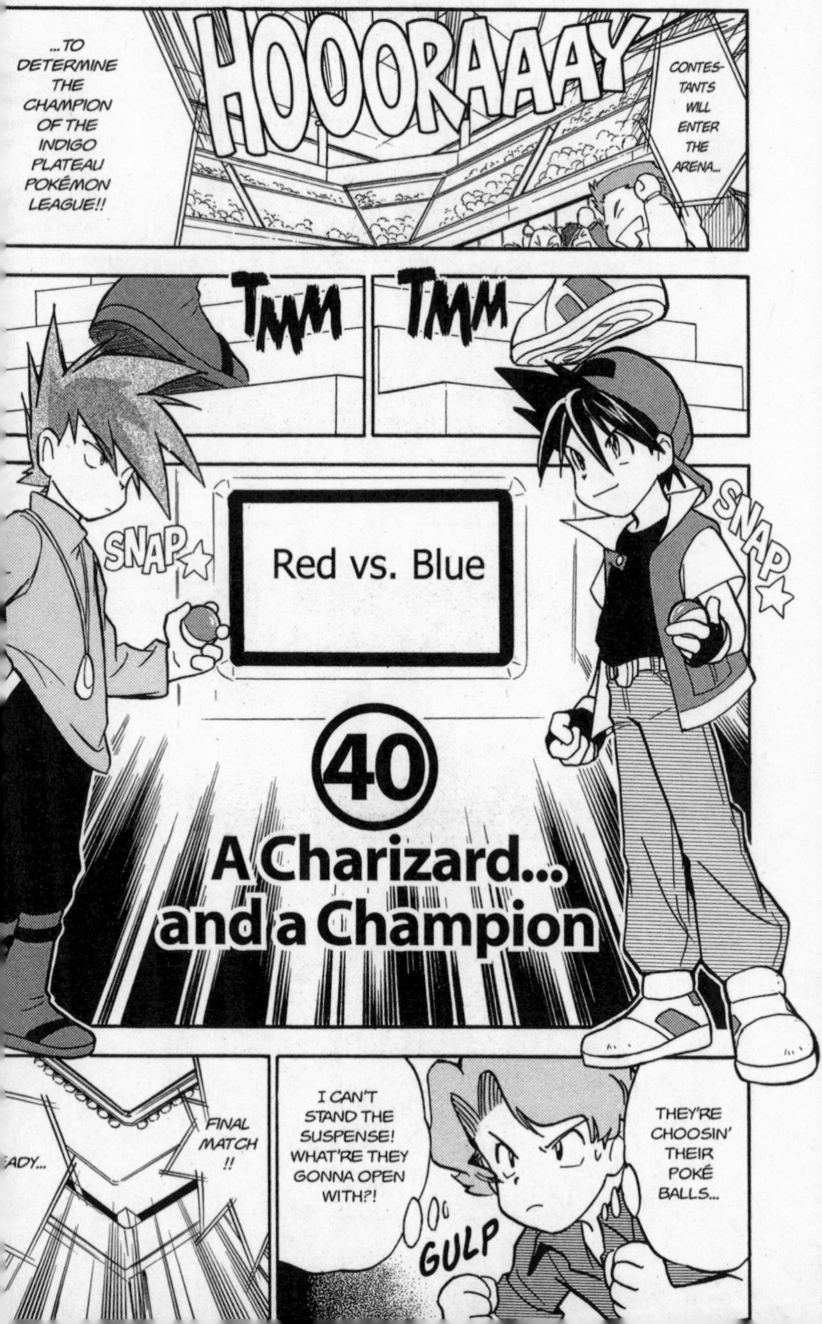

CONTESTANTS WILL ENTER THE ARENA...
HOOORAAAY
...TO DETERMINE THE CHAMPION OF THE INDIGO PLATEAU POKÉMON LEAGUE!!
TMM
TMM
SNAP
Red vs. Blue
40
A Charizard... and a Champion
SNAP
THEY'RE CHOOSIN' THEIR POKÉ BALLS...
I CAN'T STAND THE SUSPENSE! WHAT'RE THEY GONNA OPEN WITH?!
GULP
FINAL MATCH !!
ADY...

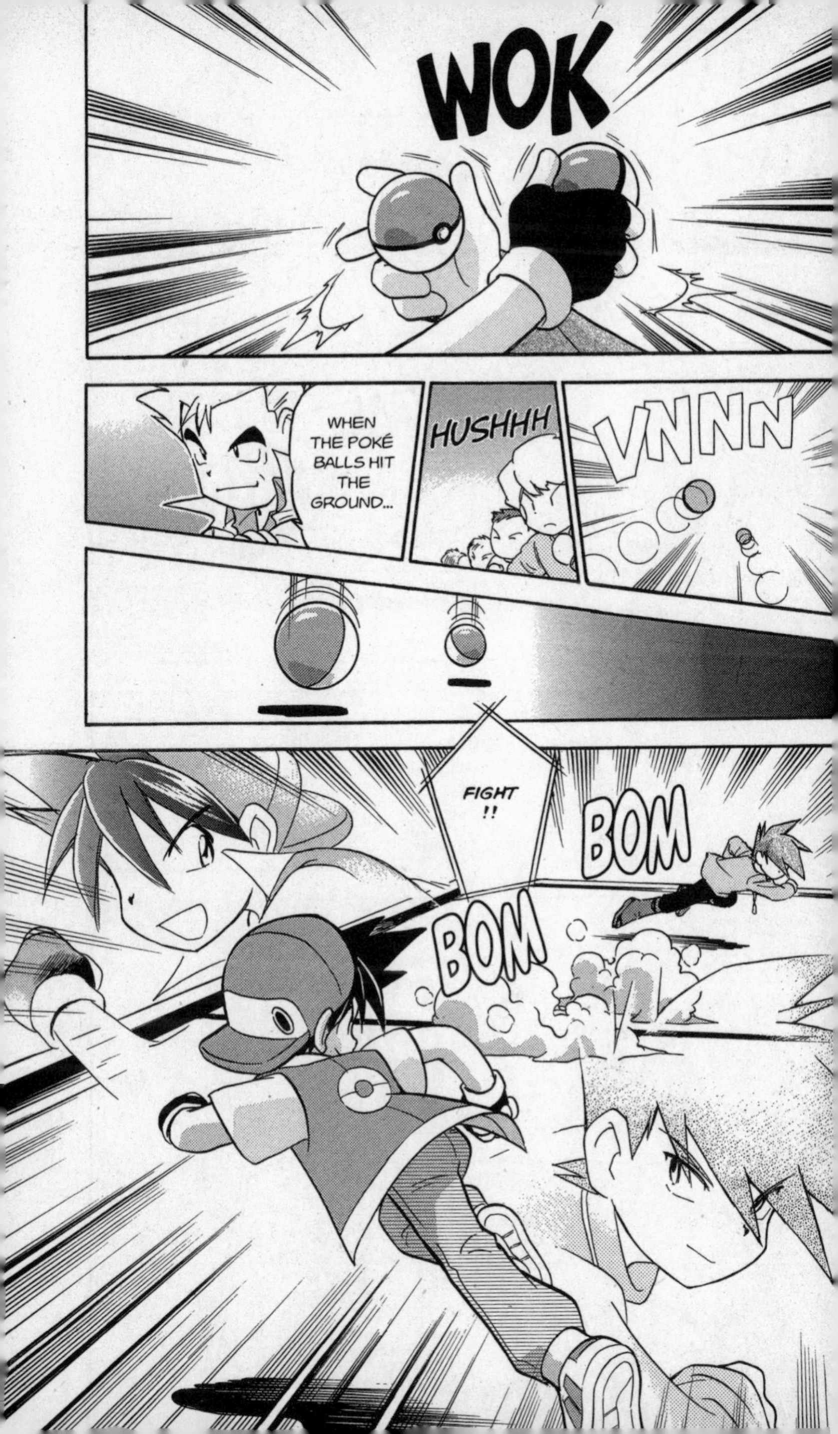
WOK
VNNN
HUSHHH
WHEN THE POKÉ BALLS HIT THE GROUND...
FIGHT !!
BOM
BOM

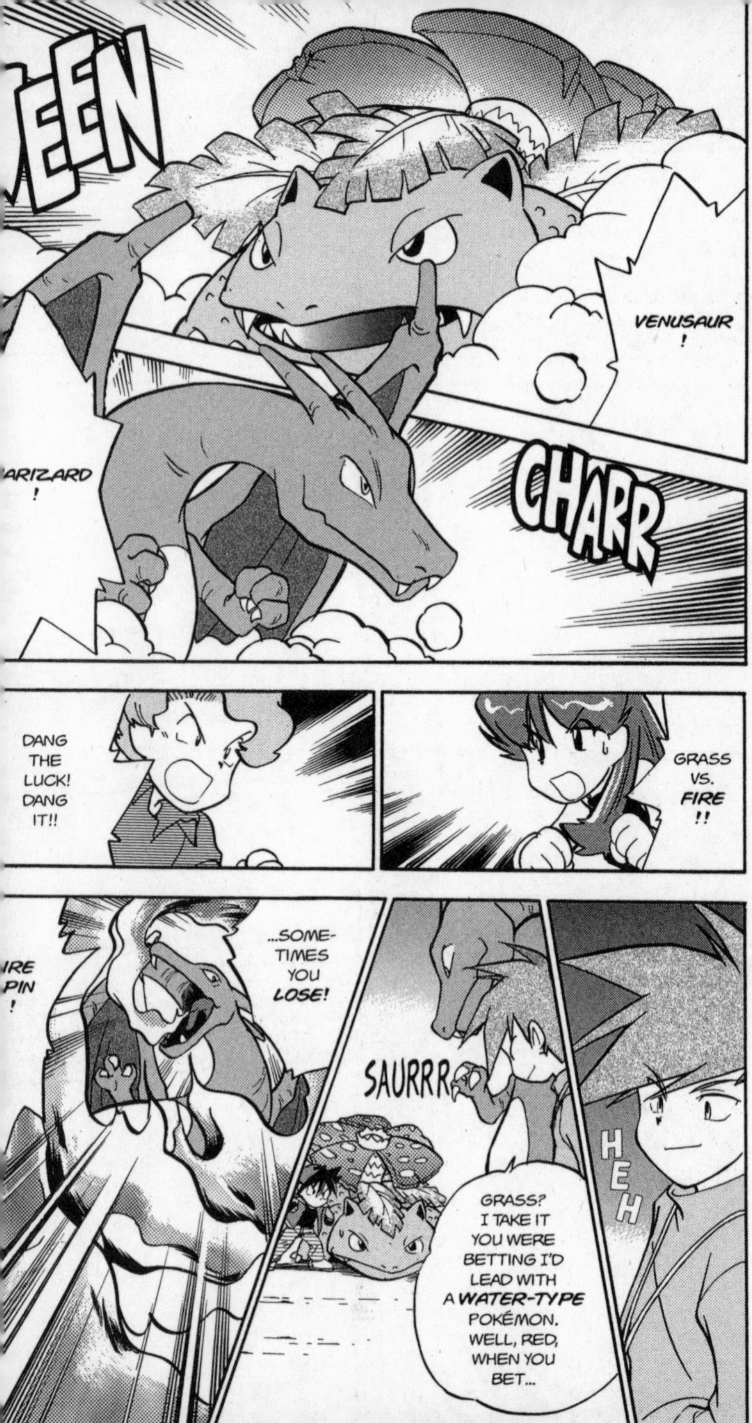
VENUSAUR !
EEN
CHARR
ARIZARD !
GRASS VS. FIRE !!
DANG THE LUCK! DANG IT!!
HEH
GRASS? I TAKE IT YOU WERE BETTING I'D LEAD WITH A WATER-TYPE POKÉMON. WELL, RED, WHEN YOU BET...
SAURRR
...SOME-TIMES YOU LOSE!
IRE PIN !

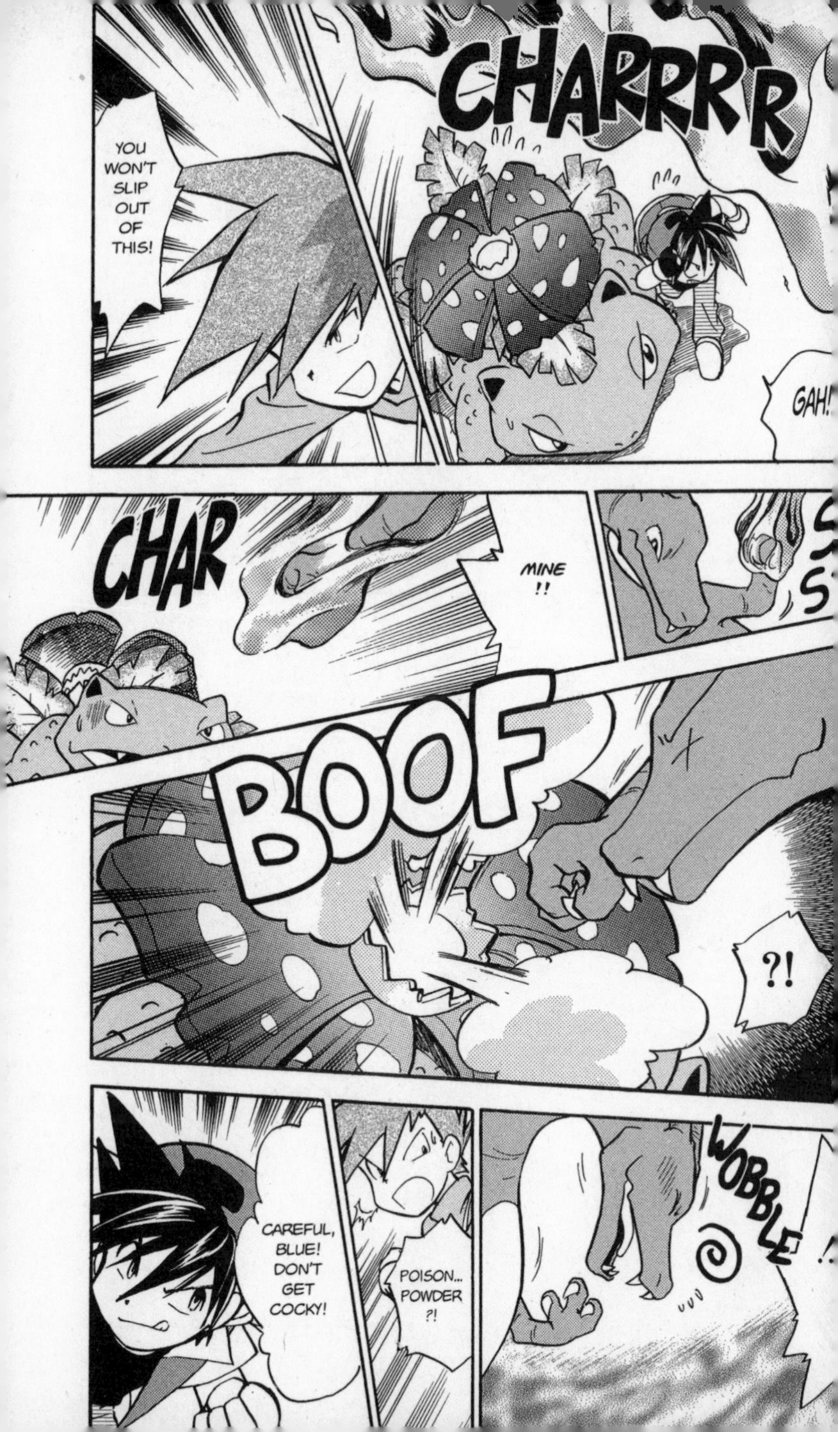
CHARRRR
GAH!
YOU WON'T SLIP OUT OF THIS!
MINE !!
CHAR
BOOF
?!
WOBBLE !
POISON... POWDER ?!
CAREFUL, BLUE! DON'T GET COCKY!

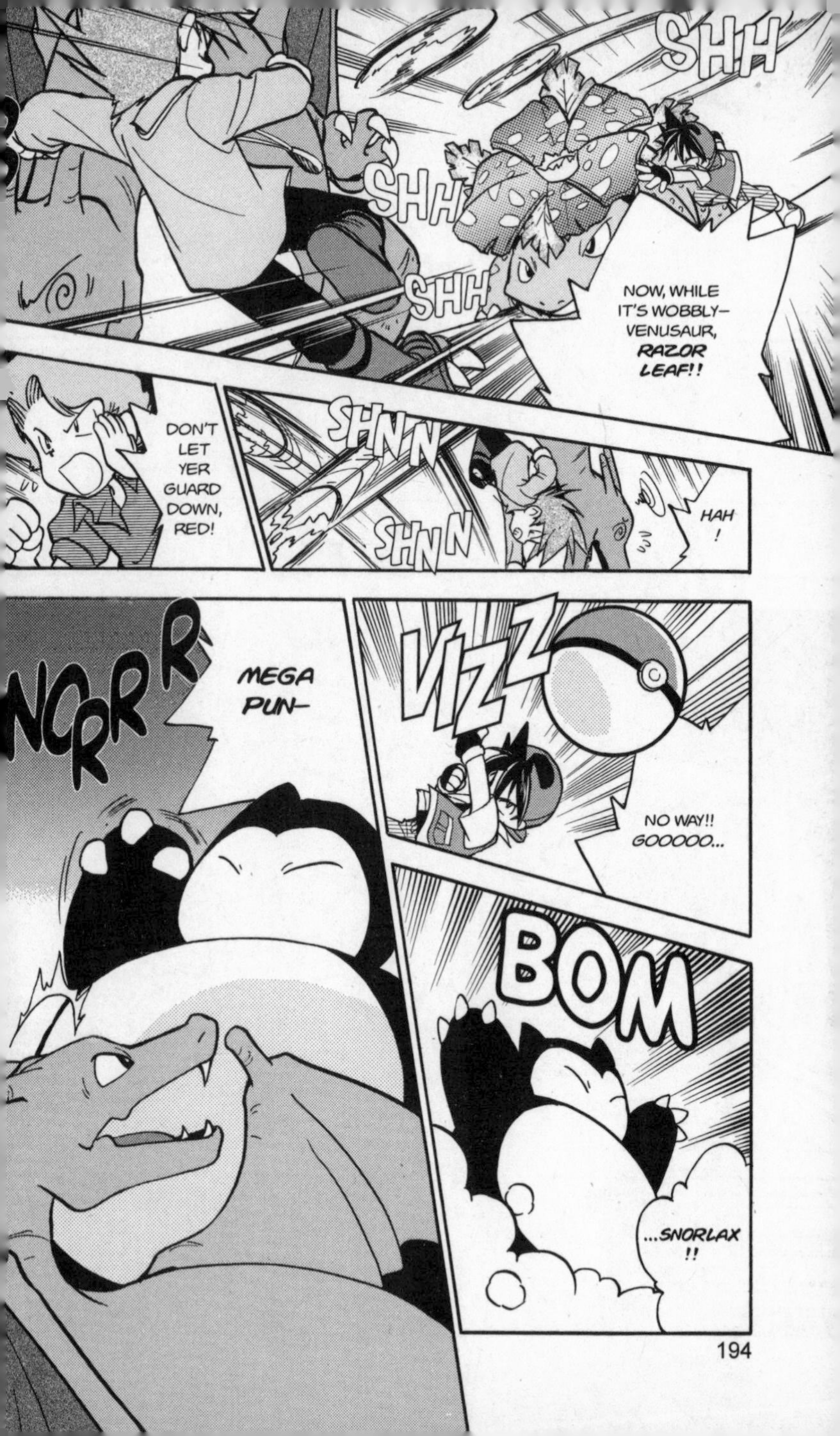
SHH
SHH
SHH
NOW, WHILE IT'S WOBBLY—VENUSAUR, RAZOR LEAF!!
SHNN
SHNN
HAH!
DON'T LET YER GUARD DOWN, RED!
VIZZ
NO WAY!! GOOOOO...
BOM
...SNORLAX!!
NCRRR
MEGA PUN—

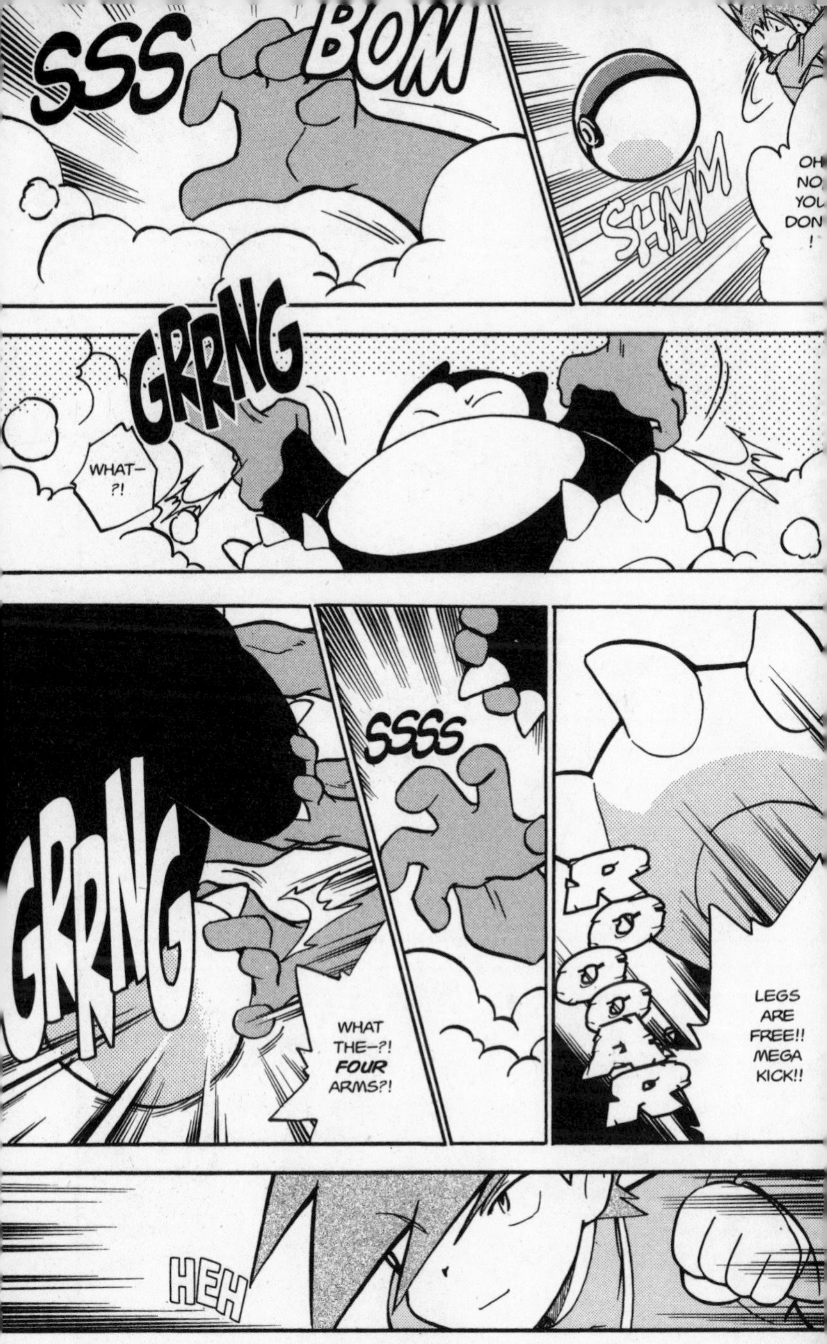
SHMM
OH NO YOU DON !
SSS
BOM
GRRNG
WHAT—?!
ROOOAR
LEGS ARE FREE!! MEGA KICK!!
SSSS
WHAT THE—?! ***FOUR*** ARMS?!
GRRNG
HEH

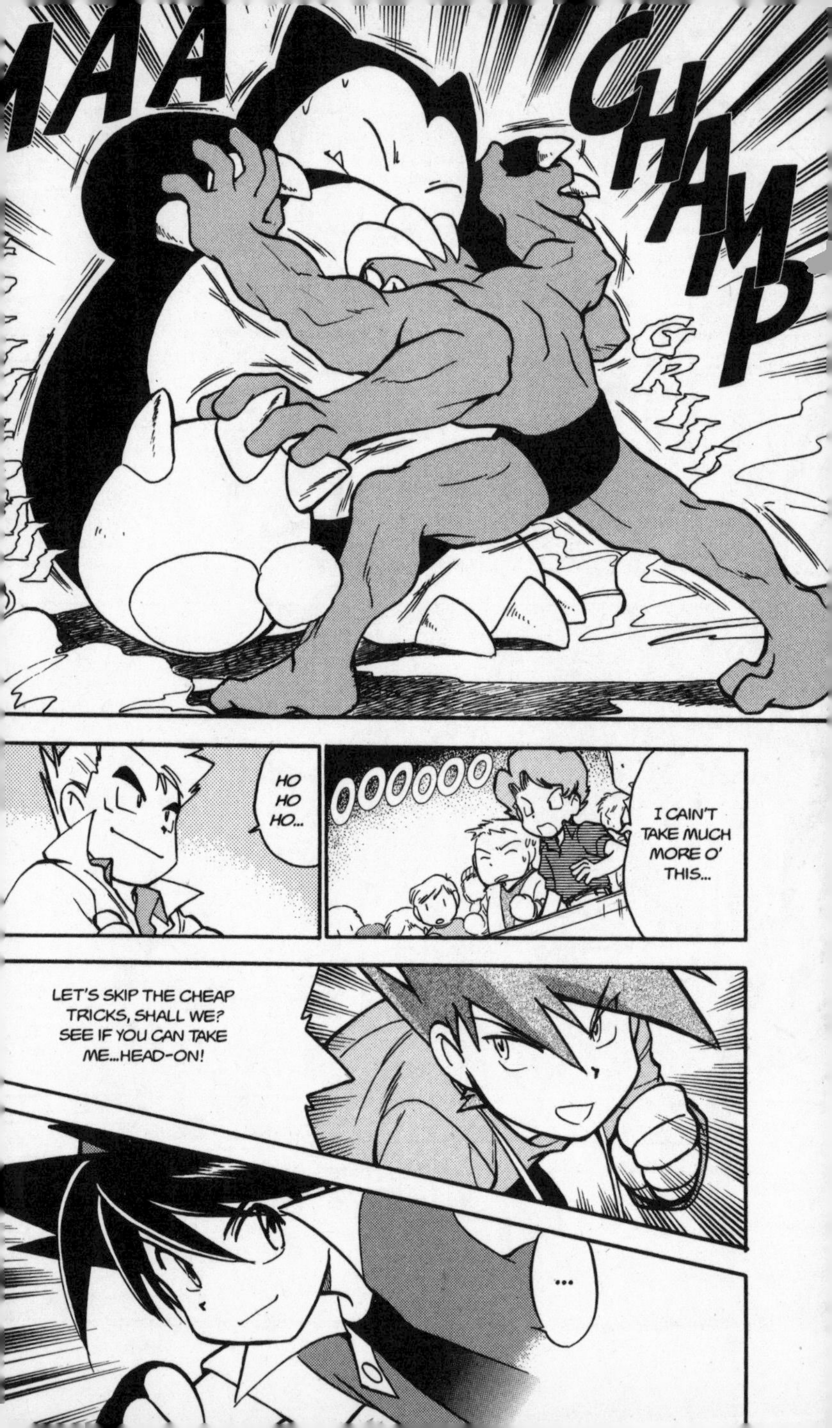
CHAMP
GRIII
AAA
I CAIN'T TAKE MUCH MORE O' THIS...
OOOOOOO
HO HO HO...
LET'S SKIP THE CHEAP TRICKS, SHALL WE? SEE IF YOU CAN TAKE ME...HEAD-ON!
...

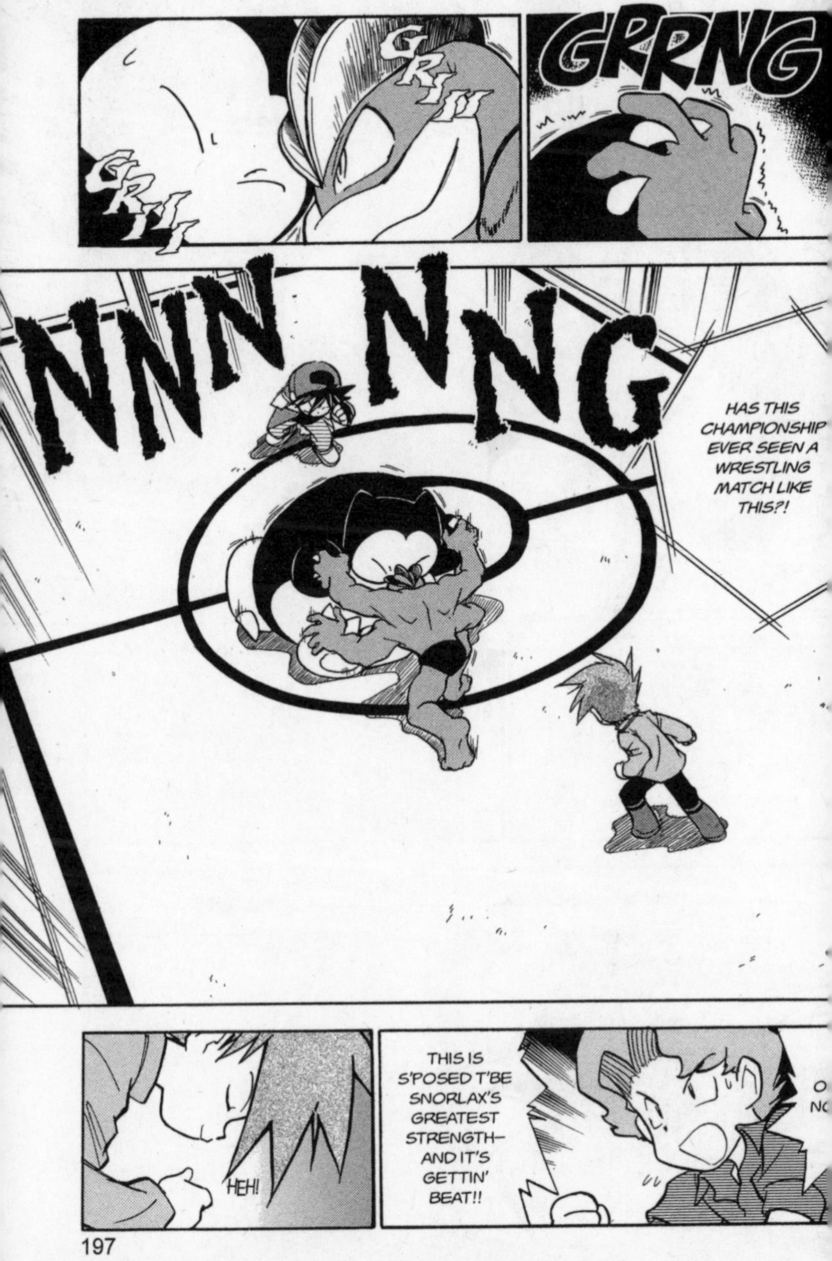
GRRNG
GRI
GRI
NNN NNNG
HAS THIS CHAMPIONSHIP EVER SEEN A WRESTLING MATCH LIKE THIS?!
THIS IS S'POSED T'BE SNORLAX'S GREATEST STRENGTH— AND IT'S GETTIN' BEAT!!
HEH!

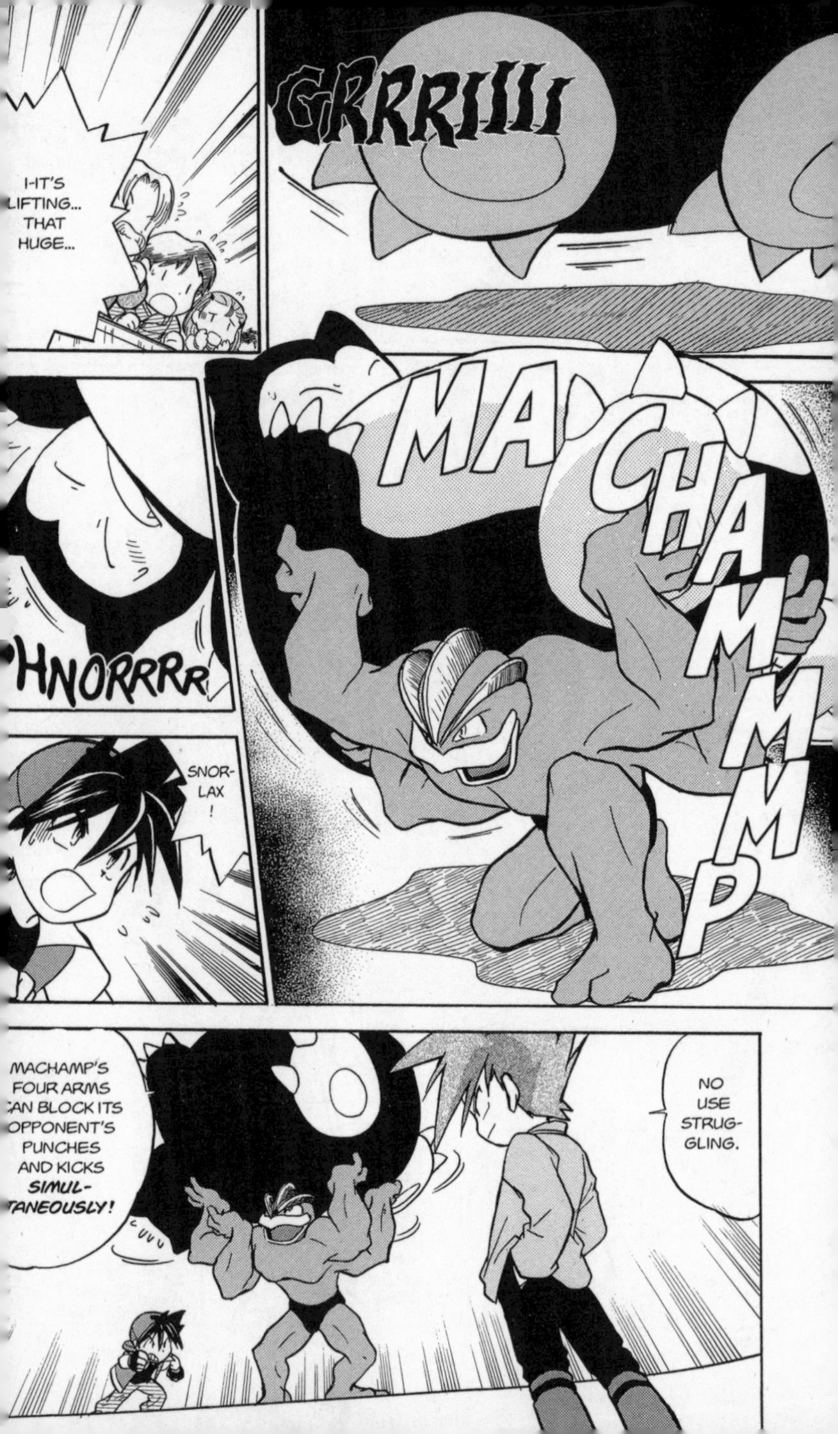
GRRRIIII
I-IT'S LIFTING... THAT HUGE...
MACHAMMMP
HNORRRR
SNOR-LAX!
NO USE STRUG-GLING.
MACHAMP'S FOUR ARMS CAN BLOCK ITS OPPONENT'S PUNCHES AND KICKS **SIMUL-TANEOUSLY!**

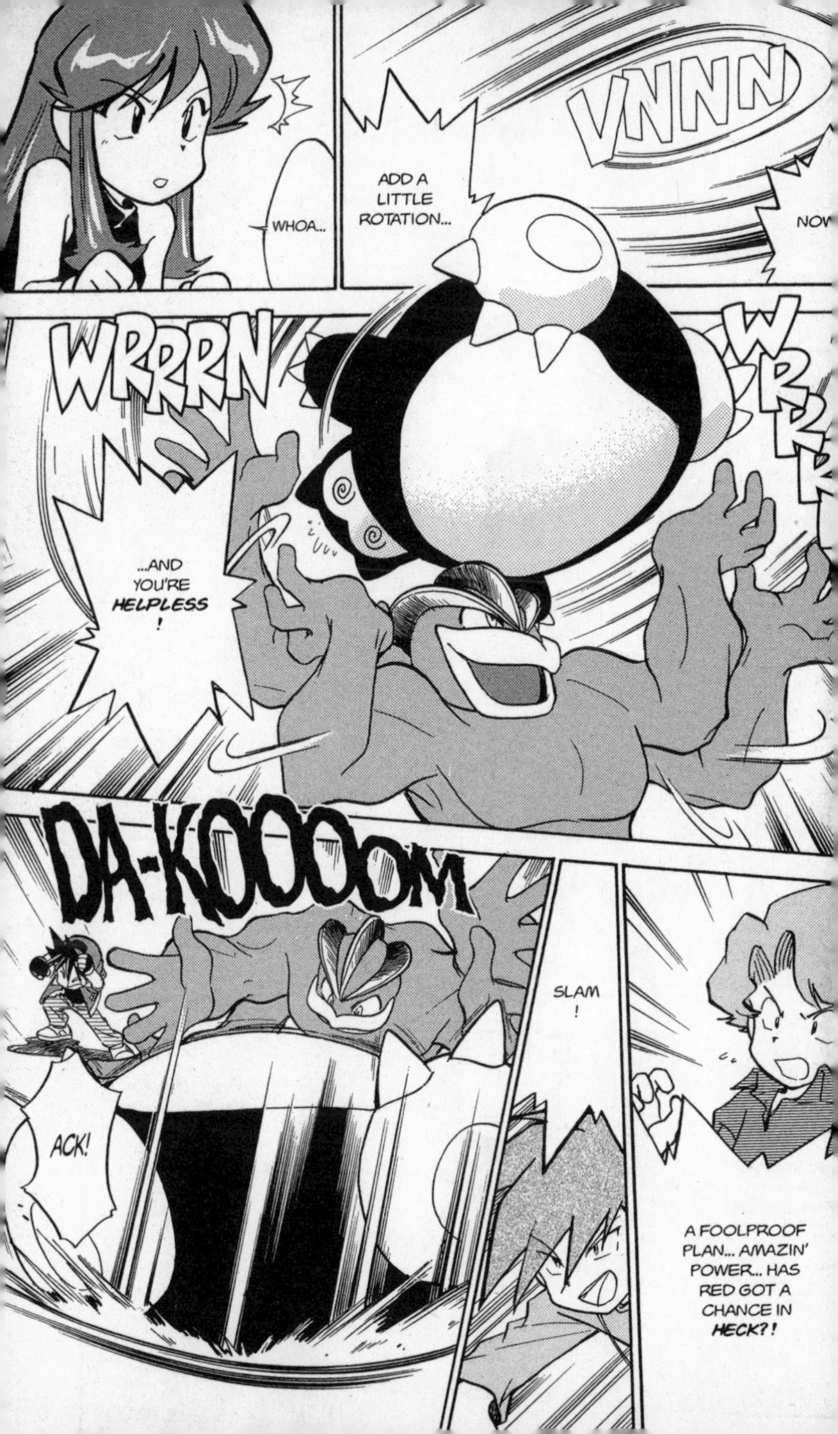
VNNN
ADD A LITTLE ROTATION...
NOW
WHOA...
WRRR
WRRRN
...AND YOU'RE HELPLESS!
SLAM!
A FOOLPROOF PLAN... AMAZIN' POWER... HAS RED GOT A CHANCE IN HECK?!
DA-KOOOOM
ACK!

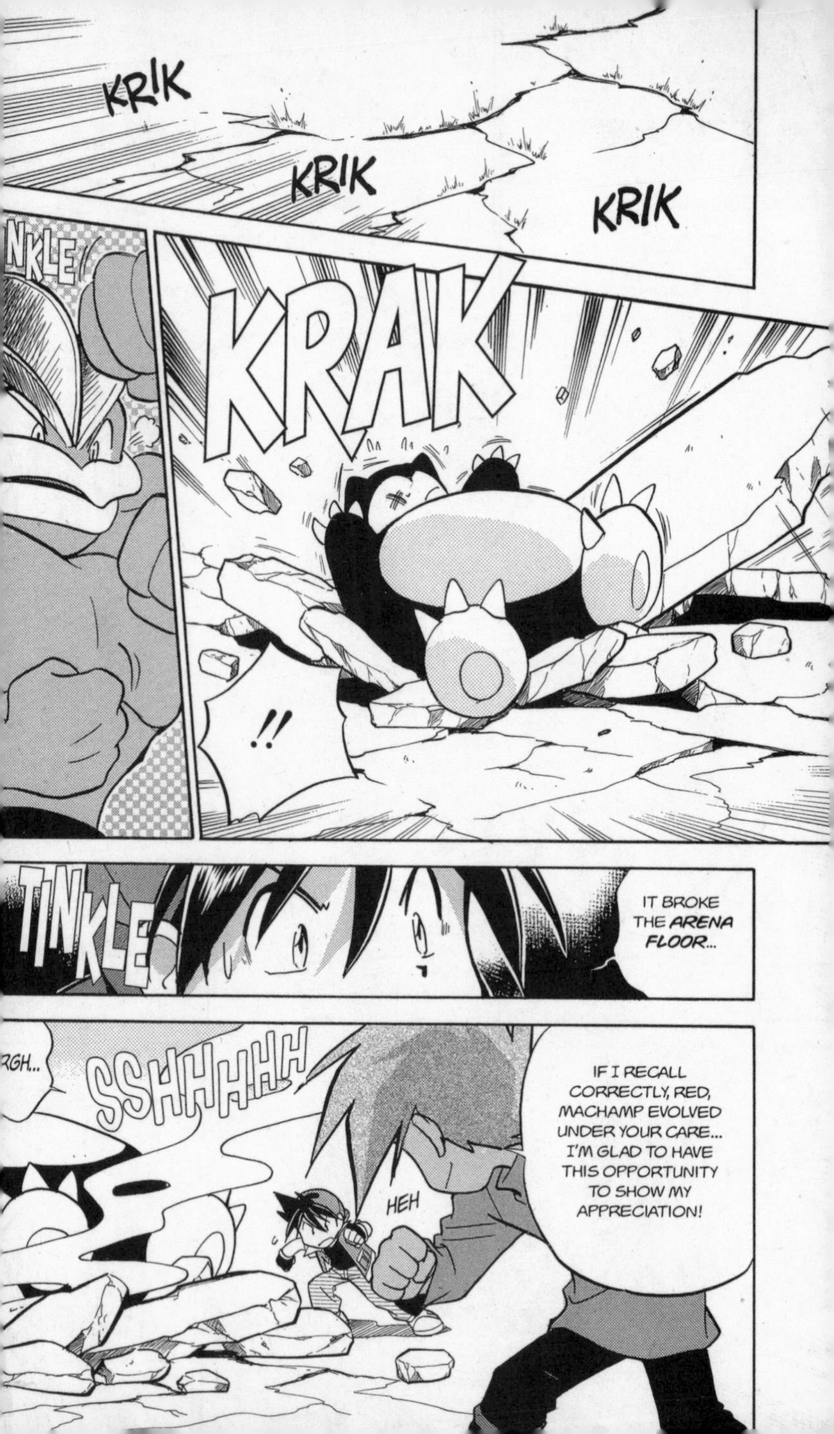
KRIK
KRIK
KRIK
KRAK
!!
NKLE
IT BROKE THE ARENA FLOOR...
TINKLE
IF I RECALL CORRECTLY, RED, MACHAMP EVOLVED UNDER YOUR CARE... I'M GLAD TO HAVE THIS OPPORTUNITY TO SHOW MY APPRECIATION!
HEH
SSHHHHHH
RGH...

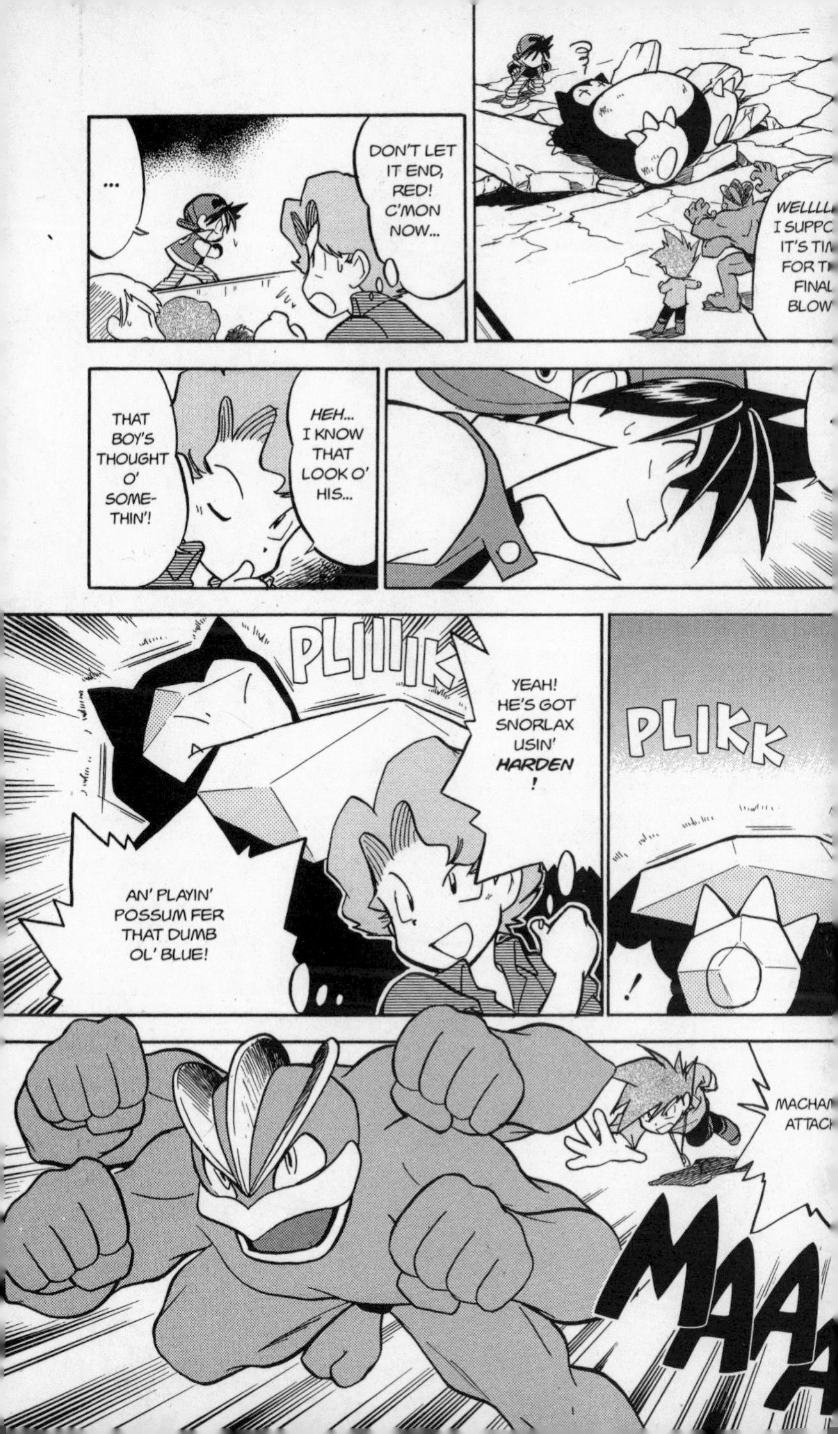
WELLLL I SUPPO IT'S TIM FOR TH FINAL BLOW
DON'T LET IT END, RED! C'MON NOW...
...
HEH... I KNOW THAT LOOK O' HIS...
THAT BOY'S THOUGHT O' SOME-THIN'!
PLIKK
!
PLIIIIK
YEAH! HE'S GOT SNORLAX USIN' HARDEN!
AN' PLAYIN' POSSUM FER THAT DUMB OL' BLUE!
MACHAM ATTAC
MAAA

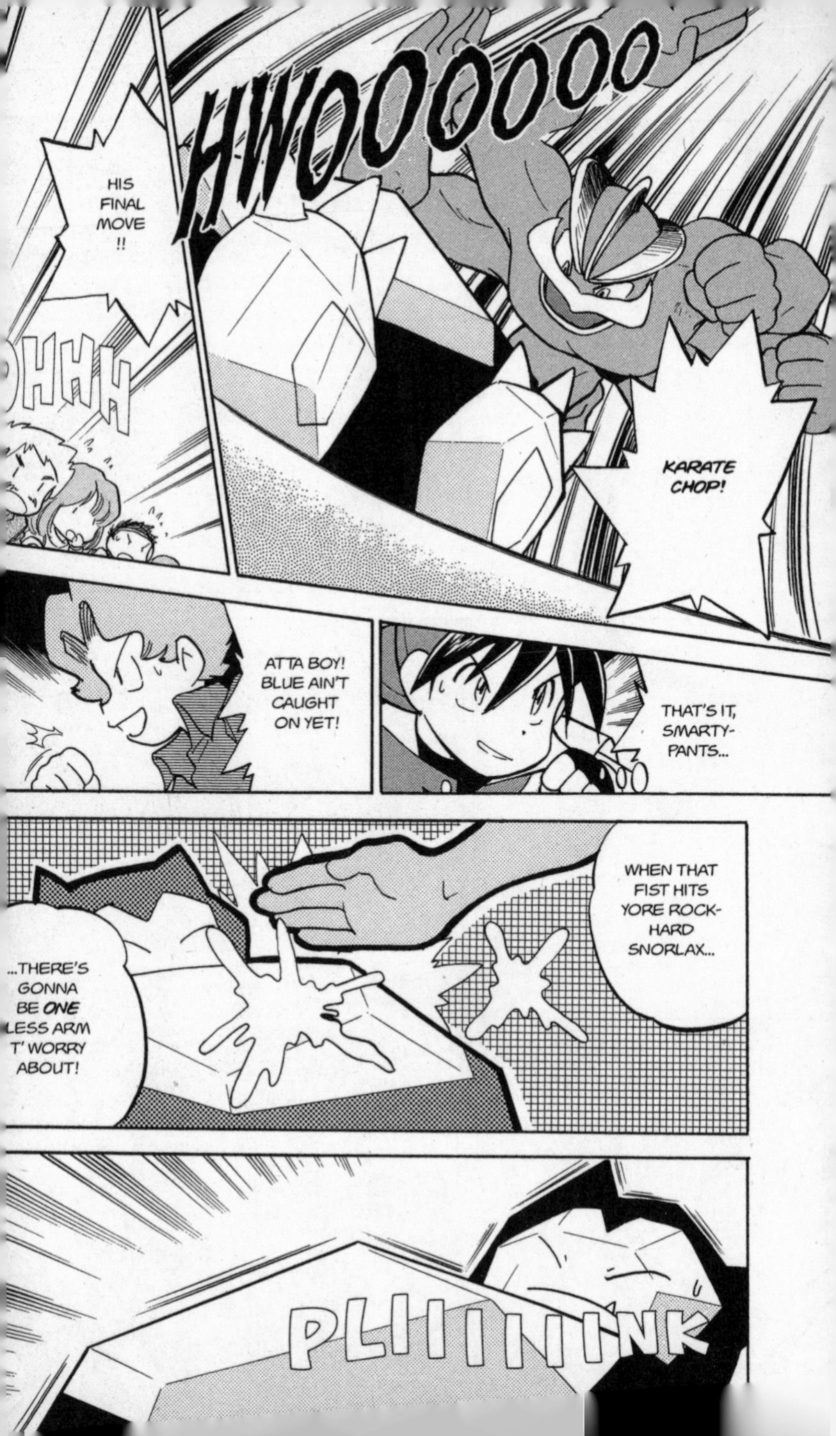
HWOOOOOO
KARATE CHOP!
HIS FINAL MOVE !!
OHHHH
THAT'S IT, SMARTY-PANTS...
ATTA BOY! BLUE AIN'T CAUGHT ON YET!
WHEN THAT FIST HITS YORE ROCK-HARD SNORLAX...
...THERE'S GONNA BE ONE LESS ARM T' WORRY ABOUT!
PLIIIIIINK

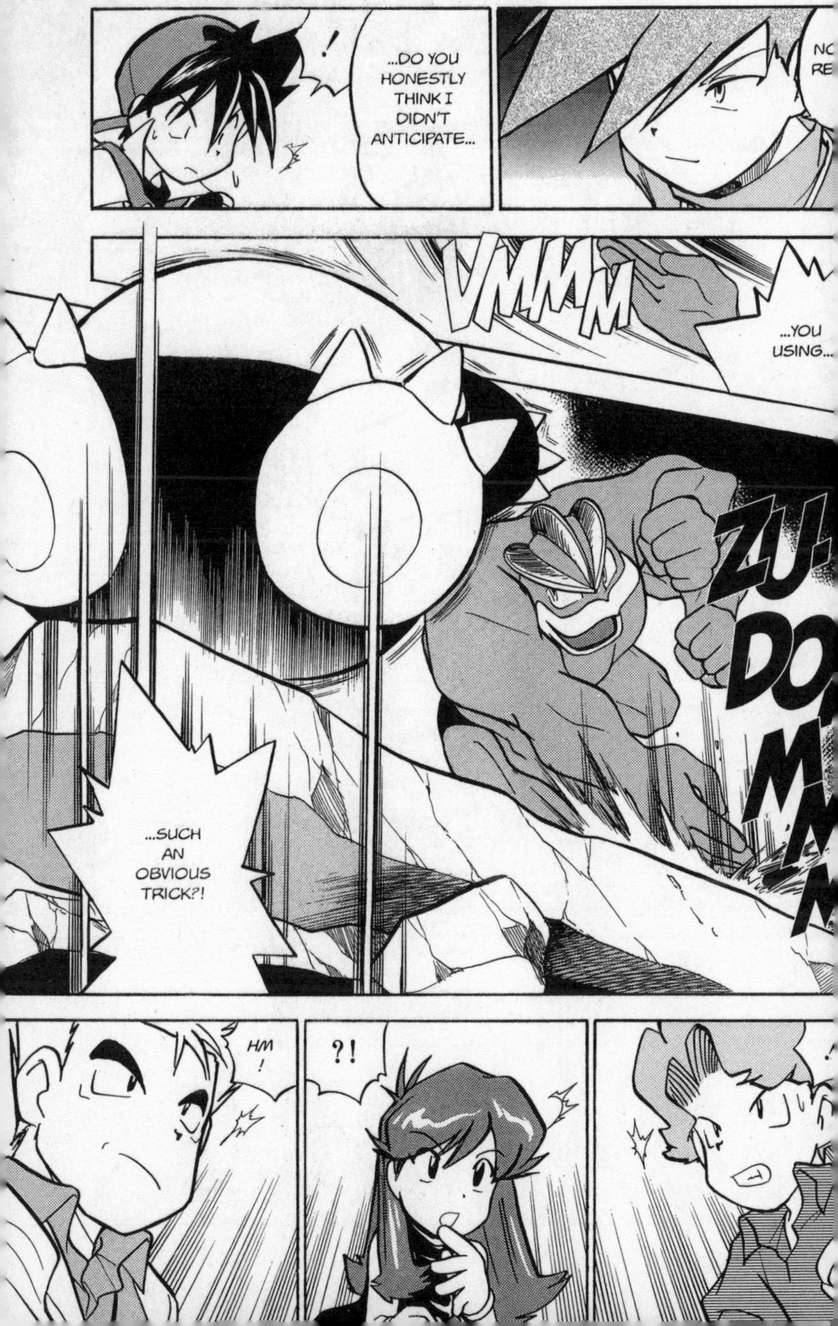
!
...DO YOU HONESTLY THINK I DIDN'T ANTICIPATE...
VMMM
...YOU USING...
...SUCH AN OBVIOUS TRICK?!
?!
HM!

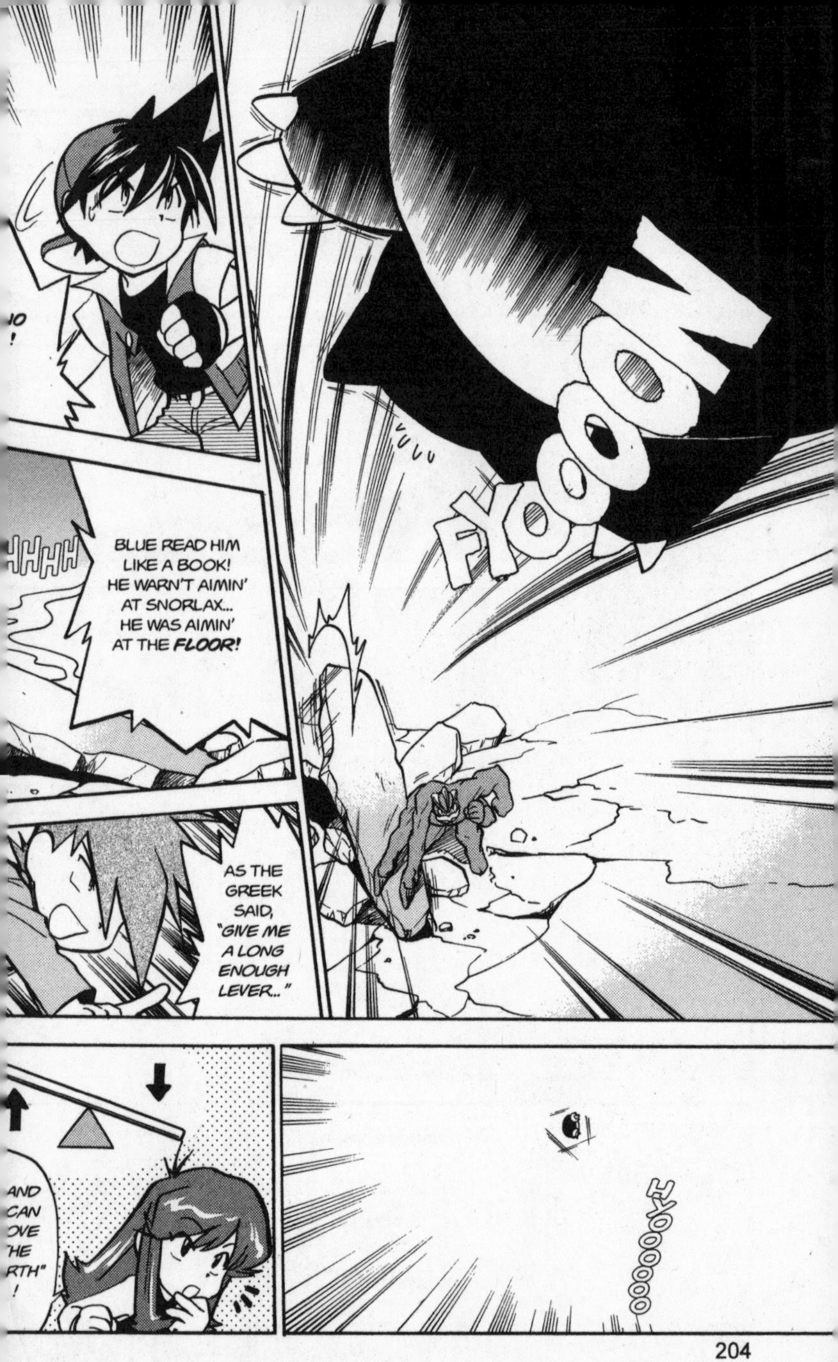
FYOOOOM
O !
HHHH
BLUE READ HIM LIKE A BOOK! HE WARN'T AIMIN' AT SNORLAX... HE WAS AIMIN' AT THE ***FLOOR!***
AS THE GREEK SAID, *"GIVE ME A LONG ENOUGH LEVER..."*
HYOOOOOOO
AND CAN OVE THE RTH" !

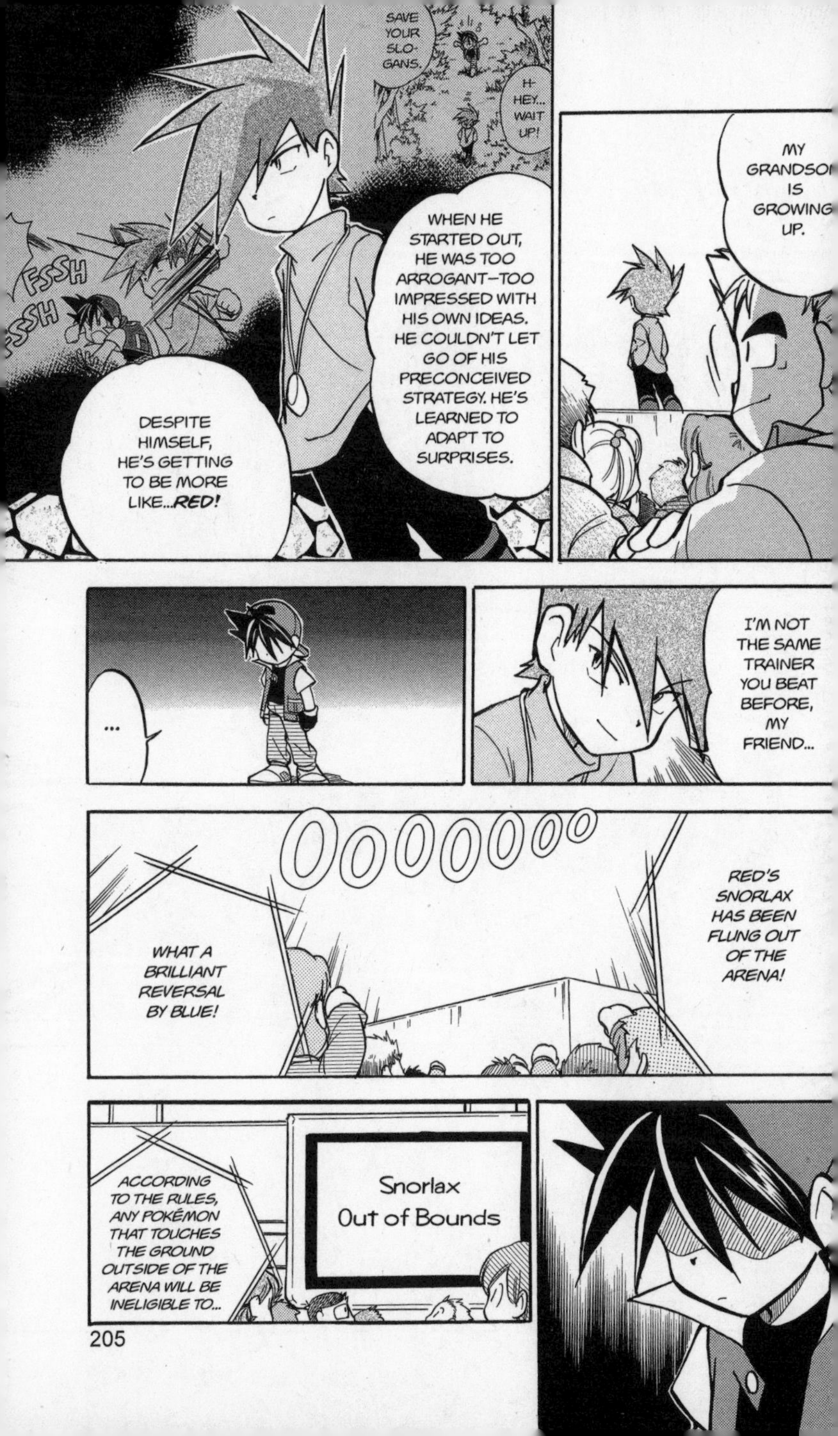
MY GRANDSON IS GROWING UP.
SAVE YOUR SLOGANS.
H-HEY... WAIT UP!
WHEN HE STARTED OUT, HE WAS TOO ARROGANT—TOO IMPRESSED WITH HIS OWN IDEAS. HE COULDN'T LET GO OF HIS PRECONCEIVED STRATEGY. HE'S LEARNED TO ADAPT TO SURPRISES.
FSSH
FSSH
DESPITE HIMSELF, HE'S GETTING TO BE MORE LIKE...RED!
I'M NOT THE SAME TRAINER YOU BEAT BEFORE, MY FRIEND...
...
OOOOOOO
RED'S SNORLAX HAS BEEN FLUNG OUT OF THE ARENA!
WHAT A BRILLIANT REVERSAL BY BLUE!
Snorlax Out of Bounds
ACCORDING TO THE RULES, ANY POKÉMON THAT TOUCHES THE GROUND OUTSIDE OF THE ARENA WILL BE INELIGIBLE TO...

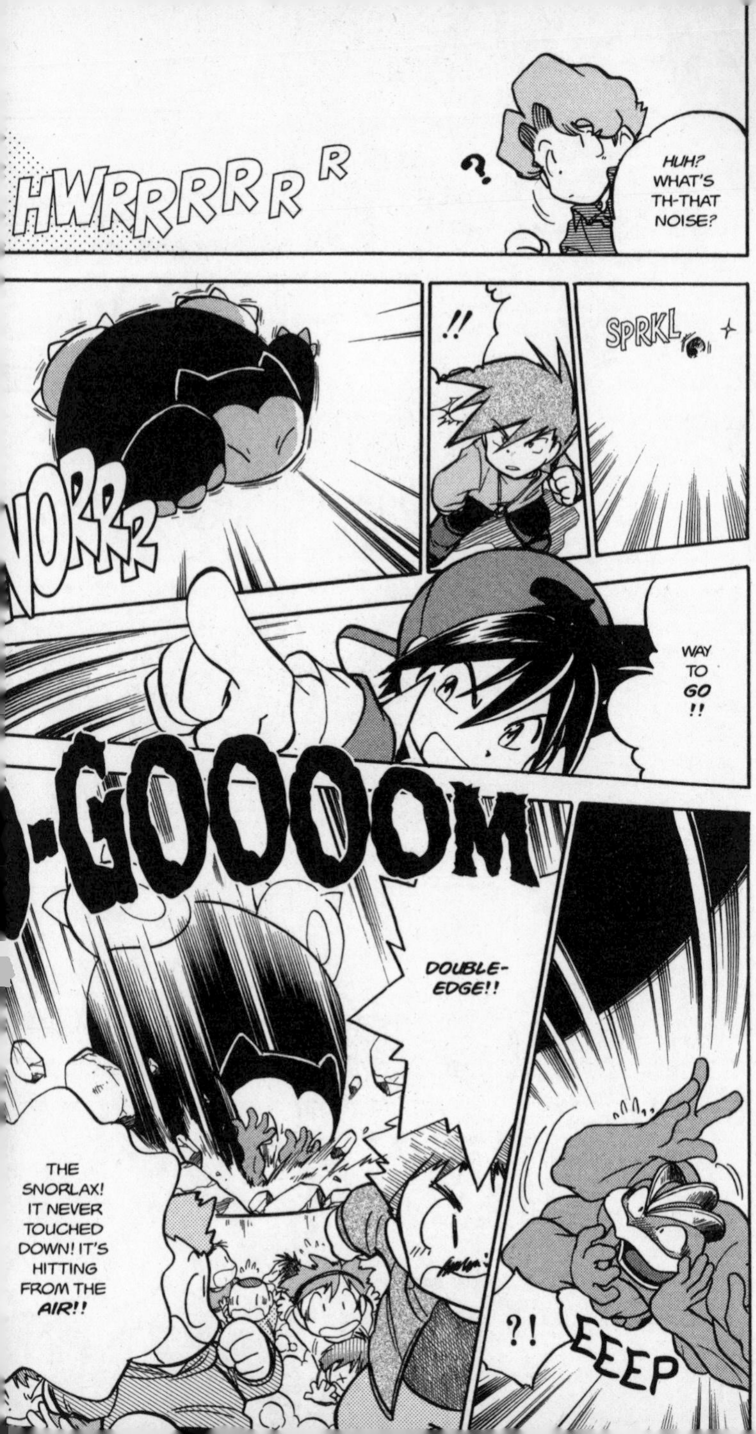
HUH? WHAT'S TH-THAT NOISE?
?
HWRRRRR R
SPRKL
!!
NORRRR
WAY TO GO!!
?!
EEEP
-GOOOOM
DOUBLE-EDGE!!
THE SNORLAX! IT NEVER TOUCHED DOWN! IT'S HITTING FROM THE AIR!!

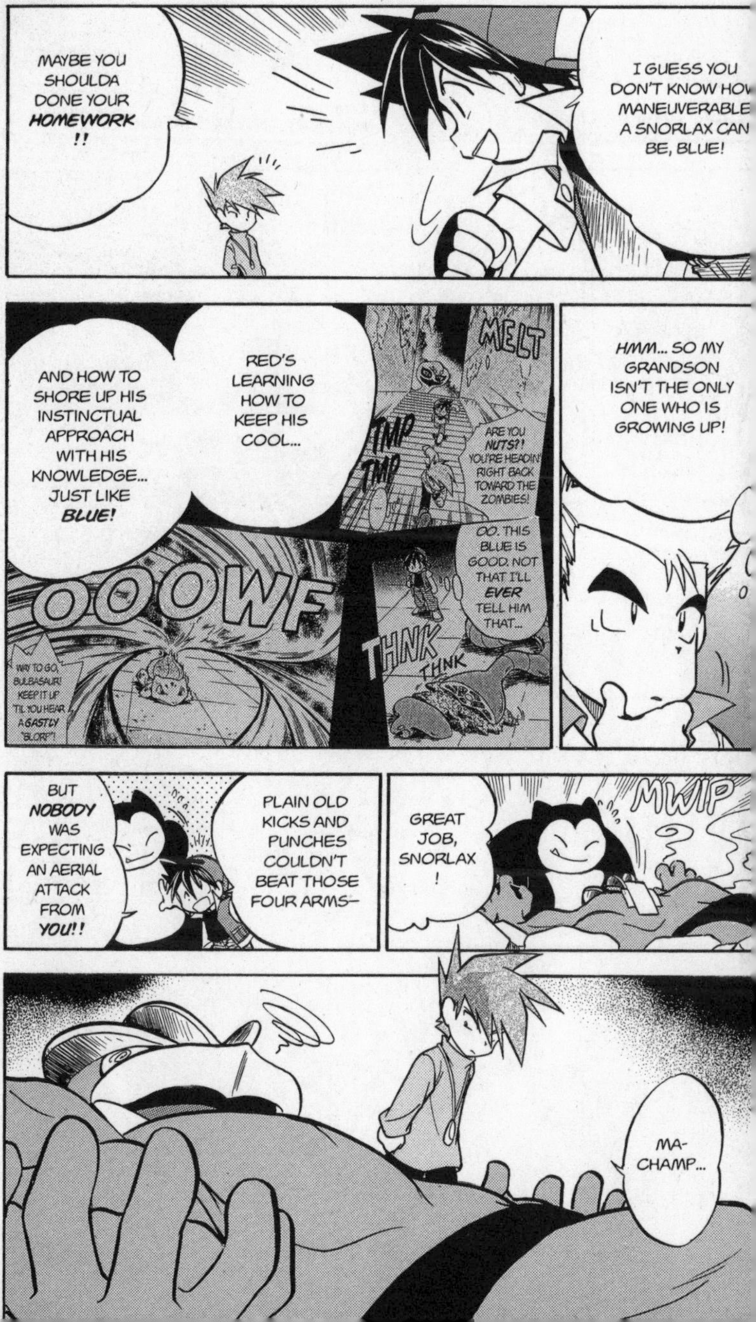
I GUESS YOU DON'T KNOW HO MANEUVERABLE A SNORLAX CAN BE, BLUE!
MAYBE YOU SHOULDA DONE YOUR **HOMEWORK**!!
HMM... SO MY GRANDSON ISN'T THE ONLY ONE WHO IS GROWING UP!
RED'S LEARNING HOW TO KEEP HIS COOL...
AND HOW TO SHORE UP HIS INSTINCTUAL APPROACH WITH HIS KNOWLEDGE... JUST LIKE **BLUE!**
MELT
TMP TMP
ARE YOU **NUTS?!** YOU'RE HEADIN' RIGHT BACK TOWARD THE ZOMBIES!
OO. THIS BLUE IS GOOD. NOT THAT I'LL **EVER** TELL HIM THAT...
THNK
THNK
OOOWF
WAY TO GO, BULBASAUR! KEEP IT UP 'TIL YOU HEAR A GASTLY "BLORF"!
MWIP
GREAT JOB, SNORLAX!
PLAIN OLD KICKS AND PUNCHES COULDN'T BEAT THOSE FOUR ARMS—
BUT **NOBODY** WAS EXPECTING AN AERIAL ATTACK FROM **YOU!!**
MA-CHAMP...

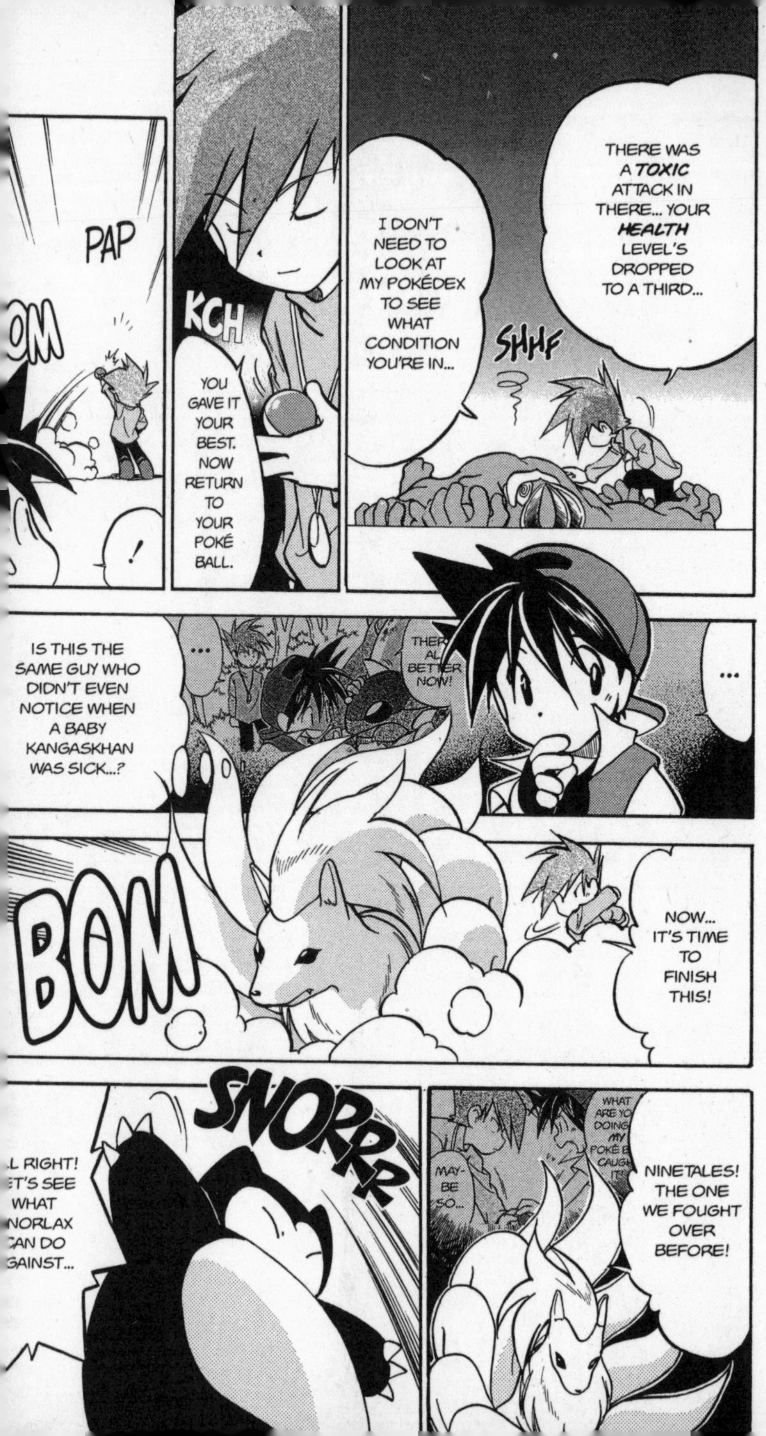
THERE WAS A TOXIC ATTACK IN THERE... YOUR HEALTH LEVEL'S DROPPED TO A THIRD...
SHHF
I DON'T NEED TO LOOK AT MY POKÉDEX TO SEE WHAT CONDITION YOU'RE IN...
KCH
YOU GAVE IT YOUR BEST. NOW RETURN TO YOUR POKÉ BALL.
PAP
!
...
...
IS THIS THE SAME GUY WHO DIDN'T EVEN NOTICE WHEN A BABY KANGASKHAN WAS SICK...?
NOW... IT'S TIME TO FINISH THIS!
BOM
NINETALES! THE ONE WE FOUGHT OVER BEFORE!
MAY-BE SO...
SNORRR

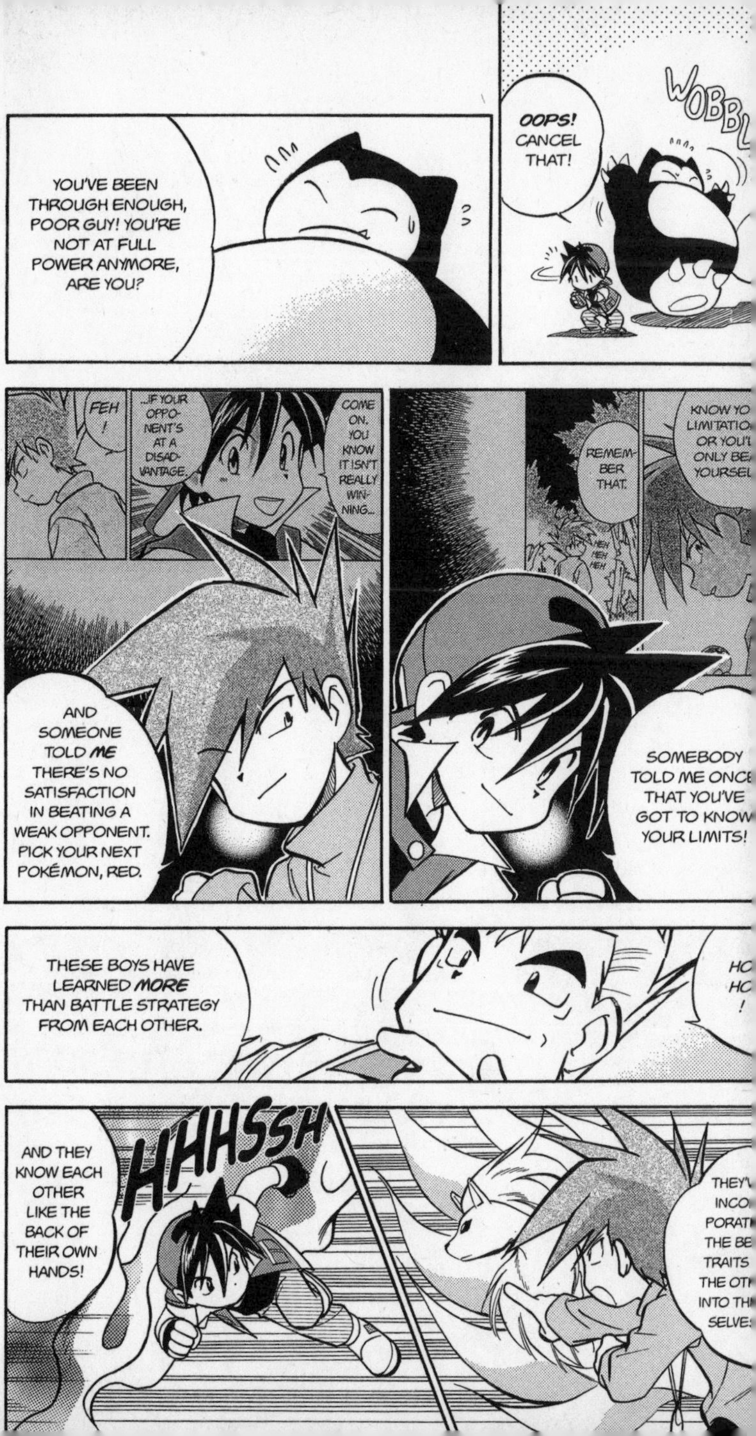

WOBBL
OOPS! CANCEL THAT!
YOU'VE BEEN THROUGH ENOUGH, POOR GUY! YOU'RE NOT AT FULL POWER ANYMORE, ARE YOU?
KNOW YO LIMITATIO OR YOU'L ONLY BE YOURSEL
REMEM-BER THAT.
HEH HEH HEH
SOMEBODY TOLD ME ONCE THAT YOU'VE GOT TO KNOW YOUR LIMITS!
COME ON. YOU KNOW IT ISN'T REALLY WIN-NING...
...IF YOUR OPPO-NENT'S AT A DISAD-VANTAGE.
FEH!
AND SOMEONE TOLD ME THERE'S NO SATISFACTION IN BEATING A WEAK OPPONENT. PICK YOUR NEXT POKÉMON, RED.
HO HO!
THESE BOYS HAVE LEARNED MORE THAN BATTLE STRATEGY FROM EACH OTHER.
THEY' INCO PORAT THE BE TRAITS THE OT INTO TH SELVES
HHHSSH
AND THEY KNOW EACH OTHER LIKE THE BACK OF THEIR OWN HANDS!

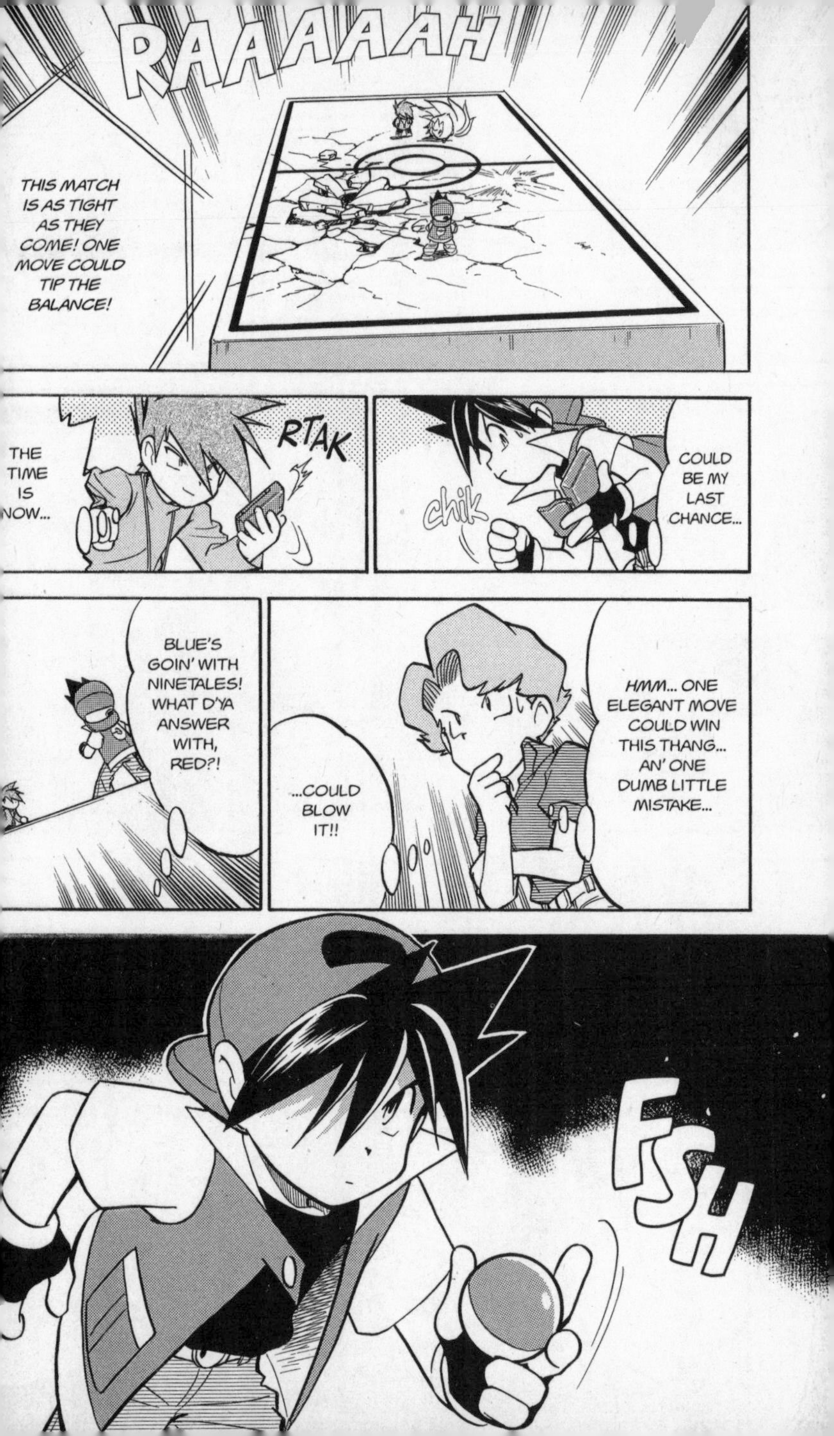
RAAAAAH
THIS MATCH IS AS TIGHT AS THEY COME! ONE MOVE COULD TIP THE BALANCE!
COULD BE MY LAST CHANCE...
chik
RTAK
THE TIME IS NOW...
HMM... ONE ELEGANT MOVE COULD WIN THIS THANG... AN' ONE DUMB LITTLE MISTAKE...
...COULD BLOW IT!!
BLUE'S GOIN' WITH NINETALES! WHAT D'YA ANSWER WITH, RED?!
FSH

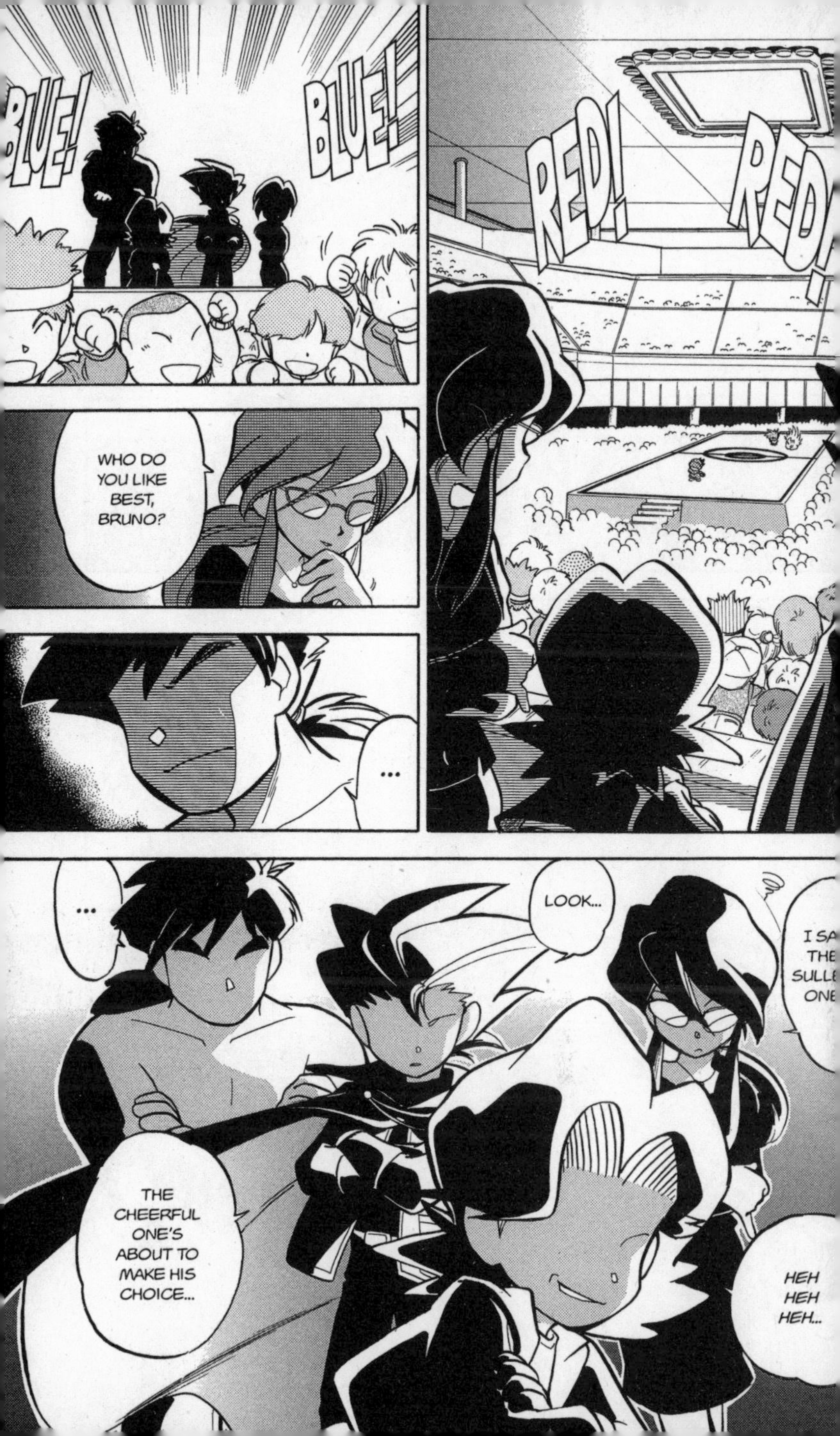
RED! RED!
BLUE! BLUE!
WHO DO YOU LIKE BEST, BRUNO?
...
I SA THE SULLE ONE
LOOK...
...
HEH HEH HEH...
THE CHEERFUL ONE'S ABOUT TO MAKE HIS CHOICE...

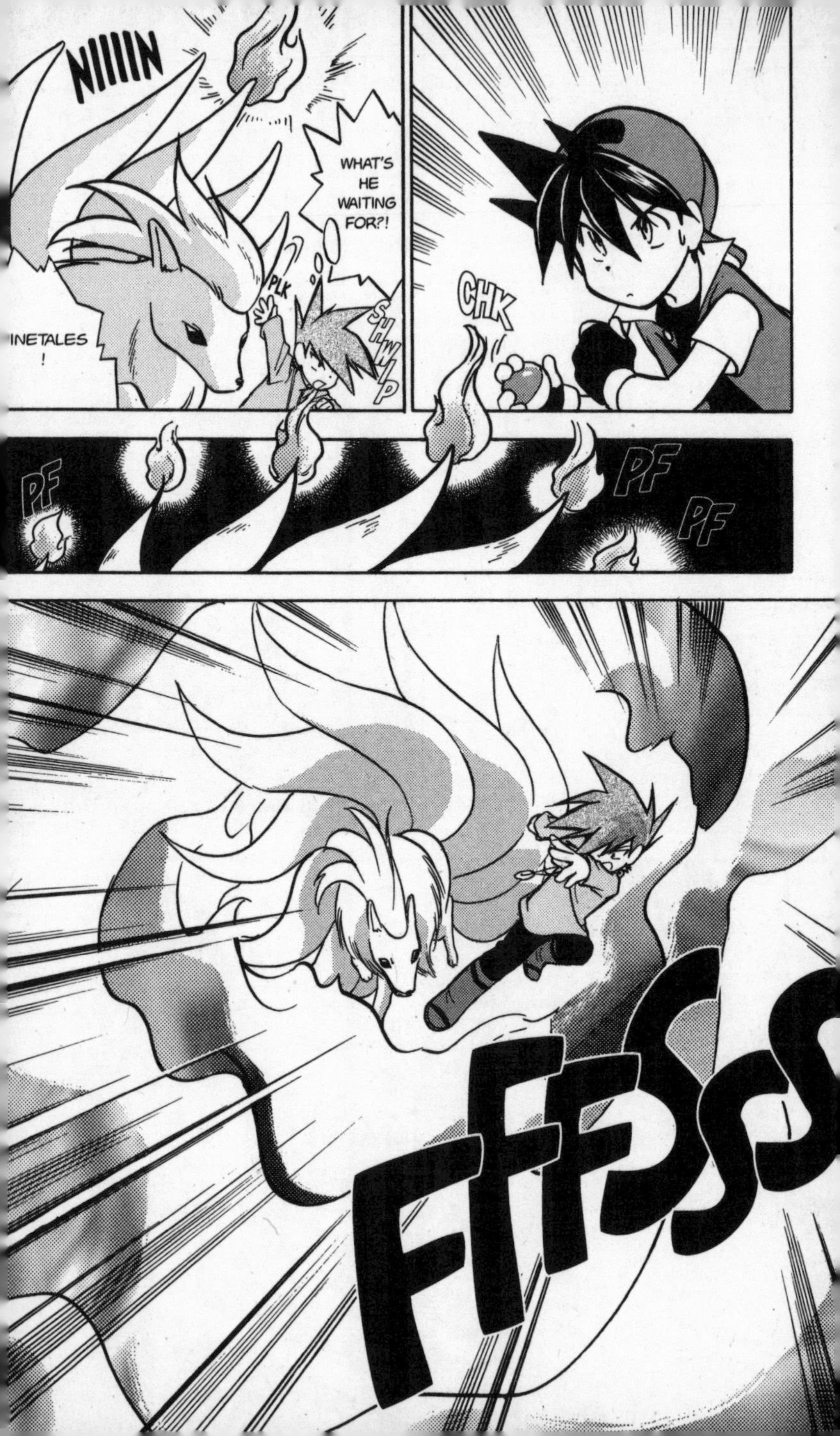
CHK
NIIIN
WHAT'S HE WAITING FOR?!
PLK
SHWIP
INETALES !
PF
PF
PF
FFSSS

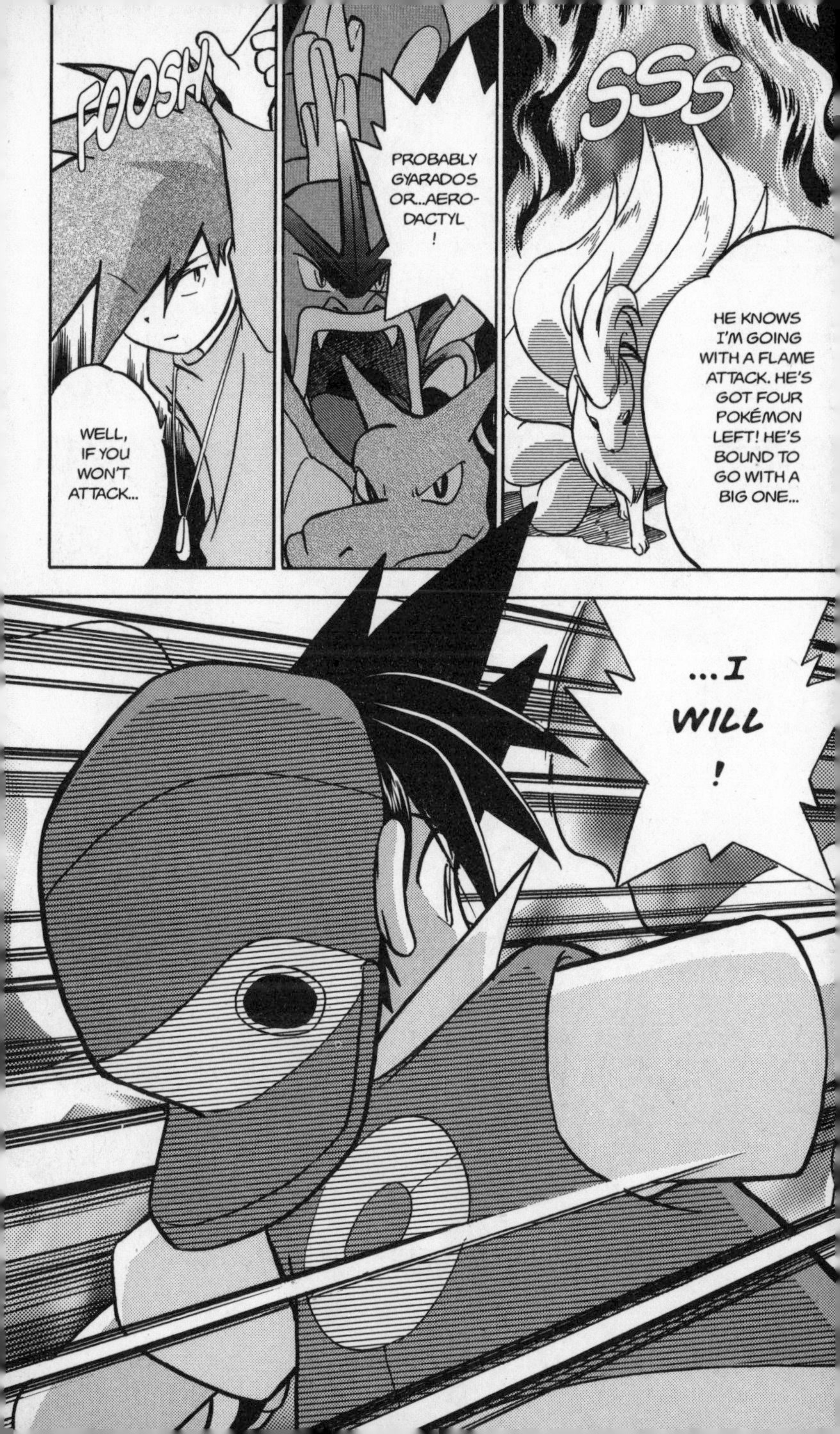
SSS
HE KNOWS I'M GOING WITH A FLAME ATTACK. HE'S GOT FOUR POKÉMON LEFT! HE'S BOUND TO GO WITH A BIG ONE...
PROBABLY GYARADOS OR...AERO-DACTYL !
FOOSH
WELL, IF YOU WON'T ATTACK...
...I WILL !

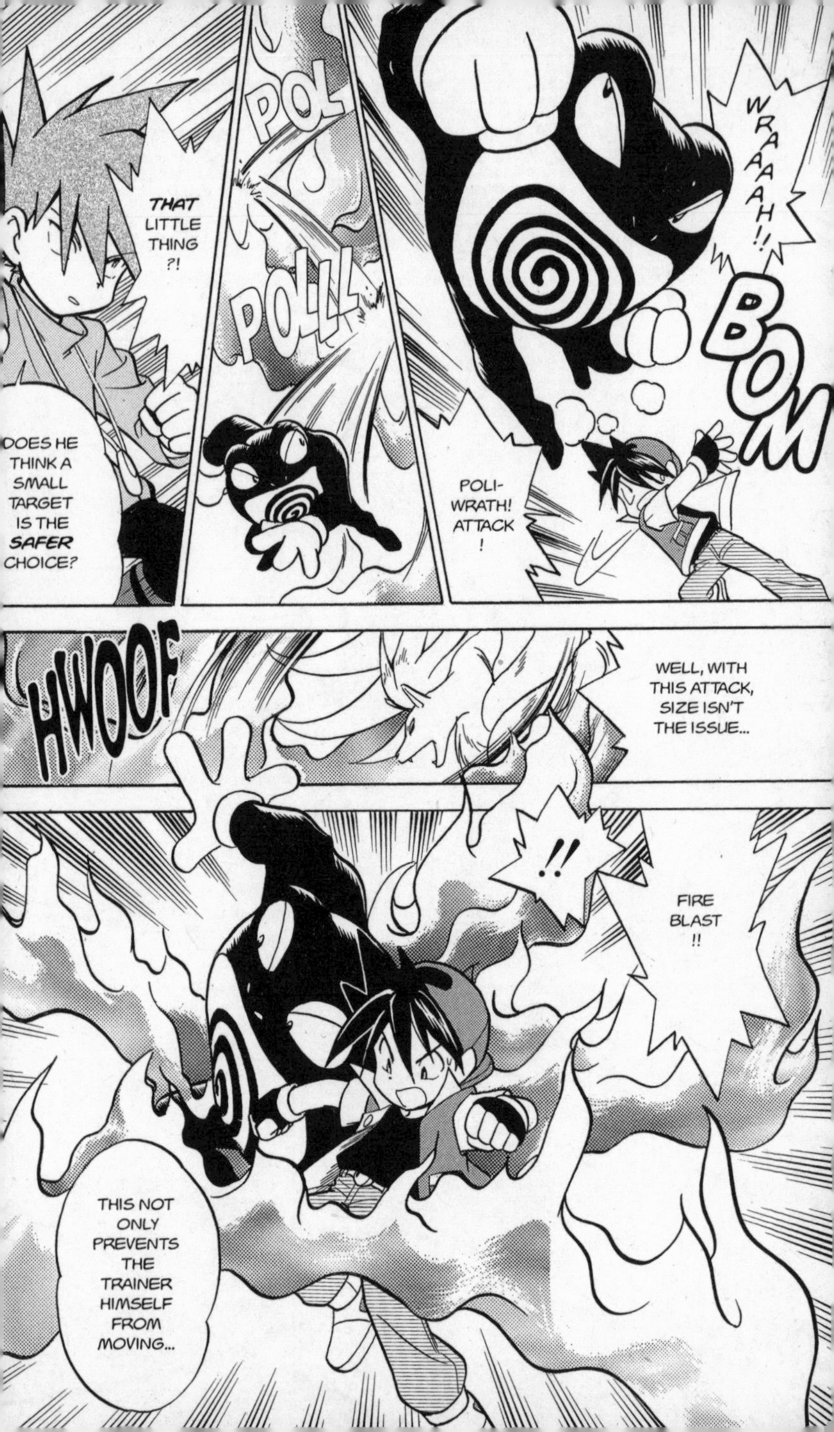

WRAAAAH!!
BOM
POLI-WRATH! ATTACK!
POL
POLLL
THAT LITTLE THING?!
DOES HE THINK A SMALL TARGET IS THE *SAFER* CHOICE?
WELL, WITH THIS ATTACK, SIZE ISN'T THE ISSUE...
HWOOF
!!
FIRE BLAST!!
THIS NOT ONLY PREVENTS THE TRAINER HIMSELF FROM MOVING...

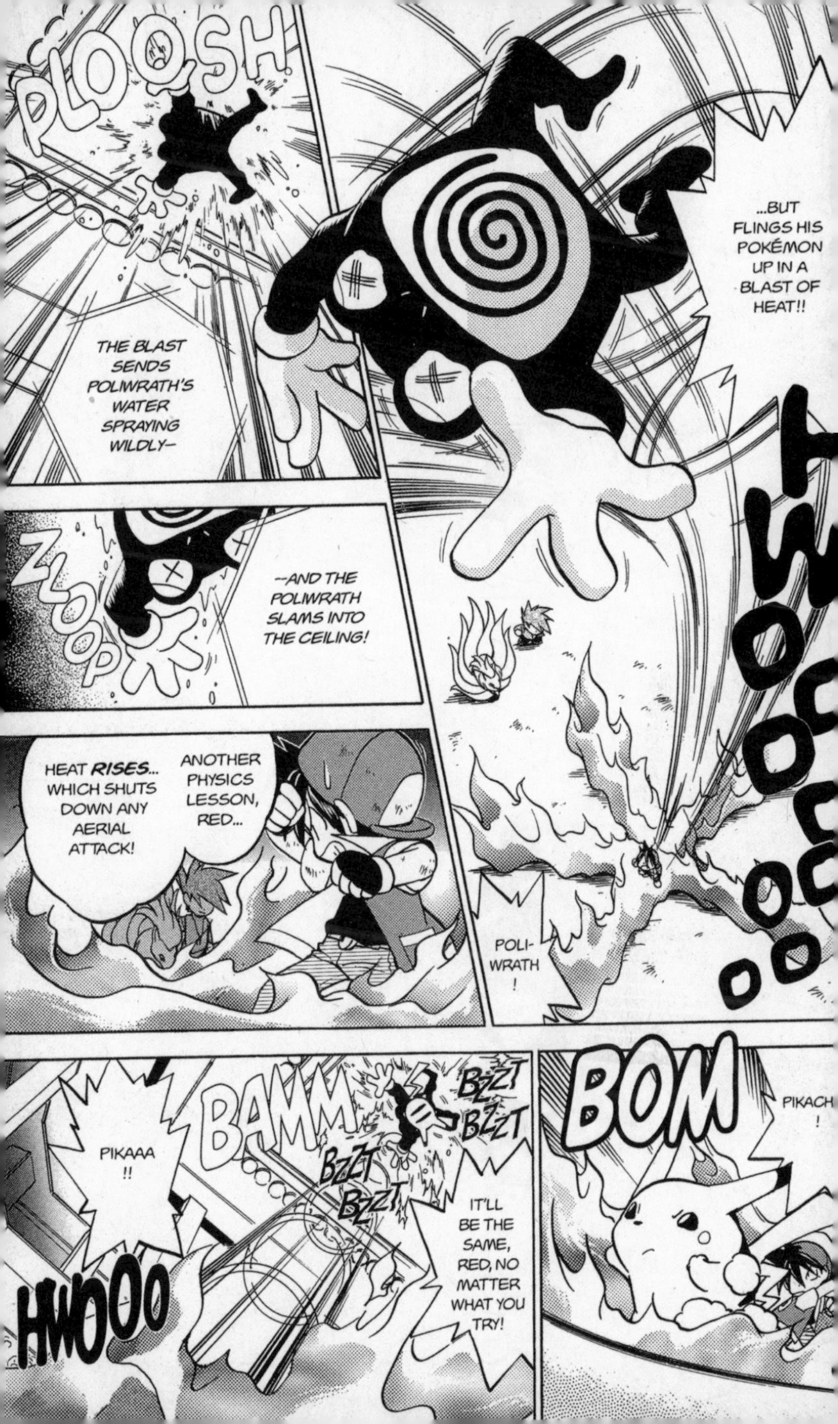

...BUT FLINGS HIS POKÉMON UP IN A BLAST OF HEAT!!
POLI-WRATH!
PLOOSH
THE BLAST SENDS POLIWRATH'S WATER SPRAYING WILDLY—
ZLOOP
--AND THE POLIWRATH SLAMS INTO THE CEILING!
ANOTHER PHYSICS LESSON, RED...
HEAT ***RISES***... WHICH SHUTS DOWN ANY AERIAL ATTACK!
BOM
PIKACH!
BAMM
BZZT BZZT
BZZT BZZT
IT'LL BE THE SAME, RED, NO MATTER WHAT YOU TRY!
PIKAAA!!
HWOOO

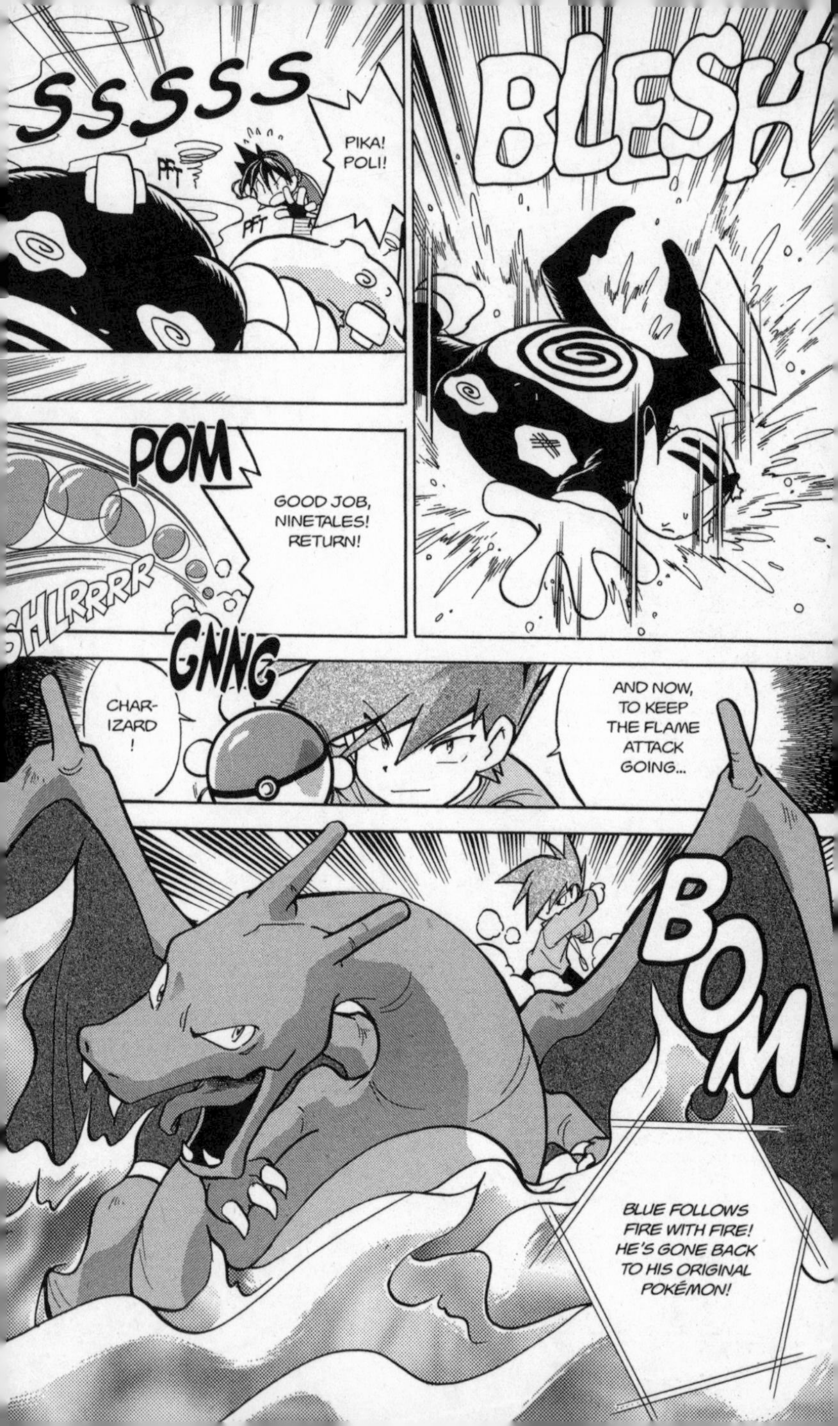
BLESH
SSSSS
PIKA! POLI!
PFT
PFT
POM
GOOD JOB, NINETALES! RETURN!
SHLRRRR
GNNG
AND NOW, TO KEEP THE FLAME ATTACK GOING...
CHAR-IZARD!
BOM
BLUE FOLLOWS FIRE WITH FIRE! HE'S GONE BACK TO HIS ORIGINAL POKÉMON!

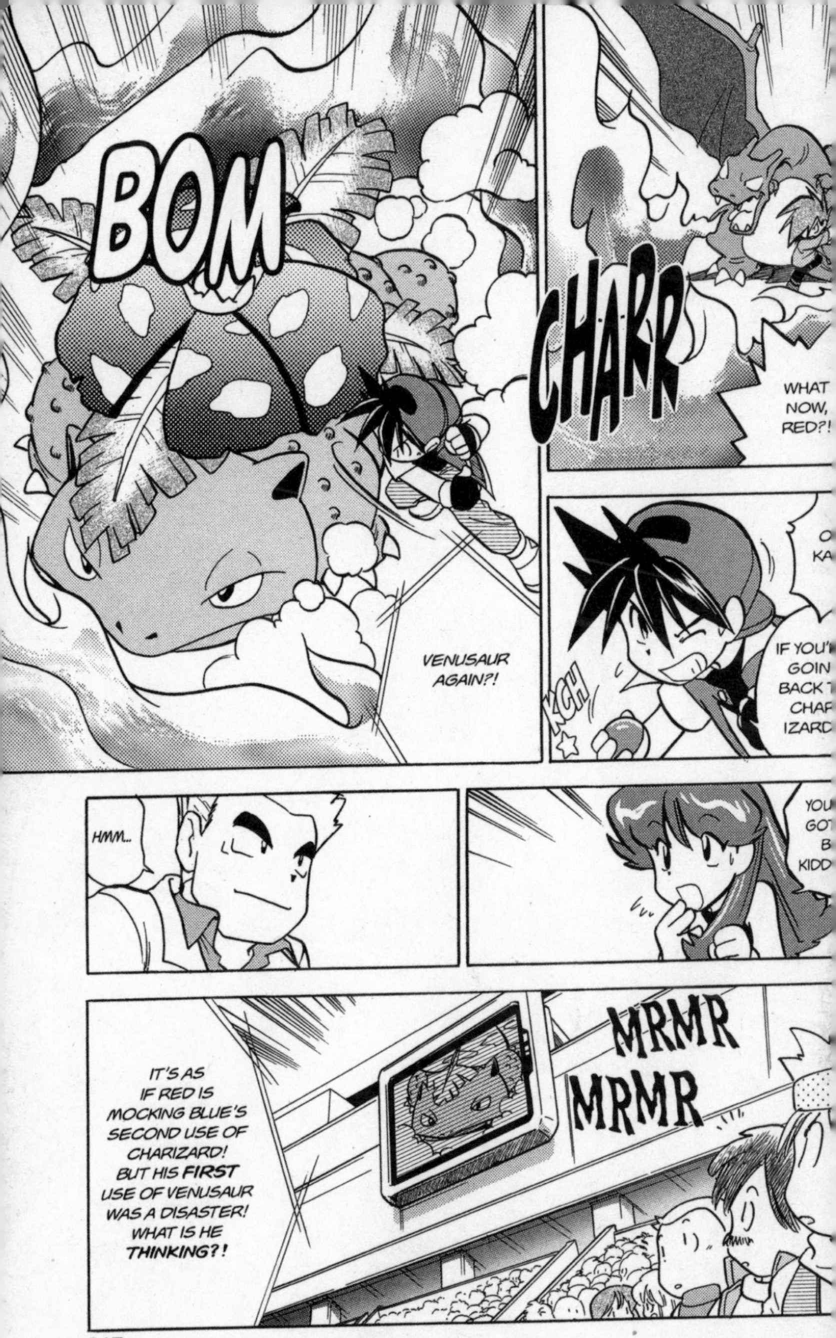
CHARR
WHAT NOW, RED?!
KCH
BOM
VENUSAUR AGAIN?!
HMM...
MRMR
MRMR
IT'S AS IF RED IS MOCKING BLUE'S SECOND USE OF CHARIZARD! BUT HIS **FIRST** USE OF VENUSAUR WAS A DISASTER! WHAT IS HE **THINKING?!**

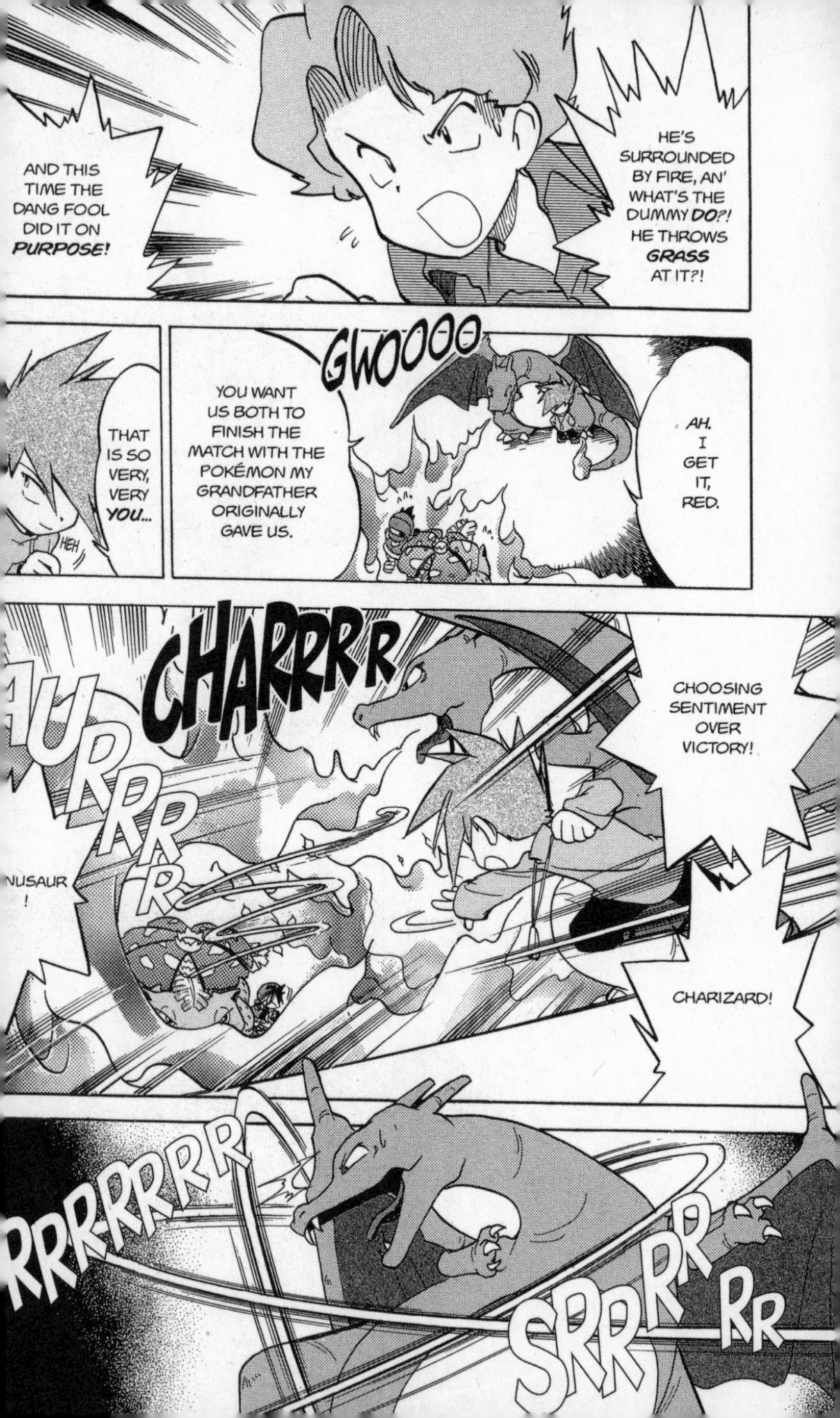
HE'S SURROUNDED BY FIRE, AN' WHAT'S THE DUMMY *DO?!* HE THROWS ***GRASS*** AT IT?!
AND THIS TIME THE DANG FOOL DID IT ON ***PURPOSE!***
GWOOOO
AH. I GET IT, RED.
YOU WANT US BOTH TO FINISH THE MATCH WITH THE POKÉMON MY GRANDFATHER ORIGINALLY GAVE US.
THAT IS SO VERY, VERY ***YOU...***
HEH
CHOOSING SENTIMENT OVER VICTORY!
CHARIZARD!
CHARRRR
URRRR
NUSAUR !
RRR-RRRRRR
SRRRRRR

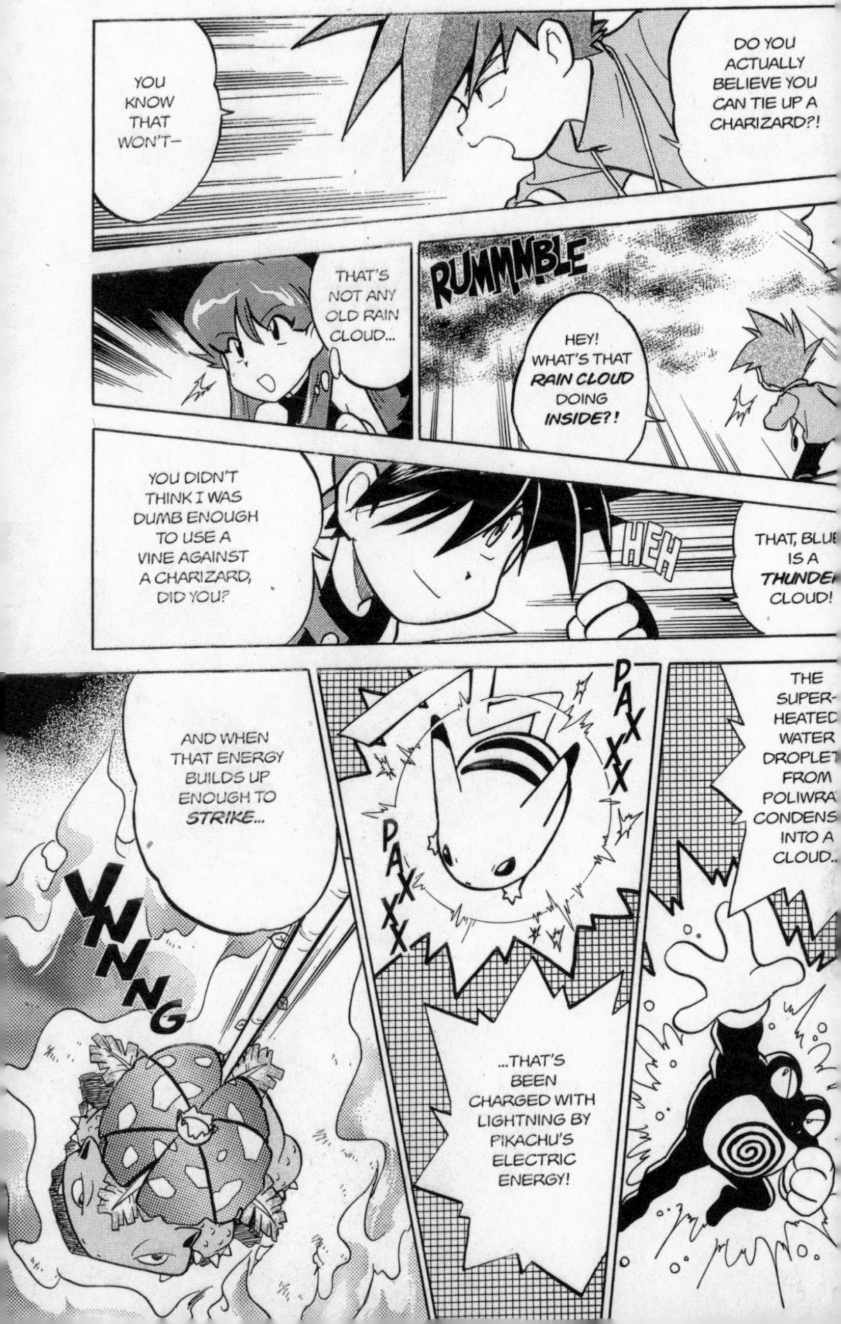
DO YOU ACTUALLY BELIEVE YOU CAN TIE UP A CHARIZARD?!
YOU KNOW THAT WON'T—
RUMMMBLE
HEY! WHAT'S THAT *RAIN CLOUD* DOING *INSIDE?!*
THAT'S NOT ANY OLD RAIN CLOUD...
THAT, BLUE IS A *THUNDE* CLOUD!
HEH
YOU DIDN'T THINK I WAS DUMB ENOUGH TO USE A VINE AGAINST A CHARIZARD, DID YOU?
THE SUPER-HEATED WATER DROPLET FROM POLIWRA CONDENS INTO A CLOUD...
PAXXX
PAXXX
...THAT'S BEEN CHARGED WITH LIGHTNING BY PIKACHU'S ELECTRIC ENERGY!
AND WHEN THAT ENERGY BUILDS UP ENOUGH TO *STRIKE*...
VNNNG

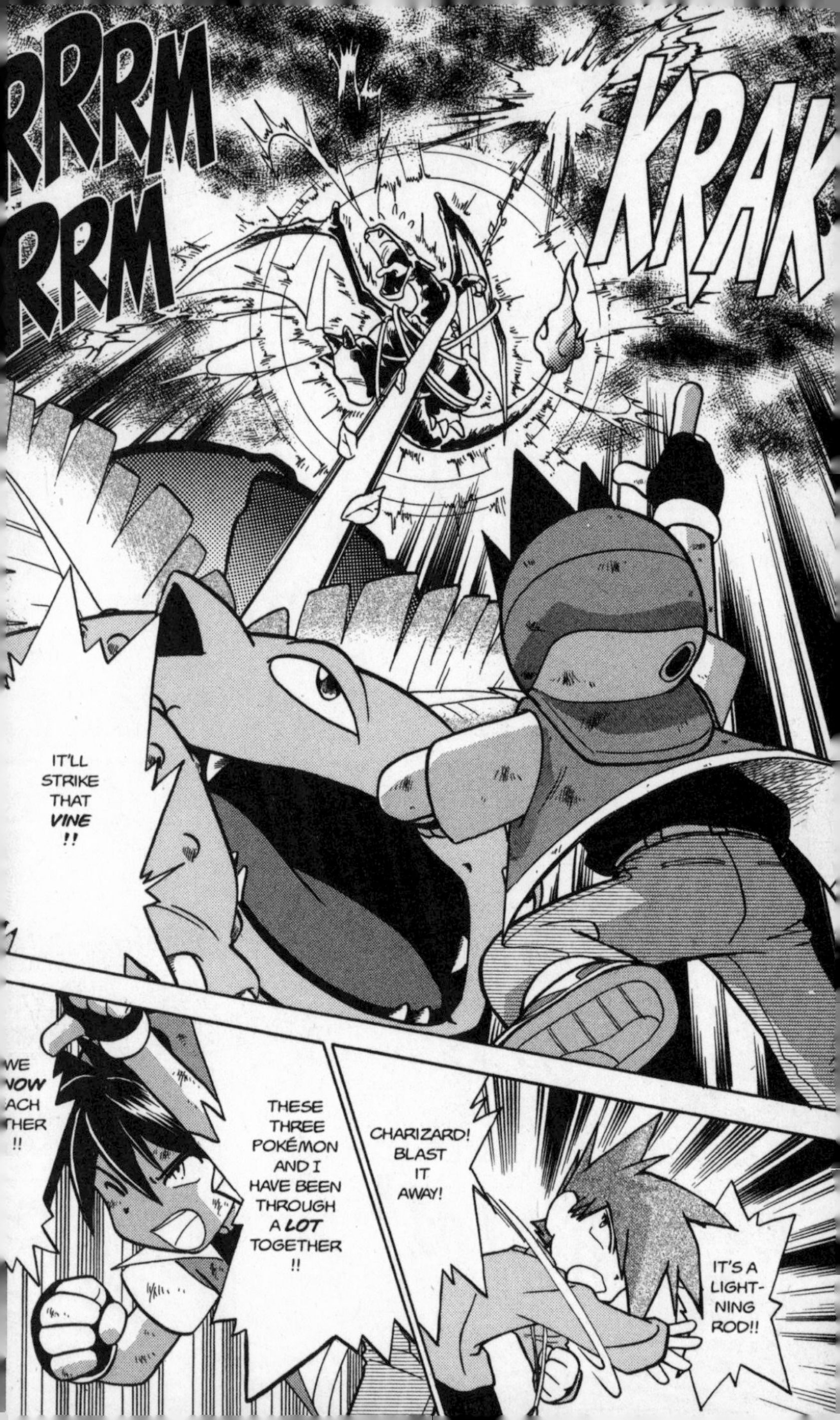
KRAK
RRRM RRM
IT'LL STRIKE THAT *VINE* !!
CHARIZARD! BLAST IT AWAY!
IT'S A LIGHT-NING ROD!!
THESE THREE POKÉMON AND I HAVE BEEN THROUGH A *LOT* TOGETHER !!
WE *NOW* ACH THER !!

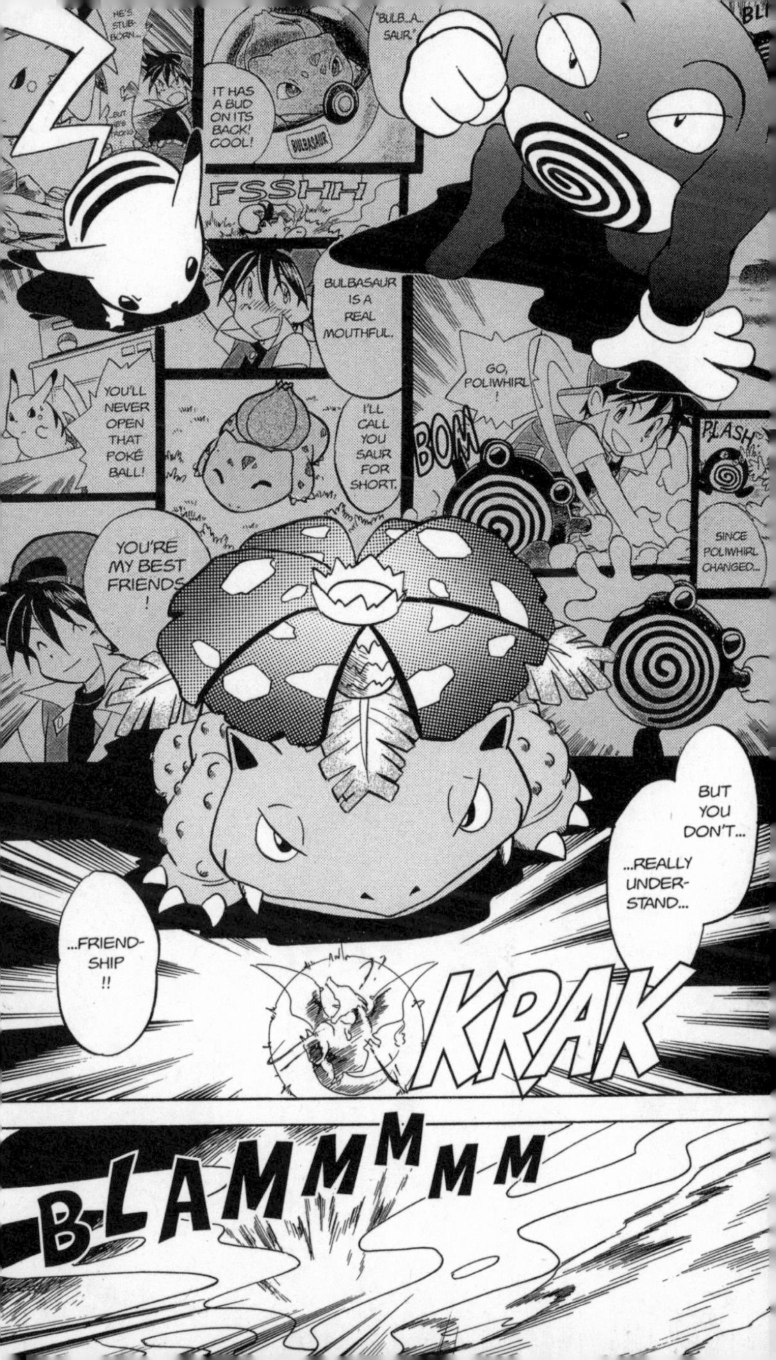
"BULB...A... SAUR."
IT HAS A BUD ON ITS BACK! COOL!
BULBASAUR
HE'S STUB-BORN...
FSSHH
BULBASAUR IS A REAL MOUTHFUL.
GO, POLIWHIRL!
PLASH
BOM
I'LL CALL YOU SAUR FOR SHORT.
YOU'LL NEVER OPEN THAT POKÉ BALL!
SINCE POLIWHIRL CHANGED...
YOU'RE MY BEST FRIENDS!
BUT YOU DON'T...
...REALLY UNDER-STAND...
...FRIEND-SHIP !!
KRAK
BLAMMMMMM

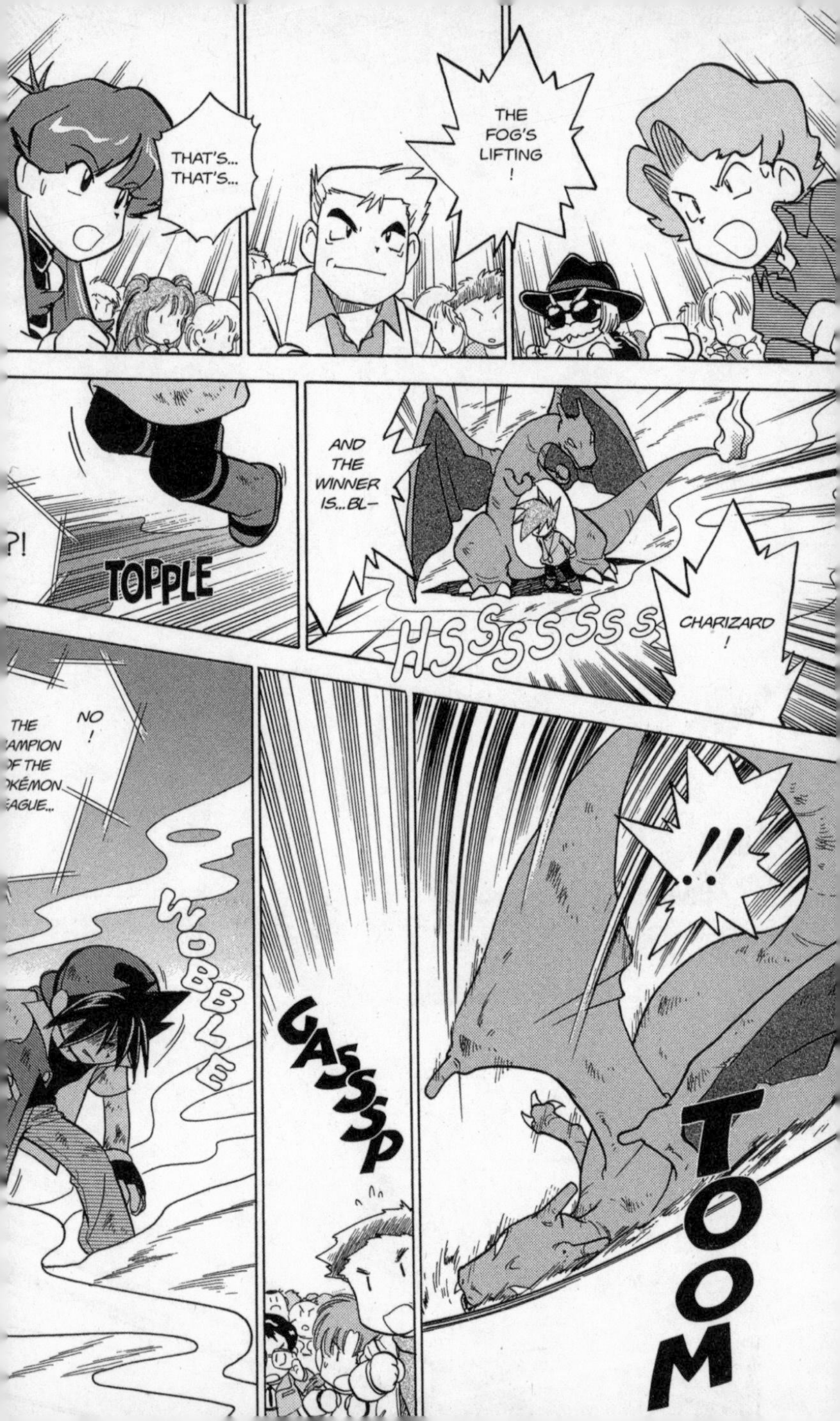
THE FOG'S LIFTING !
THAT'S... THAT'S...
AND THE WINNER IS...BL–
HSSSSSSSS
CHARIZARD !
?!
TOPPLE
!!
TOOM
GASSSP
NO !
THE AMPION OF THE OKÉMON EAGUE...
WOBBLE

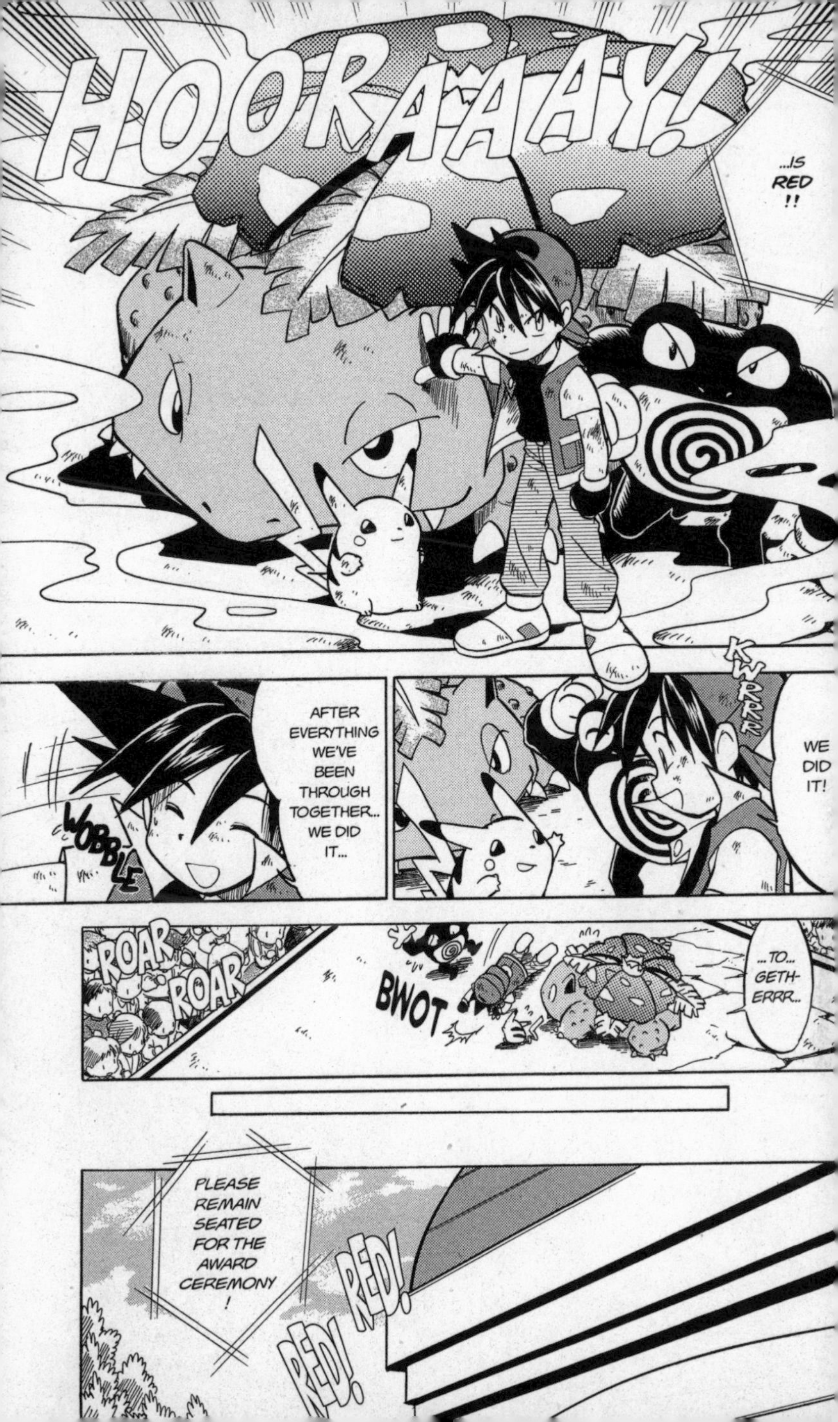
HOORAAAY!
...IS RED !!
KWRRR
WE DID IT!
AFTER EVERYTHING WE'VE BEEN THROUGH TOGETHER... WE DID IT...
WOBBLE
...TO... GETH-ERRR...
BWOT
ROAR
ROAR
RED!
RED!
PLEASE REMAIN SEATED FOR THE AWARD CEREMONY!

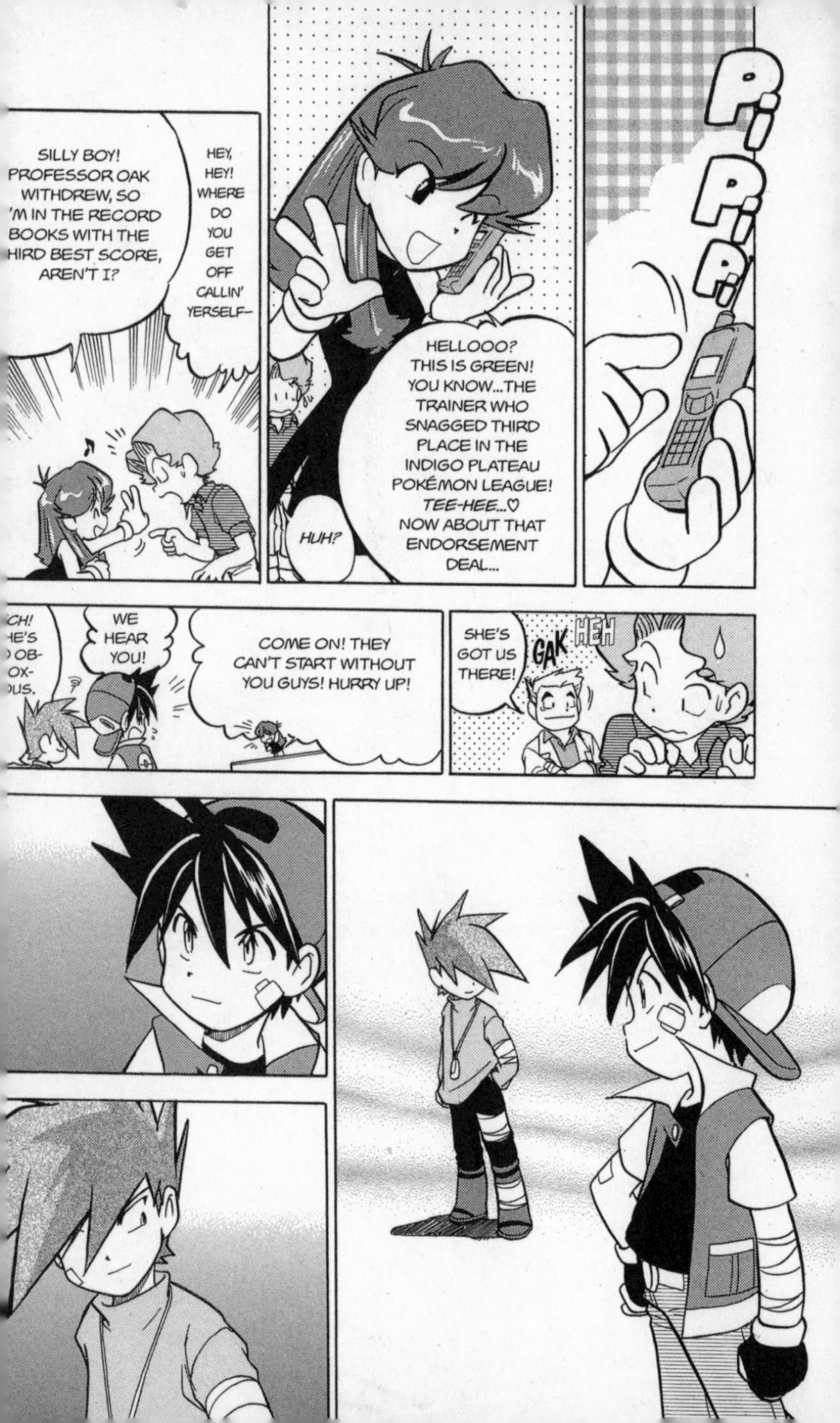
PI PI PI
HELLOOO? THIS IS GREEN! YOU KNOW...THE TRAINER WHO SNAGGED THIRD PLACE IN THE INDIGO PLATEAU POKÉMON LEAGUE! TEE-HEE...♡ NOW ABOUT THAT ENDORSEMENT DEAL...
HUH?
HEY, HEY! WHERE DO YOU GET OFF CALLIN' YERSELF—
SILLY BOY! PROFESSOR OAK WITHDREW, SO 'M IN THE RECORD BOOKS WITH THE HIRD BEST SCORE, AREN'T I?
SHE'S GOT US THERE!
GAK
HEH
COME ON! THEY CAN'T START WITHOUT YOU GUYS! HURRY UP!
WE HEAR YOU!
CH! HE'S OB- OX- US.

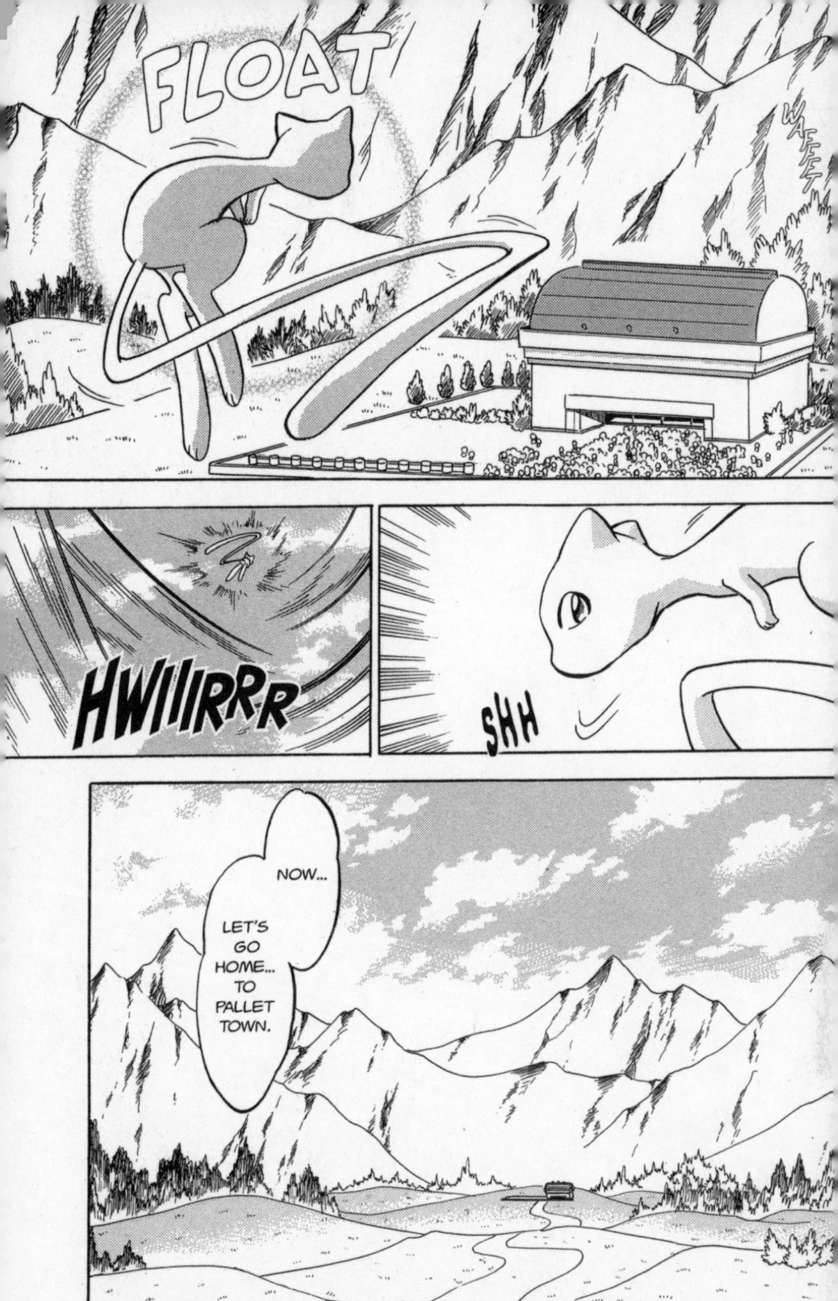
FLOAT
WAFFT
SHH
HWIIIRRR
NOW... LET'S GO HOME... TO PALLET TOWN.

To be continued in the next volume...

POKÉMON

D, GREEN & BLUE

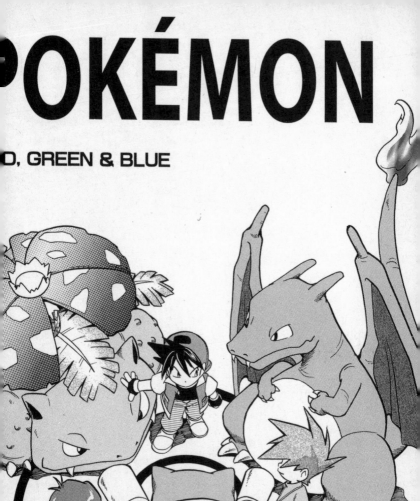

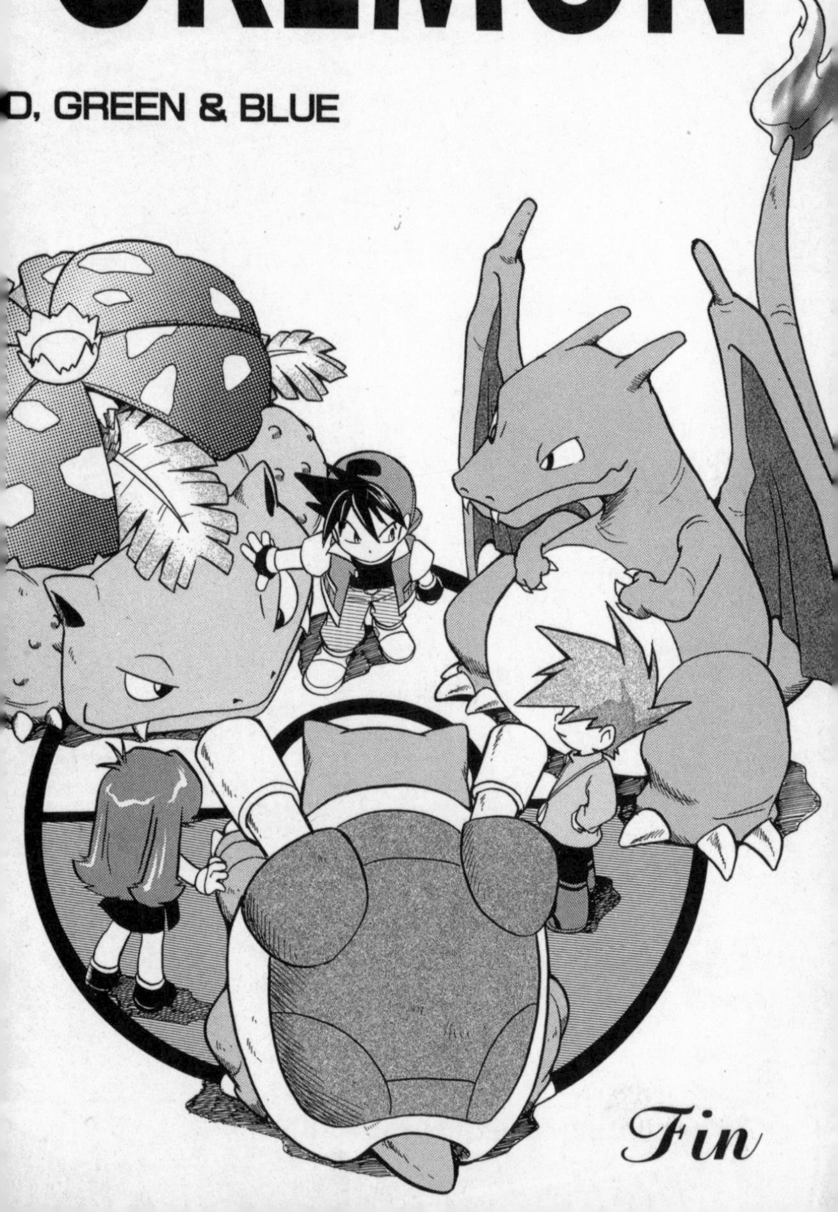
Fin

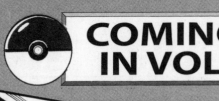

COMING SOON IN VOLUME 4!

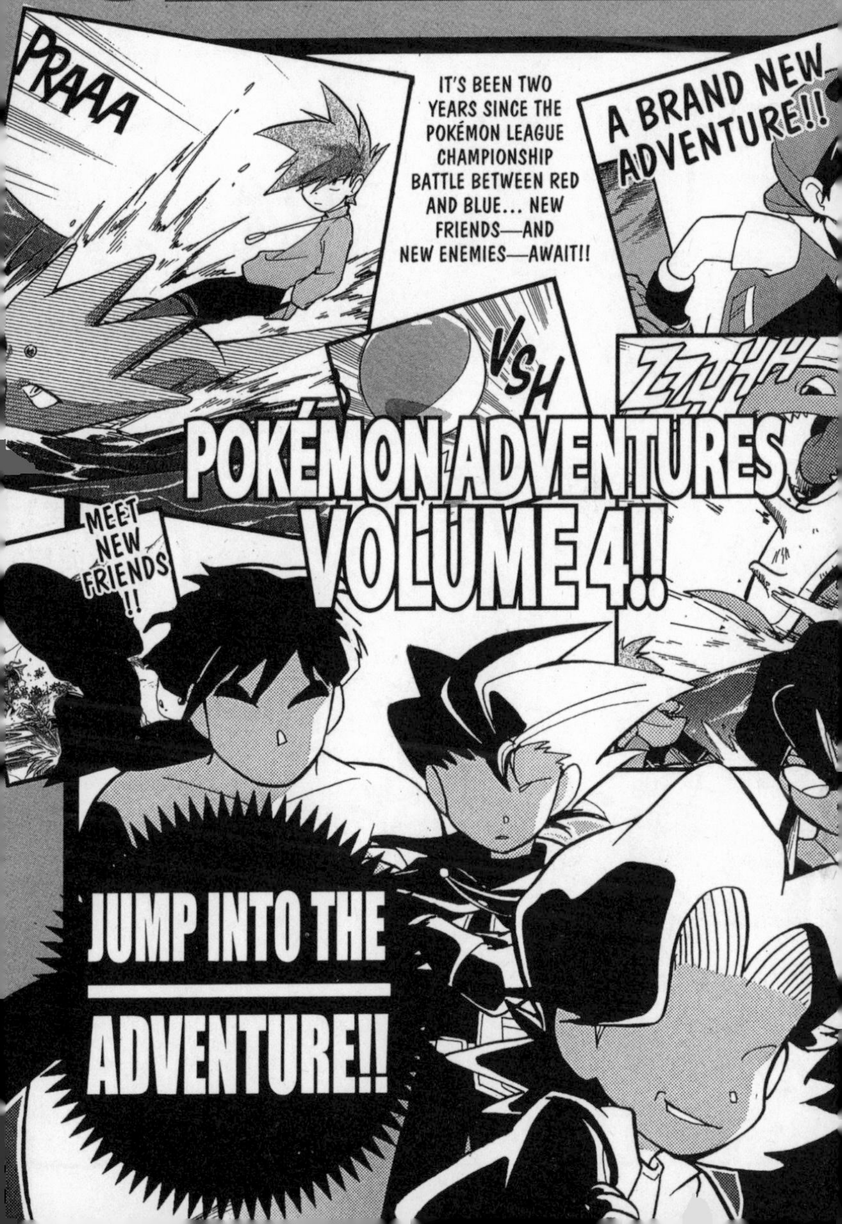

A BRAND NEW ADVENTURE!!
IT'S BEEN TWO YEARS SINCE THE POKÉMON LEAGUE CHAMPIONSHIP BATTLE BETWEEN RED AND BLUE... NEW FRIENDS—AND NEW ENEMIES—AWAIT!!
PRAAAA
ZZUHH
VSH
POKÉMON ADVENTURES VOLUME 4!!
MEET NEW FRIENDS!!
JUMP INTO THE ADVENTURE!!

ADVENTURE ROUTE MAP 3

AFTER THE BATTLE OF SAFFRON CITY, RED MOVES ON TO THE CERULEAN CAVES. TRAVELING THROUGH THE VIRIDIAN FOREST, HE DEFEATS GIOVANNI, AND FINALLY ARRIVES AT INDIGO PLATEAU!

CERULEAN CAVE BATTLE

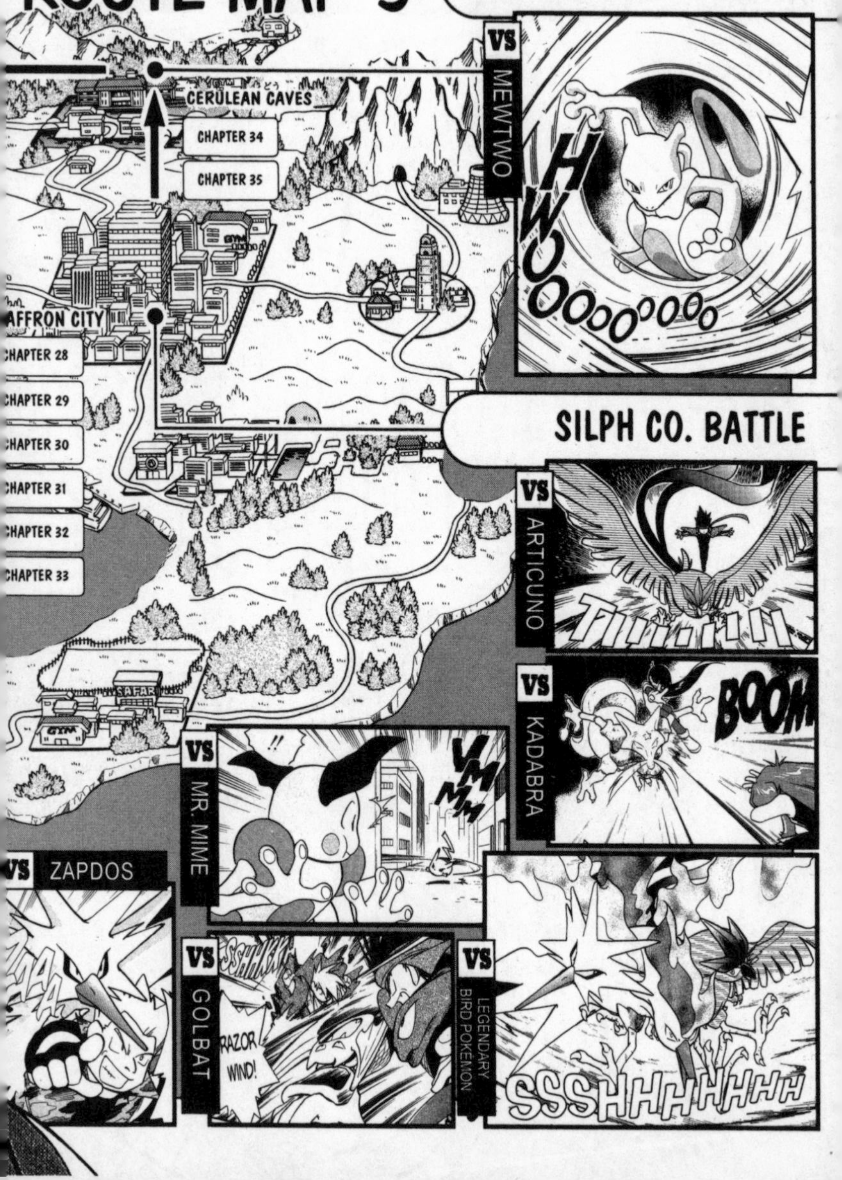
CERULEAN CAVES
CHAPTER 34
CHAPTER 35
VS MEWTWO
HWOOOOOOOOO
AFFRON CITY
GYM
HAPTER 28
HAPTER 29
HAPTER 30
HAPTER 31
HAPTER 32
HAPTER 33
SILPH CO. BATTLE
VS ARTICUNO
VS KADABRA
BOOM
SAFARI
GYM
VS MR. MIME
!!
VS ZAPDOS
VS GOLBAT
RAZOR WIND!
VS LEGENDARY BIRD POKÉMON
SSSHHHHHHHH

GOTTA CATCH 'EM ALL!!

ADVENTURE ROUTE MAP 3

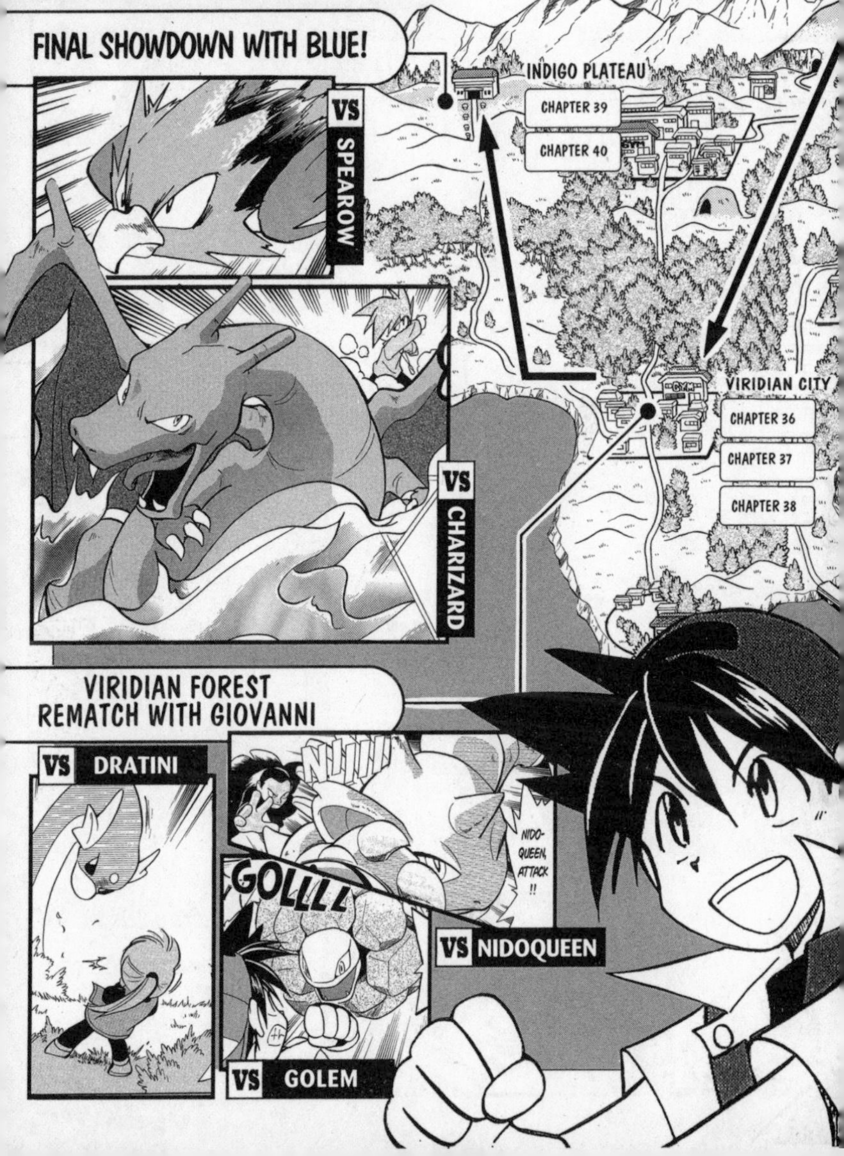
FINAL SHOWDOWN WITH BLUE!
INDIGO PLATEAU
CHAPTER 39
CHAPTER 40
VS SPEAROW
VS CHARIZARD
VIRIDIAN CITY
CHAPTER 36
CHAPTER 37
CHAPTER 38
VIRIDIAN FOREST
REMATCH WITH GIOVANNI
NIDO-QUEEN, ATTACK!!
VS NIDOQUEEN
GOLLLL
VS DRATINI
VS GOLEM

RED'S POKÉDEX!

ENCYCLOPEDIA

001 BULBASAUR
002 IVYSAUR
▶003 VENUSAUR
004 CHARMANDER
005 CHARMELEON
006 CHARIZARD
007 ....
008 WARTORTLE
009 BLASTOISE
010 CATERPIE
011 METAPOD
012 BUTTERF

TRAINER: RED
BADGES: 7
POKÉMON: 71

NUMBER CAUGHT
132
NUMBER FOUND
71

RED WON THE POKÉMON LEAGUE CHAMPIONSHIP, BUT HE STILL HAS A LOT OF POKÉMON LEFT TO CAPTURE...

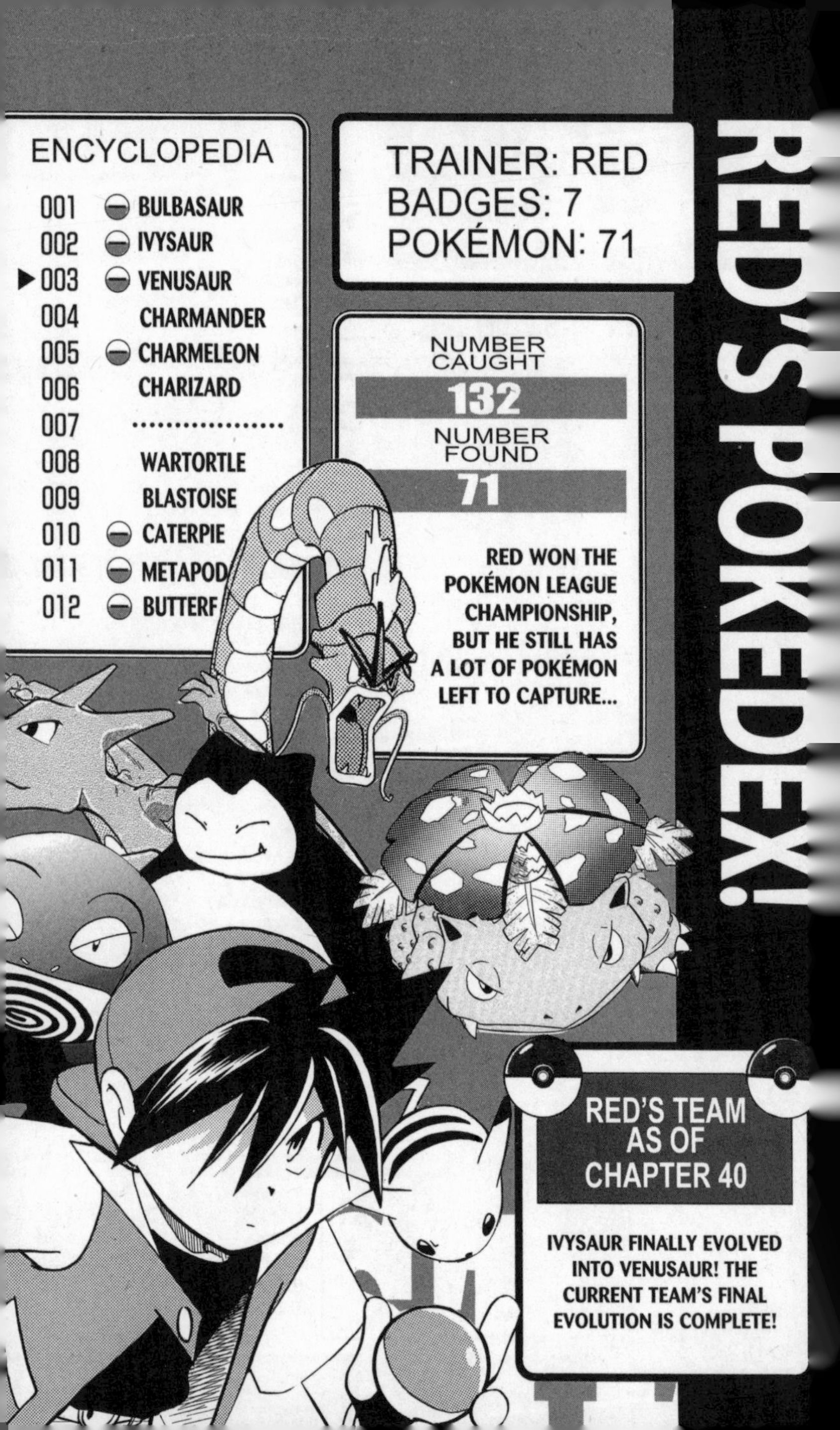

RED'S TEAM AS OF CHAPTER 40

IVYSAUR FINALLY EVOLVED INTO VENUSAUR! THE CURRENT TEAM'S FINAL EVOLUTION IS COMPLETE!

POCKE

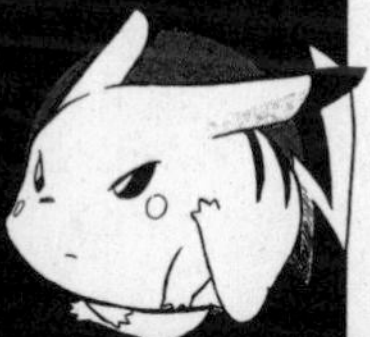

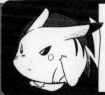

PIKACHU:L51
HP
NO.025

FURIOUS OVER THE ATTACK ON ITS VIRIDIAN FOREST HOME, PIKA WAILED ON GIOVANNI, THE LEADER OF TEAM ROCKET.

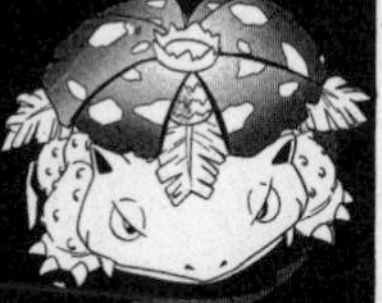

VENUSAUR:L60
HP
NO.003

IN THE DECISIVE BATTLE AGAINST TEAM ROCKET AT THEIR SAFFRON CITY SILPH CO. HEADQUARTERS, THE FLOWER ON SAUR'S BACK FINALLY BLOOMED!!

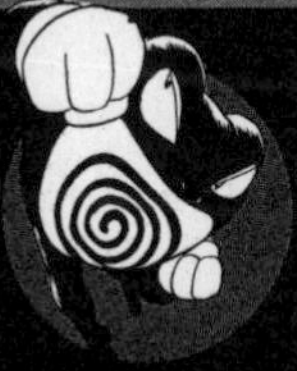

POLIWRATH:L61
HP
NO.062

POLI IS THE POKÉMON RED RELIES UPON MOST. WATCHING POLI RUSH HEADLONG INTO BATTLE IS A SIGHT TO BEHOLD!

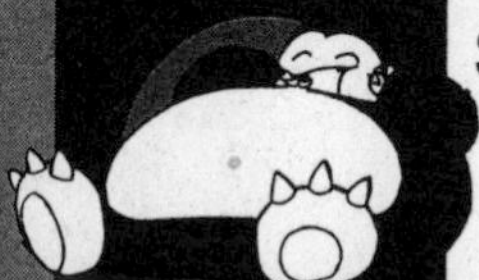

SNORLAX:L52
HP
NO.143

DURING THE POKÉMON LEAGUE CHAMPIONSHIP AT INDIGO PLATEAU, LAX BATTLED BLUE'S MACHAMP. IT'S HARD TO BELIEVE THIS HUNGRY BEHEMOTH CAN GROW EVEN BIGGER—BUT HE CAN!

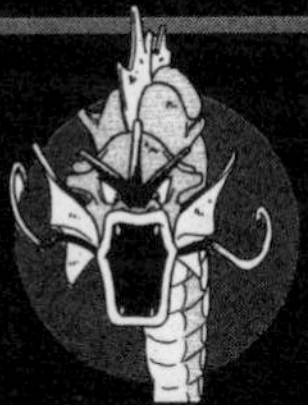

GYARADOS:L48
HP
NO.130

GYARA HAS A POWERFUL HYPER BEAM ATTACK! BUT JUST ONE LOOK AT GYARA IS ENOUGH TO MAKE AN ENEMY TURN TAIL AND RUN!

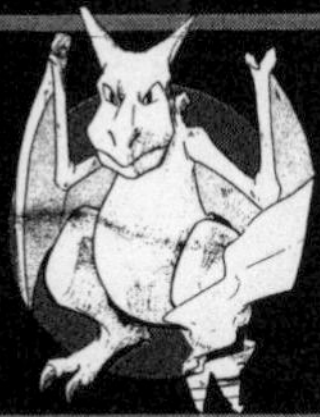

AERODACTYL:L41
HP
NO.142

AERO REALLY SHOWED ITS STUFF DURING AN INTENSE AERIAL BATTLE AGAINST MEWTWO! AERO AND RED FLY SO SMOOTHLY TOGETHER, THEY LOOK LIKE ONE CREATURE.

Message from
Hidenori Kusaka

Pokémon Adventures is already on its third volume! Now Red, Blue and Green charge into the Silph Co. headquarters of Team Rocket! What battles will unfold…?! Check out how everyone has improved!!

MWEE

Message from
MATO

One battle after another!! I gripped my pen really hard while drawing this third volume. I felt like I was the one fighting as I drew the battle scenes… Take your time to enjoy this book. We finished every chapter just barely on schedule each month!

More Adventures Coming Soon...

Pokémon trainer Red goes off on a training challenge and... *never comes back!* But a tired and tattered Pikachu manages to return home by himself. A mysterious young trainer in yellow befriends Pikachu, and together they set out to find our missing hero!

And watch out for Team Rocket, Yellow Caballero... Could they be behind Red's mysterious disappearance?

AVAILABLE NOW!

The adventure continues in the Johto region!

POKÉMON™
ADVENTURES
GOLD & SILVER BOX SET

Includes POKÉMON ADVENTURES Vols. 8-14 and a collectible poster!

Story by
HIDENORI KUSAKA

Art by
MATO, SATOSHI YAMAMOTO

More exciting Pokémon adventures starring Gold and his rival Silver! First someone steals Gold's backpack full of Poké Balls (and Pokémon!). Then someone steals Prof. Elm's Totodile. Can Gold catch the thief—or thieves?!

Keep an eye on Team Rocket, Gold... Could they be behind this crime wave?

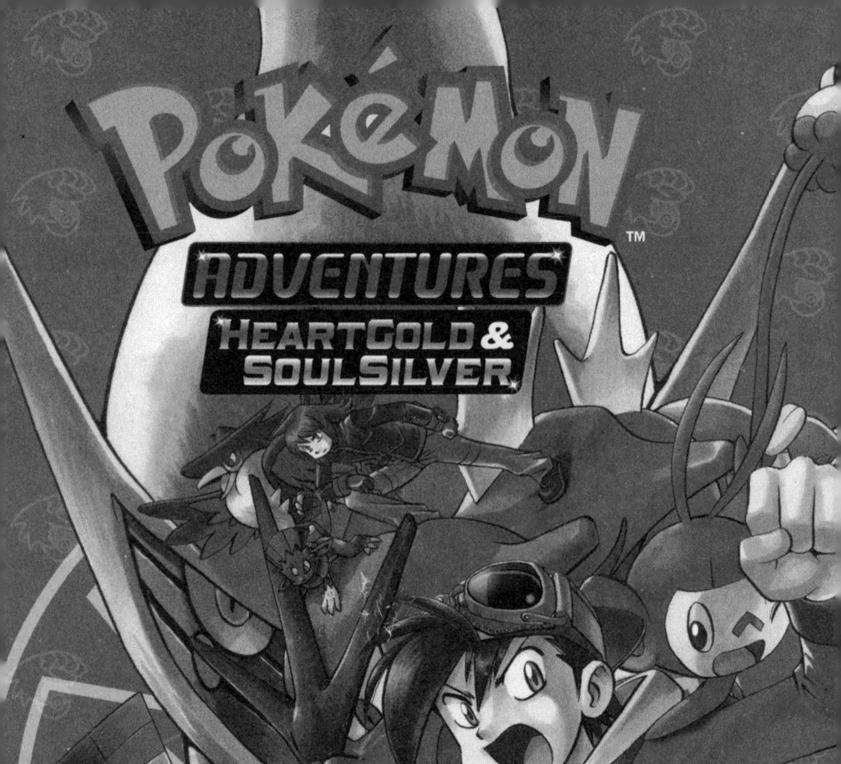

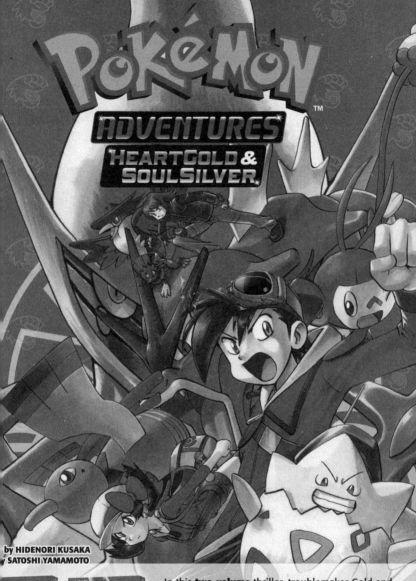

POKÉMON™
ADVENTURES
HEARTGOLD & SOULSILVER
by HIDENORI KUSAKA
y SATOSHI YAMAMOTO

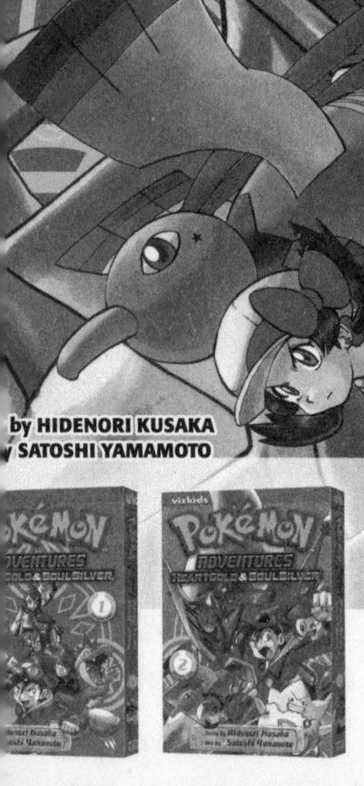

Akira's summer vacation in the Alola region heats up when he befriends a Rockruff with a mysterious gemstone. Together, Akira hopes they can achieve his newfound dream of becoming a Pokémon Trainer and master the amazing Z-Move. But first, Akira needs to pass a test to earn a Trainer Passport. This becomes more difficult when Rockruff gets kidnapped! And then Team Kings shows up with—you guessed it—evil plans for world domination!

Story & Art
TENYA YABUN

Hey! You're Reading in the Wrong Direction!

This is the **end** of this graphic novel!

To properly enjoy this VIZ graphic novel, please turn it around and begin reading from **right to left.** Unlike English, Japanese is read right to left, so Japanese comics are read in reverse order from the way English comics are typically read.

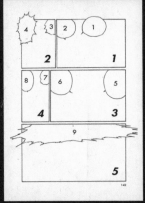

Follow the action this way

This book has been printed in the original Japanese format in order to preserve the orientation of the